Surprised by Love

Surprised by Love

Alaric's Song
SUSAN LOWENBERG

Away from Here
D.M. SNELLING

Chained to Your Heart
MAGGIE COLLIE

falling in love
HISTORICAL

SURPRISED BY

Love

FORCED INTO MARRIAGES IN LANDS FAR FROM HOME,
3 WOMEN DISCOVER TRUE LOVE.

ALARIC'S SONG · AWAY FROM HERE · CHAINED TO YOUR HEART

SUSAN LOWENBERG
D.M. SNELLING
COLLIE MAGGIE

BroadStreet
PUBLISHING

Surprised by Love

Broadstreet Publishing
2745 Chicory Road
Racine, WI 53403
Broadstreetpublishing.com

Published in partnership with **OakTara Publishers, www.oaktara.com**

Cover design by Yvonne Parks at www.pearcreative.ca
Cover and interior design © 2014 by OakTara Publishers
Cover images © thinkstockphotos.ca: Beaulieu Palace House/John Watson, 105674230; Majestic monarch butterfly on beautiful pink bougainvillea flowers/Santhosh Kumar, 17055383

ISBN-13: 978-1-4245-9915-8 ▪ ISBN-10: 1-4245-9915-6
eISBN-13: 978-1-4245-9911-0 ▪ eISBN-10: 1-4245-9911-3

Surprised by Love is a work of fiction. References to real people, events, establishments, organizations, or locales are intended only to provide a sense of authenticity and are used fictitiously. All other characters, incidents, and dialogue are drawn from the authors' imagination. The perspective, opinions, and worldview represented by this book are those of the authors and are not intended to be a reflection or endorsement of the publishers' views.

Printed in the U.S.A.

ALARIC'S SONG

Susan Lowenberg

Helena stared in disbelief at Alaric's extraordinarily handsome face. The ebony hair under his white fur cap was unfashionably long and framed his chiseled chin. His tall, muscular body was clothed in a fine wool mantle that was the same brilliant blue shade as his eyes.

He was the most magnificent man she had ever seen....

My heartfelt gratitude goes to my husband, Tony,
and my sister, Pamela, for their love, unfailing support,
and continual encouragement.

I am indebted to Richard J. Foster, for his teachings
in *Celebration of Discipline: The Path to Spiritual Growth*
(San Francisco: HarperSanFrancisco, 1998).

1

England
December 1154

"Lord Merclif, the king will see you now."

Alaric followed the servant through the crowded hall, trying to ignore the buzz of the courtiers' chatter flapping against his ears. He mounted the stairs, making a conscious effort to hold himself back and not outpace his guide. The interminable waiting had shredded his patience, and he was anxious to finally discover why the king had summoned him to Palatine Castle.

When the herald announced him, Alaric bowed low to his sovereign. Henry dominated the chamber, even though he was not physically imposing. Just the reverse, in fact. The short, stocky king was simply and carelessly dressed in loose-fitting gray breeches and a yellow woolen tunic, as if he had just returned from hunting. This was the first time Alaric had seen Henry, who had been crowned in October after the death of King Stephen.

Straightening, Alaric narrowed his eyes as he met Cardel's glance. The earl's corpulent body was draped in a deep red tunic, decorated with rich, intricate embroidery. One would think he was the king and not Henry, Alaric thought. The smug expression on Cardel's face gave him pause. What lies had the earl been feeding the king? He should have known his neighbor would be behind the king's unexpected demand for his presence. Alaric lifted an eyebrow and gave Cardel a mockingly polite nod. He scanned the rest of the solar, noticing several other noblemen in attendance.

"Merclif, Cardel has made some very serious accusations against you." Henry paced the room. "Cardel, repeat what you just told me." He waved his hand toward Alaric.

"Thank you, your Majesty." Cardel's unctuous, toadying voice caused Alaric to tighten his hands into fists. "Merclif beat my youngest son to within an inch of his life. It took Percy almost three months to recover, and he still walks with a pronounced limp. Merclif acted in a fit of uncontrollable rage, without any provocation. Merclif is clearly a danger to the peace and stability of the Mersted Valley. Your Majesty, I humbly request that you confiscate Merclif Castle and lands and give them to Percy as recompense for the harm Lord Merclif did to him."

Henry paused near a table set at the side of the solar and picked up a white knight from a chessboard, tossing it idly from one hand to the other as he moved toward

Alaric. "Merclif, what say you to these accusations?"

"Sire, I came across Percy abusing the young daughter of one of my villeins. He had severely beaten the girl. I do admit that I then thrashed Percy, but I only used the same amount of force he had used to subdue the girl. When I left him, he was able to walk and to ride back to Cardel Castle on his own. The girl was not so fortunate. She died two days later."

"Well, Cardel," Henry drawled as he paced to the table again, carefully setting the chess piece down. He picked up a black knight as he advanced toward Cardel. "Seems to me your son's beating is just recompense for the death of Merclif's villein. I see no cause for any action on my part."

"Your Majesty." Cardel's voice was smooth and silky, but Alaric could detect by the twitching of his fleshy jowls that his enemy was not so sanguine about his case now. "This is not the first time Merclif has harmed my sons or my property. His knights have trampled my fields, his villeins have stolen my sheep, and he killed my best hunting dog. His vicious falcon almost gouged out the eye of my eldest son, Gerald."

Henry paced back to the table, tossed the piece he held on to the chessboard, and continued his wandering path around the chamber. Alaric felt the king's sharp gray eyes on him.

"What say you to these accusations, Merclif?"

"Sire," Alaric spoke softly, making a conscious effort to rein in his anger, "my knights rode through Cardel's fields to retrieve the horses his knights had purloined from me. My villeins did not steal Cardel's sheep but were simply reclaiming their own animals taken by Cardel's men. Cardel's hunting dog was on my land, terrorizing my people, so I was forced to dispose of it. And as for my falcon, she was retrieving the game she had brought down, which Gerald was trying to poach."

Henry completed another circuit of the room, reaching the side table again where he picked up the white queen. As he twirled the queen in his nimble fingers, he paced into the center of the solar, between the two men. "Cardel, whence comes your title and lands?" Henry cocked his head slightly to his right shoulder.

"Your Majesty, King Stephen granted me the title of earl and the license to build my castle."

Henry turned to look at Alaric. "And you, Merclif?"

"Sire, your grandfather, King Henry the First, granted the Merclif lands and title to my great-grandfather."

"I have been informed by my advisors that this feud between Cardel and Merclif has been going on for years. The feud will end now," Henry said, the look on his freckled face unyielding. "Cardel, you have a daughter of marriageable age, do you not?"

"Aye, I do, your Majesty." Cardel shifted his weight.

"Merclif, you will wed Cardel's daughter on Twelfth Night. In this way the two warring families will be made into one peaceful family." Henry made his pronouncement as he paced back to the table and set down the queen.

Alaric clenched his jaw to keep back the protest he longed to utter. How could he marry the daughter of his enemy? What possible chance would either of them have to make a forced marriage work?

"Wyham."

"Aye, Sire."

A middle-aged man who had been standing quietly at the side of the chamber stepped forward with an easy grace. Wyham was tall and lean. The gray hair at his temple framed his patrician face and contributed to his suave, distinguished appearance.

"You will travel back to Merclif with the baron and witness the marriage between Cardel's daughter and Merclif." Henry picked up a knife from the side table. "Cardel," he said, pointing the knife at the earl, "you will provide a dowry for your daughter."

Cardel's flaccid, florid face turned even redder when Henry named the figure. "Aye, your Majesty," he agreed. The earl glared at Alaric, his rage and enmity unmistakable.

Feeling as if his own face were carved in stone, Alaric returned Cardel's look before shifting his attention back to the king.

The king paced into the center of the room and pointed the knife at Alaric's chest. "Merclif, you will provide a feast for the wedding and host your new father-in-law and your new brothers-in-law."

Alaric stood rigid, his hands closed into fists by his sides. "Aye, your Majesty."

"Now, both of you be gone from here," Henry commanded. With a detached, deliberated move, he threw the knife toward the table, embedding it in the wooden surface.

Alaric pulled his horse to a halt at the top of the hill. He took a deep breath of the frigid air and soaked in his first view of Merclif. Even the sullen, gray sky could not overcast his pleasure in the sight of the castle crowning the hill in front of him. The Mersted River, the source of security and prosperity for his family, flowed at the base of the castle mound. His great-grandfather, when building the castle, had made use of the natural defenses provided by the river by diverting it into the moat surrounding the hill. All was secure and quiet. The drawbridge was upright, just as Alaric had ordered it to be kept during his absence, and he could make out the movements of the guards on the crenellations atop the taller, inner curtain wall.

Calmness settled over him. He had been restless and agitated during the trip back from London. Plans and strategies had been scurrying around in his brain, like rats battling for supremacy. He had marshaled each idea, evaluated, weighed, and finally discarded each as unworkable, leaving him with no alternative other than marriage to his enemy's daughter. Gerald and Percy took after their father and had inherited his greed, his depravity, and his malevolent ways. It was too much to hope that the girl had not done so as well.

How could he bring such a menace into the serenity of Merclif? He had no choice. The threat Cardel's daughter posed to Merclif was outweighed by the destruction the king could inflict on Merclif if his commands were not obeyed.

Alaric heard the pounding of horses' hooves behind him as Wyham and his entourage, along with the two Merclif guards who had accompanied him to London, caught up with him. After informing Wyham that he would ride ahead to prepare the castle to receive him and giving instructions to the guards, Alaric kicked Geneir's flank, setting the horse in motion. He crested the bluff and galloped toward home. The cold wind bit his bare cheeks, the powerful horse thundered beneath him, and the rich smell of the dirt flying from Geneir's pounding hooves filled his senses.

At his command the drawbridge was lowered and the portcullis raised. Alaric nudged his horse into a walk and passed through the outer gate. As Hugh came forward to meet him, Alaric swung his leg over the back of the horse and dismounted. Although his castellan was nearing fifty, there was not an inch of fat on his broad, muscular frame. His weathered face was creased, every one of his wrinkles a testament to the number of times he had laughed with unguarded pleasure or squinted into the sun.

"Welcome home, milord," Hugh called.

"Thank you, Hugh. 'Tis good to be home."

Alaric clasped Hugh's forearm in greeting. He was at least a head taller than the older man, but he had never felt that he overshadowed the seasoned warrior. Both men turned and headed toward the stables, with Alaric leading Geneir by the reins.

"Were there any problems while I was gone?"

"Nay. 'Tis been a peaceful fortnight. How was your audience with the king?"

Alaric's mouth thinned into a grim line. "I should have known Cardel was behind the summons. Come to the solar after supper, and I shall explain everything to you and Mother."

"Aye, milord. I was just going to inspect the guards, so I will see you later at supper." Hugh bowed and left Alaric's side.

At the stables, Alaric greeted the groom and turned his horse over to the man's care. With one final pat on Geneir's nose, Alaric left and strode rapidly through the inner gate toward the donjon. The weak winter sunlight was inexorably vanishing into twilight. There was little activity in the inner bailey, as most of the villeins had returned home for the night. The huge, square, stone donjon dominated the large inner bailey and was built into the northeast side of the inner curtain wall. The door of the donjon was thrown open at his approach. Alaric thanked the guard on duty and entered the great hall, where preparations were underway for supper. He greeted each servant by

name when the maids smiled at him and curtsied to him as he strode toward the great fireplace where his mother awaited him.

"Alaric." Margaret held out her hands to him. "'Tis glad I am you are safely home."

He took both her hands in his and bent to drop a light kiss on each of her cheeks. "Thank you, Mother. I am happy to be home." Alaric released her hands and stepped back. "I have brought a visitor with me, an emissary from the king. He will arrive shortly."

Margaret's brilliant blue eyes met his with serenity. "I shall instruct Renwold to prepare a chamber for him. You had best go greet our guest."

"Aye, Mother."

Alaric smiled at her and bowed, before turning and walking back to the door. He waited on the top of the steps as the guards ushered Wyham forward. "Welcome to Merclif, milord," Alaric said.

He bowed and stood back so the couturier could enter the hall. Glancing around with pride, he tried to see his beloved home as a stranger might. The servants bustling around were well fed and cheerful. The fine white linens and the silver on the lords' table were proof of Merclif's wealth. The fire in the large fireplace dominating the west side and the giant, colorful, tapestries hanging on either side were ample evidence of Merclif's warmth and hospitality.

Alaric looked at Wyham in time to see the stunned expression on the baron's usually impassive face and knew the cause without turning—his mother's beauty had felled another victim. Smiling in amusement, Alaric turned to watch her approach. Margaret's clear, unblemished skin glowed with vitality and cordiality. Her striking blue eyes were kind and welcoming. The small amount of her ebony hair that peeked out from beneath her wimple was only slightly freckled with gray.

"Milord, may I introduce to you my mother, Lady Margaret. Mother, this is Robert, Lord Wyham."

Margaret placed her hand in Wyham's. "Welcome to Merclif, milord. 'Tis an honor to have you here."

"Milady, the pleasure is all mine." Wyham gracefully brought Margaret's hand to his lips and lightly dropped a kiss on the back of it before releasing her.

Alaric had never seen such an extravagant gesture and supposed it must be something they did at Court. He shook his head slightly. Such effete ways were beyond his ken.

"Milord, you must be weary after your long journey," Margaret said. "Renwold will show you to your chamber." She indicated the steward hovering behind her. "Please relax and refresh yourself."

"Thank you, milady, I shall." Wyham bowed and followed Renwold.

"I also must wash this dirt away," Alaric said.

"Alaric, I am anxious to hear about your audience with the king."

"I have much to tell you and Belwick. Come to the solar after supper, and I shall tell you both my news."

The heat from the brazier warmed the solar, while the heat from the wine warmed him from the inside out. Alaric took a swallow to wet his throat after all the talking he had done and leaned back in his chair. Hugh's face was grave, and Margaret's eyes were shadowed.

"'Tis possible the girl is not as bad as her father and brothers," Margaret said. "Gerald and Percy were born of Cardel's first wife. Helena's mother was Cardel's second wife."

"Helena? Is that her name?" Alaric asked.

Margaret nodded.

"Mother, have you ever seen the girl?"

"I remember seeing her once or twice when she was a babe. As I recall, she was a sweet and biddable child. Helena was sent away shortly after Cardel moved to the valley, just before her mother died. I have not seen her since she returned to Cardel a few years ago, which is hardly surprising, given the animosity of her family toward ours."

"I was only a lad when Cardel came to the valley, but as long as I can remember he has been harassing our villiens, poaching on our lands, and threatening Merclif. Why did Father not just attack him and defeat him? 'Twould have prevented the current situation."

"You must remember how it was under Stephen's rule, especially in the early years," Hugh replied. "Anarchy and lawlessness were rampant. Your father was often called away from Merclif during Stephen and Matilda's battles for the throne. He did not want to bring to our lovely valley the death and destruction he had seen in the rest of England, so he tried to live in peace with Cardel."

"Cardel has become much more brazen since Gavin's death," Margaret remarked. "I believe he has been trying to take advantage of Alaric's youth and inexperience."

"Aye, milady, just so." Hugh grinned. "He should have realized that no son of Gavin, Baron Merclif, would be easy prey. Gavin has prepared Alaric well for his duties."

Alaric rubbed his weary eyes the palm of his left hand. "Cardel's greed knows no bounds. He has tried intimidation and thievery to win Merclif's lands and property. Now he has blackened my name with the king. There is no reason to think that this marriage will stop him."

"Aye, Alaric." Hugh stroked his gray beard. "You are right. We must be on our guard, especially when he and his sons are here for the wedding."

"The best thing we can do is pray," Margaret said. "'Tis obvious the good Lord has a purpose for this marriage between you and Helena. We need but to trust Him, and everything will be fine."

"'Tis all very well to pray, Mother," Alaric responded, "but 'tis said that the good Lord helps those who help themselves. Do not worry. I have everything under control. No harm shall come to Merclif."

2

Helena crept into the deserted gallery. She had waited several minutes after her father and Gerald had entered the lords' solar to make sure they were not expecting anyone else to join them. Her hands trembled as she inserted the key into the door of the ladies' solar. Damien had not asked her why she needed to use his key, and she had been relieved that she had not had to lie to him.

Fear, like acid, corroded her composure. She dared not make a noise that might alert her father. The door opened and she slipped inside.

After her father returned from London yesterday, Damien had warned her that he was in a foul temper. Helena had remained in her room ever since, knowing her father was likely to take his rage out on her. Today, Damien had reported that the earl was in a jovial mood. She had to know what was going on—her survival depended on always knowing as much as possible of what her father was thinking and planning.

Daylight weakly filtered through the closed wooden shutters but provided enough illumination to allow Helena to find her way through the chests and barrels crowding the room. The solar had been used as a storage room since her mother's death and was full of clutter. Cautiously she made her way to the door between the chamber and the lords' solar next door. Every creak of the wooden floorboards screeched down her spine. Every beat of her heart pounded thunderously in her ears. Her nose stung with the bitter smell of her own sweat. She could not bear to think about the punishment he would mete out to her if he found her spying on him.

Helena carefully opened the connecting door a crack, just enough to clearly hear their voices.

"At first I was angry about the king's command," her father said. "But last night I came up with a way we can turn this marriage to our advantage. 'Tis amazing how a good swiving will give a man a more positive view on a problem."

"Aye," Gerald agreed. "Especially with Senicla, eh, Father?"

Both men laughed.

Helena cringed as she listened to their vile and explicit conversation. How she longed to be back in the sanctuary of her own room.

"So, what is your plan, Father? Shall we kill Merclif and take over his castle?"

"Aye, we shall."

"I was but joking," Gerald said.

"Well, I am not. We will kill Merclif and take over his demesne, but we will have to be clever how we go about it."

"What are you planning, Father?"

"You and Percy will come with me when I escort Helena to her wedding. After the ceremony, Percy and I will go home. You will stay, ostensibly to witness the bedding, and the guards will remain with you. I think five men should be enough; let me know if you think you will need additional men."

"It depends on what you plan for us to do at Merclif."

"Just so. As soon as I leave Merclif, I will return home and gather up our forces. We will ride back to Merclif and conceal ourselves a mile or so away. Once everyone at Merclif is asleep, you and your men will kill the guards on the battlements and let our troops in through the castle gate. With the element of surprise on our side, it should be an easy matter to overpower Merclif's garrison and seize the castle. When the demesne has been secured, we will kill Merclif and Helena."

Helena pressed her fist against her mouth in order to stop the scream. She must not make a sound.

"I do not understand why you must kill Helena," Gerald said. "Not that I have any objections, mind you, but with Merclif dead, the castle will be yours."

"Aye, but I will need to give Henry an explanation as to why I took over Merclif's demesne. Especially given my recent accusations against him. What better excuse than the fact that he murdered my daughter on their wedding night?"

"I see. Excellent idea, Father. 'Tis time that hideous wench was some use to us. I can just imagine Merclif's face when he sees his bride for the first time." Gerald chortled. "'Twill serve his arrogance well, that he be cursed with such a grotesque wife."

Both men laughed.

"'Twas the only consolation I had until I thought of this plan," her father said. "Once the castle is secure, I shall marry Lady Margaret, and Merclif will be mine. 'Twill be no hardship to bed the widow. In fact, I am quite looking forward to it. She is still a comely wench."

Helena slid down the wall and landed in a puddle on the floor as if a puppet master had suddenly dropped her strings. She had bitten her fist so hard that the metallic taste of her own blood sickened her. Tears chased each other to drip off her nose, dribbled down her cheeks, and slithered off her chin.

"What will you tell Helena about the marriage?" Gerald asked.

"She need know nothing about it until Twelfth Night. She knows enough not to disobey me."

"Are you not worried that Henry will take Merclif away from you?"

"That upstart will soon return to France. He will be forced to listen to the barons just as Stephen was. I have worked closely with the barons for the last few years. They will support me. After all, we English must stick together. We are too powerful for Henry to fight against."

"Ah, I see. 'Tis a clever plan. As usual, Father, you have thought of everything."

"Thank you, my boy."

There was a clink of metal. Helena pictured the two men toasting the despicable plan with their wine goblets.

"Once Merclif is secure, I will rule the entire valley."

"Aye, Father. 'Tis about time."

"If that weakling Stephan had not been so afraid of his own shadow, the valley would have been mine fifteen years ago. This track of land he granted me is almost worthless without water. Merclif has hoarded the river so his crops are flourishing, and our harvest is so poor it can barely support us. The villeins here are utterly worthless. Stephen acted like he was doing me a great favor by giving me Cardel, but he let Merclif keep the best land in the valley. I deserve more, much more than this pitiful holding."

Helena had heard this same rant from her father numerous times. He had never understood that it was his own tyranny that had so frightened and demoralized the people that they put forth little or no effort. Why should they work hard when he took everything away from them?

"Do not breathe a word of this to Percy," her father said after a short pause. "You know that the boy can never keep a secret."

"Aye, I know. You can depend on me, Father."

"I knew I could, Gerald. I knew I could. You are a son of which any man would be proud."

"Thank you, Father. I like to think that I take after you."

Helena huddled on the floor, pressing her forehead into her drawn up knees. She shrunk into herself—a doll whose stuffing had been yanked out, leaving a torn, hollow, and shriveled rag behind.

It seemed like hours before the earl and Gerald quit the solar. They had talked together a long time, refining their plan. Helena stayed alert to every word and sound the men made. Once they finally left the chamber, she waited half an hour more before she quietly slipped out of the ladies' solar, locked the door behind her, and went upstairs to her room.

Her chamber was small. When her mother was alive, it had been the storage room, and she had shared the ladies' solar with her mother. Now she slept on a pallet on the hard floor. Her one spare dress was hanging on a nail Damien had pounded into the wall. The only other object in the room was her prized lute. Helena picked it up and cradled it in her arms as she sank on to her bed.

How she longed to play the lute, but she dared not. If her father heard the music or if a servant reported to him that she was playing, she knew he would take the instrument away from her, as he had taken every other thing that gave her pleasure. She could not bear to have her lute taken from her, so had kept it carefully hidden. Music was her last refuge from the pain and heartache her life had become.

Rocking back and forth on the pallet, she mimed playing her lute. Her lips moved as she sang the words to the song, but no sound escaped her mouth. The music she played could be heard only in her own mind.

A soft knock on her door caused her to still. She counted to ten, then heard another quiet rap.

Damien.

She carefully put her lute on the floor at the side of the chamber, unlocked the door, and opened it. A look into Damien's warm brown eyes gave her a measure of calm, but she swiftly averted her eyes from his. He was too perceptive at reading her moods.

Damien entered the room, and she closed the door behind him.

"I am sorry I am so late," he said. "Your father had a lot of orders for me this morning, and then I had to supervise dinner. Here is your food."

He held out a bundle wrapped in a cloth so Helena took it from him. The cloying smell of the roast mutton caused waves of nausea to roil through her. Hastily she put the food on the floor in the corner farthest away from her pallet.

"Are you not going to eat it?" Damien asked.

"Nay. I am not hungry."

She swallowed painfully, her throat dry and scratchy, fighting to control the biliousness in her stomach. Keeping her eyes averted from his, she sank back to the floor. Drawing her knees to her chest, she wrapped her arms around them.

"You must eat, Helena." His voice was soft.

"I will eat it later." So she had ended up lying to him after all.

"Are you all right?"

He crouched beside her and placed his hand on her shoulder. His touch, as usual, gave her comfort. She glanced sideways at his narrow, elongated face, so dear to her. His expression was full of concern for her, his eyes entreating. Damien's brown bangs lay disheveled against his forehead, and his mouth was slightly parted as if he wanted to say something. A faint shading of whiskers shadowed his clean-shaven jaw.

Why could not her own brothers treat her with one-tenth the care Damien showed her? What had she ever done to cause her own father to so loathe and despise her? Was she so tainted that she deserved such foul treatment from her own flesh-and-blood?

How she longed to lean into Damien, to be gathered into his strong, capable arms, and let him deal with her problems. And she knew he would try to solve them all. He would fight against her father and his evilness with all his might. Perhaps Damien could find a way out of this horror. Perhaps he would suggest that they flee Cardel and run away together.

She gave full rein to the seductive idea of escape. Freedom. Peace. Serenity. Happiness. Maybe even love.

But where could they go where they would be safe? They had nothing—no money, no transportation, no way of providing for themselves. Her father would hunt them down with all the resources at his disposal. When he found them—and there was no question that he would—he would make them both pay. For her, that payment was likely to be a beating. She would survive a beating, as she had done so often in the past. But Damien would not survive her father's retribution. She knew he would kill Damien…and enjoy doing so.

Helena could not sacrifice her friend to save herself. She could not bear it if Damien was harmed because of her. She would have to come up with a way to help herself. She had no one to rely upon but herself. Bowing her head, she took a deep, slow, breath. Picking at the black fabric of the kirtle covering her legs, she released her dream of freedom. It was nothing but a chimera, insubstantial and fleeting.

"I am just a little on edge. I hate it when he is home." Her voice came out a mere whisper.

"I know. I know." He patted her shoulder. "He is in a much better mood today, so that at least is good news."

"Aye."

"Mayhap you can take a walk outside this afternoon. That always cheers you up."

"Nay." She violently shook her head. "Nay. 'Tis not safe."

"Calm yourself, Helena." His melodious voice was smooth and reassuring. "You need not leave your chamber today if you do not wish to do so. Do you want me to bring you anything when I come back later?"

"Nay, I am fine."

"Are you sure?"

She nodded. There was a long pause. Helena did not know what else to say to him. All her thoughts were centered on her predicament. What was she to do?

"Well, I had better get back to my duties before I am missed."

"Aye," she said.

"Helena." His voice was hesitant. "Do you still have my key?"

"Aye."

She straightened and hunted for the key on the pallet where she had dropped it. Locating it between the straw mat and the wall, she handled it to him. He patted her shoulder one more time, then stood. After following him to the door and locking it behind him, she lay on her pallet and stared up at the ceiling.

Sunlight faded slowly from the room, leaving her in darkness. Still she was immobile. She toyed with the alluring idea of taking her own life. That would deprive her father of a pawn for his scheme. After all, would not death be better than continuing to lead this miserable existence to which she had been reduced?

"Why, God? Why have You done this to me? What have I ever done that I deserve this punishment? Why have You caused me so much pain and suffering?"

Her plaintiff wail shattered the silence. But of course there was no answer. If there was a God, He had never heard her cries. He had never spoken to her or comforted her or helped her.

Suicide was a way out. But what if God really did exist? What if the priests were right? Then she would be consigning her eternal soul to hell if she took her own life. The fear of the unknown was deep and cutting. At least she knew what to expect from life on this earth. Who knew what happened after death?

Besides, suicide was craven, a coward's way out. She could not be so selfish. She had to do what she could to help Merclif.

She could not see any option other than throwing herself on Merclif's mercy and telling him about her father's scheme. At least if the baron was aware of the treachery her father was planning, he would have a chance to fight back and defend his castle. Merclif might spare her life while she knew her father would not. And at least this way she had a chance to help others.

And maybe, just maybe, she would have a chance to find some small measure of peace for herself.

3

Belwick came through the door of the donjon, and Alaric crossed the wide expanse to meet him in the middle of the hall. The tapping of their boots against the wood floor echoed in the vast, empty space. All of the servants had gone outside, leaving an abnormal quiet behind.

"Alaric," Hugh said as he came to a halt, "Cardel and his entourage are now approaching the castle."

"How many men are with him?"

"I saw five guards, in addition to Cardel's two sons and his daughter."

"Do our men know what to look out for?"

"Aye, Alaric. I have posted a double watch, as we discussed, and I gave instructions to the guards myself."

"Good. So we are as ready as we can be, regardless of what trickery Cardel has up his sleeve."

"Just so, Alaric. Just so."

"Thank you, Hugh."

The two men exchanged a long, taciturn look. Alaric read in Hugh's face his commiseration and regret. Tight-lipped, he nodded once as he grasped Hugh's shoulder in silent thanks.

Hugh bowed, turned, and strode across the hall. Alaric watched him leave before strolling back to the warmth of the fireplace where he rejoined his mother and Wyham, who stood quietly talking together.

Margaret wore her prized blue woolen mantle lined with white ermine fur. She had insisted that he wear his father's matching cloak. Alaric had submitted to her desire to treat this wedding as a festive occasion and had allowed her to make him a new tunic, also in the same brilliant shade of blue that she maintained brought out the color of his eyes. Wyham was similarly dressed in an expensive, fur-lined mantle. Both Wyham and Margaret looked at him as he stopped in front of them.

"Cardel and his family are here. 'Tis time." He held out his hand to Margaret. "Mother?"

She smiled at him and placed her hand in his. Her blue eyes were bright with unshed tears, but he knew she would not lose her composure and embarrass them both in front of their guests. They had said everything that needed to be said between the two of them earlier this morning in the privacy of the solar. Alaric could feel her deep love and unwavering support for him, so he gave her hand a slight squeeze.

Margaret walked beside him as he led her across the hall and outside. They paused at the top of the donjon steps to survey the crowded bailey. At their appearance a murmur swept through the crowd, and all eyes turned toward them. For a moment silence descended, then the crowd erupted in to a thunderous ovation.

Alaric could feel the love radiating from his people, so he raised his free hand to acknowledge their approbation. Whatever this marriage meant for him personally, whatever sacrifice he made of his own personal happiness, was worth it for them. It was his duty—nay, it was his honor—to guard and protect these people with his life.

He led his mother down the steps, and they slowly negotiated through the path the crowd made for them. Persistent applause poured over them as they walked. Seeing Phillip Talbot, the headman of Mersthrope, step forward, Alaric came to a halt.

"Milord." Talbot bowed. "Please accept the wishes of everyone in the village for a long and happy life."

"Thank you, Talbot." Alaric nodded as the village leader moved back and stepped out of the way.

The clapping continued as Alaric and Margaret resumed their procession to the chapel steps. He let go of his mother's hand, kissed her cheek, and mounted the steps, coming to a halt one step below Father Thomas, who waited at the top. Taking a deep breath he turned, ready to face his fate.

Alaric's jaw firmed as he saw Cardel's gloating expression when the earl led his retinue into the inner bailey. The man did not even have the courtesy to dismount, Alaric thought in disgust. Cardel advanced without regard to how the frozen ground made footing precarious for both the horses and the villeins in his path. The applause abruptly ceased as the people scurried to get out of the way. The earl's two sons trailed behind him. Gerald had the same heavy build as his father; one that would, no doubt, turn to fat in a few years as his father's had done. Percy was tall and thin, more a boy than a man.

Where was the girl? Alaric could not see her.

Cardel pulled to a stop in front of the chapel and dismounted. At the earl's signal, his sons followed suit, and Alaric finally spotted the girl. Her small figure was entirely covered in black, from the wimple that covered her head to the cloak that shrouded her body. Her head was bent so he could see nothing of her face.

The earl spoke to Percy, and the boy left his father's side and went to his sister's. Alaric watched closely as Percy helped the girl dismount, but he still did not get so much as a glimpse of her face.

Cardel gripped Helena's arm to pull her forward and up the stairs. "Behold your bride, Merclif."

The earl left his daughter on the steps and retreated down them. Alaric turned toward Helena as she raised her head to look at him.

Alaric stared in disbelief at her horribly disfigured face. A ragged red scar ran from the corner of her left eye down to her chin. The entire left side of her face was crisscrossed with smaller red scars, as if someone had taken a knife to her face and repeatedly slashed it.

Helena stared in disbelief at his extraordinarily handsome face. His brilliant blue eyes were furious. The ebony hair under his white fur cap was unfashionably long and framed his chiseled chin. His tall, muscular body was clothed in a fine wool mantle that was the same brilliant blue shade as his eyes. He was the most magnificent man she had ever seen.

Inwardly she shrank from the repulsion she saw in his eyes as he looked at her. So far no one but the baron and the priest had seen her ruined face, but it would be impossible to hide her appearance from the people at Merclif for long. She swallowed the shame filling her and straightened her shoulders. Taking a deep breath, she turned to fully face the assembled crowd that had become eerily silent.

As the people saw her face, she heard their gasps of shock and horror. Warriors crossed themselves and looked away. Mothers shielded their children's eyes against their skirts while they turned their own faces away from hers. A wave of revulsion emanating from the people seemed to slam into her.

"Lady Helena."

The woman's voice was strong and loud as she walked up the stairs. She commanded an enormous amount of respect as the crowd stilled, watching her. Her brilliant blue eyes, the eyes her son had inherited, were kind and gentle.

"Welcome to Merclif. I am Lady Margaret." Reaching Helena's side, she turned toward the crowd. "You will all join me in making Lady Helena feel welcome here."

She drew Helena into her arms, giving her a kiss on her right cheek. Margaret turned Helena toward the people so they could see as she deliberately kissed Helena's ruined left cheek.

Helena was used to the repugnance she had suffered from her betrothed and the crowd, but the kindness of Lady Margaret almost undid her. "Thank you, milady," she said softly.

"Alaric," Lady Margaret said in a fierce undertone, "do you not have something to say to Lady Helena?"

"Welcome to Merclif, milady." Alaric bowed to Helena.

Helena widened her eyes and blinked rapidly to subdue the tears that threatened. Steeling herself, she looked back into his eyes, but his expression was now impassive.

The baron turned to look at the priest. "Father Thomas, 'tis time to begin."

Helena rotated to face the priest as well.

"Milord, please take Lady's Helena's hand," the priest instructed.

Alaric held out his hand to her without looking at her. Helena placed her hand in his, feeling engulfed as he closed his fingers over hers.

The priest glanced briefly at her, then began to speak. "Alaric, Lord Merclif, is here to be joined in marriage with Helena of Cardel," he announced in a loud voice. "Does anyone present know of any impediment that prevents this marriage from being sealed?"

There was a pause. Helena stared at Alaric's hand, fully expecting him to repudiate her. He said nothing.

"Do you, Alaric, take Helena to be your wife?" the priest asked.

"I do." Alaric's voice was strong.

"Do you, Helena, take Alaric to be your husband?"

"I do." She could manage only a quivering whisper.

It was done. She was wed to a man who must loathe her. Helena raised her eyes to his. He no longer betrayed any emotion in his aloof features. The priest led them into the chapel and up the aisle to the altar, where he stopped and genuflected. Helena was aware of the others following them into the church.

Alaric dropped her hand when they reached the prayer rail so she glanced sideways at him and witnessed him crossing himself and bowing his head. Helena genuflected in front of the altar at the priest's signal. When Alaric knelt beside her, the priest began the words of institution. By rote she offered the correct responses and accepted the communion wafer from him. They remained on their knees as the priest spread a white veil over their heads before he intoned a blessing on their union.

She gripped her hands together before her waist, bowed her head, and silently prayed. *God, I will give You one more chance. If You really do exist, if You really are listening, then save me.*

Under cover of the veil Alaric glanced sideways at his bride. The unblemished side of her face was toward him so he could not see the ruined side of her face at all. She must have been very pretty at one time. How had she received those grievous wounds? Who could have hurt her in such a vicious manner? He felt nothing but pity for her.

Alaric dragged his attention back to the priest's blessing. When the priest removed the veil, he stood and held his hand out to Helena. She placed her hand into his without looking directly at him. After helping his wife stand, he ushered her out of the chapel, glancing back to see Wyham escorting Margaret with Cardel and his sons following them.

As soon as he reached the base of the stairs, Alaric halted. He let go of Helena's hand and scanned the inner bailey, where the servants and villagers were still gathered.

Cardel's men stood together in a group near the gate with two saddled horses. Alaric narrowed his eyes as he looked from the group up to the crenellations where his guards were stationed. His soldiers appeared to be keeping a watchful eye on the enemy. When he was satisfied all was well, he turned to watch the others exiting the church.

Margaret and Wyham came to a stop next to them.

"Earl Cardel," Lady Margaret said when he and his sons had reached the bottom of the chapel steps, "please come to the hall and join our feast to celebrate Alaric and Helena's wedding."

"Nay. Thank you, Lady Margaret." Cardel gave her a curt bow. "I may have been forced to wed my daughter to your son, but I do not have to take a meal with him. Gerald will stay to witness the bedding. Percy and I will go home."

Alaric exchanged a look with Lady Margaret and shrugged but remained silent.

"As you wish, Earl," Margaret said.

"Come, Percy," Cardel said.

The earl strode toward his men. Neither her father nor her brother acknowledged Helena in any way as they walked past her. The two men mounted their horses and rode out of the castle, barreling through a group of villagers standing in the courtyard. Under threat of the rushing horses, the villiens scattered like leaves blown by an ill wind. At the castellan's signal, the guards lowered the portcullis over the main castle gate after Cardel's departure.

Gerald, ignoring Alaric and his sister, walked over to join his men.

"Lord Wyham," Alaric asked, "does not Cardel's departure violate the king's command?"

"In point of fact, Merclif," Wyham replied, "I believe the king commanded you to hold a feast for Cardel, not that the earl had to partake of it."

Alaric made a derisive grunt under his breath, disgusted with the cavil response. He climbed back up the chapel steps so he could address the crowd. After silence descended over the inner bailey and he had their attention, he spoke.

"Everyone is welcome to join the feast to celebrate my marriage to Lady Helena."

The cheers that greeted his announcement were lackluster and subdued, a far cry from the enthusiastic response he and his mother had earlier received from the people. Alaric descended the steps and offered his hand to Helena. He kept his gaze forward as he escorted her into the donjon. Once inside he led her up to the dais opposite the door where the lords' table awaited them and pulled back the chair to the left of his.

"Milady," he said.

"Thank you, milord."

She spoke so softly Alaric could barely hear her voice. He remained standing until Margaret was seated on his right side, Wyham next to her, and Gerald on the other side of Helena. After signaling Renwold that the feast could begin, he stared unseeingly at the steward as the man directed the servants.

How were they going to get through their wedding night? If the mere touch of his hand against his bride's caused her to tremble so badly, he could only imagine her terror if he were actually to try to mate with her. Helena was obviously frightened of him. What had she been through in her past to have caused her such horrendous physical, and no doubt mental, pain?

Once the butler poured wine into the goblet he and Helena were to share Alaric offered it to her first. When she shook her head, he gratefully took a long drink before he set the cup on the table. After cutting the white bread trencher they shared into two, he gave her half, then served her the choicest cut of roasted venison from the silver serving platter in front of them. He racked his brain, trying to think of something, anything to say to her, but came up blank. Glancing at Margaret and Wyham to his right, he envied the ease with which the courtier and his mother conversed.

Alaric tried to focus his attention on his food, but he could not enjoy the stuffed roast suckling pig, normally one of his favorite dishes. As the first course was being removed, Alaric looked at Helena's trencher. She had barely touched her food and sat with her hands folded in her lap with her head bowed.

"Rather paltry meal, Merclif." Gerald's loud voice caused the rest of the company, sitting at trestle tables in front of the dais, to turn toward him. "I do not think this is quite the feast King Henry had in mind when he handed down your punishment. But, then, having to sleep with your hideously ugly wife is punishment enough for a lifetime." Gerald laughed uproariously.

The smoldering anger, hatred, and bitterness that had been churning in Alaric's gut all day flared into a roaring conflagration. Alaric grabbed the arms of his chair and pushed it back from the table.

Margaret laid a hand on his arm and leaned toward him. "Alaric." Her tone was quiet but insistent. "You must treat our guest with courtesy, even if he does not deserve it nor reciprocate."

Alaric stilled for a moment, clenching his teeth together so tightly his jaw ached. "Excuse me, ladies, Lord Wyham."

He stood and strode from the hall, into the dreary winter afternoon. Pausing on the front steps of the donjon, he took several deep breaths of the frigid air. As he drew the cold into his lungs, he let it seep into his core, trying to quench the rage before it could consume him.

His behavior in leaving his bride at their wedding feast was unforgivably rude, but if he stayed any longer, he would not be able to contain his seething anger and would beat Gerald to a pulp. That would be even ruder, he supposed. He laughed without humor. At least he had chosen the lesser of two evils with which to offend his new bride.

Once he had his temper under control, he wandered among the people, accepting their congratulations, firmly ignoring the sympathy evident in their voices and their eyes. The servants and villagers, enjoying the feast in the bailey, did not seem to feel the cold, warmed as they were by the freely flowing ale and strategically placed bonfires. He spotted Bernard on the crenellations on the inner wall and climbed the turret steps to join the knight on the allure.

Bernard's triangular face was dominated by his strong jaw and prominent nose. Like the castellan, to whom he was second in command, the senior knight was intensely loyal to Merclif.

When Alaric reached Bernard's side, he scanned the woods surrounding the castle. "Any signs of trouble?" Alaric asked.

"Nay, milord," Bernard replied. "One of the scouts has returned and reported that Cardel went straight back to his demesne without encountering anyone. The other scouts have his castle surrounded. If Cardel leaves his demesne, one of the scouts will ride back to alert us while the others trail him."

"Good." Alaric nodded. "Have guards been assigned to watch Gerald and his men?"

"Aye, milord. Sir Hugh has handpicked the most experienced men to do so. They have been instructed to make sure their quarry is not aware that they are under surveillance. Gerald and his men will not be able to make a move without our being aware of it, and they will not know they are being watched."

"Good," Alaric replied. "Keep me apprized about Cardel's movements. For now we have done everything we can to protect Merclif. We will simply have to wait and see what Cardel does."

4

An awful silence cloaked the hall after Merclif's abrupt departure, punctured only by Gerald's braying laughter. Humiliated, Helena bowed her head. She sank her teeth into her bottom lip and concentrated on the sharp stab of pain.

"Lord Gerald." Wyham's voice cut through her brother's awful mockery. "You obviously do not know King Henry very well. One thing he prizes very highly is chivalrous manners. You might keep that in mind for the future."

Helena tried to shut out Gerald's voice as he muttered curses under his breath. She could feel the covert glances of her husband's retainers as they resumed their meal and conversations. To her left, Gerald called the butler over to refill his wine. He drained his cup, burped noisily, and then wiped his mouth on the tablecloth.

"Helena," Margaret said, "I am so glad you have come to Merclif. I have always wanted a daughter, but God did not bless me with any more children after Alaric was born. Now you shall be my daughter."

The silence at the table stretched awkwardly. She needed to make some response. "Thank you, milady," Helena said.

"I have planned a traditional Twelfth Night celebration this evening, after the wedding feast. I have hired a group of minstrels to entertain us. They make a circuit in this region and are very talented. Do you enjoy music, my dear?"

"Aye."

"I quite adore music and dancing myself. Unfortunately, as my son could tell you, I was not blessed with any musical abilities, much to my regret. I always wished I could play an instrument, but I am so hopeless I cannot even carry a tune."

The smell of the rich food in front of Helena caused bile to burn in her chest and smolder in the back of her throat. Was he going to come back? She glanced over at Gerald as his teeth tore into a piece of meat, the grease dripping down his chin. Her stomach twisted as if someone were wringing it mercilessly between two closed fists. She had to warn Merclif. When was he coming back?

"Do you play an instrument, my dear?" Margaret asked.

Helena glanced furtively at Gerald. She could not reveal her love for playing the lute without risking the consequences. "Nay."

The door of the donjon swung open and she tensed. She stared as a man entered, then deflated when she realized he was not Merclif. Where was he? She had to tell him what her father was planning.

"Although I was not blessed with any musical talent, God did see fit to give me a gift for healing. I have quite an extensive herb garden under cultivation. I use the herbs to make poultices and elixirs to treat the sick and injured in the castle and the village. Are there any pursuits you particularly enjoy, Helena?" Margaret asked.

She shook her head as she pleated the black fabric of her kirtle covering her tights, smoothed it out, and then pleated it again. Head bent, she stared vacantly at her hands. Fear's cadence matched the beat of her heart.

When Alaric returned to the great hall, the floor had been cleared, the trestle tables stacked along the walls, and an apple tree brought in for the Twelfth Night celebrations. He breathed in the strong scent of cinnamon from the mulled wine filling the air as he strolled toward the fireplace where his mother stood with Helena and Wyham. Alaric bowed to the ladies when he joined them.

"Alaric," his mother said, "now that you are here, we can wassail the tree."

"As you wish, Mother."

He ignored the reproach in her tone and stood with his back to the fire as he searched the hall until he located his brother-in-law standing with his men. Gerald said something that caused the other men to roar with laughter. Everyone else in the hall seemed to be giving the Cardel group a wide berth or was trying to ignore them. As Alaric watched, a servant filled Gerald's goblet and he drained his wine in one long drink. Alaric clenched his hands into fists at his side.

"Come, my dear." Margaret took Helena's hand and led her toward the tree.

"After you, milord," Alaric said to Wyham, sweeping his arm toward the center of the hall.

The men followed the women toward the tree. They each accepted from the butler a cup filled with spiced wine and three pieces of seed cake.

Alaric stood on Helena's right side as they waited for the rest of the company to accept their cups. When everyone was gathered around the tree, Alaric lifted his cup. "Waes hael!" he shouted. "Be well!"

His retainers lifted their cups to him and replied, "Drinc hael! Drink and be healthy!"

He spoke the traditional toast in a loud voice.

"Let every man take off his hat
And shout out to th'old apple tree
Old apple tree we wassail thee
And hoping thou will bear."

A loud cheer went up as the people toasted the tree, draining their cups. Alaric ate a piece of the cake, then poured the other two pieces into the large tub in which the tree was planted. All around him his people drained their cups and tossed the seed cake at the base of the tree or put pieces of the wine-soaked cake into the crooks of the tree's branches. To Alaric, the gaiety seemed forced, a far cry from the boisterous celebrations they usually enjoyed at Twelfth Night. His people were obviously as wary and distrusting of this marriage as he was himself.

He turned to Helena, who stood looking down into her cup, appearing lost and forlorn. "Drink to a good crop, Helena. 'Tis good luck." He watched as she hesitantly took a sip of the spiced wine. "Now pour out your cup on the tree's roots."

He frowned as he watched her follow his instructions. Did they not have this tradition at Cardel? Surely it was a normal custom in most of England.

Alaric gestured for Helena to precede him as they moved away from the tree back to the fireplace. Behind them two burly men lifted the tree onto a wheelbarrow to remove it from the hall. The discordant screech of a fiddle and the shrill, metallic timbre of a psaltery could be heard as the musicians tuned their instruments.

His mother caught his arm. "You should lead Helena out for the first dance."

"I do know my duty, Mother."

She raised one eyebrow and he flushed. How could she still make him feel guilty with just one look? He was not ten years old any longer.

When the floor was clear, the musicians began a lively tune. The soaring notes of a recorder blended with the lower tones of the fiddle, while the persistent beat of a tambourine undergirded the melody. Alaric turned toward Helena, but she kept her face averted from his.

"Come, milady," Alaric said. "We must begin the dancing." He held out his hand to her.

She glanced briefly up at him, her eyes wide. Alaric felt her tremors when she placed her hand in his. Leading Helena into the middle of the floor, he greeted Hugh's wife, Elizabeth, as she took his right hand. Wyham fell into position on Helena's left, with Margaret on his other side. The rest of their dance ring promptly formed, as did two additional rings of similar size. The minstrels struck up the chorus of the song, and Alaric started the simple steps of the dance.

Pain pounded in Helena's head in a relentless counterpoint to the beat of the loud, joyous music. Helena had not been able to talk to Merclif. He had danced with her several times, but each time the dance was over, he swiftly excused himself. With all the noise in the hall she would not have been able to speak privately with him anyway. She was not just being a coward, she consoled herself. She had to wait for an opportune moment to warn him. At least they were not yet in immediate danger. Gerald and her father would strike in the dead of night.

Helena stood with Margaret and Wyham, looking around at the crowd. Wine and ale were flowing freely, and the people who had been restrained at the beginning of the evening were now enthusiastically participating in the dancing.

Suddenly six male dancers, wearing elaborate papier-mâché headdresses shaped like horns and strung with bells, bounded into the hall from outside. The crowd parted, their shrieks of laughter piercing the night. The audience clapped rhythmically as the dancers whirled faster and the minstrels played louder. The racket besieged Helena; the unruly commotion further shredded her nerves.

When the dance ceased, each of the performers pranced out into the center of the hall and took a bow. The audience applauded each one, signaling by the level of their clapping the depth of their appreciation for each participant. When the best dancer was chosen by acclamation, a hard round cake was placed on his head. After being crowned, the best beast danced wildly, trying to shake the cake off its horns without using his hands. There was much laughter and heckling as the other five dancers mimicked the best beast and the spectators wagered where the cake would fall.

Margaret leaned toward Helena. "My dear, the crowd is becoming a little too rowdy. I believe 'tis time for me to take you upstairs to your chamber."

Helena glanced at Alaric, standing next to his mother. He did not return her look, and his stoic face revealed nothing. She dreaded being alone with this warrior. He could snap her neck as easily as he now drained the wine from his cup.

"Aye," Helena murmured.

Margaret took her arm and entwined it with hers as she drew Helena toward the stairs. Cringing, Helena tried to ignore the whispers that slithered around them. She could only imagine the things they were thinking and saying.

"I had the servants bring in your clothes chest and unpack your belongings," Margaret explained as they climbed the stairs. "I have been a very happy wife and mother here at Merclif. I hope you will be the same."

When they reached the second level, Margaret led the way down the gallery along the east side of the donjon, gesturing at the closed doors they passed. "This first chamber is the ladies' solar. I have taken over this next room as my bedchamber. And this is the lord's bedchamber, which you will share with Alaric."

Margaret stopped in front of the third door, opened it, and stood back so Helena could enter the chamber. The sight of the large bed dominating the room caused Helena's throat to close. At any other time she would have found pleasure in the rich furnishings, the dark burgundy linen hangings framing the bed, and the massive fur spread over the top of the mattress. Now she could only look at the bed with apprehension and dread.

Wooden shutters covered the window located on the outside stone wall. The stone seat below the window was padded with a long, thick burgundy pillow. Helena's chest had been placed along one wooden wall next to a finely carved armoire, presumably filled with her new husband's clothes. Two wooden chairs, a settle with a burgundy cushion, and a small table completed the furnishings. A lit brazier dispelled some of the winter chill from the room.

"I thought you might feel more at ease if I attended you alone." Margaret shut the door behind them. "But if you prefer, I can call some of the other ladies to join us."

"Nay. Thank you," Helena said.

"Shall I brush your hair? That always makes me feel more relaxed."

Helena nodded. Margaret picked up one of the chairs and carried it over to the side of the room, placing it next to the small table. Turning, she held out her hand to Helena. "Sit down, my dear. At the end of a day, I always feel better when I can take off my wimple and let my hair down."

Helena joined the older woman and obediently took a seat. Margaret pulled out the pins holding the black veil over Helena's head and dropped them into a small pile on the table. Next she unpinned the band of fabric around Helena's forehead and then removed the second band that ran under Helena's chin. After removing the pins securing the mass of Helena's hair on top of her head, Margaret unplaited the braids, running her fingers through the strands to loosen them. Picking up the brush from the table, she gently pulled it through Helena's hair.

"You have beautiful hair, my dear. 'Tis a lovely shade of brown. In certain angles it shines with these gorgeous reddish flecks."

Helena tried to relax and enjoy Margaret's ministrations. The last time anyone had brushed her hair had been five long years ago, before she had been sent back to Cardel. Fortunately, the older woman's soothing chatter required no response from her.

"There." Margaret set the brush on the table. "Let us get you undressed and ready for bed. Why do you not take off your shoes and hose while I turn down the bed?"

Margaret went to the bed and pulled down the covers as Helena complied. When she was barefooted, Helena stood so Margaret could pull off her kirtle.

"Get in bed, my dear," Margaret instructed, "You can remove your chemise under the covers where you will be warm."

Helena obeyed. Pulling the bedding up to her chin, she wiggled free of her garment under the covers. Rigid, she watched Margaret as she moved about the room, but the older woman kept her back to the bed.

"I will go let Alaric know you are ready."

Waiting under the covers, Helena crossed her arms over her chest and fisted her hands on the bedding to keep it around her shoulders and hide her nakedness. She tensed when the door opened, then relaxed a bit when Margaret entered alone.

"The men will be here soon, my dear. I insisted that only Father Thomas, Lord Gerald, and Lord Wyham accompany Alaric. I did not want any of those drunken louts downstairs to intrude on your wedding night."

"Lady Margaret, you have been very kind to me. Thank you."

"You are my daughter now, my dear. I hope you will be happy here at Merclif."

The door opened and Alaric stepped into the room, followed by the other men. Helena squeezed her eyes shut when Alaric started to untie the blue wool robe he wore. A wave of air chilled her as he lifted the bedding, and she felt the mattress dip when he slid under the covers beside her. She held her body stiff and motionless, not wanting to touch any part of his naked body, and listened as the priest said a prayer to bless their marriage bed and their union. The slight sprinkling of the holy water he splattered on her face was a gentle balm.

Helena opened her eyes when the priest finished speaking and watched as the men filed out of the chamber.

Margaret went around the chamber, extinguishing all but one of the lit candles in the room. Pausing at the door, she smiled at them. "Good night, my dears." The door closed behind her.

"Milord, I must speak with you," Helena said. "My father intends to invade your castle and kill you."

"What?" Coming up on his elbow, Merclif loomed over her, his black eyebrows drawn tightly together. In the shadowy darkness she could not clearly see his face— only his brilliant blue eyes that pierced thorough her. "How do you know this?"

"I overheard my father making plans with my brother. Gerald and his men are to kill your guards and open the postern gate so my father's troops can enter the castle. My father plans to massacre you as well as your entire garrison."

"Why should I believe a word you say? This could be a trick to lure me and my men outside the castle walls and into an ambush."

Desperation filled her. He had to listen to her and act on her warning. He was her only chance to save herself.

Helena took a long, slow breath. "You do not have to go outside the castle walls to defeat my father. If you leave the castle to attack him, that will make you the aggressor rather than him. The king will blame you for breaking the peace. But if you let Gerald open the gate and let Cardel's men enter the castle, you can easily surround them and capture them inside the castle walls."

"Why are you warning me? It could lead to your father and brother's deaths."

"I have no love for my father, nor he for me. He plans to slay me and accuse you of the murder as justification for his attack. He plans to force Lady Margaret to wed him, legitimizing his holding of Merclif."

"Why do you hate your father so much?"

"'Twas he who cut my face."

5

Helena's quiet words reverberated through the still chamber. Alaric stared at his wife's face. Her left cheek had been slashed deeply from the outside edge of her eye down to her jaw. The scar had not healed well and was red and puckered. Smaller scars radiated out from the larger wound. The pain she had suffered staggered him. How could any man do this to his own flesh-and-blood?

He pulled the covers from her shoulders but felt her resistance as she tried to keep them in place. Alaric stared at Helena until she lowered her eyes and released her grip. Removing the bedding, he unveiled her naked body.

Pity filled him at the sight of her painfully thin frame. The contours of her ribs were plainly visible through her ivory, almost translucent, skin. He did not allow his gaze to linger on her perfectly shaped breasts but continued his examination of the rest of her body. Numerous scars that appeared to have been caused by the lash of a whip marred the skin of her thighs and lower legs. As gently as he could, he rolled her limp, unresisting body over to lay her on her stomach. Pushing her long, soft hair out of the way, he continued his examination. Her back, buttocks, and legs were covered in welts. Scars new and old crisscrossed her pale skin. The pain she had endured overwhelmed him.

"Your father beat you repeatedly, did he not?"

"Aye." A sob broke her whisper.

Alaric swallowed and pulled the covers up to her shoulders. His hands lingered briefly on her back before he drew away from her. Setting aside his pity for her and his anger at her father, he marshaled his concentration on the danger facing them. "Tell me again what Cardel has planned."

She rolled over onto her back, all the while keeping the bedding pulled to her shoulders. Alaric stared into Helena's brown eyes as she repeated the conversation she had overheard, feeling a reluctant admiration for her grit and her grasp of military tactics. When he focused on her intelligent eyes, he could almost forget the ruin of her face.

He heard her out in silence, then pushed the bedding out of his way and got off the mattress. Crossing the room to his armoire, he yanked out a clean pair of breeches and a tunic. He glanced back at the bed and saw her lying still, her eyes closed.

"Get dressed, Helena." Alaric had tried to keep his tone soft and unthreatening, but the sound of his voice caused her to jerk all the same. Sitting on a chair, he pulled on his hose and boots. When he finished, he stood and looked at her frozen next to the bed, covered in her white linen chemise, her arms crossed over her chest. Her head was bent, and her long, brown hair shielded her face.

Striding to the wall separating his bedchamber from his mother's, Alaric pulled aside the tapestry lining the wall to reveal the door. He knocked softly twice, paused, and then knocked again, repeating the distinctive pattern until the door opened. Margaret's ebony hair was loose, hanging around her shoulders and down her back, but she was still dressed in the gown she had worn for the wedding.

"Alaric, what is it? What is wrong?"

"Mother, come in. Helena told me her father plans to invade Merclif. I want the two of you to stay here together while I command the castle defenses. Bar both doors after me and do not open them for anyone other than myself. Understand?"

"Aye." Margaret placed her hand on his arm. "Alaric, take care."

He glanced down at her and grinned as he patted her hand. "Do not worry, Mother. I mean to finally finish Cardel, once and for all."

Sweeping through the connecting door, he closed it securely behind him. Alaric grabbed a black wool cloak from his mother's armoire and slung it over his shoulders, pulling up the hood to cover his head. Since his mother was tall for a woman, only a few inches of his breeches showed under the hem of the cloak.

He cautiously opened the outer door of his mother's bedchamber. A glance showed no one in the gallery, so he swiftly slipped out the door. Holding the sides of the hood close to his face, he walked quietly downstairs. The revelries continued in the hall, so no one paid any attention to him as he kept his head down and walked around the perimeter of the hall to the outside door. He glanced furtively around but did not see Gerald or any of his men.

Once outside the donjon, Alaric threw off the hood and sprinted for the armory, where he found Belwick, Bernard, Gordon, and two squires. The young men were helping the older knights suit up for battle by fitting them with their mail hauberks and iron helmets.

Hugh strode over to the door to meet Alaric. "Milord, I was coming to warn you. One of our scouts has reported that Cardel's garrison is amassed about one mile south of Merclif. There are approximately five knights and thirty foot-soldiers."

"Aye," Alaric replied. "Lady Helena told me her father plans to infiltrate the castle. Where are Gerald and his men?"

"Gerald retired to his chamber shortly after you did, but his men remained in the hall."

"I did not see them when I came through the hall just now." Alaric turned to his squire, who had finished assisting Bernard and now lingered nearby. "Jessup, get my armor ready."

"Aye, milord." The squire bowed and left their side.

"William," the castellan ordered in a loud voice, "go find Sir Roger and ask him where Lord Gerald and his men are, then report back here."

"Aye, Sir Hugh." The other squire left the armory.

"Hugh." Alaric spoke in a low voice so the others in the room would not hear. "Cardel's plan is to have his inside men eliminate the guards and then open the postern gate for his troops. We need to lure Cardel's forces inside the castle walls where we can ambush them so we cannot warn our guards what to expect. We need to let Cardel's men seize the battlements. I want you to reduce the number of guards on the crenellations to two only."

His gut twisted at the realization he was condemning the men to certain death, but he could see no other course of action. If he withdrew all the guards from the battlements, Cardel's men were sure to become suspicious. The sacrifice of the two guards was necessary for the survival of all at Merclif. Alaric stared into Hugh's eyes as his castellan nodded his understanding and acceptance.

"Station the rest of the men inside the turrets on the inner wall so we can trap Cardel's men once they enter the bailey."

"Aye, milord," Hugh responded. "I will go now and round up the rest of the men."

"Send for Lord Wyham and ask him to join me here. He must be a witness to Cardel's treachery."

"Aye, milord." Belwick left the armory.

Alaric joined Jessup, who held his padded aketon ready. After pulling the thick, quilted under tunic over Alaric's head, his squire pulled it down and adjusted the sleeves. Alaric accepted his padded coif from Jessup and fitted it onto his head, covering his ears with the flaps and tying the strings beneath his chin. Next came the chain mail hauberk that had sleeves to his elbows and fell to his knees, with a slit in the front and the back to allow him to move and to mount his horse. The squire took a long strip of leather, placed it around Alaric's waist, and knotted it. Pulling up some of the mail, he draped it over the belt to help distribute its weight. Then Jessup pulled the chain mail ventail attached to the hauberk over Alaric's head before raising the flap at his throat and tying it on both sides of his face to cover his neck. When his squire handed him his helmet, Alaric settled the heavy iron on his head, the brim positioned low on his forehead and the guard completely covering his nose. Last came the heavy leather gauntlets that Jessup held while Alaric slipped his hands inside.

Suited for battle, Alaric turned to look at Bernard. The knight's prominent chin was about all he could see of the man's face beneath his mail coif, until Gordon pulled up the older man's ventail and tied it. When Bernard turned toward him, Alaric returned the knight's determined look, glad to have the experienced man with him in this fight.

William returned with the news that Cardel's men were bedding down in the hall, along with the Merclif retainers. As far as anyone knew, Gerald was still secluded in his chamber. When Wyham arrived, Alaric took him to the top of the southwest turret in the interior wall, which offered the best vantage point of the river and surrounding countryside, as well as the castle grounds. After informing the king's emissary about Helena's revelations, Alaric hunkered down and waited.

Darkness was complete, punctured only by the pale light of the waning moon as it played hide and seek with the clouds. The stillness was pierced by one sharp cry, quickly muffled, and a faint scuffle. Then stark quiet descended. Alaric clenched his jaw and stared resolutely at the crenellations on the inner wall. The two Merclif guards had been taken down, and now three of the enemy took their place.

Alaric and Wyham watched as a lone man slipped out the postern gate, scrambled down the side of the castle mound, and dropped into the river. After swimming across the wide expanse of water, he reached the far bank and ran for a coppice a short distance away. Within a few minutes he reemerged riding a horse and galloped off to the southwest.

About half an hour later Alaric saw Cardel and his men approach the castle, where they dismounted under the cover of the surrounding woods. A shrill birdlike call originating from the allure split the silence. At that signal the invaders crept across the meadow, slid into the river, and swam to the castle mound. After entering the castle grounds through the postern gate, they amassed in the outer bailey, between the two curtain walls.

As soon as Cardel's men deserted the crenellations on top of the inner wall to join the rest of their troops in the outer bailey, Alaric left Wyham. He crept down the turret stairs and met Hugh at the bottom, just inside the inner bailey.

"'Tis time. Alert the men stationed in the gates."

"Aye, milord."

Hugh dispatched one man to the northwest gate and one to the southeast gate. Alaric waited with the majority of his garrison at the southwest gate, his back pressed against the cold stone wall, his sword held loosely in front of him in his right hand and the strap of his shield secured around his left forearm. Waiting, he held firm while his enemies slipped into the inner bailey one by one. Keeping a careful rein on his aggression until the majority of the attackers appeared to be inside, Alaric then rushed forward and yelled his battle cry. "Defend Merclif!"

Alaric swung his broad sword, slicing through the neck of one of the invaders. The splatter of warm blood hit his cheek as the man's body collapsed. He raised his sword again and slashed into the flesh of another infiltrator. All around him Alaric heard the grunts of the warriors as they attacked and the cries of the defeated as they died.

Seeing his men had the situation well in hand, Alaric ran through the gate into the outer bailey. The rest of his troops had swept from the other two gates into the outer ward and were relentlessly engaging the enemy. Soon the attackers were dead, wounded, or had surrendered. Merclif's victory was swift and complete.

Alaric ordered his men to take the prisoners into the inner ward. He scanned the dead bodies lying in the dirt but could see from their simple armor that none were the earl or his son. When he entered the inner ward, he found Belwick and Wyham surveying the prisoners.

"Have you seen Cardel or Gerald?" Alaric demanded.

"Neither is among the dead or the prisoners, milord," Hugh responded.

"When the battle had obviously been won by Merclif," Wyham said, "I saw one man run away, out the postern gate. When he reached the forest there was another man waiting for him with a horse. They both galloped away."

"Hugh, get a contingent of twenty men ready to ride without delay."

"Aye, milord." Belwick hurried away, shouting orders as he went.

Alaric turned back to the king's emissary. "Wyham, there can be no question of Cardel's treachery now."

"Aye. These men do not wear Cardel's colors, but I recognize two of the men who remained at Merclif with Lord Gerald."

"I am going to pursue Cardel, and if I find them, I will kill both the earl and his son."

The courtier nodded. "Aye, you are quite within your right to do so, Merclif. I will so inform King Henry when I report to him. Godspeed."

Alaric nodded and strode to where his men were gathering in the outer bailey. He mounted Geneir and led the charge from the castle.

As the first rose streaks of dawn bathed the Mersted Valley with soft light, he spotted Cardel and Gerald ahead, riding with a small group of horsemen.

After signaling his men, Alaric kicked his horse into a full gallop, giving chase. As Merclif's troops gained on them, Cardel's men turned around to engage their pursuers, their swords at the ready. Alaric rapidly assessed this diversion meant to allow Cardel and his son to escape, then shouted orders to his men.

With Bernard and two other soldiers, Alaric circled around Cardel's troops as they engaged the bulk of his men and continued in pursuit of the earl. Horses' hooves thundered over the hard-packed ground as the biting cold air slapped his cheeks, left bare by his ventail. Alaric ignored the stinging of his eyes as sweat dripped down into them and the chafing of his nose from the iron guard of his helmet. As if in unison, the cloud of his warm exhalation mingled with that of the horse laboring under him as Geneir's breath spewed from his nostrils.

Gerald's horse suddenly stumbled, throwing him to the ground. Cardel looked back once but then galloped on, ignoring Gerald's shouts for help. Alaric ordered Bernard and the other men to capture Gerald, then kicked his horse's flank, trying to wring every last bit of speed out of Geneir. The distance between him and his quarry shrunk under Alaric's relentless chase, but he was forced to turn back by the hail of arrows that fell between him and his prey. Alaric pulled up a safe distance from the archers on the battlements and watched in frustration as the earl safely entered his castle. Cursing loudly and furiously, he wheeled his horse around and raced back to where Gerald had fallen. He found his men surrounding their enemy, came to a halt, and dismounted.

"Gerald, you have a choice," Alaric said as he walked toward his prisoner. "I can either take you captive, or we can settle this now between the two of us. If you defeat me, my men will let you go."

"How can I trust you?" Gerald snarled. "Your men will slay me if I kill you."

"Unlike you and your father, my men keep their word," Alaric stated. "The choice is yours: humiliation or honorable battle."

"Give me my sword," Gerald demanded, holding out his hand.

At Alaric's nod, Bernard picked up Gerald's discarded shield and handed it to him. Retrieving the sword from the scabbard Gerald had surrendered, the knight handed it hilt first to Gerald. Bernard then directed the other men to pull back, giving the combatants room.

Alaric drew his sword and eased into a fighting stance, intently watching Gerald's every move. Gerald slashed his sword at Alaric, and Alaric raised his shield to deflect the blow and turn it aside. Alaric went on the attack, cutting Gerald's right arm, gouging his chest and slicing his left thigh. Gerald retreated under Alaric's relentless onslaught, finally going down to his knees when Alaric's vicious blow cut into his sword hand, causing Gerald to drop his blade. Alaric stood over Gerald, the point of his weapon pressed against Gerald's neck.

"Do you yield?" Alaric demanded as he kicked Gerald's sword away.

"Get it over with, Merclif," Gerald said.

"I do not kill unarmed men in cold blood. Bernard, Geoffrey, tie him up and put him on his horse."

Alaric lowered his blade and stepped back. Gerald suddenly rolled, grabbing his sword with his uninjured left hand, and sprang to his feet. Gerald threw his blade at Alaric's chest, and Alaric leaped to the side as the weapon narrowly flew past him to land in the dirt to his left. Gerald continued his forward momentum and instinctively Alaric raised his sword as Gerald lunged toward him. His blade plunged through Gerald's mail hauberk, piercing his enemy's heart.

6

Helena jerked awake, her mind cloaked in impenetrable wool. Where was she? The continued knocking on the door was rhythmic and incessant. Her neck and shoulders ached from the awkward position in which she had fallen asleep. Her eyes were dry and rough, as if someone had rubbed them with a pumice stone. Dragging herself upright on the mattress to a sitting position, she saw Margaret hurrying to the door. The distinctive knocking pattern repeated as Margaret paused, her hand on the latch.

"Alaric?" she called.

"Aye, Mother," he replied. "'Tis safe now. Let me in."

Margaret raised the bar and opened the door. As soon as Merclif entered the chamber, Margaret grabbed him in a close embrace. He briefly tightened his arms around his mother, then pulled back from her.

"Alaric, you are covered in blood!" Margaret held onto his arms as she examined his face and body.

"'Tis not my blood, Mother. I am fine."

"God be praised," she said as she released him. "Alaric, what happened?"

Merclif swept into the chamber, coming to a stop at the foot of the bed. His handsome face was splattered with blood and dirt. Wet with sweat, his black hair was matted to his scalp. The smell of his sweat and the filth staining his tunic and breeches assaulted Helena's nostrils. As the full force of his brilliant blue eyes speared her, she slowly rose from the mattress and stood before him, her arms wrapped around her waist. Trembling, she caught her lower lip between her teeth as she waited for her husband to speak.

"I have killed Lord Gerald," he stated, his eyes never leaving hers. "The earl escaped."

Helena bowed her head as Merclif's words sank into her consciousness. Gerald had tormented her almost as much as their father had abused her. She felt no grief that her brother was dead, only a sense of relief.

"Mother, I will give a full report to you and Wyham later, after I have eaten."

"Aye," Margaret agreed. "I am most anxious to know what has transpired. Tell me now, how did our men fare in the battle?"

"Two are dead. Several of the men have injuries, but none are life-threatening. Hugh has the situation well in hand, so you will not be needed to doctor them."

"Nonetheless, I will check on the wounded men myself."

"As you wish, Mother. Now, I need a bath. Renwold will see it brought here before long. Mother, please take Helena to your chamber. I will see you in the solar after I break my fast."

"As you wish, my dear."

Helena continued to stare at the floor as if in a stupor. She and Margaret had been awake most of the night waiting for news of the battle. Sleep had finally ambushed her in the early morning hours, but she felt now as if lead ran through her veins and an iron hammer pounded against her temples. Startled, Helena twitched when Margaret slid her arm around her waist.

"Come with me, Helena. Let us refresh ourselves before we break our fast. We will both feel better after we have something to eat."

Margaret guided her through the door between the two chambers.

Following Margaret into the solar, Helena glanced at Merclif, who was standing with Lord Wyham near the warmth of the brazier, but averted her eyes when she encountered his gaze upon her. Alaric so dominated the room with his power and his masculinity that he stole her wits. Margaret sat on the settle and gestured for Helena to sit beside her. Helena kept her head bent and stared at her hands clenched so tightly together in her lap that her fingers were mottled red and white.

Alaric's dispassionate words describing the battle for Merclif, his pursuit of her father and brother, and his slaying of Gerald chipped away at her composure. Helena listened intently to his words, but her anxiety about her own situation hung over her, tyrannizing her. What was to become of her now?

"Lord Wyham," Alaric stated when he had completed his account of the battle, "Cardel has wantonly and maliciously defied the king's order. I shall write to the king to explain what has occurred."

"Aye, Merclif," Wyham responded, his voice slow and measured. "I shall take your letter to Henry and give witness to these events myself."

"Given that Cardel has broken faith and cannot be trusted, the ends the king desired from the marriage between Lady Helena and myself are no longer possible."

Silence gaped, a crater separating her from her husband. Helena's heart beat an insistent cadence, clogging her throat and choking her.

"Helena."

Alaric's voice commanded her attention, and she looked up into his searching blue eyes. His chiseled jaw was clean-shaven; his ebony hair was still damp and hung uncovered to flirt with the tops of his shoulders. A charcoal gray tunic molded his upper body, the close-fitting sleeves displaying his muscular arms.

"If you could live anywhere in the whole of England, where would you go?"

"Bamchester." She hardly dared to breathe. Was it possible? Would she finally be allowed to go home to the only people who loved her?

"Why Bamchester?" he asked.

His voice was gentle and his eyes kind. The compassion he showed her now was unexpected and suspect. Could she trust him?

"I fostered at Bamchester Castle. Lady Dorothea is like a mother to me."

"Helena, would you like to be released from our wedding vows?"

"Aye," she whispered.

A single, fragile stain of hope rose in her soul. It did not matter what his motives were for wanting to terminate their marriage. The only thing that mattered was the chance for freedom that would result from his releasing her. She kept her eyes locked on his. He smiled slightly and nodded to her before turning his gaze to the king's emissary.

"Lady Helena should not be made to suffer for the treachery of her father, nor made a hostage because of his malevolence. As my mother can testify, the marriage between Lady Helena and myself has not been consummated. The marriage can easily be annulled, thus freeing Lady Helena from a union that is unwelcome to her."

"You will need the king's permission to set aside this marriage," Wyham responded.

"Aye, I realize that. When I write to the king, I will petition for an annulment. I will send a letter to Bamchester as well, asking the baron if he is willing to accept Lady Helena."

"And what of Lady Helena's dowry?" Wyham asked. "'Twas a hefty bag of coins that Cardel was required to turn over to you."

"Helen's dowry will go with her to Bamchester, to be used as she and the baron see fit." Merclif turned to address Margaret. "While we await the king's reply, Helena will need her own room. Mother, please prepare a bedchamber for her and see that she has everything that she requires."

Helena glanced sideways at Margaret as she sat beside her on the settle. Margaret's mouth was set in a straight line as she stared intently at her son. Helena dropped her own eyes back to her lap. Alaric's words withered in the silence and lingered like a wraith. After a taut, long moment, Margaret laid her hand on top of Helena's hands, her touch gentle and comforting.

"Come, my dear," Margaret said. "Let me show you to your new chamber."

She led Helena out of the solar and down the corridor, to a room at the end of the gallery, holding the door open for Helena. The chamber, located at the southwest corner of the donjon, was smaller than Alaric's but elegantly appointed. The bed, framed with dark blue hangings, was only large enough for one person. A stool sat next to a small table. The shutters surrounding the small window cut in the south stone wall were open, letting in weak winter sunlight and brisk, cold air.

"Helena, tell me about Lady Dorothea," Margaret said. "'Tis obvious you are very fond of her."

"Aye," Helena replied. "She was my mother's best friend. They grew up together in the same household. I was sent to foster with her when I was but four years old. After my mother died, Lady Dorothea became like a mother to me. I have not seen her since I returned to Cardel. My father would not even allow me to write to her."

"You must miss her very much."

"Aye."

"Then you must be looking forward to seeing her again. Until then, please consider Merclif your home, Helena."

"Thank you, Lady Margaret. You have been so kind and generous to me."

"'Tis no more than you deserve, my dear. Well, I will go get the servants to move your chest in here. I will be back in a few moments."

Helena stood in the center of the chamber, hugging herself with her arms crossed in front of her chest. Was it possible? Would she finally be free to return home? Hope started to push through the hard shell of anguish that had encased her heart in the last few years.

Alaric had defeated her father and now was setting her free. So what if by doing so he served his own purposes as well? She didn't care. As long as she would be reunited with Lady Dorothea, she could bear the stigma of being a wife cast aside by her husband. It did not matter. Alaric had saved her, and he was protecting her from her father. That was all that mattered.

Margaret came through the open doorway, leading two male servants who carried Helena's chest into the room. "Put it down against this wall," Margaret instructed, pointing to the west stone wall.

The men set the chest down, then left.

"Shall I send a maid to help you unpack?"

Helena shook her head.

"Helena, Is there anything else you require?"

"Nay."

"Well, my dear, I need to go now and check on our wounded. Will you be all right?"

"Aye."

"I hope you will be comfortable in this chamber. I will see you at dinner, then."

Helena waited until Margaret quit the room before closing and barring the door. Sinking to her knees in front of her trunk, she eased the lip open and dug through the meager pile of her possessions. She pulled a bulky package out of the chest and cradled it on her lap as she unwrapped the fabric surrounding it. When her lute was unveiled, she held it upright to examine the strings and the tuning pegs, then caressed the warm wood of the curved back with long, slow strokes.

She sank back on her heels and slowly released her pent-up breath. Pushing herself off the floor with her free hand, she stood and carried the instrument to the stool. She sat down, positioned the lute on her lap, and began to play. Tempering the volume, she continued employing the caution that had been sharply honed into her.

The mellow, dulcet tones of the strings as she plucked them flowed sweetly over her, cascading smoothly around her. As always, the beauty of the music sank deeply into her arid, thirsting soul. The tension around her heart eased as she gave herself up to the music and the words of the songs she sang. A tiny shoot of hope broke through the casing of despair wrapped around her soul and peered outside her despondency.

Alaric stood on the barbican, watching as Wyham led his men out the main gate and across the bridge, with his baggage train following close behind. The messenger Alaric had dispatched to Bamchester had departed an hour earlier. When Wyham and his entourage were no longer in sight, Alaric strode back through the curtain gate and walked around the right side of the outer bailey.

A sense of satisfaction filled him. He had successfully defeated Cardel, who would be weaker now without the presence of his oldest son beside him. Events had turned out far better than he could have hoped when the king had first ordered him to marry Cardel's daughter. Henry was sure to accede to his request for an annulment. What purpose could this marriage possibly serve the king now? Both he and Helena would be better off unchained from each other. She would be able to live with the people she knew and loved, and he would be able to marry a woman of his own choosing.

Alaric raised his hand to acknowledge the greeting of one of the grooms but did not break his stride as he continued past the stables to the mews beyond. Inside the aviary, two walls of the building were covered floor to ceiling with compartments of various sizes. Perched inside most of the cubicles were the numerous peregrines, sakers, lanners, merlins, goshawks, and sparrowhawks kept at Merclif. The muted cacophony of the birds as they called to each other and the fluttering of their feathers as they flexed their wings permeated the mews. The faint smell of blood in the air told him that he had arrived at feeding time.

"G'day, milord," the falconer said. "I didn't expect to see ye here today."

"Good morrow, Denners." Alaric walked to stand in front of Gaenor's perch.

"She's been fed, milord, so I was just gettin' her bath ready." Denners came to stand beside him. "Milord, would ye like to fetch her yerself?"

"Aye. That I would."

Alaric put on the heavy leather glove Denners handed to him, pulling the long cuff up to protect his forearm. Singing to his peregrine, he coaxed Gaenor onto his left fist and began to stroke her with his right hand. He absorbed the warmth and softness of her body as he caressed the light gray and black feathers that covered her breast. The bluish tinted feathers of her back shone even in the dull winter sunlight infusing the mews. As usual, the silent communication he enjoyed with the fierce, proud falcon resonated in the deepest part of him.

A small leather hood completely covered Gaenor's eyes, leaving her hook-tipped, slate-blue beak exposed. After untying the strings knotted behind the falcon's head and pulling the hood from her using the tassel on top, he carried her to the fresh water bath the falconer had prepared. He watched Gaenor bathe and drink as he conferred with Denners about the other birds in the mews. When the peregrine signaled she was finished with her bath by shaking the water from her feathers, he motioned for her to return to his hand.

The bells tied to the bird's yellow legs jangled as Alaric carried Gaenor back to her perch, out of earshot of Denners. The bird's sweet "ee-chup" call as he stroked her head with his finger delighted him. She turned one of her brown eyes, framed with yellow rings, toward him as if needing to scrutinize him before being blinded again.

"Ah, Gaenor," he said, "you wish to be soaring free, ready to swoop down and capture your prey, do you not, my girl? Ah, I wish it too. But duty calls today, I am afraid. Tomorrow we will go hunting. I promise."

He refastened her hood and set her back on her perch. Gaenor wailed. Her long, repetitive "waaa, waaa, waaa" cry sparked an echoing chord within him.

"Tomorrow, my girl." Alaric turned away from her and left the mews.

7

〜

"Lady Helena."

The affable voice stopped her as she threaded her way through the crowded hall. Turning, she found Renwold at her elbow. The steward, to whom Margaret had introduced her yesterday, was slim and of average height. His thin lips were spread in a convivial smile, and his close-set brown eyes were cordial.

"Lord Merclif and Lady Margaret have not yet arrived, but dinner will be served shortly. Is there anything I can get for you, milady?"

"Ah, nay. I am fine."

"Please let me know if there is ever anything I can do for you, milady."

"I shall."

With a minimum of movement, Renwold bowed to her, deftly turned, and strolled away toward the servants gathered at the entrance to the kitchen. Avoiding the eyes of the two ladies standing together by one of the trestle tables, Helena kept her head down and proceeded toward the dais. As she passed a group of men on her way to the lords' table, one of them grabbed her arm and pulled her to his chest. She stared into his wild black eyes. The rage contorting his face stunned her.

"You ugly wench," he growled, shaking her hard. "You are the reason Alan is dead. Leave." He shook her forcefully again. "No one wants you here. Even the lord has kicked you out of his bed."

Paralyzed with fear, Helena could only gape at him. As he raised his hand to strike her, she cringed back from him, her free arm coming up instinctively to ward off the impending blow.

"Wulfric!"

The shout reverberated loudly in the sudden quiet of the cavernous hall. Helena turned to watch Alaric storm toward them, her stark panic held at bay by the realization that he was coming to save her. Two knights, who had entered the hall with Alaric, followed close behind him.

"Get your hands off Lady Helena now!" Alaric shouted.

Wulfric dropped her arm and stepped away from her. Helena hugged herself, trying to still the tremors of terror racking her body. Alaric reached them, grabbed Wulfric's tunic around his throat, and slammed his fist into Wulfric's face. Wulfric went down and remained prostrate on the floor, clutching his bleeding nose with both hands as Alaric stood over him.

"Pack your gear and get out," Alaric said, his eyes narrowed to slits. "If you are on the castle grounds five minutes from now, you will be tied to a post and whipped."

Wulfric scrambled from his position on the floor, ran to the door, and disappeared.

"Bernard, follow him and make sure he leaves."

"Aye, milord." One of the knights bowed and hurried from the hall.

Alaric swiveled toward the two men who had been standing next to Wulfric during the assault. "You miserable, rotten maggots. How dare you stand around while Wulfric assaults a lady?" Intense fury was evident in Alaric's voice. "Get out. You are no longer in my service."

Alaric waited as the two soldiers rushed to get away, then raked his gaze over everyone present, soldier and servant alike. "If it had not been for Lady Helena's courageous actions, all of us would have been slaughtered in our sleep. Anyone who does not treat Lady Helena with the utmost courtesy will be flogged. Do I make myself clear?" His severe voice resonated loudly in the still hall.

"Aye, milord." The other knight who had entered with Alaric spoke clearly.

Renwold suddenly appeared next to the knight and voiced the same affirmation. Following the knight and steward's example, the other soldiers present, as well as the servants, then echoed their words.

"Get back to work," Alaric ordered when the hall fell silent again. As the hushed buzz of voices and the rustling of movement sounded again, he turned to Helena. "Are you all right?"

"Aye." Helena dropped her eyes from his and bowed her head. Crossing her arms over her chest, she clutched her hands around her forearms. Violent shudders racked her body, but she was powerless to stop them.

"I am sorry you were subjected to such horrendous treatment at Merclif." Alaric's voice was soft and gentle.

"I…I want to go ba…back to my room." Helena could not keep her voice from shaking.

"I will escort you."

When he reached out to take her arm, Helena flinched away from him. Alaric pulled his hand back from her and swept his arm away, gesturing toward the stairs. She concentrated on putting one foot in front of the other as she walked across the hall, conscious of the eyes of everyone on her, the rising and falling of her chest due to her own rapid breathing, and the clatter of Alaric's boots on the stone floor as he walked beside her.

Helena climbed the stairs with leaden legs as her heart pounded, pounded, pounded in her chest. When they reached her chamber, Alaric opened the door and stood back for her to enter.

"I will send my mother to you."

"Nay." She took a deep breath. "I just want to be alone."

"As you wish."

Helena closed and barred the door. Huddling on the bed, she raised her knees and held them with both arms against her chest.

Cold. She was so cold. She could not get warm. She willed herself to shrink, to contract, to cave in upon herself. Tears streamed down her cheeks, and she bit her bottom lip to stifle her sobs. She had to be quiet. The metallic taste of her own blood, of her fear, filled her mouth.

Margaret rushed up the stairs and met Alaric halfway down the gallery. "Alaric, Elizabeth told me what happened to Helena. How is she?"

"I do not know. She said she wanted to be alone, but I have never seen anyone react quite like that before."

"I will go to her now. We will discuss this incident later."

Margaret pushed past Alaric. She knocked softly on Helena's door, then leaned her ear close to the wood to listen to any sounds inside the chamber. Not hearing anything, she tried to lift the latch but found it barred. Attempting to keep her voice gentle and unthreatening, Margaret called through the door, "Helena, 'tis Margaret. Please let me in. No one is going to hurt you again."

Silence greeted her words.

"My dear, please let me in. I only want to hold you and comfort you as your mother would do. As Lady Dorothea would do." Margaret held her breath and silently prayed as she waited.

Dear God, please prompt Helena to open the door. Help me show her how much she is loved. She is Your child, and You love her as You love all of us, with total, overwhelming, undeserved love. You love each of us with an everlasting love. You draw us to You with loving-kindness. Precious Lord, I pray that Helena may be able to comprehend with all the saints what is the breadth, and length, and depth, and height of Your love for her.

Margaret continued to pray for Helena until the door opened. Helena kept her head bowed and turned away, but Margaret still saw the younger woman's ravaged, tear-streaked face. Margaret stepped through the door, closed it, then led the girl over to the bed. After Helena lay down on the mattress, Margaret gathered the distraught woman to her breast and cradled her in her arms.

Feeling the shudders racking Helena's thin body and seeing the silent way she cried tore at Margaret's heart as she cuddled with Helena on the bed. "'Tis all right, my dear. Go ahead and cry. Let it all out. I will not let anyone hurt you, ever again."

Margaret rocked Helena in her arms, whispering words of comfort and praying silently. After a long, long time, Helena quieted and fell asleep. Margaret remained by her side as the afternoon turned to evening.

When Helena woke several hours later, Margaret left the stool she had been sitting on and sat on the bed next to Helena.

"How are you, my dear?" Margaret stroked Helena's hair, pushing it back from her face, filled with tenderness for this poor, downtrodden girl.

"I am all right," Helena said but would not meet Margaret's eyes.

"My dear, please look at me. You are safe now. Alaric will never let anyone hurt you. He will not let anything like this happen ever again."

She nodded, still not looking at Margaret.

"Helena, none of the abuse you have suffered is your fault. Only a sick, cowardly man would hurt someone smaller and weaker than himself. The shame belongs to Wulfric and to your father, not to you."

Helena raised her eyes to look at Margaret's face. "Aye."

Margaret could tell from her tentative, desultory response that Helena did not really believe her words. "It might help if you talk about what your father did to you."

"Nay." Her eyes darted away from Margaret's. "I do not want to talk about it." Clearly agitated, her voice rose in panic.

"Ssshhh, 'tis all right. You do not have to speak of it now, if you do not wish to do so. But 'tis harmful to keep something like this bottled up inside you. Whenever you are ready to talk about it, I will be here to listen. All right?"

Helena slowly nodded.

Margaret cupped Helena's face. "My dear, do you know how much you are loved? Already, I love you as a daughter. And, of course, God loves you with a love that is everlasting, ever faithful and unfailing."

"Nay, He does not. He has forsaken me."

"Helena, God never forsakes us. 'Tis we who push Him away…we who reject and rebuff Him. God is our heavenly Father, and He never abandons us."

"God abandoned me to my father. The priests tell us that He is a God of mercy. He showed no mercy to me when He allowed my father to beat me."

"I know you have endured a tremendous amount of pain, Helena. But God is not to blame for your suffering. 'Tis your father who is to blame." Margaret shook her head. "Helena, the world is a fallen and corrupt place. The earth is decaying and dying more every day. 'Tis not the paradise God originally created for us. God gave each of us free will, and that includes the freedom to do evil. But through all the suffering we endure, the Lord is always with us—to uphold and sustain us, so great is His love for us."

Margaret could tell by Helena's downcast eyes and pinched mouth that Helena did not believe her or accept her explanation. Sighing, Margaret dropped a kiss on Helena's forehead before withdrawing her hands from the younger woman's face. "We shall talk of this again another time. Now, tell me. Are you hungry?"

"Aye."

"I will go get you some food. I will be right back."

Margaret sat with Helena while she ate a light supper of cold venison pie. Then Margaret arranged a warm bath, sprinkling the water with soothing lavender, lemon balm, and passionflower. She remained with Helena until she fell asleep, then went to Alaric's solar, where she found him sitting by the warm brazier, a goblet in his hand.

"How is Helena?" Alaric stood from his chair as she entered the room. The crease between his brows and the lines around his mouth were evidence of his concern.

Wondering if he had been brooding the entire afternoon, she lightly touched his forearm. "She has calmed down and is now asleep."

"That is good. May I pour you some wine, Mother?"

"Aye, please."

Margaret dropped on to the settle. It had always been her favorite piece of furniture in the room, and she had often occupied it when she and Gavin had been closeted together in the solar. How she missed him. Resolutely shaking off her melancholy, she accepted the goblet Alaric handed her and took a sip of the wine, letting the thick, warm liquid coat her throat.

"'Tis a good thing you told me what Helena's father had done to her," Margaret said. "If you had not, I would not have known what was wrong with her. 'Tis obvious Helena has been deeply traumatized by her father's abuse. This incident with Wulfric seems to have triggered her memories of Cardel's beatings and intensified her fears."

"Aye." Alaric stared down into the goblet in his hands.

Margaret silently offered up a prayer: *Gracious Lord, help me speak to Alaric with love and gentleness.* "My dear, I fear we are partly to blame for Wulfric's conduct," she said.

Alaric looked at her but held his tongue. She knew her son, knew that he wanted to argue the point, but that he would respect her and hear her out in silence.

"Ever since the wedding I have let her shut herself away in her chamber. It has become obvious to everyone that your marriage to Helena is not a marriage at all. 'Tis no wonder Wulfric assumed you would not care if he beat her. You need to show an interest in her, and let everyone know she is under your protection."

"Aye. You are right as usual." Alaric rolled his cup slowly between his hands.

"I should take my own advice as well. From now on, I will try to draw her out and include her in the daily routine of the castle."

"That is a good idea. Wyham said that Henry likes to travel widely in his domain. It may be several weeks before he can locate the king and bring back a reply. Even if Bamchester agrees to take Helena, I cannot convey her there until I have the king's permission to annul the marriage."

Margaret took a sip of her wine, contemplating her son, love for him flooding her heart. It had been so much simpler when he was younger. Then she could just tell him what he must do. Now she could only offer her advice and hope he would seriously consider it.

"Have you considered letting your marriage to Helena stand? Even if Henry does agree to an annulment, it will take years to secure one from the Pope. And in the meantime you are left in limbo, without a wife or an heir. Alaric, I believe God has sent Helena to us for a purpose. I believe 'tis His will that she be your wife."

Alaric lifted his goblet and tossed back the remainder of his wine before answering. "She is the daughter of my enemy. I feel nothing for her but pity. I have no desire to bed her, so how would I be able to sire an heir? I do not see how a marriage between us can succeed."

"Alaric, have not your father and I taught you better than that?" Margaret sadly shook her head. "You are judging Helena by her looks and by her ancestry, neither of which she can change. You need to get to know her as a person and look beyond her scarred face."

"I will try, Mother. I will try."

Margaret looked at her only child. He had always been strong-willed, a trait that had been intensified by the duties and obligations of leadership. Alaric's need to be in control was taking him further and further away from the only One who truly had authority and dominion over his life. Until Alaric learned to submit his will to his Creator, he would be lost.

Oh, most gracious Lord, she prayed silently, *I surrender Alaric and Helena to You and Your everlasting love. Lord, I ask that Your good and perfect will be done in their lives, and in mine as well. Dear Lord, give me the discernment to see how I can help them. And give me Your peace. Amen.*

8

The next day, Helena stayed in her room the entire morning, playing her lute and thinking about what Margaret had said about God. Was it true that she had rejected God? That He had not abandoned her, but she had been the one to push Him away?

When she was a young girl, Helena remembered being delighted in God. She had loved going to mass, experiencing the elaborate symbolic rituals, and hearing that God loved her and that Jesus had saved her from her sins. Everything had changed when her father's knife slashed her face, and her faith had withered into bitterness. If her own father did not love her enough not to hurt her, then she must be unworthy of love from everyone, even from God.

Could Margaret be right? Did God love her unconditionally? Had she turned her back on God and not the other way around?

A loud knock on her door jolted her out of her reverie. She stilled the strings of the lute and waited, hoping whoever it was would go away. A second knock reverberated against the closed door.

"Helena, 'tis Alaric. I have come to escort you down to dinner."

"I am not hungry, milord."

"Helena, the longer you hide in your chamber, the harder it will be to face everyone. You have nothing to fear. I will not leave your side."

Silence stretched between them as Helena considered his words, clutching her lute protectively in her arms. He was right. She needed to face everyone with her head held high. She was not to blame for that man's barbaric behavior. Alaric would protect her, just as he had saved her yesterday.

Helena stood, carried her lute to the chest, and laid the instrument inside. Squaring her shoulders, she opened the door.

Alaric met her eyes and gave her a slight smile. He offered her his hand so she placed her hand on top of his. The touch of his skin against her fingers sent sizzles of awareness through her.

"'Tis a lovely day today," Alaric remarked as they went downstairs. "The sun is shining and 'tis not too cold. I am going to take my falcon out hunting after dinner. I do not know if we will find anything, given 'tis the middle of winter, but Gaenor can use the exercise. You are welcome to come with us, if you would like."

"Ah, nay. Thank you."

"Perhaps you will join us another time."

When they reached the table, he drew back her chair and seated her.

"Hello, Helena," Margaret said as she approached them. She leaned over and kissed Helena on both cheeks. "I hope you had a nice rest this morning."

"Aye, thank you."

After the people settled into their seats, the priest said grace and the meal began. Helena held herself rigid and erect in her chair, hating being exposed to so many strangers. When Alaric touched her arm lightly, she flinched, and he immediately removed his hand from her.

"Would you care for some pork and apple pie?" Alaric asked. "Cook's pies are especially good."

"Aye, thank you. A small portion, please." Her stomach seemed permanently cinched and manacled.

"Helena," Margaret said, "Elizabeth and Clare will be joining me after dinner in the ladies' solar. We often gather there to work on our sewing and needlework. There always seems to be so much that needs to be done."

"Uh-huh," Helena muttered, staring at the food on her trencher.

"I would like you to join us. I have some lovely fabric that I think would make very becoming kirtles for you."

Helena thought about her two old gowns—the black one she had been married in and the gray one she wore today. "Thank you for your kindness, Lady Margaret," Helena replied when she had subdued her shame. "'Tis not necessary for you to go to the trouble and expense of making new kirtles for me, since I will be returning to Bamchester soon."

"Nonsense, my dear," Margaret stated. "A lady can always use new clothes. I insist. We will start on the new kirtles this afternoon."

"As you wish, milady," Helena conceded.

When the meal finished, Margaret immediately drew her upstairs to the solar, not allowing her to escape back to her chamber, as she wanted to do. Lady Elizabeth and Lady Clare joined them shortly afterwards. Margaret had introduced her to the other ladies the day after the wedding, but Helena had not spent any time with them.

Elizabeth, like Margaret was tall, but unlike Margaret's willowy beauty, her frame was more full-figured and robust. Her square face, resolute chin, and broad shoulders gave her a solid air of competence. About Margaret's age, with blue-green eyes under light brown eyebrows, Elizabeth was attractive in a sensible, down-to-earth way.

Helena judged Clare to be somewhere between Margaret and Elizabeth's age and her own. About her height, Clare had an ample figure that most men would term *buxom*. Whenever Helena had seen her she always seemed to be merry and cheerful.

"My dear," Margaret said, going to a chest at the side of the room, "I have a pretty moss green wool that I think will look lovely with your complexion." Margaret sorted through the fabric in the trunk until she located it. She shook out the wool and held it up to Helena's shoulders. "Clare, what do you think?"

"Aye, Margaret." Clare studied Helena. "You are quite right. That shade of green goes very well with Lady Helena's beautiful brown eyes and ivory skin."

"I know just the style for that wool," Elizabeth added. "I personally like tighter and shorter sleeves than is fashionable, Lady Helena. I find those long full sleeves just get in the way. What would you say to having sleeves like mine?" She held out her arms for Helena's inspection.

"'Twould be fine," Helena said, willing to go along with whatever these women decided.

"The bodice of the gown should be fairly tight, and the skirt nice and full," Elizabeth continued, "'Tis the newest fashion, according to my sister. She recently attended the king's coronation and all the elegant ladies of the court were wearing that style."

"'Twill be so much fun to make a gown in the latest design," Margaret commented.

"I think we should add a band of fur around the neck and the hem," Elizabeth suggested.

"That is an excellent idea, Elizabeth." Clare smiled, causing dimples to form in her plump cheeks. "A deep, warm brown will look particularly good with the green wool."

"I have just the thing," Margaret announced, going over to another chest. After a few minutes of searching, she pulled out a length of brown fur. "Alaric brought back this bear pelt after one of his hunts last spring. 'Twas from a young cub, so the fur is very soft and smooth." She offered it to Helena for her to feel.

"Aye, 'tis very soft," Helena agreed as she stroked the fur.

"'Tis perfect." Clare took the fur from Helena and placed it against the green wool. "An ivory linen chemise will look really good under this kirtle. Margaret, do you still have some of that linen we wove in the fall?"

"I believe so." Margaret returned to the first chest. "Here it is." She pulled out a length of fine ivory linen, shook it out, and held it up to Helena's neck, letting the fabric fall to the floor. "I think there should be enough left to make a chemise."

"It looks like there is plenty," Elizabeth agreed.

"Now, what shall we use for the next kirtle?" Margaret pivoted back to the chest and started to go through the material again.

"Lady Margaret," Helena objected, "one gown is more than enough."

"Helena, you need at least three or four new kirtles." Margaret pulled a piece of tawny wool out of the chest. "Clare, what think you of this for Helena?"

"Hmm." Clare took the fabric and held it up to Helena's face. "Aye, I think 'twill be an excellent color for her."

"Lady Helena, do you sew much?" Elizabeth asked as she laid out the moss wool on a table and began to cut it with shears.

"Please, Lady Elizabeth, just call me Helena."

Elizabeth glanced up at her with a smile. "Thank you, Helena, I shall, but only if you call me Elizabeth."

"Aye," Clare said. "Lady this and Lady that gets to be a bit much after a while."

The others laughed.

"Right you are, Clare." Margaret continued to sort through the fabric in the chest.

"Ah, I have adequate skill with a needle," Helena replied to Elizabeth's question.

"Than we will have you concentrate on sewing the seams, if that is all right with you?" Elizabeth responded.

"Aye."

"Margaret and Clare are expert embroiderers. I am good at creating patterns, even if I do say so myself."

"Aye, Helena." Margaret stood, holding a piece of reddish brown wool. "Elizabeth has excellent fashion sense. I am very grateful that she agreed to come to Merclif with me when I married Gavin."

"I am glad also since 'tis here that I met and married the love of my life."

Helena had never known any woman who had made a love match and was curious as to the relationship between Elizabeth and her husband but too shy to ask any personal questions.

"Aye." Margaret smiled at Elizabeth. "I was so very pleased when you fell in love with Hugh, not only for your sake, but for my own as well. 'Tis then I knew that you would remain with me at Merclif."

"Dearest Margaret, how could I ever leave you?" Elizabeth turned to Helena. "Margaret and I have been the best of friends since we were four years old."

"'Tis true," Margaret responded. "We have been closer than sisters born and bred. Now, Clare, how about this russet?"

Clare took the wool from Margaret. "Aye, 'twill make an attractive kirtle for everyday use. Margaret, do you still have that gold silk? That would be stunning on Helena."

"Oh, Clare, you are right. 'Twould be extraordinary on Helena, with her coloring."

Margaret crossed to another chest, opened it, and carefully pulled out the material. Helena followed Clare over to the chest and stood still as the beautiful silk was draped around her shoulders. With reverence, she fingered the luxurious fabric and looked up into Margaret's smiling face. She had to blink rapidly to still the tears that threatened.

"Nay, milady. 'Tis much too fine."

"I have had this silk for years now and never made use of it, since it did not flatter any of us. But on you, 'tis absolutely gorgeous."

"Aye, 'tis perfect," Clare stated.

"You might as well give in," Elizabeth said as she approached. "Margaret always gets her way."

"Aye, I do," Margaret agreed.

"I…I do not know how to thank you, milady."

"You can thank me by wearing this kirtle and by calling me Margaret."

"Thank you, Margaret." Helena's smile was tremulous.

Alaric turned from the huge fireplace, where he was talking with Hugh and Bernard before supper, and took a drink of ale as he observed Helena walk toward him. She followed behind his mother and her ladies. When the ladies joined the men, Clare went directly to her husband, Bernard, put her hand on his arm, and lifted her face. The seasoned knight lowered his head and kissed his wife's mouth lightly in greeting. Although Alaric was used to the open, natural affection the couple displayed, he could tell from Helena's stare that she was not. When she looked away from Clare and Bernard, her eyes collided with his. He maintained eye contact with her for a few seconds, watching her face as a blush infused her cheeks, before she lowered her eyes.

"I hope you had a pleasant afternoon, Helena," Alaric said.

"Aye."

"'Twas quite productive," Margaret said as she stood beside them. "We decided on four new kirtles for Helena and have started to sew one of them. How did your hunt go, Alaric?"

"We killed two deer, so that should keep us in meat for a few days."

"Excellent," Margaret replied. "I really enjoy Cook's roast venison, which we will no doubt have tomorrow for dinner."

Renwold came up to them and bowed. "Forgive me for interrupting, milord, miladies, but might I have a word with you, Lady Margaret?"

"Of course. Pray excuse me, children." She and Renwold walked away.

"Milord," Helena murmured.

Her voice was so soft that Alaric had to lean closer to hear her.

"I am afraid that my father will try to attack Merclif again. He is determined to capture your castle and very tenacious in pursuing his goals."

"You do not need to be concerned, Helena," Alaric answered as he straightened. "Merclif is almost impenetrable. It has never been captured in its fifty-year history."

"My father will not fight openly and honorably. He will use trickery, guile, and deceit."

"Aye, I am well aware of his methods and am constantly on guard against them. You will be safe here as long as you remain under my protection."

"Thank you, milord."

When she fell silent, Alaric racked his brain for another topic of conversation, well aware that this was only the second time she had voluntarily spoken to him—both times to warn him of her father's treachery. What did he usually talk to women about?

He suddenly realized he rarely had conversations with women, except for his mother. Though he had always received plenty of attention from the opposite sex, most of them had been avidly interested in either bedding him or snaring him as a husband. Never before had a woman actively avoided him. He knew only warfare and hunting, not subjects that usually appealed to ladies. Feeling completely at a loss, something to which he was not accustomed, Alaric drained his cup.

"Helena, you are in for a treat tonight," Margaret explained after supper as she settled into a chair by the fireplace. "We have a gifted jongleur here to entertain us. His name is Maximilian, and he has visited Merclif many times. We are always pleased when he entertains us."

Margaret gave a signal and a slim young man stepped into the middle of the floor. A hush fell over the hall as Maximilian began to strum his mandolin and started to sing a well-known song about King Arthur's court.

As the singing continued, Alaric found his gaze straying more and more often to Helena. The look of rapture on her face as she listened was a revelation to him. He had never seen anyone become engrossed in music the way she did. The undamaged side of her face became almost pretty, and the scarred side lost its power to repel. He was disappointed when Maximilian finished performing, because the glow that had suffused Helena's face dissipated.

Margaret graciously thanked Maximilian for his performance and introduced him to Helena. "I hope you will be able to stay with us for a while," Margaret told the jongleur.

"Aye, milady." Maximilian smiled broadly and gave Margaret a polished bow. "If it pleases ye, I can stay the rest of the week. I've several new songs to share with ye."

"That would be lovely. I am sure everyone is greatly looking forward to hearing them."

When the musician left them, Margaret turned to Helena. "My dear, it has been a long day. Are you ready to retire to bed?"

"Aye, Margaret, I am."

"Alaric, would you escort Helena to her chamber?"

"Aye, Mother."

Margaret lightly kissed Helena on both cheeks before doing the same to Alaric. After his mother left them, he offered his hand to Helena and led her upstairs, barely feeling the featherweight of her fingers as they perched on top of his closed fist. As they walked along the gallery he broke the silence.

"You appeared to enjoy the singing."

"Aye."

"When I came to your room earlier today, I heard the sound of a lute. Were you playing?"

"Aye."

"Perhaps you will honor us by performing for us one evening." Alaric came to a stop in front of her door.

"Perhaps," she murmured.

"I would enjoy it very much if you would play for us some time. I am sure that Mother and the others would enjoy your music, as well."

Helena did not respond and did not look at him. Pressuring her was not the way to win her trust. In the face of her obvious reluctance, he dropped the subject and opened the door to her chamber.

"Sleep well, Helena."

Helena stepped inside and shut the door behind her. Alaric heard her lower the bar to secure the door before he turned and strode away.

9

"**A**laric, you should take Helena for a walk on the crenellations," Margaret suggested. "'Tis such a pleasant day today."

"Aye, Mother." He set his goblet on the table and faced her. "Helena, if you are finished with dinner, we can go now."

"Milord, 'tis not necessary for you to take me for a walk. I am sure you have much you need to do."

"Nothing that cannot wait."

"There is a spectacular view from the allure, Helena," Margaret said. "You will enjoy the exercise and fresh air. 'Tis not good for you to be cooped up inside all the time."

Helena hesitated. "If you are sure…"

Alaric stood and pulled back her chair before doing the same for his mother.

Margaret gave her a kiss on each cheek, then signaled to a servant, who brought a dark brown cloak. "'Twill be fairly cold up there, so here is a warm mantle for you to use." She draped it around Helena's shoulders. "Enjoy yourselves, children."

As Margaret walked away, Alaric held out his hand to Helena with a direct look. She lifted her chin and placed her hand on his. They did not speak as he led her through the noisy hall. Once outside in the pale sunlight, Alaric released her hand and walked beside her across the inner bailey. She lifted her face to the breeze and took a deep breath. The warm smell of burning wood mixed with the cool sharp air tingled her nose.

As they strolled, Helena looked around with interest. This was the first time she had been outside the donjon since their wedding, and she had not noticed much of anything that day. The ward was a hive of activity. Along the stone wall she saw a series of wooden buildings where men were diligently working. The powerful blacksmith had a roaring fire going, and she could hear the clang of his hammer as he pounded glowing iron into shape. Next was the agile cooper assembling staves inside a metal hoop that served as an assembly jig for the barrels he constructed. Then came the dexterous cordwainer, sitting with a board upon his lap, using a knife to cut leather into patterns for shoes. Two servants carried buckets from the well in the center of the bailey back toward the donjon.

Alaric led her out of the southwest gate, through the outer bailey, and to a turret on the outer curtain wall. He stood back to let her go first, and she began to climb the steep spiral staircase inside the tower, keeping her hand against the cold stone wall to steady herself. She was glad of Alaric's comforting presence as he followed close behind her.

Once at the top, Helena felt the sting of the sharp breeze, now that they were no longer encased within the castle walls, and drew the cloak more securely about her. Alaric led her around the allure in a counterclockwise direction, nodding to each of the guards they passed. On the east side of the wall, Helena had a good view on her left of the outer bailey where she saw the stables and the mews and, on her right, the moat with the forest beyond.

They paused on the north side to observe the men training in the lists. She watched one knight gallop his horse toward the quintain and skewer the wooden dummy directly in the chest with his lance. Several pairs of men were engaged in hand-to-hand combat, using double-edged swords, axes, and spears. When Alaric resumed walking, Helena followed him around to the west side of the allure, where she could see a village in the distance, nestled close to the banks of the Mersted River.

Halting near the southwest corner, where it was relatively quiet, Alaric stood in front of one of the crenelles. His stance was relaxed with his feet firmly planted wide apart and his right hand resting flat against the stone surface of the merlon next to him. Helena stood nearby, in front of another crenelle, and studied his profile as he looked over the river. He was so handsome and virile that sometimes simply gazing at him stole her senses.

She turned her head toward the panorama spread before them. The bare branches of the trees—the brown gray oak, the silver gray hawthorn, and smooth gray beech— framed the river on both sides. In the distance, the gray green branches of the fir trees were visible. A few straggly pearl gray clouds drifted lazily overhead, blending into the pale gray sky.

Helena felt at peace for the first time in years. Even though she had only been at Merclif for a week, Margaret's affection and graciousness had transformed her. The fear that had been her constant companion was mostly absent now, and she was able to let down her guard.

"Your mother was right, milord. 'Tis a beautiful view. Thank you for bringing me here."

"You are welcome."

The silence between them was comfortable. Alaric did not seem in any hurry to leave, and Helena was enjoying the brisk air and the view too much to suggest doing so. She soaked in the serenity of their surroundings. After a while, she asked the question that had been foremost on her mind for the last few days.

"Milord, when do you think we can expect a reply from Bamchester?"

"It should take the messenger two days to ride to Bamchester. I gave him leave to spend one day there while he awaits the baron's reply. Then two days back. So, if the weather remains clear, he should be back the day after tomorrow."

"Thank you, milord."

Alaric shifted his position to rest his shoulder against the merlon. Aware of his gaze, she swiveled toward him. Tendrils of hair had escaped from her braids under her veil and gently whipped around her face as if the wind were caressing her. He smiled at her.

Helena's heart contracted at his smile—the first unrestrained smile she had ever seen on his stunningly handsome face. His brilliant blue eyes mesmerized her. The yearning that engulfed her was overwhelming. If only she were unscathed, and he was her husband in truth.

Tearing her eyes from his, she stared out over the river, afraid her desires were plainly visible. She did not want his pity, the only emotion he could possibly feel for her. She would rather be completely alone than be the object of anyone's pity. Wrapping her arms around her waist, she hugged herself.

"You must be cold," he said. "We should go in now. I need to join my men in the lists."

A tense silence loomed between them as he led her off the battlements and back to the donjon. He escorted her upstairs and opened her chamber door.

Helena hovered in the open doorway. "Milord, thank you again for the walk."

"'Twas my pleasure." Alaric inclined his head, then turned and walked away.

Closing the door, Helena sighed. She picked up her lute, sat down, and plucked the strings. As she sang a familiar love song by rote, she chastised herself for overreacting. Alaric was only trying to be friendly. He meant nothing by his smile. He must be disgusted with her standoffishness.

She would leave here soon, but in the meantime she owed Margaret and Alaric for their consideration and kindness. She no longer feared they would send her back to Cardel or that they would cause her any harm. They had proven themselves to be caring, honest, and honorable. In the time that she had left at Merclif, she would do all that she could to reciprocate their friendship.

A while later a knock sounded on her door. Helena put a shaking hand over her racing heart, drawing deep breaths to still her thudding heart. She was no longer at Cardel. She did not have to fear punishment for playing her lute.

"Helena, 'tis Margaret. May I come in?"

"Aye, of course, Margaret." Helena stood and placed her lute on the bed.

Margaret entered and shut the door behind her, then held up for Helena's inspection the green gown she had draped over her arm. "I brought your new kirtle. Perhaps you could wear it for supper tonight."

"Oh, 'tis beautiful." Helena touched the soft brown fur at the neck of the gown. "I do not know how to thank you and Elizabeth and Clare."

"You are quite welcome," Margaret said as she laid the gown on Helena's bed next to the lute. "I heard you playing. You are very talented, my dear."

"Thank you."

"Would you be willing to play your lute and sing for us tonight?" Margaret suggested. "You play and sing so beautifully. We would very much appreciate you sharing your music with us."

Helena looked into Margaret's kind eyes. Although she shrank from the idea of performing in public and being the center of all eyes, she gathered her courage, determined to repay Margaret for her generosity. "Aye, I will play for you."

"That is wonderful. I am so glad, Helena."

An hour later, when she heard the knock on the door, Helena put her hands over her waist to still the spinning in her stomach. She rubbed her hands down the front of her gown and gave the fabric one last shake. Opening the door to Alaric, she raised her eyes to his face. "Good evening, milord."

"Good evening, Helena."

She was very conscious of his gaze as he surveyed her new attire. A simple ivory linen veil covered her head. The new moss green gown hugged her upper body before dropping into graceful folds at her feet. She had not felt this good about her appearance since she had left Bamchester.

"You look lovely this evening." He offered her his hand.

"Thank you, milord."

Placing her hand in his, she counseled herself not to put too much stock in his words. He was merely being courteous. She plucked at the fabric of the gown with her free hand as she walked beside him down the gallery.

"The kirtle your mother and the other ladies made for me is very pretty, is it not?"

"Aye, 'tis most attractive. Mother tells me you are going to play your lute for us tonight."

"Aye, milord."

"I am looking forward to it."

When they reached the great hall, Clare and Elizabeth came to greet her. She followed Alaric with her eyes as he left her side to join the men, before she brought her attention back to the women.

"Helena, you look wonderful," Elizabeth said.

"I knew that color would look most striking on you," Claire added.

"Thank you so much for this kirtle," Helena replied. "'Tis beautiful."

"'Tis only beautiful because you are wearing it, Helena." Clare's dark, warm eyes were direct and sincere.

Over supper, Helena tried to respond to Margaret and Alaric's conversation but found the prospect of her upcoming performance weighing heavily. She became more silent and withdrawn as the meal came to a close.

As the last course was removed, Alaric leaned over to her. "Helena," he murmured, "you do not have to play for us tonight if you would rather not. I am sure Mother will understand."

"'Tis all right," she said, twisting her fingers in her lap. "I need to get over my fear sometime. It might as well be now."

"Aye." He sat back in his chair. "Would you like me to fetch your lute from your chamber?"

"Nay, thank you. I would rather do it myself."

I can do this. I can do this. Helena kept up the litany in her mind as she went upstairs. When she picked up her lute, she felt the old familiar fear swamp her. She hugged the instrument close to her chest. *I can do this. I can do this.*

She left her chamber and hurried downstairs to find Alaric, Margaret, Elizabeth, Clare, and their husbands waiting in front of the fireplace. The servants had removed the supper dishes and stacked the trestle tables. People sat on the benches arranged along the perimeter of the hall, their chatter saturating the room.

"I am ready, milady," Helena stated as she stopped in front of Margaret.

"I am sure you will play brilliantly, my dear."

Margaret drew Helena toward the chair that had been placed in the center of the hall. When the crowd quieted, she made an announcement.

"Lady Helena has graciously agreed to honor us with a song. Please join me in thanking her."

There was a polite round of applause as Helena sat down and arranged her instrument on her lap. Then silence descended. She raised her eyes from the lute strings and looked directly at Alaric, unconsciously seeking him in the crowd. Her eyes locked with his. She calmed, absorbing courage from the steady look he gave her. At his nod, she began to play. Her voice rose over the elaborate tune she plucked out on the strings as she sang one of her favorite love songs, "Scarborough Fair." Her consciousness narrowed and focused on Alaric as she played only for him.

When she finished, there was absolute stillness in the hall. She swallowed against the dross coating her throat. Alaric gave her a broad smile and started to clap loudly and deliberately. As if freed from a trance, the rest of the audience applauded her as well. The thunderous ovation rolled over her. Helena looked around in astonishment before returning her gaze to Alaric. Joy filled her heart and she smiled at him.

"Lady Helena," Margaret said when the applause had died down, "that was simply wonderful. Thank you so much for sharing your extraordinary talent with us. May I entreat you for another song?"

Helena nodded and plucked out another tune on the lute. She played like she had never played before and realized that sharing her music was not only a gift she offered to others, but that the pleasure of giving enriched her own enjoyment. It seemed like she played and sang for hours until she was exhilarated but exhausted. Finally Margaret stepped forward and, over the loud protests of the audience, drew her away from center stage. As the crowd dispersed, Helena drank deeply from the cup of ale the butler handed her.

"My dear, your performance tonight was superb." Margaret hugged Helena around the waist. "Thank you. I hope we can prevail upon you to entertain us again."

"I would like that, Margaret."

"Excellent."

Leaving her arm around Helena's waist, Margaret twisted slightly to welcome Elizabeth and Clare as the other women came to join them. Clare's cheerful face and wide smile caused an answering smile to come to Helena's lips. The warmth and acceptance she received from the other women overwhelmed Helena.

"Helena," Elizabeth said, "your voice is so pure, I felt as if I were listening to an angel sing."

"Truly, I do not think I have ever heard a more talented singer," Clair added.

"Thank you so much," Helena said. "I am so glad you enjoyed my music."

Alaric approached her and, after a few more words of praise and encouragement, the other women gradually drifted away, leaving the two of them alone together.

"You should be proud of yourself, Helena." He kept his voice quiet, only loud enough for her to hear. "You faced your fears, and you have emerged triumphant."

"Thank you, milord."

She smiled as his words sunk into the arid recesses of her soul. Was it possible that she would finally be able to throw off the shackles of her past and reclaim herself?

10

"This the worst snowstorm I can remember in the last ten years," Hugh said. Holding his hands out to the fire, he rubbed them briskly together. "I have instructed the guards to switch shifts every hour. We do not want them to get frostbite."

"Aye. Just so," Alaric replied.

"Milord." Renwold, the steward, approached the fireplace, a deep furrow between his close-set eyes.

"Aye, Renwold. What is it?"

"The last of the villagers have left the castle. With your permission, milord, I will instruct Cook to serve just soup and bread for supper tonight. 'Twill be too difficult for the remaining servants to prepare a more elaborate meal than that."

"That is fine, Renwold. 'Twill also help conserve our food supplies in case the storm lasts for more than a day. Have the butler keep a tight rein on the ale and wine today. We do not want the men to overindulge."

"Aye, milord. I shall do so."

"That will be all for now, Renwold. Let me know if there are any problems."

"Aye, milord." The steward bowed and left.

Alaric turned back to the castellan. "Hugh, keep a close watch on the men. With nothing for them to do today but gamble and drink some altercations may break out."

Hugh turned from the fire, bringing his right hand up to his mouth, stroking his gray beard with his forefinger on one side of his lips and his thumb on the other. "Aye. The men hate to be cooped up inside. I just hope the weather clears tomorrow."

Alaric nodded. With his back to the fire, its warmth roasting his backside while his front remained raw, he surveyed the hall. Most of the knights and soldiers sat in groups at the trestle tables throwing dice. The cacophony of their voices as they hollered when they won or groaned when they lost filled the hall. A few men lounged on their pallets on the floor. Bernard sat at a separate table with his son, Nicholas, both of them absorbed in the game they played together. When it had become clear that the garrison had taken over the hall, the ladies had retired to their solar upstairs.

"Well," Alaric drawled, "since you have everything well in hand here, I will repair upstairs. 'Tis beyond time that I go over the accounts. Let me know if anything comes up."

"I shall do so."

On his way upstairs, Alaric ambled over to Bernard's table. When the knight became aware of his presence, Bernard looked up at him, placed both his hands on the table, and started to rise.

"Milord, did you have need of me?"

Alaric laid his hand on Bernard's shoulder to keep the man in his seat. "Nay, Bernard. I just thought to see how you are faring against your opponent. I heard tell the lad is a fierce competitor at Alquerque."

Smiling, Alaric inclined his head, pointing to Nicholas, sitting across from Bernard. The ten-year-old had inherited his father's strong jaw and his mother's dark brown eyes. His dark brown hair was messy, as if he had been raking his hands through it. The board laid out between them was marked with five horizontal and five vertical lines with intersecting diagonal lines, resulting in twenty-five points. Nicholas, playing the black pieces, had a considerable pile of captured white pieces lying in front of him.

"Aye, that he is, milord." Bernard shook his head. "I need to keep my wits about me when I play against Nicholas, that I do."

As Alaric watched, Nicholas chortled and took one of his pieces and jumped three of Bernard's white pieces, leaving his father's remaining two pieces vulnerable. Bernard had no option other than capturing two of Nicholas's black pieces, leaving his last white pieces *en prise*. Nicholas quickly captured the last white pieces on the board.

"I win! I win!" the boy crowed, holding the two captured pieces high over his head.

"Better luck next time, Bernard." Alaric slapped the knight's broad back.

"I demand a rematch, me lad." Bernard arranged the pieces back into position on the board.

"Good luck, Bernard."

"Thank you, milord. I am going to need it."

Alaric left them and went up to his solar. After placing the ledger on a table, he pulled up a chair and, resting his chin on his hand, scanned the entries, checking the calculations in his head. Although he employed a clerk to compile the accounts, he needed to periodically review them to ensure the man did not defraud him. This tedious task was something he could seldom force himself to do.

Sometime later the knock on the door jerked him out of the light doze into which he had fallen. "Come in," he called.

Glancing up from the ledger, he saw his mother enter, with Helena following close behind. Pushing back his chair, Alaric stood as the women walked toward him.

"Good afternoon, ladies. To what do I owe the pleasure of your company?"

"Alaric," Margaret said, "I told Helena how you were at loose ends with this terrible storm, and she has kindly offered to play chess with you to help alleviate your boredom."

Alaric shot his mother a look, only to encounter her wide eyes and pleasant expression. Knowing he had been securely trapped, he gazed at Helena. She stood slightly behind his mother, her hands twisting into the light brown fabric of her kirtle.

"That is indeed kind of you, Helena."

"I will leave you two alone, then." Margaret cast a benign smile at each of them before leaving the solar and closing the door behind her.

"Milord, you do not really want to play chess, do you?" Helena gestured at the paperwork spread on the table between. "I can leave, if you are busy."

Alaric studied her uncertain face and gave her an encouraging smile. Margaret's efforts to throw the two of them together had been getting more and more blatant lately, and obviously Helena was being made as uncomfortable by them as he was.

Making a swift decision, Alaric closed the ledger with a snap. "Actually, a game of chess sounds like a good idea right now. 'Twill be much more enjoyable than going over the accounts."

"If you are sure, milord?"

"I am."

Picking up the ledger from the table, he carried it over to a chest stationed along the wall and left it on top. He grabbed a chair and carried it to the unoccupied side of the table he had been using.

"Please have a seat, Helena, and I will get the chessboard." He placed the board on the table between them, along with a small case. Sitting down, he opened the box and turned it toward her. "You take the white pieces, and I will take the black."

In silence, they set up the chessboard and began to play. Alaric, convinced he would find little challenge in the match, found his mind wandering. He examined Helena's face as she studied the board. The candlelight bathed her ivory skin in a soft glow. Over the last few days he had observed that she had been eating with a good appetite. As a consequence, her cheeks were no longer as gaunt as when she had arrived at Merclif.

She also seemed to be much more relaxed when in company. Her performances after supper had become the highlight of their evening entertainment. On more than one occasion he had been deeply moved by the power of her voice. Helena's joy when she sang animated her entire being, making him feel as if he were partaking in her happiness.

Studying her face, he realized that her scars no longer repelled him. Had he simply become accustomed to them with repeated exposure, or had his growing admiration for Helena made her disfigurement seem immaterial? Suddenly she looked up at him. He noticed for the first time that her intelligent brown eyes were flicked with specks of green and gold.

"Check and mate," she announced, moving her knight into position.

"What?" Alaric exclaimed.

They had only been playing for a few minutes; she couldn't possibly have beaten him. He sat up and carefully examined the board. Finally convinced that she had won, he conceded.

"Aye, check and mate, in truth." He looked up at her satisfied smile. "I demand a rematch."

"That will teach you not to underestimate a new opponent, milord." Her voice was light and teasing.

"Aye, indeed it will." He shook his head, giving her a rueful smile.

"You take the white pieces this time. I shall take the black."

"I promise you I will be on my guard now. You shall not find me so easy to defeat this time."

They set up the chess pieces and started a new game. Alaric marshaled all his concentration and needed all of his considerable skill as he battled her over the chessboard. As the afternoon wore on and the number of pieces on the board dwindled, neither could find a way to decisively beat the other. When Margaret returned to the solar several hours later, Alaric and Helena were still together, playing intently.

"Children," Margaret interrupted, "'Tis almost time for supper. I am afraid you will have to leave your game and resume it later."

Alaric leaned back in his chair, stretching his arms out over his head. "I do not think there is going to be any winner of this match. Helena, shall we declare it a draw?"

"Aye, milord. 'Tis a draw."

"Helena, thank you for a very pleasant afternoon." He started to pick up the few pieces remaining on the chessboard and put them into their storage box. "I enjoyed our game very much."

"I did as well, milord. Thank *you*." She gathered up the white pieces she had captured and placed them into the container.

"Who taught you how to play chess, Helena?"

"Lord Bamchester started teaching me when I was just a girl."

"You must still be playing regularly to have retained such a high level of skill." He put the remainder of chess pieces into the box and latched it.

"Aye. I often played with Father Michael, the chaplain at Cardel. He is an expert. 'Tis only in the last year that I have finally been able to beat him occasionally."

Alaric nodded. "That explains it. Perhaps you will play again with me tomorrow, if the storm continues." He stood and rounded the table to pull back her chair.

"Aye, I would like that, milord. I have missed my matches with Father Michael."

"Helena, I think 'tis high time that you called me Alaric."

"I would like that, Alaric." She offered him a shy smile.

"Milord," the falconer said as Alaric entered the mews with Gaenor on his arm. "Sir Hugh said John's returned from Bamchester. He's waitin' in the hall for ye."

"My thanks, Denners. Do you have Gaenor's food?"

"Aye, milord. Here 'tis."

Alaric accepted the mouse from the falconer and dangled the rodent by the tail in front of the bird. "Come, my beauty, and get your reward. 'Tis a good job you did today." He said proudly to Denners, "Gaenor brought down two gray herons and a swan today."

"Did she indeed, milord?" Denners replied. "A right good hunter she is."

"Aye, that she is."

Alaric took another mouse from Denners and offered it to the peregrine. After feeding Gaenor, Alaric watched the bird bathe, his thoughts drifting to Helena. If the news from Bamchester was what she hoped, she would soon leave Merclif. He recalled the chess game they had played yesterday afternoon. It had taken every bit of strategy he knew, but he had finally defeated her. He had been surprised he could spend hours with Helena in such a masculine pursuit and enjoy every moment.

When Gaenor was done bathing, he sang to her and offered her his arm. The peregrine stepped regally onto his fist and Alaric carried her back to her perch. After securing the hood over her head, he left the mews and entered the hall, where he found John sitting at a trestle table, eating.

The messenger stood on Alaric's approach. "Milord, I've the reply from Lord Bamchester for ye." He dug out a folded, sealed piece of paper from his tunic and handed it to Alaric.

"Thank you, John. I am glad to see you made it back safely. Did you encounter any problems on your journey?"

"No, milord. Not 'til the storm three days ago. I was on me way home and had ta stop at a tavern fer two days; otherwise I'd have been back sooner."

"Aye, 'twas a nasty storm. No matter. You are back now. Go ahead and finish your meal."

"Thank ye, milord."

Alaric nodded and turned away. After asking Renwold to send up some warm water, he headed upstairs. Once inside his bedchamber, he lit a candle and read the message. He was trying to determine exactly what his reaction was to the news it contained when a knock on the door announced the servant's arrival.

After washing and dressing in clean clothes, Alaric picked up the letter and headed for the ladies' solar. When he entered, he found Helena singing for his mother and the other women as they sewed. She glanced up at him and gave him a small smile as she played. He admired the way she looked in her new reddish brown kirtle. The color suited her. When she had finished singing, he advanced into the room.

"That was lovely, Helena. Thank you," Margaret said. "Alaric, you are back. Did you have a successful hunt?"

Helena put her lute down next to her chair and folded her hands in her lap. She looked up at him, her expression artless and cordial.

The news he had to impart would devastate her. Alaric brought his gaze to his mother's face. "Aye, I did," he answered. "Mother, I need to speak with you and Helena. Ladies—" he turned and addressed Elizabeth and Clare—"would you please excuse us?"

After they left, Alaric sat down facing Margaret and Helena.

"The messenger has returned from Bamchester. Helena, I am afraid there is bad news." He tried to keep his voice gentle as he addressed her, seeing how she stiffened as if bracing herself. "Lady Dorothea died of a stroke two years ago. Lord Bamchester died six months later. His son, Rupert, writes that he thinks his father died of a broken heart."

All the color drained out of Helena's face, leaving her deathly pale. Her despondent eyes seemed to burn into him. Compassion for Helena filled him.

"Rupert, the current Lord Bamchester, writes that he is newly married. He sends his regrets but says he cannot take on the responsibility for your care."

"May I see the letter?" Helena's voice was hoarse and strangled.

"You can read?" Alaric asked.

"Aye."

He handed the letter to Helena, then exchanged a glance with his mother. They were both silent as Helena read the message.

When she was done, she quietly refolded the paper and handed it back to Alaric. "Please excuse me," she said, then fled the room, leaving her lute behind.

Alaric started to rise to follow her but was stopped by his mother's outstretched hand. He sank back into his chair.

"She needs to grieve in private, Alaric. Give her some time before going to her."

"All right, if you think it best."

"I do, my dear. So, what do we do now?"

Alaric shrugged. "We wait for Wyham's return."

Several hours later Alaric knocked on Helena's door. After waiting long minutes with no answer, he knocked again.

"Helena, 'tis Alaric. I have brought your lute."

There was a lengthy silence before the door opened. Helena stood in the doorway, hair disheveled, face downcast so he could not see her eyes. Her face was blotchy, as if she had been crying. Alaric extended the instrument to her.

"Thank you." She did not meet his eyes as she accepted the lute and hugged it to her chest.

"I am very sorry for your loss, Helena."

"Thank you," she replied as she turned away.

"I will escort you down for supper."

"I am not hungry."

"You should eat something to keep up your strength."

"I could not. Thank you for bringing my lute."

She closed the door in his face. Raising his fist to knock again, he heard her begin to play a slow, solemn melody. The mournful sound sent a sharp, piercing arrow into his gut. Unable to listen any longer, Alaric lowered his hand and strode away.

11

At the beginning of February, Alaric was inside the mews training his new gyrfalcon. Gwylan's body was covered with light gray feathers. Her gray wings were liberally covered with dark brown spots, while her breast was lightly sprinkled with tan speckles. Small bells were tied around her feet to alert them to every movement she made. She was wearing a hood, even though her eyes had been temporarily sewn shut. With her keen eyesight stolen from her, Alaric trained the gyrfalcon through her senses of taste, touch, and hearing.

He carried Gwylan around the mews on his gloved fist, softly singing the chorus of a song he had heard Helena play.

"My King and my country I serve gladly,
Protecting the weak, pure justice I seek.
Courage, valor, and truth alone rule me,
Loyalty my guide, in honor my pride."

Alaric had identified with the song's lyrics from the instant he had first heard Helena sing them. Besides the fact that the words resonated deep inside him, he had selected the song to use in training Gwylan because it was completely different from the one he used with Gaenor. In that way each bird would know when he was addressing her specifically.

Loud shouting from the guards on the battlements penetrated the dappled serenity of the mews. Without hurrying, Alaric completed his circuit around the perimeter of the room before setting the gyrfalcon back on her perch with slow, deliberate movements. He threaded a leash through the swivel suspended from the jesses tied around Gwylan's legs, then fastened the leash to her wooden perch. When Gwylan was safely settled, he strode out of the mews, into the outer bailey. The guards on the outer curtain had relayed the information to each other until the guard on the east wall yelled down to him.

"Milord, there is a large troop of men approaching the castle."

"Has their banner been identified?" Alaric shouted.

"Not yet, milord."

Gwylan's training would have to wait for another day, Alaric decided as he loped toward the nearest turret, at the southeast corner of the outer wall. Rounding the side of the bailey, he saw Hugh standing with a contingent of their soldiers in front of the main gate. The castellan left the troops and strode toward Alaric.

"Milord, they appear to be displaying the king's standard," Hugh informed him.

"I want to see them for myself."

Hugh followed him as he climbed the steps inside the turret. Once on top of the crenellations, he walked rapidly toward the main gate. A large company of men and horses came to a stop on the far side of the Mersted River. One man removed his iron helmet, and Alaric immediately recognized Wyham.

"Hail, Merclif," Wyham shouted.

"Hail, Lord Wyham," Alaric yelled back.

"I bring you word from King Henry."

"I bid you welcome, milord." Alaric turned his head to the men standing beside him on the allure. "Guards, lower the bridge and raise the portcullis." The soldiers hastened away to carry out his orders.

"By my count there are ten knights and thirty men-at-arms," Hugh said.

"'Tis an overwhelming force." Alaric's eyebrows contracted together. "What can the king possibly have planned?"

"Only Lord Wyham can say for sure, milord," Hugh replied.

"'Tis true enough. Let us go and find out, then."

Alaric descended to the outer bailey and greeted Wyham.

"I have much to tell you, Merclif," Wyham said.

"Do you want to remove your armor before we repair to the solar?"

"Aye, that would be most welcome."

Hugh quickly went to work, disbanding the Merclif garrison and instructing the king's men where to stable their horses. After Wyham took off his chain mail in the armory, Alaric escorted the king's emissary into the hall and up the stairs. The men encountered Margaret and Helena on the gallery, and once they exchanged greetings with their guest, the women joined the men in lords' solar.

"I had quite a time finding the king," Wyham began. "He was traveling through Buckingham and Northhampton. I always seemed to be one step behind him. The foul winter weather also hindered my progress. I finally caught up with King Henry in Warwick. When I told him about Cardel's perfidy, he went into one of his violent rages. He ordered that the earldom be stripped from Cardel and that his castle be razed to the ground."

"That is extraordinary," Alaric remarked. "I had no expectation King Henry would do anything this drastic."

"Aye." Wyham took a sip of wine. "Henry has decided to bring the nobility to heel. Any castle granted by King Stephen, as Cardel's was, is to be torn down. Henry is making an example of Cardel. He means to ensure no other baron dares to defy him."

Alaric nodded. "This punishment will certainly get every nobleman's attention."

"Henry also decreed that Cardel's lands be given to you, Merclif," Wyham continued, "Upon the condition that your marriage to Lady Helena stand."

Alaric's intense gaze clashed with Helena's wide eyes. Studying her, he let the import of Wyham's words register. She would not have been his first choice as a bride, but he had come to know her character over the last few weeks. Helena was extremely intelligent and very talented. She would make him a fine wife and be a good mother to his children.

He nodded decisively, accepting their marriage at last. "Aye," he stated. "My marriage to Lady Helena will stand." He gave Helena a slight smile.

Helena dropped her eyes from his. She bent her head and clutched her hands together on her lap.

Margaret got up from her place on the settle, went over to Helena, and hugged her. "This is wonderful," Margaret interjected, her voice joyous. "My dear, I am so glad you will be staying with us always. You are like a daughter to me already."

"Thank you, milady."

"Merclif, since you have accepted the marriage," Wyham continued when Margaret resumed her seat, "I must inform you that Henry has charged me with ensuring the marriage is properly consummated so there can be no question later of an annulment."

"And just how do you propose to do that, milord?" Alaric inquired.

"There will be another bedding ceremony tonight, attended by Lady Margaret and myself. In the morning, both you and Lady Helena will need to swear before Lady Margaret, the priest, two other witnesses, and myself that the marriage has indeed been consummated."

"I agree to those stipulations," Alaric responded.

"Lady Helena, do you agree to these terms as well?" Wyham asked, his voice gentle.

Silence stretched as they waited for Helena's response. "Aye," she whispered. She did not raise her bent head.

"Thank you, milady." Wyham took another sip of his wine. "Merclif, Henry has also granted you the title of Earl. The title will be formally conferred upon you at Westminster Abbey later in the spring, but you may use the title, Earl of Merclif, now."

"King Henry has been extremely generous to me."

"Aye," Wyham agreed. "Henry is also making an example of you, so his nobles can see how he rewards those who are loyal to him."

"I would like to thank King Henry for his largesse. How can I do so in a fitting manner?"

"I suggest you send him a message expressing your gratitude, along with one of your finest warhorses. The king has a fondness for good horseflesh. As for a more enduring demonstration of your gratitude, believe me, from now on Henry will frequently call upon you to show your loyalty."

Alaric nodded. "Thank you for your advice, milord. I will do as you suggest." He took a drink of his wine. "I assume that the king sent the contingent of soldiers with you to evict Cardel from his castle."

"Aye, that he did. Tomorrow we will ride to Cardel with Henry's eviction proclamation. I require that you and some of your men accompany us. I also require that your forces act under my command. Although I shall explain to Cardel that it is in his best interest to leave peacefully, I do not expect him to do so."

"I expect you are correct, Wyham. All will be as you require."

Helena stared at her hands in her lap, tuning out the men's voices as they discussed their plans. She knew Alaric had no real desire for *her* as his wife. It was obvious that the only reason he had agreed to the king's conditions was the hundreds of acres of Cardel lands to which he would now lay claim. What options did she have? None. The king had ordered her marriage to Alaric—not once but twice. With the deaths of Lord and Lady Bamchester there was no other place for her to go. She had no say in determining her future now, just as she had not when her father had ordered her home from Bamchester nor when he had ordered her marriage to Alaric.

"Helena." Margaret's voice pierced her desolation. "We must have a special feast tonight to celebrate your marriage to Alaric. Let us leave the men to their strategizing while we make preparations."

"As you wish."

Helena felt drained and at a loss. Although she was grateful for Margaret's heartfelt approval, which put a semblance of happiness on the essentially pragmatic arrangement, she could drum up no enthusiasm to celebrate a marriage she could only dread. Standing, she raised her head only to have her gaze captured by Alaric's intense, brilliant blue eyes. With a shaking breath, she tore her eyes from his and followed Margaret out of the solar.

Helena paced her chamber. The walls confined her, constrained her, trapped her. She had not been this frightened on her wedding night, knowing that the information she had to tell Alaric about her father's plans would put all thoughts of bedding her out of his mind. But now there was no escape. She would have to submit to his possession tonight. She would be completely in his power—helpless.

She had had a warm bath earlier and was now dressed in her best gown. The lovely golden silk kirtle had beautiful red flowers embroidered around the neckline, the bottom of the sleeves, and the hem of the skirt. Margaret and Clare had spent long hours on the intricate needlework. Helena had braided her hair as usual, leaving each long plait to hang down her back. An ivory diaphanous veil covered her head, held in place by a gold circlet. She knew she looked as attractive as it was possible for her to look. Even that thought did not raise her spirits.

She would survive, she kept telling herself. She had endured enormous pain and suffering already. She could and would overcome whatever this night had in store for her.

The loud knock on the door intruded. She raised a shaking hand to her chest, trying to still the rapid beating of her heart. It was time. There was no way out. She took slow, deep breaths, trying to calm herself. The knock cracked against the door again, louder this time.

"Helena, 'tis Alaric," came his deep masculine voice.

She swallowed and walked on unsteady legs to the door. Lifting the bar, she pulled the door open. Alaric was so handsome it hurt to look at him. He was dressed in the same brilliant blue wool tunic he had worn for their wedding. The piercing blue of his eyes seared through her. As usual, when he came to escort her down to supper, he offered her his hand. She hesitated, then placed her shaking hand into his. His fingers closed gently but firmly over hers.

"You look beautiful tonight, Helena." He raised her hand and bent his head to kiss her hand. She dropped her eyes, no longer able to meet his gaze. "Come," he urged.

As they walked downstairs, the noise in the hall dissipated. When they reached the bottom step, the silence was absolute.

"Three cheers for the Earl and Countess of Merclif," someone yelled.

A deafening shout rang though the cavernous hall as those assembled voiced their approval, celebrating their lord's new title. Alaric smiled and raised his left hand to acknowledge their tribute before leading Helena to the dais.

Seated at the high table, Helena lowered her head and closed her eyes, despising herself for being such a coward. She had not always been this way. Before she had been forced to return to Cardel, she had been a happy, carefree girl. Nothing had frightened her then. She had eagerly sought out every experience life had to offer. She rapidly blinked her eyes to stop the tears that threatened to fall. *Enough self-pity,* she sternly told herself. She determinedly counted her blessings. Her life was so much better here at Merclif than what she had endured at Cardel. She already loved Margaret like a mother. Alaric was kind and handsome, and someday she would have children to love.

After supper was cleared away, musicians began to play, and Alaric led Helena into the middle of the hall for the first dance. She stepped on his toes as well as the feet of Sir Bernard on her other side. The movements of the dance confused her, so she turned the wrong way and bumped into Alaric. She raised her eyes to his, wondering if the misery she felt was evident on her face. He extracted her from the circle of dancers and led her to the side of the hall.

"I am sorry," she whispered.

"'Tis all right, Helena. You are just suffering from an attack of nerves. That is all. Everything will be fine."

They stood quietly together, watching the dancing.

After a while Margaret came to them. "Helena, 'tis time to go upstairs now."

"As you will," Helena said.

Margaret put her arm around Helena's waist and led her up the stairs. Once in Alaric's chamber, she guided Helena to a chair. Helena felt as if she were a lifeless doll as Margaret took off her veil and unwound her braids. Margaret muttered soft words of reassurance as she brushed Helena's hair. Eventually, Helena felt her rigid posture relax somewhat.

"My dear, you seem rather distressed. Are you all right?"

"I am afraid." Margaret's gentleness prompted the words to slip out of her mouth.

Margaret laid the brush down, drew up a chair, and sat down in front of Helena, taking both of Helena's hands in her own. Helena said nothing, merely stared at her hands lovingly held by Margaret.

"Helena, my dear, Alaric would never hurt you. You know that, do you not?"

"Aye," she mumbled. Helena gave Margaret the response she knew the older woman expected, even though she did not really believe that Alaric would not physically hurt her.

"Sometimes the anticipation of an event is far worse than the actual experience. I think you will find that is the case with your bedding. Eventually, you will even grow to enjoy the pleasures of the marriage bed. The physical union in marriage is one of God's marvelous gifts to us. You shall see."

Margaret stood and drew Helena up from the chair and into her arms. Cradling Helena's body next to hers, the other woman rubbed soothing hands over her back. Helena clutched Margaret's waist, hugging her.

After a time, Margaret gently pushed Helena away from her. "All right, my dear. 'Tis time for you to gather your courage and face your fears."

She took a deep breath. "Aye."

Margaret turned Helena around and unlaced her gown. She drew the kirtle from over Helena's head. Walking toward Helena's clothes chest, Margaret folded the silk and placed it inside.

"Go ahead and take your shoes and hose off and then get in bed," Margaret said over her shoulder.

When Helena had complied, Margaret came to the bed and pulled the covers over her. "Take off your chemise and hand it to me, my dear."

When Helena was naked under the covers, Margaret gently cupped Helena's left cheek and leaned down to give her a kiss on her forehead. "I will go tell Alaric that you are ready."

12

Alaric threw back the covers and swung his feet over to sit on the side of the mattress. Resting his elbows on his spread knees, he dropped his head into his hands and shut his eyes. His hands dug through his hair and into his scalp.

She is my wife.... He clenched his jaw. *Aye, she acquiesced, but she was not willing. I did not heed her fears, and I hurt her.*

His will battled with his conscience, his heart laden with guilt. Sitting upright, he turned to look at Helena, huddled on the side of the bed as far from him as she could get. Her back was to him, her knees pulled to her chest. Her long brown hair completely shielded her face. He pulled the bedding up to cover her bare back.

The cold caressed his body as he walked to the washbowl. He bent, washed his hands, then splashed the frigid water on his face. The chill in the room was no match for the ice invading his soul. He pulled on a clean pair of breeches, jerked on a tunic, and grabbed his mantle. With one last glance at Helena, he swung the mantle over his shoulders and quit their chamber.

Alaric went quietly down the stairs and through the hall, careful not to wake any of the soldiers or servants sleeping on pallets on the floor. Outside the donjon, he hesitated on the top of the steps. Taking a deep breath, letting the chilled air fill his lungs, he raised his eyes to the sky. The black of night was fading into the deepest blue. Faint tendrils of dark rose touched the bottom of the clouds hovering overhead. He dropped his eyes from the sky and scanned the top of the battlements until his gaze came to rest on the cross. As if following a lodestone, keeping his eyes on the cross, he descended the donjon steps and traversed the bailey toward the church.

When he entered the chapel, its tranquility embraced him. The gold cross on top of the altar glowed in the light of a lamp burning beside it. The only noise breaking the serenity of the sanctuary was the clatter of his boots on the stone floor as he made his way up to the altar. He dropped to his knees in front of the communion rail and automatically made the sign of the cross. Bowing his head, he closed his eyes and folded his hands together on top of the rail in the posture that was commonplace to him from years of attendance at mass.

"Forgive me, Lord, for I have sinned. In my arrogance, my greed, and my lust I have hurt my wife. Lord, I am sorry. Forgive me. In your mercy, Lord, hear my prayer."

My son, I forgive you. All your sins were paid for by My Son's death upon the cross.

Alaric let the absolution sink into his soul. Warmth filled him, chasing the cold away and banishing his guilt. Peace and acceptance flowed through him.

The sound of a door opening, then quickly closing again, returned his consciousness back to the world around him. Sitting back on his haunches, he placed his hands flat on his tights and stared up at the cross. What should he do now? How could he make this up to Helena?

Go in peace and sin no more. Love her as you love yourself.

He would start anew with Helena. Never again would he hurt her or take her against her will. He afforded his falcons more respect and consideration than he had given to his wife last night in their marriage bed. He valued and nurtured the birds' fierce spirits because that was what he needed from them. It was their spirits that made them successful hunters. Last night he had dominated and controlled Helena, with no respect for her feelings. If she were to become the wife he needed and the mother of his children, he had to give her the same care and respect he showed his falcons.

Filled with resolution, Alaric pushed to his feet. After bowing to the altar, he turned around and strolled up the aisle to the door.

Helena lay curled into a ball as she waited for day to break. She had not slept at all during the long night. Her eyes burned with fatigue. Every muscle in her body ached, and she felt numb and frozen inside.

The weight of the bed behind her shifted as Alaric turned over and sat up. She held her breath and tensed as she waited. The warmth of the bedding was pulled up to her shoulders, covering her nakedness. She listened to the splashing of the water and the rustle of cloth, then the quiet opening and closing of the door, relieved when Alaric left the room.

Alaric had saved her from her father. He had saved her from Wulfric's assault. But there had been no one to save her from him. As always, she was on her own.

She did not want to be naked and vulnerable when he returned. She pushed the covers off and stood. Swaying as her feet touched the floor, she grabbed on to the bedpost for balance. When she regained her equilibrium, she walked to the washstand and quickly washed her body.

Dawn crept through the slats of the wooden shutters, sending wisps of light into the room. Helena dressed in her green wool kirtle, trying to gain confidence from her favorite gown. Sitting on a chair, she brushed her hair and started to twist the long strands into a braid.

The door opened and Alaric entered, but he remained on the far side of the chamber from her. She swallowed. The worst was over now, she tried to reassure herself. What more could he do to her?

"Good morrow, Helena." His quiet voice seemed to fill the entire chamber.

"Good morrow, milord." Despite her intent, the greeting was weak and shaky.

"Helena, I have come to ask for your forgiveness."

Startled, she raised her eyes to his. Maintaining eye contact with her, he slowly advanced toward her. She felt like a doe, captured in the sights of a hunter, but could not pull away from the remorse she saw in his eyes.

He sank onto his knees in front of her. "I am sorry I hurt you last night. I know I have done nothing to earn your trust, but I promise I will never hurt you like that again."

He gradually reached out to her, as if giving her time to become accustomed to his presence, then took her limp hands in his own strong, warm hands. "Helena, I will try to be a good husband to you. But I cannot make our marriage succeed by myself. Will you meet me halfway?"

She stared at him, weighing his words. "I will try."

He lifted her unresisting hands to his mouth and pressed a light kiss on each of her palms. "Thank you."

She took a deep, shuddering breath as Alaric lifted his face and looked at her. A small smile spread across his lips, causing creases to form around his mouth. After releasing her hands, he rose to his feet.

"We will need to face our witnesses soon. I will leave you to finish dressing, but I will send Mother in to assist you."

Helena felt some of the lead within her heart melting away. His confession and repentance had moved her in a way she had not expected when he first walked into the chamber this morning. Her hope, which had been trampled and stomped into the ground last night, regenerated and quietly, cautiously, unfurled once more.

By the time Margaret entered the bedchamber, Helena had finished braiding her hair and had put on her hose and shoes.

"Good morrow, Helena." Margaret's smile radiated from her beautiful face.

"Good morrow, Margaret."

Margaret crossed the room and drew Helena into an embrace. "My dear, 'twould give me so much pleasure if you would call me Mother."

Helena blinked rapidly as she buried her face against the taller woman's shoulder. "I would like that very much, Mother."

Margaret tightened her arms around Helena, then released her. "Now, may I help you secure your veil?"

"Aye, please."

"I think a more formal style is called for this morning. Sit down, my dear."

Helena complied. Margaret picked up a piece of linen and wrapped it around her head, efficiently forming a wimple that covered Helena's forehead and throat.

"There." Margaret rested her hands on Helena's shoulders. "You are ready to face anything." Margaret stepped back and started walking toward the bed. "Unfortunately, 'Tis my duty to inspect the sheets for evidence." She made a small noise of disgust. "Why do men develop these barbaric traditions?"

Margaret reached the bed and drew back the covers. Helena followed Margaret to the mattress and stared at the sheet, appalled at the amount of blood staining it. She glanced at Margaret, whose mouth was pursed as she considered the bedding. Then her expression smoothed out, she briskly stripped the linens from the bed, and bundled them into a ball.

"My dear." Margaret turned toward Helena. "Please know I am always ready to listen, if you wish to confide in me."

Helena could not meet the older woman's eyes, so turned her face away.

"When I was a new bride I was quite appalled and shocked at what went on in the marriage bed. But I found, as I grew to know my husband, that there was much pleasure in the physical sharing between husband and wife. God has ordained marriage for the mutual joy of man and woman, for the help and comfort they may give each other."

She came over to Helena and laid her hand on the younger woman's shoulder. "In time, you will come to know that joy and that pleasure, my dear. Everything will work out, Helena. You just need to give it time."

Helena nodded.

"I will send a maid up with your breakfast. The men are set to leave soon, but first Lord Wyham must hear your and Alaric's testimony. Remember, my dear, hold your head up high and look them in the eye. You have nothing to be ashamed of or embarrassed about."

When Helena and Margaret entered the solar, the conversation among the men abruptly ceased and they all stood. Alaric came to meet Helena, taking her hand in his and drawing her forward. In addition to Alaric and Lord Wyham, Father Thomas, Sir Hugh, and another man she did not know were gathered in the room.

"Good morrow, Countess." Wyham bowed toward her. "I do not believe you know Sir William." The courtier gestured toward the stranger. "He is one of the king's most trusted knights."

Helena nodded to Sir William as he bowed courteously.

"Lord Merclif, would you please give me your sword?" Wyman asked.

Alaric handed over the sword, hilt first, to the older man.

Wyman took the weapon, holding it just below the guard, pommel pointed up, so it looked like a cross. He held it in front of Alaric. "Merclif, please place your right hand on your sword."

Alaric reached out his hand and laid his palm flat against the intersection of the pommel and the guard.

"Alaric, Earl of Merclif, do you solemnly swear that the testimony you are about to give is the truth, on your honor as a knight?"

"Aye, I do."

"Have you consummated your marriage to Helena, Countess of Merclif?"

"Aye," Alaric stated.

"Was your wife a virgin when she came to your bed?"

"Aye."

"Your marriage to Helena, Countess of Merclif, can never be annulled, dissolved, or set aside."

"Aye. Our marriage cannot be annulled."

Wyham handed the sword back to Alaric and waited until he had sheathed it. He turned to Helena and spoke to her in a soft tone. "Countess, were you a virgin when you came to your marriage bed?"

"Aye," she whispered.

Despite Margaret's words, she could not bring herself to look at the men in the room. She felt her face flame with her embarrassment. Alaric squeezed her hand gently, as if offering her encouragement.

"I am sorry, milady," Wyham said, "but you need to speak up so the witnesses can hear you."

Helena cleared her throat. "Aye."

"Was your marriage to Alaric, Earl of Merclif, consummated last night?"

"Aye."

"I have an affidavit each of you will need to sign." Wyham looked first at the bridal couple, then glanced around at everyone in the room.

Alaric took the document from the king's emissary and read it before signing it. He handed the affidavit and the quill to Helena. She did not examine the statement but added her own signature underneath her husband's. Once she had finished, Wyham took the document and added his own signature. When all the witnesses had signed the affidavit, Wyham took the document, rolled it up, and secured it by tying a piece of string around it.

"Merclif," Wyham said, "now that this business has been concluded, 'Tis time to depart for Cardel."

"I will be along directly, Wyham, but first I wish to take leave of my wife in private. Mother, gentlemen, please excuse us."

Alaric waited until they had all filed out of the solar before turning to her. "Helena, I do not know how long I will be gone. It all depends on how Cardel reacts to the king's decree."

"Aye." She nodded, looking at his chest. "I cannot see him giving up quietly."

"Nay, I cannot see that either. We may be in for a lengthy siege. I will send a messenger back with information as soon as possible."

"Thank you. We will be waiting most anxiously for your news."

"A small contingent of my most trustworthy men will remain here to protect the castle. They will be under the direction of Sir Bernard, so you will be safe."

She nodded. He put his finger under her chin to raise her face. She automatically tensed at his touch but then consciously willed herself to relax and meet his eyes. She was rewarded by his slight smile. He cupped her face in both of his hands and bent to kiss her. The touch of his lips was feather light upon hers, but she remained stiff and unresponsive. When she opened her eyes to look at him, his face was a polite mask.

"Fare well, Helena," Alaric said, stepping back from her.

"Fare well, milord. Godspeed."

13

Cardel sprawled in the chair and brought the wine bottle to his mouth. He upended the jug, draining the wine inside, before throwing the empty container on the floor. He put a shaking hand over his eyes. Today would have been Gerald's thirtieth birthday.

"Merclif will die!" He shouted the words in the empty solar, then staggered to his feet, kicking empty bottles out of his way. It was time he stopped wallowing in his grief and made plans. He had let Merclif go unpunished for Gerald's death as he mourned, but the best way to honor Gerald was to extract revenge.

A knock sounded on the door.

"Go away."

"Milord, I must speak with you." It was Edgar, his seneschal.

"Well, unless the castle is under attack I do not want to be disturbed."

"Milord, the castle is surrounded. There are fifteen knights and over forty men-at-arms. Both the king's and Merclif's banners are on display."

Cursing, using every vile word he could think of, Cardel wrenched the door open. "What's this you say?"

"The castle is surrounded by the king's troops. Lord Wyham says he is here on the king's business, and he is demanding entry."

Cardel ran his hand over his mouth, clutching the side of the open door in his right hand. *Think.* He had to think. "Admit Wyham, but only him. I'll see him in the hall. And send a servant with some water."

He shut the door in the seneschal's face. Grabbing a hunk of bread from the table, he tore into it and chewed. The bread in his stomach might dilute the wine enough to enable him to focus. By the time he had consumed the food, the manservant had brought fresh water. He jerked off his tunic and splashed water on his face. After drying his face and chest he pulled on a clean tunic. With measured steps he descended the stairs to the hall, where he found the king's emissary waiting.

"Lord Wyham, welcome to Cardel," the earl said. "May I offer you some wine?"

"This is not a social visit, Cardel," Wyham stated. "I come here as the representative of the king. As punishment for your treason, King Henry has confiscated your property here in the Mersted Valley. The king has ordered this castle to be razed to the ground and has stripped you of the title of Earl."

"What? I have committed no treason against the king!"

"You did willfully disobey a direct order of your king. That constitutes treason."

"I have never disobeyed the king." Cardel narrowed his eyes at Wyham.

"You attempted to invade Merclif Castle by subterfuge after the king ordered that you live in peace with Merclif."

"That is a lie! Merclif is lying for his own purposes."

"There is no lie. I clearly saw for myself the knights who invaded Merclif. Your son Gerald was seen fleeing Merclif Castle after his forces were defeated."

Cardel attempted to rein in his temper. He needed to make a good case, or he would lose everything. Spreading his hands wide, he adopted a conciliatory tone. "I had no control over Gerald, I am sorry to say. He acted completely on his own. Regretfully, his actions were misguided and wrong."

"The proof of your wrongdoing is irrefutable, Cardel. I refuse to engage in this discussion any longer." Wyham pulled a scroll from his tunic and handed it to Cardel. "This is a copy of the king's decree. You are hereby ordered to vacate the castle tomorrow at dawn. All your possessions inside the castle are confiscated. You may take with you only your personal effects. Your knights may accompany you, but the soldiers and villeins will remain." Wyham gave Cardel a curt bow, turned, and walked away.

Cardel's rage built with every step Wyham took. He barely managed to contain it while Wyham exited the hall. Once he was gone, Cardel slammed his foot into one of the dogs lying asleep on the floor. The dog howled and scrambled away. Cardel charged toward a group of villeins working at the side of the hall. He overturned a trestle table before grabbing one man by the neck. The other villeins fled as Cardel's fist connected with the man's face. Cardel held the man up and savagely pounded him, the man's blood coating Cardel's fist.

"Milord. Stop."

Langston grabbed his fist just as he was about to slam it into the peasant's face again. Snarling, Cardel dropped the villein and turned toward the steward, aiming his fist instead at Langston. The look in the other man's eyes, fearless and resolute, stopped Cardel. Stepping back from Langston and the prostrate man, Cardel shook his fist.

"I want two bottles of wine in my solar immediately. And clean up this mess."

The earl turned his back on the servants and went upstairs. As he washed his bloody hands, he contemplated his revenge on Merclif. He sat in a chair before the lit brazier and drank deeply as he considered and discarded ideas.

Several hours later, when there was a knock on the solar door, Cardel had consumed another two bottles of wine and was more than halfway done with a third.

"Father, may I come in?"

"Aye," Cardel barked.

Percy entered the solar and stood close to the door. Cardel snorted in disgust as he surveyed his youngest son. Why did Gerald have to die, leaving this weakling as his only heir? *Merclif will pay.*

"Father, I have heard the news. What are we going to do?"

"Stop hovering there like a girl," Cardel snapped. "Sit down and have some wine, like a man."

Percy picked up a goblet from the table and poured some wine into it. Then he perched on the edge of a chair, watching his father.

Cardel shifted in his seat and raised the wine bottle to his mouth, taking a long drink. "I've come up with the perfect plan, my boy. Perfect." He waved his arm expansively.

"What is your plan, Father?"

"We'll leave the castle tomorrow at dawn. We'll not give the king any reason to think we are flaunting his orders. We'll not hurt the villeins; we'll not destroy the furnishings. We'll not attack Merclif. Much as I would like to kill him with my bare hands, now is not the time. We'll go to Narhex. The house there is not as grand as this castle, but 'twill have to do." Cardel nodded and took another gulp of wine.

Several minutes passed in silence.

"Father? What will we do after we get to Narhex?"

"Huh? Boy, pay attention!" Cardel growled. "Then we wait. Let Merclif become complacent. He'll let his guard down. When he has been lulled into carelessness, we'll strike. We'll kill Merclif. Make it look like an accident. Once he is dead, I'll ride in to comfort my poor, distraught daughter. As the only man in the family, I'll take over the castle. Force Margaret to marry me. Should've been me she married, not that knave Gavin." He took another swig of wine. "'Twill be an easy matter to get rid of Helena once I'm living at Merclif. That way the king'll not be able to give her or Merclif to someone else."

"Aye, Father." Percy smiled. "That is a brilliant plan."

Cardel upended the wine bottle but only a few drops fell into his mouth. He hurled the empty container against the wall. "Make yourself useful, boy," he barked. "Send Langston up with more wine. I've some instructions to give him. And tell Sir Edgar to get the knights ready to leave tomorrow."

"Aye, Father."

"I want you to gather all the silver—spoons, plates, cups, candleholders. And don't forget the chapel. There's a lot of silver on the altar. Get going, boy."

Alaric was warming himself in front of the huge bonfire when Wyham joined him, offering him a cup of ale. He gratefully accepted and drank deeply. The cold February day had merged into an even colder night.

"There has been no movement on the crenellations, other than the routine patrolling of their guards," Wyham reported. "There has been no sign of any attempt to leave the castle, so I do not believe there are any concealed exits."

"I think you are right."

The sounds of the other men finishing their meal and settling down to sleep drifted through the darkness. Alaric took another drink of ale, savoring the subtle melding of the spicy hop sharpness and malty sweetness.

Wyham cleared his throat. "King Henry has given me leave to remain at Merclif for a while."

Alaric looked closely at the suave, older man, surprised at his uncharacteristic lack of composure. "Aye?"

"That is, if you will allow me to remain." Wyham took a swallow of ale. "With your permission, I would like to court Lady Margaret."

"'Tis not my permission you will need. 'Tis my mother's."

"Aye. I will not press my suit on her, if she is not amenable," Wyham agreed, rocking back on his heels. "Neither will I approach your mother unless you approve."

"I approve."

Wyham nodded. Alaric glanced at his face, catching the relieved smile that briefly softened Wyham's mouth before he schooled his features into a bland expression. Alaric stared into his cup. He would have to plan his own campaign to woo his wife very carefully. Amusement lightened his brooding. He might be able to get some tips from Wyham's courtship of his mother.

"I am getting too old for war," Wyham complained. "Winter cold and a siege. 'Tis the worst possible combination."

"Aye, that it is." Alaric took a drink of his ale. "'Tis hard to keep alert when watching castle walls is so tedious."

"At least the men are keeping occupied. 'Tis one good thing about a pair of dice—they can go anywhere."

The two men stood in affable silence until Alaric said at last, "I am going to get some sleep. No telling what we will encounter tomorrow."

"Aye," Wyham agreed. "Good night, Merclif."

The two men parted company, each going a little distance from the fire to find a place to sleep. They lay on the ground, rolled up in their cloaks, like their men did.

In the middle of the long night, Alaric was awakened to stand guard for two hours. He quickly returned to sleep after his shift was over.

As dawn broke, all eyes were focused on Cardel's castle. Alaric's horse pawed the ground, raising his head restlessly, his hot breath steaming from his nostrils in the frigid air. Soothingly patting Geneir's neck, Alaric felt just as impatient to be moving. As the last streak of dawn's pale red vanished, the portcullis slowly rose. The king's forces waited, the men fully alert.

Within a few moments a group of riders galloped from the gate, crossing the barbican and drawbridge. Alaric recognized Cardel and Percy at the head of the procession. They did not slow as they neared the ring of the king's troops surrounding the castle, but their stance remained unthreatening. Their hands were on their reins and no weapons were in sight. Wyham signaled for his men to make way, clearing a path for Cardel and his entourage. Alaric counted five knights, in addition to Cardel and his son, as they rode past, not acknowledging the presence of the king's forces in any way. Wyham gestured to William, who called to his side a group of five men and together they galloped after Cardel.

Wyham left Belwick in charge of a small contingent of soldiers stationed outside the walls while he and Alaric led the remainder of the men into the castle grounds. Encountering no one as they rode through the outer bailey, they rode single file through a gate in the inner curtain before coming to a halt inside. Vociferous chaos reigned in the inner ward. Men, women, children, dogs, goats, and chickens all crowded around, clamoring for attention. Narrowly missing the dog that ran under his horse's hooves, Alaric brought his fingers to his mouth and gave a shrill, piercing whistle. The uproar ceased abruptly.

"Attention," Wyham shouted before pandemonium could erupt again. "Who is in charge here? Is there a bailiff?"

"Aye, milord," yelled a man who stepped forward. His boyishly handsome face was drawn and grim.

"What is your name?" Wyham called as the man approached his horse.

"Damien Langston, milord."

"Did Cardel leave any booby traps or ambush, as far as you know?"

"Nay, milord, I do not think so."

"I want you to take the villeins into the donjon. I want everyone seated in an orderly fashion, understand?"

"Aye, milord. I will see to it." Langston turned away, calling instructions that were promptly obeyed.

As the crowd began to file into the donjon, Wyham motioned Alaric forward. "Since these are now your villeins, I will leave you to deal with them while I secure the castle grounds," Wyham told Alaric.

"Aye, milord."

Alaric ordered Jessup, as well as Roger and Gordon, to accompany him. They walked their horses toward the donjon, then dismounted, trailing the people as they trooped inside. Langston was busy organizing the villeins, ordering them to set up the trestle tables and sit down. Alaric waited until everyone was seated before calling Langston over to him.

"I am Merclif. The king has granted me all Cardel lands and villeins."

"Aye, milord." Langston bowed.

Alaric inspected Langston. He was better dressed than the others, and his intelligent brown eyes were direct. "Why did you not leave with Cardel?"

"I no longer wish to be in his service, milord."

"And why is that?"

"He viciously beat a man yesterday," Langston stated. "'Tis not the first time he has taken his rage out on someone weaker than himself."

"How long were you in his service?"

"Too long, milord. Almost two years."

"I want you to select five of the most trusted men here. I want them to gather up every article of value in the castle and bring it here. Every piece of silver, every candlestick, every dish, every pot and pan, all linens, cushions, bed hangings, everything. Understand?"

"Aye, milord." Langston bowed before retreating.

Alaric watched as the bailiff set to work, selecting and organizing the crew of workers. "Roger," he ordered one of his knights, "I want you to monitor the men. Make sure they do not steal anything."

"Aye, milord."

Alaric stood in front of the fireplace, his feet spread apart and his left hand on the hilt of his sword, as he surveyed the people packed into the hall. Muted conversations gradually started. A baby's shrill crying quickly stilled when its mother put it to her breast. Realizing there were several children crying and their mothers were trying to quiet them, he walked over to the nearest child. At his approach the mother grabbed the small boy to her, then pushed him behind her. Her fear was almost palpable.

"I am sorry, milord," she whispered when Alaric stood in front of her. "I will make sure he stops crying."

"I am not going to hurt the boy," Alaric said. "What is the matter with him?"

"He's hungry, milord. We've not eaten since yesterday."

Alaric looked around. It seemed they were all staring at him. "Is that true of everyone here?"

"Aye, milord," the woman answered.

Alaric frowned. "Where is the cook?"

"Here, milord." A large man in a grease-stained apron came forward.

"Is there any food in the kitchen?" Alaric asked.

"Aye, milord, but only Lord Cardel's food. We were forbidden to eat anything but bread and cheese."

"Take the kitchen servants and go prepare a meal for everyone. Use whatever foodstuffs you can find. In the meantime, bring in all the bread, cheese, and ale you have."

"Aye, milord."

The cook bowed. He walked through the hall, issuing orders, and gathered together several of the other servants before leaving the donjon.

Within ten minutes after they had left, several maids returned, bringing bread. The children quieted when they had something to eat.

"Where is Merclif?"

The shouted question seemed to reverberate through the hall as a quiet fell over the crowd. Alaric turned sharply to see a man in priest's robes standing at the door. The gray-haired man leaned heavily on a cane, clutching it firmly in his gnarled hand, his lined face unyielding.

Alaric walked toward the priest. "I am Merclif. Who are you?"

"I am Father Michael. Is it true you are going to destroy the castle?"

"Aye, Father. Those are the orders of King Henry."

"I need help packing up the furnishings in the chapel. Cardel has already ransacked it and taken all the silver from the altar and the sacristy." Father Michael's disgust was evident in the way he spat Cardel's name. "I want to ensure the proper handling of the rest of the chapel before any more sacrilege is committed."

"Aye, Father. I will have my squire assist you. I hope you will come with me back to Merclif Castle. I am sure Lady Helena will be pleased to have you join our household."

Father Michael's wise eyes examined Alaric's face, as if trying to divine his character. After a long pause, he nodded in acceptance. "Aye. 'Twill be a pleasure to see Lady Helena again."

"Good." Alaric called Jessup over and gave him his orders.

Wyham entered the hall shortly afterwards, informing Alaric that the men had scrutinized every inch of the castle walls and grounds and had encountered no problems. When dinner was served, Alaric instructed his men to wait until the villeins had eaten their fill. Only then did the soldiers eat, taking their meal in shifts so the castle would remain adequately guarded at all times.

At last Alaric and Wyham sat down together to eat.

"Did King Henry stipulate what was to be done with Cardel's possessions?" Alaric asked.

"Nay," Wyham replied. "They are yours to do with as you will."

"Then I will distribute the goods to the villeins." Alaric bit into a mutton chop and chewed. "I will send the villeins home to Carleigh. Cardel confiscated many acres of their farmland when he built this castle. Once it is destroyed, I will parcel out the land to them."

Wyham nodded. "Tonight, after everything is cleared out, we will tear out some of this wood and use it to construct the catapults." He gestured toward the stairs and the gallery above them.

"Then I will have some of the villeins remain behind to help with that." Alaric threw the stripped bone in his hand on to the floor. Soon it would not matter how soiled the rushes were.

Wyham took a piece of roast pork and ate it. "Tomorrow we will set fire to the interior of the castle and the buildings in the inner bailey. Once the fire has done its work, we will use the mangonels to tear down the walls."

"Aye. With any luck, we should return to Merclif Castle by the end of the week. I will send a messenger back tonight to let the ladies know what has happened." Alaric finished his ale and stood. "Let me know if you want to send a letter to my mother." With a grin, he lightly slapped Wyham on the back before striding off.

14

Helena raised her head when she heard the knock on the door and stilled her hands on the lute strings. After Alaric left, she had retreated to his bedchamber to try and regain her equilibrium. Playing her lute usually soothed her, but this morning she was too restless and fretful to enjoy the music.

"Come in," she called.

Margaret entered and closed the door behind her, giving Helena a smile. "My dear, since you are now the lady of the castle, 'Tis time for me to turn the chatelaine over to you."

Helena stood and laid down her lute as Margaret removed the ornament from her belt and handed it to her. Made of gold, the chatelaine was elaborately decorated with amethyst, aquamarines, and lapis lazuli stones. Several keys here attached to the gold chains hanging down from the oblong head.

"Gavin's mother gave this to me after we were married, and now I am passing it on to you."

Helena accepted the chatelaine and stared at it a moment, before raising her eyes to Margaret's face. "Lady Dorothea trained me in the management of a household, but I have never supervised one by myself before. Merclif Castle is so much larger and grander than either Bamchester or Cardel. I am afraid I will not know what to do."

"Do not worry, my dear, I will not abandon you. I will be happy to instruct you in all the duties you will now be assuming."

"I would appreciate that, Mother."

"I thought I would give you a detailed tour of the castle and show you which key is for which storeroom and introduce you to some of the servants."

"That sounds like a good idea."

Margaret led her down the gallery, showing her the key to the ladies' solar. "I usually lock this door at night," she explained, "since we keep all our furs and fabrics in here. I leave it unlocked during the day so Clare and Elizabeth can work in here."

Margaret led the way downstairs and to the southwest corner of the hall to a door Helena had never noticed before. She took the rushlight from the holder next to the entrance and descended the spiral staircase. Helena carefully followed, holding her hand on the winding handrail for support. It was noticeably cooler on the ground floor of the donjon. Wood pillars were strategically placed to support the wooden floor of the great hall above.

"Renwold also has a key to the door as does Alaric," Margaret explained. "There are only the three keys. We maintain tight security on the ground floor, as most of the castle provisions are stored here. Renwold guards the door whenever he has the servants bring in supplies or take them out." She held the rushlight up high so Helena could see. "We store the grain here in this first row. Wheat." Margaret walked along the row, gesturing at the neatly stacked barrels. "Barley. Oats. All of which are grown by the villeins on our lands."

Margaret turned to the next row and proceeded to walk back toward the door. "In this row we have vinegar, honey, and ale." She pointed to the butts as she named their contents. The casks of ale were by far the most plentiful and were stacked closest to the door.

"We keep the wine along the south wall." Margaret pointed out the barrels used to store wine. A series of wooden shelves were placed along the wall beyond the wine barrels, on top of which were arranged several small silver caskets.

"We keep our more costly spices and herbs here, as well as the ones we need to purchase, such as saffron, aniseed, pepper, and cinnamon. The common spices and herbs that we grow in our garden are kept in a storage room next to the kitchen. As you can see, we also store loaves of sugar and salt here, as well as our cheese."

Margaret turned and walked toward the northeast side of the basement. Again, she raised the rushlight high so Helena could see the carcasses of meat hanging from hooks attached to the ceiling.

"We store bacon, ham, salt pork, and mutton in here. In the winter we try to rely on the game the men hunt, but we do smoke and salt pork, beef, and mutton in case the weather is too harsh for the men to hunt, or they fail to find game."

Margaret turned back to Helena. "Let us go back upstairs now and get our cloaks so I can show you the kitchen and the outer buildings."

After donning their mantles, Margaret and Helena exited the hall through a door at the northwest corner and passed under the wooden pentice, walking to the stone kitchen constructed twenty feet from the donjon. The contrast of the hot, stuffy kitchen to the cold, crisp air outside struck Helena like a slap in the face as they stepped inside the open door.

The kitchen was a hive of activity as the servants prepared dinner. A huge stone oven, twelve feet in diameter, was built into one side of the kitchen. A man slowly turned the spit over one of the smaller fireplaces lining the other walls. Several men worked at wooden tables in the middle of the floor. One man glanced up and gave them a half bow, before laying the circle of dough he had rolled out on top of a meat pie. He instructed one of the other men to put the pie in the oven, then wiped his hands on his apron before coming over speak with them.

"Good morning, my ladies," he said, bowing.

"Helena, this is Laurence, our chief cook," Margaret said. "Laurence, this is Lady

Helena, Countess of Merclif. I am showing her around the castle this morning. We will come back either later today or tomorrow so she can talk to you and let you know what she will expect from you and your workers."

"Very good, milady." Laurence regarded Helena openly but respectfully. "I'll look forward to that. Would ye please excuse me now, milady? I've a lot to do still before dinner."

"Certainly, Laurence," Helena responded.

Laurence bowed again, then returned to work. Margaret led Helena through a doorway into the scullery. The kitchen and the scullery shared one interior stonewall. Several scullions, both men and women, were hard at work washing dishes, pots, and pans. Large stone sinks were built into one side wall. Water flowed to the sinks through pipes along the wall from a cistern on the scullery's roof and then drained away from the sinks into a ditch near the garden outside. The other three sides of the scullery were lined with shelves stacked with clean dishes, cups, and goblets.

Margaret and Helena exited the scullery to the outside.

"During the spring and summer we have a kitchen garden here." Margaret indicated a patch of ground near the curtain wall, directly outside the scullery door. "Of course, the garden is barren now since it is winter. Planting is usually done at the end of February, so we will start that about three weeks from now. Let us go through the gate, and I will show you the dairy and the livestock pens."

They passed through the northwest gate into the outer bailey. The dairy was located in a wooden structure built against the wall. The two women working inside looked up from their tasks and gave the visitors a quick curtsy. One maid churned butter as another poured off whey into a bowl. As they watched she added salt to the curds, then loaded them into a press. They left the dairy and went to the stables next door.

"Gavin came up with the idea of having separate stables for horses and for livestock," Margaret explained as they stood in the doorway. "Most of the cows, sheep, and pigs are raised on outlaying farms. Once a week in the summer Renwold sends to different farms to gather up enough animals to feed the castle for that week."

"I am surprised you have the dairy and stables located in the outer bailey," Helena commented.

"Merclif Castle has never been besieged," Margaret said. "Its position on this hill gives it a natural defensive advantage. Even so, given the width of the moat and the location of the stables next to the inner curtain, they are well outside striking distance of archers."

They didn't linger long at the stables, since the odor was pungent. They went back into the inner bailey using the same gate. Margaret guided Helena to the brewery, built along the west wall of the donjon. The stone building had several fireplaces where cauldrons boiled over roaring fires. The alewife stood next to a tun, mixing oats into the crushed malt. When she finished, she motioned for her assistant to bring over a pot of boiling water. The lovely smell of warm malt filled the brewery as the two women poured the boiling water into the mash tun.

"We brew about ten hogsheads of ale every week," Margaret commented as she explained the brewing process to Helena.

After watching the alewife work for a bit, Margaret led Helena back into the hall and over to the herbarium located along the east side of the first floor. "This is my favorite place," Margaret remarked as she unlocked the door and stood aside for Helena to enter. "The herbs we grow in the garden are dried and stored in here."

"I often helped Lady Dorothea in her herbarium," Helena said. "She taught me several recipes for treating aliments."

"We will have to compare recipes. I am very interested to see if Lady Dorothea knew of some I do not have."

"Aye, I would like that."

"Next door is where we spin our yarn."

Margaret opened the door and stood aside so Helena could enter. The five spinsters paused their conversations, but not their work, when the two women entered the room.

"Do not mind us," Margaret said. "I am just showing Lady Merclif around the castle."

The buzz of the women's conversation gradually resumed.

"In here we have several looms," Margaret opened the next door along the east wall. "This is where we make and store the fabric used for table linens and clothes. Helena, this is Mayda, our master weaver. Mayda, this is Lady Merclif."

"Milady," Mayda said, getting up from the loom and dropping a curtsy.

"Mayda designs our most intricate weaves," Margaret explained.

"Your work is beautiful, Mayda." Helena touched the fabric stretched tight over the loom.

"Thank ye, milady."

After leaving the weavers, Margaret and Helena went to the ladies' solar, where Margaret outlined the duties for which the lady of the castle was responsible.

Dinner the next day was unnaturally quiet. Tension seemed to grip the castle inhabitants as they waited for news from the siege. Even Margaret seemed to be affected by it. She had not said more than a few words while they ate.

After dinner was over, there was a commotion at the doors. A soldier strode purposefully through the hall, stopping when he came to Helena. He took off his helmet and bowed to her. "Milady, I have a message for you from the Earl." He handed a folded piece of paper to her.

"Thank you," Helena said. Deciding it was time she got to know the men who served Merclif, she asked, "What is your name?"

"'Tis John, milady," he replied.

"Thank you, John," Helena said.

He bowed to her. Helena glanced around, aware that the eyes of all those in the hall were looking at her. She broke open the seal on the letter and read Alaric's short message.

"All is well," she announced in a loud voice. "Cardel has surrendered his castle without a struggle. There was no fighting, and no one has been injured. Lord Merclif expects that he and his troops will return by the end of the week."

There was general sigh of relief and excited chatter, as the atmosphere in the hall lightened.

"Milord, may I have a word with you?" Langston asked.

"Aye," Alaric replied.

"I would ask a boon of you, milord. I would like to serve Merclif as a knight."

Alaric crossed his arms over his chest, studying the younger man. "Who is your father, and where did you train as a knight?"

"Milord, I am the fourth son of Sir Richard Langston. My father sent me to train with Sir John Salshill. I served him as his squire from the age of eleven until I was twenty. Unfortunately, my father died before my knighting could take place and, after his death, there was no money to pay for armor or vestures for me."

"How old are you now?"

"Twenty-three, milord."

"What have you been doing since you left Salshill?"

"I have been itinerant, finding whatever position I could. I have now earned enough to purchase a horse and armor. I am ready to become a knight, milord."

Langston's direct gaze met his. Alaric was impressed with Langston's open manner, neither too importunate nor too overconfident. He had closely observed Langston earlier in the day as the bailiff supervised the distribution of goods to the villeins. The bailiff had called most of them by name and had treated them with scrupulous fairness. As Alaric unfolded his arms, his left hand fell to the hilt of his sword and his right hand came to rest on his hip.

"Have you done any training or fighting in the last few years?"

"Some, milord."

"You may come back to Merclif with us when we leave. I want to see you in the lists before I make up my mind."

"Thank you, milord." Langston bowed his head.

"Did Cardel leave any horses in the stable?"

"There are one or two, milord, but they are both rather old and knackered."

"Tomorrow take the best one; it should get you to Merclif, at least. And release the other one to the villeins."

"Aye, milord. Thank you." Langston bowed and started to walk away.

"Langston," Alaric called.

The younger man turned back. "Aye, milord?"

"I did not see you take any of the plunder."

"Milord, I took two pieces, just as you allowed your own men."

Alaric nodded. "That is all."

Langston bowed again and walked away. Alaric turned to greet Hugh, who came to join him.

"What did the bailiff want, Alaric?" Belwick inquired.

"He wants to complete his training and be knighted."

"Are you sure we can trust him?"

"Nay, I am not. We will have to keep an eye on him. He may be Cardel's agent."

"That he may. I shall keep a close watch on him."

The next morning after breakfast Alaric supervised the dismantling of the wooden gallery as the rest of the men pulled out of the castle grounds. When enough wood had been salvaged, he had the villeins carry it outside where the soldiers, under the direction of the knights, constructed catapults while the villeins were put to work gathering boulders. When the castle grounds were vacated, Wyham ordered two men to torch the inside of the donjon as well as the wooden outbuildings.

Once the mangonels were constructed, the men began lobbing stones into the outer curtain, aiming at the same spot. When that section of the wall crumbled they targeted the one adjacent. The work was slow, dirty, and strenuous. By nightfall they had demolished most of one side of the outer wall. During the next few days, they gradually tore down the outer and inner curtain walls as well as the stone outbuildings. Alaric, aware that his original estimate had been somewhat optimistic, sent another message to Helena explaining the delay. By the sixth day the men were completely exhausted but in high spirits because the end was in sight. The donjon took another two days to destroy.

Wyham and Alaric stood in the middle of the demolished castle. Piles of rocks and rubble were all that remained.

"I have certainly learned a lot about how to bring down a stone wall," Alaric commented dryly.

Wyham kicked a small stone, sending it crashing into a larger one. "Mayhap the villeins can make use of these stones for building."

"Aye. I will have the stones cleared away this spring so we can return this land to farming." Alaric looked up at the sun. "If we leave now, we should be home in time for supper."

"Good. I am looking forward to a bath and a warm meal," Wyham said with a grin. "Not to mention seeing Lady Margaret again."

The two men walked out of the debris and instructed their men to break camp. Within the hour they were all mounted and riding toward Merclif.

15

While Alaric was gone, Margaret gave Helena detailed instructions in all household activities. Margaret felt that the lady of the castle could not direct and supervise the workers unless she had in-depth knowledge of each task. Helena had made cheese, mixed poultices and elixirs, brewed ale, and spun thread. Helena had enjoyed every task, asking detailed questions about each procedure. Working beside them, she gradually became acquainted with the women employed at the castle. The villagers, both men and women, worked one day a week at the castle on a schedule devised by Renwold. She was still amazed how Margaret knew each villager by name and hoped to do so as well one day. The village women had been reserved and aloof with her at first, until the day she had met Sadie.

Helena was churning butter when the child approached her. Sadie had been hovering next to her mother, her thumb firmly planted in her mouth. When Sadie came over to her, Helena glanced up and gave her a smile. Helena was rewarded when Sadie took her thumb out of her mouth and smiled back. In a few moments, when the little girl edged closer, Helena smiled at her again.

"Hello," Helena said. "What is your name?"

"Sadie."

"That is a lovely name. How old are you, Sadie?"

"Four." She held up four fingers.

"My, you are such a big girl."

"Does it hurt?" The girl pointed to Helena's left cheek.

"Sadie! Come here and stop bothering Lady Merclif."

"'Tis fine, Betsy." Helena smiled at Sadie's mother. "I am enjoying talking to Sadie." She returned her attention to the child. "Nay, it does not hurt any longer."

"How'd you get that?"

"A very bad man cut me with a knife." She looked steadily at the small girl.

"Must've hurt lots."

"Aye." Helena nodded. "It did. But that was a long time ago, and now it does not hurt anymore."

"Good."

Sadie came up to Helena, pressing against her leg, and reached out to touch her face. Helena stilled as the child's small fingers delicately traced the large scar on her cheek.

"'Tis kinda rough."

"Aye, Sadie, 'tis rough," Helena agreed.

Another small hand reached out to touch Helena's right cheek. "This side's soft."

"Aye." Helena smiled as the girl cupped her cheeks.

Sadie leaned over to Helena and gave her a wet kiss on her scar and then kissed her right cheek. Helena smiled at Sadie. The acceptance this small child so generously gave her touched her to the depths of her heart.

"Thank you, Sadie. Now 'tis my turn to give you a kiss."

She laughed softly as Sadie smiled and presented her cheeks to be kissed. After kissing Sadie, Helena suddenly became aware of the quiet and stillness of the normally busy dairy and glanced up to find Betsy and the two other women watching her interaction with Sadie. Helena returned Betsy's smile and nodded to the others before turning her attention back to Sadie and churning butter.

Since that day the women had treated Helena with more warmth and openness. Helena was aware the villeins would never become her friends, given the vast difference in their statuses, but she was glad they were no longer afraid of her and treated her with polite respect. She hoped that someday she would earn from them the affection they readily accorded Lady Margaret.

Helena threaded the heddle though the blue warp threads on the loom, continuing the pattern Mayda had started: over three warp threads, then under six warp threads. Next she inserted the shuttle containing white thread through the opening she had created with the heddle. After removing the heddle from the shed, she took the reed and gently pushed the welt thread down so it fit snuggly next to the previous rows. She weaved the heddle again through the warp thread, creating the shed for the next row of the pattern.

Margaret walked over to the loom on which Helena was working. "How are you doing, my dear?"

"'Tis not as easy as the other women make it look," Helena commented. "I keep losing track of the pattern."

"Aye," Margaret agreed. "The experts always make a complicated task seem simple."

Sir Bernard entered the room and walked toward Helena. She stood as the knight bowed before her. "Milady, the guards have spotted the Merclif banner and the king's banner about a league away. Lord Merclif and the rest of the garrison should arrive at the castle shortly."

Alaric was coming home. Time seemed suspended as Helena felt all the self-confidence she had regained during the last week drain away. As the silence stretched out, Margaret stepped closer to her and spoke softly to her so no one else could hear.

"Helena, are you all right?"

"Aye, I am fine," she said quietly, then turned to address the knight in a louder tone. "Thank you, Sir Bernard. That is indeed welcome news."

"Aye, milady."

"I also wanted to commend you for your diligence and vigilance this past week while the Earl was away. It has been a huge relief to know that we have all been in such capable hands."

"Thank you, milady." A smile spread across the knight's face, causing his massive chin to jut out even more prominently. "I was but doing my job. If you will excuse me now, milady, I will go and prepare for milord's return." Bernard bowed, then walked away.

Helena looked at Margaret.

"My dear, let us go to the allure where we will be able to see the men's approach."

"Aye."

"Gavin always liked to see me on the allure when he returned," Margaret reminisced as they walked. "He said when he saw my face, he knew he was home."

"That is lovely," Helena said softly. What must it be like to be loved so deeply by one's husband? It was something she would never know.

On the battlements, she stood next to Margaret, watching the approach of the troops. It was an impressive sight. Two armored knights rode in front of the procession with King Henry's banner and Merclif's banner carried by squires directly behind them. A column of men riding three abreast followed. The soldiers remained on the far side of the river as one of the knights came forward. He stopped in view of the guards on the crenellations and removed his coif. Alaric's black hair and blue eyes were clearly visible as he hailed the guards.

"'Tis Merclif. Open the gate."

The guards obeyed, lowering the drawbridge and raising the portcullis. Alaric led the men over the bridge and into the castle. When he walked his horse into the outer bailey, he glanced up and looked directly at Helena. Time stopped for her as she met his piercing gaze. He raised a hand in greeting before turning right and heading toward the stables. Helena let out a shuddering breath, her gaze tracking his progress.

"Helena, we should go down now."

"Aye, Mother." Helena followed Margaret to the turret at the southeast corner and down the stairs.

"It will be some time before Alaric comes to the hall, since he always takes care of his own horse," Margaret explained as they walked across the bailey. "And then he will need to remove all his armor."

"Lady Merclif, Lady Margaret," Renwold greeted them as they stepped inside the hall. His narrow lips curved into a slight smile that animated his usually impassive face. "Lady Merclif, water is being heated for baths, as you ordered, and Cook has supper almost ready."

"Thank you, Renwold," Helena said.

As she waited with Margaret, Helena tried to trample down her nervousness. She must not lose all the gains she had made in self-confidence and authority this past week under Margaret's guidance just because her husband had returned. She would show him that she was no longer a frightened mouse, cringing at every imagined threat.

The door to the hall opened, and Alaric entered with Wyham. Helena took a deep breath and met her husband's eyes as he strode toward them with a broad smile. Even though his black hair was matted with sweat and dirt stained his clothes, Alaric exuded masculine vigor and virility. The dark growth of hair covering his cheeks and chin gave him a rakish appearance.

"Helena." He took her hand and bent to kiss her cheek.

"Welcome home, milord."

"Thank you. 'Tis good to be home." Dropping her hand, he turned to Margaret, kissing her cheek. "Mother, I trust you are well?"

"Aye. Alaric, I am so glad you are home safely," Margaret said with a smile. "Welcome back, Lord Wyham." Margaret extended her hand to him. He bent over her hand and kissed it.

"Milord," Helena addressed Alaric, "water has been heated and supper is ready. Would you like to eat first or bathe first?"

"Bathe first. I am covered in fifth," he replied.

Helena turned to find Renwold at her side.

"Milady, I will see that everything is taken care of," he told her.

Renwold bowed and walked away. Helena breathed a sigh of relief as Alaric went upstairs. His presence overwhelmed her and set her on edge. She firmly thrust from her mind the realization that they would spend the night together, sleeping in the same bed.

Helena played her lute and sang to pass the time for Merclif's retainers as they held supper, waiting for the lord of the castle. When at last Alaric descended the stairs, she faltered. She ducked her head, not meeting his eyes, and quickly resumed singing. As she played the last chord of the song, she saw Wyham make his way downstairs. She stood, acknowledging the applause, and found Renwold at her side. He took the lute from her.

"Thank you, Renwold. Please start serving supper now."

She walked toward Alaric, conscious of his watchful eyes upon her. His hair was damp, his face cleanly shaven, and his eyes matched the brilliant blue of his tunic. She marveled again how handsome he was. He held out his hand to her as she approached. All her senses acutely tuned to him, she placed her hand in his, aware of the current that seemed to pass between them.

Over dinner Helena listened avidly to the exchange between Wyham and Margaret as he recounted for them the surrender and razing of Cardel Castle. Alaric occasionally interjected additional information, when asked by Margaret, but was otherwise silent. Helena felt strongly the tenseness that existed between them, a sharp contrast to the ease evident between Margaret and Wyham.

After supper, Alaric stood and held out his hand to her. "Come, Helena, 'tis time for bed."

She swallowed and, without a word, put her hand in his, letting him draw her up to stand beside him.

"Please excuse us, Mother, Wyham," Alaric said. "I find I am quite fatigued and wish to retire now."

After accepting their farewells, Alaric guided her upstairs and into their bedchamber. She entered first and walked away from the door, hearing him close it behind her.

"I will summon the chamberlain to assist you, milord."

"That will not be necessary. I do not need any assistance," Alaric replied. "You will not have need of a maid tonight. If you require help undressing, I shall be happy to oblige."

Helena stood immobile next to her clothes chest, keeping her back to him. He came over to her and placed his hands lightly on her shoulders. She could not control her instinctive reaction; her whole body went rigid.

His sigh seemed inordinately loud in the silent chamber. "Helena, I promise you that you have nothing to fear in our marriage bed. I will not take you again until you are ready." His voice was quiet and calm. "In time you will learn that I am a man of my word. You have nothing to fear from me." He dropped his hands from her and moved away. "I have been looking forward to sleeping in my own bed. Sleeping on the cold, hard ground loses its appeal."

The thud of his boot dropping on the floor startled Helena, and she flinched. She took off her veil, undid her braids, and brushed her hair, keeping her back toward Alaric. After removing her shoes and hose, she took off her kirtle and hung it on the clothes peg. Clad only in her chemise, she went to the bed, avoiding looking at Alaric as he stood in the middle of the chamber. As she hesitated next to the mattress, he spoke.

"Get in bed, Helena, and I will put out the candles."

She huddled on her side, as close to the edge as possible, her back to the middle of the bed. Darkness descended in the chamber as Alaric blew out the last candle. Shortly afterwards she felt the dip of the mattress as he slid in beside her.

"Good night, Helena."

At last, when he made no move toward her, she whispered, "Sleep well, Alaric."

In the morning Helena lay still in bed as Alaric washed and dressed. She had not slept well; his every movement had awakened her even though he never touched her.

Alaric came over to stand next to the bed. "Good morrow, Helena."

"Good morrow, Alaric."

"I am dressed. 'Tis safe to look at me now."

She heard the amusement in his tone as he waited. Slowly turning onto her back, holding the covers to her chest, she sat up. He smiled but made no move toward her.

"I would like for you to join me for breakfast. I am interested to hear how things have been going here in my absence."

"As you wish, milord."

"I will have Renwold send up some fresh water for you." He nodded to her and left the room.

After mass in the chapel, Helena and Alaric broke their fast together at the high table. A few of the other castle inhabitants ate their meal at the trestle tables set in front of the dais, but they were not within hearing distance.

"I noticed you are wearing Mother's chatelaine," Alaric commented.

"Aye." She swallowed a piece of bread, her throat dry. "Lady Margaret gave me an extensive tour of the castle and has been instructing me in my new duties."

Under his questioning she told him about all the tasks she had learned to perform and about taking over the supervision of the household.

"'Tis good you are learning from Mother now," he remarked when she was finished. He took a drink of ale. "She may not be living here much longer."

"What? Why?"

"Lord Wyham has asked my permission to court her."

Helena stared at Alaric. "Do you think she will marry Lord Wyham?"

"'Tis quite possible."

Feeling suddenly bereft, Helena contemplated what Margaret's departure would mean for her. Even though she loved Margaret and should want only her happiness, Helena could not help but hope that Margaret would remain with them at Merclif.

"Father Michael came back from Cardel with us," Alaric continued. "He was weary from the journey yesterday so he went directly to the chapel last night. He told me he is looking forward to seeing you again."

"I am looking forward to seeing him as well. Is Father Michael going to live here?"

"Well, with the two villages to serve now, I am sure Father Thomas could use his help."

"It might be better to build another church in Carleigh. The villagers will not be able to come to Merclif for daily mass. 'Tis too far away for them to travel."

"Hmm, I had not thought of that," Alaric muttered as he chewed a piece of cheese. "Would you talk to Father Michael and see what he thinks about building a chapel in Carleigh? And if so, whether he would be willing to serve as their parish priest?"

"Aye, I would be happy to do so."

"Good. I appreciate your assistance. Another man from Cardel Castle came back with us. Langston, the bailiff."

"Oh, that is wonderful news."

"What do you know of him?"

"Damien was my only friend at Cardel," Helena answered. "He shielded me from my father's wrath on more than one occasion. I was very grateful for his friendship and protection."

Alaric finished the last of his ale. "Langston wants to complete his training as a knight. I have not yet decided if I will take him on."

"Milord—Alaric, I beseech you to do so. Damien has demonstrated to me all the noble qualities a knight should possess."

"We will see. He will need to prove himself to me first."

16

The clang of steel striking steel filled the air as Alaric walked through the lists. Pairs of men fought each other, wielding axes and swords, the king's troops commingling with Merclif's soldiers. Alaric stopped next to Hugh, observing Langston as he sparred with Gordon. Standing with his feet braced wide apart, he rested his left hand on the hilt of his sword, unconsciously flexing and releasing his right hand down at his side.

"What do you think of Langston's skill?" Alaric asked.

"He is not very experienced, but he has a good grasp of the basic techniques. He still has a lot to learn before he becomes a knight, but he shows promise."

"What do you think of his character?"

"Langston has an easy-going manner," Hugh answered. "He has already made friends with several of the other men. He has not shirked any duty I have assigned him. For example, he worked just as hard as anyone with the mangonels."

Alaric nodded then stepped forward when he saw Gordon disengage from the younger man. Langston wiped an arm across his brow as Gordon greeted Alaric.

"I will take over now, Gordon," Alaric announced, drawing his sword.

"Aye, milord." The younger knight bowed his head and walked past Alaric as he advanced on to the field.

"Good morrow, milord," Langston said.

"Ready?" Alaric asked.

He eased into a fighting stance as Langston raised his sword and moved into position.

"Aye, milord," Langston answered.

Alaric's first few hits were tempered as he tested Langston's abilities. As the younger man easily deflected his blows, Alaric increased the pace of his attack, placing his strikes randomly to keep Langston off balance. When Langston suddenly took the initiative, attacking instead of merely defending himself, Alaric counterattacked, driving the younger man back.

Unexpectedly, the memory of Helena's pleased expression when she learned about Langston came to Alaric's mind. He swung his sword, cutting through Langston's breeches, slashing the younger man's thigh and drawing blood. Unable to defend himself against the ferocity of Alaric's attack, Langston staggered back as he tried to ward off the furious blows. He tripped and went down, lying prone on his back. Alaric pressed the point of his sword against Langston's throat as he stared down at the helpless man.

Appalled at his loss of control, Alaric jerked his sword away from Langston's neck. He never let anger rule him in battle, let alone in the lists. Shaking off his incomprehensible animosity, he reached out his left arm to the prostrate man. Langston stared up at him for a long moment, then grasped Alaric's arm and allowed Alaric to pull him to his feet.

Turning his back to his opponent, Alaric walked a few feet away. He took a slow, deep breath. This was naught but a training session, and it was time he treated it as such. When he was back in control, he turned, sword posed. "Ready?" he asked.

"Aye." Langston's voice was grim, and his breathing was rapid.

Alaric slowly engaged the younger man. When he was sure he had mastered his anger, or whatever it was that had caused his aberrant lapse, he began to fight more aggressively, testing Langston, determined to treat him as he would any other knight in training. After a few minutes he had learned what he needed to know about the less experienced man's level of skill and his strength. Alaric stepped back and sheathed his sword. Langston bent over with one hand on his thigh, gasping for breath.

"You may stay and complete your training," Alaric informed Langston.

"Thank you, milord." Langston stood and wiped the sweat off his brow with his sleeve.

Alaric nodded briskly and strode back to where Hugh and Gordon watched on the sidelines.

After Gordon left them to resume his bout with Langston, Hugh queried, "Alaric, what was that all about? I have not seen you lose your temper on the field since you were but a lad."

"I was merely giving Langston a chance to show his true colors. If he is Cardel's agent, what better opportunity could he have to do me harm?" The excuse sounded weak even to his own ears. He turned away from Hugh's skeptical glance and stared at Langston as he engaged Gordon. "I am still not convinced Langston is not Cardel's agent, so keep a close watch on him."

"Aye, milord, I shall do that," Hugh answered.

Light filtered through the stained glass windows in the chapel, draping the interior with a warm glow. Since coming to Merclif Helena had attended morning mass in the chapel each day with the entire household, but she had not let the prayers, liturgy, or Scripture readings penetrate her hardened heart. As she stood beside Father Michael, she felt the serenity of the sanctuary beckoning her.

"How are you doing, my child?" the priest asked.

"I am well, Father," Helena replied. "Lady Margaret has treated me as if I were her own daughter, and Lord Merclif has been kind and considerate."

"That is good. However, I was asking about the condition of your soul, my child. 'Tis of much more importance than your earthly comfort. The last time we spoke you had such hostility toward God. Has He eased the bitterness in your heart?"

Helena stared at the floor. The priest's words seemed to echo in the hollowness of her soul and in the hushed stillness of the chapel.

"I have been praying for you, my child. Have you been praying, as I suggested?"

"I do not see the point, Father." Helena raised her head and met the priest's wise, kind eyes. "God has clearly abandoned me and left me on my own."

Father Michael shook his head. "My child, God never abandons us. We just stop seeking Him. 'Tis why He seems so far away from you, because you have turned your back on Him. God loves you, Helena."

"No, He does not. If He did, He would never have let me suffer as He has."

"God is not the cause of evil in the world, my child. 'Tis a fallen, sinful world we have made from the paradise He created for us. Sometimes evil happens, and we suffer for it. But God is our strength and our sanctuary. He is our ever-present help in times of trouble. He permits our sufferings and then overrules them for His glory and for our good. God uses the sufferings in our lives to mold us and shape us so that we may become more like our Lord and Savior, Jesus Christ. Come, my child, we will pray together so that you may know His love and acceptance."

Helena could think of no gracious way to refuse, so reluctantly followed the priest as he made his way to the front of the chapel. The priest genuflected and went down to his knees in front of the altar. Her heart resentful and sullen, Helena went through the motions as she crossed herself and knelt beside the priest.

"Dear Lord Jesus," Father Michael prayed, "thank You for your death upon the cross where You took our sins upon Yourself. Help Helena to know that You love her so much that even if she had been the only person in the entire world You would have died for her and for her alone. Dear Lord Jesus, help Helena to know that there is no greater love than Your love for her. Help her to see that Your love is faithful and kind, that Your love will never fail her, and that You will never leave her nor forsake her. Help Helena to give to You all her burdens, all her pain, all her sufferings. Help her to present her pain and suffering to You as a sacrifice of love, a reflection of Your own sacrifice of suffering for each of us. Show her that Your grace is sufficient for her. Give her Your peace that surpasses all understanding. Give her the joy that only comes from being in Your presence."

Each of the priest's words was like a spear piercing her innermost being, chiseling her heart and stripping the hard shell she had erected. Tears slipped unheeded out of her closed eyes and dripped down her cheeks. She felt enveloped and surrounded by love and peace.

"I have always loved walking up here," Margaret remarked. "The air is always sharper and clearer, somehow. And the view is spectacular."

She stopped at a crenel to gaze at the woods in the distance and drew her mantle closer around her against the chilly air. Still in the midst of their winter hibernation, the trees remained bare of foliage with only the grays and browns of their bark visible from this distance. Margaret inhaled the robust scent of malt from the alewife's fire.

"Aye," Wyham agreed. "'Tis a relaxing retreat from the noise and bustle of the castle."

"I am glad you suggested this walk, milord. What are your plans now that Cardel has been routed?"

"The king has given me leave to remain here at Merclif for a month."

"That is good. I know Alaric will enjoy your company, as will we all."

Wyham cleared his throat. "Truly, milady, I am hoping that you and I will be able to get to know each other better."

"I would like that. I always enjoy spending time with our guests."

"Lady Margaret, Lord Merclif has granted me permission to court you."

Margaret's eyes widened, and her jaw dropped open. Seeing his gentle smile, she recovered some of her composure, closing her mouth and dropping her gaze from his. Her heart pounding as if she had just completed a race, she placed her hand over her chest to regain her poise.

"If my suit is unwelcome to you, I will of course understand and leave as soon as possible."

Margaret was stunned. She had had no inkling that the courtier was interested in her, and she had never even considered remarrying. Glancing at Wyham, who was now looking out over the countryside, she studied his face. He was a very attractive man. She had admired his sophistication and savoir-faire but knew he was completely different from Gavin, who had been first and foremost a warrior.

The idea that she could become this fascinating man's wife opened a whole new range of exhilarating possibilities for her. She felt an excitement she had not known in years. Now that Alaric had Helena, he no longer needed her to run his household. Was God calling her to serve Him as Wyham's wife rather than as Alaric and Helena's mother?

For once in her life she would be able to make a choice as to her future.

Her father had chosen Gavin for her husband and then, of course, Gavin had made all the decisions in their marriage. But it was not her desires that were important. Only God's will should decide this matter, as in all else. Was marriage to Wyham God's plan for her future? She must commit this matter to prayer and wait on the Lord's decision. Aware that she had let the silence between them drag out to embarrassing lengths,

Margaret touched his arm.

"Milord, 'tis not that your suit is unwelcome; I was simply taken by surprise, 'tis all." She waited until he turned toward her and met her eyes. "I would very much like to get to know you better, milord."

Wyham smiled. "Perhaps you should start by calling me Robert."

"Aye, Robert, I will." Margaret returned his smile.

"I must confess, Margaret, that 'twas your extraordinary physical beauty that first drew me to you. But the longer I spend in your company, the more I see your inner beauty, which has its source in your deep and genuine love for God."

"Why, thank you, Robert. One thing you must know about me is that I take my relationship with God very, very seriously. He is the most important thing in my life."

Wyham nodded. "I feel the same way. I could not contemplate taking a wife who did not share my devotion to our Lord and Savior."

"I am glad to know that we are of like mind on such an important matter." They shared a smile. "So, tell me, Robert, what exactly is it that you do in the king's service?"

"I have completed a number of assignments for Henry, mostly those requiring finesse and diplomacy. 'Tis been a long time since I carried out a military campaign like this one."

"So you live in King Henry's court?"

"Aye. I am one of his closest advisors." His tone was matter-of-fact, without arrogance or boasting. His unassuming demeanor was another element of his character that she admired. "I usually accompany him on his travels throughout the land. He rarely sends me to other demesnes, as he did in this case."

"Do any of the king's other advisors have wives?"

"Aye, quite a few do. Henry encourages his barons to marry. The wives often serve as ladies-in-waiting to Queen Eleanor."

"Do you have any family, Robert?"

"My wife died about thirteen years ago. Once she died, I did not wish to remain at Wyham Castle any longer. There were just too many memories. So I went to Normandy and ended up in King Henry's court. My son and his family live at Wyham Castle now. I have two grandsons, twelve years old and eight years old. My granddaughter is ten. How long have you lived at Merclif, Margaret?"

"I was married when I was fourteen, so I have been here almost thirty years."

"What was your husband like?"

Margaret turned to rest her back against a merlon and smiled softly. Her gaze wandered over the castle grounds as memories of Gavin filled her heart. Although their fathers had arranged their marriage, they had grown to love each other deeply. His loss had faded from the throbbing, insistent pain she had endured for several years after his death to a mellow ache she knew would always be with her.

"Gavin was a warrior. He loved Merclif with every fiber of his being and protected it with total devotion. He was just sixteen when we were married. He was such an arrogant young man then."

Shaking her head slightly, she glanced at Wyham, smiling mischievously at him. An invigorating wind swept the allure, ruffling their mantles as if inviting them to play with it. The currents of air nudged them even closer together.

"I had to take Gavin down a peg or two when we were first married. After that he was much easier to live with. We grew to love each other deeply." Margaret sighed, looking away from Wyham's warm hazel eyes, her unfocused gaze resting on the top of the donjon. "He has been gone for almost five years now, but I still miss him terribly."

After a long silence, Margaret looked at Robert. "But now that Alaric has married, and Helena is taking over the running of the household, they no longer need me. 'Twould be nice to be needed again."

Wyham stepped closer to Margaret, put his hands gently on her upper arms, and pulled her unresisting body toward him. Experiencing the full force of his charm and attention, she sank into him, absorbing him. It had been so long. She had not realized that she had missed the connection, the intimacy, of being held by a lover.

"I need you, Margaret." His voice was low and intimate.

She raised her head and met his lips as he claimed a kiss. He explored her mouth hesitantly at first but deepened the kiss when she eagerly responded to him. His arms enfolded her, and she felt as if she were the most precious thing in the world to him. She clutched him to her while sensations flooded her. His mouth was firm and commanding as he kissed her, his tongue caressing hers. For long moments she savored the taste and feel of him, before he gradually withdrew and stepped back.

Margaret opened her eyes to look at the tender smile on his face, an answering smile dawning on her own lips. Without words, he offered her his hand, and she placed her hand into his palm. They walked together side by side, continuing their stroll along the allure.

17

"Helena."

The sound of his voice stopped her, and she turned to see Langston stride toward her across the hall. He held both of his hands out to her, and she rushed to meet him, putting her hands into his.

"'Tis good to see you again."

"Damien, I am so glad you are here."

Langston stepped closer to her, keeping her hands firmly within his own. She felt his concern as he searched her face.

"How are you? Are you all right?" he asked in a low tone.

"Aye," Helena said with a smile. "I am well. And you?"

"I am fine. Merclif has agreed to my remaining here to finish my training."

"I am so glad for you. I know 'tis what you have most wanted."

"Aye. Helena, could we meet together later and talk in private, like we used to do?"

"I would like that."

Helena glanced away from Langston's face, her eyes colliding with Alaric's. His eyebrows were knit together, causing a deep furrow in his forehead. She pulled her hands out of Langston's grasp. He turned and looked over his shoulder, following Helena's gaze as Alaric advanced toward them.

"We will continue our conversation another time," Langston said.

Alaric stopped beside Helena and put his arm around her waist. Feeling as if he were trying to brand her as his, she stiffened. Alaric's possessiveness bewildered her.

"Langston, now that you have renewed your acquaintance with Lady Merclif, report to Sir Hugh to receive your instructions for the afternoon," Alaric ordered.

"Aye, milord. Farewell, milady."

Langston bowed deeply to Helena, gave a more abbreviated bow to Alaric, and walked away. Helena looked into Alaric's face to see him watching Langston disappear out the donjon door. When he turned his eyes to her, she shrank back from his scowl.

"Stay away from Langston."

He evidently took her stunned expression for assent because he strode away, leaving her standing alone in the middle of the hall.

How dare he order me about as if I were a naughty child?

Cringing inwardly, Helena glanced around. The maids clearing dishes from the nearby trestle tables avoided looking at her. She raised her chin and walked with measured steps toward the kitchen, her heart pounding loudly in her own ears.

For the rest of the afternoon, as she went about her duties, she replayed the scene over and over again in her mind. The more she recalled Alaric's behavior, the angrier she became. He had no right to chastise her like that. She had done nothing wrong.

That night, as soon as she had finished playing her lute, Helena left the hall and went upstairs to her chamber. She hastily disrobed and brushed her hair before getting into bed where she curled into a ball, with her back to the door. She willed herself to go to sleep but had not managed to do so when Alaric entered the room a little while later. When he slid into bed beside her, Helena remained immobile.

"Helena, I know you are not sleeping. Did you think to avoid me tonight?"

Silence stretched painfully between them. Helena did not move a muscle. The anger and resentment she felt at his arrogance in forbidding her to see Damien seethed within her.

"You need to become accustomed to my touch so you will not fear it."

She offered no resistance as Alaric put his hand on her shoulder and gently pulled her over to lie on her back. He stroked her hair back from her forehead, shifting his fingers through the strands.

"You have such beautiful hair, Helena. 'Tis softer than sable fur."

He continued to stroke her hair, not touching any other part of her, either with his hand or his own body. At last she relaxed under his rhythmic movements, and her eyes gradually fluttered closed. After an instant, she jerked her eyes open, staring up at him in the darkness.

"All is well, Helena," he murmured. "Go to sleep."

His touch soothed her, banishing her tension. Her burning eyes drifted closed. Languor seeped into her, and she gave herself up to slumber.

Helena came awake gradually, aware of Alaric's presence. She turned onto her back to find him propped up on his elbow beside her.

"Good morrow, Helena."

"Good morrow, Alaric."

He reached out to stroke the hair at her temple, gently brushing it back from her face, quietly humming a tune as he caressed her. At first her addled brain could not place the melody, but then she recognized his song as "*Chanson du chevalier honorable*," which she had composed about him shortly after coming to Merclif.

Alaric stroked her hair for several minutes, then put his hand lightly on her shoulder. She tensed, holding her body rigid. He lightly rubbed her arm, running his hand from her shoulder to her fingers and back again, all the while maintaining eye contact with her and humming. After a while she accepted his touch and relaxed.

He caressed her arm for a few more minutes, then rolled over and left their bed. She closed her eyes and listened to the sounds he made as he washed and dressed. When he was finished, he stopped next to the bed.

"I will see you at mass, Helena."

"Aye."

Late in the morning, Helena walked around the allure. Pausing on the north side of the crenellations, she located Damien as he trained in the lists. She watched him deftly parry his opponent's blow and then sally, driving the other man back. She sighed, wishing she were able to take up a sword and cut and slash her foes as he was doing. But her opponents were only her own jumbled emotions. They could not be banished by a sword.

"Good morrow, milady."

"Good morrow."

Helena nodded to the guard as he passed and resumed her wandering. Why should she be made to feel guilty that she had been observing Damien train? Resentment against Alaric burned brighter within her.

As she walked along the east side she saw Alaric standing outside the mews with a gyrfalcon on his wrist, and she stopped to watch him. His mouth was moving, and he appeared to be singing as he stroked the bird's feathers. She leaned forward over the stone barrier, straining to hear him over the noise of steel and horses and men that pervaded the bailey.

There seemed to be a rush of wind against her ears as she picked out the faint words he was singing.

"My King and my country I serve gladly,
Protecting the weak, pure justice I seek.
Courage, valor, and truth alone rule me,
Loyalty my guide, in honor my pride."

Gasping, she pulled back as she realized he was singing to the bird the same song he had hummed to her this morning. He was touching the bird with the same soft, deliberate strokes he had used on her this morning. She gripped the side of the wall as she stared at her husband.

Alaric carried the gyrfalcon to a perch set up in front of the mews and tied the bird's creance to it. He removed the bird's hood, all the while stroking her feathers, then backed away from the gyrfalcon and went to stand about ten feet from the bird. Denners came to Alaric and gave something to him before leaving him alone. Alaric stood with his right arm extended, and Helena finally realized he held a live mouse in his bare hand. The gyrfalcon eyed Alaric cautiously, clearly wanting the food he dangled in front of her. She shifted restlessly back and forth on her perch. Alaric merely stood still, singing the chorus over and over again. Finally, the bird flew toward him and snatched the mouse out of his hand. Brought up short by the creance, she was unable to fly away, so returned to her perch where she devoured the mouse.

Alaric walked toward the gyrfalcon, never ceasing to sing the chorus from her song. When the bird had finished eating, Alaric reached out his gloved hand to her and she obediently stepped off her perch and on to his fist. She was rewarded by the strokes of his hand on her feathers.

Abruptly, Alaric turned toward the outer curtain, as if suddenly aware of someone watching him. His piercing blue eyes met hers. He inclined his head slightly toward her in acknowledgment, a welcoming smile spreading across his face. She nodded stiffly to him and hurried away.

When she reached her bedchamber, she took off her cloak and hung it on a peg near her clothes chest. She sat in a chair and picked up her lute. Unconsciously her fingers started to pick out the melody of "*Chanson du chevalier honorable.*" Emotions tumbled over and over each other in her heart. Finally realizing what she was playing, she abruptly pulled her right hand away from the strings. She would forever now think of the song as "Alaric's Song," rather than by the title she had first given it.

Deliberately, Helena started to play a popular love song that was one of Damien's favorites. When the last chord faded, she put down the lute. She went next door to Alaric's solar and located a piece of paper and a quill-pen. She thought for a moment, then wrote the note.

Helena walked into the deserted dairy. The late afternoon sun filled the room with its dying rays but no warmth. Dust motes drifted lazily around in a shaft of light from the high window. She inhaled the smell of the cheese lying in molds on shelves along the sidewall. She turned toward the door as it opened and watch Langston slip inside and stride toward her.

"Helena, are you all right?"

"Aye, Damien, I am well," she replied, extending her hands toward him.

"I was worried when I read your note. I was afraid something terrible had happened." He gently squeezed her hands before releasing them.

"Nay, 'tis nothing like that. I merely wanted to talk with you, as you are my only friend here."

"Lord Merclif clearly disapproves of our friendship."

"Aye. I do not know why he is so opposed to it."

"Are you disobeying his orders, meeting me like this?"

"Aye. 'Tis a ridiculous order. I am a grown woman. I should be allowed to talk with my friend."

"Has Merclif hurt you?"

"Nay."

She dropped her eyes from his and turned away, going to sit on one of the stools. Langston pulled a stool next to hers and sat down.

"I do not want to jeopardize your chances with Merclif. I know that your training for knighthood is very important to you, so we will not be able to meet alone again."

"Aye. I am not worried for myself, but I fear Merclif may try to harm you if he discovers we have met."

"I do not think he will hurt me. He is nothing like my father."

"Thank God for that."

"Damien, I want to tell you how much your friendship has meant to me. If not for you, I truly believe I would be dead now."

Langston reached for her hand. "I am sorry I could not take you away from Cardel nor keep you from being forced to wed Merclif."

"It has not turned out too badly, my coming to Merclif. I love Lady Margaret as if she were my own mother. She has been so kind and gracious to me. I have taken over the running of the household, and I find that very challenging and rewarding."

"I am so proud of you." He gave her hand a gentle squeeze. "I am also glad to see you are now playing your lute before the entire castle."

"I really enjoy playing and singing for an audience. 'Tis like I have been freed. Their joy in the music energizes me. Oh, I do not know how to describe what it feels like."

He smiled at her. "'Tis clear you have enormous talent and love for music. I have always enjoyed listening to you. Mayhap you will play my favorite song sometime."

"Aye. I will sing it for you tonight."

"Good. I am looking forward to that." He paused, rubbing his thumb gently over her knuckles. "Helena." He looked directly into her eyes. "Are you happy here?"

She looked at him, aware that if she said no, he would offer to take her away from Merclif. Had that been in her mind when she had asked him to meet her? The choice lay starkly before her—to go away with Damien or stay with Alaric.

Her feelings for Alaric were such a muddle. Fear, admiration, wariness, attraction. But her feelings toward Damien were suddenly crystal clear. She loved him as a friend, as the brother of her heart with whom she had been blessed.

"Aye." She nodded once. "I am content. I will make a good life for myself here." She saw the acceptance in his eyes. "Damien, what are your plans?"

"Now I know you are well and not in danger, I shall devote myself to my training. As you know, I have always wanted to become a full-fledged knight." He dropped her hand. "After I am knighted, I shall seek out another lord to serve. Given Merclif's antagonism toward me, I do not think I have much of a future here."

"I will try to change his mind about you. He is being completely unreasonable."

"Helena." Langston's voice was gentle. "Your husband is not being unreasonable. He is protecting what is his."

She stared at him, seeing the love he felt for her in his eyes, in his smile.

"'Tis best that I leave here as soon as I can," he said softly.

"Aye." She dropped her gaze.

"Helena, if you ever need my help, for any reason, you have only to ask."

"Thank you, my dear friend."

"I had better get back." He stood. "Merclif is having Gordon watch my every move. I had to evade him this afternoon to meet with you."

"Aye, you should go." She got up as well. "I do not want you to get into trouble."

Langston put his hands on her shoulders and drew her gently toward him. He kissed each of her cheeks. "Fare well, my dear."

Helena swiped the tears from her cheeks as she watched him leave. She lingered in the dairy, giving him time to get away before she left. Gathering her cloak tightly around her against the cold February night, she walked through the deserted bailey.

The cross on top of the chapel caught her eye, and Helena slowed her steps. She wanted the acceptance she had experienced yesterday when Father Michael had prayed for her. It had been the only peace she had known in the last two days. She needed that tranquility again.

Helena entered the chapel and walked up the aisle. The gold cross on the altar glowed in the warm light from the nearby lamps. Her eyes on the cross, she sank to her knees in front of the altar. Making the sign of the cross on her forehead, breast, and shoulders, she folded her hands and bent her head. Father Michael had told her the only way she could get right before God was to confess her sins.

The priest's words echoed in her mind: *If we confess our sins, He is faithful and just and will forgive us our sins and cleanse us from all unrighteousness.*

She prayed silently, *Forgive me, Lord, for I have sinned against You. I have been angry and bitter toward You. I have blamed You for my pain and suffering. Please forgive me....*

Just then a quiet voice said, *"Take heart, daughter; your sins are forgiven."*

Forgiveness draped Helena's soul, covering and warming her. Peace invaded her mind, stilling her agitation. Serenity settled into her heart, calming her churning emotions.

18

When Helena played her lute after supper, she sang first Damien's favorite song. She felt she had never before given the words of longing for a lost love the poignancy she infused them with now. As the last note died away, she found Damien's eyes and smiled at him. He raised his cup in salute and mouthed the words, "Thank you."

She quickly averted her eyes from her friend's. When the thunderous applause trailed off, she plucked out the tune to "Alaric's Song." As she sang of the hero's valiant courage and daring in battle, she realized again how well the words described Alaric. She sang the last lines of the refrain:

"Courage, valor, and truth alone rule me,
Loyalty my guide, in honor my pride."

It was the phrase he sang to his falcon. It was the chorus he hummed when he touched her. Helena looked up into Alaric's intense gaze. She was his captive, just as surely as the wild gyrfalcon belonged to him. He smiled at her, and she felt her heart ease. She might be bound to him, but she knew he was as honorable as the knight in her song. He would do all in his power to keep her safe. She returned his smile.

When the last note of the song rang triumphantly through the hall, Alaric set down his goblet and strode toward her. The wild applause turned to groans of disappointment when Alaric took the lute from her.

"Lady Merclif is done performing for the night," he announced.

He held out his hand to her. She placed her hand in his and allowed him to pull her out of her chair. The crowd gradually dispersed as he led her through the hall and upstairs to their chamber.

"Thank you for singing that last song," Alaric said as he pulled off his boots. "'Tis one of my favorites."

"Aye." Helena drew the brush through her hair. "I know."

"Where did you learn it?"

"I wrote it myself."

"Truly? You have a rare talent for music, Helena. We are very lucky that you share it with us."

"Thank you, Alaric."

As they finished undressing, the silence between them was comfortable. When Alaric joined her in bed, he leaned over her, lightly rubbing her forehead with his thumb. Helena willed herself to relax. Moonlight filtered through the shutters, providing enough light for her to see his face.

"You are training me like one of your falcons."

He averted his eyes from her, and his lips curled slightly. He shrugged one shoulder. She stared at him in surprise. Was he embarrassed?

"Aye. 'Tis what I know. One thing I have learned from them is the virtue of patience. I hope you will be the beneficiary of the patience they have taught me."

He lightly trailed his fingers down her right, unblemished cheek before running his thumb over her lips. Alaric cupped her left cheek in the palm of his hand and she tensed when he touched her scars. As he gently traced the jagged marks with his fingers she gradually felt her tension fade under his touch. After a while, he drew back and lay down beside her.

"Sleep well, Helena."

She woke to the feel of hands on her back. Twisting, she rolled away, pulling the bedding with her.

"Helena. All is well. 'Tis me, Alaric."

Her heart pounding, her breath coming in shallow gasps, she held the covers to her chest and stared at him.

"You are safe. I will not hurt you."

Holding his hands up in front of him, he returned her look. He sat beside her, the bedding draped around his waist. His black hair lay in disarray around his forehead and cheeks; his mouth was set in a grim line.

Helena took a deep breath, closed her eyes, and slumped into herself.

"I am sorry. I did not mean to startle you."

"Nay, I am sorry."

"'Tis my fault. I should have made sure you were awake before I touched you. I will do so in the future."

She nodded, her hair hanging down over her cheeks as she bent her head. When she felt him leave the bed, she collapsed down into the mattress, putting her hands over her eyes. Tremors shook her.

I am safe. There is nothing to fear. I am safe.

She had conquered her fear by the time she heard his footsteps approaching the bed. Opening her eyes, she looked at him. He stopped a foot away from the bed.

"May I sit down?"

"Aye."

She pulled herself up to a sitting position, her back resting against the headboard. Alaric sat on the bed next to her.

"Helena, I am going to touch your shoulder now."

She nodded and kept her eyes on his as he slowly reached out and touched her. He rubbed his hand down her arm then back up again.

"Are you all right, now, Helena?"

"Aye."

"Good."

He gradually raised his hand to her face. She held herself rigid as he cupped her cheek in the palm of his hand. Swallowing the defeat in her throat, she kept her eyes locked on his. He withdrew his hand from her face and gave her a tight smile. Mute, Helena watched him as he left her side and quit their chamber.

After breakfast Helena walked toward the dairy. Today was the day Betsy normally worked at the castle and Helena was looking forward to seeing little Sadie again. As she passed through the northwest gate in the inner curtain, she saw Sadie running toward her.

"Milady! Milady!" Shouting, the child launched herself at Helena.

"Sadie!"

Helena laughed as she caught the little girl in her arms. Picking her up, she hugged Sadie tightly before giving in to her squirming and setting her down.

"Daisy had kittens!"

"She did?" Helena smiled at the child's eager face staring up at her.

"Aye." Sadie nodded. "Come see."

The little girl grabbed Helena's hand and tugged on her arm, leading her into the barn where the livestock were stabled.

"Shush! We gots ta be quiet so's not to scare the babies," Sadie explained in a loud whisper.

The girl led Helena past several stalls, where cows were placidly chewing, to a corner at the far side of the stable. As they got closer to the cat's nesting place, Sadie started to tiptoe with exaggerated care. Helena had to hide her delighted smile when Sadie turned around to look back at her.

"There's Daisy and her babies." The little girl pointed to the cat lying on her side, nursing her six newborn kittens.

"Master Halen say I can'st get any closer than this. Master Halen say I can have a kitten when they weaned. Milady, what's weaned?"

"That means the kittens are big enough to leave their mother," Helena explained. "They can eat normal cat food, not just their mother's milk."

"Oh. How long'll that be?"

"About seven or eight weeks from now."

"Oh." Sadie's disappointment was evident.

"I am sure you can come and visit the kittens every time you come to the castle. Did Master Halen say you could pick out your kitten yourself?"

"Aye." Sadie brightened, nodding.

"Then when you visit the kittens, you can study them and decide which one you think will be the best pet for you."

"Aye."

Sadie stuck her thumb in her mouth and leaned her head against Helena's side. Helena gently stroked the girl's soft brown hair as they watched the kittens. When the babies were through nursing, the cat stood, shook herself, and sashayed off, leaving her kittens behind.

"Master Halen says I can'st touch 'em, neider," Sadie complained.

"Aye. 'Tis best not to touch the kittens; otherwise their mother might mistake your smell on her babies and not feed them. You do not want that, do you?"

"Nay."

Sadie shook her head, looking up at Helena, her beautiful warm brown eyes wide in alarm.

"Sadie, does your mother know where you are?"

Sadie shrugged.

"We had better get you back to your mother before she gets scared."

"Scared? Why Mummy get scared?"

"Mothers always get scared when they do not know where their precious little daughters are."

"Oh."

Sadie cocked her head to the side, appearing to think her words over for a moment, before slipping her hand into Helena's. She tugged Helena toward the door of the barn. "Let's find Mummy."

"Cardel headed northwest when he left his castle," Sir William reported. "We kept him in our sights the entire time. He made no move to evade us or to engage us in any way. They camped out each night and avoided villages and towns. After traveling for five days, they stopped at a small manor house in the town of Narhex. I had some men gather information from the locals. The manor has been in Cardel's family for over thirty years, and he inherited it upon his father's death. We lingered a few days to make sure Narhex was his final destination, then left. We made it back here to Merclif in three days."

"Thank you, Sir William," Wyham said. "You and your men may enjoy a well-deserved rest, then leave the day after tomorrow to rejoin the king. If that meets with the Earl's approval?" Wyham looked at Alaric.

"Aye," Alaric readily agreed.

"Milord, thank you for your hospitality," William said.

"That will be all, Sir William," Wyham said.

After the knight left the solar, Alaric poured more wine into Wyham's goblet and sat back in his chair, staring blindly into the depths of his own cup.

"'Tis possible Cardel has given up," Wyham suggested.

Alaric shook his head. "Cardel will give up only when hell freezes over. He has coveted Merclif too aggressively and for too long to give up so easily. Nay, he has some plan to eliminate me. We will just have to wait and see what it is. If I am dead, he can force Lady Margaret to wed him and take over Merclif. That was his original plan."

"Over my dead body," Wyham declared.

"Let us hope it does not come to that." Alaric raised his cup and drained it.

Margaret looked over her shoulder, smiling at Wyham as he entered the herbarium and closed the door behind him. As usual, the courtier was dressed in the height of fashion, his forest green wool tunic bringing out the green in his hazel eyes. His close-fitting gray wool breeches were gartered at the knee while his tight linen hose, also gray, revealed his shapely calves.

"Good morrow, Robert," she greeted him before turning back to the worktable. "I will be done here in a few minutes."

"What are you doing, Margaret?" Wyham walked toward her.

"I am mixing some common poultices and tinctures. I like to make sure we have enough of the most frequently used remedies on hand."

"I enjoy watching you work, so take your time."

Wyham came to stand next to her, leaning his hip against the side of the table. Margaret sprinkled some elecampane root on top of the marble mortar and started to grind it using the matching marble pestle. When it was a fine powder, she added it to some honey in a bowl. She closed up the jar of elecampane root and put it back on the shelf above the worktable before selecting a jar of horehound.

"As I understand, Merclif Castle was built about fifty years ago."

"Aye, that is correct." Margaret added the ground horehound to the mixing bowl.

"When was Cardel Castle built?"

"Cardel came here about fifteen years ago. King Stephen granted him the land and the license to build his castle." Margaret glanced at him but continued to mix together the herbs and honey in the bowl.

"'Tis obvious that Merclif Castle and lands are far superior to Cardel's castle and lands."

"Aye." Margaret spooned the remedy into a glass jar. After securing the lid, she wrote out a label and tied it around the neck of the jar.

"Why did Cardel settle here? Why not build his castle on his properties in the north?"

"I do not know."

She placed the jar with the poultice on the shelf. After cleaning the mortar with a cloth, she sprinkled dried sage leaves on its surface. A redolent, refreshing scent was released as she crushed the tiny gray green leaves.

"Helena told Alaric that Cardel's plan was to kill Alaric and Helena, then force you to wed him," Wyham stated.

"Truly? I suppose such a marriage would legitimize his taking of Merclif."

"Did you know Cardel before he came to the Mersted Valley?"

"Both Gavin and Cardel received their training in knighthood from my father. I do not believe my father had much respect for Cardel. He told me that Cardel's family had approached him about the possibility of my marrying their son, but he refused them. Later he arranged my betrothal to Gavin."

"So Cardel has wanted you for years."

"Surely not." She transferred the ground sage from the mortar to a shallow dish. "'Tis not *me* he wants, but the property he thinks he can acquire through me."

"Margaret, you are far too modest for your own good. I am convinced Cardel's interest in you is very personal. He wants you in his bed."

Margaret shuddered in revulsion.

"You will just have to marry me to make sure Cardel does not get ahold of you." Wyham's tone was light and teasing.

Margaret glanced at him, smiling slightly. "Hmm. Mayhap I will."

Wyham reached for her, sliding his arms around her waist and pulling her to him. She dropped the bowl onto the table and went willingly into his arms, sliding her hands around his neck and leaning into his embrace as he lowered his head to kiss her. The heat of their leisurely kisses gradually intensified. She clung to him, savoring the feel of his arms holding her. His hands stroked up her back as he deepened the kiss. She whimpered, and he abruptly pulled back from her, moving his hands to her waist. He held her away from him, steadying her.

"Margaret, I am sorry." His voice was hoarse. "Please forgive me. I did not intend to take advantage of you. I am afraid my passion for you overwhelmed me."

Margaret stepped closer to him, dropping her forehead on to his chest, her arms curling around his waist. The solid reality of him anchored and supported her. Whereas just moments ago she had experienced the fires of desire and hunger, his arms now offered her comfort and serenity.

"There's nothing to forgive, Robert. My passion for you overwhelmed me as well. 'Tis been so long…"

Wyham cradled her against his chest. "We will take it slowly from now on," he said into her hair.

"Nay. I do not want to waste any of our time together."

She leaned back, cupped his cheeks in her hands, and pulled his head down to her as she reached up to kiss him. Margaret caressed his broad shoulders and muscular arms before slowly drawing away from Robert's embrace.

"Milord, you will have to promise not to distract me again." She was breathless, her tone playfully stern. "Otherwise I shall have to ban you from my herbarium."

"Aye, milady," Wyham said with a smile. "I will try to keep my hands to myself."

She raised her eyebrows in question.

"At least for now." Wyham's voice lost its playful tone as he continued speaking. "And, as for the danger Cardel still poses for you, I will just have to entrust you to the Lord."

"The Lord will protect us. We will continue to rely upon him and commit everything to him in prayer."

Margaret touched Robert's clean-shaven cheek, marveling again at the graciousness of God. He had richly blessed her by sending this godly man into her life, a man as dedicated to the Lord as she was herself. Their devotion to God had only deepened as they shared their faith, and their lives, with each other.

19

Alaric entered the donjon, noticing that the hall seemed much quieter than it had been the last few days since the departure that morning of Sir William and the king's troops. Feeling satisfied after the pleasant and successful afternoon he had spent hunting with Wyham and his men, he sauntered toward the steps. Margaret hurried toward him, intercepting him in the center of the hall.

"Good evening, Mother."

"Alaric, I am so glad you are back. I am worried about Helena. She has not returned yet."

"Where did she go?" Alaric frowned.

"Sadie, one of the villeins' children, is very sick. Helena has become quite fond of the girl so she went into the village after dinner to bring Sadie some medicine."

"Did she go alone?"

"Nay. A nice young man offered to go with her. I think his name is Langston."

Alaric clenched his jaw. "I will go and bring her home." He bowed briefly to his mother and strode toward the door.

"Milord." Renwold's voice stopped Alaric.

"What?"

The steward recoiled slightly. "I am sorry to disturb you, milord, but Lady Merclif has not yet come back to the castle, and supper is ready to be served. Shall we wait supper until she returns?"

"Nay. Serve supper now. Lady Merclif and I will eat later."

"Aye, milord." Renwold bowed.

He had expressly ordered Helena to stay away from Langston. How dare she deliberately disobey him? Rage built with every step Alaric took. He marched to the stables, where he found the marshal. "Saddle a horse for me."

"Aye, milord."

Alaric left the stables and headed for the armory. Belwick entered as Alaric was putting on his chain mail hauberk. Hugh immediately moved toward Alaric and helped him settle the armor over his shoulders.

"Milord, I have just learned that Lady Merclif has not returned from the village."

"Aye. And Langston is with her."

"Sir Gordon went along as well, milord. He has been very diligent about keeping an eye on Langston."

"Good. Hand me my coif."

Belwick gave the chain mail helmet to Alaric, then picked up a pair of gauntlets and held them out to Alaric.

"Hugh, this may be a ruse on Langston's part to kidnap Lady Merclif. Send three men to the village. I will not wait for them." Alaric pulled on the thick leather gloves.

"Surely not, milord. Langston appears to be genuinely fond of Lady Merclif."

"I do not trust him. He was Cardel's man for two years, after all."

"Aye, milord. 'Twill be as you command."

Alaric took the sword Hugh handed him and ignored the misgiving evident in his castellan's voice. He left the armory with Hugh at his side. Without speaking further, they split up, Hugh going toward the donjon while Alaric went to the stables, where he found his horse waiting for him.

"Saddle three more horses," he ordered the marshal as he mounted Guaire.

"Aye, milord."

The marshal released Guaire's bridle and stood back as Alaric turned the horse away from the stables. Once he was clear of the postern gate and down the drawbridge, he urged Guaire into a gallop. Twilight merged with night, but there was enough light from the waning moon for him to find his way in the deepening darkness. When he entered the village, he slowed his horse to a walk down the deserted main street. Spotting three horses tied outside a wattle and daub cottage, he headed toward them.

Rounding the side of the small house he saw Langston holding Helena in his arms, her bent head resting on his shoulder. Langston raised his eyes and steadily met Alaric's gaze. Helena, with her back to the road, seemed to be oblivious to his arrival. Pulling Guaire up sharply, Alaric jumped down from the saddle. He rushed toward the entwined couple, the sight of Helena in Langston's arms causing his already burning anger to explode into an inferno.

Gordon stepped in front of him, blocking his path. "Milord!"

"Get out of my way," Alaric snarled.

"Milord, 'tis not what you think," Gordon said in an urgent tone. "The little girl is dying. The priest is inside giving her last rites. Lady Merclif is distraught. Langston is only comforting her as would a brother."

Alaric looked again at Helena. Wrenching sobs raked her body. Her hands covered her face as she leaned against Langston's chest. The other man's arms protectively circled her upper body, and he was rubbing his hands up and down her back. Langston unflinchingly met Alaric's gaze but made no move to step away from Helena.

Alaric took a step back from Gordon and willed his tense muscles to relax. "Aye. Thank you, Sir Gordon." He cleared his throat to drive away the hoarseness cloaking it.

Gordon moved out of his way.

"Gordon, three soldiers will be arriving here soon. Head them off and send them back to the castle."

"Aye, milord." Gordon bowed and hurried toward the main street.

Alaric advanced toward Helena and Langston, drawing off his gauntlets and then pulling off his mail coif. He stood silently next to the couple, listening to Helena's heartrending weeping. Eventually, when her tears abated and she lay quiet against Langston's chest, the younger man spoke.

"Helena." His voice was soft. "Lord Merclif is here."

She raised her head. "Alaric?"

"Aye, Helena, I am here."

Langston's arms fell away from Helena as she turned toward Alaric. The younger man stepped back, releasing her. Alaric moved closer to Helena but made no move to touch her as she swiped her hands over her wet cheeks.

"Alaric, Sadie is dying."

"What ails the child?"

"She has had a very high fever since yesterday." Helena wrapped her arms around her waist. "She has been vomiting and suffering from convulsions. I gave her a tincture that Lady Dorothea used for fevers. But I do not know if it will do any good. It works best if it is administered right away, but Sadie has been fighting the fever for over a day and a half now. She is so little." A sob overcame Helena.

"Sometimes using a water bath will bring down the fever enough for the body to recover and get better," Alaric said. "I have seen it work before."

"'Tis worth a try."

"Helena, shall I fetch some water for you to use to treat the girl?" Langston asked.

"Aye, Damien."

Langston strode away, passing Gordon, who hurried back from the road.

"Milord, the men are returning to the castle."

"Thank you, Gordon," Alaric responded.

Gordon bowed and retreated, leaving them alone. Helena stared unseeingly at the cottage door. Waiting quietly beside his wife, Alaric stifled his urge to touch her, to comfort her, afraid of what her reaction would be.

Some time later, the door opened and Father Thomas came out.

"Milady, there is nothing to do now but pray," the priest said.

"Aye, Father." Helena's voice broke.

"Milord, milady, please excuse me. I will go to the chapel and pray for little Sadie's soul."

When Helena went inside the cottage Sadie was lying on a pallet in front of the fireplace, and Betsy was on the floor beside her daughter. Ogden, Sadie's father, sat at the table, staring helplessly at his wife and daughter, his face gaunt and drawn. Helena dropped to her knees next to the other woman and looked down at Sadie. The girl's cheeks were flushed, and her breathing was shallow.

"Betsy, there is something else we can try. Lord Merclif thinks we may be able to bring down Sadie's fever using a water bath. Master Langston is fetching the water. Do you have a tub we can use?"

Betsy, her eyes dull and lifeless, looked at Helena. Tears streamed down her cheeks.

Sadie's father pushed back the bench he was sitting on. "Milady, we can use the feed trough. I'll go fetch it."

"Ogden, make sure you clean it out thoroughly."

"Aye, milady."

"Betsy, let us move Sadie away from the fire and take off her clothes," Helena instructed.

The women each took one end of the pallet and dragged it back to the opposite side of the room. Helena had just stripped off Sadie's kirtle, leaving her clad in a thin chemise, when Langston entered the cottage with the first bucket of water. Alaric and Gordon followed, each with a load of water. A short time later Ogden returned with the trough and filled it with the water. After he was done, the women placed Sadie in the water, covering her small body up to her shoulders.

Dear God, Helena recited silently, *please heal Sadie and make her well. Please do not take her from us. We love her so much.*

She continued her litany of supplication as she worked over the little girl, using a cloth to trickle water over Sadie's head and trying to get her to drink some water. In the windowless hut she had no conception of how much time passed. Her consciousness narrowed and focused solely on fighting Sadie's fever and her urgent pleas to God.

Helena touched Sadie's forehead with the back of her hand for what seemed the hundredth time during the long, unrelenting battle. This time, instead of the burning heat the child had been giving off, now Helena felt only mild warmth. Holding her breath she pressed her cheek to Sadie's forehead. Helena drew back and looked more closely at her patient, noting her even breathing and natural slumber. She closed her eyes and silently prayed, *Thank You, Lord. Thank You. Thank You. Thank You.*

She opened her eyes and turned toward Betsy. The girl's mother sat on the bench. Her crossed arms lay flat against the top of the table, and her head rested on her arms.

"Betsy! Sadie's fever has broken."

The other woman raised her head. "Her fever's gone? Ye're sure, milady?"

"Aye. Come, let us get Sadie out of the water."

Helena handed Sadie into Betsy's waiting arms. Betsy dried Sadie and pulled a clean chemise over her head. Together the women carried Sadie to a mattress in the corner of the room and laid her down gently.

Helena touched Betsy's shoulder. "I will go let Ogden know Sadie is better."

Betsy grabbed Helena's hand. "Thank ye, milady. Thank ye."

"I did nothing, Betsy. 'Tis God who healed Sadie."

Smiling, Helena gave Betsy's hand a gentle squeeze. When she went outside, she found the four men surrounding a campfire they must have built on the cold ground.

Sadie's father broke away from the other men and hurried toward her. She greeted him with a joyous smile.

"Ogden, Sadie's fever has broken, and she is sleeping naturally now. Praise be to God!"

"Truly?" Ogden whispered.

"Aye, Ogden. Sadie's now out of danger."

"Praise be to God. Thank ye, milady."

Sadie's father rushed past Helena and went into the cottage. She continued walking toward the fire, rubbing her hands up and down her arms to warm herself in the cold night air. The men had all turned to look at her. She could tell from their expressions that they had heard the good news she had given Ogden.

"God has answered our prayers," Helena told them with a smile.

"Hallelujah!" Gordon said.

"God be praised." Langston smiled.

"Aye," Alaric agreed.

Alaric watched Helena disappear back into the hut. She had remained outside only long enough to share the news of Sadie's recovery with them.

He turned back to his men. "Sir Gordon, you and Langston will return to the castle now. I will escort Lady Merclif home later."

"Aye, milord." Gordon glanced at Langston.

"Milord, I would prefer to stay to help Lady Merclif in any way I can," Langston declared.

Alaric glared at the younger man. "If you wish to become a knight in my service, you will never question my orders again. Is that clear?"

"Aye, milord."

"Langston, return to the garrison and report to Sir Hugh."

"Aye, milord." Langston bowed and strode toward his horse, trailed by Gordon.

Alaric watched the men mount their horses and ride away. He stared at the dying fire for long moments, mulling over what to do about Langston. Finally, he turned, went to the cottage, and knocked on the door.

Helena answered. She held a babe in her arms, shielding the infant from the cold by pulling the blanket over its head. Would she ever hold his babe in her arms? The way things were going between them the prospect seemed more distant than ever. His resolution hardened.

"'Tis time to return to Merclif," Alaric stated.

"Nay, I cannot leave yet. I need to nurse Sadie back to health." She kept her tone low.

"Come outside so we can talk."

Helena stared mutely at him, then nodded. She closed the door in his face. Alaric's jaw flexed, and he turned his back to the door, walking several paces away.

A few minutes later, when Helena left the cottage alone and came to stand beside him, he turned to look at her. She had put on her mantle and stood with her arms crossed in front of her.

"'Tis not the job of Lady Merclif to nurse villein children. Her mother and the villagers can do so."

"Nay." Helena raised her chin. "They do not have any medical knowledge. They will not know what to do."

They faced each other. Alaric stared at Helena, exasperated with her stubbornness, while Helena calmly returned his look. The arrival of two riders broke the stalemate between them.

Lady Margaret and Wyham rode into the yard. Alaric went to grasp the bridle of his mother's horse and held the animal as Wyham helped her dismount.

Margaret hurried toward Helena. "Helena, my dear. How is little Sadie?" Margaret held Helena's extended hands and kissed her cheek.

"Her fever has broken, and she is sleeping now," Helena said with a smile.

"Oh, that is wonderful news. I am so relieved." She turned toward Alaric as he and Wyham approached the women. "Alaric, I am here to take over now. You and Helena must be exhausted, having been up all night."

"Aye, Mother," Alaric agreed. "I was just trying to convince Helena to go back to the castle when you arrived."

"Helena, you must go and rest now," Margaret insisted. "I have brought some more herbs and tinctures. I will instruct Betsy when and how to use them. We will get Gladys to come in as well. She is an excellent nurse."

"Aye, milady. Since you are here, I can rest easier, knowing Sadie is being well cared for." She glanced at Alaric.

Alaric held out his hand to her. He watched her as she briefly embraced Margaret, then accepted his help mounting her horse. As they rode out of Mersthorpe, the villagers emerged from their houses. Alaric nodded and held up his hand, acknowledging the villeins' greetings as they rode past. He glanced at Helena to see her smiling tiredly and waving to the people.

Once clear of Mersthorpe, Alaric urged his horse into a canter, looking over at Helena to ensure she did the same. Side by side they rode back to Merclif in silence. When they arrived at the stables, Alaric dismounted, then went to Helena's side to help her down from her horse. He kept her hand in his as they walked to the donjon, where

Renwold met them as they entered the hall.

"Welcome back, milord, milady." He greeted them with a bow. "The guards alerted us to your arrival so I have had warm water brought to your chamber. Food has been laid out in your solar, milord."

"Excellent," Alaric said. "Your efficiency is much appreciated, as always, Renwold."

"Thank you, milord." The steward's thin lips briefly curved into a slight smile.

"Please send a maid up to help Lady Merclif."

"Aye, milord." Renwold stood back to let them proceed.

Alaric walked next to Helena as they climbed the stairs and entered their bedroom. "Helena, I will leave you now. Please join me in the solar after you have refreshed yourself."

"Aye, milord."

20

O ver breakfast in the lords' solar, Helena observed her husband's grim expression. It made her uneasy and stole what little appetite she had. She picked at the bread in her hand, watching Alaric as he consumed a hearty amount of the cold pigeon pie. After finishing his food and draining the ale in his cup, he sat back in his chair and looked at her.

"Helena, you deliberately disobeyed my order to stay away from Langston. I cannot allow you to flaunt my commands. Your safety, and the safety of the entire castle, depends on my orders being obeyed without question."

Helena bent her head. Her joy over Sadie's recovery had dissipated under the force of his speech, leaving behind exhaustion. Feeling limp and drained, she knew she did not have the strength now to endure a confrontation with her husband.

"I am sorry, milord. I know you are angry with me, but could we talk about this later, after I have had some rest?"

"Aye, on the condition that you remain in our chamber, alone, until we do have this discussion."

"Aye, milord."

Alaric stood and came around the table to pull out Helena's chair. She followed him as he escorted her next door.

"Get some sleep." His voice was quiet. "We will talk tonight after supper."

"Aye, milord. Thank you."

Alaric did not look up from the letter he was writing but was aware of Langston entering the solar in response to his command. Silence loomed in the room. After several minutes, Alaric finished writing and leaned back in his chair, studying the younger man.

Langston stood at attention in front of the table, his hands relaxed by his side.

"Are you in love with my wife?" Alaric asked.

"Aye, milord." Langston's answer was delivered in a calm, matter-of-fact tone.

Clenching his jaw, Alaric stared at Langston, who met his gaze impassively. "I cannot decide, Langston, if you are a very brave man or merely a very stupid one."

Langston said nothing.

"If you wish to remain in my service, you will leave Lady Merclif alone."

"Milord, my love for Lady Merclif is completely pure. I seek only to protect and serve her."

"You have been listening to too many *chansons d'amour*. They are all bull. There is no such thing as a 'pure' love. If you love a woman, you want to bed her." Alaric stood, planted both hands on the table in front of him, and leaned over it to glare at Langston. "*I* will protect Lady Merclif. *You* will serve me. You are not to approach Lady Merclif. You are not to talk with Lady Merclif. You are not to be alone in her company at any time. Do I make myself clear?"

"Aye, milord."

"You are dismissed."

Langston bowed curtly to Alaric, turned, and left the room.

Helena watched Alaric as he went to a side table and poured wine into two goblets. He handed one to her and sat down opposite her. The heat from the brazier filled their bedchamber, but the warmth did not penetrate into her cold hands.

"How are you feeling? I hope you had a good sleep this afternoon."

"I am fine, Alaric. Thank you."

"Helena, I have reason to believe that Langston is an agent for your father, bent on destroying Merclif."

Helena's head snapped up. "That is not possible."

"Is it not?" Alaric's left eyebrow rose.

"Langston shielded me from my father on several occasions. He clearly abhorred my father's cruel actions. He would never act dishonorably."

"Are you willing to stake your life on that?"

"Aye."

"Are you willing to stake my life on that? My mother's life? The lives of every man, woman, and child at Merclif?"

She stared at him. "If you think Langston is such a threat to Merclif, why are you allowing him to remain here?"

"I prefer to have him under surveillance so I can counter any move he tries to make."

"What if you are wrong? What if Langston is innocent?"

"Only time will tell if he is innocent or not. He will come to no harm if he does not attack Merclif."

Helena bent her head, toying with her wine goblet.

"I must have your promise that you will not speak with Langston, and you will never be in his company."

Tears clogged her throat at the prospect of being cut off from Langston's friendship and support. She had not realized how much she had missed the comfort of his presence until he had come to Merclif. Should she fight Alaric on this? No, he was clearly not able to be reasonable about Damien.

She looked up at him, defeat heavy on her heart. "Aye."

She watched him swallow a drink of wine. He leaned forward in his chair, his forearms resting on his spread thighs, holding the goblet between his knees. He did not look at Helena for a long moment.

"Why were you in his embrace when you can barely stand my touch?" His voice was soft and unthreatening.

Startled, she looked into his piercing blue eyes. "He is not...I do not..."

Alaric sat up straight, maintaining eye contact with her. "He is not what? You do not what?"

"He is not my husband," she finally said. "I do not have to submit to him in bed."

"Do you love him?"

"Aye. Nay."

"Which is it? Aye or nay?"

"I love him like a brother, not like a...a..."

"A lover?"

"Aye."

"So you love Langston like a brother, and you find comfort in his touch. You are afraid of me, so you find my touch distasteful."

"Nay, I..."

"What?"

"I do not find your touch distasteful," she replied.

"Are you afraid of me?"

"Aye."

"Why? Do you think I will hurt you?"

"I do not think you will deliberately hurt me."

"But, given the consummation of our wedding vows, you believe that the act itself is painful."

"Aye." She dropped her eyes to the goblet in her hands.

"Most husbands would not care about their wives' fears. They would just bed their wives, disregarding their pain."

"Aye, I know." She met his eyes. "Alaric, I do appreciate your patience with me."

He gave her a slight smile. "I do not suppose it would do much good to reassure you that most of the pain was due to your being a virgin. Next time I bed you, you should not experience any pain. You might even find it pleasurable."

Feeling the heat rising in her face, Helena bent her head. "Nay, I did not think so."

There was a pause, but Helena did not remove her gaze from the cup she clutched in her hands.

"I still think the best way to solve this problem is for you to get used to my touch." He stood. "Let us go to bed, Helena. I have not slept in two days, and I am sure you are still tired as well."

"Aye."

She stood and set her goblet down beside his on the table. Silence blanketed the chamber as they got ready for bed. As usual she kept her chemise on as she slid into bed, and he waited until she was lying down before extinguishing the candles in the chamber and coming to join her. He propped his left arm on the mattress beside her and gently stroked the top of her head. He caressed her forehead, rubbing his thumb in small circles. Finding comfort in his touch, she closed her eyes. He cupped her left cheek in his hand, lightly stroking his thumb over her scars. The touch of his lips on hers caused her to stiffen beneath him. Immediately his lips left hers, and she felt him lay down beside her.

"Good night, Helena," he said quietly.

"Good night, Alaric."

When Helena opened her eyes, Alaric's intense blue eyes were locked with hers. Maintaining eye contact with her, he ran his forefinger softly over her bottom lip. She lay still on her back, wondering what he would do next. Sliding his hand gently over her left cheek, turning her face toward him, he leaned down and lightly kissed her lips. She instinctively stiffened against his touch. Instead of drawing back as he had last night, Alaric continued to delicately nibble her closed mouth. She willed herself to relax, thinking she should respond to him as much as possible so she would not exhaust his patience.

Alaric tenderly stroked her cheek as he kissed her. He caught her lower lip between his lips and gently tugged on it as his nimble lips moved systematically around her mouth, nibbling on her lips. He pulled back and looked down into her face. "Good morning, Helena."

She opened her eyes to stare at him. "Good morning, Alaric."

He stroked her face, pushing her hair back from her forehead. Cupping her cheek, he leaned down to give her another closed mouth kiss. He smiled at her before turning away and leaving the bed. She closed her eyes against the sight of his naked body.

"It looks like a sunny day today, for a change," Alaric remarked. "Helena, you are allowed to look at me. I am your husband, after all."

She choked. Her face flamed in embarrassment, and she flung her arm over her eyes. Relieved he did not say anything else, she listened to the sounds he made as he washed and dressed. Soon the mattress beside her dipped.

"Helena, 'tis safe to look at me now."

She opened her eyes to see his slight smile.

"One more kiss to last me the rest of the day. But this time, you need to open your mouth."

She stared up at him in bewilderment. Alaric cupped her face in both his hands, and he bent over her. Using his thumbs to gently pull down her lower lip, his mouth covered hers. His tongue lightly stroked her lips before he gently slid it inside her mouth. She went rigid at his invasion. He continued to kiss her, but she remained tense and unyielding. He eased back from her and sat up.

"Hmm. We will need to work on that some more tonight." His tone was light and easy, and he gave her a smile. "I will see you at mass."

Her eyes followed him as he left the chamber.

"Alaric," Helena said, "I would like to go visit Sadie this morning."

Alaric finished chewing a piece of bread before speaking. "Aye. I will instruct Belwick to assign an escort to you. You need only go to the stables when you are ready to leave."

Helena released the breath she had been holding, afraid he would refuse to allow her to go to the village. Relieved, she gave him a smile. "Thank you, Alaric."

There was a comfortable silence between them as they completed their breakfast.

"How well do you know the village of Carleigh?" Alaric asked.

"I do not know anything about it, Alaric. For the last five years, I was a prisoner in my father's castle."

"I have plans to travel there tomorrow with Father Michael. I want to acquaint myself with the village leaders as well as determine where to build the new chapel. I will leave shortly after breakfast and will not return until after dark." Alaric turned to look at her. "I am hoping that you will come with me. The villagers should get to know their new lady as well as their new lord."

Helena bit her lip as she considered Alaric's invitation. A few short months ago she would never have dreamed of showing her face to so many strangers. Now she had the experience of acceptance from the people of Merclif and Mersthrope. She not only felt stronger physically because of the regular meals she now enjoyed, but she felt stronger mentally and emotionally. She could do this. Alaric would be beside her the entire time and Father Michael would be there as well.

She nodded decisively and met Alaric's eyes. "Aye, I would like to accompany you."

"Good." He gave her a smile. Standing, he pulled back her chair so she could rise. He loosely held her shoulders and bent to kiss both her cheeks. "Have a good morning, Helena. I will see you at dinner."

She stood still as she watched him stride from the hall. When he was gone, she went to confer with Margaret about Sadie's condition and the treatment regimen Margaret had started the little girl on yesterday. After packing a basket of herbs, tinctures, and poultices from the herbarium and retrieving a basket of food from the kitchen, Helena walked to the stables. The marshal greeted her, telling her he had saddled a horse for her on his lordship's orders. Sir Roger and Matthew were also waiting for her.

When they reached the village, the people politely made way for them as Helena smiled and waved, returning their greetings. When they reached Sadie's cottage, Sir Roger helped her dismount, and Matthew carried the baskets for her. Helena knocked softly on the door so she would not wake the children if they were sleeping.

"Good morrow, milady." Betsy dropped a curtsy. She held the door open wide and stepped aside. "Please come in, milady."

Helena took the baskets from Matthew before going inside. Betsy shut the door behind her, leaving the guards outside. Helena set the baskets on the table and looked at the mattress where she could see Sadie sitting.

"Milady, milady!" Sadie excitably bounced up and down in the bed. "Did ya come to see me?"

"Aye, Sadie, I have." Helena turned back to Betsy as she took off her mantle. "How is Sadie doing today?"

"She's better, milady," Betsy smiled broadly. "'Tis a miracle. Almost as if she was never sick. Truly, I'm having a hard time making her stay quietly in bed."

"Aye, 'tis a miracle indeed."

Helena went to the mattress, sat down, and hugged the small girl to her. She pulled back so she could examine Sadie's face. "I came just to see you, Sadie. How do you feel, sweetie?"

"I fine. I want ta play. I wanna go castle ta see my kitten."

Helena placed her hand over the girl's forehead before cupping her cheek as she closely examined Sadie's eyes and skin. "Aye," she said with a smile. "You do look very well to me. You can get out of bed for a little while today. But you must not play too hard because you will get tired very easily."

"I not get tired." Sadie pushed back the blanket and got up.

Helena trailed the little girl around the cottage. Sadie showed her all her favorite places and toys as Betsy went about her household chores. After a time, when Helena noticed the child beginning to droop, she walked toward the table and sat on the bench. "Sadie, I am afraid I am a little tired. Will you sit on my lap while I rest?"

Sadie looked seriously at Helena, her head cocked to one side. She nodded. Helena picked her up and held her with Sadie's head tucked against her shoulder. Sadie put her thumb in her mouth, closed her eyes, and abruptly fell asleep.

"Milady, let me take her from you." Betsy wiped her hands on her apron as she came toward Helena.

Helena smiled at Betsy. "I would like to hold her for a little longer. I am enjoying it."

"If ye're sure, milady."

"Aye. Sadie is very sweet." Helena dropped a light kiss on the girl's head.

"Aye, that she is. Milady, ye'll be a good mother when ye've yer own children." Betsy turned back to the kettle she had suspended over the fire.

Helena contemplated the idea of having her own child, tightening her arms around Sadie's small, warm body. Her heart yearned for a baby to love and nurture, but she would not conceive a child unless she submitted to Alaric in bed. The idea of his taking her and invading her body again haunted her. Yet that was the only way to achieve her heart's desire.

She buried her face in Sadie's fine hair, thinking about the way Alaric had kissed her this morning. She had enjoyed the light kisses he had given her at first. His last kiss, however, had frightened her. It had reminded her of his invasion of her body when he had consummated their marriage.

She was grateful Alaric was sensitive to her fears and was patiently taking the time to allow her to become accustomed to him. It was not his touch so much that she feared, she finally realized. It was being under the control of someone stronger and larger than she was. Her father's abuse had seared her soul. Her only defense against him had been to hide, to make herself as small and inconspicuous as possible so he would forget about her. Whenever she had been unlucky enough to come to his attention, he easily overpowered her weaker body and had beaten her.

What was she to do? Helena silently considered. Alaric would always be bigger and stronger than she was. How long would it take for her to become accustomed to his touch? And if she ever did, would her fear retreat or would it still plague her and ruin her marriage? She knew this was not a problem she could solve on her own.

The door opened, and Ogden stepped inside, closing the door behind him. He bowed awkwardly and stood before her, fingering his cap between his hands. "Good morrow, milady."

Helena smiled at the villein. "Good morrow, Ogden. I had to come and make sure for myself that Sadie is better. I am so glad she is recovering from her illness."

"Aye, milady. Thanks be to ye and his lordship."

"Thanks be to God. He cured Sadie. As much as I hate to let this precious little girl go, I should let you have your dinner."

Helena gave Sadie one last hug before relinquishing her to her father's arms.

21

As soon as Helena returned to the castle, she went to the chapel. She fell down on to her knees before the altar, crossed herself, and bent her head. Closing her eyes, she folded her hands together and silently began to pray.

Dear Lord God Almighty, thank You for healing Sadie. Thank You for answering my prayers. Thank You for Your perfect faithfulness and everlasting love. Strengthen Sadie and make her healing complete.

Dear Lord, please heal my spirit. Remove this fear from me. I know You gave me Alaric as my husband for a purpose. I want to be a proper wife to him, but I do not know how to get past this fear. Please help me. Help me to trust only in You and to submit to Your will for my life. I know that You alone are my help and my salvation.

Helena took a slow, deep breath. *And dear Lord, help me show Alaric how wrong he is about Damien. I am so weak and spineless that I gave in even when I know he is wrong. Help me to stand up to Alaric and defend Damien.*

Helena sighed. *All these things I pray in Jesus' name, amen.*

She crossed herself but remained on her knees before the altar. As always, the serenity of the chapel soothed her. Whenever she prayed privately within these walls, she could feel strength and power flow into her.

She did not want to leave this sanctuary. As soon as she stepped out of its doors, the same old fears and anxieties overtook her, and she ended up either reacting out of fear and anger or withdrawing. How could she take this serenity with her? How could she experience this strength and power throughout her day?

Standing before the fireplace, Alaric took a long drink of the wine in his cup as he watched Helena sing a popular *chanson de geste*. She had been especially skittish around him all day. Several times he had caught her eyes on him, only to have her look away or bend her head in avoidance, her face flaming. He had thought they were making progress and that she was learning to tolerate, if not enjoy, his touch. He must have gone too far this morning, giving her a blatantly sexual kiss. Now he would have to retreat to safer territory and try to ease more slowly into greater intimacy. He tightened his fist around the wine goblet before putting it to his mouth and draining it. When Helena finished the song, he handed his empty cup to a nearby page before striding toward her. She glanced up as he approached but quickly ducked her head.

"Milady, we need to make an early start tomorrow so we should retire now."

"Aye, milord."

Alaric took the lute from her and extended his hand to assist her. He followed Helena into their chamber and lit a few more candles. Should he try kissing her again? Should he just touch her face? He unlaced the ties holding his tunic together as he considered his options.

"Alaric, could we talk for a few minutes?"

"Aye."

He drew the tunic over his head, hung it on a peg, then turned to observe her. She stood in the middle of the room, twisting her hands together in front of her waist. The look she gave him was hesitant and timid.

"Sit down, Helena." He gestured to the chair closest to her.

After drawing a chair close to hers, he sat down. He watched as she bit her lip, glanced up at him briefly, then bent her head again.

"I have been thinking about my problem."

When she did not say anything more, he broke the awkward silence. "I am sorry I went too far, too fast, this morning. I know I frightened you with my kiss. You do not have to worry, Helena. I will not kiss you again like that until you are ready."

"Nay, 'tis not that." Helena looked at him. "I mean, it is, but it is not the real problem."

He gave her a slight smile. "I am afraid I do not understand. What is the real problem?"

"Oh, I am not making any sense, am I?"

He shook his head and watched her intently, willing her to speak.

"I have been thinking a lot lately about why I am so afraid of the marriage bed. 'Tis not really you I am afraid of." She glanced up at him.

He held himself still and quiet, as he would when coaxing a wild bird to come near him. Smiling at her in what he hoped was encouragement, he silently urged her to continue.

"I trust you. I know that you will not hurt me." She bit her lip again and looked down at her hands.

"Helena, thank you for your trust. It means a lot to me."

"What I fear," she whispered, "is the lack of control over my own body."

"Does your fear stem from your father's treatment of you?"

She nodded but did not look at him.

"Perhaps it would help if you talked about what your father did to you."

"I do not know if I can." Her voice was hesitant and tearful.

"Helena, please talk to me."

If she could lance the boil that was her memory of her father's abuse and let the putrid mass drain out of her soul, maybe she would finally be able to heal.

"Tell me how he gave you the cuts on your cheek."

She took such a deep, shuddering breath that he almost felt it as well.

"He sent for me when I was fourteen. I had not seen him the entire time I was fostered with Lady Dorothea. When I arrived home, he was out hunting, so I did not see him until just before supper that evening. When I came into the hall, 'twas clear he had been drinking very heavily. I came up to him and curtsied before him, as Lady Dorothea had instructed me. He grabbed my chin and held my face up to look at me. I could see the disgust and revulsion in his eyes." She squeezed her eyes shut as tears streamed down her face. "He shoved my face away and shouted at me to get away from him."

"What happened then?" Alaric tried to keep his voice soft and encouraging.

"He drank very heavily over supper. I was hurt when my father rejected me, and my brothers ignored me. I had expected a pleasant homecoming. I went to bed early. My father jerked me awake in the middle of the night. His face…his face was contorted by rage. He dragged me from the bed and hit me. He threw me on the floor and kicked me. As I lay helpless on the floor, he grabbed my hair and yanked my head back. He sliced my cheek with his knife."

Alaric slipped onto his knees before her chair, his hands covering hers as they lay in her lap.

"I must have lost consciousness. I do not remember the other cuts he made on my cheek."

Helena was sobbing now. Alaric carefully ran his hands up her arms, touching her as gingerly as he would a wounded falcon. When she did not resist, he drew her into his arms as he stood and pressed her ruined cheek to his shoulder. Sobbing, she clutched him. He rubbed her back, trying to soothe her as the violent sobs raked her slight frame. Her torment was unbearable.

He gathered her up in his arms and sat on the chair, cradling her limp body against him as she cried. Laying his face against her head, he rubbed his cheek against the soft, silky strands of her hair. Tenderness for her engulfed his heart. Later he would plan how to avenge her, but for now he had to focus his efforts on helping her.

A long time later, her tears gradually slowed and she quieted in his arms. He knew he had to get all the poison out of her soul, if she were to heal properly and completely.

"What happened after that night?"

"I kept the door to my chamber barred at night." Her voice was expressionless as if she were numb and lifeless. "I learned to stay out of his way as much as possible. When I was not successful, he beat me. Usually with his fists. Sometimes with a whip. I became like a rat. I hid in the dark corners of the donjon. I spied on him so I could know about his plans and his movements. I lived in constant fear that he would catch me at any time. I was no match for his brute strength or his cruelty. I was completely helpless and at his mercy."

"'Tis a wonder you did not go mad."

She had to have incredible strength and depth of character to have survived the horror she had endured. Alaric felt his admiration and appreciation for her increase.

"'Twas only my music that kept me sane. I spent all my time playing and singing. Imagining a better, more beautiful world." She fell silent.

Then Alaric knew he no longer needed to prod her to recall the ugly, evil things her father had done to her. The poison had been purged from her; now she could heal. He held her securely in his arms as she gradually relaxed. When her breathing slowed and became even, he knew she slept. He carried her to the bed and removed her shoes and hose. She slept as one dead. No, she slept with the complete and all-absorbing slumber of a child. She did not rouse when he removed her kirtle or when he took her into his arms.

Warmth seeped into Helena's entire body as she snuggled her head into the hardness under her cheek. A tickling sensation against her nose awakened her from the remnants of her sleep, and she opened her eyes. Realizing she was lying against Alaric's bare chest, she gasped and reared back, bracing her hand against his waist.

"Ssshhh. Just lie back down and relax. We do not have to get up yet."

He gently but firmly pressed his hand on the back of her head, urging her head back to his chest, then tightened his arms around her. She became fully conscious of how closely she lay against his side, with her leg thrown over his naked thigh and her hand resting on his bare torso. She remembered falling asleep in his arms fully clothed while he held her on the chair, and now she was in bed with him, her nakedness covered only by her chemise.

"How do you feel?"

"I…I am not sure."

He was still and quiet as she probed her feelings. She had not realized how much it would help to tell him about her father's cruel treatment. Now that Alaric knew everything, she no longer felt ashamed or embarrassed. After telling him about the brutality she had suffered, she now realized she was not responsible for any of it. There was some evil in her father that caused him to abuse her. She was not to blame. She was not unworthy.

"I feel lighter, freer somehow," she mused.

"Do you still feel up to riding to Carleigh today?"

"Aye, I do."

"Good, I am glad." She felt his chest expand under her head as he took a deep breath. "Helena, thank you for telling me what your father did to you. It helps me understand your fears. I am sorry I have been such a domineering husband. I realize now that I have been trying to force you to comply with what I want. I have never considered your feelings at all. For that I am truly sorry and ask for your forgiveness."

"'Tis all right."

"No. No, it is not." He took another deep breath. With her ear pressed to his chest, she could hear the steady, rhythmic beating of his heart. "I have made no secret of what I want from this marriage. I want a wife to warm my bed and a son to inherit Merclif. What do you want out of our marriage, Helena?"

I want your love.

She could never say the words out loud and reveal to him her secret, most cherished desire. But she could tell him the rest of her hopes and dreams.

"I want to be rid of these fears. I want to live in peace and have a normal marriage. I want to have children to love."

"Will you allow me to give you children, Helena?"

"Aye." Her voice was a mere thread of sound.

"Thank you."

His arms tightened around her body briefly, and she felt a slight pressure against the top of her head. Had he kissed her?

"It occurs to me that a change in tactics is in order."

"What…what do you mean?"

"Since you fear losing control over your own body, it might well relieve your fears if you set the pace. If you control what happens between us in our bed. You can touch me or kiss me anywhere you choose. You would tell me where and when to touch or kiss you. What do you think about that idea?"

"But what if I do not know what to do?"

"I would be happy to provide guidance, suggestions, and instructions, if you need them. The idea is for you to be completely in charge of the situation." He paused. "Are you willing to try it?"

"Aye," she said, drawing out the simple word.

"Thank you, Helena. Your courage astounds me."

She felt his lips against her forehead, his touch feather light.

"Now, I am afraid, 'tis time to get out of our cozy bed. We have a long trip to Carleigh ahead of us."

22

Alaric, with Helena by his side and Father Michael right behind them, led the procession as they traveled to Carleigh. He kept to the edges of the newly ploughed fields so the horses would not trample the crops. After they had been riding for about four hours, he called a halt a few miles from Carleigh, near a group of trees.

After dismounting and hobbling his horse, Alaric came to Helena's side to assist her. She put her hands on his shoulders to brace herself as he held her waist and lifted her down from her horse. Once she was safely on the ground, he smiled into her upturned face before stepping back to release her. He turned to issue orders to his men as they set about preparing a makeshift dinner. When he glanced back at Helena, he frowned to see how stiffly she moved, as if she were in a great deal of pain.

"Helena, are you all right?" Alaric asked, taking her arm to steady her.

"'Tis been a while since I was on a horse for such a long ride. I will be fine."

His respect and admiration for her grew. She had not complained once during their ride. Alaric silently cursed himself. Obviously, she had been conditioned to endure a staggering amount of pain, and he berated himself for adding to her suffering.

"You need to stretch your muscles before they become too stiff," Alaric said. "Let us walk a little."

He took her arm and led her away from the men, slowing his pace to accommodate her halting gait. "Helena, I am sorry. I should have realized this trip would be too strenuous for you."

"When I lived at Bamchester, I used to ride every day. I often went on long journeys on horseback."

"Aye, but that was a long time ago. And if you have not ridden much since then, your muscles are no longer trained for it."

"I suppose so."

Alaric stopped and pulled her into his arms, using his body to shield her from his men. She rested limply against his chest as he rubbed her back.

"Do you feel up to walking back now?" he finally asked.

"Aye." She pulled back from him and started to walk.

"I will take you up before me on my horse for the rest of the trip. That should help somewhat. You will have to take short rides every day and build your muscle strength back up again."

"Aye."

A blanket had been laid out on the ground and Alaric carefully lowered Helena so she could sit upon it, then dropped down beside her. The men had unpacked the bread, cold chicken, and ale they had brought with them from the castle. Father Michael said grace and they ate. There was little talking as they consumed their meal.

When they finished, Alaric lifted Helena up onto his horse before mounting himself. He wrapped his arms securely around her and gathered up the reins.

"Are you all right?" he asked when they had been riding for a few minutes.

"Aye. 'Tis better than being on my own horse."

"Good. We will be in Carleigh soon, so I should let you know what we will be doing there. After Father Michael performed mass for the villagers last Sunday, I asked him to inform them that I would meet with them today. They are to assemble in the middle of the village at noon. I want to talk to the villeins and explain to them my requirements for their service."

"That is a good idea. I know from what Langston told me that my father treated the villeins very harshly. He required them to give him three-fourths of the grain they produced."

"Aye. Father Michael told me about that, as well. I know that Cardel also turned land that had been traditionally held by tenants into demesne land."

As they rode down the main street of the village, Alaric noted with disgust the dilapidated condition of the huts they passed. Mentally he compared Carleigh's rundown dwellings to the cottages in Mersthrope, which were in excellent condition and were an obvious source of pride to their inhabitants. Cardel's severe demands on the villeins had precluded them from maintaining their own homes in a livable state.

As he had requested, the people had gathered in the center of the village. The men milled about in a group in front of the women and children. Most of the villeins were ill-dressed and ill-kempt, their poverty another sign of Cardel's neglect. The hopelessness and hostility on most of their faces presented a sharp contrast to the pleasant welcome he always received from the people of Mersthrope.

Alaric halted and dismounted before reaching up to help Helena down. He gave the reins of his horse to one of his men and ordered them to stand aside, but to remain on alert for any trouble. He took Helena's arm and approached the villeins, Father Michael walking forward with them.

Alaric listened carefully as the priest introduced him to the village leaders, trying to commit their names to memory and to associate their names with their faces. Alaric watched each of the men's faces as Father Michael introduced the leaders one by one to Helena and noted their reaction to the scars on her face.

The man named Grentel, whom the priest had told Alaric was the de facto leader of the community, graciously bowed to Helena, neither staring at her face nor avoiding looking at her.

"Milord, welcome to Carleigh," Grentel said once the introductions were completed.

"Thank you, Grentel. I have come to Carleigh today to tell you my expectations of each of you, now that King Henry has granted all Cardel and Carleigh's lands to me." He spoke loudly so his voice would carry over the noise of the crowd.

Gradually, the people quieted.

Pausing, he looked intently into the faces staring back at him. "Father Michael has graciously agreed to take up residence here. In addition to serving as your priest, he will serve as my representative to you. He will judge and resolve all civil disputes and criminal violations that may occur. Father Michael will also assign and apportion tenant lands as well as collect and record the grain owed in service."

Alaric paused to let the villagers absorb his announcement. He saw approval on Grentel's face as the leader nodded in agreement. Approval was echoed on the faces of a few of the other men. As Alaric had expected, Father Michael was well liked here and respected for his honesty.

"The lands Cardel confiscated for his demesne will be released to you to farm as my tenants. I require that one-tenth of the grain you harvest goes to the church. I require that one-tenth of the grain you produce be paid to me as your service owed to me. The remaining eight-tenths of your crop is yours to keep."

The murmurs of the crowd grew to an excited hum. Alaric looked at the faces in front of him, noticing the pleased expressions and the relief that had begun to brighten their despair. He turned to address Grentel, as the village spokesman.

"Are these conditions acceptable to you?" Alaric asked.

"Aye, milord, they are indeed," Grentel said with a grin. "Thank ye, milord."

Murmurs of thanks turned to exuberant shouts of gratitude. Alaric smiled. After a few moments, he raised his hand for silence and the crowd quieted.

"A parish church will be built here in Carleigh. A new cottage must be built for Father Michael as well. I will supply the materials for these buildings, but I require each of you to provide your labor to construct them."

Alaric paused and looked at Grentel.

"Aye, milord, we'll gladly build the church and the cottage," the headman responded on behalf of the village.

Alaric nodded. "I would speak with your village leaders now. The rest of you are free to return to your homes and your work."

As the crowd dispersed, Alaric turned to Helena and spoke quietly to her so they would not be overheard. "Shall I find a place for you to rest while I conduct the rest of my business?"

"Nay, milord." Helena gave him a small smile. "I am fine. I would rather remain with you."

"Are you sure?"

"Aye."

The villagers wandered away, talking excitedly together, until seven men remained. Alaric walked toward the group of leaders.

"I want to locate a site for the church and for Father Michael's cottage. Do any of you have any suggestions?"

"Aye, milord." A stocky, gray-haired man spoke.

Alaric looked at him, trying to remember his name. "Udell," Alaric said. When the man nodded, Alaric continued, "Where do you suggest we build?"

"Milord, there's a level spot to the east of the village that would be a good place for the church."

The other men nodded in agreement.

"Let us go see the location, then," Alaric said.

He signaled for two of his men to accompany them, then took Helena's arm and helped her navigate the uneven ground as they all followed Udell. There was general agreement that the place, close to the village but far enough away to give the priest some solitude for his prayers, would indeed be perfect. They decided to build the cottage first, so Father Michael would have a place to live since Mass could be celebrated outdoors until the church was constructed. Alaric questioned and probed until he was satisfied with the plans and the timetable the leaders agreed on.

When they walked back to the village, Grentel offered them the hospitality of his house, which Alaric gratefully accepted since Helena seemed to be tiring. Grentel, with obvious pride, ushered them into the best-maintained cottage in the village. His wife quietly offered them hot cider and oatmeal cakes and efficiently served them.

Over the refreshments, Alaric questioned Grentel about the villagers' needs. Grentel offered Father Michael a bed in his own house until the priest's new cottage was completed. Alaric was pleased that all matters had been satisfactorily resolved and that Carleigh could now be left in the capable hands of Father Michael and Grentel.

"Milord," Grentel said when they had finished eating, "we be needin' ye to settle a dispute in the village. I've suggested several ways of resolving the mess, but none of 'em have been accepted by them that's involved."

"Tell me the facts of the case."

"Aye, milord." Grentel set down his cup and began his story. "Ye see, Falknor promised Juliana—that's his eldest daughter—to Sweting. He agreed to pay Sweting one pig as Juliana's dowry. Now Juliana doesn't want to marry Sweting, who's thirty years older than her. He's buried two wives already and has something like ten children. I don't know how many exactly, I've lost count, that I have.

"Anyway, Juliana's pregnant. She won't tell her father who the father of her babe is, even after he beat her. Sweting's demanding the pig from Falknor as payment for the broken betrothal. Falknor said Sweting should take Juliana since the babe proves she's fertile. That Sweting will not even notice one more mouth to feed. Sweting'll not take

Juliana since she's no longer a virgin. And Falknor refuses to hand over the pig."

"I want to talk with Falknor, Sweting, and Juliana," Alaric said. "Call them together in the town square, along with all the rest of the villagers."

"Aye, milord," Grentel said, pushing back his chair. "Ye and yer lady wait here. I will let ye know when everybody's ready."

"Thank you, Grentel." After Grentel left, Alaric looked at Helena. "How are you doing, milady?"

"I am fine, milord. This lovely warm cider and the delicious oat cake have revived me."

"We can leave as soon as I settle this matter."

"Aye, milord."

Grentel came back a short time later. "Milord," he said from the open doorway, "everybody's now here, just as ye ordered."

Alaric led Helena out of the cottage and escorted her down the street to the center of the village, where everyone had congregated. He released Helena's hand, leaving her with his men, and walked forward.

"Are you Falknor?" he inquired when he saw a dark-haired girl next to the man.

"Aye, milord."

"And this is your daughter, Juliana?"

"Aye, milord. 'Tis the slut."

Alaric stepped in front of Falknor, putting his face right in the villein's face. "Do not ever address her like that again. Understand?"

"Aye, aye, milord. I'm sorry." Falknor backed away from Alaric.

Alaric moved to stand in front of the girl. He put his hand under her chin and gently raised her bowed head, examining the bruises marking her face. He nodded kindly to her before stepping back. He looked next at the older man standing alone in front of the quiet crowd.

"And you are Sweting?" Alaric asked.

"Aye, milord."

Alaric stepped back and addressed the villagers. He briefly recapped the situation that Grentel had conveyed to him before turning to the principles in the dispute.

"Falknor, do you agree that this account is correct?"

When Falknor gave his assent, Alaric turned to Sweting with the same question. After he received Sweting's agreement, Alaric again addressed the crowd.

"Is there anyone else who would like to step forward with information relevant to this case, before I pronounce my judgment?"

A slim young man pushed his way through the crowd. "Aye, milord," he shouted defiantly. "I do. I'm the father of the babe Juliana's carrying."

Shock and titillation rippled through the crowd as the man went to stand by Juliana's side.

145

"Nay, Everard," Juliana said to him. "Ye shouldn't do this."

"'Tis fine, Juliana," he said. "I can't stay away from ye any more. Everything'll be all right."

"Quiet!" Alaric shouted.

When the crowd complied, Alaric looked at Juliana with the same demanding gaze he used on his battle-hardened troops. "Answer me truthfully, Juliana. Is this man, Everard, the father of your babe?"

"Aye, milord."

"Everard, do you have anything else to say to me?"

"Aye, milord." Everard stood tall and proud next to Juliana, his arm placed protectively around her waist. "I want to marry Juliana. I asked her father for permission to wed her, but he refused. I'll do whatever it takes to have Juliana as my wife."

Alaric searched the young man's face and saw the determination etched into his features. He looked at Juliana, who gazed up at Everard and leaned heavily against him. Falknor scowled, shooting daggers at his daughter and Everard. Sweting stood with his arms crossed in front of his chest.

"Here is my judgment, which will be fulfilled immediately," Alaric declared. "Everard, you will marry Juliana here and now. You will pay to Sweting Juliana's dowry of one pig."

"Thank ye, milord," Everard answered. "I'll gladly pay the dowry. But I don't have it now. I'll pay Sweting as soon as I can."

"I will give the pig to Sweting," Alaric offered. "You will owe me double service for the next five years to pay me back."

"Aye, milord." Relief infused Everard's voice. "Thank ye, milord."

Alaric watched as the young couple embraced each other. He turned to the priest standing next to him. "Father Michael, please assign to Everard two plots of land to farm."

"Aye, milord." The priest nodded.

"As for you, Falknor, I fine you one pig for the beating of your daughter."

"But, but…" Falknor's voice trailed off as Alaric continued to stare at him.

"'Tis against the law of my demesne to beat or otherwise harm one's daughter or wife," Alaric announced in ringing tones to the crowd. "Any infraction thereof will be severely punished. Do I make myself clear?"

He scanned the faces of the men in the crowd, meeting each one's eyes, silently demanding their nods of acceptance before moving along to the next. His eyes captured Falknor's last. "Do I?"

"Aye, milord." Falknor hung his head.

"Father Michael—" Alaric turned to the priest—"seems you have a wedding to perform today."

"Aye, milord. That I do."

The priest gave Alaric a nod and walked to stand in front of Juliana and Everard to begin the ceremony. When the wedding was over, Everard leaned down and kissed Juliana. When Everard released her, she came toward Alaric and curtsied.

"Milord, thank ye so much." Her voice was tremulous.

"You are welcome, Juliana." He gave her a smile. "Now go and be happy."

"Aye, milord." She blushed and hurried back to her new husband.

For a moment Alaric watched the newly married couple as the crowd milled around them. Then he strode to where Helena waited with his men. Ordering them to prepare to ride, he led Helena to his horse, lifted her up into the saddle, and mounted. He took her into his arms and led the way out of Carleigh to cheers from the villagers.

23

Margaret sat in the ladies' solar with Elizabeth and Clare, each of them sewing, their laps covered with yards of linen in disparate hues—green, blue, and red. In response to the knock on the door, Margaret called out leave to enter. Wyham came in, shut the door behind him, and gave the women a courtly bow. As always, the sight of him thrilled and delighted her.

"Good afternoon, ladies," he said with a smile. "I find myself at loose ends this afternoon with Merclif's absence, so I have come to offer you my services."

"Milord, your company is always welcome," Margaret replied. "Please, be seated." She gestured to the chair closest to her, then finished the leaf she was embroidering as he settled into it. "I am curious to know how you plan to be of service to us. Do you sew, milord?" She smiled at him.

"Nay, milady. Unfortunately, I have no skill with a needle. However, I do have some small skill as a raconteur. I would be happy to entertain you ladies with a story."

"That sounds delightful, milord." Margaret smiled at the other women. "We would very much enjoy a story, would we not?"

"Indeed we would, milord." Elizabeth's blue-green eyes twinkled as she winked at Margaret.

Clare nodded, her smile causing dimples to crease her plump cheeks. "A story will make our work so much more pleasant."

"What kind of story would you like to hear, ladies? A romantic story? A humorous story? A story about daring feats in battle? I am completely at your disposal."

"Hmm." Margaret gave him a mischievous grin. "How about a romantic story filled with humor and daring feats?"

"Ah, milady." Wyham shook his head. "You have set before me a most difficult challenge. I will try my best to please you."

He looked directly into her eyes, a sensuous smile upon his lips. Margaret found herself blushing in response to the promise in his eyes. She glanced at her friends and was relieved to see them sewing industriously. Although both of their heads were bent over their work, Margaret caught the smiles playing around each of their mouths.

"Aye, milord," Margaret said, "but the more difficult the task, the greater the service rendered."

"That is true, milady." Wyham nodded. "That is true."

He leaned back in his chair and began to spin his story. Employing all of an actor's skill, Wyham's resonant voice soon captured Margaret's imagination. Enthralled in his narrative, she abandoned any pretense of working as she hung on his every word. She noticed that Elizabeth and Clare seemed likewise mesmerized by the courtier.

When he had finished, Margaret sighed. "You are truly a gifted storyteller, milord. Your engrossing tale had everything. I do not remember when I have laughed so much. And the love story." She put both of her hands over her heart. "Ah! It was so lovely and poignant, it brought tears to my eyes. As for the daring, courageous feats of the hero, I almost swooned. Thank you, milord, for such a marvelous story."

"The pleasure was all mine, milady." He inclined his head as he bowed toward her.

Margaret stared into his amused eyes, her lips curled in a smile of pure joy. How she loved this man. It was amazing to her that she had known him for such a short time, and now she could not envision a life without him.

"Margaret, Lord Wyham, please excuse me." Claire put aside her sewing and stood. "I really should go and see what Nicholas is up to. 'Tis amazing the mischief that a ten-year-old boy can get into."

"Please excuse me as well." Elizabeth stood. "I need to check on the spinsters and see how they are progressing."

Margaret was grateful for her friends' tact, as they left her alone with Robert. Sticking her needle into the green linen she was embroidering, she placed the gown onto Elizabeth's empty chair beside her. She studied Robert's face. His hazel eyes were warm as he gazed back at her.

"'Tis a rare treat to have you all to myself," Wyham remarked when they were alone. "I shall have to take advantage of this golden opportunity." He grinned, transforming his suave features into boyish exuberance.

"Aye. What do you have in mind?"

"Ah, let me think." He stood and took her hand, pulling her from her chair. "I could take you into my arms," he said, suiting his actions to his words. "I could rain kisses all over you."

He kissed the sensitive space behind her ear, then trailed kisses down her neck before reversing course, nibbling his way up her cheek. She gripped his waist, trying to steady herself against his strong lean body, as he ignited her ardor.

"I could spend hours kissing you," he said, his mouth hovering near hers.

He captured her lips and lavished kisses on her to which she eagerly responded. Passion flared between them, the smoldering desire she always felt in his presence blazing into a conflagration. Wyham abruptly pulled back from her, cradling her head on his shoulder and holding her tightly in his arms.

"'Tis like playing with fire, I am afraid. I want you so much. Margaret, I love you."

"Robert, I love you."

"Will you marry me?"

"Aye."

Wyham raised her head and kissed her. Her joy overflowed, as they sealed their troth with their kisses. The pleasure was so intense that Margaret groaned, causing Wyham to gently ease her away from him and place his hands on her waist.

"Margaret, you have made me the happiest man alive."

He removed his hands from her and stepped away. Turning his back to her, he braced his hands on the back of a chair. Margaret went to him and laid her hand on his back. With his head bowed down, she could not see his face.

"Robert, what is wrong?"

"I want you so much, 'tis a difficult test of my self-control." His voice was hoarse.

"Aye," she said, lightly rubbing his back. She stepped back and cleared her throat. "I can arrange the wedding for the day after tomorrow. That will give Cook enough time to prepare a proper feast." She sat back down in her chair, primly folding her hands together in her lap.

"How can we marry now? 'Tis the middle of Lent."

"I am sure that if we contribute a large monetary donation to the Church, Father Thomas will grant an exception and allow us to marry."

"That is an excellent idea, my dear. I would be happy to make the donation. I just hope that I can last until Thursday." He grinned at her. Straightening, he turned the chair around and sat down. "Perhaps if I am far enough away from you, I will not be so tempted to touch you. There is something we should discuss before our wedding, Margaret." His voice had lost its teasing tone and become more somber. "I have seen how skilled you are at managing this castle. I have seen how much you enjoy interacting with the servants. You are a brilliant chatelaine."

She placed her hand over her heart. "Why, thank you, Robert. Your praise means so much to me. In truth, I have enjoyed the challenge of running this household."

"I would hate to take you away from something you enjoy so much and for which you have a rare talent. We do not have to live at court. I could give up my position with the king. We could live at Wyham Castle, and you could become the chatelaine there."

"Robert, I really appreciate your selflessness and consideration." Margaret gave him a fond smile. "I have been chatelaine here for almost thirty years. Although I have enjoyed my life very much, I find I am ready for a change. I think it will be very exciting to be at court. I am looking forward to meeting new people and experiencing a different way of life."

"Are you sure, my love?"

"Aye, I am sure."

"You have quite relieved my mind, my dear. So, we will marry on Thursday and then leave Merclif sometime next week."

"Aye." She nodded. "I will let Alaric know our plans as soon as he returns."

"Alaric," Helena protested, "I am fine. I can walk."

He cradled her against his chest and strode toward the donjon. The twilight was swiftly fading and he wanted to get her inside as quickly as possible before the cool air could chill her.

"Nay, walking would cause you too much discomfort. I will carry you up to our chamber."

The noise in the hall abated as people turned to stare at them when Alaric carried her inside. He ignored their speculative looks as he headed to the stairs, not stopping to speak with anyone, only nodding to his mother and Wyham as he caught sight of them. Renwold hurried to catch up with them as Alaric crossed the hall.

"Milord, a bath has been prepared as you requested. Food has also been provided."

"Good, Renwold. Thank you. Please send up a maid to attend to Lady Merclif."

"Aye, milord." The steward bowed and hurried off.

Once they reached their bedchamber, Alaric carefully lowered Helena's feet to the ground and held out an arm to steady her when she stumbled as she tried to stand.

"A warm bath should help relax your muscles," Alaric remarked. "I will await you in my solar. Soak for as long as you want. Let me know when you are done, and we can have our supper together."

"Aye. Thank you for your care today, Alaric."

He nodded wordlessly, still blaming himself for her pain. A knock on the door heralded the arrival of the maid, with Margaret close behind.

"Welcome home, children," Margaret said. "Helena, I have brought some herbs to add to your bath water. They should help soothe your aching muscles."

"Helena, I will leave you in Mother's capable hands," Alaric said as he made his escape.

Alaric went next door to his solar and poured himself a cup of wine. Renwold had anticipated his every need, as usual, and arranged for a brazier to warm the room, as well as food and wine. He was chewing a mouthful of cold fish when there was a knock on the door.

"Enter," he called.

"Alaric," Margaret said, "may I come in?"

"Certainly, Mother. Would you care for some wine?"

"Nay, thank you. I would like to speak with you, if you are not too tired."

"I am fine. What did you want to talk about?" He took a swig of wine as he stood next to the brazier warming himself.

"Lord Wyham has asked me to marry him, and I have agreed."

Alaric smiled at her with pleasure. "I hope you will be very happy together."

"Thank you, my dear," Margaret said, returning his smile. "I have come to love

Robert deeply. I think we will have a good marriage. 'Tis exciting, but a bit scary to be starting a new life."

"Aye, I imagine so. Wyham is an honorable man. A trustworthy man you will be able to rely on."

Margaret nodded. "Aye, you are right. I know I will always be able to depend on him."

"When is the wedding?" Alaric asked before taking another bite of bread.

"On Thursday."

"So soon?"

"Aye. We want to marry as soon as possible since Robert needs to return to King Henry's court. We will need to leave Merclif next week."

"We will miss you. *I* will miss you."

"I will miss you too, my dear. I will insist that Robert bring me to visit at least once a year."

"Aye, you do that."

There was a pause.

"Alaric, how are things between you and Helena?" Margaret's voice was hesitant. "I can tell that all is not yet right with your marriage."

Alaric stared down into his wine. "Aye. She fears the marriage bed. I am trying to be patient with her, and I think we are making some progress, but 'tis slow."

"I am glad you are being patient with her. She has endured much agony in her short life. Be gentle with her. Your reward will be a willing wife in your bed."

"Aye."

"I will leave you now, Alaric. I can see that you are tired." Margaret came to him and placed her hands on his arms. "I am very proud of you, my son. I love you." She drew him into her arms and embraced him.

"I love you too, Mother." He tightened his arms around her.

She stepped back from him, wiping a tear from her cheek. "Sleep well, my dear. Good night."

"Good night, Mother."

Alaric watched her leave the room, his heart heavy. She had been his guide and advisor for a long time. He had always counted on her wisdom and insight. Her departure would leave a large void in his life.

Helena sat in a chair by the brazier wearing a long-sleeved linen chemise that covered her from her neck to her feet. The bath had eased the soreness in her legs and had revived her. While she bathed, she had let her mind wander over the events of the day. She had been intensely interested in her husband's management of his fief and had felt such pride and gratification at his magnanimous treatment of his villeins. His cleverness and fairness in solving the conundrum that had been presented to him in the village had greatly impressed her. As had his championing a defenseless woman and punishing her cruel father. Alaric was an honorable man, and she was proud that he was her husband.

She roused herself from her daydreaming when he entered the chamber and came to stand in front of her.

"Have you eaten yet?"

"Nay." She shook her head.

He brought to her the food tray that the servants had provided, setting it down on the small table next to her chair. After he served her, he sat beside her and began to eat. As she chewed a piece of cheese, she watched him. He was so handsome with his chiseled jaw and his broad shoulders and muscular arms. She had enjoyed being held in his strong arms on the way back to the castle, never having felt so protected and cherished before in her life. His brilliant blue eyes snared her as he glanced at her.

"Mother just told me that she and Wyham are to be married on Thursday."

"Truly?"

"Aye. They will be leaving next week to return to King Henry's court."

"I will miss Mother so much when she is gone."

"I will too. She says they will visit here often, at least once a year."

"I am glad."

A comfortable silence enveloped them as she watched him consume his food. Helena tried but failed to stifle the yawn that overtook her.

"Are you done eating?" he asked.

"Aye."

"Let me get you to bed, then."

Alaric laid his cup on the tray, stood, and scooped her into his arms and out of her chair. Feeling his arms around her, she lay quietly against his chest and enjoyed his thoughtfulness. He carried her to the bed and gently laid her down. After pulling the covers up to her shoulders, he leaned down and lightly kissed her mouth.

"Good night, Helena. Sleep well."

"Good night, Alaric."

Her eyelids fluttered closed, and she drifted off to sleep.

24

As Helena ate supper she was acutely conscious of Alaric's every move, as if her entire body was in a heightened state of awareness. She glanced at her husband, recalling his words yesterday morning. The idea of enjoying greater physical intimacy with him no longer scared her. In fact, her entire body tingled with anticipation. An indistinct moan escaped her lips before she could contain it.

"All you all right?" Alaric asked.

"Aye." Helena cleared her throat. "I am fine." She took a bite of the chicken stew.

"Do you have any pain from yesterday's ride?"

"I am a little stiff and sore. But 'tis nothing. Thank you for your concern, Alaric."

"I hope you have not exhausted yourself today." Alaric took a drink of his wine, then shot her a grin. "I have plans for you tonight," he murmured as he leaned his head close to hers.

Helena's entire body seemed to go up in flames, and a vivid blush infused her cheeks. To her surprise, she was looking forward to being in his bed tonight. Her imagination had run wild since yesterday, thinking about it. "Alaric, please."

"I will try to restrain myself until 'tis time for bed," Alaric said softly, before turning his attention back to his food.

Later, when Alaric shut the bedchamber door behind them, he leaned against it as she took off her linen veil and brushed her hair.

Aware of his gaze upon her, Helena turned to look at him. "Are you not going to get ready for bed?" she asked.

"Aye." Alaric pushed away from the door. "I was merely enjoying watching you."

The smoldering in his eyes, a look of promise and expectancy, caused the fire of her desire to burn even brighter. Her fingers trembled as she untied the russet wool kirtle she wore and pulled it off her head. She settled on the bed and waited for her husband. When Alaric joined her, he lay on his back beside her with the covers pulled around his waist. In the glow of the candlelight she could see his encouraging smile when she turned toward him.

"What shall I do?" she asked.

"I would like for you to touch me." Alaric's voice was soft and unthreatening. "I would enjoy the feel of your hands on me."

Helena laid her hand on the middle of his bare chest. The warmth of his skin and the silkiness of his hair fascinated her. She lightly caressed his chest, running her hand over his well-developed pectoral muscles. Emboldened by his acquiescence, she eagerly explored his body.

"I enjoy it when you touch me, Helena." His voice was husky and mellow. "May I touch you now?"

"Aye," she whispered.

"Sit up, Helena."

She pulled herself up in the bed as he did the same. Facing each other, they were equals, neither dominating nor trying to control the other. He reached out to stroke her, the thin fabric of her chemise the only thing between them.

"Is this all right?" he asked.

"Aye," she said, her voice not much louder than a sigh.

She surrendered to the pleasure of his touch. After long moments caressing her, he slowly drew away from her and released her. Opening her eyes, she gazed at him through the haze of ecstasy he had aroused in her.

"Did you enjoy that?" he asked, searching her face.

"Aye," she whispered.

He took a deep breath. "I am afraid I will get too carried away. I think we had better stop for tonight. Unless you are ready for more?"

Helena dropped her eyes and shook her head.

"May I kiss you good night, Helena?"

She raised her head to look into his eyes. "Aye."

He cupped her cheeks in his hands and leaned over, settling his mouth gently on hers. Too soon he pulled back and released her. "Good night, Helena. Sleep well."

"Good night, Alaric."

She moved away from him and lay down on the mattress. The excitement he had induced seemed to shimmer throughout her body. She now regretted her decision to call a halt to their lovemaking. Next time, she resolved, she would stifle her fears and allow their lovemaking to come to completion.

"'Tis a glorious day for your wedding, Mother, clear and sunny." Helena brushed Margaret's hair as the older woman, clad only in her linen chemise, sat on a stool before her.

"God is indeed smiling upon us."

"'Tis His blessing on your marriage to Robert."

A knock heralded Elizabeth and Clare's entrance into Margaret's bedchamber. Elizabeth carried a length of plain linen draped over her outstretched arms while Clare shut the chamber door behind her. Happiness radiated from Elizabeth's square face, and Claire's usual lighthearted demeanor was almost effervescent.

"Margaret," Elizabeth announced, "we have something for you."

"What is it?" Margaret rose from the stool to greet her friends.

Clare whisked the linen away as Elizabeth held up a kirtle. The blue velvet gown, the exact shade of Margaret's eyes, was trimmed with soft white fur around the neck, the cuffs, and the hem. Margaret gasped, holding both hands to her mouth.

"'Tis beautiful." She came over to touch the soft velvet. "How ever did you make this kirtle? When? There simply has not been enough time for you to have made this magnificent gown since Robert and I decided to get married."

"As soon as we saw how you looked at Lord Wyham…," Elizabeth began.

"And how he looked at you…," Clare interjected.

"…we started making your wedding gown," Elizabeth finished.

"Dear friends, thank you so much." She embraced each woman, being careful not to crush the gown Elizabeth still held.

"Helena also helped us sew the gown," Elizabeth remarked.

Margaret turned back to Helena, giving her a hug as well. "Thank you, my dear."

"I am glad I could contribute in some small way to the beautiful kirtle."

"Margaret," Elizabeth prompted, "you had better get dressed. You do not want to be late for your own wedding."

"Nay. I most certainly do not."

Elizabeth carefully lowered the blue gown over Margaret's head while Clare and Helena helped arrange the material over her chemise. Elizabeth laced the gown at the back as Clare brought over Margaret's white linen veil. When Margaret was completely dressed, the other women stood back to admire her.

"You look lovely, Margaret," Elizabeth said.

"Aye," Clare agreed. "You are a radiant bride."

When another knock sounded, Helena opened the bedchamber door to find Alaric. She smiled at him, the joyous mood in the chamber pervading her heart. The sight of him, dressed in the same brilliant blue tunic he had worn for their wedding just two months ago, nearly stole her breath.

"Helena, you look lovely." His warm voice was intimate and tender.

She watched his gaze roam over her gold silk kirtle and felt for once that she really was as pretty as he told her she was. "Thank you, Alaric."

"I have come to escort Mother to the chapel," Alaric announced in a normal tone. "Is she ready yet?"

"Aye, she is," Helena answered, standing back. "Come in."

Alaric strode into the chamber. Grasping Margaret's hands in both of his, he bent and kissed her on each cheek. "Mother, you look beautiful. And very happy."

"Aye," Margaret admitted, "I am happy."

"Lord Wyham awaits you on the chapel steps. Are you ready?"

"Aye, Alaric."

Alaric held Margaret's hand and led her out of the room. Helena came next, followed by Elizabeth and Clare. When Alaric and Margaret appeared on the steps of the donjon, a loud cheer welled up from the servants and villeins milling around the inner bailey. Margaret smiled and waved to the people as Alaric led her to the chapel, escorted her up the steps, and placed her hand in Wyham's, turning her over to his care. Retreating down the steps, leaving Margaret and Wyham with Father Thomas, Alaric came to Helena's side and smiled at her before turning his attention to the wedding ceremony.

When the bridal couple emerged from the chapel after mass, another loud cheer rose to greet them. As Wyham escorted Margaret through the inner ward, back to the donjon, they were showered with shouts of approbation. Helena, following behind the bridal couple by Alaric's side, thought briefly that this was rightfully a joyous occasion, unlike their own wedding. She glanced up at Alaric. As if feeling her eyes on him, he turned and smiled at her. She smiled back. They had successfully overcome their disastrous wedding, and she hoped that they would soon have a normal marriage.

Helena woke gradually, filled with contentment and satisfaction such as she had never known before. Her head rested on Alaric's chest, her leg draped over his, her naked body flush against his. The night had been a revelation to her. The pleasure he had given her astounded her. Her fears now seemed ridiculous, and she was sorry she had wasted so much time being a prisoner of them. She now knew what Margaret had meant about the mutual pleasure for which God had ordained marriage.

"Are you awake?" Alaric asked.

"Aye."

"Good. I did not want to wake you." He rolled her gently onto her back. "I cannot seem to get enough of you."

Alaric cupped her face and leaned down to kiss her thoroughly. She eagerly responded. He drew back and pushed the bedding from her body. "Let me look at you."

In the cold light of day, she was acutely aware of the hideous scars that marred her skin. Last night, in the warm glow of the candlelight and the wine she had consumed, they had faded to insignificance in her mind. But now she felt mortified and humiliated. She desperately grabbed the covers, holding them to her chest.

"Nay," she whispered, "I am too ugly."

"Helena, you are not ugly. Let me look at you."

Responding to the entreaty in his voice, she reluctantly loosened her hands and let Alaric pull the bedding away from her.

"Helena, you are beautiful." He ran his hand lightly over her body, then traced the scars that covered her thigh with his fingertip. He looked deeply into her eyes.

"But 'tis not your body alone that makes you beautiful. 'Tis your strong spirit that shines through everything you are. The pain you endured has strengthened and molded you into the person you are today, just as the blacksmith's fire strengthens and molds iron. These are scars of battle. They are badges of honor and valor. The only shame belongs to your father, not to you. The abuse you suffered would have destroyed most women. You refused to let it defeat you. I am in awe of your courage and strength."

Helena raised a trembling hand to Alaric's face. "Thank you."

She felt her spirit heal with his words. During the past months at Merclif, her body had become strong. The time she had spent in prayer with God had restored her soul. Now his sincerity and heartfelt words had cured the brokenness in her heart. With sudden clarity she realized she loved him.

He made slow, exquisite love to her, cherishing her with his touch. Afterwards, she lay replete in his arms. She felt complete, whole, strong, and fearless for the first time in over five years.

Helena knelt at the *prie-dieu* in her bedchamber. After crossing herself, she closed her eyes and bent her head. Sadness had enveloped her after Margaret and Robert rode out of the castle a few moments ago, and she had sought refuge in prayer.

"Dear Lord, I confess to You my sins. I have sinned against You by my thoughts and my words and my deeds. I have sinned against You by failing to do what You ask of me. I confess that I have not loved You with my whole heart, and I confess that I have not loved others as myself. I am so sorry for my sins.

"Dear Lord, please give Margaret and Robert a safe journey back to the king's court. Keep them well and healthy. Please bless their marriage and the love that they share.

"Dear Lord, thank You so much for all the blessings You have bestowed upon me. You truly did have my best interests at heart when You gave me Alaric to be my husband. I am sorry for ever doubting You. I love Alaric so much. Help me to be a good wife to him. I know that he does not love me as I love him. Help me to accept that and not to yearn for what I do not have but to take joy in what I do have.

"Most of all, dear Lord, I thank You for Your love for me. In ways big and small You show me that You love me, that You consider me so worthy of Your love that You sent Your only Son to die for me. Thank You, Lord Jesus, that You died for my sins. Thank You for Your blood that washes me clean so I may come into Your presence. Thank You for Your love and Your grace and Your mercy.

"Please continue to change my heart, O Lord. Please change me. Amen."

25

"**M**ilord," Hugh said, "Roger, Geoffrey, Matthew, and Langston will be going with you today."

"Langston? Why?" Alaric pulled on his gauntlet as he looked at his castellan's weathered face.

"He requested that he be able to accompany you. He has been diligently applying himself to his training the last few weeks so I felt that he deserved the honor of hunting with you."

Alaric accepted the sword Hugh handed him while he considered the inclusion of Langston in the hunting party. The man had obeyed his orders to stay away from Helena and had been making great advancements in his training. He shrugged. "So be it."

Truth be told, Alaric had been in such a good mood since Helena had overcome her fears of the marriage bed that he could find no reason to be concerned about Langston. Helena had obviously taken his words to heart and was no longer interested in her erstwhile friend. He was pleased that his patience had finally paid off in her willing and exuberant passion.

After riding for twenty minutes, they reached the area where the head huntsman, Bardulf, had found evidence of the boar that had been frightening the villagers. Alaric signaled his men to fan out through the forest. The plan was to surround the boar, flush it out into the open, and bring it down for the kill. Alaric rode cautiously forward, concentrating his senses, alert for any sign of the animal. He could hear rustling in the woods to both sides of him as the other men spread out around him.

Swiftly the boar came crashing through the bushes, running straight at him. A fully grown male, the animal probably weighed almost three hundred pounds. Its tusks were long and wickedly sharp. As the brown, bristly beast headed straight for him, Alaric barely glimpsed the projectile hurtling toward him, coming from the grove of trees from which the boar had emerged. He instinctively turned his body mere seconds before the knife, aimed at his heart, slammed into his shoulder.

Momentum and the force of the knife toppled him from his horse, and he fell directly into the path of the rampaging boar. He shouted for his men as he rolled into a ball, protecting his head and vital organs. The boar's tusks ripped into his side, the pain from the gouging searing through him. He rolled away from the boar and lurched to his feet. Yanking the knife from his shoulder, he threw it at the boar's head, impaling

159

the beast between the eyes.

Roger burst into the clearing. Alaric watched as the knight tossed his lance at the boar still standing on its feet, striking the animal in the back of its neck. The beast gave a roar and dropped to the ground, where it remained immobile. Once Roger had downed the boar, Alaric collapsed and fell to his knees. The aggression aroused by the attack drained from his body, leaving only the burning pain behind. He clutched his side and his shoulder, trying to staunch the flow of blood. Roger came to kneel beside him. The knight pulled off his cloak to use as a pad, wadding it up and placing it against Alaric's side.

"Here, milord. Use this to stop the blood."

"Someone tried to kill me." Alaric grasped the fabric tightly against his side, using both of his hands. "He threw that knife directly at me. Search the woods. See if you can find any trace of him. He came from that direction." Alaric pointed with his head.

"Aye, milord. You should just rest while I take care of everything."

Men on horseback crashed through the brush, rapidly filling the clearing. Roger took charge, assigning Langston to search for the assassin and Geoffrey to ride back to the castle to alert the garrison of his wounds and their imminent return. At Roger's orders, Matthew stripped off his own cloak and tore it into pieces, which Roger used to bind the wound on Alaric's side. With the remaining material from the cloak, Roger fashioned another pad and placed it against Alaric's shoulder wound, binding it into place as well.

"Milord, can you ride back to the castle?" Roger asked.

"Aye. Help me up."

He grasped Roger's forearm and sluggishly stood. Matthew brought Alaric's stallion over to him and held it steady as the knight helped Alaric mount. Once in the saddle, Alaric paused, breathing heavily and fighting the pain that engulfed him. He leaned over the pommel, looking at the boar's head.

"Roger, bring me that knife." He nodded toward the boar.

The knight strode over to the animal and yanked the knife out of its carcass. After cleaning the blood from the blade on the grass, Roger brought the knife over to him. Alaric examined the weapon, searching for any clue as to its owner. The simple knife was frustratingly ordinary, the kind of tool everyone owned. He slid it into his boot.

Langston strode back into the clearing and walked to where Roger waited beside Alaric's horse.

"Milord, Sir Roger," Langston said, "I could find no trace of anyone else in the forest."

"Let us go back." Alaric locked his eyes on Langston's face. "Bring the boar."

The huntsman hastened to obey his order. Alaric turned his horse and eased it into a canter, heading toward home. Every stride of the horse jarred his body, sending pain shooting through him. By the time they reached the drawbridge, he was weaving slightly in his saddle. Alaric rode cautiously up the drawbridge, through the outer bailey and to the stables. He accepted Roger's aid to dismount, but then brushed away his assistance and walked on his own toward the donjon, past the workmen standing silent in the ward watching him. Roger remained close by his side.

Helena rushed to meet Alaric, coming to an abrupt halt before him, appalled at the amount of blood covering the makeshift bandages. Alaric kept moving toward the donjon so she fell into step beside him.

"Alaric, how badly are you hurt?"

"I shall live. I just need to wash up and get the wounds dressed properly. Roger, Lady Merclif will assist me now. Fetch Sir Hugh and send him to my chambers."

"Aye, milord." Roger bowed briefly and hurried away.

Alaric put his arm around Helena's shoulder, leaning heavily on her. "I am almost at the end of my strength," he muttered to her. "Help me get inside before I fall. Try to make it look like I do not need your help. I do not want my men to see me weak."

Helena carefully put her arm around his waist, supporting more of his weight. They walked slowly up the steps of the donjon and into the hall. The steward hurried over to meet them and accompanied them across the floor.

"Milady, all is in readiness," Renwold said. "The hot water, cloths, and the medicines you requested have all been laid out for you in the lord's bedchamber."

"Thank you, Renwold," Helena said. "I will attend to Lord Merclif myself."

"Have Sir Hugh come up to my chamber immediately," Alaric ordered.

"Aye, milord."

By the time Helena got Alaric settled on the bed, she was breathless from her exertions. She sat beside him, careful not to jostle him and cause him more pain.

"Which wound is the most serious?" she asked.

"The side, I think," he grunted. "The boar ripped me up pretty badly."

Helena untied the binding and carefully pulled the blood-soaked bandage away from his side, hearing Alaric's sharp inhalation as she did so. Blood still seeped from the large gashes that lacerated his skin. Dipping a cloth into a mixture of warm water and wine, she washed the wounds, wiping the blood and dirt away.

"I will bind this as tightly as I can to try to stop the flow of blood."

"Aye."

After folding a piece of linen into a pad, she placed it over the lesions. Taking a longer strip of linen, she wrapped it tightly around his waist to hold the bandage in place. The heavy knock on the door caused her to look up into Alaric's gray face, etched in pain.

"Enter," Alaric said.

Belwick came into the chamber, closing the door behind him, and walked toward the bed.

"What happened, milord?" The castellan's voice was calm, and his demeanor was matter-of-fact.

Alaric told them briefly and dispassionately how he had come to be injured. He drew the knife out of his boot and handed it to Belwick. "I want you to put Langston in the pit prison."

"Nay," Helena protested. "Alaric, you cannot possibly think that Damien was trying to kill you. He would never do such a horrible thing."

Alaric narrowed his eyes at Helena. "This was the first time he joined the hunt. I saw him ride into the clearing from the direction the knife was thrown. Until I have proof otherwise, I am going to hold Langston responsible."

Helena stared at her husband. "Alaric, you are making a terrible mistake. Damien would never try to hurt you. He is an honorable man."

"I would rather be sorry than dead." Alaric declared. "I cannot take any chances. Hugh, see to Langston's imprisonment immediately." Alaric closed his eyes.

"Aye, milord." Belwick bowed and left the room.

Recognizing that arguing with him now was only serving to harden his resistance, Helena pursed her lips together. Once she had the wounds on his side stabilized, she turned her attention to his shoulder, washing the cut as gently and carefully as she could manage.

"This wound is not very deep. Thankfully, it missed your heart and other vital organs," Helena said.

Alaric mumbled something indecipherable, and she realized that his strength was almost depleted. In silence she laid a pad of clean linen against his cut and bound it tightly to his shoulder, using another strip of cloth. When she was done, she washed her hands in clean water and filled a goblet with wine and brought it back to the bed.

"Alaric, would you like to drink some wine?"

"Aye."

She helped him up into a semi-seated position and held the cup as he drank from it.

"Next time I go hunting, I will wear my mail."

"Are you hungry, milord?"

"Nay." He handed her the half-full goblet and lay down in the bed.

"You should rest and regain your strength."

"Aye." Alaric closed his eyes and slept.

Helena sat in a chair she pulled up to the side of the bed, watching for signs of restlessness in Alaric that would indicate he had a fever. She knew that infection of the wound was the most dangerous threat Alaric now faced. Periodically she got up and laid her cheek on his forehead, testing his temperature.

As she watched her husband sleeping, she slipped into prayer.

Most merciful Lord, thank You for sparing Alaric's life. Please heal his wounds and restore him to health. Guard and protect him from all harm. Help him to see his accusations against Damien are completely untrue. Be with Damien and comfort and protect him. Help him to be patient and to find Your peace. Oh, Lord, help me to trust in You and wait upon You. Give me Your peace that passes all understanding. I ask that Your will be done in all things. In Jesus' name, I pray, amen.

A quiet knock disturbed her vigil. She opened the door to find both Belwick and Renwold and stepped out into the hallway so as not to disturb Alaric. The castellan's face was stoic, but the steward's thin lips were pinched into a frown.

"Milady," Belwick asked, "how is Lord Merclif doing?"

"Alaric is asleep. So far, he does not have a fever."

"God be praised," Renwold said.

"That is good news, milady." Belwick's mouth curved into a slight smile as he nodded.

"Aye," Helena agreed. "I will watch him tonight. If he does not develop a fever, and the wound on his side stops bleeding, I think he should recover quickly."

"Shall I bring up some supper for you, milady?" the steward offered.

"Aye, Renwold, that would be most welcome. Thank you." All of a sudden Helena felt tired and drained.

Renwold bowed and headed downstairs.

Helena's words stopped Belwick as he turned to follow the steward. "Sir Hugh, may I speak with you for a moment?"

"Aye, milady," Belwick replied, walking back toward her.

"In what kind of conditions is Langston being held?"

"Milady, the pit prison is under the donjon. 'Tis a space measuring three ells by three ells. Langston has a supply of candles, food, and water. Let me assure you that prisoners have never been tortured nor deprived here at Merclif."

"Thank you for that reassurance, Sir Hugh." Helena paused. "You do not think that Langston tried to kill Alaric, do you?"

"Milady, 'tis not my place to question my lord's orders. 'Tis my duty to obey them."

"I see." Helena looked down at her hands clasped together at her waist. Apparently she also was not allowed to question Alaric's orders.

"Milady, please inform me immediately if Lord Merclif's condition worsens."

"Aye." Helena raised her head to meet his eyes. "I will do so."

"Thank you, milady. I will return tomorrow morning to check on Lord Merclif."

Belwick bowed to her. Helena watched the castellan walk away, then silently opened the chamber door and went inside to resume her vigil at Alaric's side.

26

Pushing the bedding off, Helena moved deliberately so as not to shake the mattress. Once she was sitting up, she touched Alaric's forehead for what seemed the hundredth time during the long sleepless night. He continued to sleep deeply. Helena closed her eyes to pray silently.

Thank You, Lord, for Your healing power. Thank You that Alaric has no fever. Please continue to heal him and make him well. Gracious Lord, I know that You love Alaric much more than I ever could, and I know You hold him in your hands. Help me to keep trusting You. I ask that Your will, not mine, be done in his life and in my own.

A long, slow sigh escaped her lips as she exhaled.

Dear Lord, please show me a way to help Damien. I know he did not do this horrible thing. Help me to convince Alaric of Damien's innocence. All these things I ask in Jesus' holy name. Amen.

She washed and dressed with as little noise as possible, glancing frequently to Alaric's still form in the bed. He slept as one dead, he was so still and quiet. After pinning the last strip of her wimple into place, she walked back to the bed. As she leaned down to touch Alaric's cheeks, he finally opened his eyes.

"Alaric. I am so glad you are finally awake. How are you feeling?"

"Like I have been gored by a wild boar," he said, pulling himself to a sitting position.

"Thank God, you have not come down with a fever." Helena smiled at him. "I need to see if the wounds on your side have stopped bleeding. And I should change your bandages."

"Aye. But first I need to use the garderobe." Alaric pushed off the covers and swung his feet over the side of the bed.

"Alaric, I do not think you should walk that far in your condition," Helena protested. "Let me get the chamber pot for you."

Alaric paused, sitting on the side of the bed. "Aye," he said with a grunt. "Mayhap you are right."

Helena brought the empty chamber pot and set it on the floor in front of him, hovering uncertainly nearby.

"Do you plan to watch?" Alaric asked with a slight smirk.

"Nay." Helena felt the heat rush into her face. "I will go tell Renwold to bring some breakfast."

Helena hurried from the room. Before she was halfway down the stairs, Renwold and Belwick had both left their places in the hall below and were making their way toward her. Glancing down into the unnaturally quiet hall and feeling all eyes on her, she paused on the steps and smiled, hoping to reassure the servants.

"Good morrow, everyone," she announced in a loud voice. "Lord Merclif is doing well. He had a deep, restful sleep last night and is now awake. I expect him to recover quickly and completely from his wounds."

Applause broke out after she delivered the news, and she saw several people cross themselves. She waited for Belwick and Renwold as they climbed the last few steps toward her.

"Good morrow, Sir Hugh. And to you as well, Master Renwold." She smiled at them.

"Good morrow to you, milady," Belwick replied. "'Tis indeed good news you bring."

"Aye." Helena looked at the steward. "Renwold, please send some breakfast up to our chamber. Lord Merclif is hungry." After Renwold excused himself to see to her orders, Helena looked at Belwick. "Sir Hugh, would you like to see the Earl now?"

"Aye, milady."

She led the castellan back to the bedchamber, pausing outside the door.

"Please wait here while I see if Alaric is ready to receive visitors." She opened the door and slipped inside, where she found Alaric sitting in a chair by the brazier. "Alaric, Sir Hugh would like to speak with you."

"Let him in, Helena."

"Good morrow, milord," Belwick said as he entered the chamber and walked toward Alaric. "How are you doing?"

"'Twill take more than a knife and a boar to finish me off," Alaric said with a grin.

"Aye, that it will. That it will," Belwick agreed. "Milord, I have some information to give you regarding the attack against you yesterday. Perhaps Lady Merclif would excuse us while I deliver my report."

"You can speak freely in front of Lady Merclif, Hugh."

Helena moved to stand behind Alaric, facing the castellan, and caught the glance he shot her. Placing her hands on the back of the chair, she returned his look. Belwick nodded to her, then moved his gaze back to Alaric.

"Aye, milord. I have questioned Langston and every other member of the hunting party quite thoroughly. Langston vehemently denies trying to kill you.

"The men were aligned in a half-circle beside you as you approached the boar. Roger was to your right, with Bardulf just beyond him. Langston was on Bardulf's right. Geoffrey was immediately to your left, with Matthew on his other side. So Langston was the farthest away from you and had only Bardulf beside him.

"Each of the men said that when they heard your shout they rushed toward you. No one saw any one other than the men in the hunting party. Bardulf says that because of the dense foliage he lost sight of Langston while they were stalking the boar."

"So," Alaric said, "there is no proof of either Langston's guilt or his innocence."

"Nay, milord." Belwick paused, glancing again at Helena. He brought his right hand up to his mouth and stroked the beard covering his chin with his thumb and forefinger. "May I speak freely, milord?"

"Aye."

"Milord, 'tis my opinion that Langston is telling the truth. The sincerity in his eyes and voice were most convincing."

"Could be he is just an excellent liar."

"Aye, 'tis possible," Belwick replied. "But I doubt it. You know that I am not easily fooled. Langston has been extremely diligent in his training. He never questions orders. He readily takes on every task assigned to him, including the most menial. He is well-liked and respected by all the other men. None of the knights believes he is guilty."

"Thank you for your counsel, Hugh. I will take your information into consideration." Alaric shifted on the chair. "I will speak to Langston myself in a few days. Meanwhile, I want him confined to the prison. You may go now."

"Aye, milord."

Belwick bowed and crossed the room to open the door, revealing the manservant waiting in the hall. The servant stood back to let Belwick leave, then entered the chamber carrying a tray stacked with food.

"Excuse me, milord and milady," the servant said, giving them a bow. "Master Renwold told me not to disturb yer meeting with Sir Hugh."

"That 'tis fine, Stephen. Thank you," Helena said.

Moving around the chair, she noticed Alaric had closed his eyes, no doubt in fatigue. She quietly instructed the servant where to set the tray. He left, taking the chamber pot with him.

"Alaric, I should check your injuries as soon as possible to make sure they are not still bleeding."

He did not open his eyes. "Go ahead, then."

She gathered up some cloths, as well as clean water, and set them down on the floor next to his chair. Carefully untying the knot she had used to secure the bandage around his waist, she gingerly pulled the blood-soaked dressing away from the wound. After cleaning the injury with warm water and wine to remove the dried blood, she examined the wound.

"The bleeding has stopped," she announced.

Helena replaced the dressing with a clean one and secured it with a new bandage. After changing the bandage on his shoulder, she washed her hands, then served Alaric breakfast. They were both silent as they ate. Helena watched Alaric closely, alert for any signs of distress. He looked up from his cup to catch her eyes on him.

"Are you not going to plead your friend's innocence?" he asked.

"Nay. 'Twould be a waste of breath. You do not have an open mind."

Alaric grunted, setting down his cup. "I am going back to sleep."

He pushed to his feet. Helena followed him as he walked slowly to the bed and lay down. She gathered up the blanket to cover him, but he pulled it out of her hands.

"You do not have to stay with me. I am not an invalid."

"As you wish, milord."

She turned her back on him and gathered up the remnants of their breakfast, setting them on the tray. When she had her anger and disappointment under control, she strolled over to the bed to look at Alaric, who was already fast asleep.

Stubborn man, she thought. *Why does he dislike and distrust Damien so much? Damien has never done anything to harm him.*

"I wish to speak with Master Langston," Helena announced to the guard stationed outside the prison.

"Aye, milady."

Helena blinked, then endeavored to make her face impassive and hide her surprise. She had not expected her mission to be accomplished this easily, having fully anticipated a confrontation with Belwick over her plan to speak to Langston. But the guard banged on the door of the cell and called out loudly, "Langston, ye have a visitor."

Damien's face appeared in the open grill set in the top half of the door. The guard stepped back to allow Helena access, then retreated to stand at attention several yards away, facing the door.

"Helena, what are you doing here?" Langston exclaimed. "You should not have come."

"Damien, I had to see if you were all right." Helena tried to keep her voice low so the guard would not overhear her.

"I am as well as can be expected, being in prison and falsely accused of a crime I did not commit."

"Oh, Damien, I know you are innocent. Merclif has not even a shred of evidence against you, but he still believes you tried to kill him." She shook her head. "I do not understand why he mistrusts you so."

"He is jealous of me."

"What?"

"'Tis true." Langston met her eyes. "He knows I love you and want to protect you."

"But you love me as if I were your sister," Helena said, wanting it to be true.

"Nay, Helena. I love you as a man loves a woman."

"Damien, I do not feel that way about you. You are a good friend. You have been closer to me than my own brothers. But I love my husband."

The sad smile he gave her rent her heart. "I know, Helena. Do not worry. I am resigned to loving you from afar and serving you in whatever way I can."

"I am so sorry," she murmured.

"Helena, I did not confess my feelings for you to cause you hurt or grief, but to explain Merclif's antagonism toward me."

She nodded. "I am sorry Merclif has locked you in this prison. Even Sir Hugh believes in your innocence and has tried to persuade Merclif to release you, but to no avail."

"I guess I will be here quite a while then."

"In a few days I will try again to convince Merclif of your innocence. In the meantime, do you need anything?"

"Some water in which to wash and some clean clothes would be most welcome."

"I will see that you get both." Helena sighed. "I should go now, before I attract too much attention."

"Aye. And thank you, Helena."

"Take care, Damien. Do not lose hope. May God be with you."

"And also with you."

Helena walked slowly away from the prison door and around to the front of the donjon, wondering what she should do. Dismayed that Damien had voiced his true feelings toward her, she recalled their conversation in the dairy when Langston had first come to Merclif. She had interpreted his expression of love on that occasion as the love of friendship, the love of a brother for a sister. Since then she had chosen to ignore every indication that he felt more for her than that. In the face of his open declaration today, she could no longer hide from the truth.

When she reached the hall, she sought out the steward.

"Milady, what can I do for you?"

"Renwold, please send warm water and clean clothes to the prison for Master Langston."

"I am sorry, milady." Renwold looked down, avoiding her eyes. "No one is allowed to provide anything to a prisoner without Lord Merclif or Sir Hugh's permission."

"I see. Well, thank you for telling me." She tried to keep her voice calm, belying the humiliation she felt. "Do you know where Sir Hugh is now?"

"I believe he is in the lists, milady, training the men."

"Would you send a servant to ask him to come see me at his earliest convenience?"

"Aye, milady."

"Thank you, Renwold. I shall be in the herbarium until dinner time."

Helena left the chamber door wide open so Belwick would be able to find her easily. After putting on a sturdy apron, she opened the herbal Margaret had left behind and located the recipe for a tincture to treat wounds. Pulling down the jar of arnica blossoms from the shelf above the worktable, she measured out a gill onto the marble surface of the mortar. Taking the pestle, she ground the herb to a fine powder and added it to an empty jar.

As she pulverized and mixed the herbs, she chewed over her options. How was she to convince Alaric of Damien's innocence? How was she to persuade him to release Damien?

When she had finished grinding the remaining ingredients—goldenseal, comfrey, myrrh, blessed thistle, ginger root, sasparilla root and witch hazel—she added the alcohol the brewer had distilled for medicinal compounds to the herb mixture. She tightened the lid on the jar then swirled the contents around in the liquid.

A knock behind her caused her to look over her shoulder. Upon seeing Belwick, she set the jar down on the table and turned around fully to face the castellan.

"You wish to speak with me, milady?" Belwick inquired.

"Aye, Sir Hugh." She greeted him with a smile. "Please come in. I went to visit Langston in prison this morning." She rested her back against the table behind her.

"Aye, so the guard informed me."

"I do not wish to interfere with the military operation of the castle. I am merely trying to provide comfort for my friend."

"Aye, milady."

"Sir Hugh, would you please order the servants to provide Langston clean clothes and clean water in which to wash regularly?"

"Aye, milady. I will take care of that immediately."

"Thank you."

"Milady, may I offer you some advice?"

"Aye."

"You should not visit the prison again unless you have Lord Merclif's permission to do so."

Although he had couched it in terms of advice and had spoken with the utmost courtesy, it was clearly an order.

"Aye, Sir Hugh. I will do as you suggest."

"Is there anything else you require, milady?"

"Nay. Thank you, Sir Hugh."

The castellan bowed to her and exited the herbarium, leaving her alone.

27

Alaric woke abruptly late in the morning to find himself alone in the chamber. He felt only a little stiffness from his wounds as he got up to wash and dress. Seeing half a loaf of bread and some cheese left on the table, he quickly consumed it, feeling better after he had eaten. When he left the room, he walked carefully downstairs, testing his strength and stability. Servants were setting up the trestle tables for dinner in the hall, and he greeted them as they crowded around him.

"Good morrow, milord," Renwold said with a grin, bowing before Alaric. "We have all been very worried about you. How are you feeling, milord?"

"I am well. Just a little stiff and sore still," Alaric replied. "I am famished, though. How soon till dinner?"

"Dinner will be served in about half an hour, milord. Shall I bring you something to eat now?"

"Aye. Where is Lady Merclif?"

"I believe she is in the dairy. I will send for her immediately."

"Very good, thank you, Renwold."

Alaric walked briskly to the lords' table, not wanting the servants to see his weakness. As soon as Renwold set a platter with cold chicken and bread in front of him, he ravenously devoured the food. He was starving as if he had not eaten in a week. When Helena arrived shortly afterwards, he started to stand up to greet her.

"Nay, milord, do not get up." Her voice was breathless, as if she had run the entire way from the dairy to the donjon. "How are you feeling?" She sat down in her usual place beside him.

"Hungry," Alaric said before taking another bite of the chicken leg in his hand.

"Did you walk downstairs on your own?"

"Aye. I am almost back to normal, so you can stop fussing over me, Helena."

"As you wish, milord," Helena muttered.

"You can stop worrying about me as well, Helena," Alaric said as he finished off the chicken. "I have always been fast to heal."

"Amazingly so, Alaric. You were asleep for so long that I was beginning to wonder if you were more severely injured than we first thought. But now you seem to be completely recovered. I have never seen anything like it."

"What can I say?" Alaric shrugged. "I have been blessed."

After eating a hearty dinner and then instructing Belwick to bring in Langston, Alaric repaired to his solar to await his suspected assailant. Belwick ushered Langston into the room, removed his sword from its scabbard, and stood on guard with his back against the closed door.

Alaric stared at his prisoner's face, letting the silence stretch between them, trying to intimidate the younger man. Langston calmly returned Alaric's look, his eyes direct and his expression serene.

Alaric's temper ignited. "Did you try to kill me?" Alaric demanded.

"Nay, milord."

Alaric's eyes narrowed. "Admit it, Langston. Cardel has paid you to kill me."

"Nay, milord."

"Tell me the truth, and I will let you go free. 'Tis Cardel I want, not you."

"I am telling the truth, milord," Langston insisted.

"What has he promised you? Helena?"

Alaric, alert for any sign of discomfort by his prisoner, detected a slight wavering of Langston's gaze before he composed himself.

"Milord, I am not working for Cardel."

Alaric shifted in his seat and changed his tactics. "Tell me what you saw and heard while hunting the boar."

"Milord, I saw nothing but trees and brush. I heard nothing but your shout when you were wounded."

"Sir Roger sent you back to look for traces of an assailant. If you were not the culprit, why did you not find any?"

"Either the assassin was very skilled in camouflage, or I am not a very good tracker. Or, mayhap, 'twas a combination of both."

Frustrated and angry at the younger man's refusal to admit his guilt, Alaric looked at his castellan. "Sir Hugh, return Langston to his cell."

"Aye, milord."

"Milord," Langston said, "I am not guilty. You cannot keep me in prison forever."

"Oh, but I can," Alaric said. "I am lord here. My word is law. Take him away, Sir Hugh."

"Aye, milord," Belwick replied.

"Sir Hugh, please rejoin me here when you have returned Langston to his cell."

Belwick nodded, then took Langston's arm in a firm grip and led him out of the solar. When the castellan returned to the solar ten minutes later, Alaric poured him a cup of wine. Alaric waited until Belwick was seated before he spoke.

"We need to flush Cardel out. The only way to do that is to offer myself up as bait."

"Alaric…"

"Hugh," Alaric interrupted, "I know what you are going to say. Just hear me out. I will not be kept a prisoner in my own castle, nor will I wait around to see when and where Cardel is going to strike next. I plan to resume my regular activities, including hunting. I will continue to take only four or five men with me. However, there will be another man shadowing us, keeping out of sight. When there is an attack, he will blow a horn to alert the castle. You will then send the garrison out to defeat the enemy."

"In the event of an attack, you would have to hold out long enough for the garrison to reach you."

"You can assign the most experienced men to accompany me."

Belwick looked disgruntled. "'Twould be impossible to keep you in the castle, would it not?"

"Aye," Alaric said with a grin.

"In that case, your plan has merit. You will need to stay in a specific location during your forays outside of the castle so we will know where to find you."

"Aye." Alaric took a drink of his wine.

"And whenever you are outside the castle grounds, I will have the rest of the garrison close at hand and ready to ride at a moment's notice."

"That is an excellent idea."

"Alaric," Hugh pleaded, "will you at least scale back the number of hunts to once a week?"

"Four." Alaric leaned back in his chair. Hugh was now in accord with the plan, he thought with satisfaction.

"Two," Belwick said with a stern look.

"Aye." Alaric grinned. "Two it is." He raised his goblet. "To Cardel's defeat."

"Cardel's defeat." Hugh raised his cup, saluting his lord, before taking a long drink.

"Alaric, may I speak with you before you go downstairs?"

Alaric had already finished dressing and was preparing to leave the chamber. Helena hurriedly donned her kirtle as she watched Alaric walk back toward her.

"Of course, Helena. What do you wish to speak with me about?"

"Let us sit down."

Helena dreaded having this conversation with him. Although it was only three days since he had been injured, Alaric now appeared to be completely back to normal, and she felt she could delay no longer. After the wonderful night they had just spent together, she hoped he would be in a good mood. She tightened her belt around her waist as she walked over to the chair near Alaric's. Sitting down across from him, she tucked her cold, bare feet up under her skirts.

"I want to know how long you intend to keep Langston in prison," Helena said.

Alaric's amiable expression turned to stone. "That is not your concern."

"Alaric, Langston is innocent. You cannot keep an innocent man locked up in prison."

Grabbing the arms of his chair with both hands, Alaric pushed to his feet. "I will not have you telling me what I can and cannot do."

"Damien said you put him in prison because you are jealous of him."

Alaric leaned over her, imprisoning her—his hands braced on the arms of the chair in which she was sitting, his strong arms barring any escape. His menacing posture and hard look terrified her.

"When did you talk with Langston?"

"I...I..."

"When?"

"I...I spoke with him the day after you were injured."

"You expressly disobeyed my order to stay away from him?" Alaric demanded.

"I needed to find out how he was. He was locked in prison. The guard watched everything."

"Do not ever disobey me again." Alaric's voice was cold and harsh. "Understand?"

"Aye," she whispered. She shrank back in the chair, trying to get as far away from him as possible. Averting her face, she raised her bent knees up to her head, cowering into a tight ball.

Alaric pushed back from her and strode away. "I cannot have you undermine my authority in any way." His voice was now calm and controlled.

She did not look at him; she was merely glad that he had moved away from her.

"Your safety and the safety of everyone at Merclif depends on my orders being obeyed without question."

"Aye, milord," she murmured. "I am sorry."

Huddled in her chair, her head down and her arms wrapped tightly around her legs, she heard his every step as he walked back toward her.

He stopped in front of her chair. "Helena, please look at me."

She raised her eyes to meet his eyes as he knelt before her. Tears ran unheeded down her face. When he reached out toward her, she instinctively recoiled from him. He dropped his hands without touching her.

"Helena, I am sorry for frightening you." His voice was hoarse.

She swallowed with difficulty as she stared at him.

"No matter how angry I am, I will never hurt you," Alaric vowed. "You must believe that."

She nodded, unable to speak.

Alaric reached out to her again, and this time she held herself still and tense as he touched her. He gently curved his hands around her face and rubbed his thumbs under her eyes to wipe away her tears. Leaning forward, he kissed her softly. She offered no resistance but could not respond to his overture.

He sighed as he stood. "I will see you at mass," he said quietly. "We will break our fast together as usual."

Helena stared after Alaric as he left the chamber. She dragged in shattering breaths. Although she knew in her mind that he would never strike her, her instincts for survival had caused her to react blindly to his threatening posture. What had hurt the most during their confrontation was his lack of trust in her and in her judgment.

She knew with certainty that Damien was telling the truth and was innocent of attempting to murder Alaric. Alaric had closed his mind to reason and justice. She was powerless to help her friend and feared for his life. Could Damien be right? Was Alaric jealous of her friendship with him? Did Alaric think she would break her marriage vows? How could he think she would commit such a sacrilege?

As she stood, her legs were so shaky that she abruptly dropped back into the chair. The argument with Alaric had affected her more than she realized. He had lulled her into thinking she could trust him, but for the first time she questioned his actions. He had tried to intimidate her with his superior strength. She realized that he had only taken the time and effort to "train" her to make his own life easier, to have a willing wife in bed. It was obvious to her now that he cared nothing about her as a person, that he cared nothing for her feelings or opinion.

Helena took a deep breath and stood. She dashed the useless tears from her eyes. If that was the way he wanted their marriage, so be it. The love she had begun to feel for him was stupid and foolish. It only made her more vulnerable to him. She must banish it from her heart.

Alaric silently cursed himself as he stormed down the steps. He strode through the hall, ignoring his men as they stirred awake and the servants as they went about their chores. Out of the donjon, past the armory, and through the outer ward he headed toward the southeast turret on the outer curtain. After climbing the spiral steps two at a time to reach the crenellations, he headed north along the allure, ignoring the greetings of the guards he passed. He paused in front of a crenel to watch the sun rise.

Helena's concern for Langston and her unwavering belief in his innocence sent his temper to the boiling point. How dare she question his orders or his judgment? Gradually, as the brilliant pinkish orange color faded from the clouds and the sun rose across the valley, he felt his anger dissipate with the retreating darkness, leaving only regret in its wake.

What was it about Helena that roused this rage? Why was he always losing his self-control with her? He had never hurt a woman, but this morning he had come dangerously close. The realization filled him with shame. He took a deep, calming breath.

Helena had accused him of being jealous of Langston. That was ridiculous. Helena was *his* wife, not Langston's.

The quiet of the morning was pierced by the clanging of the chapel bell calling everyone to worship.

Enough, Alaric chided himself. This morbid introspection was getting him nowhere. He had work to do.

28

Alaric was not her father. He had not physically hurt her, Helena reassured herself. He had merely tried to dominate and control her.

Merely, she thought in disgust. Now she was making excuses for his awful behavior. Usually she played her lute when she was upset, but today she could not stand the idea of being in their bedchamber. Dispirited, Helena went downstairs and closeted herself in the herbarium, trying to find peace and order by following the recipes, grinding and mixing the herbs.

A firm knock on the door interrupted her. "Who is it?" she called.

"'Tis Elizabeth, Helena. May I come in?"

"Aye." Helena turned to greet the older woman as she entered the room.

"I am afraid I have come to stick my nose into your business," Elizabeth said with a determined look on her square face.

"What do you mean?"

"Helena, 'tis obvious there is some problem between you and Alaric. You barely spoke to each other yesterday, and today he is in a foul mood and you are moping. Margaret made me promise to look after the two of you." The older woman paused briefly. "I hope you consider me a friend."

"Aye, Elizabeth, I do."

"Sometimes it helps to talk about your problems to a friend."

"Aye, that is true," Helena said. It had helped enormously when she had confided in Alaric and told him of her father's abuse.

"You will find I have a very sympathetic ear. And I will hold whatever you tell me in the strictest confidence."

Helena found herself explaining to Elizabeth her argument with Alaric over Langston, Alaric's anger and threatening manner, and his lack of trust in her. Elizabeth listened attentively, encouraging Helena with gentle murmurs and understanding nods.

"Marriage is complicated," Elizabeth said when Helena had finished. "You and Alaric were two strangers tied together, and now you need to learn how to live in harmony. As you rub together, you will start to shape each other so you fit together more smoothly. Like this." She closed her fingers over her palms and rubbed the knuckles of one hand against the other until it fit securely in the indentations of its partner. She held her hands out for Helena to see. "Unfortunately, the rubbing process can sometimes be very painful." Elizabeth dropped her hands back to her sides.

"Do I not have rights in the marriage?" Helena asked. "Must I submit to whatever Alaric demands of me?"

"Well, first of all you cannot think about your rights or your pride. Marriage was ordained by God for the mutual joy of husband and wife, for the help and comfort each gives to the other. If you focus only on yourself, then resentment and anger builds. So the key is for both of you to be humble and submit to each other in the marriage."

"How can I get Alaric to humble himself?" Helena asked.

"You cannot, my dear. You can only change your own behavior and attitude."

"But if I do not stand up for myself, Alaric will just ride roughshod over my feelings. I am afraid I will simply cease to exist."

"My dear, that is your pride speaking. We are all selfish and self-centered creatures, but Jesus calls upon us to love each other and to be humble in heart. Love is a choice, an action, not merely a feeling. Being humble means that we think more about the needs of others than of our own wants and desires. Humility does not mean we do nothing and allow others to mistreat us.

"You cannot coerce Alaric to do what you want by making demands or criticizing him. If you avoid making demands, and try not to become angry or disrespectful when you discuss your feelings with Alaric, most likely he will respond in kind. If you are humble and considerate in the midst of an argument, usually the other person will calm down and respond in kind. 'Tis a very hard thing to do because our natural instinct is to be selfish and to consider our own feelings before anyone else's."

"What if he becomes angry with me again?" Helena asked. "What if he physically threatens me like he did yesterday?"

"Then you just stop talking to him and come back to the discussion some another time," Elizabeth advised. "That will give him a chance to cool down."

"What you say seems reasonable."

"Just remember that Jesus tells us to do unto others as we would have them do unto us. He tells us, 'Give, and it will be given to you. Good measure, pressed down, shaken together, running over, will be put into your lap. For with the measure you use it will be measured back to you.' You can depend upon His promises. I know 'tis much easier to offer advice than 'tis to follow it. Before you speak with Alaric, you should pray and ask God to give you humility and insight into what Alaric's most important needs are."

Helena nodded, considering her friend's words.

"Remember, a wound unattended simply festers and becomes putrid. The same thing happens to a marriage if you avoid facing your problems or withdraw from your husband."

"I do not suppose you could give this same advice to Alaric?"

Elizabeth smiled. "I do not think Alaric would take kindly to receiving advice from me. However, I can nudge Hugh into offering him some pointers on how to build a happy marriage. Hugh has often given Alaric fatherly advice in the past."

"Elizabeth, would you pray with me now?"

"I would be happy to, Helena."

Alaric stepped into the deserted mews and headed for Gaenor's perch. After donning the heavy gauntlet, he coaxed the falcon onto his hand. He stroked her feathers, singing her song. She shifted restlessly on his fist, as if she could sense his agitation.

He was a warrior. His first response to any opposition was to fight, subdue, and conquer. *Obviously not the best strategy when dealing with one's wife,* he realized in self-reproach. Guilt flogged him.

What exactly did he want out of his marriage? A willing bed partner, of course. Sons, naturally. Companionship and friendship? He had never considered that as something he could have with a woman, but now that he had started to form those bonds with Helena, he realized he wanted that intimacy with her as well. His heedless actions yesterday had probably destroyed whatever trust she had come to have in him.

"Kek, kek, kek," Gaenor screeched.

Being here in the mews had not soothed him as it usually did, and he was only upsetting the peregrine. He gently set Gaenor back on her perch; the incongruity of his care for the bird's feelings versus his lack of care for Helena's wasn't lost on him. He ripped off the heavy leather gauntlet and threw it down before leaving the mews.

He strode to the armory, donned his chain mail hauberk, took up his sword, and marched toward the lists. Seeing Gordon standing idle while the other men trained, Alaric called him over. The clang of steel as he struck Gordon's sword with his own resonated within him. Here in the lists everything was simple and straightforward, unlike the morass of his marriage. He fought fiercely, finding the less experienced knight little challenge for him. Totally absorbed in the contest, he lost all sense of time passing as he relentlessly battled the younger man.

"Pax, milord," Gordon begged.

Alaric drew his sword away and stepped back. Gordon bent over, his hands on his knees as he gasped for breath. Alaric looked around for another opponent. Spotting Roger fighting in a dilatorily manner with Matthew, he called the older knight over. Gordon hurried away as Roger came to take his place.

By the time Alaric was fighting his sixth opponent, his anger and guilt had been somewhat assuaged, and he no longer attacked as vigorously as he had to begin with. Seeing Bernard tiring, he tempered his blow and raised his sword to await a counterattack. None was forthcoming as the older knight stood, shield raised defensively. Heavy lines framed Bernard's broad nose as he pressed his lips ttogether in a straight line, accentuating his prominent chin. Bernard's eyes darted behind Alaric.

"Milord!" Belwick called out. "May I have a word with you?"

Alaric stepped back and lowered his sword. Bernard visibly relaxed and exhaled deeply as his arms holding his shield and sword fell to his sides. Wiping some sweat from his brow, Alaric walked over to Belwick. "What is it, Hugh?"

"I fear for the safety of the men, Alaric." He kept his voice low so Bernard could not overhear. "You should not take your anger out on them."

"'Tis better I take it out on them than…" Alaric realized what he was about to say.

"Than your wife?"

"Aye," Alaric admitted.

Unable to meet the older man's eyes, Alaric looked away. He realized for the first time that the lists, normally the busiest area of the castle as the men continually trained to maintain and improve their skills, were deserted. He watched Bernard walk quickly away from the practice field.

"A true knight controls his anger. He does not allow it to rule him. Not with his wife. Not in battle," Hugh admonished Alaric.

Alaric sheathed his sword in his scabbard and turned to face his mentor. Hugh was the only person, aside from his mother, from whom he would have taken such a rebuke. "Aye, you are right." Alaric clenched his jaw.

"Do you want to talk about it?"

Alaric shook his head. "She will not let it go. She challenges my judgment and questions my commands." The words burst from his lips involuntarily.

"Helena objects to your decision to imprison Langston?"

"Aye. I told her that it was not her concern. That she had to stop undermining my authority."

"Alaric, are you sure that your judgment about Langston is not clouded by personal animosity toward him?" Hugh probed. "Could it be that you are jealous of his friendship with your wife?"

Alaric's mouth scrunched into a grimace, and his hands curled into fists at his sides as he stared at the ground. The silence stretched as he considered Hugh's words. Helena had accused him of being jealous. Now Hugh was suggesting the same thing. Could it be true? "Mayhap, I am jealous."

"Marriage is a complicated business. It takes a while for a man to learn how to live with his wife. As you rub together, you will start to shape each other so that eventually you will fit together more smoothly. Unfortunately, the rubbing process can sometimes be very painful."

"Aye, that is certainly true."

"The cure for your jealousy is to spend time with Helena," Hugh suggested. "Become as close a friend to her as Langston was. Displace him in her affections."

Alaric nodded, considering his words.

"As for your authority in the castle, Helena does have a right to question it."

Alaric shot an intense, inquiring look at Hugh.

"She will be in command of the castle whenever you are away on the king's business, so she will have to make these kinds of decisions in your absence. She has known Langston for some time, so she might have a better reading of his character than you do. The question is whether you trust her judgment or not."

"'Tis not a matter of trusting Helena's judgment regarding Langston's character. There is probable cause to suspect him of attempted murder. The harm he could cause far outweighs the cost of my being wrong about him."

"You are the lord here," Belwick said. "'Tis your decision to make. Just be sure you are making it for all the right reasons."

"Aye." Alaric nodded.

"And next time you need to cool off, instead of decimating your troops, try jumping into the river instead."

Alaric laughed, his mood lightening. "I have not done that since I was a boy. An excellent idea, Hugh. I could use a cold swim."

"Take your six victims with you. They all deserve a break, after the way you trounced them."

"Aye, I will do that." Alaric slapped Hugh lightly on the back before he headed toward the armory.

Helena wondered about Alaric's wet hair as he joined her at the lords' table for dinner. He politely seated her and served some of the roast duck onto her trencher of bread. The tension that gripped her made it impossible for her to eat. Alaric, in contrast, devoured his meal with a hearty appetite.

"Are you not hungry?" Alaric asked.

Helena shook her head and silently offered up a prayer. *Dear Lord, help me to be humble and to love Alaric more than myself.*

"We need to talk," Alaric said once dinner was finished.

"Aye, milord."

"Shall we go to my solar?"

She looked at his sober face, aware he was offering her a choice, not commanding her. Perhaps he felt as keenly as she did the need to make things right between them.

"Aye."

He offered her his hand and, when she placed her hand on top of his, led her upstairs. The open window allowed sunlight to fill the chamber and the spring breeze lightly swept the room, leaving a fresh scent behind.

Alaric ushered Helena to a chair. "Would you care for some wine?" he asked.

"Nay. Thank you."

Alaric stood several yards away, feet firmly planted wide apart, hands clasped behind his back. "Helena, I am very sorry for the way I treated you yesterday. My instinctive response was that of a warrior. I set out to conquer you, with no regard for your feelings. 'Tis not an excuse, but an explanation for my behavior. I will try never to do that to you again."

"Thank you, Alaric," Helena said in relief. She had dreaded this conversation. The fact he realized how much he had hurt her eased her fear. "Your apology means a lot to me."

"I must admit that 'tis very easy for you to make me angry and lose control." Alaric shook his head. "I have never had this problem with anyone else before."

Helena felt hope rekindle in her heart. His intense feelings toward her, albeit mostly anger, must mean that she was important to him.

"'Tis natural for married couples to have disagreements, I suppose," Alaric continued. "I do value and trust your opinions, even if I do not always agree with you. I will have to learn how to respond more appropriately when you express your views."

"I did not mean to question your authority, Alaric. I was merely concerned about the welfare of my friend."

"I do not wish to discuss Langston again. My decision to keep him in prison is not up for debate."

Although his words were calmly spoken, they were nonetheless final, and Helena felt some of her hope fade. She had to accept that Alaric would not be swayed on this issue. If she continued to pursue it, she risked further damage to her relationship with her husband. She had Belwick's reassurance that Damien was being treated well in prison. There was nothing more she could do for him but pray. She must put her trust in the Lord and turn Damien over to Him.

"I see." Helena took a slow breath. "Then I will abide by your decision."

Silence lengthened between them.

Alaric cleared his throat. "I hope my brutish behavior has not entirely destroyed your faith in me. If you are able to forgive me enough to be able to trust me again, I swear that I will treat you with the respect you deserve."

Did not God require that she forgive those who sinned against her? Would He not forgive her as she forgave others?

She looked up into her husband's eyes. "Alaric, I do forgive you."

"Thank you, Helena."

The smile he offered her caused an answering smile to transform her own face. The Lord had indeed answered her prayers and brought about this reconciliation.

"'Tis a lovely, warm spring day," Alaric said. "Mayhap you would like to take a ride with me? We cannot venture far from the castle, given the continued threat from Cardel, but we can still have a pleasant ride."

"I would like that, Alaric."

29

The end of March brought the celebrations of Holy Week. Helena happily spent days preparing for all the activities from which she had been excluded for so long.

On Palm Sunday, everyone gathered in the great hall before mass to pick up a freshly cut yew or willow branch. The people then followed Father Thomas as he carried the altar Cross and the consecrated Host in a procession through the inner bailey to the chapel. As they walked, the congregation sang hosannas, commemorating Christ's triumphant entry into Jerusalem.

During morning mass on Maundy Thursday, Father Thomas celebrated the Eucharist, commemorating the new covenant Christ established with his disciples during His Last Supper. After mass, the congregation feasted in the great hall as the fasting of Lent was relaxed for this one day since the Church considered the Eucharist and fasting incompatible. Everyone avidly consumed the roast venison, mutton pie with onions and peas, cheese, and pecan tarts, delicacies they had denied themselves throughout the last three weeks of Lent.

On Good Friday the fast was resumed, with only dry bread, beans, cabbage, and salt served at all three meals.

During the solemn mass held at noon, Father Thomas, dressed entirely in black vestments, prostrated himself before the empty altar, covered only with a simple black cloth. After the lessons, chants and prayers, the priest brought forth the Cross, veiled in black cloth, and placed it on the altar. Father Thomas sang "Behold the wood of the Cross on which hung the salvation of the world," to which the congregation responded, "Come let us adore." After this liturgy was sung three times, Father Thomas unveiled the Cross. The priest genuflected and kissed the Cross, followed by Alaric and Helena, then the rest of the congregation, their adoration of the Cross symbolizing the worship due to God. The Cross and the consecrated Host were then buried in a special sepulcher in the wall of the chapel and surrounded by candles.

On Easter Eve, all the fires and candles in the chapel, as well as the donjon, were extinguished. A new fire was kindled with flint, symbolizing the Resurrection of Jesus, the Light of the World, from the tomb closed by a stone. Only the great Paschal candle was lit for an all-night vigil in the chapel.

On Easter morning the flame from the Paschal candle was used to rekindle light and fire in the castle. During mass, the sepulcher was opened and the Cross and Host were carried to the altar, restored to its previous glory. After mass the entire castle community, as well as everyone in Mersthrope, partook of the Easter feast at the castle.

Alaric and Helena wandered together through the inner ward where tables had been set up for the villagers, accepting the villagers' offerings of eggs, dyed red to symbolize the joy of Easter. In return, they offered the hospitality of Merclif in the form of an elaborate feast.

"Milady! Milady!"

The sweet, childish voice grabbed Alaric's attention as he and Helena spoke with the village leaders. He turned to find Sadie dashing toward Helena, her mother running behind, clearly trying to catch her. Helena scooped Sadie up into her arms, hugging her and twirling her around.

"Milady," Betsy panted. "I am sorry. Sadie, come here." Betsy reached out to take Sadie from Helena's arms. "Ye shouldn't bother her ladyship."

"Betsy, 'tis fine." Helena smiled, changing her hold on the little girl to brace Sadie against her hip. "Sadie is not disturbing me. Mayhap I can steal her from you for a little while."

"If ye're sure, milady?" Betsy asked, looking at Alaric and the other men who had stopped talking to watch the women.

"Aye," Helena said. "I will bring her back to you."

Betsy nodded, then curtsied toward Alaric and the village leaders before hurrying off.

Helena turned back toward the men. "Milord, gentlemen, would you please excuse me?"

"Aye, milady," Alaric said with a grin. He watched as Helena carried the little girl toward the donjon, listening to her excited chatter, before looking back at the other men.

"Her ladyship will make a good mother, if I may be so bold to say so," said Talbot.

"Aye, right you are, Phillip," Alaric agreed. "I take that as a high recommendation, seeing as how you are somewhat of an expert on the subject. Just how many grandchildren do you have now?"

Talbot rocked back on his feet. "Well, Margery, David's wife, was just delivered of a girl, so that makes a round forty."

"Congratulations!" Alaric said.

He spoke a little longer with the men before excusing himself and going in search of Belwick. He finally located his castellan coming through the inner curtain gate and walked over to intercept him. "Any trouble?" Alaric asked.

"Nay," Hugh replied. "Entry to the castle grounds was a little slow this morning since we only used the postern gate and had to search each face, but no strangers have entered."

"Good. And the guards?"

"Double guards have been posted on the crenellations, as you ordered."

"Hopefully, the Easter celebration will continue without any problems."

"Aye." Belwick nodded. "We will make sure of it."

Alaric spent a few more moments with the castellan discussing the castle defenses, then ambled back toward the table laden with venison, ham, pigeon pies, cheeses, cakes, and wafers. Picking up a pie, he took a bite and started to walk away from the table when a lad barreled into him.

"Sorry, milord," Nicholas said. "I didn't mean to hit you."

"No harm done, lad. But you should slow down, so you do not harm any of the children or women. 'Tis the obligation of a knight to watch out for others."

"Aye, milord. I'll do that."

Nicholas bowed and walked sedately for a few steps before breaking into a run. Shaking his head, Alaric turned to see Bernard advancing toward him. The knight's triangular face was creased in a frown.

"I am sorry, milord," Bernard stated when he reached Alaric. "I despair of ever teaching that boy some manners."

"Do not worry about it. I remember being ten."

"I think that Nicholas needs to start his training soon. 'Twill concentrate his energies in a more useful direction."

"Anytime you want to start his training is fine with me, Bernard. But I think 'tis not me you need to convince, but your wife."

"Aye. Clare tends to pamper Nicholas, treating him like a child rather than a man."

"Well, he is her youngest. Clare is a sensible woman. I am sure you will be able to convince her."

"'Twould be easier on her if Nicholas received his training here, rather than at another demesne. Would that be possible, milord?"

"Aye. I see no problem with that. However, it might be good for the lad to get away from here. It might help him to grow up."

"You may be right, milord."

"Discuss it with Clare and let me know what you want to do."

"Aye, milord. I will."

After her exuberant greeting, Sadie had been silent in the presence of her mother and the other grownups, but she made up for it when she had Helena's ear to herself. Helena smiled as Sadie regaled her about her new kitten, which she had finally been able to take home.

"I names her Blackie, 'cause she's all black," Sadie explained. "Blackie drinks lots of milk, but Mummy won't let me bring Blackie to the dairy when she's working 'cause she thinks Blackie will drink up all the milk for the cheese. Blackie eats fish. I likes to wrap her up in a blankie and pretend she's my baby, but she don't like that too much." Sadie scrunched up her nose in disappointment.

"Well, Blackie is not a baby anymore," Helena sympathized. "You would not want to be treated like a baby, now, would you?"

Sadie looked thoughtful for a moment before shaking her head. "Nay."

"Well, neither does Blackie. But I am sure there are lots of games you can play with Blackie that she would like."

"Like what?"

Helena had reached the great hall and sat on one of the benches with Sadie on her lap. She was not accustomed to carrying a child and had found that Sadie's weight, although very dear, had become quite heavy.

"Oh, I am sure she would like to play ball with you. And usually kittens love to be stroked behind their ears, like this." Helena tickled Sadie behind her ear, causing her to shriek and giggle. "Or you can pet her stomach, like this."

Sadie squirmed and laughed as Helena demonstrated, causing her to laugh at the child's joyous abandon. She cuddled Sadie as the animated child gradually calmed.

"I have a present for you," Helena announced.

"What is it? Let me see! Let me see!" Sadie bounced up and down in Helena's lap in her excitement.

Helena put Sadie down and took her hand to lead her to the herbarium in the corner of the hall. She unlocked the door and ushered the little girl inside. "Now, my present is very fragile, so you will need to be very careful,"

"I be careful," Sadie vowed. "What's fragile?"

"That means it will break easily."

"Oh. I be careful," the four-year old repeated.

"Good, I knew you would be."

Helena went to her worktable and picked up a small basket. The basket had a pink bow tied on the handle and was lined with straw. She knelt in front of Sadie and held out the basket to her.

The little girl leaned over the basket, careful not to touch it, and peered inside. "Ohhh," she sighed in pleasure. "They're so pretty."

Sadie reached her small hand into the basket and delicately touched one of the eggs. Three eggs, decorated in colors to please a small girl—purple with blue flowers, green with yellow dots, and orange with red stripes—lay inside the container.

"Are they real?" Sadie asked in awe.

"Aye. They are hard-boiled eggs, so you can break the shells and eat them."

"Nay." Sadie shook her head. "Not eat. Too pretty."

"Well, I am glad you like them, sweetheart. But the eggs will not keep for very long." Seeing the frown start to form on the little girl's face, Helena said, "Shall we go find your mother and show her the eggs?"

"Aye." Sadie's countenance cleared and a smile spread.

"Would you like to carry the basket?"

Sadie nodded enthusiastically and carefully took the handle from Helena. Helena followed the young girl through the busy hall, watching in fond amusement the exaggerated care with which the child walked. Once they located her mother and father in the noisy bailey, she rushed toward them swinging the basket wildly. Helena grimaced in alarm but was relieved that the eggs survived their journey intact. She left Sadie with her parents and wandered in the bailey, searching for Alaric. She spotted him talking with Sir Hugh and walked over to join them.

"Happy Easter, Sir Hugh," Helena greeted the castellan.

"Happy Easter to you, milady." Belwick bowed. "Let me congratulate you on a splendid celebration. It rivals any that Lady Margaret officiated over."

"Thank you, Sir Hugh," Helena said with a pleased smile. "That is great praise indeed."

"Aye, Helena." Alaric looked down into her eyes. "You have done a fine job."

"Thank you, milord. Most people seem to have finished the meal. I was thinking it is time for the skits."

"Whatever you would like to do is fine."

"I will go make arrangements for the mummers to perform, then. Please excuse me."

Helena smiled at the men before walking away to find Renwold. She finally located him directing servants in the great hall and spoke with him about having the mummers perform. Renwold had made all the arrangements with the men from the village who would perform the skit. It was considered bad luck for anyone besides the players to know their identities, so the mummers wore elaborate masks to depict their characters and to disguise themselves.

Helena stood with Alaric to watch the play. Saint George killed the Slasher, with much hilarity and gore. A doctor was summoned to resurrect the Slasher, but before he did so, he offered up a hilarious boast, claiming to be able to cure the pains of old age and broken bones, not to mention wives who make their husbands miserable:

"If any man has got a wife
That makes him weary of this life,
Scolding and bawling about the house
The same as if the Devil was turn'd loose,
Let him bring her here to me,
And I will cure her instantly,
For with one pill I'll make her civil,
Or I'll send her headlong to the Devil."

After the doctor revived the Slasher, the play was over. The mummers accepted
applause of their audience as well as coins from Alaric. The feasting lasted long into
afternoon, with more skits, dancing, and merriment. By the time dusk fell, many of
men were too drunk to walk home and were allowed to sleep off their overindulge
in the hall. Families with young children were the first to leave the castle grounds
the trek home. Helena found she was quite fatigued by the time she accompa
Alaric upstairs.

"That was fun," Helena said as she walked into their chamber before Alaric.

"Aye," Alaric agreed. "Thank you for all your hard work, organizing the feast."

"You are welcome," Helena replied with a smile. "I enjoyed it."

She went to her clothes chest and retrieved the basket she had decorated for Al
The basket was trimmed with blue and silver ribbon. Inside, lying on a bed of st
were the five eggs that she had decorated especially for him. This was the first pre
she had ever given him, and she was unsure how he would react. After all, Easter
were not exactly manly.

"Alaric?"

"Hmm?" he muttered as he hung his cloak on a peg.

"I have made something for you." She extended the basket to him as he turne
face her. "Happy Easter."

Alaric took the basket with a bemused smile. She waited anxiously as he picke
an egg dyed green with yellow stars. Silence stretched as he carefully replaced the g
egg and picked up the blue one with white stripes. He looked up at her wi
delighted, boyish smile.

"These are amazing. I have never seen such beautifully decorated eggs before. T
are very intricate. However did you make them?"

"First, I made a pin prick in the shell and drained out the egg so it would
longer. Then I melted some beeswax and applied it to the shell before dipping the
into dye. When the dye had dried I melted the wax off the egg."

"Helena, thank you so much."

"I am glad you like them."

Alaric set the basket down on a table. "May I give you a thank-you kiss?"

"Aye," she whispered.

Alaric gently took her into his arms and lowered his head to kiss her. She lea
eagerly into him, sliding her hands around his waist as he kissed her. Much too s
for her, he reluctantly drew back and cleared his throat.

"I have something for you," Alaric said, releasing her.

He opened his clothes chest and pulled out a small wooden box tied with a g
ribbon and handed it to her. She could not remember the last time she had receive
gift. Smiling, she untied the ribbon and took off the lid. She stilled when she saw

gold cross pendant lying inside the box. The cross was studded with jewels—brilliant rubies, emeralds, and diamonds sparkled in the candlelight.

"Oh, Alaric," she breathed, stunned. "'Tis beautiful." She looked up at his smiling face. "Thank you."

"You are welcome," Alaric said. "Shall I put it on you?"

"Aye."

She turned and lifted her wimple so he could fasten the necklace around her neck. The gold chain was long so the cross pendant lay between her breasts. She touched it in awe, still not able to believe he was giving her such a costly gift.

"Do I get a thank-you kiss?"

"Aye."

She dropped the pendant and pivoted to face him. Putting her hands on his waist to steady herself, she raised her face to his while he lowered his head to meet her. She kissed him with all the love that filled her heart. Gradually she drew back from him and met his searching eyes. Sliding her arms around his waist, she laid her head on his shoulder as he enclosed her in his arms.

30

Alaric rode at the head of his men, leading them through a dense thicket of trees, all the time scanning the woods for any sign of danger. After sending the huntsmen back to the castle with the dogs and the stag they had slain, he lingered in the forest with his men, hoping to attract attention and end the waiting. Spring had filled the bare branches of the trees with fresh green leaves, but the cold rain had turned the day gray and miserable. Alaric shook his head to clear away the rain dripping from his coif into his eyes and down his neck.

He was tired of this endless waiting. It had been two months since the attack on him. If Cardel didn't make a move soon, he was considering taking the fight to him in Narhex. He sighed, chiding himself. As satisfying as that course of action would be, it was out of the question. He had no proof Cardel was behind the assassination attempt. Although Langston had been interrogated several times, he still resolutely maintained his innocence. Alaric was beginning to feel guilty for Langston's long incarceration. Helena had not broached the subject of Langston since their violent confrontation at the beginning of March, but he knew she was troubled about her friend.

Thoughts of Helena warmed him. He had taken Hugh's advice and been courting his wife. Whereas before, when he had been training her to accept his touch, he had only been concerned with her physical reaction, he now found himself vitally interested in all her feelings. He shared activities with her that he knew she would enjoy—riding, taking walks along the allure, playing chess. Mostly, they talked.

Mindful of his castellan's counsel that Helena would be in command of the castle should he be away or if something should happen to him, he started educating her about the garrison and the castle defenses. He found her an apt and keenly interested pupil. She had an excellent understanding of tactics and strategies, no doubt honed by her own harrowing experiences.

With his mind occupied, Alaric let his vigilance slip. He rode unsuspectingly into the trap. A rope sprang up from the thick underbrush, smashing into Geneir's chest. The horse reared back, furiously pawing at the air. An arrow slammed into Alaric's calf, another into his uncovered arm. Geneir's front hooves crashed down, the violence of the movement sending Alaric tumbling to the ground.

The quiet forest suddenly reverberated with the screams of horses, the shouts of men, and the clank of steel as hordes of men in tattered garments ambushed them. Staggering to his feet, Alaric drew his sword from his scabbard. He dispatched one assailant with a sharp stab to the chest, only to have two other men rush him. He swerved, avoiding one blade, and engaged another. Slashing and hacking with his sword, Alaric heard the cry of a horn. Merclif had been notified of the attack. Belwick would immediately dispatch the castle garrison, as they had planned. They just needed to hold out until help arrived.

He glanced back to see how his men were faring. Two were on the ground, dead. Roger and Gordon were off their horses, trying to make their way toward him. Alaric retreated toward his men, parrying the attacks aimed at him, shouting orders as he went. When he reached Roger and Gordon, they stood in formation, their backs to each other.

Wave after wave of the attackers assailed them. Gordon went down. Alaric and Roger stood back to back, fighting for their lives. A blade escaped Alaric's vigilance, slicing into his neck.

Time ceased to have meaning as they battled against overwhelming odds. Alaric saw Bernard, who had been following them and who had joined the battle after sounding the alarm, take a mortal blow to the chest.

Fiercely Alaric fought. A sword cut his thigh…another, his arm. Roger fell under the brutal barrage. A sword cut into Alaric's waist, finding the opening in his mail, and sliced up through his chest. He staggered under the lethal hit and collapsed to the ground. Blow after blow assaulted him as he lost consciousness.

The thunder of hooves filled the air as Belwick raced into the thicket. The few remaining attackers were cut down as they tried to flee. Frantic, Belwick scanned the carnage. Dead bodies were strewn on the ground, and it appeared as if no one was alive but the men who had just arrived.

"Alaric," Belwick shouted.

Anguish tore at him as he quickly dismounted, issuing orders to his men. They searched through the corpses, separating the ambushers from their own.

"Sir Hugh!" Matthew yelled. "'Tis Lord Merclif."

Belwick rushed to where the young soldier knelt next to Alaric's prone body and dropped down on one knee beside his lord. Alaric's body was shrouded with so much blood it was almost impossible to see his injuries. Laying a shaking hand against the uninjured side of Alaric's neck, Belwick closed his eyes in prayer as he felt for a pulse. Hope returned when he detected the faint beating of Alaric's heart.

"He lives," the castellan announced.

Belwick's long years of experience took over as he shouted orders. After stripping the mail and outer garments from Alaric, Belwick applied a tourniquet to Alaric's thigh to stop the flow of blood, while Matthew pressed his cloak against the wound on

Alaric's chest. The castellan dispatched Geoffrey to ride to the castle to prepare them to treat Alaric. He instructed four soldiers to fashion a stretcher to carry Alaric and ordered the rest of the men to lay out the bodies of their fallen comrades. Belwick put Sir Ralph in charge of the men who remained behind, searching the enemy dead for signs of their identity and affiliation.

It was a slow journey back to the castle as the four men carefully carried the stretcher. Belwick and Matthew had managed to bind up the most serious of Alaric's wounds, but Hugh was well aware that Alaric hovered near death. In agony, Belwick silently berated himself. He should have argued with Alaric more strenuously when he had first proposed this rash plan. The thought of Alaric's death was unimaginable.

Helena waited on the crenellations above the main gate, searching for any sign of Alaric's return. Geoffrey had reported the ambush and that Alaric was grievously injured. She had prepared everything she would need to treat him. Now all she could do was to pray and to wait.

"Milady, they're coming." The guard's agitated voice cut into her prayer.

He pointed toward the band of men emerging from the forest, carrying a stretcher. Anguish filled her as she watched their painstaking progress. When they drew closer, she could make out Belwick walking beside the litter, his attention firmly fixed on Alaric.

Dear God, keep Alaric alive, Helena silently prayed. *Heal his wounds. Please let him live.* She repeated the litany over and over in her mind.

When the men crossed the drawbridge, Helena raced down the turret steps and out the main gate to meet them. The sight of Alaric's blood-soaked body slammed into her, and she faltered, agony engulfing her. She raised tortured eyes to Belwick.

"He is near death, milady," Belwick said in a hollow tone, the depth of his own grief apparent in his drawn, gray face.

Lord, give me strength, Helena prayed. *Help me know what to do. Please heal Alaric. Let him live.*

She walked next to the stretcher, on the opposite side from Belwick, as the men carried Alaric through the main gate and through the outer ward. All activity in the inner ward stopped when they entered. All eyes were fixed on Alaric. The unnerving quiet was oppressive, overflowing with sorrow. Father Thomas joined the entourage as Alaric was carried through the hall and up the stairs.

When they reached the bedchamber, the four of them—Helena, Belwick, Father Thomas, and Renwold—lifted Alaric's limp, unconscious body from the litter and laid him on the bed. The stretcher-bearers quietly filed out of the room. Father Thomas began to administer last rites to Alaric as Helena removed the strips of cloth wrapped around Alaric's chest, revealing his most serious injury.

"We have to stop the bleeding." Alarmed, Helena looked up at Belwick where he stood beside her. "We cannot cauterize this wound. 'Tis too close to his heart. What if I sew it up? Do you think that will stop the bleeding?"

"'Tis worth a try," Belwick replied.

When Renwold fetched the sewing supplies, she heated the strongest sewing needle in the brazier to clean it before she started to piece Alaric's jagged flesh back together. She inserted the needle deeply into the skin on one side of the gash and brought it up through the opposite side, knotting the individual lengths of thread.

Belwick worked closely with her, cutting the threads after she completed the stitches and handing her new pieces of thread. Father Thomas, when he had finished administering Extreme Unction to Alaric, left his bedside and went to the *prie-dieu* at the side of the room. The priest's muffled prayers could occasionally be heard, providing a soothing counterpoint to the tumult and commotion surrounding her as she treated her husband's injuries. After she finished sewing Alaric's chest wound, she and Belwick uncovered the deep wound on his leg. It was still bleeding freely.

"'Twill have to be cauterized," Belwick stated.

"Aye," Helena agreed.

She checked Alaric's pulse. He was still alive. How much more trauma could his body endure?

Belwick put his knife in the brazier. As they waited for the knife to heat, Helena carefully washed Alaric's chest wound with warm water and wine. She then washed the wound on his thigh, clearing away some of the blood for the cauterization. After testing the knife, the castellan instructed Renwold to hold Alaric's lower body still while Helena held his upper body, then he laid the flat side of the blade directly against the gaping wound. Even though Alaric's unconscious body arched as he instinctively recoiled from the pain, Helena was easily able to hold him immobile. She almost wept when she realized the extent of his weakness.

The smell of burning flesh assaulted her nostrils before Belwick pulled the knife away and covered the wound with a cold, wet cloth. After returning his knife back into the glowing brazier, the castellan returned to the bed and lifted the cloth.

"I need to do it one more time to cover all of the wound," Belwick explained, his voice hoarse.

Helena and Renwold resumed their positions holding Alaric's unconscious body still as the castellan cauterized the remainder of Alaric's wound. His battered body lay motionless under this new assault. Helena determinedly blinked away her tears as she unwound the cloth that had been placed around Alaric's neck wound. Relieved to see that the bleeding from this lesion had ceased, she gently washed the laceration and applied a poultice to it to guard against infection before bandaging it securely around Alaric's neck, making sure it was not tight enough to interfere with his breathing.

Once his major injuries had been treated, she spread the poultice on the wounds on his chest as well as his thigh and bandaged them. She and Belwick then washed and treated the remaining abrasions, cuts, and gouges that covered Alaric. A long time later, the last gash and lesion treated, Helena numbly sank to her knees beside the bed. She raised anguished eyes to Belwick's haggard face.

"What happened?" she asked. The mutilation that had been inflicted on Alaric staggered her.

"Alaric was hunting with four of his men," Belwick responded. "A fifth man was shadowing them, to warn the castle if there was trouble. It appears that they were taken by surprise and ambushed. When we arrived, there were only five of the attackers still standing. We killed them all. Alaric was the only one of our men still alive when we reached them. Bernard, Roger, Gordon, Walter, Edmund…they are all dead. Every man fought valiantly."

"Bernard is dead," Helena whispered. "Clare and Nicholas will be devastated."

"Aye. All our men perished. All were courageous and experienced fighters. They had no chance. They were ambushed by an overwhelming force. We counted over thirty attackers."

"There were six men against thirty?" Helena was appalled, incredulous that Alaric had managed to survive the savage onslaught against him.

"Aye. Alaric and his men were able to kill twenty-five of their attackers before we arrived. Milady, I have ordered that the bodies of Merclif's dead be brought back to the castle with all reverence."

"Have you specified they are to be brought to the chapel?" Father Thomas asked. He had left his prayers to listen to Belwick's account. When the castellan nodded, the priest turned to her. "Milady, if you will excuse me, I will go see to our dead."

"Aye, of course, Father."

"Milady, I will also say mass for Lord Merclif and arrange a prayer vigil around the clock."

"Thank you, Father."

The priest touched Helena's hand lying on the bed next to Alaric's inert body. "Lord Merclif is in God's hands now, milady."

Helena nodded, her eyes resting on Alaric's white face.

"Milady," Belwick said after the priest left, "I have also instructed that the enemy dead be searched to see if they carry any identifying markings. I need to go now to see to the castle defenses."

Helena raised her eyes to Belwick's. "Aye, Sir Hugh. Thank you. For everything." She did not have the words to express her gratitude to this man who loved Alaric as if he were his own son.

Time ceased to have meaning for Helena, as she concentrated all her energies on Alaric. She stayed close to his side, monitoring him and administering medications. Elizabeth came in, offering to help, but Helena declined. She could not bear to leave Alaric. Throughout the long night Helena watched as Alaric's strength ebbed dangerously. She was helpless to do anything for him but pray. Over and over again, she pleaded for God to save him.

With the dawn a raging fever engulfed Alaric's tortured body. Helena roused the servant sleeping outside the chamber, sending him for cold water and cloths. After stripping the sheets off Alaric, she bathed him endlessly with the water to cool him.

"Milady," Belwick said, "how is Alaric?"

Helena raised burning eyes to the castellan. "I do not know if he will live. Please send for Lady Margaret."

"Aye," Belwick said. "I will send a messenger immediately."

Helena's consciousness dwindled to Alaric. Her arms and hands ached with the strain of wringing out the wet cloths and plastering them to his body. She urged tinctures down his throat and bathed his wounds in wine to stop the infection.

"Helena," Elizabeth said, "you must eat. You must rest."

Helena looked up at the older woman who had become a good friend. "I cannot leave him."

"Helena, you have not eaten nor slept in more than two days. You must keep up your own strength, or you will be useless to Alaric."

Helena looked at Alaric. Despair and hopelessness filled her weary mind. She had ferociously battled the fever that ravaged him. She had prayed endlessly to God to heal Alaric.

"I am a skilled nurse," Elizabeth said. "I will take care of him while you sleep. If there is the slightest change in his condition, I will wake you. Let Clare take you next door to Margaret's old chamber."

"Aye." Helena allowed Clare to lead her away from Alaric. Suddenly remembering the loss the other woman had suffered, she gripped the widow's hand. "Oh, Clare, I am so sorry for your loss. Sir Bernard was a valiant man, and I know that Alaric will grieve for his loss."

"Thank you, Helena."

Clare settled Helena into a chair and brought her cold venison, cheese, and bread.

"You should not be waiting on me," Helena protested. "You must take care of yourself."

"I would rather help you and Lord Merclif since I can do nothing more to help my Bernard. 'Tis better to focus on helping others."

"How is Nicholas faring?"

"He is bearing up as well as can be expected."

"Clare, please let me know if you need anything. Anything at all."

"Aye, Helena, I shall." She put a piece of bread in Helena's hand. "For now, you must eat."

Helena, rung out and limp as a rag doll, mindlessly followed Clare's gentle orders. Clare helped Helena bathe, dressed her in a clean chemise and tucked her into bed, then remained by Helena's side as she slept.

"Alaric!" Helena woke abruptly. "I must see Alaric."

Helena accepted Clare's assistance as she dressed before hurrying back to her husband's side.

"There has been no change," Elizabeth informed Helena. She stepped back from the bed to allow Helena to minister to Alaric.

At Elizabeth's insistence, the women fell into a routine. Helena nursed Alaric through the long, dark nights, when his strength was at the lowest, and he was most in danger. Elizabeth nursed him during the morning hours when Helena slept. Fever continued to devastate Alaric's weak body. He alternated between burning up and shaking with chills. He became delirious, thrashing about and speaking gibberish. Helena held him to still his movements and to prevent his wounds from reopening.

"Sir Hugh, have you been able to identify the assailants?" Helena asked during one of Belwick's regular visits to check on Alaric's condition.

"Nay, milady," Belwick replied. "Although they wore ragged clothing and did not wear armor, their weapons were such as only knights and men-at-arms would have. There is no doubt in my mind that Cardel ordered his men to disguise themselves as vagrants and to attack Merclif."

"But you have no proof?" Helena asked.

"Nay, milady." Belwick shook his head, his mouth set in a grim line. "I do not."

Desolation as black as the dead of the night filled Helena's soul. Alaric's emaciated body was so weak and frail. How could he endure any more pain and agony?

"Dear God," Helena pleaded for the hundredth time, "do not let Alaric die. Please heal him."

Despair crushed her spirits. She laid her head against the pillow next to him.

"I love you. I love you. I love you," she chanted. Tears wrenched her body as she sobbed out her misery and torment.

31

Helena roused from the stupor caused by her storm of weeping. The light of the candles bathed the chamber in a warm glow. Something had changed. What was it? Alaric's body was no longer a furnace burning beside her. Her heart froze as she reached a shaking hand to his throat, fearing that he had died. The slow, steady beat of his heart against her fingers sent blessed reassurance flooding through her.

She sat up in the bed and closely examined Alaric. His breathing was no longer laborious; his skin was neither cool nor hot to the touch. He appeared to be sleeping naturally.

"Thank You, Lord," she whispered. "O, gracious Lord, thank You. To You belongs all glory and honor and praise. Thank You for answering my prayer and sparing Alaric's life."

As she held her hand to Alaric's cheek the realization flooded her that she had not trusted in God at all during his illness. Pleading and cajoling, she had beseeched Him to spare Alaric and heal him, wanting only her own will to be done. She had not committed Alaric's life to God's loving care.

"Oh, Lord, forgive me for not trusting You, for not fully surrendering Alaric's life to You. I know You love him so much more than I ever could. I know You have a plan and a purpose for his life, as well as for my own. Please forgive me for not trusting in Your love or in Your plan. Most merciful Lord, help me to surrender my will to Yours and to seek to do Your will always, in every circumstance. Amen."

Leaving the bed, Helena pulled up a chair next to it and closely observed Alaric as he slept. Finally freed from the awful burden of fear and worry, she relaxed enough to be able to contemplate the danger still facing Alaric.

By the time the new day dawned, and the rising sun warmed the chamber, she was convinced that Alaric was out of danger. When Elizabeth quietly entered the chamber, Helena turned to greet her with an ecstatic smile.

"How is he?" Elizabeth asked, as she had every morning for the last fortnight.

"Elizabeth, I think the crisis has passed. See? Alaric is sleeping peacefully. The fever is gone."

Elizabeth felt Alaric's skin to see for herself. "Oh, Helena, I think you are right. This is indeed cause for celebration."

"Elizabeth, I do not want anyone to know that Alaric is getting better."

"Why ever not?"

"I have been doing a lot of praying and thinking while I was watching Alaric this morning. I have an idea I need to discuss with Sir Hugh. Would you ask him to come here? And please do not let him or anyone else know that Alaric is out of danger now."

"As you wish, Helena, but I would like to hear your plan as well, if I may."

"Aye, aye, of course."

Within a few minutes Elizabeth returned to the chamber with her husband. Belwick's face was set. He was obviously preparing himself to hear the worst.

"Sir Hugh, Alaric is much better," Helena said without delay. "His fever has broken, and he has been sleeping naturally since the middle of the night."

Belwick's grim face dissolved into a broad smile. "That is very good news, milady."

"I am now convinced that Alaric will recover, but I want everyone to think that he will die."

"What?" Belwick asked. "Why?"

"We have no evidence that my father is behind the attacks against Alaric. We need to have proof before we can arrest him and bring him to King Henry for justice."

"Aye," Belwick agreed, his eyes narrowing on Helena's face.

"Cardel's plan must be to kill Alaric and then take over Merclif."

"Aye, that is what Alaric and I have surmised."

"If we say Alaric is dead and hold a funeral for him, my father would be bound to hear about it. He would come to Merclif and try to take over the castle. I could confront him and get him to admit he ordered the attack on Alaric. With you and Lord Wyham as witnesses, we would be able to arrest him."

"Hmm. 'Twould be risky for you, milady. You would be in danger, confronting Cardel by yourself."

"Nay," Helena said. "I would be here in this chamber, supposedly prostrate with grief. You, Alaric, and Lord Wyham could listen in on the conversation from Margaret's room next door. With the door open and the tapestry down, you will not be seen, but you will be able to hear everything that is said in this chamber and be able to protect me if my father tries to harm me. I could also have a weapon—say a knife—to defend myself against him, if necessary. Sir Hugh, I have been doing a lot of praying this morning. I truly feel as that this idea is God's will."

Belwick nodded, stroking his beard. "Your plan has merit, milady. It goes against my grain to just sit back and let Cardel attack Alaric at will. 'Twould be good to flush him out, like the beast he is."

"Aye," Helena agreed. "We cannot put my plan into action until Lord and Lady Wyham arrive. It would be cruel to let Lady Margaret think that Alaric has died."

"Aye. They should arrive in the next few days."

"Good. Alaric will also need to recover and regain his strength before we confront Cardel."

Belwick nodded.

"So we should wait until Lord and Lady Wyham arrive. Then we will announce that Alaric has died. We will make sure the entire Mersted Valley knows about his death, so we will hold a funeral for him to make it look convincing. You and Elizabeth will tell everyone that I am prostrate with grief and that I will not leave this bedchamber. That will cover up the fact that Alaric is really alive and will allow food to be brought here."

"'Tis a very clever plan, Helena." Elizabeth spoke for the first time since bringing her husband upstairs. "We will need to maintain our current routine. Although Alaric may be out of danger, he will still need a lot of nursing."

"Aye, Elizabeth," Helena responded. "You are correct. And we must make sure that no one besides you two, Renwold, Father Thomas, Margaret, and Lord Wyham know the truth."

The next two days passed quietly. Helena found she had the easiest job, since she never left the bedchamber and devoted all her energies to Alaric's continued recovery. Her co-conspirators, on the other hand, had to contain their relief at Alaric's steadily improving health and instead had to act solemn and downcast around the other inhabitants of the castle. Alaric, who slept a tremendous amount, as he had when he recovered from his previous wounds, had not yet been informed of her plan.

Late in the afternoon, Elizabeth came into the chamber to inform Helena that Margaret and Wyham were approaching the castle with a contingent of the king's troops. They were shown into Alaric's bedchamber as soon as they arrived. Helena rushed to greet Margaret, embracing her.

"Mother, Alaric is better," Helena said. "He will recover."

"Thanks be to God," Margaret breathed. She pulled out of Helena's arms and went to Alaric, laying her hand on his cheek as he slept. "The way everyone was acting, I feared he was on his deathbed."

"He is," Helena stated.

She explained her plan to Margaret and Wyham. Playing devil's advocate, Wyham probed and quizzed her, trying to find flaws in her strategy, but she was able to respond to every objection he threw at her.

"Helena, I do believe your plan will succeed," Wyham finally concluded.

"Aye, I hope so," Helena replied. "My only concern is allowing enough time for Alaric to recover fully before we force the confrontation with my father."

"I do not think we should delay any longer," Wyham said. "It will take a few days for the news of Alaric's death to reach Cardel and for him to marshal his forces to take over the castle. 'Tis best to announce Alaric's death right away."

"We can say tomorrow that he died during the night," Helena suggested.

"Aye," Wyham agreed. "I will go now and confer with Sir Hugh. I want to know what plans he has made for Cardel's arrival."

"Tell me what happened to Alaric," Margaret implored Helena when Wyham left. "Sir Hugh's message was not very detailed."

Helena related to Margaret how Alaric had been ambushed, the nature and extent of his wounds, and his recuperation. They sat by the bed talking quietly, Margaret's eyes rarely leaving Alaric's face. Wyham returned before supper to tell the women that Belwick agreed they should put Helena's plan into action immediately.

That night, Margaret and Helena remained closeted with Alaric in the bedchamber, as if they held a vigil over his dying body. Father Thomas was summoned in the early morning hours, purportedly to administer last rites, and was informed of the plan to entrap Cardel. After a few half-hearted objections over the deception of performing a sham funeral, which Wyham neatly deflected, the priest agreed to participate. Ironically, on the day he would publicly be pronounced dead, Alaric stirred and returned briefly to consciousness long enough to greet his mother and to consume some broth.

"'Tis heartrending," Elizabeth reported after dinner. "Everyone in the castle is overcome with grief. 'Tis very difficult for me to watch the anguish of the people without telling them Alaric is alive."

"Elizabeth," Helena said, "I know this is very hard on everyone, but it is absolutely imperative that no one but the eight of us know the truth."

Helena remained secluded with Alaric as the castle community grappled with the news of his demise. On the day of his funeral, Helena left him in Elizabeth's care as she sat next to Margaret during mass. Helena wore a heavy veil covering her face, leaning heavily on Wyham's supporting arm and speaking to no one. She watched in silence as an empty coffin was lowered into the ground. After Alaric's burial, Helena returned to their bedchamber as Elizabeth spread the news that she was overwhelmed with grief.

Helena and Margaret shared nursing duties. Belwick and Wyham were the only visitors allowed. Everyone took care not to inform Alaric about the plan, waiting until he had completely regained his strength.

Alaric opened his eyes, the pain swamping him again, the waves pulsing through his body. Even the simple act of sitting up seemed beyond his present capabilities. Helena and Margaret had both counseled him that his recovery would take time. It was easy for them to tell him to be patient—they were not the one lying here weak and broken.

He hated this weakness, hated being powerless, hated being dependent. Hated this fear. What if he died? What if he did not regain his strength? What if he were crippled?

Suffering was new to him. Of course, he had been wounded before, but nothing like this. Pain consumed him until he ceased to function, ceased to exist. How he hated his helplessness.

"Alaric, you are awake." Helena came to sit next to him on the mattress. "Would you like some porridge?"

"Nay." Even turning his head to look at her hurt.

"Alaric, you must eat to regain your strength."

"I am not a babe. Do not tell me when to eat."

"As you wish."

Confound it. He could not even piss without help. "Get Stephan."

"What do you need? I will help you."

"I do not want you. Get Stephan." He closed his eyes.

"I will call Renwold."

"I told you to get Stephan."

"I will be right back, Alaric."

Finally, she was doing what he asked. Bile seized through his chest. He was not a child.

Then the door opened. Renwold was trailing Helena. Rage burned within him. Could she not follow a simple direction?

"Helena! I told you to get Stephan."

"Stephan is not available, Alaric. Renwold will help you."

"Get out! Out, Helena, out!"

She turned away and rushed toward the door. When Renwold, who had remained close to the exit, moved to follow her out, the flame within him exploded again.

"Renwold, get over here. Now!"

"Mother."

His voice caused Margaret to break off her prayer. She opened her eyes and looked at her son. His eyes were still clouded, and the pinched lines around his mouth and between his eyebrows bore testimony to his continued suffering.

"How are you feeling, Alaric?"

"How do you think I feel? I am in pain, and I cannot move without causing myself more pain."

"Do not take that tone of voice with me, Alaric." Margaret tried to keep her voice quiet and without heat. "I have had enough of your surly attitude this week past. Your injuries do not excuse your bad temper. Especially toward those of us trying to help you. Especially toward Helena, who has tended you with unselfish devotion and dedication."

Her son refused to meet her eyes, looking instead over her shoulder, his mouth set in a mulish line.

Margaret silently prayed for guidance. She needed to approach this with gentleness and love. "Alaric, I know you are afraid…"

He jerked his head back, his eyes burning into hers. "I am afraid of nothing."

"Are you not, my dear? Are you not afraid of dying?"

She looked steadily at him until he sighed and closed his eyes. He seemed to slump into himself as he leaned back onto the pillows.

"Alaric, you almost died, but God was merciful. He heard our prayers and spared you. My dear, you have no need to fear death. You were baptized as an infant, and I know that you believe in the Triune God. You have been saved by God's grace. You have His gift of eternal life."

"But I have not been a good man, and more often than not I have failed at being a good husband." The misery in his voice speared her heart.

"Alaric, you cannot add anything to your salvation by your own works. We can never be good enough to earn our salvation. Jesus has done it all for us. He paid the penalty for your sins with His death on the cross. Our salvation is by God's grace alone. 'Tis His free gift to us.

"But, once we have been saved, our correct response to God's love is to surrender all that we are, and all that He has given us, back to him. All your life, you have made your own plans and lived by your own will. I fear for you if you do not surrender yourself completely to your Lord. I believe God allowed your severe injuries to get your attention. He wants all of your heart in total submission to Him."

"Submission? Surrender? I might as well have died, if that is what God requires of me."

"I know 'tis hard for you. You are used to being in control, to being a leader of men, and you are not accustomed to submitting your will to another's. Denying yourself does not mean losing your identity. Jesus tells us that 'he who finds his life will lose it, and he who loses his life for my sake will find it.' God created each of us with unique characteristics and personalities, and He treasures our individuality."

"Why should I submit to God?" His tone was no longer sullen, but rather perplexed and questioning. "You already said that I am saved, that I am going to heaven and nothing I do will affect my salvation."

"Nothing you do, except completely disowning God, will jeopardize your salvation. But is not your refusal to surrender to God a sin against Him, a rejection of Him? Because He first loved us, do you not want to love Him and serve Him? Jesus proved that real leadership is found in humility, and real power is found in submission to God and in service to others."

Margaret waited, giving Alaric time to think about her words, praying that Alaric would open his heart and his mind to the truth.

"How do I submit my will to God?"

"'Tis like taking a fealty oath to the king. Submitting your will to God is the duty you owe Him. But such a submission must be made out of love, not obligation. Just as each time the king calls on you for service and you must do what he requires of you, so too the Lord will call upon you, through His Holy Spirit, and tell you what service He requests of you. But unlike the king's demands, God makes requests that you are free to ignore or to disregard. 'Tis a daily, continual process to deny yourself and to submit your will to the Lord. Submitting your will to God frees you from yourself, frees you from the need to always be in control. Surrender to the Lord brings freedom and peace."

She smiled tenderly at him. "Alaric, I can see that you are tired. Just think about what I have said. Better yet, pray about it and ask God to give you the gift of discernment. I will continue to pray for you. Alaric, I love you."

"I love you too, Mother."

32

Alaric pushed the bedding out of his way and stood. When his shaking legs buckled, he grabbed onto Helena's shoulder while she put her arm around his waist to help support his weight. He gritted his teeth, sweat breaking out on his forehead. "'Twould appear you were right. I am still too weak to walk by myself. Please help me get to the chair."

Helena held him as he walked the few steps to the chair and eased him gently down into it.

"I am still weak as a baby," he muttered. He laid his head back against the chair and watched as Helena returned to the bed to strip off the linens. "What are you doing?"

"I am taking advantage of your being out of bed to change the sheets."

Alaric watched her silently for a few moments before speaking. "Helena, I am sorry for my rudeness. I am not used to being an invalid."

She finished her task before coming to his chair and dropping onto her knees before him. "I was so afraid you would die." She took his hands in her own. "Please try not to push yourself too hard. I fear you might have a relapse."

Alaric raised her hands to his lips, dropping a kiss on each of her palms before releasing them. "Thank you for your care."

"You are welcome." She smiled at him, then rose to her feet.

"I hope you will not take this the wrong way, but I find I need some time alone."

She frowned down at him. "I am not sure that is such a good idea."

"I will be fine. Just half an hour."

"Only if you promise not to move from that chair."

"I promise."

"As you wish, then. I will be back in half an hour."

Alaric watched her gather up the dirty linens and, with one last searching look, departed. He sighed as the door closed behind her. He had had a lot on his mind since his mother's visit yesterday. All night long he had mulled over her words. At first he had been defensive and resistant. He saw now that he had reacted to God's call on his life with defiance and resentment. He did not want to give up his own will to his Creator. Facing the fact he was so selfish and self-centered had hurt.

His mother was right. Everything he had done in his adult life had been the result of his own will, his own desires, his own ideas. He had never consulted with God, never requested His guidance, never waited on His plan, never trusted his life to Him.

The only times he had turned to God was when his own guilt and shame had overwhelmed him. He would ask for God's forgiveness and, once it was granted, he would go his own way once again.

Control. He had to be the one in control. If things did not go his way, he reacted with anger and resentment, lashing out at others in frustration when they did not do as he decreed. He had hurt Helena in his attempts to rule her, and he had willfully caused the death of Bernard, Gordon, Roger, and the others. Guilt engulfed him.

"I am so sorry, Lord. I have resented You. I have been proud and arrogant. I have put myself and what I want above You, above others, even my own wife, even above the lives of the men who serve me. Please forgive me."

The words of a familiar psalm came to him:

Create in me a clean heart, O God,
and renew a right spirit within me.
Cast me not away from your presence,
and take not your Holy Spirit from me.
Restore to me the joy of your salvation,
and uphold me with a willing spirit.
Deliver me from bloodguiltiness, O God,
O God of my salvation,
for you will not delight in sacrifice, or I would give it;
you will not be pleased with a burnt offering.
The sacrifices of God are a broken spirit;
a broken and contrite heart, O God, you will not despise.

"Lord, break my spirit. Break my willfulness. Conform my will to Yours. You alone are worthy of my obedience. You alone are holy. I rededicate my life to You. I ask that Your will be done in my life as it is in heaven. All this I pray in Jesus' name, amen."

Feeling as if he had just climbed an enormous mountain, he leaned his head back and rested in the chair. Peace pervaded his soul—a peace such as he had never known.

Alaric looked at his mother. "I thought about what you said yesterday, Mother. You were right. I have been like a willful, selfish child. I have asked for God's forgiveness, and I have asked Him to change me."

"Oh, Alaric." Margaret clasped his hand in both of hers. "I am so glad. 'Tis been my prayer for a long time that you would seek the Lord's guidance and that you would trust in Him and not rely solely upon yourself."

"'Tis hard. I did not want to admit how arrogant I am. I needed you to point out my failings to me."

"Pride and the desire to be God is the oldest sin. 'Tis the sin Satan used to tempt Adam and Eve. We, all of us, are beset by the old Adam. We need to daily submit our will to God's. It does get easier the more we do so, the more God changes our hearts."

Alaric nodded.

"Now that you have humbled yourself before God, the next step is to humble yourself before others. The Lord calls upon us to love others as we love ourselves. That means putting the needs of others before our own selfish wants and desires."

Raking his free hand across his mouth, Alaric reflected on her words. Humility would be even more difficult for him than submission. He was used to being in command, having others serve him. How would he be able to serve others?

"You can do none of this on your own," Margaret said. "Pray and rely upon the Holy Spirit to continue to change you."

"Mother…" It shamed him to admit this to her, but he knew that if he did not unburden himself of his guilt, it would continue to tear him apart and might eventually destroy him. "…I am still haunted by the deaths of my men. In my arrogance, thinking I could conquer anything, I deliberately put my men in danger. I caused their deaths."

"Alaric, have you asked the Lord for forgiveness for your part in their deaths?"

"Aye."

"Do you not believe Him when He says that when you confess your sins, He removes them from you, as far as the east is from the west? That if you confess your sins, He is faithful and just and will forgive your sins and cleanse you from all unrighteousness? You must trust Him and rely on His promises."

"Mother, please continue to pray for me."

"I always will, Alaric. I always will."

While Margaret stayed with Alaric, Helena took a walk on the allure with Wyham. Every time she left the confines of the bedchamber the sadness that pervaded the whole of Merclif, from the great hall to the inner bailey and the lists, oppressed her and made her feel guilty. Everyone had been extremely solicitous of her supposed state of mourning, treating her with gentle sympathy as if she, in her fragile state, would shatter with the least provocation.

"I am so sorry we are putting everyone through this suffering," she remarked to Wyham when they were out of earshot of the guard.

"'Tis an unfortunate result of your plan, my dear." Wyham commiserated with her. "The people's grief will soon turn to joy, when this is all over."

Raising her face to the sky, Helena breathed deeply of the fresh spring air. Life had become even more precious to her since Alaric's near fatal injuries. She rejoiced in the light breeze caressing her cheeks, the warmth of the sun on her skin, and even in the faint scent of manure from the livestock stabled below. Helena returned her gaze to Wyham's face. "When do you think my father will come?"

"Belwick sent out spies to Cardel's estate in the north. Cardel left Narhex two days ago with a large force. We believe he will be here in a few days. I have proposed to Belwick, and he has agreed with me, that I should leave Merclif with the king's men while Margaret remains here with you. 'Twould be natural for her to remain behind to comfort you. After making a public departure, we will surreptitiously return to Merclif and remain hidden. The soldiers will camp out, concealed in the woods, while I sneak back into the castle. They will provide support and backup for Merclif's troops when Cardel strikes."

"How soon will you leave?"

"Tomorrow."

"We need to tell Alaric about our plan soon. It is getting harder and harder to keep him in our bedchamber. Thankfully, he has almost regained his full strength."

"Aye," Wyham agreed. "Belwick and I will come to your chamber this afternoon to explain to him our course of action."

"Good. I think he will accept the idea better if it comes from both of you instead of just myself."

"My dear, your plan is brilliant. You have an excellent tactical mind."

Helena smiled. "Thank you for your kind words, milord."

"Alaric, where are you going?"

He paused with his hand on the latch of the door and looked over his shoulder at her. Helena rushed over and inserted her body between Alaric and the door.

"I am heartily sick of these four walls. I am strong enough to go downstairs."

"Nay, you must not."

"Why not? You can walk by my side, if you think I am likely to keel over."

Helena pressed her hands lightly to his chest. "Alaric, please. You must not leave this chamber. Lord Wyham and Sir Hugh will be here soon to explain everything."

"What is going on?"

"Please, Alaric, will you just wait until they can explain?"

"All right."

Helena breathed a sigh of relief that he had yielded to her wishes so easily. There has been a marked change in Alaric lately. Not so much his physical condition, but his mood had improved tremendously. It seemed to have stemmed from that time she had left him on his own three days ago. He was less demanding, less dictatorial, more appreciative of her efforts.

"Have I told you lately how grateful I am for your care of me?"

With her back pressed against the door and her hands still on his chest, she gazed up into his brilliant blue eyes. The gentleness of his voice and the heat in his eyes caused her to catch her breath. He bent his head, and his lips settled over her parted mouth. His arms went around her, and she sank into him, into his tenderness, into his care.

"Helena," the voice came through the closed door, "'tis Wyham and Belwick."

"Oh, my goodness," Helena whispered. "Just a moment, milord."

"You look thoroughly kissed, but otherwise presentable," Alaric murmured, giving her one more lingering kiss before stepping away from her. "We will continue this later. Go ahead and open the door."

She watched him walk toward the chairs, envying him his composure, as she moved to open the door. If Wyham or Belwick noticed her flushed face, they politely ignored it. The men had visited Alaric during his convalescence, but never before together.

Alaric returned their greetings, gesturing for them to be seated. "So," he said when everyone was settled, "Helena tells me you have something to explain to me. I must confess, I am very intrigued."

Wyham laid out the strategy the three of them had devised, making it clear the original idea had been Helena's. Alaric listened intently, all trace of his earlier amusement gone. He closely questioned both Wyham and Belwick as to the details before falling into contemplation. The others remained quiet, letting Alaric think.

"'Tis a good plan." Alaric looked at Helena. "Wyham is right. You do have an exceptional tactical mind. However, your plan involves a very real threat to your safety. 'Twould be unconscionable for me to put you in any danger."

She met his gaze. "Alaric, the danger to me is minimal. You will all be close by, should my father turn violent. I will have a knife with me as well."

"Would you be able to use a knife against another human being?"

"Against my father? Aye, I would. Alaric, I need to do this."

A few months ago she had been frightened, fragile, broken. Today, she felt strong and resolute. She knew that with God's help she could do anything. She truly believed this was God's plan for her life. She needed to face down her greatest fears, to see her father brought to justice for his brutality and treachery. Then she could bury her past.

"All right," Alaric said, "but I will give you instructions in using a knife while we wait for Cardel to arrive."

Helena nodded. "Aye, that is a good idea."

"So." Alaric looked back at Wyham and Hugh. "I am dead. 'Tis a passing strange thing to grasp."

"Aye," Belwick said. "And you have been greatly mourned by everyone, from the bravest soldier to the lowliest kitchen boy."

"Let us hope Cardel arrives soon then," Alaric said. "I would have this finished."

33

"**C**heck and mate," Alaric declared.

"Aye, you win," Helena said. "This time."

"So, are we even yet?"

"Nay, I still am one game ahead of you. Would you care to play another game to even the score?"

"Nay." Alaric pushed back from the table. "I am far too restless. I would like to get out of this chamber. If Cardel does not arrive soon, I may have to disguise myself and sneak out of here at night."

Alaric paced to the window and stood looking over the moat and the surrounding countryside. Since he had fully regained his strength, he had been like a caged bear. The endless waiting grated on him. He was a man of action, so the patience required now did not come easily.

"I know this confinement is difficult for you. Dinner should be here soon. Perhaps after dinner you could continue training me."

He turned away from the window. The view was too restrictive to afford much information as to what was occurring around the castle. His gaze fell on Helena as she gracefully moved around the chamber, putting the chess pieces and board away.

She had been with him throughout most of the days of his captivity. He had learned much of humility and service from her example. A silent prayer formed in his mind, something that happened more and more often lately.

Thank You, Lord, for giving me Helena as my wife. 'Tis only now that I see how You have worked Your good and perfect will in my life, despite me. She has been such a blessing to me. Please keep her safe. Lord, I am trusting in You. In Your love for her and in Your love for me. I ask that Your will, not mine, be done in her life and in my own. In Jesus' name, amen.

Helena went to answer the door to admit Margaret, Elizabeth, and Renwold as they entered with trays of food. Ever since Alaric's recovery, Margaret and Elizabeth had eaten with them to help disguise the amount of food a supposedly frail, distraught Lady Merclif was consuming. After the door closed behind Renwold, Margaret opened the connecting door to her chamber and Wyham joined them. Margaret and Elizabeth watched the others eat, as had become their practice. They would eat later so the men would have enough food. When they were almost finished with the meal, another knock sounded on the door.

"Lady Merclif," Belwick's voice rang out. "I need to speak with you."

Alaric abandoned his food and stood as Helena let Belwick into the chamber.

"Milord, Cardel's forces are approaching the castle."

"How many men does he have?" Alaric asked.

"There are five knights and about thirty men-at-arms," Belwick replied.

"A siege force."

"Aye, milord."

"Is everything ready?"

"Aye, milord."

"Good. We proceed as planned."

Belwick bowed and left the chamber.

Margaret and Elizabeth began to gather up the dishes and remaining food, stacking them on the trays. Wyham pushed back his chair and stood. Helena sat frozen in her seat, staring down at her hands.

"Helena," Alaric said, breaking into the commotion, "'tis not too late to change your mind. You do not have to confront your father. We can carry out the plan without your participation."

The room was suddenly quiet. Helena looked up to see everyone stilled, their eyes on her, waiting for her response. She was so grateful for everyone's encouragement and support. Shaking herself out of her immobile state, she drew in a deep breath and met Alaric's eyes. "Nay. I am ready," she stated.

Alaric's eyes searched her face. "Aye." He nodded. "You will be fine."

Movement resumed. Helena assisted the other women clearing the meal from the table, while Wyham helped Alaric don his chain mail hauberk, which Belwick had smuggled into the bedchamber. Alaric went next door with Wyham to do the same for the older man. After Margaret and Elizabeth carried the trays from the chamber, Helena pulled the table and chairs to the side of the room, setting the scene for the confrontation with her father.

Alaric reentered the bedroom, leaving Wyman in the other chamber. He strode to Helena and gently drew her into his arms. She rested her head on his shoulder as she gratefully absorbed the comfort he offered. They did not speak as he held her.

Belwick paced along the crenellations above the main gate, watching the troops approaching the castle. The portcullis was down over the main gate and the drawbridge was up. Guardsmen and archers were aligned around the battlements, and the remainder of the garrison was strategically stationed in the outer bailey. The castle was ready for Cardel's assault.

Cardel drew to a halt on the far side of the river. "Hail the castle," he shouted.

"Hail, Lord Cardel," Belwick replied.

"So you know who I am. I will see my daughter, Lady Merclif."

"Aye, milord. You may enter the castle. Leave your men outside."

"Nay," Cardel bellowed. "My daughter is a widow. She bore her husband no son. My daughter's protection and property falls to me now. By rights Merclif is mine. Open the gate."

"Nay," Belwick called. "I will not admit your men unless Lady Merclif gives the order."

"I will enter the castle with my knights," Cardel conceded. "The men-at-arms will remain outside while I talk to my daughter."

"One knight may enter with you," Belwick yelled.

"All five," Cardel shouted.

"Two, no more," Belwick countered.

Cardel, clearly displeased, sat rigid on his horse. "Agreed," he finally yelled. Wheeling around, he rode back to his men, issuing instructions.

Belwick watched as Cardel's forces retreated from the riverbank. When the enemy force was far enough away, and Cardel returned with two mounted knights, Belwick ordered the drawbridge to be lowered and the gate to be raised. He also ordered a green flag to be hoisted over the castle once Cardel was inside. This was the signal for the king's troops hidden in the woods to advance and surround the attackers.

Cardel and his entourage rode into the outer bailey, where Belwick waited with several soldiers.

"Please dismount, milord," Belwick said, "and I will show you and your men to the stables."

Cardel complied. An edgy silence pervaded the bailey as Belwick led the way to the stables. The marshal and his assistants quickly came forward to take charge of the horses.

"Your knights may remain here while you speak with Lady Merclif," Belwick said to Cardel.

Cardel's eyes narrowed. "Now see here. I am in charge now. You will be taking your orders from me."

"Not until Lady Merclif agrees," Belwick stated. "Until she turns the castle over to you, you are a guest at Merclif."

"How do I know this is not a trap?" Cardel demanded. "I must have my knights with me to protect me."

"The knights may accompany you inside the donjon," Belwick conceded. "However, you must meet with Lady Merclif alone. She has been distraught since Lord

Merclif's death and has remained secluded in her chamber."

Cardel pursed his mouth. "Aye. Edgar, Denis, come with me."

Belwick led Cardel and his knights through the southeast gate in the inner curtain and up the donjon steps, two of Merclif's soldiers following close behind. The hall was deserted as Belwick escorted the enemy up the stairs to Helena's bedchamber. He paused outside her chamber and knocked on the door.

"Lady Merclif, Lord Cardel wishes to speak with you."

They waited a few moments in silence until Helena opened the door. Her face was pale but composed as she faced her father.

Helena was surprised to find her father was so short. He had taken on such huge dimensions in her fears that she had not realized he was merely an old man.

"Milord," Helena said, "please come in."

She stood aside, holding the door wide. Cardel paused in the entrance, searching the chamber, before he stepped inside. Helena closed the door behind him, shutting out the other men. She stayed by the outer door as Cardel inspected the room. When he finally came to a halt in the middle of the chamber and turned to face her, Helena stepped forward a few paces but remained well out of reach of her father, as Alaric had instructed her. Fear closed its clammy hands around her heart. She took a deep breath, remembering Alaric's training.

"You will feel fear," Alaric had told her. "But you must not let Cardel see your fear. That will give him control over you. Breathe deeply. Keep your eyes steady and your face expressionless."

"Why are you here, milord?" Helena asked her father, trying to follow Alaric's instructions.

"Since Merclif is dead, I have come to protect you, Daughter."

"I do not need your protection."

"You no longer have a husband, so your guardianship reverts back to me. Since you bore no heir for Merclif, the castle rightly belongs to me as well."

"Would it not be up to the king to decide what happens to Merclif?" Helena asked.

"Henry is not here, while I am. You are in my power." Cardel advanced toward her. "If you do as I command, I will not harm you."

"Why do you hate me so much?" The words seemed to burst from her.

"You are a faithless slut, just like your mother." Cardel sneered. "She sent you away before it became apparent you were her bastard. But once you returned, I took one look at you and knew you were no spawn of mine. I slashed your face so no one would want to look at you."

Cardel's words stunned Helena. "Who was my father?"

"Some worthless, landless knight. I have long forgotten his name." Cardel shrugged. "I got rid of him. Strangled him with my own hands. 'Twas most satisfying."

Horror gripped Helena as she stared at his evil face. Out of the corner of her eye she caught a slight flutter of the tapestry covering the concealed door. The movement focused her mind back on her real mission here.

"You killed Alaric as well. You ordered the ambush that led to his death."

"Aye. After he escaped my first attack, I decided that the second time I would employ overwhelming force, to make sure he died."

"Did you use Langston to make the first attempt to kill Alaric?" Helena asked.

"Langston?" Cardel scoffed. "That milksop? Whatever gave you that stupid idea?"

"So Langston was not here at Merclif spying for you?" Helena asked.

"Nay. Enough of this drivel. You will order your castellan to turn the castle over to me. You will make it clear to him that I am now the rightful owner of Merclif."

"She cannot do that as I am still alive," Alaric stated as he entered the chamber from the concealed door. Alaric drew his sword, advancing toward his enemy.

Wyham followed close behind. "Your full treachery has now been exposed, Cardel," Wyham declared. "You are under arrest for the attempted murder of Lord Merclif. I will take you to King Henry for his judgment."

Cardel snarled and lunged toward Helena, grabbing her arm. He pulled her in front of him, holding a knife to her throat.

Alaric and Wyham halted.

"One more step and she dies," Cardel barked.

"You stinking coward," Alaric said. "Let her go and face me like a man."

Cardel dragged Helena back toward the door. "She is my guarantee of safe passage out of here."

Alaric advanced toward Cardel, but with her in danger between them, she knew there was little he could do. His eyes seemed to bore into hers as if he willed her to act. Helena calmed as Alaric's training filled her mind. He had shown her how to use an opponent's superior strength against him. He had taught her to be merciless when facing the enemy.

Raising the knife she had concealed against her skirts, she grasped it with both hands as she dug it into the hand Cardel held at her throat. With all her strength she pushed the knife down into him, forcing his hand away from her. Cardel yelled and flung her away from him, into her husband's path. Alaric jumped over her as she sprawled on the floor and trapped Cardel against the closed door, his sword at Cardel's throat.

"Drop the knife," Alaric ordered.

Cardel threw the knife down. Alaric kept his blade at Cardel's throat as he pulled the older man's sword from the scabbard at his side. Alaric stepped back slightly, a sword in each hand.

"Wyham, get the rope so I can tie him up."

"Nay," Cardel gasped. "Nay."

He brought his fist up to his chest, as he fought for breath. Helena stared as Cardel slumped to the floor. Alaric stood over his enemy, both swords poised over the man's body. When Cardel did not move, Alaric went down to one knee beside him.

"Wyham, take this sword while I check him."

Wyham left Helena's side and went over to Alaric, taking Cardel's sword from his hand. He remained on guard as Alaric put his hand to Cardel's throat.

After a moment, Alaric stood. "He is dead." He looked over at Helena. "You are bleeding. Are you all right?"

"What?" Feeling dazed and unsteady, Helena raised her hand to her throat to find a trickle of blood. "He must have cut me." She pulled her hand away and stared down at the smear of scarlet on her fingertips.

"Helena, will you be all right?"

"Aye," Helena whispered.

"Wyham, take care of her."

"Aye, I will. You go ahead."

Alaric pulled the chamber door open.

Ralph turned from his post guarding the door and gasped. "Milord! You are alive!"

"Aye," Alaric responded. He glanced toward a gaping Matthew and the two dead bodies lying on the gallery floor. "What happened here?"

"Sir Hugh gave us orders to make sure Cardel's men did not go into the chamber. When they heard sounds of a struggle, they attempted to enter. Matthew and I stopped them."

"Good. Cardel is dead. Remove his body from the bedchamber immediately. Then take all three bodies out of the donjon."

"Aye, milord," Ralph and Matthew responded in unison.

"Where is Sir Hugh?" Alaric asked.

"He is securing the castle, milord," Ralph replied.

Alaric went down the stairs into the empty hall. He strode through the deserted inner bailey toward the stables. The servants and villeins had been instructed to remain in the unused lists in the outer bailey, protected from danger, during the confrontation with Cardel. A few of his men-at-arms were standing in front of the stables with the marshal.

The stable master was the first to spot Alaric. He gave a shocked exclamation and crossed himself. "'Tis a ghost!" he cried.

"'Tis no ghost," Alaric said. "I am as alive as you."

"God be praised!" the marshal exclaimed.

"Geoffrey," he addressed the soldier who stood with his mouth wide open, "where is Sir Hugh? What is the situation?"

The young man snapped to attention. "Sir Hugh is on the crenellations, above the main gate. I know not how the battle in front of the castle is going, milord."

"My thanks."

Alaric headed toward the southeast turret on the outer curtain and rapidly climbed the stairs to the battlements. Ignoring the shocked exclamations that greeted his appearance on the allure, he headed directly toward Belwick, who stood over the main gate.

"How goes it?" Alaric asked as he halted next to his castellan and surveyed the battle scene on the far side of the river.

"Cardel's forces are defeated. The knights put up a fight but were quickly dispatched by the king's troops. The men-at-arms swiftly surrendered when the knights were killed. Victory is ours, milord."

"Good."

Dead bodies were strewn across the meadow. Two soldiers were trying to corral the horses while the majority of the king's men disarmed the enemy force. A group of Merclif troops crossed the drawbridge to assist in the capture.

"Since the castle is secured, you may let the servants and villeins return to their work," Alaric said.

"Aye, milord."

"And Hugh, please make an announcement that I am very much alive. I do not want anyone else to mistake me for a ghost."

"Aye, milord," Belwick said with a slight grin.

"Release Langston from prison. Ask him to come to my solar at his earliest convenience."

"Langston has been exonerated?"

"Aye."

34

laric strode through the empty hall and up the stairs. Now that he knew the castle was secure, he could focus his attention on Helena. When he opened the bedchamber door, he found Helena seated with his mother attending to her injury. Wyham stood nearby.

"How goes it, Merclif?" Wyham asked as soon as he saw Alaric.

"Cardel's forces have been soundly defeated." Alaric crossed the chamber and knelt in front of his wife's chair. "Helena, how are you?"

"I am fine."

Her face was pale, but composed. A bandage was wrapped around her neck. Alaric shot a questioning look at his mother.

"The bleeding has stopped," Margaret informed him. "Luckily, the cut is not too deep nor did it sever a major artery. I have cleaned the wound and applied a healing salve. She should recover well, but it will leave a scar."

So Cardel had given her one more scar. Alaric should never have let her face Cardel. The sight of her in his power had twisted Alaric's gut. Looking back into her eyes, he noticed for the first time the serenity that filled them.

"I faced him, Alaric," Helena said. "I did not cringe. I did not hide."

"Aye, you faced him like a warrior. And you defeated him. You did not let your fear conquer you. You controlled your fear and used your training to attack Cardel. Helena, I am very proud of you."

A smile spread slowly on Helena's lips. "Aye, I did."

Alaric lifted her hand from her lap and pressed a kiss on her palm. After gently returning her hand to her lap, he stood. Keeping his eyes on her face, he marveled at her air of dignity and tranquility. The things she had just learned from Cardel must have shaken her, but she gave no sign of any disquiet.

"It must have been a shock to learn that Cardel is not your father," he stated.

"Aye," Helena agreed. "But 'twas a relief as well. I never understood why he hated me so much. And I dreaded the idea of passing his evil blood onto our children."

"What do you want to do about this information?" Alaric asked.

"May I make a suggestion?" Wyham interrupted.

"Aye, by all means," Alaric said, turning to look at the older man.

"I believe it would be a mistake to make public the fact that Helena is not Cardel's daughter. It brands her mother an adulteress. It calls into question the legitimacy of your marriage. And it jeopardizes the transfer of Cardel's lands to Merclif."

Alaric considered the diplomat's arguments. He looked at Helena. "'Tis up to you, Helena. What do you want to do?"

"I have no need for anyone else to know the truth. The people of Merclif have already accepted me. 'Tis enough that I know I am not his daughter."

"As you will," Alaric said. "Only the four of us will know the truth."

"Milord," Helena stated, "there is another truth Cardel spoke that does need to be made public. Damien Langston is innocent of attempting to murder you."

"I have already given orders for Langston to be released from prison, and I will make a formal, public declaration of his innocence. Helena, I ask for your forgiveness. You were right about Langston's innocence from the start. I confess that I let my jealousy of your friendship with him get in the way of my sound judgment."

"Thank you, Alaric. Your confession means a lot to me. I do forgive you. Does this mean that you now trust me? Will I now be able to speak with Damien?"

"Aye, you shall. 'Tis another thing for which I ask your forgiveness. I should have trusted you to keep our marriage vows and not given in to my unreasonable jealousy. I should not have tried to control you and deny you your friendship with Langston."

Helena stood and came to him, putting her hands on his upper arms. He looked down into her face and felt the warmth of her radiant smile. Losing himself in her eyes, he experienced a tremendous weight being lifted from his soul.

"Alaric, I do forgive you."

"Your forgiveness is more than I deserve."

But then he had learned that forgiveness is not something one can earn. Not from another and not from God. Forgiveness was a precious gift that God gave freely. Forgiveness was a gift that He enabled His people to give each other.

He gathered her into his arms and held her against his chest. Closing his eyes, he savored the joy of her forgiveness and the peace that enveloped him. He kissed her head, rubbing his cheek on her silky hair. When he lifted his eyes to his mother's face, he saw her incandescent smile and the approval in her eyes. Feeling overwhelmingly blessed, he offered silent thanksgiving to his Lord.

At Alaric's command, Belwick opened the solar door and stood back to let Langston enter. Then he closed the door, leaving the two of them alone. Standing in front of the window with his feet braced wide apart, and his hands clasped behind his back, Alaric surveyed his erstwhile prisoner.

"Please come in, Langston," Alaric said. "I trust that Sir Hugh has informed you of what has occurred here today."

"Aye, he has."

"I owe you an apology."

"Aye, you do."

"Langston, I am sorry I imprisoned you for a crime you did not commit. And, although I know I do not deserve it, I ask for your forgiveness."

"How did you learn the truth?"

"Helena confronted Cardel to get him to admit his guilt in the attempts on my life. She specifically asked him if he had employed you to kill me. He told her he had not. Helena, at great risk to her own life, solicited the truth from Cardel. 'Tis due to her courage and bravery that you are a free man."

Langston smiled. "'Tis just like Helena to think of others before herself."

"Aye. You are very lucky to have her as your devoted friend."

The younger man nodded. "I know."

"Langston, I will make reparations to you for your imprisonment," Alaric stated. "I will provide you with the armor, sword, and horse deserving of a fine knight. I will arrange a knighting ceremony for you here at Merclif. If you do not wish to have me knight you, I am sure Lord Wyham would agree to do so. If you no longer wish to serve me, I am sure Lord Wyham would be able to find a place for you in the king's service."

"Do you wish me to leave here?"

"I leave the decision entirely up to you."

"And if I stay at Merclif, am I allowed to be in Helena's company? Am I allowed to speak with her?"

"Aye."

"I agree, then. I will be knighted by your hand, and I will remain in service to Merclif."

Alaric nodded once. "Let us go downstairs so I may make an announcement regarding your innocence."

Alaric gestured for Langston to proceed out the door and down the stairs. As the crowd spotted Alaric and let out a rousing cheer, he stopped halfway down the stairs and smiled at his people's joy in his resurrection. The hall was packed with men-at-arms, servants, and villeins. It seemed as if the whole community was present. His wife, his mother, and Wyham stood in front of the fireplace at the side of the hall. Alaric held up his hand, trying to bring order and silence to the throng so he could speak. Gradually, as soldiers nudged their comrades, mothers shushed their children, and superiors rapped subordinates, the hall quieted.

"'Tis good to be alive," Alaric proclaimed in a voice that rang through the hall.

A hearty cheer greeted his statement. Several people yelled out their pleasure.

Again, Alaric held up his hands asking for silence. "I am sorry my fake death caused so much grief and anxiety for you. As Sir Hugh has no doubt explained, 'twas done to lure Cardel into coming to Merclif so he could be defeated once and for all."

Another cheer roared through the crowd. When quiet was restored once more, Alaric continued speaking.

"This clever plan was devised by Lady Merclif. We owe the safety of the castle, and everyone in it, to her intelligence, bravery, and courage. Thank you, milady." Alaric formally bowed deeply toward Helena.

The crowd turned to look at her and applauded her long and loud. Helena, clearly embarrassed, nodded and raised her hand in acknowledgment. Gradually the people settled down and returned their attention to him.

"During her confrontation with Cardel, Lady Merclif got him to admit that he had attempted to murder me twice. Cardel also revealed that Damien Langston had no part in the first attempt on my life. I have unjustly accused and falsely imprisoned an innocent man, for which I am truly sorry. In order to make amends, I will soon knight Langston with all due ceremony. Langston has agreed to remain in service at Merclif."

Several men pushed their way through the crowd to reach Langston, who had remained at the base of the stairs. They greeted him enthusiastically, slapping him on the back to congratulate him. Alaric waited for the general tumult to die down again before concluding his speech.

"Our victory this day is cause for celebration. Renwold, break out the wine and the ale!" Roars of approval greeted his words.

Alaric was mobbed as he threaded his way through the crowd. It seemed as if everyone wanted to touch him to assure themselves that he was indeed alive. He deeply regretted having put his people through the uncertainty of his fabricated death and was now glad to be able to compensate them with his time and attention. By the time he reached Helena's side, he was overwhelmed with the love showered upon him by his people.

"Thank you, Alaric," Helena said as soon as he reached her.

Smiling at his wife, he accepted a cup of wine from a servant and surveyed the celebration going on around them. He braced himself as he spotted Langston approaching. Entirely ignoring Alaric's presence, the young man's attention was focused solely on his wife.

"Helena," Langston said.

"Damien," Helena exclaimed, holding out both her hands to him.

"Thank you, dear friend," Langston said. One at a time he raised her hands to his lips and kissed them.

"I am so glad you are free, Damien," Helena said.

"I know it is entirely due to you, milady," Langston replied. "And for that I sincerely thank you."

Helena held his hands a moment longer before dropping hers away from his. "So you finally get your wish to become a knight."

"Aye," Langston, said, pleasure evident in the smile he gave her.

Alaric turned away. This business of trust still came hard for him, but he was determined to show that he did indeed trust his wife. Leaving her with her friend, he strode away from the fireplace and found Belwick.

"Are all the prisoners secured?" Alaric asked his castellan.

"Aye," Belwick answered. "What are we going to do with them?"

"I want them interrogated tomorrow. If they show no loyalty to Cardel, and are willing to return home without their arms, they may be released."

"As you wish, Alaric." Belwick took a drink of his wine. "We discovered the body of Cardel's son Percy among the dead."

"So the Cardel line is finished."

"Except for Lady Merclif, of course," Belwick said, as if pointing out the obvious.

"Aye." Alaric's eyes sought her out across the crowded room to find her engaged in an animated conversation with Langston.

"'Tis a bitter thing to be proved wrong," Belwick remarked.

"Aye." This business of humility was hard as well. Alaric said a silent prayer. *Lord, give me strength. Help me to be as humble as Jesus was.*

"Alaric, 'tis a strong man who admits his mistakes, especially in so public a fashion."

"Thank you, Hugh. Let us just hope that I also may learn from my mistakes."

"Aye. So when are you going to admit you love your wife?"

"What?"

"'Tis as plain as the nose on your face. Do you think that loving your wife makes you a weakling?"

"Nay."

"Your father was no weakling. In fact, he was the strongest man I have ever known. He was strong in both body and mind. And he loved your mother. He loved her with an intensity evident to everyone who knew them. Do you think I am weak, boy?"

"Nay."

"I love my wife. It happens to the best of us, Alaric. And a good thing, too. 'Tis love that makes life worthwhile."

Alaric stared at Hugh's back as he strolled away. Mayhap he had once thought that love made a man weak, just as he had once thought that submitting oneself to God would annihilate him, and that humility meant mortification.

But now he knew the truth, and the truth had set him free. Free to love his wife. Free to serve his people in humility. But most important of all, free to submit his will to the Lord.

Helena pushed her way through the crowd, marveling anew at the love everyone had for Alaric. From the lowliest villein to the hardened men-at-arms, all were loyal and dedicated to their overlord. She finally located Alaric talking with several of his men. When she approached him, she laid a hand on his forearm and smiled up at him. He returned her smile while the men greeted her. Gradually the other men drifted away, leaving her alone with Alaric.

"It has been a very eventful day," Helena said.

"Aye, that it has," Alaric agreed.

"'Tis good to be among everyone, after being in seclusion for so long. You must be very gratified at the joy everyone feels that you are still alive."

"Aye." His crooked smile was self-abasing. "'Tis a passing strange thing, to be raised from the dead."

"I know it was hard for you to admit you were wrong about Damien, especially in front of the whole assembly. Thank you for being so gallant and making your confession in public."

"'Tis the least I could do, since I made my accusation so public."

Love for him flooded her. He was all that was honorable, noble, and valiant. He epitomized the heroic knight of her song. The lyrics played in her head.

"My King and my country I serve gladly,
Protecting the weak, pure justice I seek.
Courage, valor, and truth alone rule me,
Loyalty my guide, in honor my pride."

Silently, she praised God. *Thank You, Lord, for giving me Alaric for my husband.*

Alaric leaned close and murmured in her ear. "'Tis time to retire. I would celebrate our victory in a more intimate manner."

The heat of passion seared though Helena at his words. Her gaze met his, and his intense blue eyes ensnared her. Unconsciously, she licked her upper lip and saw his eyes blaze in response.

"Aye," she whispered. "That is an excellent idea."

"Are you well enough?" He lightly touched the bandage around her throat.

"Aye, I am fine."

The powerful need she had for him dwarfed the residual pain from her wound. She took his hand and walked with him upstairs to their chamber, to their bed, to their bliss.

35

"I need to visit Mersthrope and Carleigh so all the villagers will know I am really alive," Alaric said over breakfast the next morning. "I plan to ride to Mersthrope this afternoon and Carleigh tomorrow." He took a bite of cheese and ate it before continuing. "Would you care to accompany me?"

Helena paused in eating her bread to answer him. "Aye. I would like that. 'Twill be good to be outdoors again. I know you were bored to tears, being confined to our chambers for so long."

"Aye, that I was. Thank you for keeping me company when I was in my grave."

She laughed. "'Twas my pleasure."

"Are you up to the four-hour ride to Carleigh?"

"Aye, I think so. My muscles have toughened up considerably, with the short rides we have been doing."

"You can always ride double with me, if you get too tired riding alone."

"Aye, thank you, Alaric." Helena smiled at him.

"I am interested to see what progress they have made on the chapel in Carleigh."

"Oh, I forgot to tell you. Father Michael sent word shortly after you were injured that the chapel was finished, and he was waiting for you to recover so you could attend the consecration. With everything that has happened lately, I forgot to tell you about that. I am sorry."

"Do not worry about it." Alaric took a drink of his ale to wash down the bread he had finished eating. "I will send a message to Father Michael to schedule the consecration for tomorrow, when we will be there."

"Aye, that is a good idea." Helena wiped her mouth.

"I need to talk to Clare as well. I did not see her last night at the celebration, nor this morning. How is she doing?"

"I know she must have been devastated by Bernard's death, but she has been unfailingly supportive and sympathetic to me during your long recovery. She was one of the few people who knew the truth about your 'death.' I felt it would be too cruel to let her believe that you had died as well. I did not want her to think that Bernard's sacrifice had been in vain."

"Thank you for that. Would you ask Clare to come see me in my solar?"

"Aye, I will do so."

Alaric stood and pulled back her chair. "I will see you at dinner, Helena. I hope you have a pleasant morning." He leaned over and gave her a kiss on each cheek.

She watched Alaric stride through the hall. When Wyham intercepted him and the two men went upstairs together, she headed to the kitchen to consult with the cook. She would give the men some time to talk before locating Clare.

Alaric led the way into his solar and shut the door after Wyham. "Thank you, Robert, for all your help with Cardel."

"I am glad to be of service," Wyham replied. "Unfortunately, your mother and I need to leave Merclif tomorrow, now that everything with Cardel has been resolved. I have been away from court too long already. And the king's troops need to return to their regular duties."

"Please give my thanks to King Henry for sending his men. They were a great help in defeating Cardel's forces."

"I will do that. I will also report to him what has transpired here. There is still the matter of what to do with Cardel's northern estate. I will try to persuade the king to grant it to you and Helena."

"I do not want it. I have no need of more land, and 'tis too far away to manage properly."

"One can never have too much land. If you do not wish to keep it, you can always sell it."

Alaric shrugged.

"Alaric, I hope you will not mind if I consider you and Helena as my children. I have come to love both of you."

"Nay, I do not mind, and I am sure Helena would benefit from a loving father figure."

"Well, I am considered a fair judge of character and relationships between people, so I wish to offer you some advice. Whether or not you wish to take it is entirely up to you."

"That sounds ominous."

"I did not mean it to. I only wish to urge you to tell Helena that you love her, as soon as possible."

Alaric turned away from Wyham's perceptive gaze. "'Tis hard to open up my heart to her when I do not know how she feels."

"You do not think she loves you? I have seen the two of you together. 'Tis you she confides in, 'tis you she turns to for support and comfort, 'tis you she loves."

"You truly think she loves me?"

"Aye, I do."

Alaric considered Wyham's words. Did Helena love him? Every indication was that she did. She generously responded in their marriage bed. She had devotedly nursed him though his injuries. She had faced Cardel's evil to protect and defend him and Merclif. But if she loved him, why had she not told him so?

He slowly nodded. "You have given me much to think about."

"Good," Wyham said.

After Wyham left, Alaric spent some time in prayer to fortify himself before his interview with Clare. With the help of God, he had discarded the load of guilt he bore for Bernard's death, as well as that of Gordon and Roger and the others, but the temptation to resume that mantle of blame was ever present. The more time he spent in prayer, the easier it was to claim the forgiveness his Savior offered.

The knock on the door called him back to his responsibilities. Rising from his chair, he went to open the door.

Clare's usually jolly face was composed and sedate as she dropped into a curtsy. "Milord, Lady Helena said you wished to see me."

"Aye, Clare, please come in." He closed the door after she entered. "Please have a seat." He gestured toward the settle.

She took a seat, clasped her hands in her lap, and looked at him.

After bringing a chair over and setting it in front of the bench, he sat down and returned her look. "Clare, I am so sorry for your loss. Bernard was a good, honorable man and a valiant warrior. I deeply mourn his loss. I am completely to blame for his death. I foolheartedly led him and the others into danger. 'Tis something I will regret for as long as I live. I am so sorry."

"You are not to blame for Bernard's death, milord. He knew the dangers he faced as a knight, as a warrior, and he willingly accepted them. His greatest joy was serving you and protecting Merclif."

"He gave his life for mine. Does not Jesus Christ say that there is no greater love than this, to lay down your life for your friends? I will try to always be mindful of Bernard's sacrifice for me."

Clare gave a small, sad smile and nodded. "I know Bernard is now with Jesus in heaven. That knowledge makes my pain bearable. He is with our Savior now—there can be no greater joy than that—and I will see him, when my time on earth is over."

"Aye." Alaric cleared his throat. "What would you like to do now, Clare? You have a home here at Merclif for as long as you want. I will support your family and ensure that your futures are secure. If you need anything, anything at all, you have but to ask."

"Thank you, milord. I would like to remain at Merclif. 'Tis been my home for a long time. I think I can still be of service to you and Lady Helena." She hesitated. "There is one thing I would ask, milord."

"Just name it, Clare."

"If you could but be an uncle, or an older brother, to Nicholas…'tis what he so desperately needs right now."

"I would be honored to do so. I know Bernard thought it was time for him to begin his training. 'Twould help focus his grief and his energies. Is that all right with you?"

"Aye. I think that is what he needs right now."

"I will see to it. Is there anything else you require?"

"Nay, milord. Thank you."

Margaret cornered him after supper, requesting a private word, so they repaired upstairs to the lords' solar. After pouring wine into goblets, he handed one to his mother, then sat beside her on the settle. Taking a sip from his own cup, he turned to observe her. "I have not had a chance to ask you how you are enjoying the king's court."

"'Tis very interesting and exciting," Margaret replied. "I have made friends with several of the wives of Robert's associates. I am very happy, Alaric, even though I miss you terribly."

"I am glad you are happy," Alaric said with a smile. "I miss you as well. I can always count on you to give me a severe kick when I need it."

"I am sure that Helena will be willing to provide you the same service if you but listen to her. 'Tis good to share your faith with your spouse. You will grow closer together as you grow closer to the Lord."

"I have not yet spoken to Helena about the change God has wrought in me."

"Why not? I have seen her own devotion to the Lord, especially when she was nursing you back to health."

"'Tis hard to share my feelings." He looked into the dark purple depths of his cup.

"Who better to share your feelings with than your wife? Alaric, do not let your pride get in the way of a full, loving relationship with Helena. 'Tis as important for you to surrender yourself to her as you have surrendered yourself to the Lord. Love is a choice you make to put your spouse's feelings and needs before your own. Love is more than just a feeling...'tis action. Respect, consideration, and humility."

"Have you been talking to Robert about this?" Alaric asked.

"Robert? Nay. Why do you ask?"

"This morning Robert asked me when I was going to admit that I love Helena. Last night Hugh asked me the same thing."

"Good. Well?"

Alaric gave her a blank look.

"When are you going to admit you love your wife?" Margaret clarified.

"How can I know if what I feel for Helena is love?" Alaric sat with his forearms braced on his thighs, holding his wine goblet between his spread knees, his head bent.

"What do you feel for her?" Margaret probed.

"I admire her intelligence, her courage, her talent. I want her to be happy. I desire her." He sat upright. "I am a warrior. I am not used to delving into my feelings."

"Aye, I know." Margaret gave him a sympathetic smile as she patted his knee. "'Twas the same with your father. It took me five years to get that stubborn man to admit he loved me. I hope you will not make Helena wait that long. Just think of all the happiness and contentment you will miss. Alaric, love does not make you weak. On the contrary, it makes you strong and powerful. Love completes you and enhances you. 'Tis nothing to fear."

"'Tis if love is not returned." Alaric took a large gulp of wine.

"Helena loves you, Alaric. 'Tis plain to see whenever she looks at you."

"Then why has she not said so?"

"As you just said yourself, 'tis hard to admit one's love when one is not sure it is returned. You must give Helena some indication that you share her feelings before she will tell you she loves you. One of you must take a risk if you are to enjoy the full blessings of marriage."

Alaric nodded but said nothing.

"Well." Margaret stood. Alaric stood as well. "Enough soul searching for one day."

"Amen to that." Alaric raised his cup to toast his mother's words before draining it and setting it on the table.

Margaret took him in her arms. "Alaric, I love you. I know you will do what is right."

"Aye, I hope so. I love you too, Mother."

"I will pray for you. You must commit your marriage to the Lord."

"I will, Mother. I will."

Langston intercepted Helena when she walked through the hall after dinner. "Helena, can we talk?" he inquired.

"Aye, Damien. I am sorry I have not been able to spend time with you since you were released. There always seems to be so much to do."

"I know you are very busy."

"Never too busy for a friend. Shall we take a walk on the allure? 'Tis one of my favorite places. You can see the entire valley. 'Tis quite spectacular."

"I would like that," Langston said, holding out his arm to her.

Helena chattered lightly, telling him about her visits to the villages of Mersthorpe and Carleigh as they strolled through the inner bailey toward the turret in the outer wall. Once they were on top of the crenellations, Helena felt as she always did, as if she were on top of the world. Looking out over the beautiful valley spread below them, she marveled again at the intense colors—the brilliant cerulean of the sky, the glistening white of the billowing clouds, the myriad shades of green—that God had used to paint their world. As they ambled along the west curtain wall, Helena smiled at the guard and waited for him to pass by them before turning to Langston.

"Damien, how are you really? You do not look any the worse for your long incarceration."

"I am fine. Sir Hugh made my imprisonment bearable."

"I am glad. I spoke many times with him to make sure you were doing well, since Alaric had forbidden me to speak with you. Well, that is all in the past now and should be forgotten. On a happier note, I was thinking we should hold your knighting ceremony next Sunday. Is that all right with you?"

"Aye." Langston smiled at her. "The sooner the better, as far as I am concerned."

"We will need to make new clothes for you. Lady Elizabeth and Lady Clare are very skilled with the needle. I am sure they will be able to complete your vesture in time. I will speak with them this afternoon."

"I do not want to put you to any trouble, Helena."

"There is no trouble, Damien. You deserve to have a proper knighting ceremony. I will speak with Alaric to make sure these arrangements meet with his approval."

"Aye, you had better get his permission. I would not be surprised if he changed his mind about knighting me."

"Alaric would not do that. He always honors his word."

"I am sorry, Helena. I did not mean to offend you."

"I know. I am the one who is sorry. You have not been well treated by Alaric. I intend to make up for it."

"'Tis not necessary." She just looked at him until he shrugged and gave in. "As you wish, milady." He gave her an elaborate bow.

They resumed their stroll on the allure. Reaching the north side, they had a good view over the lists where Alaric was training with his men. Helena stopped to watch him, admiring his muscular body as he fought.

"Have you told your husband that you love him?"

Helena looked up at her friend with a rueful smile. "Nay."

"Mayhap you should do so. Then he might no longer want to take off my head every time he sees me. Come to think of it, you *had* better tell him before the knighting ceremony, when his sword will be in very close proximity to my neck."

Helena laughed at his teasing. "Aye, I will do that."

"Are you happy?"

"Aye, Damien. I am very happy." Helena smiled at him. "I hope someday you will find someone to love as deeply as I love Alaric."

"Aye, I hope so too."

Langston offered his arm to her. She placed her hand on his, and they continued their stroll.

36

Alaric pulled Guaire to a halt near the thicket of hawthorn trees and turned to look at Helena. Not wanting an audience for his discussion with his wife, he had already given orders to the guards who accompanied them to station themselves discreetly nearby. After dismounting, he went to her side and helped her down from her horse.

"This looks like a good place to take a walk." Alaric placed her arm through his.

"'Tis a beautiful day today."

"Hmm," he murmured. Just how did he go about telling his wife that he loved her? The fear that she did not return his feelings was still present. He would much rather be facing an enemy in a fight than this conversation. He was a warrior, not a poet, for Saint Peter's sake. It was still hard to humble himself, but he had to take the risk. Their whole future depended on this conversation, so he had to handle it properly. That was why he had chosen to have this discussion with his wife outdoors, rather than in the intimacy of their bedchamber. He did not want Helena to feel obligated to return his words of love if she did not feel that way toward him.

Gracious Lord, he prayed, *give me the words. Help me to open my heart to Helena. Thank You for giving her to me as my wife. Help me to be a loving, supportive husband to her. Help me to be humble and considerate of her. Amen.*

"Alaric, is something bothering you?"

"Nay. I just have had a lot on my mind lately, 'tis all."

"Do you want to talk about it?"

He halted next to the river and stared into the distance, gazing at the beech trees lining the meadow, but not really seeing them. Perhaps it would be easier to talk to her if he was not looking directly at her. Conscious of her pressed against his side, he took a deep breath. "I had several long conversations with Mother while I was recuperating."

"Aye?"

Taking heart from her encouraging tone, he laid his hand over hers as it rested on his arm. "She pointed out to me that I have been willful and headstrong. That I was insisting on being in control, rather than submitting my will to God. I did not want to listen to her at first, but eventually I realized she was right. I tried to control everyone around me—not only the men at my command, but also you, my wife, as well. Helena, I am sorry. I am trying to surrender my will to the Lord, but I have not yet completely mastered this. I suspect I never will, in this life."

She squeezed his arm. "Aye, I do not think such a trait can ever be mastered this side of eternity."

"'Tis been a struggle, but one that becomes easier every day. I find the more I rely upon God and ask Him to change me, the more He conforms my will to His own."

"My own struggle has been to accept that God really does love me. When the man I believed was my father did not love me, in fact abused me and showed me nothing but hatred, I decided I must be unlovable. That I was not worthy of having anyone love me. It was your mother who taught me that the Lord does love me. He loved me so much that He died for me."

Alaric turned toward her and cupped her face in his hands. "Helena, you are worthy of love. I love you with all my heart."

As she gazed up at him, he saw the tears pool in her eyes.

"You love me?" she whispered.

"Aye. I bless the day that the Lord gave you to me. Helena, my dearest love, my beautiful wife, I promise to love you and cherish you, for the rest of our lives."

The tears spilled over on to Helena's cheeks. "Oh, Alaric, I love you."

"Then why all the tears?" He smiled at her, tenderness overflowing his heart, as he gently wiped her tears away with his thumbs.

"I never thought you could love me. I am so ugly and deformed."

"Nay, you are not ugly. You could never be ugly to me. I forbid you to even think that again. Understand?"

She smiled at him through her tears. "Aye, milord."

"Oh, Helena, I love you so much."

Alaric captured her lips, wrapping his arms around her and gathering her tightly to him, sealing their love with their kiss. His joy and happiness was so overwhelming he wondered if his heart would burst. He reveled in his wife's arms, rejoicing in her love.

On the last Sunday of May, Helena woke gradually to sunlight streaming into their chamber. Alaric was sitting in a chair, putting on his hose and shoes. She marveled again how changed her relationship with him was, now that they had openly declared their love for one another. Every day was a delight; every day was spent in harmony and sharing.

Helena threw off the covers and started to sit up, only to be brought short by the wave of nausea and dizziness that caught her unaware. She gingerly lay back down, waiting for the sick feeling to pass.

"Still abed?" Alaric teased, coming over to sit down beside her.

"Alaric, I feel a little dizzy. I think 'tis from hunger."

"Probably. I did give you a thorough loving last night. It undoubtedly used up all your strength. Shall I go get you something to eat?"

"Aye, please. Just some bread. 'Tis all I want."

"All right." He leaned down and lightly kissed her. "I will be right back."

Helena waited in bed until Alaric returned with a tray of food and two cups of ale. He set the tray on the floor next to the bed and handed her a large piece of bread. She gratefully took a bite and ate it. Alaric chewed on the rest of the bread as he watched her.

"Feeling any better?" he asked.

"Aye, a little."

"I found I was hungry as well," Alaric remarked as he bit off another piece of bread. "Breakfast will be no doubt be late today, what with the knighting ceremony after mass. 'Tis good to have some food now."

Helena declined his offer of ale and determinedly ate the rest of the bread. Feeling her stomach settle, she cautiously sat up and stood.

"Are you all right now?" Alaric asked.

"Aye, I am fine now. I just needed to eat something."

She washed quickly and slipped on a clean chemise, then sat down to pull on her hose and shoes. "Are you waiting for me?" she asked. Usually he left their chamber to attend to castle business before mass.

"Aye." Alaric lounged back on the bed. "I spoke with Hugh when I got the food. There is nothing requiring my attention this morning, so I will escort you to mass."

She smiled at him and donned her best kirtle, the gold gown with red embroidery. When she finished tying the laces, he came up to her and smoothed his hands down the arms of the gown.

"You look beautiful," he said huskily.

"Why, thank you, milord." She twined her arms around his neck.

Alaric bent to kiss her, leisurely exploring her mouth before drawing back. "That will have to keep us until later."

"Aye." She sighed. She reluctantly stepped out of his arms to brush and braid her hair. After securing the diaphanous ivory veil on her head with a gold circlet, she turned to Alaric. "I am ready."

He held out his hand to her and dropped a light kiss on the hand she extended to him before escorting her out of the chamber.

When they reached the chapel, they saw Langston standing in the center aisle, at the base of the steps leading to the altar, upon which his new armor and sword rested. He bowed deeply to Alaric and Helena as they paused in front of him, before taking their places in the front row on the right side of the chapel. Helena smiled at Damien with pride and happiness. She glanced at Alaric's face after she took her seat. He greeted her with a small smile, one eyebrow raised. Her joyous heart full of her love for him, she gave him a smile before turning her attention to the mass.

She had not seen Langston since yesterday at supper. Last night, he had completed a silent, all-night vigil in the chapel. This morning he was to have had a ritual purification bath, attended by Hugh and Ralph, before dressing in the white vesture that Elizabeth and Clare had made for him. Helena thought Damien looked very handsome in the elaborate garments the women had designed, but not anywhere near as handsome as Alaric, dressed in his own brilliant blue tunic.

After the entire congregation had filed in and sat down, Langston turned to the altar and genuflected. He then took his seat in the front row on the left side of the chapel, joining Hugh and Ralph, who were already seated. Helena listened intently to Father Thomas's sermon exhorting the young man to the duties and obligations of a knight: to be loyal to God, his king and his overlord, to protect the weak and helpless, and to honor women. After his sermon, the priest blessed Langston's armor and sword.

"May the Lord bless the one who carries this sword, so he will use it only with honor and righteousness." Father Thomas made the sign of the cross over the sword lying on the altar. "May the Lord bless the one who wears this armor and shield, protecting him from all harm." The priest likewise made the sign of the cross over the armor and shield as he spoke the blessing.

After mass, Alaric held Helena's hand and led her from the chapel. Langston exited after them while Hugh and Ralph carried his armor, shield, and sword out of the chapel. The rest of the congregation filed out of the church and arranged themselves around the inner ward. Helena had ordered the ward cleared and cleaned for the ceremony. Colorful banners hung from poles placed around the bailey, adding to the festive mood. After everyone was assembled, Alaric climbed the steps of the chapel and addressed Langston, who stood before him.

"Damien Langston," Alaric stated, his voice carrying to the furthest reaches of the inner ward, "you have completed the rigorous training required of a Knight. You have proved yourself to be honorable, loyal, honest, and courageous. Don your armor. Take up your sword."

Hugh and Ralph, attended by two squires, carried the armor forward. While the squires held the armor, Hugh and Ralph ceremoniously dressed Langston. A solemn, expectant quiet filled the bailey as the spectators watched the robing ritual. Hugh and Ralph pulled the chain mail hauberk over his head and settled it over his shoulders. They placed the mail coif on Langston's head. One by one, they held out the gauntlets into which he placed his hands. Ralph knelt to fasten the spurs on his boots, after which Hugh buckled the scabbard around his waist and handed him the sword. The older men stepped back, and the knight candidate turned to face his overlord.

Alaric came down the steps to stand in front of Langston. "Please kneel."

Langston knelt on one knee before the Earl and bowed his head. Alaric pulled his sword from the scabbard at his side and placed the blade of his sword flat on top of Langston's right shoulder.

"In the name of God," Alaric declared, "and St. Michael and St. George, I dub thee knight; be brave and loyal." Alaric placed his sword flat against Langston's left shoulder as he completed the accolade. He sheathed his sword and extended his hands to Langston, who placed his hands into Alaric's.

"My lord," Langston declared, "I pledge to you my fealty, my loyalty, and my obedience. I will serve, protect, and defend you and your family to the best of my ability. So help me God."

Hugh handed the shield to Alaric. Alaric released Langston's hands and took the shield, offering it to the new knight.

"As a token of my duty to you," Alaric stated, "and the protection I owe to you, I give to you this shield. May God guard you and protect you in my service." Langston took the shield, bowing to Alaric. "Arise, Sir Damien," Alaric instructed.

When Langston got to his feet, a resounding cheer swept through the audience. Langston walked toward Helena, who had been standing at the base of the chapel steps, closely observing the rite. He went down on one knee before her as she offered him her right hand. After placing a kiss of fealty on the back of her hand, he then stood and bowed deeply to her. She graced him with a smile, her joy and pride in him filling her heart. His solemn face dissolved into a broad smile in return. Langston stepped away, accepting the congratulations of Hugh, Ralph, and the other men who crowded around him.

Helena walked toward Alaric. He turned to her, offering her his hand. Smiling at him, she placed her hand in his.

The boisterous celebration carried over to the elaborate feast at dinner. Wine and ale flowed freely as the revelers consumed roast beef, ham, venison, meat pies, cakes, wafers, and cheese. After eating their fill, everyone adjourned to the lists to watch Sir Damien exhibit his skill and demonstrate his prowess.

"I do not know how Damien and the other men will be able to fight, after that huge meal," Helena remarked to Alaric as they stood beside the lists.

"'Twill not be very serious fighting," Alaric commented. "The wine and ale would merely have served to make everyone more relaxed."

Langston walked into the middle of the lists with Ralph, speaking to him. When Ralph nodded, Langston left him and walked toward Helena. He dropped down on to one knee in front of her and looked up at her, his love for her clearly showing in his happy face. A hush fell over the crowd at this unusual, slightly scandalous, behavior.

"Milady," Langston spoke, "I would fight as your champion. Would you grace me with a small token I may carry into battle?"

Mortified, Helena cast a helpless look at Alaric. He nodded to her in reassurance, his eyes clear as he returned her look. Realizing it would cause more of a scene to refuse Langston's extraordinary request than to comply, Helena swiftly took off her veil and handed it to the young knight.

"My friend," Helena said, "I know you will fight with honor."

"Aye, milady. Thank you."

Langston accepted the veil and stood, smiling broadly. He bowed deeply to her and returned to the lists. As he walked, he tied the veil around his upper left arm. When the buzz of the crowd rose, Helena knew the audience must be speculating on Sir Damien's outrageous behavior.

"Alaric," Helena whispered frantically to Alaric, clutching his arm, "I had no idea he was going to do that."

"Hush, Helena, do not worry. Everything is fine."

He cupped her scarred left cheek and bent to give her a thorough kiss. It was the first demonstration of passion he had ever displayed toward her in public. She leaned into him, completely absorbed in the kiss, forgetting they had an audience. When Alaric pulled away from her, he hugged her to his side before turning to watch the contest already underway. Helena looked around at the faces of the villeins surrounding them, seeing approval and acceptance in their eyes.

She leaned against Alaric as she watched the competition between Damien and Ralph. Even to her untrained eye it was clear that Damien was doing a better job than Ralph. At first she suspected that Ralph was letting Damien win the contest, as it was his day, or that maybe Ralph had had too much to drink over dinner, but finally she realized that Ralph was earnestly fighting his best but was outmatched by Damien's superior skill.

When the battle finished, with Langston the clear winner, a resounding cheer greeted the new knight's achievement. Damien left the field, coming toward Helena. She stayed close to Alaric's side, his arm around her waist, as Langston dropped to one knee in front of her, untied her veil, and extended it toward her.

"My humble thanks, milady," Damien said, looking up at her.

Alaric reached over and took the veil from Langston's outstretched hand. "Sir Damien, you have fought well. You have honored Lady Merclif with your devotion."

"Thank you, milord." Damien stood and bowed before walking away.

"Here, milady." Alaric took the gold circlet from her head, draped the veil over her hair, and replaced the circlet.

"Thank you, milord," Helena murmured.

With her heart full of Alaric's romantic gesture, she tried to concentrate on the next competition between Gregory and Matthew but found her gaze wandering to Alaric's face instead as he intently watched the battle.

"Do you wish you were fighting today?" she asked him as they waited for the next pair of combatants.

"Nay," Alaric said, looking down into her eyes. "I am more than content to be here by your side."

37

Helena dozed in bed, hearing the sounds of Alaric's ablutions, but not really conscious of them. She had been so tired yesterday after the tournament that she had fallen asleep as soon as she went to bed. When Alaric quietly let himself out the chamber door, she hazily appreciated his thoughtfulness in letting her sleep. Eventually she decided she really had to get out of bed, so she pushed back the covers and tried to sit up. A wave of dizziness swamped her as nausea churned in her empty stomach. She quickly lay back down, willing the sickness to pass.

This cannot just be hunger. She had eaten like a horse yesterday, both at dinner and at supper. Tentatively she touched her flat abdomen. *Could it possibly be?*

After waiting until the nausea and dizziness diminished, she gingerly got out of bed. She called a servant to bring her a piece of bread and ate it before trying to wash and dress. As she went about her usual activities that morning, she was in a daze. She felt Alaric's questioning look more than once but merely smiled dreamily at him.

That afternoon, she sat with Elizabeth and Clare in the ladies' solar, playing her lute while they sewed.

"Helena," Elizabeth said, "are you all right? You seem to be very distracted."

Helena looked up to find both women's eyes on her.

"I, um…" She bit her lip. "I am fine."

The more she reflected on her symptoms and the timing of her last cycle, the more convinced she became that she was indeed pregnant. She wanted to tell her friends her joyous news, but she felt Alaric should be the first one to learn she was with child.

Elizabeth and Clare smiled at her, resuming their sewing and their conversation. Helena went back to picking out the new tune she was trying to compose. A little while later the door opened, and Alaric walked into the chamber.

"Good afternoon, ladies," he said in his deep voice. After exchanging greetings with Elizabeth and Clare, he looked at Helena. "Milady, I would like to speak with you."

"Of course, milord." She put the lute down by her chair and stood.

Alaric led her to his solar. "I received a message from Wyham." He handed her the letter. "He has informed King Henry of Cardel's attack and his death. Wyham has persuaded the king to give Cardel's northern estate, Narhex, to you."

"To me? Not to you?"

"I told Wyham I did not want Narhex. 'Tis too far away and will be difficult to administer. I suppose you could sell it."

"So Narhex is mine?"

"Aye," Alaric said. "Read Wyham's letter for yourself."

When she had finished reading the letter, she stared sightlessly at the tapestry that lined the wall, thinking about this development.

"Have you ever been to Narhex?" Alaric asked.

"Nay." Helena shook her head.

"Do you know anything about it?"

"Nay. Alaric, I would like to give the estate to Damien."

"Why?"

"We do not need the money it would bring if we sold it. You have more than enough land to manage here," Helena reasoned. "I think Damien is in love with me."

"Aye. 'Tis very clear to everyone that he is."

"'Twould be good for him to be gone from here. He needs to find a woman who will return his love. I owe him so much, Alaric. If not for Damien's protection, I truly believe Cardel would have killed me."

"Aye. That is a good idea. It might be better for Langston if he were not constantly in your presence. His unrequited love for you could so easily turn bitter. We could grant Narhex to Langston as compensation for his extraordinary service to you. That way he can hand the fief down to his son. There is nothing like the incentive of preserving one's property to spur a man to take a wife. But before we make this decision, I think we should pray about it first."

"Aye, you are absolutely right. We should pray."

"Come, my love."

She placed her hand in Alaric's outstretched one and walked with him over to the settle. Sitting side by side, hand in hand with her husband, she closed her eyes to concentrate on her Lord as she rested her head on Alaric's shoulder.

"Dear Lord, most gracious and merciful God," Alaric prayed, "thank You for all the blessings You have showered upon Helena and me. Thank You for the love You have given us. Thank You for the devotion and service that our people have given us, and thank You for Damien Langston's fidelity and friendship. Dear Lord, please show us if it is Your will that we grant Narhex to Langston. We ask that Your will be done in our lives and that we base our actions and decisions solely on Your will.

"To You we give all glory and honor and praise. You alone are worthy of our praise. Holy, holy, holy, You are the Lord God Almighty, who was and is and is to come. The whole earth declares the glory of Your name. In Jesus' name we pray, amen."

"Amen," Helena echoed.

She felt a peace descend over her. These times that she and Alaric spent together in prayer had further cemented their love for each other, as well as their love for the Lord.

After a long, contented silence, Alaric spoke. "I feel an overwhelming peace with this decision, Helena. I think we have God's answer. What say you?"

"I too feel the Lord's peace. I believe it is His will that Narhex be Damien's. I think you should tell Damien what we have decided. I do not wish to tell him by myself."

"I will send for Langston, and we will tell him together."

They spoke lightly of inconsequential matters as they waited for the young knight to arrive. When Sir Damien entered the chamber, he bowed and stood quietly, while Alaric informed him of their decision.

"I will send a contingent of men with you to help you get settled in at Narhex," Alaric offered. "I require one-tenth of your profit from the estate as your annual payment to me. If you realize no profit the first few years, then no payment is required. Do you have any questions?"

Langston appeared to be stunned by this good fortune. "Nay, milord."

"I would like a report of the conditions you encounter at Narhex. Do you read and write?" At Langston's nod, Alaric continued, "I think you should be able to leave for the north the day after tomorrow. Is that acceptable?"

"Aye, milord."

"Well, I believe we have covered all the details," Alaric said. "You may leave and begin to make preparations for your journey."

"Milord, thank you for this extraordinary honor." Langston looked at Helena. "Helena—milady—I do not know how to thank you for this incredible opportunity."

"Be happy, Damien." Helena came to him and took his hands. "Thank you, my friend, for your love and protection."

He nodded. With a glance at Alaric, Langston bent to kiss each of Helena's cheeks. He released her hands, bowed to both of them, and left the solar. Helena turned a watery smile toward Alaric. He strode to her and wrapped her in his arms. She hugged him tightly and laid her head against his chest, accepting his comfort.

Later that night, Helena lay replete against Alaric's bare chest, reveling in the warmth of their passion.

"Alaric?" she said softly.

"Hmm?" came his languid reply. He held her closely to him, one hand lightly caressing her back and shoulders.

"I am carrying your child."

His hand stilled. Abruptly he rolled her over onto her back and looked intently into her face. "Say that again," he insisted.

"We are going to have a baby."

Helena's joy overflowed at the look of wonder on his face. Alaric pulled back from her, throwing the covers away from them to inspect her body, placing his hand over her flat abdomen. Her heart swelled at the reverence in his touch.

"My babe grows inside you?"

"Aye. 'Tis too soon for him to show. He or she will be born right before Christmas."

"Are you happy about the babe?"

"Aye, very happy," Helena affirmed. "And you, Alaric?"

"You have made me the happiest of men," Alaric vowed. "Helena, I love you."

"Oh, Alaric, I love you so, so much."

"Helena, I love you with all my soul."

Alaric made sweet, soul-shattering love to her, demonstrating his love, his devotion, and his commitment to her and to their child in his every touch.

As they rested in each other's arms, basking in the afterglow of their lovemaking, Helena offered up a prayer of praise and thanksgiving to God for the infinite blessings He had bestowed upon her. A husband who loved her as intensely as she loved him, a child to love and nurture, a home filled with peace and friendship. All the pain she had endured in the last five years had long ago faded into insignificance in light of the abundant love with which she was now surrounded.

About the Author

SUSAN LOWENBERG, the associate dean of the library in a private arts college, is also the author of *The Tournament* (OakTara) and the nonfiction work *C.S. Lewis: A Reference Guide 1972-1988* (New York: G.K. Hall, 1993).

Susan has a BA in English and French from California State University, Dominguez Hills, a Masters in Library Science from the University of California, Los Angeles, and an MBA from Bradley University, Peoria, Illinois.

She and her family live in Southern California.

www.susanlowenberg.com ▪ www.oaktara.com

AWAY FROM HERE

D.M. Snelling

Stephen turned his face toward the fire, wondering what had changed over the last few hours. Could Catherine have possibly become sensible? Had she resigned herself to the fact that she would be sailing on to Quebec? Had she given up her fight?

He tipped his head slightly so he could see her out of the corner of his eye. She was brushing her hair, which was her routine, undoing the curls and sweeps of shimmering brown and letting them unfurl on her shoulders. She looked so much younger when her hair was down…so delicate and sweet. He looked away with a pang of remorse.

My deepest thanks
to Bishop W.R. Felton,
who, with love and patience,
taught me how to get on the horse,
grab the reins, and ride.

1

France, 1641

If Stephen Marot could have predicted what lay ahead on the road to Elbeuf, he would have taken a different way home—a shorter, more direct path through the woods and not the leisurely road along the Seine. Then he never would have heard the angry voices or seen the huddle of men. If he had known how the misplay of events that night would change his life, he would have stayed at the inn some twelve miles away. His urge to return to his own bed moved him on. He would not sleep in it that night. He would never sleep there again. Stephen knew too much and had done more than he thought himself capable of doing. The news he now had to bring Judge Charles Compeaux would be devastating: his son was dead.

"I don't understand this, Judge Compeaux," said the tall, formal man as he removed his hat and entered the house.

"Please, Henry, don't ask any more questions," the elderly judge pleaded. "I don't have time to explain any further. Just trust me."

Judge Henry Ponte looked at the retired Honorable Judge Compeaux. Henry's mentor in the early years, Judge Compeaux had been tough and demanding. Henry had learned much of his trademark decisiveness from him—judging by the rules and allowing no exceptions. Henry enjoyed the reputation it gave him. He straightened his back and smiled inwardly. Any intimidation he'd felt was totally gone now as he saw the wrinkled old man in his nightclothes so desperate for a favor.

"If I can trust anyone, it is you," Henry said, "but asking me to do something like this in the middle of the night is highly unusual."

"It is highly unusual, yes," Judge Compeaux answered, "but not illegal or unethical." He moved Henry from the anteroom of his home into the parlor by the lit fireplace. The carved, leggy furniture cast shadows about the room and almost hid the couple standing there.

"You know Catherine," he said as he held out his hand for his daughter.

She stepped from the shadows toward the firelight and took her father's hand. She was pale and trembling.

Henry shot a look at Judge Compeaux, but the voice of the other figure answered before the question could be asked.

"She's been ill, Judge Ponte. Pardon me, I am Stephen Marot." Stephen respectfully nodded toward the judge.

"He is the man who will be marrying my daughter, Henry. His father has been in this area his whole life. They are all stone masons…reputable tradesmen."

Henry eyed Stephen's stocky, stiff frame and his hastily groomed appearance. "A tradesman? This is your only daughter. I would have expected you to select someone in good social standing—,"

"Love," interrupted Judge Compeaux. "These two have fallen in love, and I am too old now to wait for someone more suitable. There are few men to choose from unless I want her with an old man like me."

"I will take good care of her," said Stephen as he moved toward her. "We are grateful that you have come here to perform the ceremony."

"Ceremony? Nonsense. I've merely brought the appropriate documents for you to sign and I've only done that as a favor to Judge Compeaux."

"We are grateful, Henry," Judge Compeaux said. "In other circumstances we would have had a fine wedding, but our poor planning has forced this to be done in haste. They must leave quickly to arrive at port before the ships leave for New France. Their wagon is loaded and ready to go as we speak."

"New France?"

"Henry, please."

The judge pulled two documents from his leather pouch and spread them on the writing table. Judge Compeaux and Stephen signed them both.

"I will see you out, sir," said Stephen.

"I shall see myself out," replied Henry. "I will be by in a few days. We will visit then."

"Yes, my friend, of course."

The three stood still as they listened to Henry's steps disappear and the door close.

Stephen's stiffness loosened into a slump and a groan. "We must leave now."

"Father, please," wept Catherine. "Please don't send me away. What have I done?"

Charles pulled his daughter to him and buried his face in her soft, brown hair. "You have done nothing, but this is how it must be. Stephen will take care of you. It is all for the best."

"What about you, Father? What will they do to you?" She continued to weep.

"We will sort out the whole mess, my child. If you are here, they will look no further for a culprit. Stephen has offered to take you away from all this. It is the safest thing we can do right now."

"Why would they see me as a culprit?" She lifted her head and looked at her father. "What have I done?"

"Don't worry about any of it now. You must be leaving."

"You can't do this to me, Father. Please. I am a grown woman. You can't treat me like a child. If we are in trouble with the authorities, I should know why. I should stand up and face the charges with you. It's not too late. We can tear up the marriage papers, and I can stay here with you. I love you, Father, and I love Gaston. You know that."

Charles looked at Stephen, and Stephen imperceptibly shook his head no.

"I must tell her, Stephen."

"Father, please tell me." Catherine kept her eyes on him as he sat her in the chair and knelt beside her.

"Stephen has brought us some terrible news, Catherine. You must promise me you will be brave when you hear it."

Catherine's eyes widened as she nodded.

"Yesterday your brother…" Charles's voice halted. Stephen stepped forward but Charles raised his hand. "…your brother is dead."

"What? You must be wrong. He will be home tomorrow. He told me so."

Charles took her hand in his and held it to his heart. "Catherine, listen to me. Your brother is dead. He was stabbed last evening during a robbery."

"Oh, no!" Catherine gasped. "Not Jean! Please, Father, tell me this is a lie."

"It is not a lie. I wish it were." Charles's voice broke.

"Who did this? Who is the criminal? Who murdered my brother? Tell me!"

"Your brother caused his own death," said Stephen. "He was killed during an ambush. He was the criminal."

"You liar!" she screamed as she stood. "If this is true, then where is my brother's body? I want to see him."

"He couldn't bring him here," said Charles. "The authorities have to bring him. We can't behave as if we know anything. We need time to sort things out."

"What things do we need to sort out?"

"We don't have time for this, Judge Compeaux. We must leave now if we are to reach the ships in time." Stephen went to Catherine and took her arm.

"Jean may have been involved in other crimes. He may have killed someone before," said Charles as he stood, then crumpled into the chair, given over to grief.

"It can't be so," said Catherine. "I know it isn't true. Gaston went with Jean this morning. He would never let anything bad happen to him. He loves me, and he knows I love my brother."

"I am sure Gaston is a part of all this," Stephen said coldly as he stood over Catherine. "That is why we must leave. You, Gaston, and Jean were always together. Whatever one has done the others are implicated. It's safer if we leave now."

"This is all lies. Father, this cannot be true."

"Don't make me say it again. Just believe it is so." Charles sank further into the chair. "Go, Catherine. You must go."

"I can't leave you, Father. Who will take care of you? If I am implicated in this lie, then you will be too."

Charles lifted his head and straightened as much as his elderly frame would allow. He took his daughter into his arms. "My Catherine, I have taken care of you these many years since your mother died. I shall surely be able to take care of myself. I have a reputation of good moral character that, I am heartbroken to admit, did not flow through my blood to your brother. You will be safe in New France, and I will be here working to clear your brother's name. When all is settled, I will send for you."

"Oh, please, Father, promise me you will bring me back."

"I promise, my daughter." Charles squeezed her tightly, then stepped away. "Go now, quickly."

2

Stephen woke with a jolt. Once again he lay in sweat, lungs aching from fear, mind aching from his nightly terror. The dream pressed against his chest like a curse, causing him to strain with every breath. Images swirled through his mind in a sickening motion. He held himself very still until the dizziness left, then sat upright.

The hold of the ship was dark and the air stifling. Too many people shared the same space. French soldiers and settlers, Ursuline nuns and Jesuit priests, trappers and the ship's crewmen all breathed the same stale air whenever they were in the belly of the ship. Three months at sea. Three months of rations, sickness, and boredom.

The further they sailed from France and the closer they were to New France the fewer nightmares Stephen thought he would have. But the dreams got worse. Sometimes the essence of them would linger into the daylight, and he would spend a better part of the morning forcing them away. He found it hard to let the mental pain go. There was little work to do on the ship to engage his mind, and he hadn't developed any skill for small hand work. Some of the travelers carved beautiful figurines to keep busy. Stephen looked for anything to lift—bales, kegs, trunks. He was willing to move whatever needed to be moved.

Stephen lay back down on his mat. The ocean pushed and creaked against the wood hull of the ship but could not overtake the sound of the passengers breathing and stirring. One man coughed. Several snored in different pitches. A young child fussed, refusing her mother's whispers to go back to sleep. The mother lit her lantern and tended to her child. Someone cursed.

Rolling onto his side, Stephen gazed at Catherine. The soft light skimmed across her sleeping form. She was so beautiful and delicate he feared he might crush her if he ever held her too tightly. She brushed out her wavy brown hair every night before she went to bed, and it took on a life of its own in the lantern light, moving and sparkling as Catherine breathed. Her cheeks glowed, too, in this magic light. Stephen traced the shape of her face with his eyes—forehead, eyes, nose, and chin in lovely proportion.

He closed his eyes and tried to picture her smiling. She had a beguiling smile. It was the one thing that first drew him to her. He tried hard to think back to the days when she was carefree in France…when she was adored and admired by many less fortunate in beauty or presence…back before they wed, before their lives changed. He almost succeeded in the mental task of picturing her smile, but the strength of her sadness was

247

fixed upon her face—ominous and ever-present. The few times a smile seemed about to appear, it was chased away an instant later. No matter what his antics or kindnesses were, they failed to make Catherine happy.

He opened his eyes again as the woman with the child turned down the wick in the lantern. The light dimmed, gave one last flicker, and died. All was black again. He rolled onto his back and stared into the darkness. The muffled sounds in the hold resumed their haunting rhythm. The air grew thicker. Stephen clenched his fists and jaw in nervous succession. He didn't want to fall asleep again that night, but he couldn't lay in the dark and wait for the endless hours to pass. Carefully, he made his way around sleeping bodies to the ladder that led to the deck. He climbed up, pushed open the hatch, got out, and quickly closed the hatch again.

The night air was exceptionally cool and clear. Stephen wrapped his coat tightly around his bulky frame and tucked his large hands under his arms. He was adequately built for his work as a stone mason. Nothing about him suggested that he should have chosen a softer trade. His hair was dark, coarse, and straight. It was often moved out of place by wind, work, or a quick turn of his head. His nose and jaw had strong, straight lines and were handsomely set. Though his general appearance was of rugged warmth, his eyes were pale blue. Not the blue of a warm summer sky, but the blue of snow or ice. They were appealing and deep and consistently betrayed him.

The crewman on watch stood. Seeing that it was Stephen, he nodded. "No sleep again? You should have my job."

Stephen nodded in return and walked to the side rail.

The moon was high and scattered chips of light across the water. It made a silhouette of the second boat in the tiny fleet. The third boat had been separated during a storm weeks before. The captain said the ship was probably still headed for Quebec, but the talk of the sailors was that the ship had sunk. Everyone hoped the captain's assessment was right. That ship was loaded with supplies for the new land and goods to be bartered with the Indians for fur when they arrived at the port town of Tadoussac.

"I see the call of the ocean air has drawn you from your slumber, Stephen."

Stephen jumped and turned toward the voice.

"It's just me…Jacques." The tall, sandy-haired, black-robed priest chuckled.

"You must announce yourself more subtly, Father. I fear I aged greatly with your bold address." Stephen laughed stiffly.

"I am truly sorry, indeed," the young priest apologized. "I didn't expect to see anyone on deck but a few sailors. And, please, call me Jacques. I feel uncomfortable having a friend refer to me as Father," he continued, speaking freely in his usual friendly manner. "The Father in my title is still quite new to me. Sometimes when people address me as such, I look around to see to whom they are speaking."

Jacques was in good humor, which was in character for him. He always had a pleasant look around his mouth, and his small brown eyes had a spark in them, leading one to think that he had a tendency toward mischief. In the three months they had been together on the ship Stephen had never seen that mischief played out. It was, quite possibly, a remnant of his past before he had put on the black robe. Stephen liked this Jesuit priest…a man his own age, yet filled with a deep peace. When he was near Jacques, he thought that maybe he, too, could possess some of it.

"Of all the times I could pray," Jacques continued, "I feel most compelled to pray in the early morning just before the sun rises. Judging from the moon I would say I rose too early."

"Yes, morning is hours away."

"Maybe that is just as well. It will give us time to talk."

"What would you like to talk about, Father…eh, Jacques?" Stephen asked, swiveling back toward the rail.

"We've become rather friendly during this long journey, and I do like you, Stephen. I also know that you guard your privacy." His voice had taken on a more serious tone.

Stephen stared intently at the ocean, not wanting to meet Jacques's gaze.

"Please do not think I am prying out of idle curiosity, for I ask this out of friendship."

"Go on," Stephen said nervously. "Ask what you will."

"You had another dream, didn't you?"

Stephen took a quick breath inward. "Dream?"

"Yes. I know you have them. Even when you don't awaken, I can see it in your face while you sleep. You mumble and thrash about."

"You stay awake and watch me sleep?"

"No, I don't. But there are times when I awaken. That is when I noticed you. What is wrong?"

"Wrong?" Stephen searched for a reply. "Ah, now, Jacques, I can scarcely remember the dreams. As you said, I don't even awaken sometimes. Possibly it is the slop we have to eat that plagues me at night. Yes, that is most likely the source of my thrashing about." Stephen continued to stare at the sea. It hadn't occurred to him that anyone would have noticed.

"I am sorry," Jacques apologized. "I have overstepped the bounds of our friendship. Please forgive me."

"Oh, no," said Stephen, realizing his response was taken as a rebuke. "You have done no such thing. I was merely surprised at what you said." For a moment he wanted to be candid with the priest. "It is really nothing." He shook off the urge to tell all with a shudder. "It's this journey. It was taken on an impulse. I don't quite understand why I did such a thing. I made a very good living in France as a mason. I had built some impressive stone buildings and bridges. They were not grand palaces, but they were impressive. Then a fellow told me the government was recruiting masons and other builders to build New France. I had known that France was eager to populate its land across the sea, but I had never considered going. I was told it would be a great opportunity since France was promising incentives of money and livestock to those who would settle there. Still, I was not in need of either of those things. Then, one day, it just sounded like a good idea, and here I am. I'm not accustomed to doing anything on impulse. I find it quite disturbing."

"And Catherine?" asked Jacques.

"What about her?" Stephen asked with increased guardedness.

"Was she happy to join you on this journey?"

Stephen paused to retrieve the story he had told so many others on the ship. "It was very sudden for her, too," he began. "Neither of us gave it much thought. Her brother had died just days before we departed, and she was still quite upset. She regrets this move far more than I, though I think she is beginning to warm to the idea."

Stephen shook his head at himself. *"Warm to the idea"*? He knew it was obvious to all that Catherine had deep regrets about the journey.

"Is there a problem...something beyond this move to New France?" asked Jacques.

"Why are you asking me all these questions?" Stephen asked sharply as he pivoted toward Jacques. The knot in his stomach tightened.

"I can see that you are not a happy man, Stephen."

"I am as happy as I care to be."

"But what about Catherine? She is sorrowful beyond a brother's death. Her soul is discomforted and anguished. Perhaps I can help you both."

"Father Jacques, I thank you for your concern, but you are imagining more than there is." Stephen's square jaw tightened and shifted as he worked to keep his confession inside. "We are simply a man and woman recently wed, trapped on this ship in an expanse of water so great that we have not seen land for months. We haven't had time to adjust to each other, much less the multitude of others who are on this journey as we are." Stephen turned back to the ship's rail.

"I will pray for you and Catherine." Jacques put his hand on Stephen's shoulder. "God knows and sees all things. He watches over you both."

"Thank you, Father," said Stephen, hoping that God had looked away that night in France.

3

The next day came to life slowly as the sun melted its way through the sea's mist. One by one the travelers arrived on deck, moving the stiffness from their bones as they began their morning tasks. Soon the women had the breakfast hot and ready to serve.

Stephen put a heaping spoon of gruel in his mouth and swallowed before it had time to rest on his tongue. Several more hurried bites and the gray mush was cleaned from the bowl. He smacked his lips together and reached for the water jug.

Jacques approached, staring at his own bowl of mush. "Ah, Stephen," he said as he shook his head, "it is times like this that I wonder why any of us…nun, priest, soldier, or settler…has subjected himself to three months of sea rations." He twisted his thin mouth to the side and furrowed his brow.

"Unfortunately, I am hungry enough for another bowl," said Stephen as he stood.

"Awk!" screeched Jacques. "The ultimate horror!"

"A person must eat to keep his strength, Father Jacques." Stephen laughed. "You never know when you may have to run around the ship."

"My only running is to be ill over the side of the ship!"

Stephen smiled as he walked to the pot of gruel. It felt good to have a moment of frivolity and absence of serious talk. Perhaps if he sustained it long enough, he would forget everything that had happened in France.

He wanted to start a new life. Catherine frequently reminded him that she would return to France as soon as her father straightened everything out. Stephen would nod in agreement. He didn't tell her he had no intention of returning.

Catherine quit stirring the pot of lumpy gruel and handed the ladle to the woman standing next to her. "I simply cannot do this today. I fear I am going to be sick again."

The woman huffed and grabbed the spoon. "Yeah, it's always the same with you, isn't it? You're just too delicate to do your share of the work."

Catherine ignored her taunt and went to the opposite side of the ship, away from the passengers and crew who were clamoring for the same dreary food. Her stomach had not been right since they'd left France. She ate as much as she could, but some days it was impossible. It had little to do with the motion of the ship, though there were some days when the weather and waves took their toll on everyone.

Catherine went to the rail and faced the wind. She closed her eyes and breathed deeply, convincing herself that the ocean air was refreshing. An occasional mist of water sprayed up from the sea and sprinkled her face. The water dried off quickly, leaving a fine dusting of salt on her dry skin. In France she would have run to wash the caustic salt from her face and apply her expensive oils and perfumes, but her skin had now been subject to months of salt, cold, heat, and wind without any remedy.

"Catherine," Stephen murmured from behind her, "are you ill?"

"I am as well as can be expected, Stephen," she said with her eyes still closed.

"Surely there is something I can do for you...to make you more comfortable. Please, Catherine. It pains me to see you this way."

Catherine took a deep breath and opened her eyes. The same endless seascape of blue stretched out in front of her.

"Catherine, would you please talk to me?"

Catherine turned and regarded him with a weary gaze. "Talk about what? I've heard you talk. I've heard my father talk. Talk doesn't change anything. I am still here on this floating prison. My brother is still in the grave. Gaston is still in France, and I am still your wife under duress. What does talk change?"

Stephen looked around to see if anyone was within hearing distance and lowered his head when he saw several travelers watching them. "You best not talk so freely when people are around," he said quietly. "We are going away from France for your protection until the whole matter gets settled. If you keep talking out loud like this, people will get suspicious."

Catherine turned back to the rail. "You asked me to talk, Stephen. I'm trying to be strong, but I don't understand any of this." She closed her eyes tightly as tears pushed their way through. "I know you married me to protect me, but I don't even know what I'm being protected from. I only want to go home...to be with Father and with Gaston. I don't mean to hurt you, Stephen, but we both know this marriage was not born from love."

"Yes, I know," Stephen said as he closed his own eyes.

He chided himself for imagining that the act of consummating marriage would be rewarded with a reciprocal feeling of love. He couldn't let those thoughts run wild again. They had to be tamed. He had to be in control of himself.

Stephen turned and walked back to where Jacques was sitting, keeping his eyes averted from his fellow shipmates.

"Have you returned with no mush?" Jacques joked.

"I thought wiser of it by the time I reached the pot, Father Jacques. The bowlful I ate earlier began to settle and weigh me down." He forced out a half-hearted chuckle and sat down.

"It's all right," said Jacques. "We have all been through a lot on this ship."

"Yes, we all have." Stephen sighed. "May I ask you a question?"

Jacques nodded.

"I know why I am on this ship enduring all this…misery…but why are you here?" asked Stephen.

"We, the priests and nuns, are on a mission to the Indians of New France. Quebec is our first destination, as there is a good-sized population of Huron Indians being served at our mission."

"I know that is what you are all going to do," interrupted Stephen, "but why are *you* going? Were you forced to go because you are a priest?"

"Oh, no," laughed Jacques. "I volunteered. I begged. I prayed that God would be able to use me in this hostile frontier."

"I don't quite understand your eagerness."

"It is not that complicated. I simply desire to do something for God because he has done so much for me. Not in repayment…that's impossible. It's more a form of thanksgiving. Believe me, Stephen, I was not always a priest."

"I had a feeling that you were not."

"I was from a poor family. I had no father to speak of. My mother did what she could, but it was never enough to put any decent food on the table. Now that I think of it, it shames me to take our beloved sea rations so lightly. But that is another confession. The Jesuits were very good to us and provided food and support on more than one occasion. They were kind to my brother and me. Well, matters improved for my mother when she was hired on as permanent help for one of the wealthier families around. That left me and my brother to fend for ourselves. We were old enough to get by doing heavy labor and foolish enough to spend our earnings on strong drink and merriment.

"Then I met Angeline. She was the most beautiful, kind girl who ever existed. No more foolishness for me. She was going to be my bride. But the very night that I was going to ask her father for her hand in marriage I got a very unsettled feeling. Being the deep thinker that I am, I was sure it was a stomach illness."

He laughed. "As the evening progressed, I started thinking more and more about those Jesuit priests. I couldn't shake the thoughts of how they literally saved our mortal flesh and how they talked to us about the salvation of our souls. I knew I couldn't marry Angeline if I was only right with my flesh. I needed to be right with my soul, too. I didn't ask her father for her to be my bride. Instead, I went to the mission and learned of Jesus the Christ. I embraced him fully. When I told Angeline, she became cold toward me. She said she would have no part of this folly. Then it was as if my eyes became clearer than they had ever been. I knew that she and I were not meant to be together because I was meant to serve the Lord with abandon."

"You are a rare person, Jacques. I cannot imagine there are many like you."

"Oh, I am nothing. There are many priests who have gone before me, who have suffered much so that I can minister upon the foundation they have laid. They are the truly amazing people of a great calling." Jacques gave Stephen a mischievous grin. "Now that I have told my story, I am entitled to inquire of you."

"I have already shared too much of my uninteresting story," replied Stephen.

"Ah, but I have made the rules for our conversation, and I insist you patronize me for just a while longer," laughed Jacques. He was not going to be dissuaded from the opportunity to learn about his new friend and his sorrowful wife. "I shall make it easy for you. Tell me about Catherine. What was she like back in France?"

The playful tone in Father Jacques' voice was calming, and Stephen willingly submitted to the conversation. He leaned back against the parcel he was sitting by and began to speak.

"She was happy, mostly. She was always very friendly and always polite...a true lady. I had first seen her when I was a young boy. My father, also a stonemason, was building her father's house. We teased each other in fun. As we grew older, our stations in life dictated that we would never..." Stephen stopped, realizing that his ramblings were leading him to reveal more than he dared.

Jacques looked at Stephen questioningly; then, to Stephen's relief, he asked about Catherine's mother.

"I don't know much about her mother. She died when Catherine was young. I've never heard her mention her. I think she was too young to remember."

"Tell me about her brother...the one who died. What was his name?"

"Jean...Jean Compeaux." A shadow came over Stephen's face as he spoke his name. He adjusted himself nervously against the parcel, then sat up and fixed his eyes on the toe of his boot. "He wasn't very old when he died, just a few years younger than Catherine. She loved him."

Stephen glanced up at Jacques, then down at his boot again and waited for the next question. He was unwilling to offer more than he was asked and would probably not answer anything but the most benign questions...*What was his line of work?...Was he married?...What did he look like?*

Jacques said nothing more.

"I really must tend to my chores." Stephen stood, still averting his eyes from Jacques. He felt the priest watching him as he walked away.

Stephen got no more than twenty paces when the excited shout of the sailor stationed in the lookout boomed, stopping him midstride.

"Land! Land! There it is!" The sailor pointed toward a dark ripple on the horizon. "It's land, I say. Beautiful land!"

A cheer went up as nearly all the passengers ran to the side of the ship. Mothers held up their young ones to see above the rail this long-awaited sight. They had to squint to view the black ribbon that the same sailor now said were mountains. No one doubted him.

"People! People!" called the captain, his hands raised in the air to quiet the joyous group. "The land that you see is Newfoundland, near the mouth of the St. Lawrence river. It is very good news for us here today, but I must remind you that it is far from our destination. You still have almost a month more of sailing before you will reach the city of Quebec."

The reminder quieted the group somewhat, yet all seemed encouraged. They were closer to their new home. Stephen looked to see if Catherine had shown any sign of excitement over the event but could not find her on deck.

"She went below after the sighting," said Jacques as he put his hand on Stephen's shoulder. "She'll be alright. Things will work out fine. You will see."

As the dreary days passed, the two ships sailed the long, cold distance around the northeastern coast of Newfoundland. The excitement that took the travelers upon the sighting of this land was now replaced with an overwhelming sense of monotony and, for some, a twinge of regret. The tall, black cliffs of the coastline seemed impenetrable and bleak. The captain said that Quebec was not such as this now that it was early spring, but was lush and green. Still, some were skeptical.

Catherine kept to herself, much like she had for most of the journey. Stephen continued his attempts of comfort but was met with the same unyielding sadness. He settled in for the rest of the trip, resigned to the fact that her heart was locked away from him.

After many days the ships entered the Strait of Belle Isle, carefully maneuvering around the icebergs floating slowly out to sea. Large mounds of white dwarfed the ships. Navigation was so treacherous that the captain asked for prayer from the priests and nuns. Four of the nuns stood on deck and prayed continuously until the icebergs had been passed. They then spent time thanking God, who had answered their prayers, not only for safety, but for the survival of the third ship, which was spotted just beyond the last iceberg. It looked no worse for the lone journey. After the crewmen's well-being was confirmed, they continued their journey along the black coast of Labrador.

To the settlers' relief, the mainland's chilly gloom slowly gave way to ever greener shores as they neared the mouth of the mighty St. Lawrence River. The ships sailed easily into the river's mouth, but travel down its wide throat was treacherous. Navigation around sandbars, whirlpools, and sharp, menacing rocks sorely tested the captain and crew.

The heady smell of pine and cedar began to fill the air as the ocean disappeared far behind. Wildflowers and brush lined the now sloping riverbanks, occasionally dipping their thirsty fingers into the blue-green river.

Stephen often lingered on deck, enjoying the sights and smells he had never experienced before. He envied the settlers who had purposely set out to build a life in Quebec. The men with their wives and children were happier than he had ever seen them. They were so near to their destination. All they had been dreaming about was close at hand. He could see it in their eyes, in the way they acted toward each other. He wished that this had been his dream. It seemed so much more purposeful than running away from France.

Finally, the announcement was made. By dawn of the next day they would be at Tadoussac—a trading post located where the Saquenay River spilled into the St. Lawrence. From there the settlers would take smaller boats up the river to Quebec as the larger ship would go no further. With that news the excited passengers readied their goods and bed down for the night. Even though they would spend nearly two more weeks sailing up the river, this was surely a sign that their exodus was nearing an end.

Stephen had remained on deck after everyone had gone below for the night so he could be alone with the quiet night sky. It was not long before he unwillingly fell asleep. The sailors on duty let him alone. He spent the better part of every night on deck anyway, and they were glad to see him finally sleep. It wasn't until very early, before the sun rose, that his torment began....

Stephen grabbed the thick rope that tightened around his neck. His head throbbed and his airless lungs ached as he struggled to loosen it, but the weight of his body only pulled the slipknot tighter. Through the buzz in his ears he could hear the frenzied crowd calling for his death.

"Kill him! Kill him!" ebbed in and out as they began to pull on his kicking legs, tugging to ensure the noose would do its job....

"You're dreaming, Stephen. Wake up."

Stephen opened his eyes and violently pushed the hands on his shoulders away. His eyes darted back and forth, his mind trapped in distortion for a moment before grasping on to reality. He brushed the hair back from his sweating brow, then covered his face with shaking hands.

Jacques sat next to him. "Do you want to tell me why you have these nightmares?" he asked softly.

Stephen took his hands from his face, brushed his hair back again, and sighed. "We've spoken about this before. It's this trip...or the food...or both." His voice trembled slightly. He took several deep breaths to calm it.

"I may have believed that before, but I don't now." Jacques paused. "There is a darkness that comes over you at times, as if you are wrestling with something deep inside where no one else can see. It's more than just this trip or Catherine."

"If you have such insight, then why don't you tell me what my problem is?"

Stephen snapped. "Or why don't you ask your God why I can't sleep without visiting hell?"

Stephen stood, stomped over to the rail, and hit it forcefully with his hands. He was angry that he had a nightmare, angry that Jacques had noticed, angry with himself and angry that God had let any of it happen.

Jacques went to him and gently put his hand on his shoulder.

Stephen was quiet as he looked out at the river sparkling from the moon. It was still there…still peaceful. It had stayed within its borders and quietly continued on its way. Jacques was like the river. He still had peace, no matter how rude or reckless anyone was to him.

"I'm sorry, Jacques," he finally said. "I get crazy when I wake up from a dream. I didn't mean what I said. I do think it is the trip. Maybe it is a form of seasickness. We will be in Quebec in two more weeks; then I'm sure they will stop."

"Maybe so," replied Jacques.

4

Tadoussac harbor was alive with canoes and other small craft as the three ships from France came into view. Like a parade welcoming victorious soldiers, the inhabitants of Tadoussac cheered, whooped, and shot their guns into the air. In the water, on the shore, and on the decks people were scurrying to do their jobs or positioning themselves for a better look. The shoreline was covered by an assortment of characters waiting to make a trade. Indians and French fur-trappers alike waved to the ships in excited celebration. This was the payoff for the long winter month's trappings. Their skins of marten, beaver, and fox would be traded for European delights. Woven fabric, beads, brass cooking pots, and brandy were the most popular items for trade. Some tribes, more sophisticated and cunning than the others, had developed a keen business sense and became the middlemen for Indian groups of the interior.

These Indians more often dealt with the Dutch, as the latter would trade firearms; something the French would not dare.

The strip of shoreline that was called Tadoussac was freckled with tree-bark teepees hastily erected wherever there was a space wide enough to fit. In the middle of them stood the only permanent building—a dingy log hut that appeared to be the social hub of the barbaric little town. Behind the crop of teepees was a dense growth of trees with several paths cut into it that led to fertile hunting grounds and to fellow tribesmen and their families.

"One can scarcely imagine this harbor was deserted just a few days earlier," said Jacques as he took in the view. "And now look…a city of teepees…people everywhere…all here just for what these ships can do…bring goods and take furs. I am sorry to say none of this excitement is on our behalf."

"Are these the people you came here to help?" asked Stephen.

"Yes, we have come to serve the Huron and, hopefully, the Iroquois. The Huron are the friendlier of the two."

"They don't look like they need too much help to me."

"You are looking at one exciting day. You don't see the other days. These men have wives and children who get sick and hungry. Entire villages have been killed by fighting with other tribes. I have heard accounts of tortures, cannibalism, and such barbarity I cannot repeat it to you. They need the hope of salvation."

For the first time Stephen noticed sadness come over Jacques's face as he looked at the people in Tadoussac. The mischievous spark in his eye was gone and moistness formed there. Stephen knew for certain that Jacques's desire to serve these people was something deeper than following the Jesuit crowd or doing what was expected of him. His desire was born out of compassion for the soul of the Indians. Stephen suddenly felt awkward standing by him, as if he were invading something holy; yet, at the same time, he was honored to be in his presence.

"Stephen Marot," the captain's voice boomed into the air.

Stephen jumped and turned in one quick movement. "Yes, sir."

"I must speak to you regarding your wife. She has approached me on more than one occasion about returning to France on this ship. I have told her any such plans must be made by you. So, what is your plan, Marot?"

"Ah…no," Stephen answered in stunned disbelief. "We are going on to Quebec as planned."

"Then please inform your wife. I am tiring of her persistence."

"Yes, sir, I shall," he said as the captain turned to leave. "Where is she?" Stephen asked aloud as he looked at the crowd on deck. "What is she thinking?"

"Stephen, calm down. You know the state of mind she has been in," said Jacques. "I'm sure once she sets foot on solid ground she will forget about going back to France. Who could possibly bear four more months at sea?"

"Her sorrow has made her mad." Stephen threw his hands in the air.

"As your dreams have made you," said Jacques.

"Why do you say such things? What have I done to make you pursue this subject? My wife is going mad with grief, and you confront me on these silly nightmares."

"Because one day you will tell me what you are trying so hard to keep hidden," said Jacques. He held Stephen's gaze for a moment, then turned and walked toward the other missionaries who were readying their goods for departure.

Stephen wanted to call after him and explain away the seriousness of his dreams, but he held his tongue. It would do no good. He didn't believe the explanations himself. Besides, he couldn't risk saying anything he may regret, no matter how compelling the priest could be.

Stephen shook his head in amazement and disgust at how quickly his countenance had changed from awe and honor to anger and confusion. He used to be steady and calm back in France. He had the ability to face a difficult situation with logic and resolve. Now, with one little word, he could be turned upside down. He wanted to grab Jacques and beg him to deliver him from the demons that plagued him. He sighed again, hoping for some control to come over him, a fleeting strand of who he had been before.

"Perhaps one day I will tell you everything, Father Jacques," Stephen whispered to himself.

The three ships pulled as close to shore as possible before anchoring themselves against the river's flow. The sailors ushered the passengers and their goods onto a smaller boat that was then lowered to the river by strong cords. In a few moments they were on shore. The ship's crew followed close behind. Solid land felt wonderful. Many of the passengers wept openly with joy for what was to come and with sorrow for what they had endured to get this far. The people who had mingled freely on the ship divided once again into their respective groups. The priests gathered in a clump of black, the nuns in a clump of white. The soldiers met together briefly, then spread out through Tadoussac. The settlers gathered together, frightened and awestruck at this strange new place.

The crewmen, however, had much work to do before they could enjoy the land and join in with the trappers, who were already breaking open the liquor brought from France. They gruffly demanded that every man assist with transferring the goods destined for Quebec onto a three-masted barque and several large canoes.

While the men were busy loading, the women stood together near the shore, keeping the children within arm's distance. The celebrating of the trappers grew louder as the liquor flowed freely and an occasional glance at the huddle of women had turned into frequent leers and unsavory comments. The men worked faster as the women huddled closer.

Catherine was frightened and fascinated at the scene that, in France, would have been nothing to think about. Here, on this primitive shore, it was barbaric and raw. The men were strange and rugged and vulgar. They were not worrying and consumed with their struggles but were celebrating the day. She stared intently at the crowd of grizzly Frenchmen and sleek Indians and turned her head away only when a suggestive comment was made to her. But, like a child overcome with curiosity, she turned her eyes back to the scene.

"Mademoiselle," said a rather young man who dressed more like a Frenchman than most of the people at Tadoussac. Catherine stiffened as he walked toward her. "Pardon me." He bowed slightly. "But I could not help but notice your interest in the surroundings here at Tadoussac."

"Yes, this is a very fascinating place," she replied nervously.

"Fascinating, indeed! Such sights you would never see in France. Ah, but it is still French blood in our veins. We are very loyal to France. Even some Indians are very loyal to France. Do you see that Indian standing over there by the fire?"

Catherine nodded.

"He will be going back to France with me. He is very concerned with how to behave when he meets a French lady. I have taught him how to be gracious, but still, he worries. That brings me to ask if you would be so kind as to speak to him?"

"What?" Catherine gasped.

"You do not even have to speak to him, if you prefer. Just let him introduce himself so he can overcome his fear of meeting such a beautiful lady as yourself."

Catherine looked again at the tall, slim, Indian. He also dressed more like a

Frenchman than many in Tadoussac, but his black hair and eyes were darker than any Frenchman's, and his skin had a bronze glow that made him look like exotic royalty stuffed into commoners' clothing.

"Just for a moment," she replied. The young man held out his arm and Catherine took it as they walked toward the Indian. Several other men gathered around, laughing and howling, as Catherine approached. The Indian she was to meet stood in the middle of the men. He, too, must have found the event amusing; a crooked smile scrawled across his face.

"He doesn't look nervous about meeting me," said Catherine as her pace slowed. "He appears quite amused."

"Oh, Mademoiselle," replied the young man as he gently pulled on her arm, "you are mistaken. He is scared silly." The young man let out a loud laugh and pulled her toward the crowd that had gathered only to have her arm pulled more forcefully from him.

"These women are to be left alone," said Stephen as he held onto her arm. "*All* of them."

The young man paused, his eyes scanning Stephen's muscular frame and clenched jaw. "Monsieur, you are new to this place. You will be surprised at how many of those women do not *want* to be left alone." He laughed, then quickly added, "But if this is your woman, I do apologize. We were all taken with her great beauty and merely wanted to meet this goddess from beyond the sea."

Stephen turned back toward the group of settlers, dragging Catherine by the arm as the trappers burst into another gale of laughter. His rage concentrated in his hands; one clenched in a fist at his side, the other encircled Catherine's arm. His strides were double the size she could manage, and she struggled to keep pace.

"Stop!" She tried to free her arm. "Stephen, I said stop! You're hurting me!"

Stephen abruptly stopped and turned toward her. His eyes narrowed and his other hand grabbed her free arm. "I'm hurting you? Just why is it you think my only desire is to hurt you? Do you know what those men could have done to you? They haven't seen a French woman for a year…maybe longer. Didn't you consider that it could possibly be even worse than our wedding night?"

Stephen looked in her eyes. Anger and fear stared back.

"Maybe not," he said as he took his hands from her.

He walked back to the boats. There was still much work to do before they could rest.

Night settled on Tadoussac with a damp chill that made everyone cold to the core and sticky and wet on the surface. The giant bonfire helped to dry things somewhat, but the side facing away from the flame remained uncomfortably damp. The noise from the trappers had begun to taper, and the group from the ship settled down into smaller groups, yet remained close. Catherine helped some of the other women settle their children to sleep, and when her task was done, she was urged to get a good rest for the next leg of the journey to Quebec. Though no one was too excited to be on a boat again, they were less excited at the idea of delaying their travels for such a place as this.

Stephen stared into the fire, which warmed his face and hands slightly hotter than was comfortable. It felt good, just the same…something intense he could control with only a move of his head. He had made a bed for Catherine next to where he sat, but he did not expect her to lay in it or even to come near. All he could do was provide what she needed. Her accepting anything from him now was out of his hands.

"Is this for me?" asked Catherine as she smoothed out the bedding.

Stephen turned to look, thinking his ears had deceived him. "Yes, if you want it."

"Thank you," she said through a polite smile.

Stephen turned his face toward the fire again, wondering what had changed over the last few hours. Could she have possibly become sensible? Had she resigned herself to the fact that she would be sailing on to Quebec? Had she given up her fight? He tipped his head slightly so he could see her out of the corner of his eye. She was brushing her hair, which was her routine, undoing the curls and sweeps of shimmering brown and letting them unfurl on her shoulders. She looked so much younger when her hair was down…so delicate and sweet. He looked away with a pang of remorse for how he had treated her earlier.

"Catherine, about today…I am sorry. I didn't mean to be so rough." He cleared his throat and lowered his eyes. "When I looked over and saw you being made sport of by those men I just…"

"Oh, Stephen." She touched his arm. "I know you were only watching out for me. I am the one who needs to apologize for being so foolish."

"What?" Stephen turned toward her. Had his desire caused him to distort what he was hearing?

"Don't look so surprised. I did some thinking today and remembered how you were back in France. You were a fair man, never taking advantage of anyone. You were kind and gentle. I had never known you to be anything but gracious to me. You were my friend. I realized that, despite whatever reason you have for bringing me here, you are still a fair man. I know that if I just explain matters, you will understand."

"Understand what?" he asked with suspicion.

"Why, I think we should get back on the ship and return to France."

Stephen let out a short laugh and shook his head. "So that is what you want to explain. Catherine, you know that this is for the best." He looked in her eyes again, expecting to see some determination for her cause. The same familiar tears were there instead. He gently took her hand, sorry again for his words.

"Catherine, listen to me. I am a mason. The others and I will build towns to rival any in France. We'll build even better ones. You tell me how you want the buildings to look, and I will build exactly to your liking. I will build you a grand and glorious house. You will grow to love it there, and one day you will forget about France."

"I will never forget France," she spit as she tore her hand from his. Anger came back with a violent rush. "It is not the towns or the buildings I care about. You took me away from the people I love. I couldn't even bury my brother. I was delirious with grief, yet you married me and took me away. Why? Why didn't you just leave me alone? Why did my father let you take me away before my brother's funeral?" Her lips trembled as she fought her tears.

Stephen turned back to the fire. He had no reply. What she said was true, and he could not answer her questions. Not now. He threw a stick into the fire and watched it sizzle and burn up to nothing.

"You took from me something I had promised in my heart to another," she whispered.

"You speak of Gaston," he stated, hoping she would disagree.

"Yes. We planned to marry before…"

"Before this filthy beast married you. Is that what you really want to say?" he asked, not wanting to hear the answer.

Catherine buried her face in her arms. Her shoulders shook with emotion.

"That is how you see me, isn't it? You can't see that I loved you. You only see the filthy beast." Stephen stood and paced between Catherine's huddled form and the lapping fire. His anger rose again, covering the pain that was there a moment ago. He took a deep breath and let it out slowly. "I'll tell you who the beast is, Catherine." He issued his words in a controlled monotone, not allowing the anger to escape unbridled. "It is Gaston. You were not the only one in all of France who thought he was faithful to you."

"You are wrong!" Catherine put her hands over her ears. "I don't believe you."

Stephen quickly knelt in front of her and pulled her hands away. "Yes," he said, his words losing their control. "Everyone knew he had a woman in every town he traveled in, but I didn't tell you because I didn't want to hurt you. He doesn't love you."

"Why are you doing this to me? You are being so cruel." She wearily hit his shoulders with her fists and finally buried her face in his shoulder. Her weeping was no longer silent but given over to moans.

"Please forgive me, Catherine," he whispered into her ear. "I don't know what has come over me. It has to be the months at sea. It has made everyone on edge. Please forgive me."

Catherine continued to weep. Stephen looked at the other settlers spread out around the bonfire and settled down for the night. They had come to expect Catherine's episodes of weeping and paid them no attention.

Stephen dozed off and on throughout the night and was surprised when he woke with the sun completely above the horizon. Some people were moving about, preparing to leave, but many were still in the early stages of waking after the first night on dry land. He was surprised, too, that Catherine was still lying next to where he was, though she was curled up with her back to him in an unsubtly protective fashion. He hesitated to wake her but knew he had to. He shook her shoulder.

"Wake up. We have to leave now."

"Oh, I can't go," she mumbled as she curled up tighter. "I am not feeling well."

"It won't work, Catherine. You are coming with me no matter what," he said as he pulled the blanket off of her. Her clothing was damp and stuck to her body. She trembled as she wrapped her arms around her knees.

"Ah…maybe you slept too close to the fire and got overheated. Come now," he said as he sat her up. "There, do you feel better?"

Catherine lurched forward and wretched.

Stephen enlisted the help of a nun to clean her and make her as comfortable as possible. By midmorning all who were headed for Quebec were on the boats and ready to set sail…including Catherine. Her vomiting had subsided, yet she would wretch every time she smelled the salted cod stored on the boats. Unfortunately, the fish soaked in vinegar would be the mainstay of their diets for the next two weeks.

Catherine and Stephen were assigned to one of the two large canoes with the nuns, a sailor, a soldier, and Father Jacques, who had requested that he be there to support them both. Traveling in the large canoes was a challenge to all. Tempers flared more often than the entire time at sea. The nuns and priests and those who "believed" spent much time in prayer in order to stay focused on their mission. It had become far too easy to murmur and complain.

Catherine tried to care for herself, but soon the illness overtook her and all her energies were spent on maintaining some kind of health. When that failed, she just lay on the bottom of the canoe and shivered. The nuns did their best to make her comfortable and practiced what medicine they knew. Whatever she had would have to run its course. They prayed she would have the strength to endure it.

Stephen tried to tend to whatever she needed but was limited by the nuns, who were only too willing to practice what they were trained and called to do. He could only look on, helpless and guilt-ridden. It crossed his mind to bargain with God for Catherine's health, but he didn't think he had anything to offer. He knew Jacques was praying for her. He knew the nuns were, too. God would surely move on their request without a shaky offer from him.

Days and nights passed slowly on the river, and sometimes it seemed as if the boats made no headway at all. The St. Lawrence became the enemy, continually flowing away from their destination. The harder it pressed toward the sea, the harder the men worked to move the boats toward Quebec. The battle was fierce, but everyone knew they would win. They were not so sure of the battle with the unseen enemy; the eyes that were surely watching them as they traveled so vulnerably on the water. The river was the Iroquois' friend and, if they wanted to attack, would have no trouble doing so. Some of the settlers on board refused to believe the tales about Iroquois attacks, especially after seeing some Indians up close at Tadoussac. It was easier to deny the possibility than harbor the pain of fear.

The Jesuits and Ursuline nuns knew the stories to be true as they had seen the recollections of torture written by the victim's own hand. They were aware of the price paid by those who went before them and equally aware of the price they may have to pay. Fear was not a stranger to them. It often knocked at their hearts, but they were well-practiced in turning it away.

5

The early morning sun beamed across the sky, dripping light from the treetops and bidding a glorious welcome to the vessels on the St. Lawrence. An array of birds joined the greeting with a bright melody that swelled and waned with the precision of a conductor's wand. Even the air seemed to greet the passengers with unusual clearness. They had reached Quebec.

Lofty Cape Diamond projected its stony face into the flow of the river, boldly announcing its presence. At the base of the cliff were a handful of unimpressive warehouses and wooden tenements that looked all but abandoned. A zigzag of worn earth led the eye up the side of the cliff, finally resting upon a fortress built of earth and logs. It was from there a cannon rang out, signifying to all of Quebec that the boats had arrived.

People gathered at the top of the cliff and filed down the path. Leading the procession was Governor Montmagny, complete with an entourage of soldiers in military dress and armed with muskets. Close behind was Father Vinmont, Superior of the Quebec mission. Several priests followed him. Like the priests on the boat they were in black, but their robes were faded and worn. Settlers in dress ranging from rugged to dapper joined in the parade, waving their arms and calling out greetings.

Fur-trappers and their Indian companions were also on the scene, though they were reserved and disgruntled. The settlers' arrival only meant that the town would grow, sending their profitable prey further into the vast woodlands of the continent. Their only hope was that a bevy of single Frenchwomen had been sent aboard for marrying, as had been sent in the past. Opportunities in Quebec for unattached women had been heavily advertised in France. Families with too many mouths to feed were glad to have someplace to send their unmarried daughters. The financial incentives offered by the government didn't hurt, either. Unfortunately for the men, no available women had ventured to make the trip this time.

The final group in the band of welcomers was the nuns. Their long white robes were dyed nut-colored to hide the dirt that came with serving in an unrefined environment. They greeted their fellow nuns as a flurry of Indian girls raced about their feet, finding it hard to keep their enthusiasm contained.

Stephen lifted Catherine from the boat and steadied her on the shore. Though her health had improved, she was still weak and became exhausted with the least amount of exertion. The sickness had been hard on her, taking from her too much weight and color. Her eyes had become dark, dry, and looked in need of sleep, even though they had had plenty of it for many days.

Catherine was glad to be off the boat and standing on solid ground again. The land seemed to give her strength as she felt the warmth of it radiate on her skin. She refused Stephen's insistence that she sit, preferring to stand while listening to the Governor's welcome.

After a round of personal greetings, Governor Montmagny mounted a crate and held up his hands to quiet the new arrivals. The nervous and excited chatter fell to silence as he began his address.

"We who have tread upon this land before you offer our heartiest and most sincere welcome. I have no doubt that you have suffered at sea, your heart longing for your new home and, perhaps, mourning for the old. Some of you have lost loved ones along the way and have faced the tiresome journey alone.

"But your sojourn is now over, for you have placed your feet upon the solid ground of Quebec. Your children, their children, and generations to come will remember you as the brave pioneers of this great new land. Each one of you has securely set for yourself a place in history."

The newcomers stood silent, tears dotting the eyes of many.

"I can see that some of you have acquaintances or contacts here and are not in need of immediate quarters. Father Vinmont will direct those of you who are here in missionary capacities to your posts. And let me add a word of gratitude. Your faithfulness and servitude has been, in the past and surely in the future, a most important part of Quebec.

"Those of you in the employ of the current fur trade monopoly, the Company of the Hundred Associates, will be aided by those with whom you have had previous contact.

"And those of you who have come to this land to start life anew will find that our residents are extremely hospitable and willing to lend their aid whenever it is needed. Many will provide you with temporary lodging if space allows. If there are any not adequately sheltered in the city of Quebec, we will provide temporary housing at the fort."

Murmurs of relief spread about the crowd at the governor's assurance of housing. The talk on the boat had been that many would have to reside in hastily built lean-tos until they could construct a home of their own.

The governor continued and the crowd quickly hushed.

"Before you find your abodes, I must issue instruction—yea, even caution—about life in Quebec. You have heard of Indian attacks. I tell you they are, unfortunately, true. Though possibly not to the extent the rumors have told them to be.

"When Champlain came to make a prosperous settlement of this land he befriended a group of Huron Indians. As circumstances came about, he found himself defending them in a battle. In the midst of the fight he killed some Iroquois warriors with his musket. What Champlain didn't know was that he had provoked a great enemy, for the Iroquois are many and mighty. Now we, the settlers of New France, are the objects of their vengeance. The Hurons, which you have seen in Tadoussac and here among you, have been especially victimized.

"We have had very few attacks at Quebec, and, though the Iroquois now possess muskets, we have always managed to come through the attacks victoriously. Even so, it is advisable to be adequately armed whenever you wander beyond the protection of the fort.

"But now, I am sure you are all eager to find lodging, so I will not keep you any longer. Once again, welcome to Quebec."

The crowd clapped and cheered as the governor made his way back to the fort, leaving most of his soldiers behind to direct the activities on shore.

"It is true," said Catherine weakly as she touched Stephen's arm. "The rumors about the Indian attacks...I didn't believe them...but they're true."

Before Stephen had time to move, Catherine's eyes rolled back and her knees gave way, bringing her abruptly to the ground.

Catherine stretched long and hard on the narrow cot before opening her eyes. Her pleasant expression from a sweet dream fled as she scanned the strange, dingy room.

"Good day, Madame Marot."

Catherine turned toward the soft, feminine voice. Its owner was an older woman sporting a gentle smile and simple bonnet of gray hair cut short and practical. Her skin was lined and baked by the sun, but her light blue eyes suggested that her skin was naturally fair. Her ample weight and many years hadn't stooped her sturdy frame and seemed more like a clever disguise as she quickly moved across the room and seated herself on a wooden chair near the bed.

"You have had quite a rest. I trust you are feeling better?"

"Umm...yes...yes, I am," Catherine replied as she sat up.

"You fainted yesterday. Do you remember?"

"Fainted? Oh, yes...during the governor's welcome speech." Her cheeks blushed at the thought of such a spectacle. "Did you say yesterday?"

"You were brought here yesterday morning, and it is now approaching midday. You had a fever and just needed to sleep it away. Any boat journey needs a good deal of recuperation afterward." The woman let out a hearty laugh and patted Catherine's hand. "Don't you worry, dear. You'll get your land-legs back very soon."

Catherine took her hand away and glanced around the room. "Where is Stephen?"

"He is already talking with the governor and a few other fellows about building projects. He is very excited about being here. I thank God that people with such skills as your husband are coming to Quebec. You must be very proud of him."

"Excuse my ignorance, but who are you?"

"I am Madame LaPointe. My husband and I worked the land here in Quebec. My three sons work it now that we have grown weak in our arms and gray on our heads. Corn, beans, and squash," she said with obvious pride. "But now that is being boastful, is it not? I do tend to talk on about such things, so while I have my head let me show some hospitality."

She got up from the chair and moved to the adjacent wall, where the small hearth held a low flame and a kettle of thickened stew. She stirred the meal, bending over slightly to catch the aroma. "This will help to keep your feet on the ground," she said as she ladled a healthy portion into a wooden bowl.

Catherine blushed again at the reference to her fainting, then straightened her back. "I'm sure I will have no more trouble." She eagerly accepted the bowl.

"Your husband said you ate almost nothing for the last two weeks. Be assured, my dear one, that I put no salted cod in the stew. It is venison, vegetables, and gravy."

The delicious smell of the stew reached out to meet Catherine, and she started to eat it furiously.

"You had best slow down. When a stomach has been empty as long as yours, you've got to break it in slowly, or it will come back on you."

Catherine paused and wiped a drop of gravy from her chin. "Yes, you are right. Thank you for this delicious stew and for whatever else you have done."

"It was the least I could do. I am just so happy to have such good people settle here in Quebec that I want to help out whichever way I can. I know how hard it can be."

"When did you come to Quebec?" asked Catherine, wondering how long this woman had endured life in such an uncivilized place.

"Twenty-one years ago, in 1620. This town was almost nothing then. Although it isn't much now, either, when you compare it to France. Only one other family had made a profitable go of it by settling here. For most everyone else it was a matter of simply surviving. It still is. But we are growing, though only by a few families per year." Madame LaPointe sat back down and adjusted herself in the chair, wriggling her shoulders to set her bones and muscles in comfortable order.

"My boys have been a tremendous help over the years. We could not have survived without them. We have seven children all together. Two of my daughters are married and living in France. I receive letters from them every year when the ships come. I have many grandchildren from those two!" She laughed. "That is very good, as there are not many women here for my boys to choose from. I wonder at times if they will ever marry."

The smile left Madame LaPointe's face. "My third daughter came to Quebec with us. She was a fine girl...kind and gentle with such a sweet singing voice. On the ship she would sing in the evening, lulling our fears and sicknesses to sleep. Her voice comforted the dying, too. Many did not live through our first year here in Quebec. They would ask for her to serenade them through the gates of heaven. She died not many years after we came. I still miss that dear young girl. I know it won't be long before I hear her sing before the throne of the Almighty."

Madame LaPointe sat silently for a moment, but just as quickly as her reverent mood came, it was replaced by a mischievous chuckle. "Now my youngest son is a different tale. He was always entertaining some wild notion. Papa would get so upset with him that sometimes leaving his presence was the only way he could keep from shaking the boy. Ah, but if a mother could have a favorite child, he was mine. The boy had spirit. I knew he would never be content raising crops and livestock, but I did not expect him to abandon it at such an early age."

"Where is he now?" asked Catherine.

"When he was but seventeen, he set off with a group of fur-traders. He said, 'Mama, you know I was born different from you all. I cannot sit still here on this farm any longer. Please bless my leaving.' What could I do but bless my dear boy and try to explain it to his father? Papa took the news better than I had imagined. I think he, too, knew the boy was burning to be off on his own. He comes home once a year during the summer when it is trading time. He has grown into such a capable man that his father is now very proud of him. He has finally accepted the truth that his son can be a good man without having to be like him.

"My family is much like Quebec, itself. Papa and I are like its founders, desiring to see Quebec and all of New France prosper and grow. My hard-working boys are like the settlers that have come—not to make an easy profit from furs or to indulge in the wild living of some fur-traders, but to work honestly and faithfully tilling the ground. As you shall see, this rocky ground is not always hospitable to your farming plans.

"Then, of course, there are the fur-traders. They are so much a part of New France that it seems they were here before the Indians! They would descend upon our town in the spring for trading. Quite often they turned quiet Quebec into one big brothel, drinking in the street shamelessly with their Indian friends and conducting themselves rather loosely with the girls from town. But please do not think that I would raise such a son," she added hastily. "Just as there are undesirable characters in any group, you will also find good people in the most unlikely places. Oh, I am sure he does not live as virtuously as the Jesuits, but he does not cause me any shame."

Madame LaPointe adjusted her shoulders again and sighed, squinting her eyes ever so slightly to sharpen her gaze on Catherine. Her pleasant look, once again, dimmed. "Unfortunately, part of settling a community in a strange new place is that death too often comes early. Unlike the fur-traders who visit us only once a year, death is a constant companion. The nuns in the hospital at the base of the cliff see death by the score as Indians crawl in half dead with the diseases we brought with us. Many of us die from the same scourge…like my daughter. Yet, I fear the ravages of disease are nothing compared to the tortures of the Iroquois."

"I thought the governor said that Quebec was always victorious in their dealings with them," Catherine said.

"Yes, it is true. But at what point do you call it victorious? Is it when we kill ten Indians to their killing of eight Frenchmen? Or is it when a lone farmer is butchered in his field, but the fort is not attacked? Maybe it is being killed instantly instead of being taken away to endure tortures. That is what we hold to as victorious." Madame LaPointe leaned forward and intensified her gaze. "Always be on your guard, Catherine. They are everywhere and nowhere, so silent and quick that many could not even take aim with their muskets before they were cut down."

Catherine shuddered and paled at Madame LaPointe's words.

"I am sorry. I must be frightening you with all this talk."

"I am not frightened." Catherine straightened her back again and lifted her head a little higher in defiance of fear. "I am simply weakened from the long journey."

"Such a spirited one I have not seen since my son left to become a fur-trader!" Madame LaPointe laughed, once again placing her hand on Catherine's.

This time Catherine did not pull away but smiled gently at the friendly old woman.

"Don't ever lose that spirit, but don't let it blur your judgment, either." Madame LaPointe gave a satisfied sigh and slapped her knees. "It is clear to me that you are most definitely on your way to recovery, so I must be off. Even though I am old, I still have to feed my men. What they will do without me I shall never know." She stood quickly and sprightly, then gathered her cape.

"Go?" asked Catherine. "Your family lives with you here, don't they?"

Madame LaPointe laughed. "My child, I do not live here. You do."

"Me? How?"

"The Jesuits secured it for you and your husband. No one has lived in it since Pierre died. He was a good man. An Iroquois tomahawk split his skull while he was exploring the woodlands west of here. He never did have a wife, which is obvious when you look about this house. I'm sure she would have insisted on a few niceties."

Catherine scanned the tiny one-room house again. Everything in it—walls, ceiling, floor, and hearth—was colored a dreary gray. She couldn't tell if it was weathered wood and stone or if Pierre had intentionally painted it so. The furniture consisted of the cot she had slept on, one wooden chair, and a rough-hewn table barely big enough for two plates. On one wall by the hearth hung three shelves, which appeared to have been freshly dusted and stocked with flour, dried beans, and other food staples. The bottom shelf also housed two cups, two bowls, and two plates. On the floor along the wall opposite the cot was a bedroll, hastily tucked between the crates and parcels she and Stephen had brought from France.

"Do all those who arrived here yesterday have quarters such as this?" asked

Catherine.

"Governor Montmagny is a very good and pious man, yet he overestimates the kindness of his people. Only a few families have the space to house anyone, and a portion of them have no desire to do so. The fort is not equipped to house many, either. So, as disgusting as it may seem, you have the nicest quarters of all your shipmates."

"Oh," Catherine said, not caring that her face displayed her disappointment.

"Don't let this one little thing discourage you," Madame LaPointe continued. "Even though I told you of the darker side of Quebec, there is much that is good here. Most of the people are kind, the air is clear, and there is so much to look forward to in the years to come. Your husband will probably build you a grand house very soon. He cares very deeply about you. You can see it in his face. You are a very lucky woman, Catherine."

An image of Stephen on their wedding night flashed through Catherine's mind. She shuddered. "The grandest house I know of is back in France. There is no replacement for that."

"You are right. We always have special memories of our childhood home," Madame LaPointe encouraged. "But you will have another home here in which to make memories for your own children."

Madame LaPointe gave her a smile and promised to visit her the next day.

Catherine followed her out the door and watched her walk down a worn path that disappeared into a patch of woods. She stared after her for a time, then gazed across the weathered tree stumps that dotted the little yard in front of the house, sticking up like demonic fingers out of the dirt. For a second she imagined poor Pierre chopping the trees, tired and sweating with aching muscles and big dreams, building his little house…only to be viciously murdered by an Iroquois.

Catherine shuddered and dashed back inside, bolting the door.

6

"This has been a pleasure, Monsieur Marot." The thin, pale man grasped Stephen's hand with more vigor than expected. "You are more than we had hoped for in both skill and experience. You are by far the most eager of anyone I have met! I would have thought your first few days in Quebec would be spent recovering from the journey and settling your own affairs instead of meeting with us."

"It was an honor to meet with the planners of this city and to be included in their discussion so soon after my arrival," said Stephen with formal politeness. "To be in conversation with Governor Montmagny regarding the building of Quebec was far more than I expected. I assure you, Monsieur Fonte, that I am most eager to put my hand to building. It has been too long since I've been able to build, and I sorely miss it."

"Ah, yes." Monsieur Fonte laughed in agreement. "I remember how excited I was to use my skills after the long journey to Quebec. Forced idleness can be great motivation. Pace yourself, Stephen. We have a great deal of work ahead of us. The governor's plans are quite aggressive and—"

"Aggressive but achievable," Stephen interrupted. He was feeling wholly optimistic for the first time in months and did not want Monsieur Fonte to utter any word that might diminish his zeal, no matter how realistic the word might be. "With time, materials, and manpower the plans for the city can be accomplished."

"It appears that you and Governor Montmagny are of like mind as it pertains to building," Monsieur Fonte said with a grin as he walked with Stephen down his curved stone walkway from his house to the dirt avenue. "I think we will all work together quite well."

Stephen nodded in agreement and farewell and began the short walk down the avenue and the longer walk up the untamed path to his own home. The day was an excited whirl of events: the meeting with the governor, the builders, the blueprint for the city streets of Quebec, the planned homes and buildings, the churches and hospitals. He could see them so clearly even though they were only lines on paper or verbal descriptions. He was glad to have a grand, ambitious project to look toward. The long day of ideas and planning for the future had been like a needed medicine. He felt something within breathe again after being shut up for so long. It was a part of who he knew himself to be.

Monsieur Fonte had understood his feelings on a surface level…the joy of doing what one was trained to do…but he didn't know the extent to which Stephen felt relief. Stephen was careful not to let his excitement loosen his tongue. He answered the questions as to his past succinctly, not giving any more information than was necessary and certainly not mentioning anything personal. Fortunately, the men gathered at the meeting were focused on building and appeared to have no interest in Stephen's personal affairs.

The sun was tucking itself behind the tree-laden horizon as Stephen approached the clearing around his little house. He slowed his steps and watched as the earth's blues and greens were dimmed by a sky of translucent rose. The cooling air revived the crickets that had lain unnoticed during the day, sending them into a pulsating rhythm that echoed through the dusk.

Stephen stopped and closed his eyes, breathing in the cool, clear air. The scent of trees and warm earth was a new delight. There was none of the heavy perfumes France used to cover up the stench of a crowded city. Even when Stephen traveled out of the French cities he could not remember the air being as pleasant as it was in the new land. The overall effect of the moment—the sky, the air, the sounds, the satisfaction of a day's work—was incredibly peaceful. Stephen didn't want to move from his spot at the edge of his newfound homestead, lest he break the wonderful spell, but he walked on.

A smaller path broke off the main trail and rose slightly as it led to the little house. The front of it appeared as basic and dreary as the inside—gray and flat with one small window placed at eye level on the left and a sturdy, well-built door on the right. The other three sides were continuous logs fused together by gritty chinking.

Stephen turned the latch on the door and pushed. The door moved slightly, then stopped against the wooden plank that bolted it shut from the inside.

"Catherine, it's me…Stephen." He put his ear to the door and listened for her approach, stepping back when he heard the plank being lifted. All in one instant he hoped for the best, that his moment of peace would continue, that Catherine would be well and pleasant, that all things past had been forgotten, and that all would be good in his world.

Catherine opened the door.

"Catherine, you look well," he said as he entered the house.

"Yes," she said coolly and turned back to the kettle on the hearth. She added more water to the stew that had become thick and pasty from simmering all day, reconstituting it to a palatable level.

Stephen walked to the middle of the room. He wished there was somewhere more he could move to, but six steps in any direction would place him at a wall. "Whatever you have there smells wonderful." He sniffed the air. "Did you make it?"

"Of course." She swiveled toward him. Stephen winced at her sarcastic glare, immediately wishing he had stayed outside. "After I woke up from being terribly ill, I went out into the woods and shot a deer, gutted it, and dragged the poor thing back here. Then I scrounged around for some forgotten vegetables in the ground. All this just so you could come home to this terrible, little place and have fresh stew!"

Stephen swallowed hard and pasted on a painful smile. "I guess it was a foolish question. I remember now. Madame LaPointe's son, Louis, said that she had left you healthy and with a good supply of stew."

"When did you see her son?"

"In town today. I was on my way to meet with some people and he crossed my path. He's a fine fellow. He works his family's farm here in Quebec...very friendly." Stephen was surprised and encouraged by her sudden interest. "I have good news, Catherine. I have already found work. It is far more than I had hoped."

Stephen sat on the edge of the little table and continued to talk more freely as his excitement from the day revived. "For the immediate time I will be working for the Jesuits. They provided this house, which is less than an hour's walk from their mission. They said a man named Pierre used to live here."

"Yes, I heard about Pierre," she said, turning back to the kettle.

"The Jesuits acquired the house and planted wheat and corn in the clearing right out behind us. It's not a huge field but big enough to give us plenty of produce. It is as if they knew we were coming and arranged everything to the smallest detail. Did you know that they had been praying for someone to help them build a hospital?" he asked, not allowing time for her to answer. "They need a church and homes. I also heard some talk of a school to teach Indian children. I will be kept busy for some time. They will pay me as they can, though they couldn't commit to any sum. I understand. I would have offered to help them for nothing since their endeavors are all for noble purposes. They are letting us live here and giving us the garden produce. All they ask is a small portion of the harvest and our attendance each Sabbath for mass. It sounds reasonable to me."

Stephen paused. When Catherine made no attempt to speak, he continued. "I also had the opportunity to meet with the other builders and even spoke with Governor Montmagny about plans for the city. He has great vision for Quebec. I am encouraged by all I have seen and heard today."

Catherine ladled some stew into a bowl and handed it to Stephen. "That is all very exciting, but who will be tending our crops?"

Stephen looked at her with a puzzled expression, then realized why she was asking. He sat in the chair and spoke in a more cautious tone. "I will, essentially, but you may have to tend them for a time." Catherine opened her mouth to protest, but Stephen continued. "The Ursuline nuns desperately need a building to use as a hospital, and I have offered to assist in the construction of it. Right now they are in one of those tattered buildings at the base of the cliff and, with the recent Indian attacks, we have to get them into a building closer to the fort." Stephen stopped abruptly, remembering the last time Indian attacks were spoken of in her presence. "But I have been out all day and have not seen one Iroquois or heard of any attacks," he said in a hasty attempt to relieve the tension. "I think the people's concern is quite out of proportion to the actual threat."

Catherine gave an irritated sigh and pivoted toward Stephen. "If you treat me as if I will faint at every mention of Indians, I will go out and drag one back here by the hair! The only reason I fainted yesterday was because I was ill. As you can see, I am perfectly fine now. You certainly did not think I was so frail, leaving me here with a perfect stranger." Catherine bit her lip to stop it from shaking. "Now you ramble on about building this and building that, like I don't even matter at all. You haven't asked once what I want."

Stephen pushed his bowl of stew aside and stood as Catherine quickly turned back to the pot of stew and wiped her eyes.

"Oh, I am so tired of crying, but that is all I can do," she said as she felt him come closer.

Stephen reached out one hand to touch her shoulder. Then, in reflex, he put it back at his side as she faced him again.

"I know you are excited about being here," she said with a subtle plea, "but you must understand that I don't care. I didn't care on the boat or at Tadoussac. I never will care."

Catherine put her hands on Stephen's arms and commanded with her eyes that he look and listen to her intently. "Don't you see that I will never be happy here with you? My life is in France. That is where I long to be. I won't survive this desolate place. If the Indians or disease don't wipe us out, then I will surely die of a broken heart." A heavy weight of frustration swept over her and her knees weakened as her tears came unhindered.

Stephen caught her in his arms and let her cry into his shirt. For a moment he wanted nothing more than to take her back to France so she could be happy, so she could be away from this primitive place, so she could be with her father and with the one she loved.

Gaston. The sound of his name in Stephen's head made his stomach instantly lurch. If all remained the same, except that Gaston would disappear from her life, Stephen would not hesitate in finding some way to send her back to France. But there was such darkness in Gaston that, as long as he was in France, Stephen couldn't willingly let Catherine return. Though at times he was confused in the matter, he knew then, in that moment of her neediness and pain, that he loved her…in the past, the present, and in the time to come. It was as if his love for her had a power all its own beyond what he could understand. It didn't make sense to his logical mind. It wasn't practical or sensible or productive. It wasn't necessary to sustain his body, but he knew he would die without her.

"I know it's hard to understand," he murmured as he gently stroked her hair, "and sometimes I don't understand it myself, but what I did, marrying you and bringing you here, I did because I believed it was the right thing to do." Stephen brought his head close to hers and felt her soft hair brush against his cheek. He closed his eyes and let the warmth rush over him. His arms ached to consume her, to hold her tightly and feel her yield to his embrace. He could feel her weeping stop and her head move from his cheek, her warm breath rising up, touching his face. Without conscious thought his head turned toward the warmth, his lips grazed her cheek, then pressed against her mouth....

Instantly his cheek burned, and he stumbled backward.

"No!" Catherine yelled as she brought her sleeve to her mouth and wiped the feeling of him away. "You touched me once when I was out of my mind with sorrow for my dead brother. I cannot allow you to touch me again when my heart belongs to Gaston. It won't be long, and my father will send word that we can go back to France. Then we can end this charade."

Catherine pulled her shoulders back and tipped her head upward. "In spite of how I appear to you now, I have grown strong inside over the past months. Surviving that ocean voyage has shown me that I can survive almost anything. I am even stronger this minute than I was the last. See, Stephen, I am no longer crying before you, and I chide myself for having done so at all. You know that I will only love Gaston, not you. Look at yourself," she said in disgust, placing her hands on her hips. "You have to steal a wife! You have to take what is not yours! I know Gaston will come for me. He will find me. And when he does, I hope he puts you in the ground. Then you can rot and see if anyone cries for you!"

Stephen's heart stopped beating for what seemed an eternity. He did not move. He did not breathe. He watched her look at him with fear and hate in her eyes. The pain of it went deep within his chest and twisted his insides into tortured knots. Suddenly, his lungs took in a breath and his heart crashed back into beat, shaking his body. He turned and walked out the door, shutting it firmly behind him.

7

〜

S livers of light penetrated the thick forest, casting random pools of brightness where Stephen lay. He breathed in slowly and with great effort, working the heavy air into his aching lungs. A mist had risen from the damp forest floor, draping nature in an eerie shroud and soaking deep into his bones. His mind acknowledged his aching before he had even left his sleep. The cue of morning light began the birds on their haunting melody that echoed through the trees, making the intervals of silence much more noticeable.

Stephen opened his eyes and lay still for a moment, letting the strangeness of his surroundings remind him where he was. "The woods," he whispered as he took another labored breath and propped himself on one elbow.

The sunlight that had streaked across his face began to flicker, as if an object was being passed through it. Back and forth the shadow moved. There was no breeze to explain it away. The air was still and suffocating.

"Who is there?" he called. No one answered.

Stephen slowly stood, shielding his eyes from the sunlight with his hand. "Who is there?" he asked again. Still, no one answered. There were no footsteps, no breathing, no sound other than the haunting bird song. He moved cautiously toward the object that was passing through the light. A few steps closer and Stephen was overcome with sickening horror. The body of a man hung from a tree branch, his head tilting unnaturally to the side.

Stephen desperately wanted to run but continued his slow pace toward the body. The man's face was turned away from him, but there was something about the cut of the clothes, the color of the hair, the largeness of the hands…something familiar. He slowly extended his hand toward the body, every muscle ready to retract in a second. He took hold of a pant leg to turn the body so he could see its face.

"Oh, God! No!" Stephen screamed. He turned and ran several paces, then fell headlong to the musty ground. "No…no! It can't be. I am here. I am alive." He turned and looked at the body again. It had Stephen's face, his form, his hands. Stephen turned away again and frantically scrambled to his knees, folding his hands together so tightly his knuckles pressed white against the skin. "Let this not be. Release me from this hell. Oh, my God, my God, answer me!" he sobbed. "You can't answer me. You cannot even hear me. My sins have done this!" Stephen buried his face in his arm and moaned, slamming his fist into the ground.

"I must take the body down," he mumbled into his sleeve. "Yes, I'll take it down and bury it. No one else will see it…."

Stephen slowly raised his head. The morning light no longer flickered in his eyes but poured into the little clearing in a steady beam. The ground was dry except for little

278

droplets of dew that stubbornly clung to the occasional tufts of grass. He looked at the tree where his likeness had hung. The man was gone.

"A dream," he whispered. "It was all a dream."

He lay back on the grass and put his hands to his eyes, pressing hard to block out the images that had been there. For a brief moment he felt relief. Upon his next breath he felt anger. "God in heaven, why do you plague me so? I am tortured in the day by what haunts me in the night. It should not be! Surely, you have the power to release me from this hell, but you continually choose to leave me here. I fear you have forgotten me or simply do not care at all." Stephen clenched his fist at the sky. "I am cursed of God!" he shouted, then wept, then lay still as an icy chill washed over him. "There...I have said it. It is hopeless now."

It was a short walk back to the little house, but it left him so breathless and weak that he fell against the rough wood door, regaining his balance just as Catherine opened it.

"Where were you?" Catherine asked as Stephen brushed past her into the house. "I was worried."

"I spent the night in the woods not far from here. I simply came to get my musket and do some hunting," he replied in a controlled monotone.

"About last night," she continued. "I didn't intend for you to take up sleeping in the woods. Everyone says you always have to be careful of the Iroquois."

Stephen picked up the gun and headed toward the door.

"Stephen, would you say something?"

"Later," he said as he closed the door. His large steps took him quickly down the path and into the woods. He had no intention of actively pursuing any object of a hunt but moved his eyes amongst the trees in case an animal should happen to present itself. He felt some sort of honesty with the compromise. It struck him as humorous that he should be concerned with keeping a small truth when he spent so much energy deceiving others about so much.

The sun ate up any dew that remained along the pathway in the woods and blazed where it could through the tree branches. Stephen felt stronger as he walked through the dappled sunshine. He fixed his mind on the effort, listening to the crunch of leaves and twigs under his feet, feeling his legs lift and step, seeing the color of the leaves as they were touched by light, of feeling the warmth of it. The tightness around his chest and neck loosened as his mind became proficient at the game. For a time he felt that he did not exist outside of what he could see, touch, hear, and smell. He had no thought or emotion. He was void. There was a peace in that. It was not a happy peace. It was not a reflective peace. It was somber and grave and dull...but it was peace.

The pathway led him easily through the woods and onto a clearing by the cliff that ran alongside the St. Lawrence. He squinted as the sun poured unhindered on the water, making it impossible to look directly at it until his eyes adjusted to the light.

279

"Greetings, Stephen," came a voice a short distance off.

A group of black robes approached on the trail to the east, each man panting in varying degrees from the trek up the moderate incline.

"Father Jacques, is that you?"

"Yes." Father Jacques appeared from behind the group. "Good morning." He nodded to his fellow priests, and they continued on the trail without him.

"Out for the hunt, I see." He eyed Stephen's musket.

"Yes, Jacques, but I'm not sure of the trails, and I ended up here."

"It is a beautiful view." Jacques sighed as he looked out over the waterway. "I am grateful to be standing here on solid ground and not on that ship. It will be a long while before I could ever set foot on another one. I don't know how those sailors do it year after year."

Stephen silently agreed that he would never be back on that ship. "I'm glad you happened by, Jacques," he heard himself say. Once again, the humble priest's mere presence stirred something inside Stephen. "I need to talk to you."

"You look troubled. Is Catherine all right?"

Stephen swallowed hard. "She is well. Her strength is coming back quickly."

"Oh," replied Jacques. "What is wrong, then?"

"It is about the dreams…" Stephen's head spun again at the image of himself hanging from the tree.

"Sit down." Jacques took Stephen's arm and led him to a large rock by the cliff. "Tell me about the dreams. They haven't gone away, have they?"

"I must confess to you that the dreams are not occasional, and they are not because of sea rations or sea sickness or any other excuse I have offered. I have been plagued most every night by these terrors." His words poured out, and he did not care to stop them. The dull, solemn peace he had as he walked was gone, and the hideous feelings returned. Fear overwhelmed him, making him speak as if he were gasping for air.

"Last night I saw myself hanging from a tree. Someone had hung me by the neck, and I was dead. Someone is always trying to kill me in these dreams. Every night I am being executed. I called out to God, but He did not answer me. Jacques, it is as if I visit hell every night. On the ship I tried to stay awake, but I could not. I would fall asleep and dream. I am never free from them." The horror of the memories swirled within his throat, nearly choking him.

"Why is God afflicting me so? Surely, He is trying to render me mad. He wants me as insane as the nightmares to which I am chained. Sometimes, before I go to sleep, I fear that I will be hopelessly lost in one of them. Trapped forever. That shall be my hell. Never dying, never waking. Merely existing in agony." He trembled, fearing that he already sounded mad.

"Stephen, I had no idea you were under such torment." Jacques's face was wrapped in regret. "When did these dreams start?"

Stephen hesitated. "When I left France."

"What happened that would cause this? Was it marrying Catherine in haste? Why has your conscience pursued you to such a degree?"

Stephen stood and paced back and forth. "Perhaps it was marrying Catherine so quickly." He felt himself pull back, as if some power within had sucked all emotion and openness into a door and shut it tight. He stopped pacing and looked back at the river. "I really can't say…uh, I don't know. Jacques, I am sorry once again. I have made myself to appear quite unstable. I really don't know what comes over me."

"Don't do this. Don't pull back. Tell me what really plagues you. What happened in France?"

Stephen swiveled toward Jacques. "No. Don't *you* do this," Stephen said with surprising force. "Trust that I will tell you what I need to tell you, no more."

"Then what can I do for you? You give me a little piece here and there. Am I to put it all together and make some sense of it? You have come to me for help, and I want to help you, but tell me how?"

"Ask God to release me from this torment. He will listen to you."

"Stephen, He will also listen to you."

"Do you not understand even yet? I have called to Him, and He doesn't hear me. My sins are so great that He cannot hear."

"What sins? Tell me," Jacques pleaded.

"Will you help me?" Stephen stepped backward, taking himself out of confidential proximity. "Will you pray to God on my behalf?"

"I believe there is something deeper that you are not telling me. It may be that this matter is something God will rectify only after you have done your part."

"And what may that part be?"

"Confession."

"Then I am doomed." Stephen turned toward the river and crossed his arms. "Good day, Father Jacques."

"I'm not refusing to help you. God is not either. Do you understand that?"

"Yes, I understand. The remedy for my torment begins with me," he answered once again in dry monotone. "I hold nothing against you. Good day, Jacques."

Stephen continued to stare at the St. Lawrence as Jacques left to join the other priests. The glare of the sun on the water was nearly blinding, leaving vacant spots of light in his vision. The possibility of falling over the edge of the cliff crossed his mind. Instead of moving back from the edge, he toyed with the idea. Would it be so awful to deliberately throw oneself down the long stretch of earth? To find peace, at last, in death?

No, he knew it would only offer a speedy plunge into the very horrors he so desperately wanted to be free from.

8

The young buck fell with one shot, and Stephen instinctively let out an excited whoop. He scrambled over the thick brush and fallen tree to reach the deer. "Good shot," he rewarded himself. "Right in the neck." He unsheathed the hunting knife he had found in the little house and drew his arm back. Then, with full force coming from his shoulder, he drove the knife through the tough skin just under the rib cage. With a sawing motion he split the buck's belly open and let the contents spill onto the ground. The smell made Stephen back up and turn his head.

He worked to clean the inside of the deer. When the job was done, he removed his outer shirt and wiped his arms and hands as best he could. He then took the shirt and tied it securely around the buck's small rack and proceeded to drag it toward the path that led to the little house.

The smell of fresh blood was nauseating as it wafted up in the heat of the open carcass. It dried quickly on his forearms; yet, where it pooled between his fingers, it glistened deep red. He couldn't look away from his hands. The sticky sensation of the deer's blood caused his insides to tighten. His arms and back ached from dragging the deer's weight, but he continued to move quickly toward the clearing.

Catherine and Madame LaPointe were standing by the garden when Stephen finally reached the yard. His undershirt was stuck to his body from sweat and deer blood, and his hair was equally drenched from the hideous effort.

"Greetings, Madame LaPointe," he called after catching his breath.

"Stephen, what a fine hunter you are!" she replied. "You have done well. You have been here little more than two days, and you are already out for the hunt. Most people are worth nothing for weeks because of sea legs."

"Please, you give me too much credit. This poor young buck practically offered himself to me. I almost tripped over him."

Madame LaPointe laughed, and her whole rounded body jiggled in response. "You are modest, too. Catherine must be very proud of you."

"Oh, yes, of course." Catherine walked around Stephen to look at the deer.

"What?" he asked, surprised at her friendly tone.

Catherine came close to Stephen with her back to Madame LaPointe. "Now, there you are, being modest again." She squinted and tipped her head.

"Oh," he said, deciphering her look. He would play along.

"Your wife tells me you have not eaten yet this day, and it is past noon. If we are to keep such capable young men as yourself, we must feed them." Madame LaPointe laughed. "You hang up that deer, and we will find you something to eat."

"I will be with you in a moment," Catherine called to Madame LaPointe as the woman walked toward the house. "I'm just going to get some water so Stephen can wash." She went to the well by the garden and drew up a bucket of water while Stephen tied a rope around the deer's neck and hung it from a sturdy limb. A piece of his nightmare flashed through his mind as he tied off the rope.

"You look awful." Catherine poured some of the water into a wooden basin placed on a tree stump. "And you smell. Where did you have to go to get this deer?"

"What are you doing?" he asked in a low tone as he dipped his hands into the basin. "What kind of game are you playing?"

"I have been thinking about us...our situation...and I think it would be best if people here think we are happily married. I don't want anyone giving us advice or sympathy or being busy where they don't belong. If we are hiding here, waiting to return to France, then I think pretending everything is as it should be would be wise."

"Everyone on the ship knows we aren't happily married. You wept most of the journey, and we showed little affection to each other."

"I am sure we are not on their minds," said Catherine. "They are all probably consumed with surviving in this horrible place. I am referring to the people who have lived here and have nothing better to do than meddle in other people's lives."

"That is a very negative assessment of the people here. You don't even know them, except for Madame LaPointe, and she is very kind." He watched the water in the bowl turn red. "Get me fresh water...and that scrub brush over there."

Catherine emptied the bloody water from the basin and poured in clear. "Here is some soap, too." She pulled a small hunk from her apron pocket and handed it to him along with the worn scrub brush. "It seems that poor Pierre did clean up on occasion."

"Can't you even speak kindly of the dead?" He did not look up from his hands.

"I was speaking kindly. Now, is it agreed that we behave as if everything is well when people are around?"

"It is agreed. Whatever you want. Get me some more water."

"Your hands look clean. Take that bloody shirt off, and you'll be fine."

"I'll take my shirt off. You just get me more water. This blood is dried on. I need to scrub more."

Catherine refilled the basin and Stephen continued to scrub.

"What is wrong?" Catherine asked. "Are your eyes failing you? Look at your hands. There's no blood."

Stephen rubbed more soap on his hands and arms and scrubbed again with the brush. He knew how hard it was to remove blood. He remembered the night in France when he had scrubbed his hands. He remembered how the blood had soaked his shirt, sticky and red. He scrubbed that night, too. Hard. The blood would not wash off.

"Stephen," said Catherine as she pulled his hands from the basin, "the only blood in the bowl is yours. Look!" She held his hands to his face. They were scrubbed raw.

"Your meal is ready," called Madame LaPointe from the doorway. "Come now, you must be starving."

"Yes, I am," he called back to her.

Catherine offered him her apron to dry his hands on and looked intently at him. "Stephen, are you ill? Did something happen?"

"My food is waiting." He stalked toward the house.

Stephen ate the meal ravenously, grunting and nodding to Madame LaPointe's talk of preparing for winter. It seemed a long way off to him, but she assured him that gathering time was short, and winter was long in Quebec.

As he was finishing his meal, Monsieur LaPointe and two of his sons rolled a small wooden cart up the path and stopped outside the door. Each one of the LaPointe men picked up a haggard chair from the cart to carry it inside. Just one of the burly sons could have carried all three chairs, but they split the labor. Monsieur LaPointe seemed to have the most difficulty, his squinty gray eyes showing just above the back rail and not much more than half his shin showing beneath its legs. He walked with a step and shuffle, his right foot not completely making it off the floor.

The two sons waited for their father to enter the house and followed him in, each nodding their greeting to Stephen.

"You have found the chairs." Madame LaPointe gestured happily. "I knew we hadn't burned them. They are not very pretty, but they sit well."

Catherine smiled. "They will do fine. Thank you."

"Stephen," Madame LaPointe continued, "you remember my sons and my husband, but I do not think they have had the pleasure of meeting Catherine."

"No, we have not met," said Catherine.

"I am Monsieur LaPointe." The old gentleman bowed his already stooped frame.

"And I am Louis." The tall, sandy haired young man was rugged, handsome, and uncannily resembled his mother in looks and personality. "This is my little brother, Lucas."

Lucas, slightly darker and smaller than Louis but with his same rugged looks, gave Catherine a polite bow.

"It is so good to meet you," Catherine replied. "You have all been so helpful to us. I don't know how to repay you."

"Having you and Stephen settle in Quebec is payment enough." Madame LaPointe again commandeered the conversation. "It gives me hope for this land. You are a reminder our work has not been in vain, that there are others in France who believe in Quebec. When your children are born here, they will be true products of Quebec."

"Now that we have chairs, please, won't you all sit for a moment or two?" Stephen held a chair for Madame LaPointe and then Catherine. "Madame was instructing me on providing for the winter months. Contrary to my actions today, I am not much of a hunter." He rubbed his raw hands. "I would think if one had a net, he could fare well with fish from the St. Lawrence. Yet I saw very few men on the river."

"You won't see many there in the future, either," Louis muttered. "Lauson owns the river."

"He does not own it, Louis," the elder LaPointe corrected. "We must not be passing on false information."

"I would say that owning all the fishing rights to the river is the next best thing. Let me explain." Louis leaned forward with his elbows on the table to denote the seriousness of the following news. "The Company of the Hundred Associates is the fur-trade monopoly in all of New France. I am sure you know that having traveled such a great distance with some of the associates. In order to keep the monopoly, it was bound to send four thousand colonists here before 1643. Four thousand!" He laughed. "It is quite obvious to anyone that they failed miserably. We cannot have more than 200 French souls in all of New France. You see, if the company brought in that many settlers it would ruin their business. Land would be used for farming; the animals, along with their hides, would move further inland; and it would be virtually impossible for them to enforce their monopoly.

"So what they did was grant tracts of land to several individuals under the condition that *they* would bring out settlers to work the land. They knew it was too expensive a proposition for most of the grantees to bring people here. By some conniving, Lauson, who is the son of a former Company president, acquired a large tract of land south of the St. Lawrence, including most of the islands and all the fishing rights in the river. He has not brought in one settler."

"What about the rivers that flow into the St. Lawrence?" asked Stephen. "It may not be convenient, but I would think they could supply you with plenty of fish."

"The inconvenience is great, indeed, when you consider losing your scalp for a few pounds of fish," Louis replied. "The Iroquois are all over the riverways and woodlands. One cannot venture far without thinking. You must always be ready for an attack, and that is best done by staying at home."

"It appears that this town is destined to fail," said Catherine.

"That is contrary to the truth." Monsieur LaPointe's serious face tilted slightly upward in indignation. "The hardship Quebec has faced and shall continue to face is solid proof that she is to stay. Whatever assails itself upon this town has never taken hold. Disease, dishonest men, the English, or the Indians have not been able to stop this city. You can be assured, Catherine, that this town will become the home of many, and they shall claim it with pride." He gazed at her sternly for a minute, then looked away, releasing her from the reprimand.

"But for the task before us now," said Louis, breaking the silence with a light-hearted tone, "you will need some help putting up the meat and repairing the house. I am sure you are unaware of how this roof above us leaks. Pierre was going to fix it, but..." Louis shrugged.

"Thank you for the offer, but I am sure I will be able to take care of these things alone. I have put up meat a few times before and—"

"Stephen," Louis interrupted, "you have just spent three months on a boat. If you don't rest, you will be worthless. Then think of all the work you will be to us." Louis laughed.

Lucas shook his head and blushed.

"We will be by tomorrow to take care of these things, unless you still refuse our assistance."

"How can I refuse your help under these circumstances?"

After a bit of trivial conversation, led mostly by Madame LaPointe and Louis, the LaPointes left the little house. Stephen stood in the doorway and watched the family disappear with their empty cart down the path. Suddenly he was tired. He tilted his face toward the sun, which was still high but starting to move slowly to the west. The warmth felt good. His muscles started to loosen, reserving just enough tension to keep him standing. *Yes,* he thought, *it has been a long journey. Too many hours with nothing to do but stare at the horizon and hope to see land. Too many sleepless nights. Too many dreams.*

"Stephen." Catherine's urgent voice broke into his moment of quiet. "Did you hear what those people were saying? No fishing, dangerous hunting, long, cold, winters, and those Iroquois! Don't you see? This town is without any hope. This awful shack is ready to fall around us, too. We need to leave on the next boat heading back to France. There is no other way. You see that, don't you?"

"The next boat back to France is yours, Catherine," he said, still standing in the doorway with his back to her. "But don't think you have won some great battle with me, my dear wife. The next boat back to France won't be here till next spring."

Catherine wailed and threw herself on the cot, cursing him between sobs until she drifted off to sleep. Stephen drew the blanket up over her shoulders, being careful not to wake her. He took the other blanket and laid it on the floor. He was too weary now to even remove his shoes.

9

It was not the season for rest. The sun shook everyone out of bed earlier each morning as midsummer quickly approached. Once one was up, the business of the day would begin. Much work was needed to make the little house more livable, and the garden demanded a great deal of attention.

After hesitating and complaining, Catherine finally resigned herself to working in the dirt and weeds. She was surprised to find some enjoyment in the task. She likened it to the fine ladies of France strolling among the flower gardens with their baskets, carefully snipping at the stems to collect colorful bouquets, and being admired for their civilized earthiness.

Her own venture into earthiness was not so civilized, but on occasion, Stephen would stand by the garden while she worked and compliment her efforts. She did her best to obviously ignore him and give the impression that she detested the job. It was her act of rebellion. No one suffered by it, though, and when Catherine was in the garden alone, there was peace.

Being in the garden also gave her time alone to dream of Gaston. She imagined him striding valiantly up their path, bursting through the door and declaring to Stephen his intentions to take her back to France. Stephen would have no choice but to let her go. He would see how much Gaston loved her and would do anything for her. At times her imagination continued on to a fight to the death between Gaston and Stephen. Of course, Gaston would win.

But even with the dreams of Gaston saving her, she was bothered with the continued pain of her brother's death. Many times she told herself she had mourned long enough, and that nothing anyone could do would bring him back. She had recovered from the loss of her mother quickly, her father told her that, but mourning for her brother seemed to be endless. She couldn't understand the mysterious circumstances surrounding his death. How did he come in contact with the killer? Why was he attacked so viciously? Everyone liked him. He had no enemies that she knew about. He was fun-loving and carefree. He was so young. She tried to put the questions away and dismiss the whole affair as a random act of cruelty by some heartless beast, but she could not get the pain of it to subside.

Stephen chose to ignore Catherine's moodiness, assuming anything he could say or do would only irritate her. He had plenty to do to keep busy as long as there was daylight. The roof on the little house leaked so fiercely the majority of it had to be replaced. Even with Louis's help, the repairs were so extensive he wished he would have just built a new house. The results of the labor would have been more rewarding.

No matter what task he was faced with, his mind was on Quebec. Governor Montmagny had excavated the city streets, but they remained vacant-looking, like a skeleton of what is to be. Stephen pictured the streets paved with cobblestones and lined with buildings, flat stone walks leading to the houses, shops built of gray block, and steep, red roofs standing like sturdy soldiers with crimson plumes. He envisioned mansions with great brick walls and dazzling gardens, churches with far-reaching spires that could be seen for miles, and, perhaps in the center of it all, a palace keeping a watchful eye over its city.

He was ready to put himself to the task of building Quebec and his visions of what it could be spurned him on. Monsieur Fonte kept in contact with him, sending messages inquiring when he would be able to begin. He sent word back that he would assist with the hospital the day after next Sabbath. Catherine complained that she was still too weary to go to mass, but Stephen insisted.

The bargain with the Jesuits was that they would attend mass each Sabbath, and they had already missed several. It was time they kept their end of the deal. Curiosity was Stephen's major motivator, though. Yes, he would hold to his agreements, whether spoken or in writing, but he wanted to hear what the priests would have to say in such primitive surroundings. Mostly, he hoped his mere presence in the chapel would drive the nightmares out of his soul. The work and plans of building Quebec helped relieve the constant nagging of them, but any quiet moment would bring the dreams to life.

Sabbath day dawned, and after performing a few necessary chores, Stephen and Catherine readied themselves for the chapel service. Stephen was clean, shaved, and dressed within moments as Catherine moved slowly about the little house, lazily digging in the one trunk she had brought from France. Stephen was irritated at her slowness, sure that it was meant solely to aggravate him. Not to give her the benefit, he waited outside without saying a word.

Catherine readied herself behind the makeshift partition Stephen had made for her by her cot. She was uneasy baring herself even if Stephen was not in the house. She wanted to keep as much distance as she could between her nakedness and anyone else. There was no one who would be her protector in this strange new place…no one who really knew her heart and her fears. She had to protect herself until the day she would return to France.

Catherine made one last complaint about going to the chapel as she appeared from the little house. She looked more radiant than Stephen ever remembered. It made him furious. He had managed to feel nothing more than irritation and guilt about her for weeks, seeing her so mournful and angry. Now he had to wrestle with other feelings, seeing her in beautiful fabrics and ribbons, her hair brushed to its most silky sheen and fastened with pearls. He longed for her to smile at him.

"If we must go, then let us be on our way," she said as she brushed past.

Jacques greeted them at the door of the makeshift chapel. The fort was used for mass ever since the chapel had been destroyed by fire. The plan was to rebuild, but there were other priorities.

"How good to see you again," said Jacques. "I am afraid we have all been too busy to visit since our arrival. We will have to make an effort at it. I miss your company, my friend." Jacques looked at Stephen with a questioning look.

Stephen smiled and nodded back an all-is-well. "And I miss your company, Father Jacques."

"Catherine, you look more beautiful than words can describe. Obviously you are completely recovered from your fever. No one ill has such a glow."

"I am doing well. My strength has returned. With all the fieldwork I have been doing lately, I think I may be stronger than I have ever been," she replied, suddenly blushing and guiltily glancing at Stephen. "Thank you for your concern. Are you performing mass today?"

"Oh, no. I will be listening to Father Vinmont with the rest of you."

"I hope someday to hear you, Father Jacques," she said.

"And I hope to please you by doing so…someday."

Catherine took Stephen's arm to keep up appearances, and they entered the building. Ten benches were lined up, five on each side, with an aisle down the center. They were plain and hard and had no back to them. At the front of the room was a taller bench on which sat candles, an ornate cup, and a large book of Scriptures with a tapestry marker hanging from between the pages. They chose the bench closest to the door and sat down. Stephen moved over slightly so he would not touch Catherine. Even the possibility of doing so was a distraction.

Father Vinmont entered the room and the soft chatter ceased. He walked up the aisle to the taller bench and faced the people. He smiled and welcomed everyone, then read from the book of Scriptures. When he was done with the passage, he closed the book and began telling how Jesus came to save their souls.

Stephen leaned forward to focus on the Father's words.

Father Vinmont continued to speak, despite varying degrees of attention from his audience. Stephen, unused to the whole concept of preaching, struggled to focus on what was being said. The Father would say something that sent Stephen on a whole new trail of thought. By the time he brought himself around, he had missed much of what else was preached. What he did hear fascinated him and caused him to want to hear more.

Catherine fidgeted on the hard bench, uninterested in anything the Father had to say. She scanned the room and made a mental note of the parishioners. All were scrubbed clean and had on their best clothes. She could tell some of the men were uncomfortable, tugging with their finger at their buttoned collars and self-consciously patting their combed and parted hair.

The wives of the employees of the fur-trade monopoly were the best dressed, wearing black and muted colors of fine fabrics, their hair adorned with clips and broaches. Catherine put her hand up to her own hair, feeling the pearl combs that held her hair in place. Her father had given them to her when she was twelve years old. They had been her mother's. She pulled her shoulders back and held her head up a little higher.

Then she noticed Madame LaPointe sitting on the bench closest to the front. Her husband and sons sat with her. The gentle woman glowed. It was the look on her face, a gentle smile that displayed how much she loved being there, loved her family, loved the words she was hearing, that intrigued Catherine. She softened her posture and smiled.

As Father Vinmont was closing the service, two soldiers standing in the back of the room exchanged a few muffled words, then quickly left. Stephen turned to see what the commotion was when he heard the sound. At first it sounded like a bleating animal from a distance. As it came closer, everyone in the room turned toward the distinct sound of a woman screaming in horror. A collective gasp filled the room.

Stephen and several men ran out of the building to aid in whatever way they could. They weren't sure why the woman was screaming, but each one suspected the worst…Iroquois. They followed a group of soldiers as they went out beyond the west wall that surrounded the fort and headed toward the scream.

A woman was running toward them through the long, open field, arms swinging with an air of hysteria. Her face was red, and her eyes were wide with fear. "They killed him! They killed him! They killed my husband!" she screamed, pointing behind her to a cluster of woods.

"Iroquois," said a soldier flatly. "Are they still there?" he asked the woman, but she could not answer, being totally given over to sobbing.

"Head out!" he called to the others. The soldiers immediately obeyed the command and, with muskets in hand, moved toward the cluster of trees that surrounded the woman's farm. Stephen felt compelled to follow them, not knowing what gruesome sight he might come upon. Curiosity propelled his feet forward.

It was a few minutes' run before they reached the farm. The soldiers slowed their pace and held up their muskets, ready to fire. Stephen felt foolish for being there unarmed and quickly moved next to one of the soldiers. The air was still, and all was quiet, except for a few farm animals that mooed and clucked in upset. It didn't matter that it was quiet. The Iroquois often struck without making a sound. Stephen shuddered. This was a modest farm, with a few animals, a well, and some sheds. Freshly washed clothes lay in a basket, waiting to be hung over a line to dry. Boards were in the process of being nailed together to make a trough. The hammer lay some feet away, hurriedly discarded.

The soldier in charge assessed the area, determined that the Indians had gone, and ordered the group to spread out and look for the woman's husband. Stephen's eyes shifted rapidly between the ground in front of him and the grove of trees that bordered the area on three sides. His ears listened intently for a rush of feet, a war whoop, or a single crunch of grain under a moccasin. With chilling uneasiness he felt that *he* was the invader, walking dangerously on a nation's primitive ground.

"Over here! He's over here!"

Stephen's heart beat hard as his feet carried him slowly toward the soldier and his hideous find. He needed to look and see how gruesome life in Quebec could be.

The man was lying face down, arms spread out and one leg bent as if he died running. A tomahawk pinned him to the ground, nearly splitting his skull in two and leaving him in a pool of blood. Stephen's stomach lurched at the sight.

"Get a blanket from the house and wrap him up," said the soldier in charge to one of his subordinates. "It looks like the bloody savages have declared war on us, men. I expect there will be more attacks...and bloodier ones." He looked down again at the corpse. "I see there are definite benefits to being in church on the Sabbath. Poor fool." With that, the soldier led the group back to the fort.

The churchgoers had emptied into the yard to hear of the latest attack and try to comfort the new widow, who would not be comforted. Stephen shook his head at what horrors the woman had seen. It would be a long time before the woman could receive any comfort. He wondered if she had any grown children to help her take care of her farm and to prepare for the winter. Would she have to leave her farm? Would she leave

Quebec? He looked at the woman again with increased pity. Her life would be changed forever.

"Stephen, did you see her husband?" Catherine touched his arm to gain his attention.

Stephen nodded and put his arm around her to comfort himself. She did not pull away. They stood and watched the people move about and talk to each other with renewed urgency and horror, giving opinions on what should be done about the problem. They hoped whatever the governor decided to do would be done quickly and efficiently.

One thin, frail-looking Jesuit speaking with Father Vinmont said the Jesuits must go to the source of the evil. They must attempt to win the Iroquois to the cause of Christ.

A chill took Stephen upon hearing of such a plan. It would be death, indeed, for any Jesuit who would attempt such a feat. He knew Jacques would be among the first to volunteer, refusing the temptations of fear.

They walked home with the LaPointes in silence. Even the jovial Louis said nothing. The Indian attacks they hoped would diminish were becoming more commonplace. This weighed heavily on the LaPointes, for they had many years invested in Quebec and longed for a time when they would not have to fear for their lives. They were afraid of the impact the attacks would have on the new settlers. The future of Quebec depended on a steady stream of settlers coming to live, farm, and raise families there. They did not want them returning to France or sending word to others that the way of life in the new country was inhospitable and dangerous.

The rest of that day Stephen pondered the message Father Vinmont gave and how that could possibly apply to the incident with the Indians. What of the man cut down in his own field? Should he not be avenged? He certainly couldn't be saved from the slaughter. And what of himself? Was he doomed to hell? If salvation entailed complete surrender and disclosure, then getting into heaven would be impossible for many...himself included.

The stoic soldier was right in predicting the rage of the Iroquois. That very night he was killed in the same manner as the man in the field...quickly, quietly, and without a chance to fight. He would have labeled himself a "poor fool" if he had the breath. No one else thought of him in such a way, though, for they all knew it could have been them.

Father Vinmont performed the funeral service for the two men, ending the rite with a prayer for the salvation of the Iroquois. Several residents stirred, uneasy with the words of charity that invaded their meditation. Stephen was among them, lifting his head as if seeing the Father speak the words made them easier to hear. He could not help but think that the best way to deal with the Iroquois would be to eliminate them.

One of the settlers seemed to speak for the majority when, after the funeral, he exclaimed, "I say we send them to hell with our muskets!"

It was obvious that the Jesuits had the nobler attitude, and most, if not all of the rest, considered them to be too generous with their benevolence.

"I cannot understand the barbarity of man," Jacques said to Stephen as they stood beside the freshly covered graves. "It seems so impossible that one should kill at random with no consideration for that man's soul. They may have sent those two to eternal damnation. I cannot help but be hesitant with my prayers for the salvation of the Iroquois and swift with my prayers for their defeat. It is unsettling to me to have such thoughts, yet I seem to hold onto them."

"I don't know what to say to you, Jacques," Stephen said after an awkward silence. "Your view of life is so different from mine. I tend to agree with the other settlers…kill them before they kill us. You see people as countless souls looking into the jaws of heaven or hell. Despite the struggle you are having, I am sure you will act true to your faith."

"Ah, but acting and knowing that it is a part of your character are two different things. I will not be content until self-sacrifice and unconditional love are second nature to me. There are times when I think I have attained it, concerning the Indians, or at least so near as to touch it. Then I read a letter from a fellow Jesuit serving in the interior and learn of the degradation and mockery they are forced to suffer, and my self-acclaimed holiness is dashed to the ground. I end up despising those I came here to serve."

"I am not one to offer you condolences, Jacques, for I have never gone above your most sinful state. I am not one to debate theology with you, either. You know I am ignorant in the matter. Yet, I must say, it seems to me that you are setting too high a goal for yourself. If you are courageous enough to act with the highest degree of morality under any circumstances, no matter if it is from compulsion or genuine servitude, then it should be good enough."

"That is precisely where my problem lies," Jacques explained. "It is not what you do, whether good or evil, but what is in your heart. Sometimes I wonder if I truly want to serve the Indian people, or if I just act the part because of my fellow priests."

"You confuse me."

"Think of a child who accidentally breaks his mother's finest vase while washing it. Is he made evil by his act, no matter how unintentional it was? Then look at the servant who does many things for his master but secretly despises him. Does the act of obedience make him a good person?"

"Your examples are very simple compared to the complexities of life," said Stephen. "There is so much good and evil in everyone that you cannot expect any single person to be totally one or the other, including yourself."

"There is more to this, Stephen...much more than I can even put into words."

"Why are you so concerned with being good?" asked Stephen. "Why do you place guilt upon yourself for not being overzealous where the Iroquois are concerned?"

"It is something that comes from within, a desire to please God." Jacques's brows furrowed. "No, it is making myself smaller and God larger, letting him show kindness and mercy to others through me."

"I do not understand this. Every time I learn something of God it raises more questions, and they are more complex and baffling than the ones that had been answered."

"You shall never know all the answers," said Jacques. "Some things must simply be believed."

10

The sun blazed steady and strong as soon as it cleared the horizon and promised another day of summer heat. Jacques took out his handkerchief and wiped sweat from his neck and brow as he made his way up the trail from the mission toward Stephen's little house. He took off his black robe and rolled up the sleeves of his white shirt, exposing as much of his arms as he could. From outward appearances he now looked like any other man, trudging along on a hot day.

The black robe was a mysterious garment. When a man put it on, he was thought to be calm, gentle, longsuffering, wise, and part of God's inner circle. Some who wore the robe even believed that it was true. Jacques was very much aware that it was only a robe and did nothing for the man who wore it. He didn't struggle less over his purpose for being in Quebec when he had it on, and he was still as passionate for God when he took it off.

He reached the Marot house and wiped his face again before knocking on the door.

"Father Jacques, how nice of you to come by," called Catherine as she appeared from the garden, wiping the dirt from her hands onto her apron.

"Catherine, good morning." He walked toward her, admiring the garden that was full and lush. "You have done very well with this. I must say I am impressed."

"To be honest with you, Father, I am also impressed. I had no inkling I could take care of a field, much less actually enjoy doing so. But don't tell anyone I told you this, or I will be forced to deny it." She laughed. "It has been a pleasant diversion for me."

"It has been a very productive diversion, also." He smiled at her, and she blushed.

"If you've come to see Stephen, he is not here."

"Has he gone to meet with Monsieur Fonte about the hospital?"

"I don't know. He doesn't tell me where he is going." Catherine's smile disappeared, and her eyes nervously shifted to the ground before returning to Jacques. "He often leaves our house in the morning as soon as he awakens. I don't know why. It is as if he wakes up nervous and upset. Then, after he has been out…somewhere…he returns and behaves as if nothing is wrong."

Jacques closed his eyes and imperceptibly shook his head. He should have known that Stephen was still plagued by his dreams and would not tell him. Stephen was resistant to his advice of confession and did not want to hear it again. Jacques wondered for an instant how he could have believed all was well with Stephen even if he insisted that it was.

"Father, he has told you something, hasn't he?"

"We talk, Catherine, but I don't know anything that will help you. I don't know where he goes, either. Perhaps he is with Monsieur Fonte. There is much that goes into building a hospital."

"But there is something disturbing him. He has talked to you, I know that. What has he told you, Father?"

"Whatever I discuss with anyone is confidential, Catherine. I can't tell you what he has said to me…not that he has disclosed much of anything."

"Father, please listen to me. I am not asking you anything for idle curiosity. I am concerned about Stephen. I have to live here with him, and if he is not right, I need to know." Her eyes teared. "I'm sorry. This is all very hard. Even though we have been in Quebec for almost two months now, I am still longing for France. Please understand."

"Catherine," he said, taking her dirty hand into his own, "Stephen is very private. He has revealed very little to me. I wish he were more disclosing."

She frowned, pensive. "I understand, but has he said anything to you about how we came to be married?"

"He told me that soon after you were married, you left for Quebec. It was easy to observe on the ship that you were not happy but very sorrowful."

"Did he tell you why I was not happy?"

"It was because of your brother's death," he replied.

Catherine sighed and gently took her hand from Jacques. "Yes. I was sorrowful for my brother's death."

"What can I do for you, Catherine?" asked Jacques, feeling inept at deciphering her cues. Women were illogical to him, and he had learned, from failed attempts at ministry, that being direct with the opposite gender was safest.

"There is nothing you can do for me, except to watch after Stephen. He is beginning to concern me. I know we did not have an easy time aboard the ship, but he has become more aloof than I have ever known him to be. At times he is very distracted."

"The work of Quebec has that man distracted, to be sure. He is eager to build and raise a city like no other. Catherine, I am convinced that God has brought him here, to Quebec, for a mighty purpose. He has a great hunger to build. The leaders in Quebec must be very excited with his motivation."

"Yes." Catherine sighed. "I understand that even Governor Montmagny is impressed with Stephen. "But I am still…"

"Be assured, Stephen will be fine," Jacque said with a deliberate smile. "Like many young men, he is wrestling with thoughts of God, family, and the magnitude of his decision to settle in New France. Give him time, Catherine." He patted her shoulder. "Go about tending your home and your field. Think about the goodness of God. Say a prayer for Stephen. That will be your best course of action."

Catherine nodded in timid agreement. She would do as the priest suggested. She was not one to disobey without just cause. Catherine was surprised by her concern but unmotivated to curb it. In all her attempts to straighten out her mind and heart she failed. She hated Stephen and needed him at the same time. She despised Quebec and loved the freshness and productivity of her little field. She felt suspicious of the people in this strange land, yet was irresistibly drawn to the LaPointe family. She wanted to keep everything surrounding her secret, yet she wanted to tell Father Jacques the whole story. Catherine hoped that Stephen had. Then she could someday tell all to Father Jacques and be rid of the tightness that had held her heart for so long.

"Did you see which way Stephen went this morning?" Jacques asked as he turned his head to view the paths that led from the clearing.

"Yes, I did. Every morning he heads down that path into the woods." She pointed to the little trail that led east from the clearing. "I have been tempted on occasion or two to follow after him into the woods, but I fear the Indians."

"If they are Huron, you have nothing to fear. We are working closely with them, and I am finding they are rather friendly, gentle folk." Jacques peered toward the trail.

"I don't think, if I met up with an Indian, that I would take the time to ask if he were Huron or Iroquois," Catherine said with self-amusement. "Father, if you will excuse me, I must return to my chores."

"Yes, of course," he answered without looking back at her.

Jacques moved toward the path that led into the woods with an ache in his stomach for Stephen. "Where are you, my friend?" he whispered. "Lord, let me find him, for I cannot help but feel the compassion You have for him."

Jacques prayed as he followed the path. It disappeared into brush and weeds, only to appear again some feet away. He hoped it was the same path. If he were a woodsman or the Indian who had been born here, he would be able to track Stephen's footsteps with ease.

Jacques kept his eyes to the ground but saw nothing. He wondered what he would say if he did find Stephen. If pride were a virtue, Father Jacques would say that understanding men was his best quality. But Stephen was a mystery. His first inclination when he met Stephen was to let him alone and wait for him to approach first. But God would not let him forget Stephen and placed him on his heart and mind many times a day. So Jacques relinquished himself to the task of watching over him.

The trail led deeper into the woods. Just at the time Jacques was considering turning back, he saw Stephen. He was leaning against a large tree with his eyes shut and his chest heaving. Stephen looked up as Jacques made his way toward him, then quickly wiped his eyes with his sleeve.

Jacques halted. His own eyes threatened to become moist. He cleared his throat and continued to move toward him. "Stephen." He opened his mouth to say more but could not bring anything to mind that would give his friend comfort without sounding trite and patronizing. He sat on a fallen tree across from him.

"I've become quite a mess," Stephen said slowly. "I don't know what more I can do."

"The dreams?" asked Jacques.

Stephen nodded. Torment wrote itself across Stephen's face, casting a gray pallor that caused him to look older than his years. The corners of his mouth turned tightly downward, the creases deepening as he continued to speak. "Some mornings it takes all my strength not to slay myself. I fear I am going mad, Jacques. I cannot bear this much longer. Oh, God, how I want this to end."

"Can you tell me now what demon is chasing you?"

Stephen closed his eyes and leaned back into the tree. The gentleness of Jacques's voice was soothing to his ravaged soul. Just as the man had great peace, so his voice contained the same. Stephen wanted that peace more than ever, but no matter how hard his soul reached out, he could not obtain it.

Stephen sighed in resignation. "I will tell you." He turned his head and looked intently at Jacques. "Please, Jacques, do not tell anyone what I say."

"You have my word."

A dark shadow came over Stephen's eyes as he pushed away the curtain of pain. "I have committed a hideous crime." He paused and listened for a response from Jacques. Hearing nothing, he continued. "It happened back in France, but of course, that is obvious. I was a good day's journey from home, finishing a commission of work, and had sent my hired man ahead with the wagon. I lingered to settle business, so it was early evening when I plodded home alone on my horse, enjoying the night. The moon and stars were especially bright. I remember that, for I could see quite a distance.

"On the road just outside of a small village I happened upon a group of men. I could make out five of them from their silhouettes. Three were on their horses. A fat man and one who seemed familiar were standing on the ground. Though most of what they said was muffled, I heard enough to know someone was being accused of a wrongdoing.

"Not wanting to involve myself in the matter and to avoid any chance of being robbed, I led my horse across the shallow creek that ran alongside the road. A border of trees hid me from their sight, yet I could still see them.

"As I passed, I recognized one of the men…his voice, actually. It was Jean, Catherine's brother. Surely, I could not go on in case he needed defending, so I turned back across the creek. As I dismounted, I saw a glint of metal and knew someone had drawn his weapon. I drew mine.

"When I neared, I saw their faces. Jean was obviously drunk, taunting the fat man with laughter and belittling his efforts to lay hold of some money. Gaston was there. He was Jean's closest friend. That was to Jean's detriment, for anything Gaston touched was ruined. He is evil and conniving. I had warned Jean about him, and I had warned Catherine also." Stephen looked again at Jacques, wondering if he saw deeper into his statement.

Jacques lifted his head and eyebrows slightly to signal that he did.

Stephen continued, "Gaston remained mounted and was quietly letting Jean antagonize the man. Then everything seemed to happen at once. The fat man swung his knife, catching Jean's coat. Gaston dismounted and joined me in combat against the two strangers, who had also slid off their horses. I saw Jean lunge forward, slashing the fat man's arm. I got away from the man I was struggling with and rushed to help Jean. As soon as I reached him, Gaston and the other man had stumbled into us. It was chaos…arms, legs, hands flying everywhere. I was struck time and again, and I could not tell by whom.

"Then the most sickening feeling came upon me. I felt my knife enter something thick, stopping at the shaft. Blood oozef sticky and warm on my hand. Jean looked at me. He knew. He knew I had stabbed him." Stephen closed his eyes to blot out the picture. He could not keep his calm as the images forced their way through.

"I felt him go limp in my arms. I prayed that he would not die. He kept looking at me. He didn't close his eyes or say a word. Then he let out his breath and died. I laid his body on the ground and looked up. Gaston was gone. I, alone, faced the three men. They had put their weapons away. I didn't know what to do or say. I just knelt next to his body. The fat man shouted at me and accused me of murdering Jean so I could take the money for myself.

"I swear I know nothing about any money. I can only guess that it was come by illegally and that Gaston had ridden off with it."

Jacques was silent.

"I have never before killed anyone. Believe me, Jacques. I was a simple mason. I lived an honest life."

"I believe you," he said. "Is that why you are on this ship, to escape the authorities?"

"As much as I could tell, no one other than the men present knew that it was I who killed him. I quickly left the scene after the man accused me of murder, but I left Jean with my dagger in his belly. The dagger was a gift from my father. My initials are engraved on it. I suppose it is only a matter of time before Gaston points that out to the authorities. That is why I married Catherine in haste. I couldn't let her find out that I had killed her brother, and I couldn't let her continue to see Gaston. News of his death came to her shortly after the ceremony. She didn't see him or attend his funeral because I had hurried us to port to save myself. I convinced myself that the marriage was as real in heart as it was on paper and moved to consummate it as she wept for her losses. I have proven myself to be a pitiful coward."

"Not a coward," said Jacques. "If you were a coward, you would not have become involved at all. From what you tell me, Jean's life was destined to end that night."

"Perhaps, but I do not believe that I was to be his executioner. Now I am being executed almost every night in my dreams. I know I deserve as much. I've killed and lied and deceived. I have run away from just consequences. I have forced myself upon a woman who now despises me." Stephen blinked away the emotion in his eyes. "Jacques, do you have a remedy for me now?"

"You didn't intend to harm him. You are innocent for lack of malice."

"It is true I did not intend to harm him. Yet it was my dagger that took his life and my hand that put it there. I have settled that within myself. You do not need to comfort me on that account. But tell me, please, how to be delivered from these nightmares."

"Confession is the only way I know, Stephen. Confess to God and ask forgiveness, then confess to Catherine and ask forgiveness from her, also."

"Isn't confessing this to you enough? I couldn't bear to tell Catherine that I murdered her brother. I couldn't face it. I would rather die. At every turn I am faced with a nightmare. I understand that you want me to reconcile with God and those I have wronged, but that is something I am unable to do. Please, Jacques, pray to God on my behalf."

Jacques looked into Stephen's troubled eyes and was sorrowful at the condition of his soul. He knew Stephen would continue to be tormented until he came to the place of confession.

"Yes, my friend, I will pray for you."

11

The quiet discontent that had been felt throughout Quebec had become loud and demanding. Though the growing season was proving to be a profitable one, winter loomed only a few short months away, and most everyone was too afraid to venture very far to hunt. The increase in clashes with the Iroquois was wearing heavily on Quebec, and large numbers of settlers wanted to leave. Governor Montmagny tried diligently to keep the spirits of the people alive, but even he had trouble believing his own encouragement. He, more than anyone, wanted the situation resolved but had little power to do anything about it. He promised to send for more French soldiers on the next ship and to speed up construction on a wall to surround the city. This seemed to satisfy most of the settlers for the time being, but they all knew danger lurked everywhere. Each day that passed without an attack from the Iroquois was just one day closer to when they would.

Until the soldiers could be sent for, each man was responsible for the safety of his own family. Those who had large farms always had muskets at their sides whenever they were in their field. If one Indian attacked them, they had a chance of surviving. If a group of them wanted to terrorize the farmers, they would find little resistance. Those who owned stores and lived near the fort had the best advantage in the event of an attack. The soldiers were just a scream away. Even so, it only took a few seconds to die at the wrong end of a tomahawk. At least they would be less likely to be taken hostage.

There was not much Stephen could do to secure his home. He put a stronger bolt on the door and fixed bolts to the window shutters. In spite of his efforts, if anyone wanted to get inside, it wouldn't be difficult. The only other task was to teach Catherine to use the musket. If it were not such a serious matter, Stephen would have found the training humorous. Catherine was knocked backwards every time she fired. She was no match for the power of the gun. Time after time she landed on the ground. After days of practice she could load it and fire. She never hit the target, but the volley of pellets landed somewhere in the vicinity of her aim. They hoped that would be good enough.

Stephen's work of constructing a hospital was hard and tiring, but incredibly rewarding. He was finally doing what he was skilled at doing and working with people of like mind. Few had masonry or building skill, but their willingness to participate in the project was impressive. Unfortunately, the time they could spend participating was limited since all of them had to take care of themselves and their families.

Stephen felt the urgency of the project. He was fearful for his own home, which was located relatively near to the fort, but he could not imagine the fears of the nuns living in the hospital at the base of the cliff. They were vulnerable there and feared what the Iroquois would do to them if they were captured, yet they stayed on. They continued to care for the sick, mostly Huron Indians who were stricken with white man's diseases.

The summer months kept Catherine and Stephen busy with chores that never seemed to be finished. They were both glad for that, though one would not admit that to the other. Life had become a functional routine of rising early, working hard, and falling asleep early. The animosity Catherine had felt toward Stephen dissipated into tolerance. She was not a fool. She needed him for protection and sustenance until they could return to France. In a way, she knew he needed her too. It was not for the obvious womanly duties of cooking, cleaning, or even tending to their crops. Stephen could survive without help in any of these things. But there were times when Catherine saw flashes of fear and helplessness in his eyes. It had nothing to do with Iroquois, disease, or hardships of Quebec. It was more sinister and frightful. She knew he found a margin of comfort when he looked at her. He did not tell her what caused his pain in spite of her asking. She quit pursuing the answer but did not quit pondering.

Catherine now visited town more frequently with Stephen. The news of discontent tickled her ears, and she felt drawn to any negative conversation. She wanted to know that there were others who wanted to go back to France as much as she did. When she talked with some of the other settlers, she found initial agreement. When she pushed the issue, she found that even though they may be disgruntled, very few were willing to give up their stand in Quebec. They had worked hard to get there and would not give up easily. Catherine was shunned several times by a few who were deeply loyal to Quebec and verbally reprimanded by one husband who didn't want his wife any more discouraged than she already was. The social slights bothered her, but she couldn't deny the fact that she lived to leave Quebec and return to her life and love in France.

Catherine didn't bring the subject of leaving up to Stephen anymore since she had his assurance that she could leave on the next ship back to France. Most of her conversations with Stephen were about the activity in town, the LaPointes, and preparation for winter.

Catherine continued to spend most of her days in the garden. After she cleaned up her little house, she would gather her large basket, a knife, and her trusty musket and head outside. She never worked feverishly, preferring to weed and pick at her leisure. She stopped every now and then to daydream. In spite of her relaxed approach to gardening many of the vegetables were ripening and needed to be picked and put up for winter. The picking was easy, requiring little skill. Preparing it to last for months required knowledge that neither she nor Stephen had. Madame LaPointe, once again, was gracious and helpful, teaching Catherine everything she needed to know.

Madame LaPointe was fast becoming Catherine's friend. Catherine felt at ease around her and enjoyed listening to her stories about her children and her childhood. Even the stories about the early days in Quebec held her spellbound. If she could have come to Quebec under different circumstances, she may have even enjoyed those stories being her own. As it was, she listened to Madame LaPointe as if she were reading aloud from one of her books. Catherine knew that one day she would have her own litany of interesting adventures to share with her family and friends about the time she spent in New France. She hoped some of them would be pleasant. But for now her pressing task was to stay alive and heap up provision for the winter months.

Catherine was pleased with her garden. Produce abounded and needed to be harvested faster than her lackadaisical approach afforded so she set her mind to the task with fervor. She didn't want any produce to waste on the vine.

Catherine ran her hand along the small bush, catching the green beans and pulling them from their stems, being careful not to uproot the plant. The bushy rows of green had to be harvested almost daily. When her basket was full, she walked her harvest to the little house, emptied the basket into a tub, then returned to the garden, passing though her many rows of corn. The cornstalks were green and high, towering over her head as she walked between the rows. It was like a growing maze, and she imagined if she went to the left or to the right she could easily get lost. She was tempted to test her silly theory but opted to keep her eyes fixed on the beans at the end of the row.

She didn't notice the footsteps that mirrored her own until she stopped to retie her apron. She listened carefully. The steps were medium-paced, muffled, and uncertain. It was not the sound Stephen made with his heavy boots or the sound of Madame LaPointe's spry steps. Catherine's heart raced to her throat as she quickly crouched low to the ground and looked between the stalks of corn in an attempt to see the intruder. She looked toward the row of beans where she had been picking to see the musket laying where she had left it. Still crouched low, she crept toward the gun. Her heart pounded frantically. She had to get the musket before the intruder saw her.

When Catherine reached the end of the corn, she paused. She dared not go into the open in case she came face to face with an Iroquois, but she knew the musket was her only hope of survival. She listened carefully to discern which direction the steps were coming from, but the sound was distorted as it came through the rows of corn. With a deep breath she lunged forward and grabbed onto the musket, pulling it back to where she was hiding. Her hand tightened around it.

A flash of buckskin and the glint of sunlight off glossy, black hair appeared between the rows. She held perfectly still. The footsteps stopped. Then, after a moment, they began again, moving closer to where she was. She opened her mouth to scream, but her own hand reached up to cover it. She steadied herself and raised the musket to her shoulder, watching the moccasined feet approaching through the cornstalks. She dared not fire until he was a few feet away.

Her hands were sweaty on the gun. She felt her finger twitch with readiness as the intruder came closer. She could hear his breathing. He was close enough. Catherine gritted her teeth and quickly stood, head cocked, with one eye closed as she had been taught, and fired the gun. The man in buckskin crouched and sprung at her, catching her waist and knocking her to the ground.

"What are you doing?" screamed the man as he pinned her shoulders to the ground and sat on her. Catherine closed her eyes and turned her head. She didn't want to see the tomahawk speeding toward her scalp.

"What are you doing?" the man breathlessly repeated.

Catherine slowly turned her head and opened one eye and then the other. "You aren't an Indian," she said in surprise.

"I'm not? Thank you for pointing that out to me," he replied, still holding her to the ground.

"Why are you dressed like that?" she demanded. "What do you want with me? My husband will be back any time now. He always comes home about this time. Who are you?" she asked as she attempted to free herself from his grip.

"I am Eliot LaPointe." He tightened his hold. "Surely my mother has told you about me."

"Eliot LaPointe? The fur-trader?"

"Yes."

"Well, Eliot LaPointe, let me up!" she yelled. "How dare you creep around here dressed like an Indian, scaring the life out of me! You are lucky that you are not the one lying in this cornfield with a hole in your chest. Now, let me up!"

"Madame, I was not creeping around. I came walking in full view. How was I to know you find amusement by hiding in cornfields and blasting people as they walk past? I will let you up if you promise not to touch that musket…" Eliot lurched backward and met with a strong fist to the jaw.

"Catherine, are you all right?" asked Stephen with alarm and breathlessness. "Did he hurt you?" He extended his hand and helped her to her feet. "I thought he was an Indian." Stephen panted as he looked at Eliot lying still in the corn, blood from his split lip trickling down his chin. "He's a white man."

"He is Eliot LaPointe." She bent over him. "Did you have to hit him so hard?"

"Aggh," he said in disgust. "The next time I see some man in buckskin pin you to the ground I'll be sure to get his permission to hit him."

"If he had been an Indian, I would have been dead." She shuddered.

Stephen bent over and picked up Eliot in his arms. "We can at least get him out of the garden. Run up ahead and get a chair from the house. Maybe we can prop him up and make it look like we have an Iroquois over for dinner."

Stephen set him on the chair Catherine had brought from the house and patted his face to wake him.

"Whoa!" he said as he came to and blocked Stephen's hand. "Enough, enough! What hit me?"

"I did," said Stephen.

"My mother didn't tell me you folks attacked people for fun."

"Attacked?" asked Catherine. "Who attacked whom, Monsieur LaPointe?"

"From where I stood it looked like you were doing the attacking," Stephen said to Eliot as he sat on a tree stump.

"I was merely delivering baked goods from my mother. If you look in the garden, you'll probably find them." Eliot rubbed his jaw. "You have got a strong punch, Monsieur Marot."

"Please, call me Stephen. I would feel compelled to apologize for the beating if I did not feel it was deserved."

"And I would apologize for knocking down your wife if I did not feel that it was necessary to save my life. You may call me Eliot."

"Oh, look," said Catherine as she came up from the garden. "Madame LaPointe did send us baked goods." She held open the cloth that held the pulverized pastries. "Do you care for some, Eliot?"

"Ah, no, thank you."

"Stephen?"

"I will have to decline."

"When did you arrive in Quebec?" Catherine picked at the larger chunks of pastry.

"A few days ago. I was at Tadoussac some time back to trade my pelts. We must have been there at the same time. I think you were the only shipload of settlers to land this year."

"Tadoussac! What an awful place…awful people." She sat on a grassy patch of ground near Eliot and continued to pick at the pastry pieces. "Just awful!"

"Fur-traders are not what you would call the socially elite, but most are harmless…unless you've got fur for skin."

"Do you really live with those men?" she asked.

"Catherine," Stephen admonished, "perhaps Eliot would prefer to remain private with complete strangers."

"Nonsense," he replied. "My mother has told me so much about you both that I feel as if I know you well. To answer your question, I did not live with the French fur-traders. I have spent this last year with a band of Huron Indians."

Catherine gasped.

"They are very good in the woods. They were here long before we came and know this land up and down and backwards. You couldn't pick better people to spend the winter with."

"I heard rumors that the Huron didn't fare very well this past winter between lack of food and the Iroquois," said Stephen.

"The band I was with did better than most. Other Huron have not been so fortunate. I've heard that some had to eat the rawhide thongs in their snowshoes to survive. Others ended up with smallpox. Considering that, I say we did rather well."

"At least the Huron are not as barbaric as the Iroquois." Catherine shivered.

"I disagree with you on that point," Eliot said. "You must understand that all the natives of this country have lived in the same manner for centuries. They know no other way. Look how difficult it is for you to adjust to living here, and you are not trying to change your way of life. You are just trying to fit it into a new setting. The difference between the Iroquois and any other tribe is that their vengeance is on us. To be more accurate, their vengeance is on anyone who is not Iroquois. They are also more clever and more daring; thus, they are more in number."

"How could you live with such goings on?" Catherine blurted out.

"Catherine…" Stephen shook his head as a cue to stop her interrogation.

"I am not one to back down from an honest question." Eliot took a piece of pastry from the cloth and popped it in his mouth. "The Indians I was with were not too eager to attack anyone, though they did what was necessary."

"What do you mean 'necessary'?" asked Catherine.

"They defended their own people however they had to. For example, one day, about midmorning, a few months back, a small group of Iroquois ran into our camp. They were whooping and throwing spears and tomahawks. I suppose they believed they could surprise us and slaughter us all, even though we were twice in number. We were all taken by surprise. We quickly picked up our weapons and fought as best we could. Being a novice warrior, my job was to watch over the women and children. I was to blast the attackers with my musket as they came near." Eliot's face lost the animation it had carried, turning solemn and stony.

"Did you protect them?" Catherine asked.

"I was quite shaken at the events. I fumbled when I loaded my gun. A woman was running to me. A young woman. She was running toward me because I was going to protect her. Just as I reloaded my gun, a spear struck her through her back and pinned her to the ground at my feet. She raised her arms to me, but I could do nothing. I was frozen. It seemed like hours as I watched her die. I know it was only seconds. I couldn't have helped her. The guilt plagues me just the same. In the end we slaughtered our attackers."

Eliot took a deep breath and sighed. "I think I've revealed more of my life than I cared to." He stood and smiled, bringing life back into his face. "Stephen, I am here to offer my assistance if you should need anything. Mother said you were settled in, and by the looks of your homestead, I see she was right. Still, if you should need anything, just ask. I will be here in Quebec for another month; then I will go back to the vast interior," he said with a comical wave of his hand.

Stephen nodded in gratefulness. "I am impressed with your generosity. The entire LaPointe family has been more help than you know."

"My parents came here many years ago, but they still remember the very hard, early times. They have helped many new settlers, and I am convinced that they are the reason so many have stayed. Remember my offer of assistance."

"I will, thank you," said Stephen as Eliot turned down the path rubbing his jaw.

Stephen stoked the fire and watched the orange flame lick the bottom of the heavy black pot. Catherine was quiet as she prepared the evening meal, stopping every so often to stare into the distance.

"Weighty thoughts, Catherine?" He poked at the fire.

"I was thinking about Eliot. He does appear to be full of spirit, as Madame LaPointe said. I simply cannot imagine choosing to live with the Indians, whether Huron *or* Iroquois." Catherine brought a bowl full of freshly chopped vegetables to the kettle and threw them in. She stirred the contents well, then hung the ladle back on the hook. "I felt badly for him," she said as she sat on the chair by the table. "It must be awful to carry around the guilt of someone's death."

Stephen stopped poking the fire and gave complete attention to what she was saying.

"It wasn't anything he did," she continued. "He was in an impossible situation and did the best he could. He has to forgive himself."

"Do you mean that?" He winced as soon as the words were spoken.

"Of course. Do you think otherwise?"

"No. I think you are right." He rubbed his damp hands on his pants and stood. He walked over to Catherine, then back to the fire.

"Is there a problem? Did you want something?"

"No, no…just pacing." He poked at the fire again. He could scarcely believe the direction their conversation had taken. The simple fact that Eliot had come to their house that day and said what he did must have been an act of God. To have Catherine feel compassion for Eliot's circumstance and then to actually talk about it was a sure sign that the time had come to set matters straight. He didn't know whether to be relieved or to be angry. He was not prepared to disclose his secrets but afraid to let the opportunity pass. He knew Jacques had prayed for him but didn't expect this to be the answer. He set the stick down.

"Catherine, I have something very important to tell you." He continued to stare into the flames under the kettle.

"What is it?"

He closed his eyes to summon his courage, then stood and faced her. The glow from the fire lit sparkled in her eyes. The shadows in the room softened her edges. She looked like a painting—a beautiful moment caught in time. He couldn't possibly tell her what he had done. How could she understand that he was the one who killed her brother?

He sighed. "I have been making plans for a new house. I was going to surprise you with it, but I thought maybe you would find some relief, knowing you would not have to live here forever."

"When do you plan on building this house?" she asked.

"Next spring, as soon as the ground thaws."

"Oh." She moved to the kettle and stirred the contents once again, then turned toward Stephen. She was calm and steady as she looked straight into his eyes. "How will that benefit me, Stephen? If you like this house, then stay here and save yourself some work. I will be gone in the spring. Remember? I'll be on the first ship back to France. You said it yourself. I am going, and nothing will stop me. You could build a palace, and I would still go. Please don't make any plans with me in it. You have already done enough damage."

"Yes, I have done enough damage." He lowered his eyes from her stare and moved back to the fire, relieved he had not confessed.

12

Autumn came with a bracing chill and a sweep of magnificent color. The trees gave up their leaves to make a thick carpet of yellow, orange, and crimson over ground that had become dry and brown, yet the trees kept enough to create a breathtaking view throughout all of Quebec. Nature was dressed beautifully, and its perfume was a clear, brisk, icy smell. It was a refreshing, colorful time when the heat of summer had passed, and winter white had not yet grabbed hold with its frigid fingers.

Most all the harvesting had been done, and the produce put up whichever way was deemed best for its type and expected length of storage. The farms were void of any green and looked unkempt, like a lazy man with cornstalk stubble and masses of brown grass hair, cut but not yet baled. Sturdy squash lay in no set pattern, brightly colored and defiant even as the vines they grew from had browned and withered. The farmers could now slow their pace. Their shelves and cellars were full. They had beaten winter.

Just as the fields were made bare by harvesting, the town of Quebec was equally quiet and bare by the departure of its most colorful occupants, the fur-traders. Their ruckus and carousing had filled the streets with life, though not the kind of life many of the decent folks of Quebec appreciated. Even so, none of the storeowners discriminated against their money. The fur-traders spent it freely as long as they had it. They didn't have much use for it when they went inland, which was where they were all headed.

The remaining people of Quebec busied themselves with winterizing their homes and pantries. Stephen and Catherine did what they could to obtain provisions that would last the long winter. It took a great amount of planning to assure a winter without hunger or hardship, and often hardship would overrule even the best-laid plans. Some winters were harder than others to survive, depending upon the severity of the weather and the amount of meat-on-the-hoof for hunting. The shops in town had many empty shelves not long after the goods had arrived on the ships. Those who had not planned ahead would fare the worst. Stephen had to pay well over the normal price for the few items he'd overlooked, when he could convince the owners to part with them. He would have to be more careful with his planning. The amount of money he had brought from France would not last another year. He was glad he did not have to provide food and shelter for any livestock, though a mule would have made his life easier on many occasions.

The late October day started out with the sky threatening the first snow of the season, but by afternoon the old man of winter receded and the golden sun of autumn returned to warm the cheek of bundled humanity. Catherine knew these days would be few in number and that even this may be nature's last kind touch until spring. That thought alone motivated her to head down the path to the LaPointes' homestead. She didn't know what she would do once the harsh winter set in. She never had much tolerance for the cold. Certainly, she would not dare venture to the LaPointes' in the winter months, and she would desperately miss Madame LaPointe's company.

Catherine took with her a small woven sewing basket filled with thread and a circle of fabric that she had been embroidering. "Just a little something fancy," she would say when asked what it was. It wasn't anything purposeful that she was making, but it was something to keep her hands busy when she visited Madame LaPointe. The elder, in contrast, kept her hands busy with a multitude of mending, breaking from the monotony every so often to skillfully add stitches to her own version of "a little something fancy." Catherine supposed Madame LaPointe had been working on the lacy shawl for months, her other chores always being a priority.

Catherine also carried the musket. It had become part of her wardrobe, like a handbag, but bulkier and more necessary. She had not had the opportunity to fire it, except for the unfortunate incident with Eliot, and she hoped she never would. Yet she was confident she could adequately lift, aim, and fire if the need ever arose.

The Indian attacks had lessened considerably since most of the tribes had gone inland to go about their seasonal work of trapping for furs and antagonizing each other. French fur-trappers were with them, living as the Indians had for centuries, taking Indian wives and having children. Eliot remained behind the great exodus while waiting for a companion to recover from an illness. They both would then join the band of Huron with whom they had been living.

Catherine enjoyed Eliot's talks of adventure. She listened intently as he dramatically told of vicious animal attacks or creeping so close to an Iroquois camp that he could have reached out and taken one of their spears. Eliot used his whole body when he told a story—his eyes widened, and his arm flew wildly with punctuated stabs in the air. He didn't stay seated, either, jumping at an intruder or crouching low as he described how he stared down a bear. Eliot amused Catherine with his animated facial expressions and his voice that varied in tone and pitch with each word he spoke.

Madame LaPointe sometimes cringed and told him to stop. She couldn't bear to hear how close to disaster her son had come. In Eliot's absence Madame LaPointe and Catherine laughed over his probable exaggeration of events. It seemed to ease Madame's mind.

Stephen did not appreciate Eliot, making excuses to leave the few times he had stopped by. To him, Eliot was foolish and irresponsible, certainly not suitable company for Catherine. Yet, even with the unflattering opinion he had of Eliot, he could not deny the man's willingness to help. Eliot never came to their little house without offering to work. Madame LaPointe's glowing reports of her son, or his brothers' stories of when he was a child, did not ease the concerns that rose in Stephen.

What bothered him most was how Catherine spoke of Eliot. She would ask Stephen if he thought Eliot resembled Jean. "The way he moves his hands," she would say, or, "Did you hear how he said that? He sounded just like Jean." Stephen refused to acknowledge any resemblance to her dead brother and accused her of being morbid. He suggested she stay away from the LaPointes' until Eliot had left, citing him as stirring up memories of Jean. She laughed at his suggestion, visiting them as often as she could.

Long, narrow flower beds on either side of the LaPointes' stone path had, during the long, warm days of summer, greeted the visitor with fragrant patches of white, pink, and pale yellow. Now they simply waved the visitor on to the front door. Catherine rapped twice, then opened the smoothly sanded door, calling out a greeting to Madame LaPointe and any other LaPointe who may have been present.

Madame, the only one home, returned Catherine's greeting with a cup of steaming tea and an offer to sit down. Catherine chose the dark green upholstered chair positioned at a diagonal in the small but comfortable parlor. Madame LaPointe sat next to her mending basket on the sofa. It was an ornate piece with the arms and legs made of a deep rich wood. A pattern of vines and leaves had been beautifully carved into them, as well as a wood piece that ran along the top of the back. The rest of it had been made with smooth fabric in muted shades of red. Gold braiding outlined the seat and back, giving the sofa a definitely royal character. A table, a lantern, two pictures, and a rug completed the room.

"I enjoy your home so much." Catherine ran her hand over the upholstered arm of the chair. "It reminds me of my home in France. The hovel I live in now reminds me of one of the outbuildings."

Madame LaPointe laughed and picked up her mending. "Dear Catherine, you must remember I have lived here for over twenty years. I waited a long time for these nice things. You will have nice things, too, just like in France."

Catherine stood with her cup and walked around the room, running her hand over the ornately carved frames around the paintings—one of Madame LaPointe's father, who was a sea captain, and the other of her mother, a cold-looking woman who bore little resemblance to her daughter. She touched the carved wood of the sofa, the softness of its fabric, the smoothness of the brass on the lantern, the lacy roughness of the curtains. She sighed and looked out of the window. "Do you ever, even for a brief instant, want to return to France?"

"The only things in France that I long for are my daughters and their children. It matters not whether I go there or they come here. France itself does not pull on my heart any longer."

"I still miss my father and…" Catherine turned from the window. "But I have told you that before and will not bother you with it again." She returned to the green chair and took a sip from her cup. "How is Eliot's friend, the one who is ill? Has he recovered enough to join the trapping party?"

"Why did I know your change of subject would involve Eliot?" Madame LaPointe laughed.

Catherine blushed. "He reminds me so much of my brother. I imagine that is why I have such a fondness for him. If Jean were here, I think he would be doing the things Eliot does. I think they would even have become good friends." Catherine sipped again from the cup, and she frowned. "Stephen says I am morbid for thinking Eliot looks and acts like Jean." She studied Madame LaPointe's face. "Do you think I am morbid?"

"Hellooo…," interrupted a nasally sing-song voice from the front door. A second later the owner of the voice burst into the parlor. Reneé Nicollet, a tall, gangly woman in her early years of marriage but the middle years of life, had married an employee of the fur-trade monopoly right before he set sail for Quebec. He was older than she by at least a decade. Having been recently widowed, he'd quickly married her so he would not have to suffer loneliness in the land of so few women. She was a homely woman with no great potential in beauty and less in personality, though clearly she believed she had reached a measure of stature in both areas. Catherine had met her at the chapel but did not have the opportunity to socialize with her beyond a polite nod of introduction.

"Oh, Madame LaPointe, I have heard the most glorious news."

Reneé brushed past Catherine and seated herself on the vacant portion of the sofa. She nodded at Catherine, then continued in breathless excitement, "Monsieur Nicollet just told me that word has come from Tadoussac. There is a ship headed here at this very moment!"

"What?" Catherine set her cup on the little table.

"Is that tea, Madame LaPointe?" asked Reneé.

Catherine leaned toward the woman. "Please, tell us all that you have heard."

Madame LaPointe poured Reneé a cup of tea, gave it to her, and patted her knee. "Take a sip and a breath, then tell us all about your news."

Reneé took one long sip. "What I said is true. A ship is headed here, to Quebec."

"This is very late for traders," observed Madame LaPointe. "Most of them have left for the interior. I wonder what brings them?"

"Oh, Madame, does it matter?" asked Reneé. "I just hope and pray they bring decent fabric and fancies to this…community."

"Surely, there is some word as to why the ship is coming," said Madame LaPointe.

"My husband told me a man named Maison…Maisonneuve, I think it was…and a party of about forty are going to try to settle on a tongue of land to the west. If there are any goods for sale, I am sure they will drop them off here. There is nobody upriver to buy anything. It thrills me to think that my new gown might, at this very moment, be floating toward me!" She waved her hand in delight and nearly spilled her tea.

Excitement flooded through Catherine. She could not have hoped for such good fortune. Instantly she started working out the details of her escape upon the ship. To her understanding it was very late in the year for sailing, but to Catherine it was perfect timing. Her prayers had been answered, for God had sent her the ship to take her back to France, to her warm, cozy home, her friends, her father, and Gaston.

"Oh, my," said Catherine with feigned alarm, "I have forgotten some of my mending. I promised Stephen I would repair his good shirt today, and I have left it at home. I'm sorry, but I must return home and finish my tasks." She gathered her basket and musket, then turned back toward Madame LaPointe, who appeared puzzled. "Oh, I almost forgot to mention it, but Stephen asked me to find out if Eliot could come by this afternoon. It seems he needs his help with a few things. Could you please give him that message?"

"Certainly, dear," Madame LaPointe replied.

Catherine smiled at the two women and left. She couldn't keep her feet from running back to her little house. She worked out the details to her plan on the way. She would quickly pack her most necessary items in her bag. By then Eliot would arrive, and she would explain everything to him. She was sure he'd take her to Tadoussac, where she would board the ship that would return to France.

"I am going home, home, home," she sang as she haphazardly stuffed her dresses into her bag. She grabbed her pearl combs, her brush, and one of her books and put them in also. "That's it." She placed her bag by the door and looked outside. "Where are you, Eliot? I'm counting on you." She went to the food shelf and took a parcel of dried meat and fruit and squeezed it into her bag. "That should be enough for the trip. Moving with the river's current we should arrive at Tadoussac in just a few days, if not sooner." She reviewed her plan to make sure she had taken care of the details, then sat at the table with a piece of parchment, ink, and quill, and began a letter.

Stephen, she wrote, *the opportunity has arisen to sail back to France. I have taken it.* She stopped writing and put the quill pen back in the ink. "That sounds awful," she mumbled as she balled up the paper. She was surprised how little emotion she felt while writing the letter; she was more concerned for the writing style than the content.

"Eliot! What took you so long?" Catherine rushed to him as he appeared in the doorway.

"What is wrong? Is Stephen hurt?" he asked.

"No, it is I who need your help so desperately."

"What's wrong? Mother said Stephen needed my help."

"That is what I told her. I didn't want to answer any questions about why I needed you."

"It seems to me you are playing a game and haven't informed me of the rules. What is so important that you needed to bring me here under a cloak of secrecy?" he asked in his usual exaggerated manner.

"I am not playing a game, Eliot. I need your help to reach Tadoussac. There is a ship there, and I must be on it before it sets sail for France."

"You cannot be serious about this," he said incredulously.

"Please, I am sure you would have no trouble getting me there. I have my things packed. I have food, too—at least three days' worth. I am ready to go," she pleaded.

"You can't just decide one day to leave. It's not a pleasure trip; you know that."

"I have not decided this in one day. I never wanted to come here. I cannot tolerate another day of life here, knowing there is a ship waiting to take me home. I must get away from here…from Stephen. Oh, Eliot, please understand how important it is that I be on that ship to France." Tears filled her eyes. "I have to leave here."

Eliot took hold of her shoulders and looked intently at her. "Is Stephen mistreating you? Does he hurt you?"

Catherine shook her head.

"I cannot help you unless you tell me."

"He does not beat me," she said softly. "It is worse."

"Worse? What could be worse? Tell me, Catherine."

"He brought me to this horrible place against my will!" she shouted, tears running down her cheeks. "He married me when I loved someone else and made me be his wife. Do you understand? His wife! He defiled me when I loved someone else. I have to leave."

Eliot let go of Catherine's shoulders and stared at her.

"Will you take me to Tadoussac? We need to leave soon before the ship leaves. Stephen has even said I could go back to France on the next ship."

"He has? Then why aren't you begging him to take you?"

"He is not as experienced as you in this country. If he took me, we would never get there."

"Woman, you are mad. If there is a ship at Tadoussac, it will be long since sailed by the time we reach it and, dear Catherine, do you have a boat in which to get to Tadoussac? Do you have any money to pay your way? Did you forget how long it took for you to sail here?"

"Can't you find a boat? You must know someone with a canoe who would lend it to you. As for the money, I'm sure I can arrange something with the captain. My father can pay him when I arrive in France. I must leave here. Please, Eliot, you can take me to Tadoussac. It will work out."

"You make your life sound like agony. I don't understand your thinking at all. You say you have been defiled? You are not defiled; you are Stephen's wife. What did you expect him to do?" he asked in astonishment. "He does not beat you, he does not torture you, he provides for you. What is it you want from him?"

Catherine turned her back to him.

"I think you have misread me to think that I would be part of this plan of yours. I am adventurous, this is true, but I am not foolish. I see nothing in what you have told me to warrant such an irrational action. I suggest you put away this foolishness and be the best wife to Stephen that you possibly can. Maybe that is why he is so irritable," he said with a laugh. He turned her toward him and kissed her forehead. "I will always come to your assistance when I can. You know that, or you would not have called on me. Sometimes the best assistance is showing someone their error."

Catherine wiped her eyes and said nothing.

"Is there any other thing I can do for you since I am here?"

"Yes," she said. "Tell no one of this."

"I will tell no one." He kissed her forehead again and left.

Catherine kicked her bag. "Oh, what a fool I am! What was I thinking? I will never return to France. I'm trapped here with no one on my side. Gaston, oh, how I need you now. You are my only hope for rescue. Dear God, send him to me. Don't make me live without him." She started to weep her familiar tears again. She crumpled onto the cold floor and gave herself completely to sobbing.

"Catherine," whispered Stephen as he gently shook her. "Catherine, are you well? Why are you sleeping on the floor?"

Catherine sat up quickly and scanned the room. It was dark except for whatever light Stephen's lantern gave. "Oh, I just lay down by the fire and…" She looked at the cold, gray hearth. "Well, I was going to start the fire, but I didn't have any wood, and I was so tired from…from chores that I must have fallen asleep." She rubbed her eyes and, feeling their puffiness, turned her head from Stephen. "Would you start a fire, please? I will get you something to eat."

Stephen stepped outside to fetch some of the wood he had cut and stacked up against the side of the little house. He returned with his arms full of the dried logs and stacked them again neatly by the hearth. In a few moments he had a full-bodied fire lighting up the room. He extinguished his lantern and hung it on a peg by the hearth.

"I will leave a stack of wood here by the hearth whenever I am away. I'm sorry that I had overlooked that simple thing. I should have considered it, now that the days are so much shorter and cooler."

"That would be helpful." She cut open a sturdy squash and scooped out the seeds and the stringy middle.

"I'll bring in some more." He walked back to the door but stopped before reaching it. "What is this?"

Catherine turned and gasped as he picked up her bag.

"Are you going somewhere?"

"No, I'm not going anywhere." She frantically tried to think of a reason her bag would be packed and by the door. "With the weather turning cold, I thought I would pack away my cooler dresses. When I was done, I realized I had packed almost all my clothes." She wiped her hands, then took the bag from him and put it behind the cloth partition. "I don't think I'm quite ready for the long, cold winter."

Stephen examined her face for a moment before heading outside to get more wood. He stacked the wood with the rest, then used a long metal poker to adjust the burning logs in the hearth. "I came home by way of the LaPointes' today," he said as he walked to the table and sat on the chair closest to the fire. "Madame said Eliot had come here to help me as I had requested. Do you know anything about this?"

Catherine stiffened. "Oh, that." She laughed as she measured the cornmeal into the wooden bowl. She continued to prepare the cornbread with her back to him, adding water and stirring with such vigor that her voice shook. "It was all a misunderstanding. I merely said that, with winter coming, you might accept his offer of help. I don't know what you need to accomplish before the first snow. I told Eliot of the mistake when he stopped by." She spooned the lumpy mixture onto a flat stone. "He said to tell you he would be willing to help. I felt foolish that he had come over for nothing."

Catherine placed the stone on the ledge above the fire and turned back to the table. Stephen had his back to her and his head down as if looking at something. She bit her lip as her heart raced. It was the letter she had left on the table. Her mind swirled with every possible reaction. She knew he would be angry, but how angry? She waited for him to move or say something, but he continued to look at the note.

"Are we ready for winter, Stephen?" she asked to break her tension.

"What?" He turned, and she saw him slip the parchment into his pocket.

"Are we ready for winter? Will you need help with anything?"

"Ah…I believe we are," he said softly, studying her face, her eyes.

She looked to the ground nervously.

"If we are lacking in anything, I am afraid I don't know what it is," he continued. "I've never had to prepare so much on my own for winter."

Stephen went to his stack of belongings along the wall and took out several rolls of paper tied with cord, then unrolled them on the table. Without saying any more he fixed his attention on the drawings of the city and the buildings that were to be. Catherine waited for a minute more before she finished preparing the meal. Stephen consumed every morsel as she lay silently on her cot behind the cloth partition.

The walls of the tunnel were gray and damp. Beads of moisture fell frequently, stinging the open wounds on Stephen's back, lashed forty times as his arms were stretched out before him. The blood oozed thick on his raw flesh, slowing to a stop, only to be opened again by the gloved fist of a soldier. He walked along the tunnel's path to a hazy light up ahead, an orange light like a fire, but nothing burned. He knelt before the woman who was seated on an iron throne in the midst of the light. On her lap was a thick rope tied in a noose. Her hands stroked it as if it were a cat.

"What can you say to me now, Stephen Marot?" Her voice echoed through the tunnel. "Have you considered your crime?"

"I have," he said. "Jean Compeaux died by my hands."

"So be it." She stood, placing the rope around his neck, and tightened the slipknot, tighter and tighter.

He put his hands to the rope but could not get ahold of it. "Please," he choked out. "Please, grant a pardon. I did not mean to do it! Please, I did not mean for it to happen!"

"Stephen, Stephen," said the woman with the rope, "wake up, Stephen. You're dreaming." She began shaking him with the rope, pulling him back and forth.

"Forgive me," he pleaded. "Please, forgive me."

The woman let go of the rope and placed her hands on his cheeks. "I forgive you. Wake up, Stephen."

Stephen drew in a deep breath as the noose fell from his neck. The woman still held his face. Her voice was suddenly soft and comforting. She brought her face closer to his. "Stephen," she whispered.

He met her lips as she leaned close and pulled her to him in a rush of emotion....

"Stephen!" yelled Catherine as she dug her nails into his cheek and pushed him back onto the floor.

"Wha...What?" he stammered as he looked around the room. "What happened?" He shook his head and blinked hard.

"Don't you know?" she asked as she stood above him.

"No, I must've had a dream," he slurred. He put his head in his hands and moaned. "My head...it hurts." He turned onto his side and drew his arms and legs up tightly. He felt a heavy blanket being pulled over him, and a wave of warmth as the fire was stoked back into life.

13

"Did you run into a wild animal, Stephen?" Jacques pointed to his cheek.

Stephen put his hand to the deep red lines. "I think you could say that." He had forgotten about the marks as he busied himself with the construction of the chapel. With the hospital finished the men had been focusing on the chapel and were making good progress. More than the expected handful of builders arrived to assist in the labor. Some offered to help because they were overwhelmed with charity, and some were just tired of meeting in the fort. Harvest time having passed was a great asset to the project; otherwise the chapel may not have been past the first course of stone. The priests assisted when they could, and some were quite capable in construction, out-swinging and out-shoveling even the sturdiest of settlers. Jacques held a middle ground, being neither a hindrance nor an architectural genius.

Stephen took a bite from a small loaf of bread and washed it down with a swig of water from his jug, then offered it to Jacques.

"Did Catherine make those marks?" Jacques asked as he took the jug from Stephen and put it to his own mouth.

"It would be my guess."

"Don't you know?"

"Well, it was the strangest thing. I was having a dream, I know that."

"I am sorry, Stephen," said Jacques.

"This dream was not as horrible as some of them. I was dreaming that I was at the mercy of a queen, and she put a noose around my neck for murdering Jean." He instinctively put his hand to his throat as his heart quickened. He thought he could talk about the dream without a reaction, but his visceral response overrode his logic.

"It's strange how the feelings rush upon me." He wiped the sweat from his hands on his pants. "It is as if I am suddenly back in the dream, and for a moment I have no control of events. It is just for a brief second, but my fear is that one day it will be longer—that I will have no control over myself and might do something horrible."

His mind flashed to the sight of the gleaming St. Lawrence from the cliff and how close he had been to stepping off and plunging into the deep water. He wiped his hands again. "In this dream, after the queen put the noose on me, I started to beg for mercy, saying that it was an accident that Jean had died. Then, slowly, the dream started to take on a more realistic quality. It gained depth and form. When I touched the queen, she touched me back, and I felt it. The queen loosened the noose and touched my face. The she drew near and kissed me."

"Catherine?"

"It must have been. I was jolted from my sleep by a burning sensation on my cheek. I vaguely remember it. I was awake for but a moment before drifting back to sleep. Catherine didn't say anything about my cheek this morning. I did notice her looking at it, though. She must have done it while I was dreaming."

"That is most peculiar," said Jacques.

"What puzzles me most is why she scratched me. Do you think the queen in my dream was really Catherine? Not the part with the noose, but when she drew near to kiss me?"

"That is very odd," said Jacques. "I suppose it could have been her. Perhaps she woke to your mumbling and was overcome with compassion at your misery."

"I am very confused. That very night she had packed her bags and tried to convince Eliot LaPointe to take her to Tadoussac."

"Are you certain?"

"Yes." Stephen capped his water jug and donned his thick gloves. "I stopped by the LaPointes' on my way to the chapel this morning and spoke with Eliot. He was hesitant at first, but when I presented the evidence of what I knew, he confirmed it. He said he told Catherine of the folly of her plan. Then he made a point of saying that he would be there to help her whenever she needed him, as if it were a threat to me. When he said that, I wondered what Catherine had told him. I assure you, Jacques, I have conducted myself properly concerning her. Perhaps too properly."

Jacques tightened his black wool cloak around himself. "Tadoussac...that must be the settlers destined for Montreal."

"Montreal? There is nothing at Montreal."

"As was the case here at one time. We had heard that a man named Maisonneuve was planning to set up a mission there. God bless that man and those with him." He briefly closed his eyes. "What concerns me is how late in the year they are arriving. They would no sooner reach Montreal, and they would be beset with cold and snow. The wind is already laced with bitterness." He pulled his coat tighter.

"You are right," said Stephen. "And Quebec does not seem too friendly as of late. The people here are very discouraged with the struggle and the attacks by the Iroquois. If Montmagny had not sent word for more soldiers, I'm sure no one would have remained. I hear the murmuring from those who assist me with the building and, I must confess, I'm concerned, also. Do you suppose soldiers are on that boat?"

"I don't know. If they are, then it was by forethought. I am sure Montmagny's message has not yet reached France. I don't want to sound pessimistic, but I fear the people here will be less than cordial to the newcomers," said Jacques.

"I can understand it, Jacques. The harvesting and labors of the summer are over. We have all stocked what we could to survive the winter. Now a group of people arrive late in the year, too late to venture to Montreal. They will have to have a place to wait out the winter. Who will be called on to provide for them? We will. These people could not have chosen a worse time to come."

"I am sure they started their journey with zealous fervor and, perhaps, some ignorance of how long the journey would take. They aren't to be blamed. They should be admired. Montreal is a most dangerous place to settle. They will be unprotected from Indian attacks directed at them and will be promptly in the middle of Indian attacks between the tribes."

"And they are to be admired? Jacques, what purpose is there to a group of people getting slaughtered?" asked Stephen as he stirred the thick mortar.

Jacques turned in the direction of the St. Lawrence and gazed far off at the gray-blue sky. His brows were furrowed, and his mouth turned down slightly at the corners. He stood still for a moment, then slowly walked away. Stephen wondered if the priest had even heard his question.

The builders continued working on the chapel at a rapid pace, cutting block, making mortar, stacking stones and cutting posts. By midday most of the men had their coats off and sleeves pushed up, letting the cold breeze dry their sweaty skin. The chapel was near completion. It would not be as grand as Stephen had envisioned, but it would be functional and a definite improvement over their temporary meeting place in the fort.

The men responded well to Stephen's direction and quickly finished any task they were given. They had been well primed by the short summer and harvest seasons to work quickly as long as there was daylight. Weak-willed men didn't bother to come to New France. They wouldn't have survived. Camaraderie abounded with the settlers as long as each did his share, but any display of laziness brought rapid rejection. Unmerited gifts of generosity were rarely given.

The sun grazing the treetops was a sign for the day's work to end. By the time the men's tools would be collected and the area around the chapel was cleaned of debris, there would only be enough light left to find one's way home. Stephen watched closely as the tools were returned to the cart. He had been a mason long enough to know the value of his tools and did not want anyone taking liberties with his possessions. The workmen knew of his watchful eye and made sure all tools were returned. Not that they would have taken them anyway. The men respected him enough to deny any thieving impulses.

Suddenly the boom of a cannon rang out...once, twice, three times. Everyone froze and listened for a sound of alarm—an Iroquois war whoop or the scream of their victims. Stephen's heart pounded wildly as the image of the slain man in the field flashed in his mind. People at the fort and those along the cliff started to talk and shout excitedly, their exuberance eventually becoming clear to the ears of the workers. A collective sigh of relief flooded the men.

"A boat has landed! Come on!" called a young man as he ran past them.

"The day is almost done," Stephen said to the men. "Pack up your tools, and let's go greet the newcomers."

The men gathered up their tools and put them in the wagon in which the large field stones were transported, then followed the steep path that led to the shore of the St. Lawrence. Stephen waited until the last man had deposited his tools, then made a trek around the chapel, picking up stray tools and stacking rocks and lumber. After he was sure the work site was in order, he went back to the wagon and heaved the last of the tools onto it.

A second later Stephen heard an ominous *crack* as the wagon's wooden axle gave way under the weight of its contents. The back of the wagon crashed to the ground, smashing its rear wheels and sending several large stones tumbling out with force. Stephen knew he was in the wrong spot as soon as he heard the crack but failed to get more than one step away before two stones knocked him off his feet and the third large stone rolled onto his leg. Sharp pain gripped his foot and raced up his leg to his hip joint. He instinctively tried to jerk his leg free, but it did not move. The action sent his muscles into spasms. His right leg was pinned to the ground. He closed his eyes tight and cursed fluently through clenched teeth. He knew the intense pain he felt would only increase when the shock of the moment was over.

Stephen looked around for someone to help him and called out, but no one was close enough to hear over the shouts of the party at the St. Lawrence. He took it upon himself to push the stone off with his left foot, increasing the injury but freeing himself from his awkward position. He hollered as the stone rolled off of him, and the blood and sensation rushed to his extremity. He lifted his foot, wincing with every flinch of his muscles, and moved it into the light so he could take account of his injuries. He grit his teeth again and tried to flex and point his foot, a tip he'd learned from a fellow mason to tell if one's ankle was broken, though he couldn't remember if not being able to do so was a sign of a fracture or a sprain. Either way, he was unable to move it beyond the slightest degree.

He unlaced his boot and, with both hands and a single swift movement, pulled it off. His foot began to swell instantly, and in a few minutes was twice its normal size. Several large cuts on his lower leg and ankle oozed blood. He took off his shirt and wrapped his foot, knotting the sleeves tightly around his ankle. Pulling himself up by the side of the collapsed wagon he stood on his one good foot until the throbbing in the injury lessened somewhat. He slowly brought the foot down and attempted to bear a portion of this weight on it. Shooting pain raced up his leg. His knees buckled, and he found himself on the ground again. Rolling onto his back, he listened to the sound of a city greeting a boatful of new people. They were welcomed just like Stephen had been welcomed. The Quebec people remembered when they had come and extended these pioneers the same honor. Stephen wanted to be there, too. He wanted to see what it was like to be on the other side of the greetings, but forging the steep path was impossible.

The sun was half hidden by the trees when Stephen was finally standing with the help of a pole that rolled from the broken wagon. He would have to welcome the newcomers tomorrow. For now he had to begin his challenging journey home if he wanted to reach it before dark.

Catherine knelt on the floor with a basin of warm water and washed the blood and dirt from Stephen's swollen foot. "Did you see anyone from the boat?" she asked without looking up.

"I wasn't in any condition to hobble down the trail to the shore, and I didn't wait around for them to come up and say hello. Ouch!" he yelled as he jerked his foot out of her hands.

"I think it may be broken. Maybe you should see the hospital nuns tomorrow. They could do something for it. I'll go with you and help you walk."

"I managed to walk here by myself. Besides, all the nuns would do is wrap it, and I can do that much. I'm sure it is only a sprain." He grimaced as he tried the point-and-flex test again.

Catherine dried her hands on her apron and stood. "Let me wrap it, then," she said as she disappeared behind the cloth partition. Stephen heard a snip, then a ripping sound, another snip and more ripping. After a few minutes Catherine returned with a handful of pale blue cloth strips.

"Catherine, that was your dress. Why did you rip your blue dress?"

"Your foot needs to be wrapped," she said plainly.

"But your dress; it's not as if there is fabric to spare in Quebec. You may not see another piece of fabric or a new dress for a year."

"Please, hold your foot still." She gently placed it in her lap. "I have other dresses. It is nothing to even make note of."

Stephen watched her as she worked the soft blue cloth around his foot and ankle. She rarely displayed tenderness toward Stephen, but there was caring and gentleness in the way she tended him. He wondered when she was going to bring up the subject of returning to France or mention that she still loved Gaston.

"There," she said as she looked up. Stephen saw her glance at his cheek, and he instinctively put his hand to it. She looked back down at his blue wrapped foot and cleared her throat. "You were dreaming again last night."

Stephen continued to look at her.

"I've heard you moan in your sleep many times. Last night you were calling out. You looked so scared."

Stephen felt his face redden and then pale. He was confused with the softness of her voice and fearful of her discovery of his restless nights.

"Are you afraid of something?" she asked.

"No, I am not afraid of anything. If I was dreaming as you say, then I don't remember it," he lied. "All I know is that I must have scratched myself accidentally." He leaned back in the chair and carefully lifted his foot from Catherine's lap and set it on the floor.

"Stephen, you were calling out. You said, 'Forgive me,' over and over. Forgive what?"

"As you said, I was dreaming. I told you I don't remember anything."

"You're lying, Stephen." She stood, gazing down at him. "I am neither blind nor stupid. I have seen how you act some mornings. You are pale, like you are right now. You don't eat. You just run out the door without saying anything."

"You have quite an imagination, Catherine."

"Admit it, Stephen. You don't like it here anymore than I do. Why don't you say it? Maybe then you can sleep without groaning and thrashing about." Her voice had an unnerving calm to it.

Stephen pushed himself out of the chair and shifted about on one foot to get his balance. "Have we, even once, said more than two words to each other without you bringing up France?" he asked, trying to maintain his own calm. "We have discussed it to the death. I said you could leave when the boat comes in the spring, but you continue to push, then I get upset, then you get upset, then you cry..." Stephen stopped himself from saying more. He could feel the frustration rise.

"It is all I ever think about, Stephen. Is it so strange that I talk about it? Is it so inconceivable that I would take any opportunity to go home?"

"Please, Catherine, I don't want to talk about it anymore. You've said your piece; now let it rest."

"You can't just—"

"Stop!" he shouted. "I can't do this anymore. I can't hear about you leaving over and over. I can't keep giving you the same answers." He set his injured foot on the floor to steady himself. It throbbed and ached up into his hip. He closed his eyes tight and clenched his teeth.

"Stephen," she said. He could hear her move toward him but was startled when he opened his eyes and saw her hand moving to his face. His arm quickly rose to stop her from making contact with his cheek.

She withdrew her hand and put it to her mouth. "You do remember," she said softly.

Stephen brushed his hair back with his hands and locked his fingers behind his head. He wanted to sit down, for the pain; yet he wanted to stomp out the door and disappear.

"You remember your dreams. Why would you lie about them?"

"What does it matter? What concern could you possibly have regarding my dreams?"

"I am not heartless." Catherine reached out to touch his arm, but he stepped back.

"What are you trying to do? What game are you playing now?"

"I'm not playing a game. You were once my friend. Can't I show some concern for you?"

Pain covered Stephen's face as he moved forward and grabbed Catherine's shoulders. He couldn't tell which emotions moved inside of him, but they spun and twisted and made his stomach burn. "Do you want to know what I dreamt of last night? I dreamt a beautiful woman, a queen, put her hands on my face and leaned toward me. Then she kissed me." He watched Catherine's face redden at his words. "You can't do this to me, Catherine. If you hate me, then hate me."

"I'm sorry," she whispered. "Please, let go of me."

Stephen loosened his grasp, and she stepped back. He let his hands drop wearily at his sides. He realized he had been hoping in that moment that she had found a place in her heart that was warm toward him. He was suddenly very tired. "I need to sit down."

"Wait there. I'll bring a chair over to the fire." She quickly took a chair from by the table and set it behind him. "There, sit." She stood back and watched as he lowered himself to it without touching his wounded foot to the ground. He looked different...tired and pale and worn.

14

Stephen joined the men and women gathered outside the fort along with the group from the boat. Most of the new arrivals were present—almost forty men and four women. Each one had determination etched into their faces. It was obvious they were committed to one goal only: their mission.

Most of the settlers had already spoken to them, probing them for news from France. A few fortunate ones discovered they had a common acquaintance in France that instantly transformed them from strangers to family. The rest of the people of Quebec settled into their own small groups of friends and mumbled complaints about this group who had dared to venture to New France at such an inconvenient time of year.

The crowd hushed as the voices from inside the fort raised to an angry pitch.

"That sounds like Montmagny," said Stephen to the man standing next to him.

"Who is the other man I hear?"

"That's Maisonneuve. They have been arguing all morning."

"About what?"

"Montmagny is trying to convince this other fellow to settle here in Quebec instead of going on to Montreal. He's using every argument he can think of," the man said with a pessimistic chuckle. "Maisonneuve is not going to give in. I have never heard Montmagny behave in such a way. He is acting like…a jealous child. I think he wants to control all of New France, not just Quebec."

"That sounds out of character for Montmagny. Maybe there is another reason why he is fighting so hard to keep them here."

"Not from what we've heard so far," the man said as he nodded toward the fort. Their voices could, once again, be heard through the walls of the fort.

"Stephen," said Jacques as he approached him from behind, "what happened to you?" He looked down at Stephen's bandaged foot. In one shake of his head he managed to say, "I'm so sorry this happened to you, and if I could change matters I would." Jacques had given him those condolences more than once.

Stephen smiled at Jacques's response to his misfortune. "I am embarrassed to tell you what happened, but for the sake of a good laugh I will disclose it to you. Of all the places I could have been standing, I chose the very spot that one of the chapel building stones decided to rest upon. That rock moved faster than I could and, well…" He lifted the blue bundle and shook his own head. "It hurt beyond belief yesterday. You may want to pray in front of the chapel today and clean up the choice words I left laying around." He laughed.

Jacques joined in the brief chuckle.

"The pain is bearable now. If I walk on just my heel, I can get around fine."

"For a man with an infirmity you certainly are in good spirits."

"You will be amazed by this, Jacques, but I woke up this morning determined to find some happiness in my day. I realize it is still morning, but I have managed to keep a friendly look on my face."

"I am glad for you. Just remember this: unless the Lord is the reason for your joy, it will not last."

"Well, thank you for that word of encouragement, but I think I could have gone about my day without that information and been quite content."

"I'm sorry." Jacques laughed. "I have not yet become a master at timing my nuggets of truth."

"Father Jacques, you are forgiven. Look, I am still smiling." Stephen exaggerated a toothy grin, and both men had a hardy laugh.

"So, my damaged friend, do you need help with anything?"

"If I should happen to encounter anything too much for my lame condition you shall be the first person I call upon for help. Perhaps someday I will be able to return the favor."

Jacques returned the comment with a smile and a firm slap on the shoulder. "I certainly hope not!"

"Tell me, Jacques, what do you think of this situation between Montmagny and Maisonneuve?"

"Maisonneuve is going to start a mission in Montreal no matter what Montmagny says or does. It doesn't matter to him what the risks are. He and the people with him have counted the cost and decided they were willing to pay the price. They will not be swayed to any other opinion."

"Is there anyone anywhere in New France who supports their effort, or are they alone in this venture?"

"Lauson has granted Maisonneuve most of the land at Montreal, except for the far western portion and the right of fishery within two leagues of the shore. All they have to do is give him ten pounds of fish each year."

"What?" Stephen asked in surprise. "From what I've heard, Lauson does not give anything away."

"What I have said is true. Maisonneuve even has a signed confirmation from the King."

"Well, they surely can't head there now. They will have to stay in Quebec until spring, but where? Listen to the people mumble amongst themselves. They aren't willing to part with what they have so these latecomers can feed during the winter."

"That is all taken care of, too," said Jacques. "Early this morning a very generous man named Puiseaux offered them the use of his home. It is rough but very large. As for food, we, at the mission, will help as we can. The portion we have received from your garden will help. We should not forget that God is our provider."

"I believe you are right on that account. It sounds as if…" Stephen's eyes darted over Jacques's shoulder.

"What is it?" asked Jacques, quickly turning around.

"Ah, it must be my imagination." Stephen strained to see across the crowd and along the street where people were beginning to go about their business. "I thought I saw someone I knew from France." He continued to look until he was assured that he had scanned every face before he returned his attention to Jacques. "Did you see the people when they arrived yesterday?"

"Yes, I did."

"Look at them standing over there. Is that everyone who was on the boat?"

"I couldn't say. Maybe. There were forty men and four women. Maisonneuve is inside, so…" Jacques whispered as he counted the group. "I count thirty-seven men. Two of them are not there. Why do you ask?"

"Does one of the two who are not there have dark hair and strange brown eyes?"

"Stephen, after a three-month sea voyage, they all have strange eyes," Jacques said. "Besides, I don't remember what they all look like. There were forty of them."

Stephen rubbed his chin and looked again at the crowd. "The odds are too great that he would come here now," he mumbled.

"Who?" asked Jacques.

"Gaston."

"Catherine's Gaston? The man who was there the night Jean was killed?"

"My eyes are playing tricks on me." Stephen put his hand on Jacques's shoulder and used him to turn on one foot. "I best return to work on the chapel before I am no good at all."

"Please be careful, Stephen. You worry me."

Stephen brushed off Jacques's concern with a wave, then instantly felt a pang of conscience for dismissing it. He knew he was more than fortunate to have Father Jacques' friendship. He turned to recant, but Jacques had already joined the group of missionaries in deep conversation.

Stephen hobbled the short distance to the chapel, continuing to look for the face he'd caught a glimpse of earlier. He hoped it was someone who resembled Gaston, therefore dispelling any idea that the menace had come to Quebec. If he could not find the familiar face, he wouldn't rest until he had confirmation that Gaston was still in France. There was too much harm that he could cause if he were to follow Catherine. Too much hell that he could stir into Stephen's life. Stephen could not trust Gaston to stay away, for his very nature was evil.

327

Stephen's new condition prevented him from physically assisting with the construction of the chapel, but he could still give direction to the other workers. He soon discovered they were competent to complete the task without any further interference from him. He watched as the last course of block was hoisted, stone by stone, onto the top of the walls. The building was now ready for a roof. This meant the end of Stephen's involvement with the building as men adept at constructing roofs would now take over. He stepped away from the chapel and admired the uniform lines and sturdy construction and was pleased. He would return home early and satisfied.

Stephen looked toward the fort. The crowd was breaking up and going its way, and the group of travelers was being helped onto a large wagon, ready for delivery to the kindly Monsieur Puiseaux. He was relieved to see that one of the men on the wagon had Gaston's build and hair color. He watched as the wagon pulled away, and its passengers were jostled down the road toward their winter home.

Relief washed over him as he headed toward his own winter home. The day had been tiring with the added effort of his disabled walk. He was eager to sit in front of the fire and do nothing. Idleness was much more enjoyable when one had well earned it. He was anxious, too, to be near Catherine. Frustration lost to curiosity with the new tenderness he was seeing in her. He reminded himself that it could be momentary, like a blink. Being near her while it lasted was his consolation.

The dusty road stretched a small distance through the town, flanked by necessary merchants and brothels. His mind was on the trail beyond and the home at the end of it when, from the corner of his eye, he glimpsed a figure moving along the street. The familiarity, once again, gripped Stephen's attention. He turned to look fully at the man. It was not the man in the wagon. It was Gaston. He still had that self-assured swagger that was his trademark. It instantly made one feel smaller when in his presence and, even from a distance, made Stephen want to cower.

Stephen watched as Gaston entered a tavern and disappeared behind the plank door. His heart raced. He did not think that Gaston noticed him. If Gaston had, Stephen was sure he would have made it known. Gaston would not have traveled such a great distance just for a woman. He had plenty of women in France. But he would travel that far to torment someone, to get even for disrupting his plans, or to lay the blame of a murder on someone.

Stephen walked as casually as he could toward the tavern. Before passing the door, he stepped into the shadows of the alley between the tavern and the general store next to it. His heart continued to beat at a rapid pace as he waited for Gaston to pass. He didn't know what he would say or do to him, and he almost hoped that he would not even pass by the alleyway. He would rather deal with Gaston on a different day after he'd had time to find out why he was in Quebec.

It was nearly twenty minutes before he heard Gaston's familiar laugh and his footsteps as he left the tavern. Gaston stood for a moment outside of the building, then, having chosen his direction, walked past the alley. With a burst of nervous energy and anger Stephen lunged forward, grabbed Gaston by his coat, and yanked him into the shadows. He pushed him forcefully against the side of the building so hard that his head bobbed back and struck it with a thud.

Gaston said nothing as he shook his head clear.

"What are you doing here?" Stephen demanded.

A smile slowly spread across Gaston's face. "Stephen Marot. Why didn't you come to greet me when I arrived on the boat? It would have been nice to see a sinner's face after being on that boat full of saints."

"What are you doing here, Gaston?" Stephen pushed on his chest harder.

"There is no need to get violent, though I know you are a man prone to that sort of behavior." Even in the shadows his eyes unnerved Stephen. "Since we are on the subject of violent behavior, where is that lovely dagger of yours? You know, I have always had my eye on that, but I knew you would never part with it. Or did you?"

Stephen was silent.

"Oh, I remember." Gaston commandeered the confrontation to make Stephen the victim. "The authorities have that little gem. If I remember correctly, your initials are on the handle, and Jean's blood is on the blade." He pushed Stephen back.

"What have you told them?" asked Stephen.

"Me? I have told them nothing, my dear friend."

"Why? I'd think implicating me would give you great pleasure."

"Now, Stephen, if you are hung for murder, then what fun would it be for me? What would it profit me?"

"What do you want from me?" demanded Stephen as he stepped toward him again.

"I don't quite know yet, but when I find out, I'll certainly inform you. I know what *you* wanted, Stephen. Is Catherine everything you expected?"

Stephen rushed forward and pushed his arm against Gaston's throat, slamming him against the building again. He hated Gaston and his filthy references to Catherine. All he wanted to do that moment was to push harder on Gaston's throat, to see his face turn red and watch him struggle against his arm, struggle for air. He wanted to feel *his* body go limp and have *his* eyes looking into his own the last second of his life. Then he would be rid of Gaston. No longer would he be a threat to him or Catherine. He could do it, right there in the shadows. No one would know.

Fear suddenly seized Stephen. He let go of Gaston and stepped back. He closed his eyes tight as great flashes of light crossed his eyes and his chest heaved as his lungs worked to keep up with his pounding heart.

"You never did have any nerve." Gaston rubbed his throat. He quickly moved toward Stephen and sent his boot heel crashing down onto his wrapped foot.

Stephen let out a howl and dropped to the ground, clutching his leg.

"In just the little time I have been here I have found out where you and my beautiful Catherine live," said Gaston as he looked down upon Stephen. "I have thought of her often on that long, lonely sea voyage…her hair, her lips, her soft skin. She has many charms." He crouched by Stephen's head. "I will come to visit you one day, Stephen. When? I don't know. You won't know, either. I will get what I want from you, dear friend…and from Catherine." He laughed and walked out from the shadows and onto the street.

Stephen lay in the alley, forcing himself to breathe slowly. The pain throbbed from his foot up to his knee. He felt the blue cloth becoming moist with blood and loosening. He didn't want to look at his foot. He didn't want to see that it was too damaged to walk on. He had to get home. Gaston could be on his way there.

He rolled onto his knees, then brought his good foot under him. He held onto the side of the building and stood, holding his re-injured foot off the ground. Taking a deep breath, he put the bloody bundle on the ground. The pain shot a fiery line up his leg as he put weight on it, and his whole body responded in throbbing. He carefully moved toward the street. Seeing no one, he hobbled out of the shadow and down the street to the path that led to his little house. His eyes watered as he moved. He didn't stop to dry them. Simply kept moving to the little house, step by faltering step.

The yard around the house was quiet, and he could see a sliver of light from between the window shutters as it competed with the dusk. A few more steps and he would burst through the door, hopefully to find Catherine alone and unaware that Gaston was in Quebec. He placed his wounded foot on the ground and lifted his arms slightly to help his body move forward, keeping the momentum of his uneven gait. That proved to be the last step his bloodied and swollen foot could manage. It crumbled helplessly beneath his weight, and the pain pushed a loud cry from his throat.

"Who's there?" called Catherine from inside the house.

"It's me, Stephen," he gasped.

Catherine unbolted the door and stepped outside to find Stephen on the ground just two steps away. "What happened to you?" She held onto his arm as he tried to stand again. He said nothing as he grit his teeth and hopped into the house, plopping into a chair and letting out a groan.

"Stephen, what happened to your foot?" she asked as she looked down. The blue wrapping was soaked with blood and dirt and had loosened, revealing the open wounds. "Did you drop another block on it?"

"Clumsy, am I not?" he said with relief. It was obvious by Catherine's attention to his wound that she had no knowledge of Gaston's presence in Quebec.

He leaned forward and started to unwrap the loosened bandage as Catherine filled a bowl with water she had heated for washing.

"Let me do it," she said as she knelt by the chair. Catherine gasped as the blue cloth fell to the floor and revealed Stephen's mangled foot. It was mottled with purple, red, and green, swollen and bent inward. The gashes, which had been cleaned and healing that morning, were reopened and filled with dirt and blood. The thick red fluid trickled down and splattered on the floor.

"This looks awful." Carefully she placed his foot into the warm water.

He tightened and drew a quick breath through his clenched teeth.

"If you aren't more careful, you'll end up killing yourself. I didn't know being a mason was so dangerous."

"The only way I'll kill myself from now until spring is around here. The mason work on the chapel is finished. I think the fine folks of Quebec can finish the roof without me."

"Do you mean you'll be here?"

"Yes, for good or bad we will have to tolerate each other for countless hours each day."

Catherine was quiet as she dabbed at his wounds with a rag, then threw the bloody water out the door and refilled the bowl with more clean, warm water. "You soak your foot while I make you something to eat."

Stephen closed his eyes and let his head drop forward. He could hear Catherine's dress rustle as she moved about and the soft sounds of her humming a tune he had known from his past, long ago. The throbbing in his body subsided, and his muscles relaxed. He was glad to have made it home, glad Gaston hadn't come, glad he didn't have the guilt of another murder on his conscience. *To know the beauty of a smile…*he remembered the words now…*to know the peace of home…these are the treasures of life.*

The sun was high by the time Stephen woke and higher still before he was ready to do anything productive. His foot was so tight it felt as if it would burst through the skin. Catherine had torn more fabric from her dress and rewrapped it again. The bleeding had stopped and left only small patches of dried blood on the blue fabric. She demanded that he go to the hospital nuns and see if they couldn't prescribe a better remedy. He refused, insisting they had done everything the nuns would say to do.

Stephen spent most of the day in the house by the fire carving a crutch from a conveniently shaped stick that Catherine had found. He occasionally reached over and threw another log on the fire to chase an early winter chill from the house. They didn't talk much. Catherine busied herself with her daily chores and would periodically sit at the table and read from her book. Stephen positioned himself so he could see out of the window. It offered a limited view so he would hop to the door and peer out, then hop back to his chair by the fire. When questioned, he said he needed a breath of fresh air.

The sun had set the same way it had risen, with Stephen fast asleep in the chair by the fire. Catherine spread his bedding on the floor and retired to her cot behind the partition.

15

"Stephen, what are you doing sitting out here?" asked Jacques as he approached the little house. His sandy hair was tossed back by the cold breeze exposing red ears, nose, and cheeks. His hands would have been chilled red, too, had he not stuffed them into the deep pockets of his heavy wool coat.

Stephen leaned forward, bringing the tilted chair onto all four legs. "Good afternoon, Jacques. I was just taking a break from chopping wood."

Jacques looked at the huge pile of chopped wood stacked neatly against the side of the house and a second one started along the edge of the woods.

"You have enough wood for four winters. Why are you chopping more?"

"The trees were already downed and…" Stephen sighed. "It is an excuse to be outside to keep an eye out for Gaston." His eyes briefly scanned the pathway to his house then looked back at Jacques.

"So you did see him in town yesterday."

"Yes. He is the menace he has always been. I was right to fear him."

"Has he told the authorities?"

"No, not yet. He has decided to play some sick game with me, keeping me wondering what he'll do, where he'll show up."

"I think I know where he's shown up," said Jacques. "I was visiting the LaPointes' yesterday afternoon, and I saw a man that looked just as you described—tall, dark hair, strange brown eyes."

"Yes, that must have been him," Stephen said, alarmed. "What was he doing there?"

"He was talking to Eliot and the man Eliot will be trapping with. From what I heard, Gaston, if that was him, had known Eliot's friend back in France. They were laughing and carrying on as if they had been good friends. He seemed nice enough, certainly not the rogue I had imagined. This friend was back to health, and they were all preparing to leave…"

"Gaston was going with them?" he interrupted.

"Yes, I believe that was their plan."

"But Gaston isn't to be trusted, no matter how he appears. That is why he is such a menace. He is all the gentleman but only to meet his own wicked ends. He can't leave with them. I know he was involved in something lawless the night Jean died and I am sure he took whatever money I was accused of taking. There is no telling what he will do here." Stephen grabbed his crutch that was leaning against the house and stood. He was agitated and insistent. Gaston had to be dealt with, and who better to do so than Jacques and himself? He hoped Eliot would have sense enough to see the truth; he had when Catherine had tried to ally himself to her mission of returning to France. "We've got to tell Eliot not to go with him." He began to hobble toward the path.

Jacques grabbed his arm. "It will do no good to go to the LaPointes' now. They left yesterday."

Stephen cursed and threw his crutch to the ground.

"Eliot is a very smart and resourceful man, Stephen. He will be able to take care of himself, no matter what Gaston should decide to do," said Jacques as he bent over to pick up the crutch. "And consider how many years he has spent as a trapper in the woods. Gaston has just come from France. Do you really think he will do anything to jeopardize his only means of survival?"

"Perhaps you are right." Stephen moved toward the little house. "He will be away from Catherine, and that is good. Maybe leaving with Eliot will be the best thing he could do. Maybe he will never come back. The Indians might be his end."

"Stephen! No matter how you feel about him, you should not wish death upon anyone."

"Not now, Jacques. I don't need to be reminded what a wretch I am. I tell myself that often enough."

"How are things between you and Catherine?" he asked as he helped Stephen to the chair.

"I don't know how they are between us. It is the strangest thing, but every now and then I catch her looking at me. If it were contempt or tolerance in her eyes, I could say that matters are the same between us. But it's neither. I don't really know what it is. Curiosity, maybe?"

"Curiosity about what?" Jacques stuffed his cold hands back into his pockets.

"About what has happened to me, why I brought her here. Maybe she is wondering if there may be something more between us than simply living side by side. It could be anything." Stephen tilted the chair back again. "She has even shown me some kindness in that she wrapped my foot and put a measure of softness in her voice."

"That is good, Stephen."

"It would seem so," he said flatly.

"Why are you less than excited about her softening?"

"This is insane, Jacques, but the nicer she is to me, the more I abhor myself. When she spits fire at me with her tongue, I feel that I am justly punished. Yet, with even the smallest hint of kindness she shows I am confused. I just want to get away…away from myself. The pain of what kind of a person I have become weighs greatly on me." He sighed. "Does this make any sense, or have I lost any reasoning I may have had?"

"You are feeling your guilt. You can't think or reason your way around it. You can't run away from it. You can't justify it."

Stephen felt the firmness and sincerity of Jaques's words. Jacques believed what he said. His goodness caused a stab of pain. "Jacques, I have not dismissed what you have told me about confession. I tried to tell Catherine about Jean. I was so close to disclosing everything but I froze. I couldn't tell her."

"God will give you another chance to tell her. Don't let it pass you by."

"I'm afraid I am a great disappointment to you."

"Never." Jacques stepped toward Stephen with serious intensity in his eyes. "Don't ever say that. You will never be a disappointment to me."

"I am a great disappointment to myself. Sometimes I have to search my memory for something I have done that has been good." Stephen lowered his eyes. "All I can think of is that I loved Catherine once, in purity, with caring and kindness. I loved her when she only saw me as a friend. I loved her even when she loved someone else and, if that person had not been Gaston, I know I would have let her go."

"You will find that you are still that person, Stephen. When you have done all you need to do, you will find yourself again."

Stephen brought his hand to his eyes and pressed gently with his fingers. "I am suddenly very tired. I think I chopped myself into needing a nap." He brought the chair onto all fours again and stood, holding onto the crutch. "Oh, Jacques," he said suddenly, "I apologize. I have gone on about myself and haven't even asked why you came by."

"I came by with sad news. Monsieur Fonte has died. I was told he went in his sleep."

"The first time I met him, when he showed me the plan for the building of Quebec, I could tell he did not have long. It is Quebec's loss that he has passed."

"That is not all. Do you remember the man who was killed by the Iroquois when you first arrived? The one you saw in the field?"

"How could I forget?" Stephen said with a shudder.

"His widow hung herself yesterday."

Stephen closed his eyes and tightened his shoulders.

"Living here without her husband was too overwhelming," said Jacques. "There will be a funeral for both of them. It seems that death is a frequent occurrence in Quebec."

Stephen nodded and quickly became dizzy. He grabbed Jacques's shoulder.

"Are you all right?"

"Yes." Stephen shook his head clear. "I just got dizzy for a moment. I'll be fine. I think the pain in my foot has worn me out."

"I thought you said the pain had lessened."

"It had until I reinjured my foot yesterday."

"Oh, Stephen, you must be more careful."

Stephen expected Jacques to inquire about the incident and was greatly relieved when he didn't. He wasn't eager to admit to his friend that he had been ready in his heart to kill Gaston. Surely, by anyone's standards, Gaston was justified in his action of self-defense. "My foot has hurt all the more since then."

"Then I agree with your plan to rest, but please be careful. I have seen more than one person lose a limb from this sort of thing."

"By tomorrow it should be almost as well as before I injured it."

"I pray you are right. I will stop by tomorrow and see if you are feeling better."

Jacques put his hands in his coat pockets and disappeared down the path. Stephen was glad Jacques had been on the ship with them and was his friend. He knew much of their relationship was based on the priest's unending goodness and his own neediness. Was it possible to be a good friend to this man of God? Could Stephen ever add anything of substance that Jacques didn't already possess? *Perhaps once this nightmare is behind me, I will find I do have something worthwhile to offer him.* He supposed Jacques would rebuke him again for that thought, insisting he already offered him much.

Stephen made his way into the house. Warmth from the fire blanketed him and enticed his sleepiness. He sat down at the table and fell asleep without hesitation.

Stephen didn't wake until Catherine set his plate before him. The aroma wafted upward and caused his stomach to lurch.

"I'm sorry, Catherine, but I can't eat this. I don't feel so well." He pushed his half-eaten meal away from him.

Catherine picked up the plate and sniffed at it. "I ate it, and I feel fine."

"It's not the food. I just feel tired and weak. I can't seem to shake it." Stephen wiped his forehead with his sleeve. The dizziness returned and caught his eyesight with it, making the room appear to spin. He took two deep, slow breaths and rested his head on his folded arms on the table.

"You don't look very well, either. Let me see your foot." She moved toward him.

"No, no." He waved her away. "My foot is fine. I think I just need some sleep. I'll get my bedroll and—"

"Please," she interrupted, "sleep on my cot tonight."

He looked at her and wondered again at her acts of kindness. Her eyes appeared sincere and her mouth, drawn up in a slight smile, looked innocent and eager to help. "That's really not necessary," he said.

Catherine put down his dinner plate and went behind the partition. She brought out the cot, positioned it by the fire, and spread his bedroll on it. "There." She stood, hands on her hips. "It's too late to argue."

Stephen took off his heavy wool shirt and slid from the chair to the cot. He covered himself up to his chin, except for his bundled foot, which dangled over the edge of the cot. He mumbled a "thank you" and within seconds drifted off to sleep.

The room was large and empty, the ceiling domed. Bright white light reflected in every direction from the polished gold ornaments set in the white walls. At one end of the room sat a woman on a golden throne. As Stephen approached, his footsteps echoed in pulsating hollowness. The woman was dressed in black and brown with harsh lines and a high collar. Upon her head was a crown of hammered gold encrusted with rubies that did not sparkle. Her eyebrows were severe and her mouth was a single line painted red. She leaned forward and squinted at Stephen.

"So you are the low one who has been sent to me." She sneered. "You do not look impressive. Have you anything that would warrant sparing your life?"

Stephen knelt and bowed his head. "I have no possessions to offer. I live in a humble dwelling, and I have spent what little money I had. I have no livestock. I have no children."

"What talents do you have that I might be interested in?" the woman asked.

"I am a fine mason. I have built many strong, beautiful buildings. I could build you a castle, a splendid palace," he said with eagerness.

The woman leaned back and laughed. "A fine mason? Turn around and look!"

Stephen turned his head and saw a large scene upon the wall. The picture moved slowly, showing one building after another that Stephen had constructed. Each building was crumbling; stones lay scattered on the ground.

"See how sturdy those buildings are? Ha! You have nothing. You are nothing. I commend you to death by hanging."

"No!" he screamed as he turned back. "Surely I must be of some value."

"What might that be?" she asked.

"I am a human being, a person who can love…who can care. Isn't that worth a great price?"

The woman laughed again. "You are also a person who lies, deceives, and is capable of murder. Isn't that worthy of death?"

Stephen opened his mouth to continue to plead his case, but no words came out. All that could be heard was the woman laughing as he was being led to the gallows….

Catherine paced back and forth between the fire and Stephen. She wrapped her arms tight around her and rubbed away an imagined chill. She kept her eyes on Stephen, pacing faster when he would moan and grimace. She was afraid to wake him. Sweat glistened on his forehead, beaded, and rolled onto the bedding, yet his body shook with chills. She gently placed another blanket on him and stoked the fire.

Catherine desperately wanted morning to come. Stephen had said Jacques would be stopping by to check on him, and she prayed he would come early, as soon as the sun rose. She didn't know what to do for Stephen. She tried to remember how he and the nuns had taken care of her when she was so ill on the boat, but her memories of it were spotty.

Catherine walked to the door and opened it a crack. An icy wind blew in and caused her to shudder. The night sky was still dark. "Oh, God, speed morning on its way."

"What are you doing?" Stephen whispered.

Catherine jumped and turned. "Stephen, you startled me." She closed the door and slowly walked toward him. "Are you all right? You were moaning."

"Oh." He closed his eyes again. "I don't feel well. I think I'm awfully sick. I hurt everywhere, and I'm so cold." He pulled the blankets up to his chin and continued to shiver. Catherine placed another log on the fire and coaxed it into flame. The room warmed quickly, causing Catherine to perspire, but Stephen continued to shiver.

"I don't know what to do for you, Stephen," she murmured. She took a step toward him, then another, ever so cautiously approaching the man who, by law, was her husband. She feared him and hated him and yet now, so sick and helpless, felt a strange attachment to him. She knelt by the side of the cot and, with a shaking hand, wiped his forehead with the hem of her skirt. He opened his eyes, and she could tell by the slight movement of his eyebrows that he didn't understand. He closed his eyes again.

"I'm sorry," he said softly. "Can you forgive me?"

"Forgive you for what, Stephen?" There was something more in his voice than a general apology. "Stephen…"

He had fallen asleep again.

"What haunts you, Stephen?" She gently touched his hair, then pulled her hand back. She couldn't help the warmth and concern she was feeling for him. It frightened her. It was not at all what she had wanted. She wanted to detest him right then. She wanted to scream at him and say that if he had not brought her here, none of this misfortune would have happened. She didn't want her love for Gaston to change or her strong desire to return to her home in France to be set aside.

She stood and resumed her pacing. "God, send Gaston to me," she whispered. "Take me from here soon. Oh, God, I want to go home to France. I don't want to feel this." She stopped her pacing and looked down at Stephen. He was helpless, fast asleep in his torment. Catherine could tell that, even in his sickness, his dreams persisted. She wanted to cradle and comfort him but dared not even bend down close to him. "Please, God, rescue Stephen." She wept.

A loud rap at the door snapped Catherine out of her sleep. A moment later the rap was heard again.

"Stephen, it's Jacques. Are you there?"

"He's here," called Catherine in relief. She stumbled as she untangled herself from her blanket and hurried to open the door. She didn't intend on falling asleep but was relieved that she had. Waiting through the night for Father Jacques to arrive in morning had been torment.

"I'm so glad you are here, Father Jacques. Stephen is sick. I've never seen him like this." She drew the priest into the house and closed the door behind him.

Jacques handed her his coat. "He said he didn't feel well yesterday." He went to Stephen and knelt on one knee beside the cot. "Stephen, tell me how you are feeling."

Stephen moaned and sleepily opened his eyes. "Jacques, I'm not doing so well." He swallowed hard before speaking again. "It is a great effort to even open my eyes."

"Close them then, my friend. I will get you some water; then you can rest." He put his hand on Stephen's cheek. "He's burning up. We've got to get these blankets off him and move him back from the fire." Jacques quickly tossed the blankets into the corner.

"I didn't know what to do," Catherine said as she looked on from near the door. "He looked so cold. He kept shivering, and I—"

"Get some water," Jacques interrupted, taking charge. "He has sweat out most of his fluids. The bedding is soaked."

Catherine poured water from a jug into a cup and handed it to Jacques.

"Stephen," he said, lifting the sick man's head off the cot, "drink this." Stephen took several swallows, then nodded to say he had enough. Jacques handed the cup to Catherine without looking up and lowered Stephen's head back onto the cot. "Help me move this cot back," he commanded.

Catherine jumped at his words and grabbed onto the cot near his feet. With Jacques at his head they lifted the cot and moved him back several paces from the fire. Stephen cried out as his leg slid off the cot, bringing his bandaged foot swiftly onto the floor.

"How long has he been this way?" Jacques asked. His tone unnerved Catherine.

"He went to bed immediately after he ate the evening meal. Well, he didn't eat much of his meal. He said he couldn't. I went to bed shortly afterward. Then he started moaning and talking in his sleep. That is what woke me." Catherine started to pace again. "What is wrong with him?"

Jacques crouched down by Stephen and gently put both hands under his lower leg and foot. "I'm going to lift your foot onto the cot, Stephen. Take a deep breath." Stephen breathed in and Jacques carefully raised his foot. "It feels hot right through this wrap. Get me a knife." He held out his hand. His eyes were fixed on Stephen's leg, red and swollen above the blue cloth that encircled his foot.

Catherine put the knife into Jacques's hand and stepped back. "What are you going to do? You're not going to hurt him, are you?"

Jacques slipped the knife under the bottom of his pant leg and pulled upward. Grasping the cut fabric with both hands, he ripped the pant leg up past Stephen's knee.

He placed the tip of the knife under the knot in the blue dressing and sawed it loose. Carefully he unwrapped the cloth, tugging slightly as it stuck to itself and to his foot.

Catherine put her hand to her mouth.

"Oh, my God in heaven," Jacques whispered as he looked down at Stephen's mangled foot. A large gash ran lengthwise down the front of his foot pulling open wide in the center over the bone and exposing ground flesh and a mixture of liquid brown and green. Stephen's toes were mottled black and blue. Within seconds the swelling from his leg descended and the entire foot enlarged. A rancid smell radiated upward. Stephen groaned as horrendous throbbing seized his foot.

"I'm going to wash your foot, Stephen. It will hurt but just hold on to the cot. I will be as gentle as I can, but I must clean it."

Catherine warmed a basin of water and Jacques carefully lowered Stephen's foot into it. He used a soft cloth and wiped the open areas clean, then patted the foot dry and gently placed it back on the cot. Stephen was sleeping again. Jacques carried the basin to the door and threw the water out. He closed the door again and leaned against it, his eyes closed and his mouth moving with a silent prayer. "I don't know what to do," he said at last. "I haven't seen any cures other than time or…"

"Or what?" she asked.

"If time doesn't stop the poisons from spreading, the only thing that will is to take off his foot."

"Oh, no, Jacques, you can't do that," she pleaded as she moved to him and put her hands on his arm. "I have heard stories—the horrible pain…the blood! They bleed to death. There has to be something else we can do."

"I just don't know what."

"How much time do you think it will take, if time is what will cure him?"

"I don't know that either. A few days, I would guess—at least to judge which way the wound will progress. But then maybe that will be too late to do anything. He is very sick right now." Jacques walked to the cot and looked down at Stephen. He was beginning to shiver so that even his jaw shook. "I will go back to the mission. Someone there may have other ideas. The nuns at the hospital may be able to help, too."

"No, let me go." Catherine stepped toward him. "Please, I can't be left here with him. I have proven that I don't know what to do. He would feel more comfortable with you here. I'm sure of it."

Not waiting for an answer, she grabbed her cloak off the peg by the door and bundled herself tightly. "Father Jacques, Madame LaPointe has told me stories of her early days here—how she has helped take care of people who have become ill or injured. She took care of me when we first arrived. Perhaps she will know what to do."

"Go and get her then, but please, be careful. Bring the musket."

Catherine grabbed the musket from the corner and went out the door.

16

J acques poured hot tea into an earthen cup and sat in the chair Catherine had set by
the fire. He kept the flames low to keep the little house from overheating. The
warm cup felt good to his cold hands. He touched Stephen's arm. It was cooler than
it had been before. Jacques set his tea down and covered Stephen with a thin blanket.

"Thank you," Stephen said, his voice breathy and soft.

"I didn't realize you were awake." Jacques crouched by his head and smiled.

"I have been, now and then. It is just too much effort to make it known." Stephen's
eyes flickered open, and he smiled. "Thank you for coming by. I think Catherine was
worried."

"Yes, I think she was." Jacques's smile faltered. He looked at the floor, then at
Stephen's foot rewrapped in another bundle of blue. The festering discharge had soaked
through the bandage, making it wet and sticky along the top.

Stephen opened his eyes again and looked around the room. "Where is she?"

"She went to get Madame LaPointe. Catherine thought she might know of a way to
heal your wounds."

"Did she take the musket?"

"Yes, she did. She will be fine. It is you we need to tend to."

He waited as Stephen's face made motions to speak again, but the look gave way to
sleep. Jacques was silent as he watched Stephen breathe. His chest rose and fell faster
than his own, slowing gradually, settling into a pace that signified he had fallen into
deep sleep. Jacques was worried at how dark Stephen's eyes had become and how the
paleness of his face chased away the stubborn tan of summer. His hands twitched every
so often, and he turned his head as his eyes tightened. Jacques knew Stephen was in
pain...pain and torment...even though it did not wake him.

Jacques poked at the fire and added a log to sustain it. The fire held his gaze as it
danced about the log licking it into flame. "Dear God," he whispered, "what will it take
for Stephen to come to You? He lies here suffering, and You are ready to take away all
his burdens. You have done it for me so many times." A deep sadness swept over him.
"I pray that this is not unto death. Spare his life, Lord."

Jacques knelt again beside the cot and gently laid his hands on Stephen's leg. He
closed his eyes, summoned any measure of faith he had to come forth, then dove with
abandon into prayer. His mouth moved fervently, yet he didn't utter a sound.

The morning passed slowly, the sun hidden for the most part by low, vague clouds.

Stephen woke several times and looked around the room for Jacques. Spotting the priest, Stephen would feebly smile, then close his eyes and begin a short rest until the pain or the dreams would cause him to grimace and moan.

Jacques judged it to be midday when he stepped outside for a breath of clean, crisp air. The smoke from the low fire made his breathing feel labored. The smell of ice was in the air, and the feel of it stung his face. Small gusts blew brown, dried leaves across the little yard and pinned them against the edge of the woods. The other priests at the mission wouldn't miss him today. He had told them he would be visiting the sick.

Jacques had seen plenty of sickness and death in France. But nothing had prepared him for the infirmities in Quebec. The Huron who filled the hospital had every kind of symptom: fever, chills, spots, coughing, delirium, and unconsciousness. He visited many of them, praying for them and giving them last rites, but he did not sit vigil at their bedsides, watching as they ebbed in and out of life. Now he was by his friend's side and every physical change, no matter how slight, caused Jacques alarm. Most of the sick and dying he saw were more willing to listen to him tell of Jesus. The closer they were to the line between life and death the more eagerly they accepted Christ. He didn't understand Stephen's stubbornness.

He also didn't understand the persistence with which he pursued a friendship with Stephen. They had little in common, but a bond had formed. Sometimes he felt as if he were Stephen's guardian angel, sent to keep watch over him. Whatever the connection, Jacques knew there was purpose in it.

Jacques took another breath of cold air and went back inside. Stephen's breathing had become more labored, and his chills had returned. He wanted to cover him with blankets, as Catherine had, but knew it would only send his fever higher.

Stephen stirred and opened his eyes just enough to make out Jacques's form. "What is happening?" he asked between breaths. "I don't understand why I feel so awful."

Jacques squeezed Stephen's hand. "It's your foot. It has poisoned your blood."

Stephen sighed. "He will take me out one way or another."

"What do you mean?" Jacques bent closer to be sure of what Stephen said.

"He did this to me." Stephen started to shiver again. "Jacques, I'm so cold." He folded his arms over his chest and continued to shiver. His jaw shook as he spoke. "Where is Catherine? She can't know. She can't know."

"Remember, Stephen, I told you that Catherine has gone to fetch Madame LaPointe to help you. Tell me, what can't she know?"

"When I saw Gaston in town…"

"Calm yourself. She has no idea he was even here, and now he is gone."

"You don't understand." Stephen grabbed Jacques's sleeve and looked him squarely in the eyes. "When I saw Gaston in town, I was going to kill him. For an instant I was going to kill him." Stephen dropped his arm back onto his chest. "I don't know what stopped me."

"You're not a killer. That is why you stopped."

"When I let go of Gaston, he ground his boot heel into my foot. He is killing me, and he isn't even here."

Jacques stared at Stephen lying on the cot—the poisons, hour by hour eating away at him, the guilt consuming him. Jacques stood again and turned toward the fire in the hearth. Tears welled in his eyes. He dried them quickly, for he knew they would help no one. He drew the chair up close to Stephen and sat in it.

"Now it is time that you listen to me, Stephen." His voice was even and calm but demanded attention. "You will not be able to hide from what happened in France. Look around you. Everything that has happened will remind you. Simply being in Quebec reminds you. And Catherine will, one day, find out what happened the night that Jean died. You are lying here because of what happened in France. It's not going to go away. It will plague you by day, and it will plague you by night. I have been sitting here, watching your face as you sleep. It twists and grimaces with your nightmares. If you continue on as you are, you are a fool."

"I fear it is too late, Father," Stephen said as his eyes closed again.

Jacques gently shook his shoulder, but Stephen did not stir. Jacques sat back in the chair and resumed listening to his friend's every breath.

The figure draped in black moved toward Stephen. A just scale was in his hand. One side was weighted down. An icy chill washed over Stephen as the figure came closer. He looked intently at the scale as it was brought before his eyes.

"Look," the breathy voice of the figure said to him. Suddenly the weighted side filled with blood and overflowed its edges. Stephen tried to wipe the blood off of his hands as it spilled, but he could not. "Repayment is demanded of you now, Stephen Marot," the voice said as it came nearer...

"No...no, please," Stephen groaned as he turned his head from one side to the other.

Jacques moved from the chair by the fire and knelt by the cot. "Stephen, wake up. It's just a dream." Jacques shook his shoulders more vigorously this time.

Stephen opened his eyes. They were eerily dark and sunken. He looked at Jacques for a long moment as if trying to recognize him, then groaned. "This is too much to bear," he whispered, his throat raspy with thirst.

Jacques took the cup of water he had set by the cot and brought it to Stephen's mouth. Stephen turned his head away, but Jacques kept the cup in place until he had taken several swallows.

"Jacques, they are coming to get me," he continued after catching his breath.

"There is no one here but you and me. You were dreaming and—"

"You don't understand," Stephen interrupted with weary urgency. "Every time I close my eyes, they come for me. I have to pay for what I've done. Don't you see?"

Jacques was halted by Stephen's words. He had seen fear and delirium in the sick before. It was a sign that the malady in the poor soul's body would soon overtake him. He, himself, was seized with fear and overwhelming inadequacy for this task. "No, Stephen, I do not see. Please rest. You need your strength to heal."

"They come for me every night…every night…whether I remember them or not. They are there to capture me, to hang me. My accusers…" Stephen grabbed Jacques's arm with a surprisingly tight grip. "Keep me awake. Don't let me fall asleep again," he pleaded breathlessly.

"I will keep you awake; just rest, please."

Stephen released Jacques's arm from his grip, and his whole body loosened in response. He closed his eyes again and continued to speak. The sound of fear had left and was replaced with slow, tired words. "My head feels strange, Father. It is as if it was in a cloud. I think I am not doing so well."

"You are strong. You will make it; I know you will." Jacques's voice quivered. Being called "Father" by Stephen set his heart on edge.

"You have always been good to me. Always."

"Come now, Stephen, you must continue to fight this battle. I know you have much to do. You can't lose your hope."

Stephen looked at Jacques with the same sunken eyes. "I cannot feel my leg. I know it is there, but I cannot feel it. That is not good." A tear welled up in his eye, hung for a moment, and splashed onto his cheek. "I am frightened. I don't know how to do this. I don't know how to die."

Jacques's tears came again, and this time he didn't try to stop them. "You are not going to die, my friend. You have too much left to do in this world. You will see tomorrow and the next day and many more after. You will be here with me to face anything this land can throw at us. If God allows it, you will even see me preach one day. I will bless your children and watch them grow with you. We will see this city spring up with buildings crafted by your hand, Stephen. Your time to go is not now. Do you hear me?"

"It is as you say, Father," he slurred as he fell back into sleep.

The sun was setting. There was still no sign of Catherine or the help she went to retrieve. Stephen rarely came to his senses now. The smell of death was heavy in the room, and Jacques fought intensely to keep the fear of it away. He unwrapped the foot

343

again, repeating the washing he had done earlier. The redness had moved further up Stephen's leg and the open gash was purulent. Jacques could barely stand the smell of the infected flesh. He left the wound open and sat back by the fire. He was sickened by what he knew must happen next.

"God, I don't want to do it," he prayed. "I don't want to take off his foot. I wouldn't know how…how much…where to start." He stared at the unwrapped wound. "But I can't sit here and watch him die." He forced himself to stand and walk to the cupboard. "Lord, give me courage."

Jacques rolled up his sleeves and his emotions with it and grabbed the knife off the shelf. The firelight gleamed off the blade. He walked to the fire and stuck the knife in the flame until the heat spread up to the handle. He turned toward Stephen and spoke to him flatly. "I have to do this, Stephen. Can you hear me?"

Stephen moaned but did not open his eyes or say a word.

Jacques held the knife above the ankle and with the other hand grasped Stephen's leg below the knee. He closed his eyes and drew in a deep breath. His hand remained poised for a moment, then for longer. He let out the breath and stepped back from the cot. "I can't do it," he said to himself. He stuck the knife in the fire again. He looked intently at Stephen. He knew his friend was unaware of what was going on.

Jacques stood at the cot again, this time with the point of the knife at the bright red flesh on the top of the injured foot. He took another breath and swiftly brought the knife down around one side of the gash. Stephen let out a yell and thrashed about on the cot. Jacques tried to explain what he was doing, but it was to no avail. So he held Stephen's leg down with as much force as he could while he slid the knife along the other side of the gash. Blood immediately filled the slits and trickled onto the cot. With the tip of the knife he removed the poisoned piece of flesh and threw it on the fire. The flames made it spit and sizzle, sending a putrid odor into the air. Jacques took a ladle of very cold water from the bucket outside and poured it over the foot. The blood thickened, making bright red strings as it was washed away.

Picking up the knife, Jacques stuck it in the fire again. He laid the hot blade on the cuts on his ankle and pressed down. The smell of burning flesh made him turn his head. He moved swiftly to clean the wounds, removing as much infection as he could see. Stephen moaned and then was very still except for his rapid breathing, which shook the entire cot. Jacques took some of the blue fabric Catherine had left on the table and wrapped his foot tightly, bringing together the edges of the wound as closely as possible.

He stuck the knife in the fire again to burn off the flesh and blood that clung to the blade. He rechecked the cloth on Stephen's foot to make sure it was not soaked through with blood, then stepped outside the little house. He hung his head and fell to his knees, his shoulders shaking with sobs.

17

The door to the little house rattled, then three sharp raps sounded.

"Father Jacques...Stephen...it's me."

Jacques rushed to the door and unbolted it. Catherine and Louis LaPointe rushed in with a sprinkling of white powder following.

"What took you so long?" Jacques demanded with obvious irritation. "I was afraid I would have to leave and search for you."

"Father, please don't be harsh. When I first arrived at the LaPointes', no one was home. I waited for hours until they came," she said breathlessly as she removed her coat. "It has gotten so cold. It started snowing just before we arrived here."

"What did Madame LaPointe say to do? Why isn't she here with you?"

"She was too weary to come, so she sent Louis back with me. Madame LaPointe gave me this paste. She said it would work." She handed Jacques a clay jar with a tight-fitting top.

Jacques pulled it off and looked at the green-gray mash.

"I've seen it work many times." Louis stood over Stephen. "His leg looks bad."

"Louis, it is much worse than what you see," said Catherine.

"Mother said if it doesn't work, someone will have to take off his leg," said Louis.

"It will work," Catherine insisted. "Father, please, would you put it on his foot?"

Jacques knelt on the floor at the foot of the cot. "Oh, my friend, I pray this heals your wounds." He set the jar on the floor and carefully lifted Stephen's leg. He motioned for Louis to hold it up while he unwrapped it.

Catherine gasped. "What did you do to him?"

"Catherine, are you so blind?" Jacques snapped. "Look at him. I had to do something. I should have taken his foot off hours ago, but I couldn't bring myself to do it." He surprised himself with his tone. "Don't question me now. It will do no good."

Catherine moved to the far side of the room and looked on quietly as the two men tended to Stephen's foot. Once they had unwrapped his foot, Jacques picked up the jar and scooped out the mash. It was cool and thick. He smeared the paste onto the opening on the top of his foot. He rubbed it back and forth several times. The mash adhered more to his fingers than the wet, raw skin. He applied the paste until the wound was totally covered. More mash was put on the smaller cuts on his ankle.

"Now wrap it back up tight," said Louis as he continued to hold Stephen's leg. "Stephen isn't moving at all. How long has he been like this?"

"He said he couldn't feel his leg by late afternoon. Yet when I cut into his foot, he nearly threw himself onto the ground in pain. He hasn't moved much since."

Louis looked at Stephen's face, then back at Jacques. "This doesn't look good."

"Please don't tell me what I know already. I am trying to deny it as best I can."

Catherine stared at the wall in front of her. Stephen had repaired the crumbling caulking between the logs soon after they arrived in Quebec. She touched the smooth, hard material. He had worked tirelessly to fix this place while she recuperated, and he didn't complain. "This just isn't right," she whispered. More than ever before, she wanted to turn back time.

"Catherine," said Jacques. It startled her to turn and see the priest so close. "I want to apologize for the cruel way I spoke to you earlier. I have treated you abominably," he said gently. "I was out of my mind with worry for Stephen. I have to tell you I was scared. I didn't want to be here alone and not know what to do. I think how you were here all night with him so sick. I am ashamed to say the least. Please forgive me."

"Oh, Father," she said, tears welling, "you are forgiven. I am so afraid, too. I don't know what I'd do here without..." She caught herself. "I just don't know anything anymore."

Jacques drew her near him. Her heart poured out in weeping like it had not done in months, for there was someone to comfort her. She couldn't have let Stephen offer her comfort when she wept for France. She couldn't let him comfort her for anything. He was an enemy in her quest to return home. She wept from the agony of being away from her father and France. She wept from becoming so ill on the journey. She wept from the death and disappointment of living in Quebec. She wept for Stephen's life.

The pain felt for Stephen was beyond her understanding—so close to the pain she felt for her brother. An attachment had been made against her will during the hard summer months. She didn't understand it. Maintaining her position as an unwilling victim in the whole event was her stead. Cruel reality gripped her now. If Stephen died, she would be alone for the winter. Knowing the LaPointes would be her salvation, for they would watch over her until spring when the ships came. She would abandon the little house and move in to their home. But there was more in her heart that would be abandoned if he should die...something new and tender. She could not put a word to it. It was just felt.

Catherine wiped her eyes on her sleeve as she stepped back from Jacques. She caught Louis's eyes and he quickly looked downward, as if embarrassed he had invaded her private world. She forced a soft smile. "I have a pot ready for some tea, and I'd made bread fresh just the other day. Please sit down and let me serve you."

Jacques and Louis sat at the table while Catherine prepared them a meal. She was glad to occupy herself with something rote. When the food was put before them, Jacques rubbed his eyes and then bowed his head for prayer. Louis watched him for a time and then gestured at Catherine that perhaps Father Jacques had fallen asleep.

"I did not fall asleep," said Jacques, "though I think I could without much provocation. And Catherine, you have been up since yesterday. Please lie down and get some rest. Louis and I will stay the night here by Stephen."

"Yes, go to sleep," added Louis. "Stephen's in good hands, and I know how to brew an excellent pot of tea, so we will be fine."

"Perhaps you are right. But do wake me if there is any change in Stephen."

Both men nodded. Catherine went behind the cloth partition and wrapped her blanket tight around her. She lay on the floor and looked at the ceiling. The fire flickered warm reflections on the rafters. Watching them sway hypnotized her into thick sleepiness. She blinked slowly and more slowly until her eyes remained shut.

It was not long after Catherine fell asleep that Jacques fell into slumber also. Louis stoked the fire to warm the room and lay on some bedding he'd found stored in the corner of the house. Moments later the rhythmic rubble of his snoring filled the room.

Catherine's sleep was restless. Her mind kept waking her with all that churned inside it, and the noise from Louis prevented her from falling back to sleep. What raced through Stephen's dreams when he lay groaning and thrashing in the middle of the night, almost every night? She wondered. She couldn't fathom how he'd managed to get up in the morning and work as hard as he did. Weariness covered her, but she couldn't go back to sleep.

She got up from her bed and went to where Stephen lay so still on the cot. Sweat clung to his hair and shirt and glistened on his forehead. His leg had been propped up on rolled bedding. Only a small amount of blood had seeped through the blue dressing.

Catherine ladled some hot water out of the kettle by the hearth and put it in a basin. Taking a fabric scrap from her needlework basket, she dampened it when the water was cool enough to handle. She hesitated, then placed the damp cloth on his forehead and brought it up into his hair. She dipped the rag again and brought it back to his hair, wiping the sweat from his head and behind his neck.

"Thank you," he whispered.

Catherine jerked in surprise. "Stephen, I'm sorry. I didn't mean to wake you." She dropped the rag back in the basin and moved away from him slightly.

He squinted hard to look at her. "Where is Jacques?"

"He is sleeping at the table. Louis LaPointe is here also. Can you hear his snoring?"

Stephen looked at the table to confirm her statement.

"Madame LaPointe gave us a paste to put on your wound. She said it would heal you quickly. You will be walking around this little house in a very short while."

He closed his eyes. Catherine could see moistness in them.

"What is wrong, Stephen?" She moved closer again. "Please tell me what's wrong."

He lay still. A tear rolled off his eye and disappeared into the bedding. She put her hands over her face and muffled her own soft cries. When she brought her hands down, he was staring at her, his eyes reflecting the firelight, making the dead ice blue come to life. His eyes were asking a question. She dared not answer lest she was mistaken.

"Why?" he finally asked.

"I don't understand, Stephen. What do you want to know?"

"Why are you crying?"

The words instantly wounded her. Had she been that cold that he thought it unusual for her to weep for someone so ill?

"What decent person wants another person to die? I was weeping because you are so ill. No matter what I have said in anger, I care about your welfare."

"Catherine, if I should die…"

"No, please don't say it, Stephen," she whispered intently. She moved closer still and put her hands on his arms. "I have realized something far more frightening than being in Quebec is being here without you." Her voice choked. "You have to get well. What would I do without you here? I wouldn't be able to survive. I would die before spring came. I would die in this awful place. Please get better for me."

"I must learn to stop imagining things," he said hoarsely as he closed his eyes.

"Imagining what?"

"That there was another reason for your sadness."

"I have never lied to you, Stephen," she said softly. "I have been awful and cold, yes. But I have never lied to you. Do you want me to start now? I don't know what I am thinking or feeling other than what I have just told you."

"Lies…" He struggled to open his eyes again. "I have told lies. I have told you a lie."

"About what?"

Stephen let his heavy eyelids win the battle. "Will you forgive me?"

"Forgive you for what?" She waited for him to answer. She put her hand on his shoulder to shake him awake but just gently rested it there. She didn't want to know what had been told to her as a lie right then. Another day she would pursue it.

Catherine sat in the chair by the fire. Her head slowly moved toward her chest as the warmth of the fire wrapped around her. Sleep finally took hold.

The colors in the little house began to slowly appear as the sun crept its way up the icy-blue sky. Louis's snoring was squelched as he coughed and repositioned himself. Jacques and Catherine remained asleep, each in their own chair. Suddenly all were startled with a crash and a moan.

"Stephen!" shouted Catherine as she jumped from her chair. Jacques and Louis were instantly on their feet, staring at the overturned cot. Stephen lay face down on the floor with the bedding wrapped around him like a shroud. He was perfectly still.

"I seem to have gotten slightly tangled," he finally said.

"Oh, my friend," said Jacques with a relieved sigh as he knelt and helped him to sit up on the floor. "Thank God. For a moment I thought…well, are you feeling better?"

"Except for this headache I've just received, I am feeling much better." He put his hand to the red mark on his forehead. "I would like something to drink."

Catherine brought him a cup of water while Jacques and Louis helped him back onto the cot.

"You should still lay here," said Jacques. "Put your foot up on that bedroll."

"My foot," said Stephen cautiously. "It's still there?"

"Yes," replied Jacques.

"I thought…" Stephen turned his head away from them. He wiped his eyes and turned back. "Was I dreaming? I thought you had a knife and…"

"I did. I was going to take off your foot, but I couldn't bring myself to do it."

"But the pain?"

"I cut out the poisoned part. You're going to have quite the scar."

"I have my life, Father…at least for today," he said solemnly.

"If you are awake and talking after last night, I would say you are on the mend," said Louis as he grabbed his heavy coat. "I must get back to the farm and let everyone know you are well. My mother isn't feeling too well as of late. She was sorry that she couldn't come to tend to you. Your improvement will be great news to her."

"Please thank her," said Stephen. "And tell her I will be over to help with what I can as soon as I am able."

"You know she'll refuse." Louis laughed. "But she will make sure you're well fed for making the attempt." He left the little house.

Jacques put on his own heavy coat. "I must go, too," he said as he fastened the last button. "I am sure my fellow priests are wondering what has happened to me. I need to show myself to them, so I am not classified as having been martyred."

"Oh, Father," said Catherine, "that is not funny in the least."

"After the last day, everything is appearing as humorous. I am so greatly relieved."

"Thank you for your help, Father. Thank you for your prayers and understanding."

She closed the door and latched it behind him. Stephen was asleep again on the cot by the fire. It was safe now to cover him with a blanket and stoke the flame.

18

Stephen walked with a limp through the snow to the pile of wood he had stacked along the trees. The cold made his foot stiff, and it pained him to put pressure on it. His skin had finally grown over the gash and made a thick depressed scar. He had been fearful for a long time that he would lose one or more of his toes, but their gray-blue color and chill eventually opened up to warm and pink. The limp and scar was the only remaining malady.

Stephen was more relaxed than he'd been since they had left France. Gaston being off with the fur-traders reassured him that winter would be free from any harassment. Catherine did not mention Gaston anymore, nor did she persistently mention returning to France. But he knew it was frequently on her mind. When spring came, he understood that this little piece of quiet existence would be over. She would not pass by the opportunity to return to her home.

Stephen stacked several pieces of wood into his arms and headed back to the house. The landscape had softened with the snow. The tree stumps were hidden in white, and the little gray house stood out against the stark snow. A steady stream of smoke puffed from the chimney, telling all that warmth greeted them on the inside.

He nudged the door open with his shoulder and kicked it closed after he was inside. He set the wood by the hearth. Taking a stick, he pushed the burning logs into the center of the fireplace and placed several new ones on top, arranging them so they stayed in place as they burned. Once the flames were lapping at the newcomers, he reached up and stirred the stew Catherine had made for him. It was nearing evening, and he was tired from the events of the day.

Madame LaPointe's illness proved to be a lingering type and had sapped her of her strength. Catherine had promised her that Stephen's injuries posed no threat any longer and that her greatest desire was to be by her friend's side and nurse her to health as best she could. Anyone who saw Madame LaPointe knew that she was nearing the end of her days, but no one said it to the kindly old woman. Catherine announced to Stephen that she would be spending much of her time at the LaPointes' home, tending to her and helping as she could. Stephen didn't argue against the plan; he let Catherine do as she pleased. He would have felt wrong for not letting her go. She prepared food for him for several days and started a pot of stew to simmer for when he returned from accompanying her to the LaPointes'.

It was a long journey by foot, especially with Catherine's bag, Stephen's limp, and the freshly fallen snow. They were both exhausted. Louis greeted them at the door and ushered them in with unexpected good spirits. Monsieur LaPointe greeted them soon after and took their coats and Catherine's bag. They expected sadness from him, too, but received his usual polite friendliness. Catherine was led into Madame LaPointe's room, where Lucas had just finished stoking the fireplace. The wood made a cheerful snapping. Lucas blushed as he bowed in greeting toward Catherine.

"My dear Catherine," said Madame LaPointe with the same jovial tone she always had. But her round face was puffy, as were her hands that lay across the blankets. Her breathing was heavier than normal, and her eyes revealed her concern. "Come sit by me," she said as she patted the bed.

Catherine sat on the edge of the bed and held Madame LaPointe's hand.

"How are you, Catherine?" the old woman asked.

"How am I? Oh, Madame, I am fine. Why are you so concerned with everyone? Please tell me how you are faring."

Madame LaPointe laughed heartily, which set off a coughing spell. Catherine stood and looked at the door as Lucas entered.

"I am here, Mother." He grabbed the cup from the little table at her bedside, lifted it to her lips, and she took a sip between coughs. He helped her lie back onto her pillows. Her chest rose and fell with a jerky motion, setting the fluid in her arms to shaking.

Suddenly the veil of her jovial nature was lifted, and Catherine could see the suffering. "Oh, Madame," she said with sadness.

Madame LaPointe continued to struggle for breath as Lucas put more pillows behind her back. She closed her eyes as if concentrating on breathing slower. After several minutes, her breathing slowed and the wheezing could not be heard.

"She has spells," said Lucas in a serious tone. He was the first LaPointe to speak gravely. "We have a mixture of herbs and berries in this cup that we give her when she has trouble. It silences the coughing, but it doesn't remedy her condition."

"My condition is that I am old, Lucas," she said breathlessly.

"Madame, please don't talk," urged Catherine. "I am going to stay with you until you are better. I have talked with Stephen, and he agrees that it is a good plan."

"I cannot take you from your husband," she protested.

"You need someone to nurse you."

"I have my boys and…"

"And nothing." Catherine put her hands on her hips. "Your boys have livestock to take care of, and Monsieur LaPointe is not as strong as he used to be. I have no children, no livestock, and a capable husband. It would be shameful for me not to help you after all you have done for us. Stephen even brought me here today with my bags."

"He is here? Please, send him in," Madame LaPointe said with a fond smile.

Catherine retrieved Stephen from the parlor. When they entered the bedroom,

Madame LaPointe motioned for Catherine to remain outside.

"Stephen, come closer," she said, reaching out her hand to him.

He came near her, took her hand in his, and kissed the top of it. "Madame, what can I do for you? Please don't hesitate to ask me for anything. If it were not for you, we wouldn't have survived our first days here, and I wouldn't have survived my injuries."

She smiled at him with tenderness, the way a true mother would smile at her own child. "God would have kept you, my son. You have a purpose for being here, in spite of what your original intent was for coming." She saw the question in his eyes. "I know there is a reason you came. You are trying to hide from something. That doesn't matter now. You are here, and I know God sent you."

"You have such high hopes for me, Madame."

"I don't have high hopes for you, Stephen. My high hopes are set on Quebec and what people like you can do for this place. That is why God sent you here. You are a leader. You have skills. Buildings and commerce are waiting for you to say the word, and they will nearly spring up on their own."

"I am honored that you have that much faith in my words," he said humbly. He knew he was in the presence of someone wise and sent from heaven. He couldn't protest or retreat. Accepting her words was his only option. "I will work hard at building this city. It will be grand, Madame. I promise you this."

"Thank you," she whispered. She brought his hand to her cheek. "Take care of Catherine. She will make a good wife one day."

Stephen smiled and stood as Madame LaPointe's eyes closed.

"Pay me no mind, Stephen. I'm just resting my eyes. Please send Catherine in."

Stephen brought Catherine back to the room, but Madame LaPointe had taken her weary eyes to full slumber.

Catherine stepped backward and gently closed the bedroom door. "I will stay until she no longer needs me," she said flatly.

"You will get no argument from me. I will stop by every few days to check on matters." He bid farewell to the LaPointe men and headed back to his home.

Stephen ladled the stew into his bowl and sat at the table. He didn't mind being alone as much as he thought he would. Good ease filled the little house instead of lingering tension. Catherine had been more aloof since his illness, and he tried to figure out why. He only remembered bits and pieces of that time and tried to figure out what happened that pushed her further away, especially since he had felt her tenderness toward him. His fear was that he might have told her he was responsible for Jean's death. But he dismissed it every time it entered his mind, knowing that if he had told her, she would have confronted him with it now that he was well.

Stephen finished his stew and added several more logs to the fire. Morning would come quickly, and he had volunteered to help the nuns at the hospital. Sick Hurons had poured into the new hospital, and the nuns and priests were worked to exhaustion. Catherine protested his going. But now that she was gone, he had no reason to remain at home. If he should contract something from the sick, she would not be affected by it.

The smell of death permeated the new hospital, and the nuns and priests were worn and haggard. Stephen instantly regretted coming. He looked over the sea of cots filled with the sick and the hunched backs of the priests as they tended to them. The nuns moved quickly between the cots, bringing and taking medicine and wastes. There was nothing he was equipped to handle in this infirmary.

"Why are you here?" asked the nun. She was tall, thin, and straightforward in her approach. She didn't have time for proper etiquette.

"I'm here to help…if I can," he stammered.

"See that bucket and mop?" She pointed toward the far corner. "Start at that end and mop your way through the hospital. And don't let the smell of vomit cause you to donate your own." She gave him a doubting look, then went back to her patients.

Stephen walked past the rows of sick Indians to the bucket and mop. The water was already used but short of being filthy so he stuck the mop in and began his task. He kept his mind on finishing and not what he was mopping up. The water was replaced many times before he finished.

Jacques was with the other priests giving last rites and doing anything else that needed to be done. Stephen tried to get his attention, but the priest was focused on the people who lay dying in front of him. The task seemed overwhelming.

Stephen followed any order he was given without thinking much about it. He could barely fathom the mass illnesses spread out before him. The deep despair and suffering sidestepped any rational answer to the question of why. As soon as one patient would die or become well enough to walk, his bed was given to another. It was a seemingly endless process. Periodically he would have to find a clean spot to sit and rest his foot, which throbbed with overuse.

"Stephen, I haven't had much time to speak with you as of late," said Jacques as he sat next to him. He looked pale and tired. His hair was in need of cutting and his chin had been left to whatever hairs appeared. "How is your foot?"

"Almost as good as new," Stephen replied. "I am not going to complain about a sore foot after being in here. What disease do these people have?"

"Our diseases," he replied. "The infirmities our French bodies have grown used to are killing them."

"How can that be? I have never heard of such a thing."

"I do not understand it, but I do see the effects. I don't know if I am ministering to them out of duty or guilt."

"Jacques, you still question all of your motives," Stephen said casually as he rubbed his foot.

Jacques was silent for a moment; Stephen could feel him tense.

"I meant nothing harmful by the comment, Jacques. You know I esteem you."

"No harm taken, Stephen. How is Catherine? I haven't had opportunity to see either of you for weeks. I feel as if I have totally lost touch with you both."

"Catherine is staying at the LaPointes to nurse Madame LaPointe either to health or…"

"I had heard she was doing poorly. I visited her not long ago, and she had taken to bed rest. Her heart doesn't tolerate much activity anymore. I am glad Catherine has decided to help her."

"It is noble of her," said Stephen. "It is also more peaceful at home with her away. She has been more distant since my illness, and it has me wondering."

"Wondering what?"

"Perhaps you would know. Did I confess anything to her while I was sick with fever?"

Jacques was silent again.

Stephen wondered at the tension. "What is bothering you, Jacques?" he finally asked.

Jacques started to stand but quickly resumed his position next to Stephen. His small brown eyes became smaller with intensity and ire. "Why do you continue on with this charade?" he demanded. "How can you play with your own salvation and her heart as you do? Look around, Stephen. What do you see? Death and disease everywhere. And yet you find enough leisure in your spirit to think you can play with life. Well, you can't. This is not a game."

"I don't think this is a game, Jacques," he protested.

"Then why are you consumed with keeping a secret that is only hurting you? There is no point."

"But Catherine…"

"Catherine has no idea who you are. You have spent too much of your energy fighting off night demons and avoiding the truth. You have belittled Catherine by assuming she wouldn't understand. She stood by you and cared for you when you were almost dead. And I had the absence of mind to scold her. I am ashamed of that." Jacques stood and looked down at Stephen. "And right now I am ashamed of you."

At a loss what to say, Stephen looked after Jacques as he stalked back to the patients. Then Stephen stood, asking the first nun he saw what else he could do.

The few days that Catherine anticipated spending with Madame LaPointe had turned in to months. She returned to her own little home on occasion for respite, though she found it less relaxing than being at the LaPointe farm. She enjoyed the rich conversation and activity of the family, and they, in turn, enjoyed her humor and spirit. Those were characteristics she forgot she had. She was a daughter and a sister at the LaPointes. She loved being both.

Her time with Stephen was more tolerable taken in small amounts. She chided herself for being so foolishly taken with Stephen while he was ill. Certainly now that he had recovered he didn't need her and made it plain that it was so. He was still sullen and quiet when he woke in the morning and didn't seem to have any need to share what tormented him with her. Every tender motion she made in her intimate shyness was looked at with suspicion. She took it as rebuff and ceased to make herself vulnerable. After being away at the LaPointes, she was relieved that her head became clearer and she focused again on leaving for France in the spring. She hoped Gaston was still waiting. Surely her father would have told him that she would return.

"I love the spring, Catherine," said Madame LaPointe. It was effort for her to talk. Her breathing became labored with the slightest of exertion. Over the weeks her health moved between being restored and being bedridden. When her puffiness subsided, she was strong enough to walk to the kitchen and have her meal. When it came back, she was confined to her bed. It never completely went away.

"It is still too soon to yearn for spring," Catherine said as she busied herself with her needlework at Madame's bedside. "It has been a mild winter, though. Perhaps spring will come early."

"Perhaps it shall." Madame became quiet and stared off into the room.

Catherine noticed the distance the elderly woman had gone in her mind and waited for her to return. "What were you thinking?" she finally asked.

"I was thinking about how I will miss spring. I will miss the flowers and the freshness of the air. I will miss Eliot when he returns."

"Oh, Madame, please don't speak that way."

"One cannot afford to pretend here, my child. Certainly not when death knocks."

Catherine put down her needlework and sat on the edge of the bed. "I don't want you to go, Madame." Her voice wavered. "You have been the mother I never knew. I know it is selfish for me to want you here, but that is how I feel. I don't want to lose you." Catherine took Madame LaPointe's hand in hers. "There is no one here in Quebec who could ever replace you."

"I am not ready to leave today. I have not said my good-byes. But I know I will leave soon. You will do well without me, Catherine. You are a strong woman. Most people can't see that because you don't let them see it. I can sense it in you."

"Oh, I am not strong. I have done little but cry ever since I came here."

"You have grown in your suffering. That is the most powerful kind of strength. That is strength that goes down deep and is not easily uprooted." Madame LaPointe smiled and closed her eyes. "Is my husband in the house?" she said softly. "I would like to see him."

Monsieur LaPointe was quick to enter the room when Catherine beckoned him. She watched as the little old gentleman pulled the chair closer to the bed and took his bride's hand in his. He stroked her puffy hand and looked intently at her as she spoke.

Catherine left the room and gently closed the door behind her. She put on her heavy coat, wrapped it tightly around her, and stepped outside the front door onto the snow-covered walkway. The old stems of summer flowers that lined the path were still buried in white. She hoped Madame LaPointe could see spring again—just one more time. Her heart told her, though, that it would not be so.

Louis and Lucas were carrying bags of grain to the cows and donkeys that lazily meandered from the corral to the barn with nonchalant ease. Catherine looked at the two men who were so faithful to the LaPointe farm and Madame's legacy. Madame told them often how proud she was of them. She often kidded each spring that their brides would be marching up the steep hill to Quebec as soon as the boats landed. Though she made it light, it was truly her desire each year. She prayed fervently that God would send her boys good wives. Maybe this spring her prayers would come true. Yes, Madame loved spring.

"Catherine, good afternoon," Stephen called as he reached the LaPointe farm. He looked toward the barn and waved his hand at the LaPointe men. "Catherine," he said, turning his attention back on her, "what are you doing standing out here?"

"I needed some clean, cold air. I've become quite melancholy with Madame preparing her heart to pass away."

"She knows her time is near?" he asked.

"Yes, she knows." Catherine turned into the cold wind and let it dry her sudden tears. "She is a brave, wonderful woman. I am so glad to have known her."

Stephen looked at Catherine and saw a bravery of her own. He wondered for a second where it had come from or if it had always been there. "You have been good to her, Catherine."

"It was the least I could do. I, really, am the one who has been blessed by being here." She looked at Stephen directly. "Why have you come by?"

"I came to see how you and Madame LaPointe were. It has been several days since I was by."

"It seems you were here only yesterday. Time must be moving faster than I realize. Stephen, have you seen Father Jacques? He has not been here for some time now."

"It is the strangest thing. I had been looking for him in recent weeks. He has not been to the hospital or in town. I was very concerned. When I spoke with Father Vinmont at the chapel last Sabbath, he said Father Jacques has gone into seclusion."

"Seclusion?" Catherine looked puzzled.

"Father Vinmont said seclusion was a time away with God with no other distractions."

"I am surprised he did not tell you. You have such a strong friendship."

Stephen looked down and cleared his throat.

"What if we need him here for Madame LaPointe?"

"I told Father Vinmont about Madame. He said he would send a priest here soon."

"I do hope Father Jacques is well. He does so much for all of us."

Stephen looked at the ground, remembering Jacques's last words to him. "Catherine, when this is over…I mean, when you come back to the house…we must talk. There have been so many things happening to us, so many things that have passed."

"When this is over, Stephen, perhaps we can."

Stephen left without seeing Madame LaPointe. Monsieur said she was fast asleep, and he didn't want to chance disturbing her.

Stephen strode home in the same footprints that had brought him to the LaPointes. The steps were very different now. They had promise and fear in them. He could barely believe that he had held out the offer of disclosure to Catherine and that she, tentatively, took it.

Father Jacques's words rang again in Stephen's head. He could not shake the idea that he had shamed his friend. He didn't know if he could even be classified as a friend anymore. How could one man be so lost in his own turmoil that he lost sight of the entire world around him? He didn't know. He wasn't sure if he wanted to know.

Yet he committed in his heart to confess to Catherine before spring came…before the ships from France came.

Stephen brought more wood into the house with him and restarted the fire. The little house cooled off quickly once the fire went out. Even with the thick logs and repaired caulking, there were plenty of cracks to let the cold in. Stephen lay on the cot for the night. He used it every night that Catherine spent away. He didn't bother building one for himself, finding it only slightly more comfortable than the floor. Jacques's words and stern tone continued to play over in his mind. How could he have been such a fool and not have seen it? How could he have let the one true friendship he had slip away? Why did he disregard Jacques's help for so long?

"In deed, in debt, indescribable," crowed the bony judge as he peered down over his high bench at Stephen. "You defend yourself…Ha! In trouble, insane. To the gallows with you, beggar."

"For what crime?" Stephen pleaded.

"Insubordinate, ingrate, inquiring. Let me tell you…murderer."

Two cloaked henchmen moved toward Stephen and grabbed his arms. Stephen tried to fight them off with his fists, but they neither flinched nor wavered in carrying out their duties of justice. Swiftly he was led from the judge's chambers to the gallows in the square. A rough rope was placed around his neck, and a cloth bag was placed over his head.

"Inconsequential, indifferent," said the judge as the gallows floor opened.

Stephen felt himself plunge through the floor, only to snap back at the end of the rope. He jerked up once and then back again, snapping the bones in his neck. Lights flashed brightly for an instant, quickly turning to black. He heard no more. Saw no more.

Felt no more.…

Stephen could not tell that he was awake. The thick smoke from the fireplace filled the house and made the scene surreal. He put his hands along the wall until he recognized what he was feeling, then made his way to the door. Once the door was opened, he spilled outside and lay on his face in the snow.

"Oh, my God, no," he wailed, beating his fist into the frozen ground. He gave himself over to groaning and tears until his breath couldn't be caught. He rolled onto his back, and the early morning sky pulled him fully out of his sleep. He took a deep breath and began coughing until most of the smoke expelled from his lungs.

Smoke billowed out of the house and hung low in the cold morning air. Stephen jumped to his feet and ran back into the house, opening the door wide and flinging open the window. Something had blocked the chimney and caused the slow-burning flame to billow smoke into the house. He was fortunate that he was alive.

Finding the smell unbearable, he chanced that nature would not wander into his house as he left the door and window open. He hoped, too, that the weather would stay calm. He put his heaviest clothes and boots on, fastened his coat tightly, and set out for the LaPointes' once again.

"Catherine, Mother would like to see you now," said Louis as he wiped his eyes. His chin quivered and the look of it caused Catherine to falter. She put her hand on his shoulder and took a breath. She could say nothing to him.

The room was softly lit as the lantern and the rising sunlight gently wrestled for dominance. Both sources cast a warm glow on Madame LaPointe's face. Monsieur sat on the bed and brushed her gray hair from her forehead.

"Catherine, I have said my good-byes now," she whispered. Even with a gentle voice her breathing became labored.

"Shhh, Madame, save your strength," Catherine said.

"Why would I waste the last few moments I have being quiet? You know me better than that."

Madame started a coughing spell and Catherine looked to Monsieur for the cup of herbs and berries. He shook his head and looked down. She was beyond any good that it might do. Catherine waited for her coughing to subside and wiped the pained tears from her eyes.

"You haven't said good-bye to Stephen, Madame. Your time can not be now."

"My dear, I said good-bye to him weeks ago. I touched him and felt his spirit strong," she said slowly and softly to conserve her last bit of strength. "Take care of him. He needs you more than you know."

"Please, now is not the time to leave us, Madame," Catherine pleaded. "I know you could stay longer if you desired it. Please, desire to stay."

Monsieur LaPointe turned his head and wiped his eyes while he held his wife's hand tightly. He turned back to Catherine, silently demanding that she look at him. "She is tired, Catherine. She is weary of the struggle." He gasped imperceptibly as his wife squeezed his hand and shut her eyes.

"There is no one on earth who wants her here more than I. She was the bride of my youth. My heart always rested safely with her. She has served and loved her family well. But she is tired now." He looked at her with love and sadness in his eyes. The sun cleared the barren treetops and sent light flooding through the misty glass pane onto Madame's restful form. "It is time we let her go."

Madame LaPointe's body slowed into death in the presence of her loved ones. Her chest no longer fought against itself to catch a single breath. Her face was relaxed, and her mouth turned up in a gentle, restful smile.

20

Louis and Lucas kept the fire burning over the plot of ground for a full day. The heat and ash penetrated into the frozen earth and brought the smell of it to life. They dug down as far as they could, then started another fire on top until they had the hole deep enough for their mother's coffin. Monsieur LaPointe had been making the box since Madame told him that her time was near. He believed what she said and dutifully prepared the way.

In the winter many of the dead were either burned or preserved for burial in the spring when the ground had thawed. The LaPointes agreed that winter would not stop them from giving Madame a proper funeral and her final resting place. She would be laid in the earth next to her beloved daughter, who had died many years before. It was a beautiful place on the LaPointe property, and Madame diligently had kept nature from invading the space where her daughter lay. She made sure each spring that flowers would bloom there.

The priests from the mission arrived shortly after Madame had passed and tended to her body. She was placed in the coffin and brought to a building on the property and rested there until the grave was ready. In the early morning of the funeral Louis, Lucas, and Stephen brought the coffin to the grave and slowly lowered her in.

By midmorning the people of Quebec began arriving. Carts drawn by oxen, horses, and donkeys pulled into the LaPointe farm. Some came on foot. Father Vinmont and his fellow priests arrived with several of the nuns from the hospital. They came to give their respects to a woman who had always done what she could to keep the hospital functioning. Even Governor Montmagny came with his entourage of soldiers. Before long the quiet little area where the grave lay open was surrounded by people.

Father Vinmont began the service with the story of Madame LaPointe. Catherine tried to listen but found it difficult to concentrate. Her mind was on the empty place that was now in Quebec and the hearts of those who knew her well. She wondered how many of the people there really knew her or just knew of her. She felt sorry for those who only knew of her. They had missed something wonderful.

The Father finished his eulogy with a prayer and motioned for Monsieur LaPointe to place the first shovel of dirt upon the coffin, followed by his sons. Catherine couldn't watch the scene and tried not to hear it. The sun was warm that day and the sound of snow falling in wet clumps from the trees made music in the air. Its pleasantness drowned the thud of the dirt. *Perhaps spring will come early for Madame,* she thought.

Stephen watched the face of Louis and Lucas as they shoveled their spades full of dirt on the coffin. Sadness burdened their shoulders as they stepped back alongside their father. He hadn't thought of his own parents for months. One hasty message sent to them before he departed France was all he had left them. Did they wonder if he was dead or alive? Was there someone there to console them? Did they think he had become an outlaw? He had always been a good, respectful son. One decision in his life had turned him into a shallow, self-centered person. Or perhaps he had always been that way, and circumstances pushed it to the surface.

Stephen searched the faces of the people gathered there in hopes that he would spot Jacques. He had to talk to him. Everything Jacques had told him before was starting to become clearer. He knew he had to tell Catherine what happened that night in France. He knew he had to confess. Then the dreams would stop. He would feel real again. If Madame LaPointe's words were true, then he could build Quebec with abandon.

Jacques's support was all that was missing right now. He wished he had respected it while he had it.

The visitors began to disperse at the same rate that they came. The cart and hoof tracks left muddy ruts on the dirt paths around the farm. Stephen watched as they left, hoping Father Jacques would be uncovered as the crowd thinned. He was not there.

Catherine offered to prepare the LaPointe men an evening meal, but they refused and urged her to finally go home and rest. It had been a long journey for them all.

Catherine was quiet when she returned home. She went to the cupboard and took out the cups Madame LaPointe had given her when they first arrived. Stephen brought the fire to life and soon had hot water for tea.

"I wouldn't have made it without her," she finally said. "She was like a mother to me. I didn't understand how much she meant until she became ill." Catherine looked at her tea and pushed it aside. "I think I will lie down for the night. I am no good to anyone right now." She started to move back from the table when Stephen reached out and placed his hand on hers.

"Catherine, before you go, I must tell you," he said, forcing himself into tenderness, "I am humbled by your service to Madame LaPointe. What you did was a heroic act that I imagined myself to be capable of, yet when put to the test, proved that it is not in me." He didn't want to let go of her hand but could feel her discomfort.

Catherine looked bewildered. "Thank you. I really must rest my head. It has been a very long time since I could give myself over to exhaustion. I intend on doing that tonight."

Catherine disappeared behind the partition, and Stephen remained at the table. The little house was too small to hide in any more.

Stephen and Catherine spent the remainder of the week getting back into a routine that was comfortable for both of them. The mood was somber as the pain of Madame LaPointe's death lingered, though each day that passed made the sadness easier to bear.

Stephen waited for a more opportune time for his confession. Perhaps when Catherine was light enough to laugh, she would be ready to hear his story. How cruel a reward that would be.

Since Monsieur Fonte's death, Montmagny had been trying to convince Paul Lebec to take over supervision for the building of Quebec. He had been resistant, not wanting to spend the time, but his planning skills were superb. The governor finally persuaded him with much pomp and flattery. Monsieur Lebec's first order of business was to call a meeting with all the skilled tradesmen in the city.

Stephen went to the fort earlier than the meeting called for to look at the structures that lined the streets nearby.

Catherine took the opportunity to travel with him. She had not been to town since Stephen's injury and was anxious to see if anything had changed. She wondered if everything would look different simply based on how she felt. The last few months had made her strong. She felt the difference within herself. Her heart, which raced before with any wind of change, remained steady. She smiled when she remembered Madame LaPointe's words to her. She knew now that she was right. Suffering had given her a deep strength.

Stephen left Catherine visiting with a group of women who had gathered outside the chapel and continued his meandering through the few streets of Quebec. His ideas from the previous summer remained viable. Nothing had changed, which sparked his excitement all the more.

While he surveyed the land and the buildings, he tuned his eyes to finding Jacques. It had been many weeks since the priest had gone into seclusion, and Stephen could not imagine that Jacques could be away from the work he loved so much. He was surprised that someone could hide themselves away in such a small community and not be seen for such a length of time. He had eased his concern for Jacques by periodically asking the other priests about him. The report was the same each time; Father Jacques was well and tending to his spiritual needs.

The air was particularly warm for the time of year, and people had ventured outdoors more. Folks who lived just beyond the fort came to the main street and chatted with the friends they had not seen for some time. There was excitement as people shared the news of the winter and talked of the work ahead when all the ground had thawed. Several of the workmen who assisted Stephen with the chapel stood and admired the work their hands had done. They agreed that during the coming summer they could build twice as many structures if the Iroquois kept away.

"Have you heard of any attacks yet? I have been concerned with the weather being warmer than usual," inquired Stephen.

"I saw their footprints near the edge of the woods at my place," said one of the men. "Fresh as could be right there in the mud."

"How many do you figure?" asked another of the builders.

"I would say five, anyway. I didn't venture into the woods to see if there were any more. Those Iroquois would just as soon slit your throat as let you breathe their air."

"But are you sure they were Iroquois?" Stephen asked. "I heard every other tribe is running scared of them. Maybe it was some Huron Indians coming here for a little safety."

"Are you willing to take the chance? I say we had better get ourselves more prepared than ever to defend ourselves. Once those rivers to the St. Lawrence open up, we'll be crawling with Iroquois."

"The St. Charles is already starting to thaw," said another. "And I've heard other folks say they've seen evidence of the Iroquois moving in. We're just sitting targets if we don't do something. The nuns at the hospital said the Huron are dragging in half dead because of the Iroquois."

"You mean they've attacked them and they survived?" asked the first man.

"No, the Iroquois have them running scared. They have no food. One said they had resorted to eating tree bark to stay alive. The Iroquois attack almost every camp they make."

"And to think those crazy missionaries are going to Montreal. They will be right smack in the middle of war parties. What can they possibly be thinking?"

"They go because they feel compelled by God to go," called a man from behind the group. Stephen knew the voice. "Wouldn't it be far more dangerous to live outside the will of God than to go where He leads you?"

"Pardon me, Father," said the man. The other men nodded in polite agreement and the group started to disperse.

"Jacques," said Stephen as he limped toward him, "it is so good to see you. I have worried about your absence. It didn't seem like something you would do. Every time I came to town or went anywhere I searched for you. I asked the other priests and they always said you were alone seeking God. I have missed you, my friend."

"Whoa, Stephen, slow down." Jacques laughed. His brown eyes had their sparkle back. "It is good to see you, too."

"You look well, Jacques."

"I am well."

"Pardon my asking," Stephen said as they started toward the chapel, "but you have been away for much of the winter. How could you seclude yourself in prayer for that long?"

"I haven't been secluded the whole time. I did spend several weeks in intense prayer and searching my heart. But after that I wholly devoted myself to the service of those at the hospital."

"The hospital?"

"Yes," he replied. "You would have found me there if you would have looked. It is such a sad situation, yet a blessing, too. The Huron Indians and other tribes have come in by the droves, sick and starving. They are a beaten people. But it is that very reason why they are so open to learning of Christ. All their resources for building a future are gone with the Iroquois after them. That is causing them to look at eternity as a quickly approaching thing."

"Jacques, don't you think that they are saying what you want them to say so you will protect them?"

"I don't see how much protection we can offer them. More than they have in the woods, I suppose. But I have seen the change in their hearts. Granted, not all who profess Christ are sincere. I would like to think the majority is. I have seen the changes."

Stephen touched Jacques's arm and stopped him from continuing toward the chapel. "I have missed you. Why didn't you come and see me or send word that you were out of seclusion? I have so much to tell you."

"I had to get my mission straight, Stephen. I was sent here to minister to the Indians, and my heart was all tangled up with you and Catherine. Not that I regret the time I have spent with you, but I fear it was a diversion for me...an excuse to neglect the reason I came here. I had such a hard time loving the Indians when I heard and saw the things they had done. I saw the situation as us against them. I had to deal with the fact that I could not give myself to them fully."

"Jacques, you never allowed me to sway your opinion toward the Indians. You always took the moral high ground. It grieves me that you had to seclude yourself to see that."

"It wasn't just that. I was so consumed with your life and the torment you had that it caused me to act against what I had spent years bringing under control. I was becoming irritable toward you. My patience was waning with your struggle, and that should not have happened."

"I was pig-headed," Stephen said. "I don't blame you for being sharp with me. I deserved far more than you gave."

"I not only snapped at you, but I was harsh with Catherine for no reason. The animosity that lives and breathes between the two of you caused me to become irritated with everything about her. Whether I displayed it or not, it was in my heart. Catherine at least had the honesty to be truthful to herself and to you. She never tried to pretend something that wasn't. I admire that in her, yet I think that irritated me the most. It was a reminder that I was less than honest with myself."

"Once again you are being too harsh on yourself."

"Are you still so blind, Stephen? Don't you see yourself in anything I have just said?"

Stephen studied Father Jacques. He looked clearer and brighter than he had for a long time. He was focused. It could be seen in his stance and the way he spoke.

"I had so much to tell you…so much I was going to make right. But I stand here wondering if anything I purpose to do will come to any good." He continued to look intently at Jacques. "I fear I have lost all sense. Perhaps I have let guilt erode my senses and too many nightmares damage my thinking."

"Father Jacques," called a priest from the door of the chapel, "Father Vinmont is ready for you."

"I am sorry, but I must go, Stephen."

"But, Jacques, what plans do you have now? Will you still be put away from us?"

Jacques laughed and put a reassuring hand on Stephen's shoulder. "I am going to continue to work at the hospital when I can and perform my duties at the mission. There is a fellow priest, Father Jogues, who had been ministering to the Huron up the St. Lawrence at Huronia. He will be returning there this summer with supplies. I hope that I am ready in my heart to go back with him."

"Jacques, travel to Huronia is incredibly dangerous. It's in the middle of the worst tribal fighting."

"Yes, I know," he replied.

Stephen watched Jacques disappear through the chapel doors. His heart sank as the priest's plans resounded in his head.

The meeting for the building of Quebec was brief and straightforward. Paul Lebec had little to add to the plan that Monsieur Fonte had previously laid out. Stephen was quiet during the meeting. Nothing struck him as needing a comment. Perhaps if his mind wasn't contending with his conversation with Jacques and the state of his own affairs, he would have had something to say.

Catherine was waiting outside the fort with several of the other women who had come into town with their husbands for the meeting. When Stephen emerged from the meeting, he acknowledged Catherine with a nod, and they began the journey home. More hours of daylight afforded them a leisurely walk back to the little house.

Catherine had enjoyed the opportunity to converse with the other women, listening to their struggles and joys and sharing her own on a casual plane. She didn't explain about her sorrows, for fear of the kept secret restrained her. She was growing unsure of the need for secrecy. But until she understood the reasons herself, she would remain silent.

Catherine wasn't sure whether the slower stroll was because of Stephen's distracted mood or if his foot was paining him. His limp was more pronounced than on the journey to town, but he denied any increased discomfort. She looked at him closely. He had the answers to her questions and to the secrecy of them being in Quebec. She wanted to ask him everything that had puzzled her, but he needed to be willing to give her the answers. She gambled that this would not be the day to approach him. Perhaps tomorrow would yield the truth.

Little was said by either on the journey back to the little house. The usual routine was embarked upon returning: Stephen would build a blazing fire, and Catherine would prepare the meal. And, according to routine, neither would speak beyond the necessary. The day came and went, each one keeping to their own corner of the house.

Stephen ran hard, barely noticing the branches as they slapped against his chest.

His shirt was ripped and bloodied. Welts formed on his skin. He ran harder, pushing his strong legs to maneuver over fallen trees without losing speed. His lungs burned as they gulped air. He wanted to look back to see how close they were—the men with the rope—but he couldn't risk it. His eyes were fixed on the woods in front of him. There was no path to follow. He had to keep running.

A pain suddenly seized him in his side and threw him forward to the ground. He struggled to his feet and stepped out, but the pain brought him to his knees. Something warm had soaked his shirt. Stephen put his hand to his side and felt the warm blood. He had been shot. He struggled to his feet again and moved forward. He could hear their voices now.

The pain shot through his body with every step. His legs trembled, faltered, and sent him crashing to the forest floor again. He could hear the men. He could hear the crunch of twigs and leaves under their feet. Stephen tried to push himself up off the ground, but his legs wouldn't move. He could hear them breathe now...their footsteps slowing...stopping...

Catherine lay on the cot and listened to Stephen thrash about on his bed. She hadn't awakened to his dreams for quite some time. Her sleeping mind had gotten used to his turning and moaning in the night. She didn't know why she had awakened this night. Perhaps the full moon shining through the tiny cracks in the door and window kept her sleep light. The anguish of his deep moan surprised her. Months ago it caused her concern. Then it transformed into irritation for the interruptions of sleep. Now it caused her sorrow. Something had deepened in her, and she was too tired to convince herself that irritation was the better emotion.

Catherine donned her robe and moved out from behind the partition. The fire had dimmed to glowing embers and a small flame that showed itself sporadically. She stepped around Stephen and placed two more logs on the flame, coaxing it to a blaze. The light from the fire illuminated Stephen's form. He lay on his side with his legs drawn up, his hands clenched behind his head. He moaned again.

Catherine knelt by his back. She hesitated waking him. He was often sullen and strange after waking from a dream, and she did not want the sorrow of that in the night hour. He moaned again. Placing her hand on his shoulder, she gently shook him. He did not respond beyond another moan. She shook him again, and he released his clasp and turned onto his back. His head turned side to side, intense pain on his face.

Catherine shook him more vigorously. "Stephen, wake up," she said, becoming more fearful with each second. Fearful for what he was enduring, yet more fearful for what may occur when he awoke. She didn't want to be alone with him, feeling as incapable of tending to his soul's torment as she did when he was racked with fever. "Please, Stephen, it's only a dream."

Stephen opened his eyes. They were wild with fear as he looked at her shadowy form. "I did not mean to…," he blurted out. "Believe me. I did not mean to kill him."

"Stephen, you are still sleeping." Catherine tried to put her hands on his face.

He backed away in fear, still caught in the dream. "No…no, you cannot take me."

Catherine's heart raced. "Stephen, please," she pleaded, "it's me. Wake up." She turned so the light of the fire touched her face. "Do you see now? It's just me."

Recognition crept onto Stephen's face, and his ice blue eyes brimmed with tears.

Catherine placed her hand on his rough cheek that was wet with sweat and tears. He put his hand on hers and kissed her palm. He looked so gentle and helpless in the firelight. She hadn't seen him tender since he was ill. His pretense and isolation were discarded in that moment, and she was moved with compassion.

"Catherine," he said with regret in his voice, "I cannot continue with my life one more day with the heaviness I have in my heart." He took her hand from his face and held it in both of his. "I must tell you something that will be hard to hear."

Fear grabbed at Catherine's throat. She wanted to tell him that she didn't want to know what he had to say. Whatever it was could be said tomorrow or the next day. It could be told to her when Father Jacques was with them to make sense out of it. She didn't want to hear something hard from this man in the thick of the night.

"Catherine, please don't be afraid," he softly said as he kissed her hand again.

The gentility in his eyes pulled the words from her mouth. "I won't be afraid. Tell me what you will."

"I must first apologize to you for these months. I have been so cold toward you. I've been so confused. I suppose you still despise me, and I cannot put blame on you for that. I deserve any rebuff you give."

"Is this the hard thing you have to say?" she asked.

"I wish it were. I don't know why I am wasting my words. I guess fear is overtaking me as I speak."

"Please, just tell me what you have to tell me. You said you couldn't go on without baring your heart."

"Catherine," he said, looking at her squarely, "I have murdered a man."

"What?" She tipped her head slightly, unsure she had heard him clearly.

"The truth, my beautiful Catherine, is that I killed your brother. I killed Jean."

Catherine knelt, frozen. She stared at him as tears pooled and spilled from her eyes, her chin shaking with emotion.

"I am sorry, so very sorry. Please know that I did not plan it or ever want it to happen. It was an accident." He let go of her hand and pressed his hands onto his eyes. "I am haunted by the memory day and night. I did not mean for my knife to pierce him. I wanted to help him. But it all happened so fast."

She got up and moved to the fireplace. With one hand on the hearth and the other at her side, she spoke toward the fire with purposed control. "Was there no robbery?"

"I suppose there was. There was mention of money. I know nothing of it, really. I just happened by on my journey home after working. Jean sounded in trouble, so I stopped to help him. Before I could understand anything, a fight ensued. The men drew their knives. I drew mine and somehow...I don't know, Catherine. I was pushed or bumped into and my blade..." He stopped speaking when he saw Catherine's shoulders stiffen. Stephen stood and moved toward her.

"Please don't," she said.

"I believe Jean was in trouble that night. I know he was. The men he was with acted as criminals, and Gaston did, too."

Catherine turned sharply to look at him. "Gaston was there?"

"Yes, he was part of the whole event."

"Gaston was there, witnessing the murder of my brother, and you whisked me away before he could come to me?" Her tone moved from control to indignation and contempt.

"No, it wasn't that way. Catherine, Gaston is evil."

"You tell me you murdered my brother, but that my beloved Gaston is evil? What sense can you make from that?"

"Please understand...Gaston is somehow to blame for all of this. I know that to be true. I know it in my gut."

"Why did you bring me here? What purpose could you have in doing that?"

She looked at the tormented man she had been forced to marry in haste at her father's urging. He stood facing her with his broad, muscular shoulders bent in resignation and his hands hanging powerless at his sides. She was suddenly sickened.

"Oh, how hideous and vile you are! I have been defiled for your own purposes."

"No, that isn't true. I never meant to hurt you. I've always loved you."

"No." She started to pace in front of the hearth. "Don't say that. This is all a game to you, a sick game from a sick mind. You took me and consummated a marriage that was a lie. You consummated a marriage, not in a marriage bed, but on a cart along a dusty road while I was sick with grief." She shook her fists in the air and screamed. "I hate you, Stephen Marot! I hate you!"

Shame washed over Stephen like a consuming wave. He fought it with all the strength he had, for he knew it had the power to consume him unto death. The pain of it hammered at him. He stepped back from Catherine and breathed deeply, summoning what power he had from the hidden fibers of his character.

"I loved you, Catherine. I love you now. I have regretted that night with every waking and sleeping moment since. I have not touched you again. I did not defile you in the sight of man because I am your husband. But I know I defiled you in your own eyes. For that I am truly sorry. But I am not sorry for loving you and protecting you from Gaston. He is wretched and evil. He was not faithful to you, yet you were the only one who did not know it. He mocked your love every time he took another woman."

"You are a liar. He loved me and only me. He told me so. And I loved only him."

"He is the liar," Stephen said as he backed further away from Catherine. The turbulent wave in his head had crashed and washed back out to sea, leaving tumbled sand and quietness. "I have finally told you what consumes me. Now you know that I am paying a price each night the dreams come. I pay over and again for the price of a life. Mine has been tormented as recompense for Jean's."

Catherine gave herself over to tears. "How could my father have let you take me?"

"He had suspected Jean was involved in wrongdoings long before that night. When I told him what had happened, he encouraged me in my plan. He feared for your life and your reputation. He feared Gaston."

"You lie again. You lie about all those I love."

Catherine continued to weep by the fire. She didn't want to think about it anymore. She didn't want to feel it anymore. She didn't want to despise Stephen anymore. If sorrow produced deep strength, as Madame LaPointe professed, then the morning light would bear witness to a woman of great courage.

21

Spring came rushing in with several warm rains that carried away the lingering snow. Rivers ran high and fast. Green-yellow buds sprouted under the tender care of the sun opening into leaves of rich green. The air was fresh with the smells of spring. Catherine was eager to till up the garden, which surprised even her. She knew it would be the only thing to occupy herself now that Madame LaPointe was gone.

She hoped Eliot would return from trapping soon, as many of the other men had done already. Sad news would await him. His sorrow would be even greater in that he did not attend her funeral. She knew the pain of unsatisfied grief and the pall that lingered until it was resolved.

Her anticipation of his return was tempered with the memory of their last meeting. She wondered what had caused her to behave in such a fashion. How ridiculous to think Eliot would take her to Tadoussac without Stephen's knowledge. She should have been forthright with him, or with any sailor who could have sped her away on the ships. That time and opportunity had passed, but another one waited ever so closely. Soon the ships would come in. Spring arriving was as a promise that would be kept. She would return to France on the first boat that left Quebec.

Building projects boomed as soon as the ground thawed, and Stephen was busy from morning until the sun began to set. Most of the construction was reinforcing the protection around Quebec. Attacks were on the rise, and every day someone had a tale to tell or a body to bury.

Maisonneuve and his forty missionaries badgered Montmagny daily to set sail for Montreal, but the governor insisted that it was too early in the year to start a settlement. Finally, Maisonneuve declared he would go with or without Montmagny's blessing and that he would set sail the next day.

Most of Quebec watched as Maisonneuve, forty missionaries, several soldiers, Montmagny, and enough experienced seamen to navigate the governor's brigantine, set their course for Montreal. They waved, a little more reluctant to see them go than they had thought. The more people at Quebec, the safer they felt.

The city was on edge the entire time Montmagny was gone. He was the leadership a city under imminent attack needed. Also, the soldiers he took with him would be sorely missed if the city should come under attack. Montmagny and his soldiers did return safely. But the general feeling was that the forty who would settle at Montreal would never be seen again.

Stephen was not immune to the feelings that ran through the city. He heard more than he cared to hear as he worked in town each day. Not only had he begun scanning the horizon for Iroquois but for Gaston. It was only a matter of time before Eliot and Gaston returned. Stephen was eager to talk with Eliot and warn him of the evil of his new companion, though by now, Eliot might have discovered that on his own.

Stephen didn't really know why he feared Gaston after disclosing everything to Catherine. The only damage he could do to him would be to tell the authorities that their stonemason was a murderer. They would either try him in Quebec or send him to France to face their magistrates. It would be his just reward. The damage to Catherine would be more heinous, but Catherine was out of his control or his protection. She rebuffed him every time he attempted to reason with her. She had her heart and mind set on France and Gaston. The only hope Stephen had was that she would leave for France before Gaston returned. He would do the best he could to protect her without her awareness until that happened.

The sun rose late that morning, being restrained by a thick band of clouds. Cloudy days were difficult for Stephen. His foot ached with the dampness of the air and took longer in the morning to warm up. He fashioned a cane for those days. It also helped him with the long trips into town. He had hoped that one day his foot would be restored to its normal condition, but complete restoration was elusive. The skin and bones had set and healed into the form it was. He would have to work with what he had. How close he had come to losing his foot made the condition of it now a small burden to bear.

By the time it reached midmorning, the clouds disappeared and bright sun flooded Quebec.

Catherine wrapped her shawl around her and went to her garden. There was still much to be done to prepare it for planting. Stephen offered to help, but she wanted none. She enjoyed the quiet and peace of her outdoor space.

Catherine had just picked up the hoe that Stephen had made for her last year when she heard familiar footsteps approaching from behind her. She spun around and shouted, "Eliot! You're back!"

"And it is good to be back. I'm glad you don't have corn to hide in this time, Catherine." He laughed.

"But you still sneak up on a person," she replied. "It is so good to see you. I've missed you terribly. How long have you been in Quebec?"

"Only a few days. We've been at Tadoussac trading. That's another sad story I shall tell you someday." He laughed again.

"We?" she asked.

"Eliot, welcome back," said Stephen quickly as he approached from the house.

"Stephen," Eliot greeted with a nod.

"I am so sorry about your mother," Stephen continued. "What a shock it must have been to come home to such sad news."

"Yes, it was very sad. She lived a good life and had many years. I am glad she went peacefully. We know this land can take its toll. I see you must have had a run in with it," Eliot said, pointing to the cane.

"I hurt my foot sometime back. It's fine now, except for a little limp. I only use this cane when I plan on walking a distance, which is what I intend to do now. I have to do more work on a building in town. Let me walk down the path with you." Stephen took Eliot by the elbow and started away from the house.

"But, Eliot, you just got here," Catherine pleaded. "Won't you stay for a little while?"

"Well, I…"

"I am sure he has things to do, Catherine," Stephen interrupted. He looked at Eliot and gave a slight nod, his eyes telling Eliot to agree.

"Yes, I do have a number of things to attend to. I will call on you again soon."

The two men walked down the path until they were out of sight of the house.

"What is on your mind?" Eliot said as he pulled his arm from Stephen.

"I didn't want you to say anything in front of Catherine. Tell me, what was the name of the man who went with you to trap?"

"Henri? He has been my friend for years. Why do you need to know?"

"No, the other man. The one you had just met."

"Oh," he said and shook his head. "His name is Gaston."

Stephen cursed and kicked the dirt. "Where is he now? Is he in Quebec?"

"I don't know where he is. We split from him shortly after we set out. He went with a small group of Huron that split off from the band we were with. Took himself an Indian wife, I hear. With the Iroquois on the rampage I don't expect any of them to last long by themselves, though many of the men were exceptional woodsmen. Maybe they will survive. I take it this man is not a friend of yours?"

"You understand me right. He is like poison to me…and to Catherine. She does not know it, though."

"Catherine." Eliot nodded in understanding. "So he is the man she wanted in France."

"She told you?"

"When she wanted me to take her to the ship she told me. It's all folly, Stephen. You don't need to be concerned. Gaston is long gone. He may even have been someone's dinner months ago. It happens, you know."

Stephen shuddered. "He didn't say anything to you about Catherine?"

"No, not her in particular. Women he talked about. The man has no conscience, I am sure. We were glad when he split from us. I pity the Indians he went with. I can see why you took Catherine away."

"Unfortunately she doesn't see it that way."

"Does she know he is here?" asked Eliot.

"No, and I don't want her to know. Can you imagine how knowledge would play on her heart? It would be a disaster. I just hope he doesn't come looking for her."

"Have you seen him? Does he even know that you and Catherine have settled in Quebec?"

"He knows." Stephen lifted his foot. "My little run-in with Quebec was actually a run-in with him. I've never seen anyone so purposefully vicious."

"I will keep your secret, Stephen. But I don't think you will have to worry. I think he is long gone. New France is a very big place. A very dangerous place."

"I hope you are right. Please let me know if you see him…or even hear about him."

"I will," said Eliot as he took the trail that led to his home.

Stephen continued on toward town. His insides ranged from agitated to relieved at the news Eliot brought. He counted Gaston short of nothing when it came to survival, especially when there was someone ripe for harassing. Stephen had his woman, and he had Stephen's secret. That proved to be a caustic mix.

Just as Stephen arrived in town, a crowd started to gather outside the fort. Someone mentioned that Montmagny was going to give a speech and urged Stephen to listen. A moment later, Governor Montmagny stood on the podium and raised his hands for silence. He looked paler and thinner than on previous occasions, and the drawn look to his face gave evidence of a streak of sleepless nights.

"I am not going to charm you with eloquent prose today. I am going to get straight to the matter at hand. We have lost some settlers recently to Iroquois attacks."

"Some?" heckled a voice from the crowd. "I would say too many!"

"Yes, even one of us is too many, but if you insist on the interruptions I'll have you thrown in the stockades. What I have to say is very important, and I need your full attention." He paused until all were silent, then continued.

"We have stationed soldiers at some of the areas we felt were inroads for the Iroquois to travel close enough to us to cause trouble, especially the river Richelieu. Obviously, we underestimated the cunning of this people, and their attacks are only increasing. We are under siege."

Murmuring went out over the crowd.

Montmagny raised his hands again. "Silence, please. Several days back I received word that our good King has heard our request and has sent us forty soldiers. They are, right now, making their way up the St. Lawrence from Tadoussac."

The crowd cheered, and Montmagny did not bother to silence the jubilant crowd before speaking again. He simply raised his voice. "With the troops that are arriving soon and plenty of able-bodied volunteers from among you we will be able to erect a fort by the river Richelieu in a week's time. We need you if we are going to stop this attack on our settlement."

Montmagny got down from his podium and went back into his office, shutting the door behind him.

"Sounds like a plan that will work," said the heckler.

"Iroquois are too crafty for that," said another man. "They'll find a way to get to us. I think the best thing is for us to pack up and go back to France."

The man's statement drew a volley of comments.

"I have spent too much time and sweat into building this place to leave it all behind now. This is our chance to do something for our children and ourselves. Yeah, it is hard, but we knew that before we ever left France. I'm staying." Most of the crowd agreed.

Stephen heard what the men said, but it was as if he were hearing it through a bottle. All he could think of was the ships that were coming…and the ships that would be going back to France. Catherine would be on one of them.

22

"I wondered when we would be seeing you again, Jacques," said Catherine as she saw the priest heading toward her from the path that led to town. "Welcome." She dusted her hands off on her apron and stood to greet him.

"Once again, your garden is thriving." He waved a hand toward the rows of green sprouts. "It is exciting to see the vegetation spring from the ground. You have done well."

"Thank you, Father. Please, may I offer you a cup of tea?"

"Yes, I would enjoy a cup." He scanned the property, then eyed Catherine.

"He should be here any moment," she said, reading his look. "He just went a short ways into the woods to set some traps."

"I have something I would like to tell the both of you. But for now, I am thirsty for that tea."

Catherine laughed and entered the house to get Jacques and herself cups and a tea strainer. She ladled the water that was being kept hot on the open fire outside the little house and poured it over the tea leaves.

"I grew this tea last year," she said as she handed him his cup. "It is my special blend." They each sat on adjacent tree stumps.

"Mmm…very good Catherine," he complimented as he savored his first sip.

"Well, it was just a variation on Madame LaPointe's tea." Sadness brimmed in her heart.

"You miss her, don't you?" he asked.

"Yes, I do. She was the only thing that kept me sane last year. I learned so much from her. I believe I am stronger for having known her."

"I have noticed that change in you. You are more settled."

"Oh, Father, do not take me wrong. I am more settled in who I am and what I am doing. I am not more settled in Quebec."

"I understand," he said as he looked long at her. "Then you still desire to return to France."

"Yes, I do. As soon as the ships come. Stephen and I had discussed it before winter came."

"I am surprised that Stephen is in agreement." Jacques took another sip of tea.

"He is not in agreement, but he said I could go. I think it would be best for him if I were not here. I have brought nothing but sorrow to him, I am sure."

"He loves…" Jacques stopped himself from finishing.

"But I cannot say without a doubt that I love him. I know that love is not everything in a marriage union, and people marry all the time who barely even know each other. But I have always had a dream, Father. I dream of marrying someone I have known and loved for some time. Someone who cherishes me and who I do likewise. I want to be a real wife in my heart, soul, and body."

Catherine focused on her cup to hide her eyes and emotion. "I know that sounds frivolous, especially with people being killed almost daily here in Quebec. My dream sounds like complete fantasy." She looked up directly at him with sudden boldness. "It is not a fantasy in France. It is what I almost had there. I want to return."

"Have you spoken about this with Stephen recently? Surely the ships will be coming soon. It is best not to surprise the man."

"I will speak to him very soon. Perhaps even today."

"I hope you will talk about many things that concern you both. Confession and openness will only bring about healing of the soul, no matter how much it hurts in the process."

"Father, I know Stephen has confessed much to you. I am certain of it. He has also told me some things."

Jacques looked at her with puzzlement. He wanted to ask the question but dared not lest he was mistaken.

"He told me about the night that Jean was murdered," she said to answer the question.

"Catherine, I am sorry. You had to know the truth, and Stephen needed to tell it. I am proud of him for doing so." He set his cup on the ground and shook his head. "So much has changed, Catherine. I thought I knew so much about life and serving mankind, but I miss even the most life-changing event in my friend's life."

Jacques smiled and put his hand on hers. "Someday I will achieve genuine servitude. One thing I have learned is to not place excessive pressure on oneself for missing the mark. Thank God for grace and mercy. They have become my greatest companions! I trust you will do the right thing, Catherine. Stephen is a good man. I know you can see that. He is becoming better every day. With his confession to you his nightmares must have stopped."

"I must admit they have either become less intense, or I am no longer waking from them. There are still times in the morning that he behaves as if he has had one. Something still plagues him, Father. I cannot understand him or solve whatever bothers him."

"Jacques," called Stephen as he appeared from behind the little house, "I had been thinking of you just moments ago. I have kept my eye out for you whenever I have been in town, but I think we are always on different roads."

"That is probably the case. It is surprising not to be able to find someone in such a small community. I have looked for you in chapel, also."

"That is to my shame," said Stephen as he stood before them. "I have put my work and my distractions ahead of my commitment to the priests at the mission. I vow to you now, in complete repentance, that I shall be at the next chapel service and every one thereafter."

"Good. I am glad to hear that and so will the other priests."

"I know that is not what brings you by, Jacques. What is on your mind?" asked Stephen.

"You know me well. Let me begin. I have been in much prayer regarding this matter, and I am excited and a bit frightened at the same."

"It's about Father Jogues's mission at Huronia, isn't it?" Stephen's mouth drew tight in seriousness.

"Yes. Another priest and I will be accompanying him back at the end of the week."

"Father," Catherine said softly, "I have heard about this mission. It is a dangerous place, a dangerous journey."

"Dangerous?" questioned Stephen, giving way to his own staged answer. "It's not dangerous, it's suicide!" He started to move away but paused before he could take a step. "I'm sorry." He exhaled. "I am out of place to behave this way toward you. I just can't bear the thought of you putting yourself in such a vulnerable place. I know your faith is strong but with the Iroquois on a rampage you will all be prime targets."

"I have grown to love you, my friend," Jacques responded in an even, gentle tone. "But in this area the division between us is wide. It is easier for me not to discuss this with you than to have to justify my decision with you in an area you do not understand. So I will not justify myself. I will tell you this has been my prayerful decision. I have felt and known this for quite some time." Jacques looked at Stephen and Catherine. "You could at least bid me safe travel and best wishes," he finally said.

"Of course, Father. I bid you much success and a speedy return," said Catherine. Her eyes were moist. "We love you and will miss you terribly."

"Jacques, I…I don't know what to say," said Stephen. "I can't imagine Quebec will be quite the same without you. I know I will not be the same without your friendship."

"We will always have our friendship. That will never end." Jacques picked up the cup and handed it to Catherine as he stood. "Thank you for the tea, dear Catherine. God protect you in all that you do and everywhere you go."

"Stephen, will I see you on the day of my departure?"

"You could not keep me away." Stephen quickly embraced Jacques, then stepped back and wiped his eyes. "Thank you, Father Jacques. Thank you for everything."

Jacques disappeared down the path he came on.

"I cannot understand his deep faith," said Catherine solemnly. "I pray one day that I would."

"This is heavy news," Stephen replied. "I am comforted by the fact that Father

Jacques seeks God for all things, though I do not understand it at all. This hasn't been an easy choice for him, I am sure. He shared with me his struggles before. Ha...he shared with me. I am the last one he could have had a deep conversation with."

"You dismiss yourself too readily, Stephen. You were never like that back in France."

"I was not like many things that I am now. At least that is what I supposed. If I have learned one thing in this whole journey, it is that I am not what I thought I was. The pressure that has come from this whole nightmare has pushed all my outward flesh away and exposed my true character. I have to tell you, Catherine, I am not impressed with myself."

"I am impressed, now." She moved closer to him. "You are finally being a real person with me and with yourself. If your true character is exposed, then it can be changed...refined. I wonder if we will ever understand things as deeply as Father Jacques. It seems his character had been refined long ago. I believe only goodness remains."

"There is a matter that we need to discuss," he said as he stood in front of her, silently demanding she look into his eyes. "If my character is to be refined, then I must be forthright toward you and your desires. You know that the ships will be coming to Quebec soon. I have been stubborn in the past, hoping that you and I could..."

"I know," said Catherine.

"You desire with your whole being to return to France, and I would be cruel to stand in your way. I know of the pain of having a dream thwarted, and I would not want that for you. I will send you with a letter of agreement to dissolve our marriage union. I surely think an annulment would be offered in our case. You will be free to marry again."

"Oh, Stephen."

She wept. She was confused if they were tears of sorrow or joy. Logic would say they were tears of joy at receiving the desires of her heart. At that moment she doubted that logic knew either.

"I don't know what to say. I thank you for making this easier." She reached up and put both arms around his neck. "Thank you," she whispered.

Catherine wanted to tell him that he would do well in Quebec without her, that he was made for that place, that perhaps with her gone, his nightmares would completely stop. She wanted to reminisce about the first months after they had arrived. She wanted to laugh with him about the hard times. She wanted to connect her experience with his and savor it with him. There would not be much time to do that. She would soon be leaving him for her beloved France.

Stephen pulled her arms from his neck and held her hands. "We will be civil, then, until the ships come. We will do what we can to ready the garden and to pack your things. There is just one thing I ask of you."

"What is that?" she asked, willing to give him anything.

"Please do not put your arms around me. Don't be tender toward me. Don't give me any sign that I may have won any small space in your heart."

The request stunned Catherine. Her heart felt as if its reins had been suddenly jerked back. She couldn't understand why she even felt it. "I will do as you request, Stephen."

Catherine turned back to the fire and removed the kettle that had simmered dry. She would concentrate on France now—on France and on Gaston, who would surely be waiting for her when she returned.

Stephen mindlessly went about his duties around the little house. He tried not to think about the day when Catherine would leave. At random moments his heart would tell him that he still had time to woo Catherine. Then he reminded himself that Gaston was still in Quebec and was still a threat until there was proof he was dead. Stephen could not change that even if he managed to win over Catherine. And that, alone, was an insurmountable feat.

Stephen pushed the ax blade across the flat stone time and again, making tiny sparks shoot from the blade. Every few strokes he would check its sharpness by running his thumb across to the edge. Several more cycles and the ax was ready to use. He looked at the fallen trees at the edge of the woods and took a deep breath. He flexed his arms and looked at them again. All desire to chop them into burning-sized pieces left him. He visually measured the wood stacked alongside the little house and determined that the need to cut more wood was not imminent. He leaned the ax against the already stacked wood.

"Catherine," he called to her over his shoulder, "I'm going to check my traps."

"But you just set them," she replied.

"I will check them anyway. The rabbits don't know how long the traps have waited for them. Roasted rabbit will be a good meal tonight."

Stephen followed the little path. He had placed the traps not too far from the woods' edge. He didn't want to be deep in the woods with the Iroquois in an uproar. The sun was beginning a slow descent to the west, casting beautiful shadows. Shades to jewel greens spread a blanket of tranquility over the place.

"This is beautiful, God," he heard himself say. He stopped on the path and listened to the woods; the hush of the leaves way up on the treetops, filtering down to where the breeze didn't blow; the melody of a thousand different birds, each singing his lazy tune; the trickle of a little stream, meandering through the rocks and leaves.

"This is what Father Jacques must feel always," he said to himself. "The peace I wished would transfer to me if I were by him long enough." Stephen closed his eyes and breathed in the fragrant air. His mouth moved with words that didn't make a sound.

Stephen returned to the little house without a rabbit or even having checked the trap. The sun was starting to touch the treetops and cast a warm pink glow across the sky. He looked at it for a time, then went into his little house and went to sleep.

The remainder of the week passed quickly. There was more work in preparation for Catherine leaving than either of them had expected. Stephen continued to work on the buildings in town and fortifying the area around the fort. Once again he and Jacques missed each other in the busyness. The day had finally come when Jacques would head with the other missionaries to Huronia.

Twelve canoes were loaded with supplies and bobbed as the occupants boarded. Some canoes sat so low it looked as if the water would come right over the edge. Most of the travelers to Huronia were Hurons—men, women, and children. Thirty-seven people in all. Father Isaac Jogues, Jacques, and one other priest were surrounded by the other priests from the mission as Father Vinmont prayed for them before they began their journey. Stephen stood back away from the group but kept his eyes on Jacques. He was reassured by how peaceful he looked. This surely must be a mission that had been knit into his heart. He felt honored that he had been his friend. The group in black broke up and Father Isaac Jogues was helped into the canoe.

Stephen approached Jacques and put his arms around him. "God bless you, Father."

"God bless you, Stephen. Here," Jacques said as he reached into his pocket and handed him a piece of paper. "I was afraid I wouldn't see you before I left so I wrote my good-byes in a letter."

"I would have swum after the boat if you left without me seeing you, my friend. Jacques, I can never tell you how much you have changed my life. I know I have been the most exasperating man you have tried to reach. Please believe, it has not been in vain. I listened to you. I have pondered and wrestled with what you have told me over and over again. It exposed in me things I did not want to see and set before me the man that I truly want to become. Your words of truth have become a part of me. Your faith has become my faith. One day, when you return, I pray you will see a man who has become what you have demonstrated all the while I've known you."

Jacques looked at Stephen knowingly, as if he had anticipated his words long ago, and now they came as no surprise. "My son, you have come to know God. What greater gift can there be?"

"I believe there is no greater gift," Stephen answered.

"Take good care of Catherine while you can, Stephen," Jacques said as he was urged to board the last canoe.

The caravan of boats pushed off from the shore and paddled upriver toward their mission at Huronia. Stephen watched as they disappeared from view, then climbed the steep path up the side of the precipice along with the remaining priests. They were excited that Father Jogues was on his way back to his beloved Huronia with supplies to help the sick and needy Huron. Stephen still could not join in their excitement but would not speak ill either.

The climb was difficult for his foot, so he decided to rest for a few minutes before heading back to his home. He found a spot of grass to sit on and a sturdy shade tree to be under. He unfolded the paper that Jacques had given him and began to read.

Stephen, My Friend,

It is late at night as I write this. The moon is high tonight and shines brightly. The stars are brilliant, too. It is a beautiful sight on the eve before my departure. Tomorrow I go and will journey far from the people I have come to love. But tomorrow night I will look up at the sky and see the same stars and the same moon. It will let me know that we are not that far apart.

I have been blessed by knowing you and Catherine. I have been blessed by being a part of Quebec. But God has called me to another place. I think you are beginning to understand. As for the dangers I may encounter, Christ has already endured anything I could possibly encounter…even death on a cross. I do not know whether I am blessed or cursed not to have suffered for the sake of Christ. I am finally willing to endure anything for His cause. He will give me all the strength I will need. His blessings are never ending when He dwells within.

May God be with you always,
Father Jacques

Stephen carefully folded the paper and put it in his pocket.

23

It was barely a week after Jacques and the twelve canoes began their journey up the St. Lawrence River to Huronia when the ship carrying the King's promised soldiers arrived. The boat received the largest fanfare Stephen had seen. The settlers were excited that their help had finally arrived. Governor Montmagny wasted no time in updating the new arrivals on the events around Quebec and his plan to halt the Iroquois by building a fort by the mouth of the Richeleu River. He planned to leave in three days' time. The soldiers protested greatly amongst themselves but followed the orders they were given. The citizens of Quebec were summoned by Montmagny's assistant to report to the fort the following day, as plans for the resistance of the Iroquois would be explained.

"I know what the plan is already," said Stephen as he spread currant preserves on his bread. "The plan is to load up every able-bodied man and set sail for the Richeleu River."

"That is the talk going around," said Catherine as she stood in the open door of the little house. The cool breeze combed through her hair, chasing away the heat of the day. She closed her eyes and breathed in the fragrance in the air.

"I may refuse to go," he said.

"Why wouldn't you go? It sounds like something you would find great reward in doing."

"There are a lot of reasons." He took another bite of the bread. "One reason is this: who will protect the people left behind? Who will protect you, Catherine?"

"I will be fine," she answered.

"What about the protective construction around Quebec? There is still much to be done. Are we to just leave it unfinished and start a new project?" He took one last big bite of the bread and washed it down with a cup of water.

"You will not be gone forever. I'm sure the walls and buildings will still be here when you return."

Stephen turned in his chair and looked at her standing there, her form lovely and soft. "But will you?" he finally asked.

Catherine turned toward him. "I thought this was all settled with you, Stephen. We were going to be civil and carry out our plan. You cannot change your mind now."

"I have not changed my mind. I will keep my word to you." He dropped his eyes and looked at the table. It was too hard to think with her gazing into his eyes. "What is the real truth, dear Catherine, is that I don't want to leave you here in this house and then come back home to nothing. For whatever reason, I need to bring you to the shore. I need to see you get on that boat and sail away. If the ship leaves before I return, it will seem as if we parted without matters settled. It sounds crazy, I know." He looked at her again. Softness covered her as the light from outside cast a halo around her form. "Do you understand, Catherine?"

She was silent for a moment. He could see the silhouette of her shoulders rise and fall as she breathed. He had to remember these images and memorize her voice. He had to be able to resurrect the smell of her hair washed in perfumed soaps and the salty smell of her skin after laboring in the garden.

"I do understand," she answered softly. She gazed at him for another moment, then turned back to the gentle breeze.

The next morning a crowd of Quebec's men stood outside the fort as Governor Montmagny took his stand and began to speak.

"I have called you all here because of the urgency of the times," he began. "Several boats will be leaving for the Richeleu River tomorrow morning, and I need at least 60 men of Quebec with me to build a fort there. You will be provided with arms if you need to leave what you have with your families. There will be soldiers remaining behind to protect your loved ones. The men among you who are solitary have no excuse for remaining behind. We need to band together to bring a halt to our citizens' bloodshed. If we work hard, and I am sure that you will, we will have the fort built in one week. Then you can return to Quebec with the confidence of knowing the Iroquois inroad to this area has been destroyed."

With that statement the once skeptical crowd cheered.

Montmagny raised his hands. "I am counting on you all to be a part of this defensive move and will be waiting at the boats at sunrise."

"Tomorrow is sooner than any of us expected," shouted a man from the crowd. "We have to think about our families. It takes some preparation."

"While we prepare to leave our families in ease, the Iroquois continue to head this way in masses," Montmagny responded. "I do not think we can afford to give them one more day in which to bring us closer to an attack. We must depart at sunrise."

The crowd continued with their discussion of the speech and the petition for their labor. Most agreed that it was a good plan. It didn't matter if they agreed or not…the call to service had been sounded.

Stephen agreed it was a good plan but could not bring himself to sign his name for duty. He had to be sure the ship would not leave before he returned. He approached one of the soldiers standing by the fort and caught his arm before he went inside.

"Sir," he said as he quickly let go of his arm. The defensive look in the soldier's eye caused Stephen to immediately assume a submissive posture. "Please, could you tell me if the ship will set sail for France any day soon?"

"Do you plan on being on it?" the soldier asked in a gruff voice.

"No, sir, I do not. But someone I love does. I don't want to come back from Richeleu and find her gone."

"Heartbreaking, eh?" He laughed. "Rest your mind, man. Montmagny has ordered the ship to remain in port until he returns from Richeleu. That boat isn't going anywhere."

Stephen started home at a rapid pace. There was much to do before he left in the morning. He wanted Catherine to be well set while he was gone. He stooped down on the path and picked up a long stick. He had left his cane at home, for his foot had not been paining him for quite some time. Now it throbbed. He walked on it lightly the rest of the way to the little house.

Another warm, sunny morning greeted the men who had gathered at the shoreline. Several boats were loaded with supplies and Montmagny's brigantine was stocked and ready to go with Montmagny and his soldiers aboard. The surprised workers quickly boarded the boats with their own meager supplies and pushed off toward the Richeleu River. The men, with strong arms from building and working their land, propelled the boats upriver with greater speed than they anticipated. They would arrive the next morning.

Another morning dawned as a copy of the previous two. The sun set the sky a clear light blue and reflected off the vivid green of the trees. Heavy foliage graced the water's edge, sparkling with dew, and birds of varying voices sang a bright tune to the men on the boats. The river's current strengthened as they neared their destination. The Richeleu River was just beyond the small peninsula that jutted into the St. Lawrence. The men were excited and relieved that they had arrived with great speed and no mishaps.

As the first boat cleared the wooded peninsula their jubilant chatter fell silent. The second boat did likewise. Their heads were turned toward the shore. The remaining boats quieted in anticipation. Stephen's hand gripped the boat's edge in readiness as his boat slowed as it rounded the peninsula. He kept his eyes on the trees, straining to see what was beyond them. His eyes widened as he saw what quieted the boats before him.

Along the river's edge were placed long wooden stakes. Many footprints marred the narrow strip of sand. Stephen made his eyes follow the stakes' forms from the sand up their knotty bark to the tops, where the bloodied heads of travelers, who had come by not long ago, rested. Stephen tried to look away, but his eyes were fixed in the horror of the scene. They passed from one severed head to the next. They were Huron. He recognized one as having been on the trip to Huronia with Jacques. He prayed that this poor man had strayed away from the party. His eyes moved to the next one—another Huron and then another. A white man was next, the priest who accompanied Jacques.

All of Stephen's insides knotted up so tightly that he felt pain throbbing at his core. He looked again and tears filled his eyes so thick he could not see any more. He blinked slowly and opened his eyes again. It was Jacques.

"Oh, no…no," Stephen whispered. The voice in his head let out a long, violent scream while his jaws clenched in agony. "God, my God…why?" Then his mind stopped thinking, and his gut became numb.

The boats were pulled up on the shore, except for Montmagny's brigantine, which was anchored close by. The bodies of the slain men were scattered around the clearing, their clothing ripped from them. Blood had soaked the ground where they lay. Along the wood's edge several trees were stripped of bark and the gruesome attack was engraved in carved drawings. From this primitive pictorial they were able to learn that Father Isaac Jogues had been captured. They shuddered with the thought of his captivity. The men who lay dead on the beach had the better lot.

The stakes were quickly brought down and the heads placed in a gruesome pile. A large grave was dug and the bodies and heads were placed in it. They did not take time to place the head to the right body nor lay all the slain in neat fashion. They did not want to be the next victims. The soldiers, who had seen blood and battle, could not make any comment of the sight. This was beyond anything they had seen before. The workers could barely breathe.

After the bodies were all placed in the grave, Stephen's mind and heart came back into being. Sadness and loss overtook him, and the pain was more than he had ever known or imagined. He fell to his knees, unable to stop the tears and deep pain from coming out in wails.

A while later he felt a hand on his shoulder. He opened his eyes and saw the boot of a soldier.

"Was he a friend of yours?" the soldier asked softly.

"Yes," Stephen choked, "a very good friend."

"It is sad. Very sad," said the soldier. "We have a lot to do here, man. There will be time to mourn later." He stuck a shovel in the dirt by Stephen. Stephen looked at it and knew what he had to do. He wiped his face on his sleeve and took hold of the shovel and joined the men as they heaped dirt on the bodies. A large cross was made and stuck into the dirt alongside the grave, and Montmagny said a prayer. A blast from the muskets signified that they had been laid to rest.

The rest of the day they set about chopping down trees and clearing the ground, setting fire to brush, and digging up roots. Stephen couldn't get the image of the shoreline that greeted them out of his mind. On more than one occasion his stomach quivered and threw up its contents. He was not alone.

The sunset and campfires dotted the clearing. Twenty of the one hundred took night watch and paced the perimeter of the camp with their muskets ready. They certainly didn't want to become as the men they buried that very morning. Stephen adjusted his pack under his head and settled in for the night. He closed his eyes, but the images of Jacques too easily tread across his eyes. He looked up at the stars and remembered the letter Jacques had given him. He touched his pocket and heard the crinkle of paper. He had kept it in his shirt pocket but had not read it again since Jacques first gave it to him. He took out the paper and turned toward the fire so he could read it. He silently mouthed the words. Tears filled his eyes as he whispered, "I do not know whether I am blessed or cursed not to have suffered…"

"Oh, God, I pray that Jacques did not suffer. I pray his death was swift and unforeseen…that he went from peace on this earth to instant presence in glory." He put his head back down on his pack and looked up at the sky. "You were supposed to be looking at the sky now, Jacques. It would remind you that you were not so far away."

This light of the moon cast a celestial haze across the night sky. The stars were bright, scattered across the milky dust. The night was quiet and serene. "Maybe you are closer now than ever."

The days passed quickly as the men cut trees to shape and began building palisades. The work proceeded in record time to the surprise of the workers, but right on schedule for Montmagny. He stated time and again that this would be the salvation of Quebec and in his great concern for its citizens he wanted it done quickly. Montmagny spent most of the days upon his brigantine, coming ashore frequently to check on the progress and shout encouragement to the men who worked so feverishly to execute his plans. The Iroquois were never far from any one's mind. There was always a group of soldiers on duty whose sole concentration was to look out for Iroquois. They surrounded the construction site pacing, looking, and listening.

Every day for nearly a week they watched the woods and the river in anticipation of an attack. They assumed the Iroquois were not far away and might even be close enough to have been entertained by the men's response at seeing the massacre. Any memory of that first day sent chills through a person.

The fort was near completion. The wall surrounding the buildings was strong and, hopefully, adequate to fend off any Indian attacks. The buildings were done but needed reinforcement at the bases. Wells and troughs would have to be created after the soldiers have officially moved in. The men were glad that the project was almost over and busied themselves with the finishing details. Their nerves were on edge, and each day that passed gave them dread that they were one day closer to an attack. They had only one more day's work ahead of them. Then they could return home. With that in mind they continued their work without complaint.

Suddenly, without warning or hunch, a volley of shouts pierced the air. Stephen had never heard such a sound before, but his instinct told him quickly that what they had feared had come upon them. They were being attacked. Wave upon wave of Iroquois poured out of the woods. They were organized and in one accord as they flooded the perimeter of the fort.

The soldiers along the palisades fired their muskets as fast as they could while yelling to everyone inside to get their guns. Workers scrambled for their muskets and climbed the wall, firing into the rush of Iroquois. Stephen lifted his musket to aim and didn't even get off a shot before the man next to him fell backward with a bloody hole in his chest. Stephen aimed quickly and shot. Loaded and shot again, and again.

The Indians fearlessly approached the fort, running and screaming in such a way that sent waves of fear through the air. In spite of the men's best efforts some Iroquois reached the wall and scaled it as if it were a garden fence. They stuck their guns through the loopholes that were meant to aid the men and fired at them. The soldiers were quick to fire back from above. Their Iroquois bodies fell to the ground with another kind of scream.

As quickly as they came, they left, disappearing into the thick woods. All was quiet again. Once the men realized what had just happened they cheered in victory.

Montmagny watched the scene from his brigantine, shouting orders no one could hear. When the battle was over, he set across the short expanse of water and arrived on land with a speech of praise ready. "Good work, men." He paced excitedly. "You do not realize the magnitude of what just occurred here. If this attack had come earlier than today we would not have been ready. The one hundred of us against the two hundred or more of them would have been a disaster. But the fort and its palisades have proven to be sturdy and an ample defense. We lost one man. Our hearts are with his family. But we must rejoice that only one man was sacrificed while ninety-nine are standing here today. The courage with which you have all fought makes me proud to be among you."

He finally stood still, took a deep breath, sighed, and looked around at the men. "Magnificent." He saluted them all, then went back to his boat.

The man who was killed was buried and the work on the fort continued with more effort than before. Another day's work and the fort would be as secure as possible. Then they could all go home.

24

The journey back to Quebec was swift because the river current ushered them along in less than a day. Most of the men were jubilant with their accomplishments of the week. They had fulfilled Montmagny's plan for the protection of the citizens of Quebec. Though much success was achieved, Montmagny still had the unpleasant task of informing Father Vinmont that his priests and Huron missionaries had been martyred. The loss would be painfully felt but would only solidify their resolve to reach this wild and vicious people.

Stephen resisted the joy of his comrades. His mind finally had enough quiet and stillness to think upon the events of the week. He wondered if Jacques had been wrong about his calling to go to Huronia. It seemed so heartless of God to lead them to a place in the wilderness to be slaughtered in such a horrible fashion. And why would God even care about such an evil people as the Iroquois? Their whole intent for existing seemed only for the joy of watching suffering and death.

There had to be some sense to make out of it all, but Stephen could not think of any. Perhaps the devil was alive and at enmity with mankind. He imagined that would be what Jacques would say. It would be all the more reason for him to persevere with the truth. Sadly, Jacques never had the chance to accomplish what his whole heart was set on doing. The devil himself had stopped the missionaries' plans by spewing his vulgarity across the shoreline and consuming the flesh of those who were pure in heart. One thing that was certain in Stephen's mind was that Jacques, no matter what he may have endured, would confess Christ with his dying breath.

That thought strengthened Stephen. Depth of conviction was a compelling quality in a man, and he'd had the opportunity to see it firsthand in his friend. It rose to every challenge and never wavered, even though Jacques talked of himself as weak. Yet he was proven strong and true in the battle. Stephen was proud of his friend, Father Jacques, who gave his life to serve a people who didn't know his God. He had accomplished what his heart was set on doing. Stephen sat up straighter in the boat and fixed his eyes ahead at the shoreline of Quebec. He had a story to tell and a woman's heart to win.

It was late in the day by the time the last man set his foot on the solid ground of Quebec. A few folks who had been near the shore gathered to cheer them back home. No one expected them back so soon. Montmagny disembarked with as much royal fanfare as could be mustered by the crew. All were weary and exhausted from the week's labors.

Stephen looked at the sky and judged the time. It would be almost dark when he reached his little house. His foot had been paining him since before he left on the trip and was surely tender now. All the men were encouraged to spend the night at the fort, but Stephen wanted to get home as soon as he could. He had much to tell Catherine. A year of vague intentions and deceit upon deceit had to be reconciled. He felt as if somewhere on the journey he had awakened and found himself in the midst of a multitude of mistakes.

Why did he ever hide what had happened that night in France? Did he not have enough faith in Catherine to trust that she would believe him? Why did he tie such an incriminating noose around his own neck with lies? He had laid a good foundation of mistrust for Catherine. It was inevitable that she pull away from him. He had to win her heart now with complete honesty. He didn't know how much time he would have before the ships would sail for France. He didn't bother to ask.

He used his cane to climb the steep path from the shore to the fort, then leaned heavily upon it as he made his way up the familiar path to his home. He wanted to see Catherine. Perhaps he would hold her, and she wouldn't pull away. Maybe she would run to him and embrace him. He knew he would tell her he'd loved her long before they had left France and would vow to love her and care for her for the rest of her life.

Dusk fell quickly. Stephen was limping, and his pace was slower as he reached the clearing where the little house stood. A fire burned in the pit he had made with stones in the center of the yard. Its flames licked and snapped at the black pot that hung above it, steam rising into the heavy air. As the gray of dusk settled into night the fire glowed warm across the yard and spilled into the house. The door was open, and the lantern was burning.

Stephen stopped to catch his breath. He wanted to be tall and straight when he saw Catherine again. He wanted to be able to speak to her with fullness in his voice. He wanted his heart to be ready for whatever her response would be.

He moved closer to the little house and stopped again. He heard the low rumbling of voices talking. His mind searched for familiarity of tone or a logical explanation of who would be at his house at this hour. He quietly moved closer, sensing that something was not right. He listened to the voices again.

It was a man. It was Gaston. Stephen's heart raced. Gaston appearing while he was away hadn't even entered his mind. Guilt and regret seized him, and he wrestled it away in an instant. It would do him no good now. He had to deal with the situation rightly.

Stephen made his way to the door of the little house. Catherine was behind the partition. He could hear her low voice but could not tell what she was saying. Gaston was sitting on the chair, pushed back to rest on two legs. His hair was longer, obviously not cut during his winter of trapping, though his face was clean-shaven. A long pipe was held between his thumb and forefinger, and he lazily put it to his lips and inhaled slowly, held it for a moment, then blew the white smoke into the air. His clothing looked like what was worn by the trappers at Tadoussac: part Frenchman and part Indian. The lantern light illuminated his face. Even from a distance Stephen could see that evil remained in his eyes.

Stephen set down his cane and stood in the doorway, blocking the light from the outdoor fire.

Gaston took the pipe out of his mouth. A grin crawled across his face. "Stephen, you have returned so soon?" he asked in sarcasm.

Catherine's rustling behind the partition stopped and for a moment she didn't move. Stephen looked at Gaston and saw that any answer would entangle him in vicious conflict.

"Are you surprised beyond words, my friend?" Gaston asked.

Catherine stepped out from behind the partition and put her hand on Gaston's shoulder. She looked flushed and ashamed, not ready for the encounter. She looked at Stephen, and her eyes said all her heart had to say. She attempted to put it into words anyway.

"Gaston has come for me, Stephen. I knew he was waiting for me." She looked away to ease the discomfort. "I know this isn't what we thought would happen..." Her words fell to the ground as she turned from him. "It was a surprise for me, too, that Gaston should arrive at my door. But he has come to escort me back to France. That is safer than going alone, isn't it?"

"Catherine, no, it is not safe." Stephen stepped toward her. "You think you know this man, but you do not. He is a liar and a manipulator. He has been playing with your heart for as long as you have known him."

"He has thought of nothing else but rescuing me. He has cared for my father while I was gone and got aboard the first ship that sailed for Quebec. How can that be a cruel man? He has proven his love for me with his actions. How can I disregard that? He has come so far for me."

Gaston put the pipe back into his smirking mouth and brought the chair down on all fours. "Yes, you see we were meant to be." He squinted at Stephen. "Don't you have anything to say?"

Stephen tried to search her eyes for a sign of weakness, but she kept them from him. He turned his gaze upon Gaston. The evil of his persona enraged Stephen.

"I had hoped you were lost in the interior, Gaston, maybe eaten by the Iroquois' dogs. That would be fitting for your kind," he said as he moved closer.

Gaston laughed.

"Stephen," said Catherine, "Gaston has come to help us...to help me."

"Don't be fooled, Catherine. He is only out for what he can pillage and destroy. There is rottenness in his bones. He has been in Quebec since last fall. You can ask Eliot, or maybe his Indian wife."

"No more lies," she cried. "Why do you make this difficult?"

Gaston stood and put his arm around Catherine's shoulder. "It is his guilt that makes him speak so. He is torn apart because he murdered your brother. I was there. I know. I saw the whole thing, dear Catherine."

"You are wasting your foul breath," Stephen said, holding in his anger. "I have disclosed everything to her. You will not use that against me."

"Did you tell her how you stabbed him in the stomach and then ran off with his money?" Gaston asked with one eyebrow raised.

"You are a filthy liar. Can't you be honest about anything?"

"Stephen, is this true?" asked Catherine.

Gaston answered for him. "Of course it is true. Why do you think he whisked you away to France? What sickness comes up on someone to kill a man, take his money, and lay with his sister?"

Stephen's anger burst through his control and sent him rushing into Gaston and slamming him up against the wall. Catherine ran into the yard and covered her ears as she sobbed and begged them to stop.

"You are disgusting," Stephen said with his teeth clenched. "You are sick and evil. I can't even ask why you came here because I know it is for sport." Stephen clenched his fist and threw it into Gaston's belly. Gaston let out a muffled groan and leaned over slightly. Stephen brought Gaston's head up again with his forearm against his chest. Gaston looked at him again with a defiant stare.

"This reminds me of the last time we met," Gaston said. "Remember in town when you attacked me? It went something like this…" He lifted his foot and brought it smashing down on Stephen's.

A burning pain shot up Stephen's leg, but he would not give into it. He pushed harder against Gaston's chest.

"Yes, this does bring back memories," said Stephen. "I remember that I was ready to kill you in that alley; to rid the earth of your stench."

Stephen stepped back, and Gaston slouched forward, then stood again. "But somewhere in my being there was decency, that you know nothing of, that said it was not my hand that would be your downfall. God will judge you, Gaston."

"Let me tell you something, my friend," Gaston said as he straightened himself. "After Jean was murdered by your hand, I had no choice, being the noble man that I am, to go to the authorities and tell them everything I knew."

"You did what?" Stephen turned his head and saw Catherine appear again in the doorway.

"I could even describe for them the man who murdered Jean. It was just a matter of giving them a little hint at the initials on the dagger."

"Gaston," said Catherine, "we must go. We must leave now. Please take my bags." She lifted the lantern from the table. "A ship is leaving for France tomorrow. We will be on it. I wish you could see us off, Stephen. You know this is what we had planned all along." She caught her quivering breath. "I'm so sorry, Stephen," she whispered. "Please wish us well."

Stephen looked at her and knew she didn't understand anything he had been trying to say. Her mind was spoiled by Gaston's poison. He had hoped her heart would be open for him, but it appeared the doors were shut tight.

"I cannot wish the two of you well, because there is nothing but evil in Gaston." He stepped toward her and touched her arm. She looked down and pulled away. "But I know that my faithfulness cannot outshine what lies he has put in your head. I pray this will not be your end, Catherine."

Catherine glanced at him with a question in her eyes, then proceeded out the door.

"Do you hear that, Stephen my friend? Catherine is eager to be gone from here. What torment did you put her through this long, long year?" Gaston laughed again as he reached behind the partition and grabbed Catherine's two bags. When he got to the door, he pivoted toward Stephen. "Never underestimate me, Marot," he growled.

Stephen watched as they walked away from the little house...the lantern light bobbing along the tree stumps and the trees, finally consumed by the night. The fire in the yard still licked and snapped at the kettle.

She was gone. The little house was empty of her.

And so was his heart.

25

Noise from the brothel spilled into the streets of sleepy Quebec. Short verses of drinking songs were started, only to end in mistakes and laughter. The masculine gaiety was punctuated by occasional shrill squeals from the women inside.

"It sounds as if the fun is just beginning, Catherine my love," said Gaston as he approached the building. "I will get you settled in my room; then we will join the merriment."

"Oh, Gaston, I can't bear to be around all those people tonight. It has been such a full day. I didn't expect you to come for me. It was such a shock. And I didn't expect Stephen to come back before I even had time to think…"

Gaston stopped and turned toward her. "Did you have to think about us? Were you unsure of my love for you?"

"No, not at all. My thoughts about you have kept my sanity all these months. That has not changed." She stepped toward him and touched his cheek. "I needed time to know what to say to Stephen. He has been as good as he can to me, Gaston. It was his work and skill that has kept me alive so I could be with you here and now." She leaned into his body and rested her head on his chest. "Oh, Gaston," she said softly, "I need you so."

"That's my girl." He kissed the top of her head. "Let's get your bags up in my room and get you settled."

Catherine smiled wearily, put out the lantern, and followed him into the brothel. Smoke hung in the air, and the smell of sweat and alcohol combined in an acrid mix. Gaston nodded greetings to several of the men and ignored their waves for him to join them. Catherine stayed close, following his back through the maze of revelers. She didn't like the place. Eyes from many of the men followed her in either curiosity or lust. She pulled her arms in closer to her body as she walked.

A large, blond-haired man noticed Gaston and pushed through half the room to heartily greet him. "Gaston!" he said with surprise in his voice. "I cannot believe this is you! I gave you up for dead months ago. You are a cat with many lives. You will run out of them one day." He slapped Gaston on the back, then wrapped his thick arms around him in an embrace.

"I will always be around, Barnabé. Don't ever doubt that." Gaston laughed. "Where is your woman?"

"She is with her tribe. I have come into town to be a Frenchman tonight." He scanned the room and eyed Gaston. "And where is your woman?" Barnabé looked puzzled for a moment as Gaston gave him an urgent, imperceptible shake of his head.

"Barnabé, I would like to introduce you to my beautiful lady from France," he said as he moved aside and revealed Catherine.

"What is this? A lovely Frenchwoman." He winked at Gaston. "I will never be able to outdo you at anything." He laughed gruffly and dissolved back into the crowd.

"Come now," Gaston said to Catherine. "Barnabé is a good man. Crazy, but a good man."

Catherine followed Gaston up the narrow stairs to the second level of the brothel. Several doors lined both sides of the hallway. Gaston walked to the last door on the right and opened it, throwing the bags inside. He went to the dresser and lit the lantern that rested there. The soft glow dusted the room, illuminating the dresser, a small bed, and one chair.

"You rest now, Catherine." He ushered her into the room. "I am going to speak with Barnabé about a matter."

"No, please, don't leave me here. There is so much I need to think through. I need you with me tonight, Gaston."

"You think too much. Go to sleep." He put his hand on the doorknob and started to leave.

"There are things I must know, Gaston. Please stay with me."

Gaston moved toward her and put his hands on her shoulders. "My dear frail one," he said as he gazed down upon her, "you know you always get yourself tied into knots over silly things. You are with me now. Go to sleep, and in the morning we will talk." He kissed her head again and left the room.

Catherine stared at the closed door. Her stomach and heart had become entwined and agitated. In all her daydreams of Gaston arriving to rescue her she never imagined it as such. She didn't ever wonder what it would be like if her passion for him would have less flame, or if his suave French demeanor would be washed with Indian dress. She looked at the blank, flat door. She didn't imagine being led to a brothel and left in a room alone.

Catherine went to the bed and pulled the blanket back. She dusted off the debris left from the previous guest and lay down. She pulled the blanket up tight beneath her chin and turned onto her side. The noise from below billowed into the room from the floorboards.

Her chin quivered and gave way to her heart before her eyes did. She stared at the door and let her tears fall onto the bed. Her greatest desire was to return to France and to be with Gaston, yet she could not understand the sorrow that gripped her. Something was askew in the puzzle. She didn't feel as she ought. Gaston didn't act as a man come to rescue his woman, and she could not feel relief that she was free from

Stephen. The fire would be burning in the little house now, she knew. Stephen would be spreading his bedroll on the floor in front of it. He would have made sure everything was safe before he went to sleep. He would have leaned the musket in the corner, ready for any intruder.

She remembered the look he had every night before she went behind her partition…a longing gaze, not for her body, but for something deeper. Catherine let the noise from below drown out her thoughts and serenade her to sleep.

"Catherine, my woman from France," came the hasty melody from beyond the door. She sat up just as Gaston stumbled into the room. "Ah, my woman, my woman…you wait for me!" He closed the door and moved toward her with an inebriated swagger. "Let's talk now, Catherine." He sat on the edge of the bed and playfully leaned into her. "Tell me whatever you will, my woman."

"You're drunk." She smelled the rancid alcohol permeating the air.

"You are so wise." He brushed her hair off the back of her neck and placed his lips there.

"Gaston, please, don't." She shrugged him off of her. "It is almost morning. Look, the sun is ready to rise. Why did you stay away all night?"

"I am a rugged man. I go to sleep after I have sown all my energy. You didn't want me to sow it with you, did you?" He ran his hand across her shoulders and down her back. She had longed for his touch since the day she left France, and now it appalled her. She pushed back the covers and stood facing him.

"I must ask you something that has been puzzling me." She stepped back as Gaston stood and moved toward her. "What did that man downstairs mean saying he thought you were dead months ago?"

Gaston stopped and let out a laugh. "I had known him in France. He had not seen me for a long time. I had been too busy trying to find you."

"But he said he thought you were dead months ago. Why would he say that if you just arrived in Quebec?'

"I told you, the man is crazy. I don't take into account anything he says." Gaston moved toward her again.

She stood still for a moment, but fear moved her back. "He asked you about your woman. Why? Why would he think you had a woman?"

"Because I speak only of you. Is it strange that I should have you always on my mind when I came so far to recapture you?"

Catherine felt the door behind her as Gaston continued to move closer. She tried to see the look in his face that had won her heart in France. Her imagination participated in the effort, trying to take any trace it found and bring it to life. It was gone. Gaston pressed against her, his breath, warm and sticky, pouring over her face.

"You have waited so long for me, haven't you, Catherine," he murmured as he brought his mouth close to hers. Revulsion rose, and she turned her head. She felt his hand slide up her arm as he put his mouth to her ear.

"No." She pushed against his chest. "This isn't right!"

Gaston took her face in his hand and turned it toward him. His eyes were red and piercing. His hand squeezed tight and pressed on her jaw. "You should take your lessons from the Huron women." He sneered. "They were glad to do my bidding and eager to be my wife. It was a challenge to choose just one." He pressed his body harder into hers. "You know I'm a man of great appetite."

His mouth moved toward her again, and she fought against it. Gaston stepped back and shook his head. "You are not worth the effort anymore, Madame Catherine Marot. It is good that I had my fill tonight. You leave me not wanting more." He staggered to the bed and fell across it. "Come lay next to me, and I will not touch you, dear Catherine," he slurred. "We have many more nights for you to make love to me."

Catherine's heart was pounding. She looked at the man whom she had loved and was sickened. It was inconceivable that he had been so vile back in France. Quebec must have soured his soul to the point of this depravity. But if there was nothing innately evil in the man, how could he become as he was now? Perhaps Stephen had told her the truth. She rested her head against the door and listened to his wet snoring. She had never felt more violated in her body than she did then.

When sunlight streamed through the streaked windowpanes into the little room, Catherine picked up her two bags, straining with their weight. She quietly left the room, not wanting him to waken. As much as she loved him in France, she feared him now. If he were to get on the ship with her, she would have to leave. The vessel would not be large enough to ease the chill of his proximity. She could not miss the boat to France. More than the thought of a life with Gaston was the pull of her homeland.

Mist rose from the grassy areas and billowed in the sunlight. Her footsteps echoed in the emptiness. Comfort had disappeared, and wisdom had vanished. She wished Madame LaPointe was here to guide her. She always found comfort in the wise old woman. Her faith in Quebec and the people who settled there carried her through the hardships. But it was more steadfast than that. Madame LaPointe gave people something that lived beyond mere words. Catherine knew the woman imparted something in her that made her strong enough to walk away.

Catherine continued down the road toward the clearing where the cliff jutted into the St. Lawrence. She had made her way up the rough steps one year earlier. Today she would make her way down them and onto the boat that would begin the long journey home.

26

The shoreline was deserted, but activity was apparent on the boats. Goods were packed neatly on each of the three boats and would be transferred onto the ships at Tadoussac. All the labor in readying the boats and supplies was done the day previous so they could set sail by midmorning. The captain requested all passengers and crew to be on board by daybreak, but Montmagny halted the order. Too much had happened of late, and he did not want to set sail too early. If anything else had to be loaded, it could be done that morning. He gave allowance for the overlooked and unplanned.

Catherine sat on a makeshift bench that had been placed by the shore and put her bags next to her. She sat in angst, hoping and praying that Gaston would remain asleep until after the boats had left. If the captain had his way, they would be far downriver by now. Catherine knew she was vulnerable to any wind of change as long as she was in Quebec. The only sure thing now was France. Nothing else seemed to make any sense. She could barely piece together the events of the last twenty-four hours and was afraid to spend any more time thinking of it. She didn't want anything else to change. This boat to France was what she had waited and longed for. She couldn't risk missing it in a moment of confusion.

The shoreline came to life body by body. A priest and several nuns gathered on the shore, each with a bag in tow. The Company of a Hundred Associates supplied passageway to a middle-aged couple who felt Quebec was beneath their means. It was obvious to all who remotely knew them or even saw them that the lack of niceties was too much to bear. They were leaving with their dignity intact and a somewhat skewed but fairly good report would be brought to the Company's head in France. Several settlers gathered, too, looking worn and beaten by the experience. Catherine wondered if she looked like them. Right at that moment she felt like them.

People continued to gather on the shore and wait for Montmagny's procession to signify that the boats were ready for departure. Catherine wanted to stand and pace, but her legs and eyes were heavy from the previous night. She closed her eyes briefly. She dared not leave them shut long as sleep would surely come.

But, against her will, it came....

"Catherine," called a voice that gently woke her from sleep. Catherine jumped, and her heart raced. She looked at the boats and sighed relief that they were still there. Then she looked for the voice.

"Catherine, I've come to see you off as I promised." Stephen stood looking at her. Relief flooded her, and she restrained sudden tears.

"Oh, Stephen, I'm so glad you came," she said as she took his arm to stand.

"You couldn't keep me away. You know I had to see you get on the boat, or I would always wonder…" He surveyed the people gathered there. "Where is Gaston?"

"I hope and pray that he is still drunk and sleeping."

"I don't understand."

"You were right about Gaston. I think everything you accused him of doing he is capable of. I didn't see it before. I don't know why…"

"Did he hurt you?" Stephen interrupted, concerned pain drawn quickly to his face.

"No, but I saw that he could. I don't know what happened to him to cause such a change."

"He has always been as he is now. In France he was able to hide his intentions under mock propriety. Here, where a man is stripped of pretense, his evil intent was laid bare. I know my heart has been laid open for all to see. I cannot hide, either."

"Yes, Stephen." Her tears could no longer be held back. "You have laid your heart bare, and I have tried to understand mine. I thought I knew it well…now I don't know."

Stephen reached for her, but she stepped back.

"Please don't. It will only make this harder," she said.

"But Catherine…"

"I must leave on these boats. Over the last year this was the only thing that made any sense. It has not changed. I cannot give it up on a hunch that something could be greater between us than this desire to return to my home and my father. Can you understand what I am saying?"

"I understand the strength of a heart's desire," he said softly. He took her hands in his and kissed them, then held them to his cheek for a moment.

A ship's crewman cleared his throat and gruffly told Catherine her bags had to be loaded now if she wanted them. She nodded. Then they followed the man to the boats.

Stephen took her hands again and gazed at her with softness and resignation. "I know you are wiser and stronger than the day we arrived here. I trust you will, one day, find love and happiness in France." He reached into his shirt and pulled out a sealed parchment and placed it in her hand. "This is a letter of agreement for the dissolution of our marriage." He closed her hand around it. "Please forgive me if I cannot watch you board. I thought I was stronger of heart than I am feeling now." Stephen kissed her hands again. "Please know that I love you, Catherine," he said, looking long into her eyes.

"I know," she whispered.

She watched as he turned from her and moved slowly toward the captain, who had been waiting by the boats. After speaking to the man briefly, Stephen took another parchment out of his shirt and gave it to him. He hung his head and made his way up the incline, away from the shore and away from the boats that would take her home.

Construction was underway by the time Stephen reached the building site, and he wasted no time in joining the other men. There was still much to do to protect Quebec from the Iroquois attacks. Stephen was glad for the opportunity to be consumed with the task. He had pondered his life enough the past few weeks that he didn't want to think anymore or mourn anymore. He was glad he had not told Catherine of Jacques's death. She would have enough to occupy her thoughts those many months at sea.

Montmagny's fanfare sounded, then a musket shot. The boats had set sail. Stephen looked down from his perch upon a stone wall and saw the three boats moving into the middle of the St. Lawrence, then catching the swift current and disappearing from view. Catherine had left Quebec. Stephen did not let his mind feel the pain his heart was in. There would be a later time to deal with it. Perhaps by then the intensity would be gone. He scooped mortar from the bucket and slapped it on the stones. There was work to be done.

He balanced himself on the scaffolding and signaled the men below to begin hoisting the next stone up on the wall. Two men pulled on the rope and raised the heavy stone that was secured in a sling to where Stephen waited. He grabbed the rope and positioned it above the mortar and signaled again to lower the stone. He slipped the sling out from underneath the stone and tossed it over the wall for the next stone.

"Hey," called one of the workers below. "You about hit someone with that filthy thing."

"You are all filthy already," Stephen called back to them. "What should it matter?"

"Not this one," the man replied.

Stephen looked over the wall to see what foolishness the men were playing. He caught his breath, then looked out at the river again. The boats were gone. He looked back down at the ground.

Catherine stood looking up at him, her two bags at her side.

"I searched my heart, Stephen," she shouted up to him, "and I tried to find any place within it where you were not. I searched my memories to find happiness without you, and I couldn't find any. I looked to my future, and I could not see me without you. You are my home, Stephen. I love you."

Stephen gazed down at her as tears filled her eyes. He couldn't stop them from filling his own.

About the Author

D.M. SNELLING is an artist and author with a passion for history and its meaning for us today.

Residing in Minnesota, she has worked in the health care industry for over 20 years, as well as authored numerous books, plays, and dinner theater productions with a ministry perspective.

Her award-winning murals and artwork are displayed in many homes and public establishments. Her thought-provoking writings are geared to inspire the reader to seek deeper spiritual meaning.

www.dmsnelling.com ▪ www.oaktara.com

CHAINED TO YOUR HEART

Collie Maggie

Katie thought about the big man in their cell at Newgate. He didn't complain or shout his innocence to anyone who would listen. He simply served others any way he could. By watching him, Katie felt hopeful in a strange way. His acts of kindness seemed to confirm that the future would somehow get better. Then and there she made a decision. No matter what the future held for her, she would be strong. She would make it through—somehow.

Red studied the girl. She captivated him. Eighteen or twenty with a slim build, she looked fit and seemed to have a delicate, gentle manner—a sharp contrast to their surroundings. To Red, she was of a ray of sunshine. Something stirred within, a familiar longing. It took him a while to figure out what that longing was. Over the years he had tried to tell himself that one day he would have his own land and family. One day he would have a family who wouldn't leave him. His mind continued to chase the elusive and impossible dream....

To Bonnie Blue, my dear friend who first pushed me to write this story.
I'll never forget your sweet spirit and grace.

Audrey, without you I would still be staring at my computer like a deer in the
headlights, trying to figure out where all the quotes and commas go.

My friends and family in Christ at Living Hope Church:
your encouragement, love, and prayers have made this possible.

Most of all to my Jesus, thank You for my salvation and for adopting me.

1

Kathryn Elizabeth Brady

The Year of Our Lord, 1864
Newgate Prison, England

Any hopes or dreams Kathryn Elizabeth Brady once had were gone, and she'd only just turned eighteen. Her future was a fearful thing now. She had heard about Newgate as a young girl and the horrors that dwelled there. People went in but never came out. Prisoners were treated horribly, and disease ran rampant. England had many prisons or gaols, as they were better known, but Newgate was the most notorious of all. And here Katie sat in the middle of it.

Never in her wildest dreams would she have believed she would one day be locked in a communal cell twenty feet long and fifteen feet wide, along with twenty-five other men, women, and children. Their only light came from small windows, built near the ceiling, and covered by metal grating. Any available fresh air stayed at the top. A few lanterns burned but proved useless. Off the large room were two smaller rooms, one of the areas for the women and one for the men. A few chamber pots and buckets lined the walls. In the three days Katie had been there the rooms had not been cleaned. Most prisoners sat with their backs against the block walls. Others tried to sleep on the hard floor covered by filthy, matted hay.

Katie scanned the prison cell. A rat scurried across the floor, forcing her to curl her legs up. She pressed against the dank wall. The small boy and girl lying next to her for warmth stirred in their sleep. Looking down on them, she was filled with compassion. She stretched her skirt over them in an attempt to keep them warm.

Leaning her head back and closing her eyes, Katie tried to deny her surroundings. She couldn't be here. She would wake up, and it would be a horrible nightmare lingering only in her memory. But her other senses proclaimed the reality of her situation. The smell of mildew, vomit, and human waste mixed with the scent of dirty bodies overwhelmed her. Words from her past came to soothe and comfort.

"All right, Katie, hold on. Hold on tight to what ya believe and who ya are."

They were the words of her beloved Gran, who could always ease Katie's mind whenever she felt frightened. But now she needed more than words. She longed for her home—for Papa and Gran.

Just then the great iron doors opened, and the gaoler mercilessly shoved a stout woman through them, causing her to sprawl facedown on the floor. A "whuff" came out of her. She lay motionless until the gaoler closed the doors. Slowly lifting her head, she scanned the cell with fiery eyes, like a trapped animal. With dark hair speckled with gray, she appeared to be in her midforties and looked like she had lived a hard life.

The children jerked awake and started whimpering. Katie put her arm around them reassuringly. A man said something crude to the older woman while others snickered, then grabbed the woman. With a growl the woman reached up, pinching the man in the most sensitive of areas and twisting with all her might. The two of them rolled, kicking and swearing.

With one good push the man freed himself. "All right, ye old cow. If that's the way you want it!"

"Ya ever try an' touch me again, ya stinkin' scum, and ol' Mary will crack yer 'ead!" she screamed back.

Laughter erupted at her words. "Ye better listen to the ol' girl, Pete, or we'll be diggin' your grave!" quipped another man.

The woman got to her feet facing the group of men. With her hands stretched into claws she braced herself for another attack. She wouldn't win, but she would take a few down and leave a scar or two.

"Ah, she ain't worth it, Pete," another man piped up. "Besides, there be better tastin' fish in 'ere than that ol' whale." With that said, all the men turned to eye Katie.

The children pushed themselves flatter against the wall, clinging to each other as Katie slowly stood. Her heart tore at her ribs as her knees threatened to buckle.

Two of the men stepped closer. The dark one with matted beard led while the man with brown hair sneered at her, showing broken, black teeth. Their stench washed over them and anyone else near.

The older woman ran to Katie, standing in front of her. "Why, ya filthy blokes! It be not enough to grab poor ol' Mary, is it? Ya gotta try and put the hurt to this wee lass besides! Well, I ain't 'avin it, ya 'ear me?"

Katie was surprised at the sudden fear on the men's faces. She followed their gaze until it fell on the giant of a man standing behind Mary. Big Red, as the men called him, stood head and shoulders above the rest. His expression caught and held their attention. Without a word the men stepped back as their laughter died in their throats.

The older woman straightened and smiled. "Ya blokes learn'd, did ya? Ol' Mary don't take nothin' from scum like ya. It be best ya learn it now if we be locked together in this 'ole of Satan's!"

Once the men were seated, Red returned to "his" corner. Katie was amazed how quietly he moved in spite of his size. Even though no words were spoken, the men heard Red loud and clear. There would be no more trouble of that kind with him in the cell.

Mary stood without seeing the large man standing behind her. Pushing her large bosoms up proudly, she straightened her crumpled dress. Brushing her hair away, she proceeded to put her arm around the young woman. "No need for ya to worry, lass. Mary won't let them scruffs touch ya in any way. Ya be safe with me 'ere."

Katie felt lightheaded. Slowly she slid against the wall to the floor. Sitting next to her, the older woman turned a wary eye on the bunch of foulers, just in case they needed another lesson.

Red watched until he was certain the trouble had passed. In the two weeks he had been in Newgate, all had been quiet, but when this young woman came in, the other men took notice. He'd felt trouble brewing. He studied the girl. She captivated him. She looked to be eighteen or twenty with a slim build but looked fit. She seemed to have a delicate and gentle manner about her in the way she handled the two children. To Red, she was of a ray of sunshine.

Red turned his gaze on the young ones. He guessed the girl to be four and the boy, maybe six years old. A week after he arrived, they came in with their mother, who seemed ill with a cough. Within days she died, leaving her children behind. He had tried to reach out to them, but they were too frightened of him. He was relieved when the young woman came to the cell. The children seemed drawn to her. She didn't hesitate to share her meager portions of bread and gruel with them. It was foolish of her to do so, but Red believed she knew that and gave anyway.

Katie was finally able to breathe normally again. With her head on Mary's shoulder she listened to the older woman as she babbled on about her life. How fate had slapped her upside the head, landing her in this unfortunate situation. Katie's mind wandered in spite of the chatter. Why had that man stepped forward to help? What did it matter? She was simply grateful he was there.

Her attention returned to the woman. Smiling, she thanked her for her protection and introduced herself. "My name is Katie. Did you say your name is Mary?"

Returning her smile, the woman answered, "Aye, 'tis Mary, miss. Why, it was fittin' ol' Mary would step in. Us ladies got to stick together, be what I am thinkin'.'"

Katie nodded in agreement. She wondered why Mary would talk about herself in the third person, but it added to her charm.

Mary went on. "Ya seem too fine a lady to be 'ere. What would ya be 'ere for, if ya don't mind me askin'?"

Katie shrugged. "I was accused of stealing something I did not take."

Mary nodded. "Aye, that has happened to meself once long ago. Now I 'ave done enough to make up for that one time of falsehood. I wish I could tell ya that ol' Mary be 'ere because of a falsehood now, but I cannot." Her shoulders seemed to stoop a little with her confession. Katie didn't push for an explanation.

The two women stopped talking. Before too long, the older woman was dozing, her head bobbing back and forth, threatening to hit the wall. When two small children wiggled in between her and Katie, Mary jerked awake.

"What this be? Why in this troubled world would ya be here for? Babes should be in their mum's bed. Just come betwixt ol' Mary and the lass. We keep yas warm as can be."

Soon the young ones were snuggled in and sleeping as if they had no troubles at all. Mary looked at Katie with questioning eyes.

Katie quietly explained, "When I first arrived, the children were petrified of everyone. I coaxed them a little, and soon they came to me. When I asked about their mum, they told me she had died here before I came. The poor wee ones. I don't know how long they've been here. I feel somewhat responsible for them now, but what am I to do? I don't even know what is going to happen to me."

Mary regarded the children with sadness. "Aye, what is to be done? I 'ear babes are given o'er to the workhouses. Terrible places they be. Queen Victoria, bless 'er 'eart, be easier on us poor than ol' King George was, but they got to go somewheres."

Katie noticed a small, dirty piece of cloth in Mary's hand. The older woman stroked it as if to soothe herself. Katie wondered about it, but other things crowded in. Closing her eyes once more, she thought again of her beloved Gran and her stories about Ireland.

"It be the prettiest land ya e'er see," Gran would say, *"but rocks grew where potatoes wouldn't. It be a 'ard life for sure. God made it up to us by making us Irish, and placing us in the most beautiful place except for heaven. County Mayo 'tis where all yer people come from, Katie. They were fishermen and farmers, the lot of 'em. Not a one owned 'is own land. It came to be that we all 'ad to leave our 'earth and 'ome. Still brings a tear to me eyes thinkin' on it."* The dear old lady would wipe her eyes, loudly blow her nose, and sadly smile. *"It be a 'ard thing to remember on."*

As Katie dreamed of the woman closest to her heart, she dozed, picturing Gran rocking in her creaky old chair and talking softly of things that mattered most to her. *"Ya know, Katie Elizabeth, life 'tis all about choices that are made. Whether by ya or someone else, it doesn't matter. What does matter is making good choices and how ya decide to live through the choices made. The biggest choice ya will e'er make is whether to be a-walkin' with Almighty God or not. You need Him in yer life, lass."*

Katie stirred in her sleep. Her sweet dreams of Gran disappeared and were replaced by dark shadows and the demon-like voice of the "black princess," Tess.

"Katie, where's my blue gown with the lace? Why do my things seem to disappear all the

time? Get my pearl bobs over there and hurry. My hair is a mess. Fix it!"

Katie ran in circles trying her best to please her young mistress, but could not.

"You are getting more useless as time goes on. Why can't you appreciate your position? My mother should never have allowed you here. You are useless!" Miss Tess screamed.

Miss Tess's mouth got bigger and bigger until only a massive black hole remained, and Katie fell into it. Down, down she fell as slimy hands grabbed at her...

Katie jumped herself awake. For a split second she couldn't remember where she was. As the fog lifted, any sense of relief she might have felt was gone. She had awakened from one nightmare into another. Frantically she tried to remember her dream about Gran. The dear old lady's Irish brogue came back to her, but what was it she had said about choices? It was something about God— that far-away being with white hair. Katie always imagined Him with one big eye that saw every sin and a long finger to point it out. Almighty God, who never spoke to her or seemed to acknowledge her existence. Then again, she never acknowledged His existence either.

But for the first time, Katie wanted to feel close to Him. She wanted to believe He was real and could help her. There was no one else now. She had never felt so alone. The lowest time in her life had been losing Gran and Papa...until now. How she longed for that faith—that belief in a Being who would love you no matter what—that seemed to come so easy to Gran. Where did that faith come from? Did God pick and choose who received it?

With a sigh, Katie leaned back against the wall. What did it matter? She didn't have it. Katie tried again to recall Gran's words but could not.

Her second dream was a different matter. She remembered it all too well. It was because of the "black princess" that Katie was here. How could Tess have done such a thing? As long as Katie could remember, Tess seemed to hate her. Tess was capable of cruelty, but to this degree? How could she have told such a lie?

The fact Lord and Lady Wilson would allow such disaster to befall Katie caused the worst pain of all. They must have known she would never have betrayed their trust. But they had to believe their own flesh and blood over a maid...didn't they? Still, they knew what Tess was like. They should have believed Katie when she told them she had not taken the necklace. It was obvious to everyone that Tess was jealous of Katie's relationship with Lord and Lady Wilson. Couldn't they see it, too?

Katie remembered the day Papa had secured a position at the Brick House for her. Oh, the excitement his news brought. Brick House was the name given to Lord and Lady Wilson's manor. It was huge and covered in red brick, thus the name. It seemed a palace with many large windows and beautiful lawns.

Papa, their head gardener, took great pride in his job. He made sure the grounds and gardens were at their best. He even had a staff of six men working under him. There was pride in that, too. Papa was a hard worker. He worked as if Lord Wilson was looking over his shoulder, though he never did. Papa had proven himself to be an honest man. When Lord Wilson approached him about Katie working in the house, it only took Papa's word for Katie to get hired.

Yes, she had been excited, but frightened, too. To work at Brick House was an honor in itself. Employment was so rare for the Irish, and being Katie's first job made it very special. She couldn't believe she would be making money of her very own...a farthing a week! Dreams of all the grand things her earnings would buy consumed her. She would buy linen and a new bonnet for Gran. Papa could get a new plow along with a pipe. Oh, the wealth they would have.

"Katie," Papa started, "Lord Wilson's daughter is home from school, and he wants you to be her maid. You're both the same age. Won't that be a fine thing?"

Katie had never really had a best friend, except for Gran. Did she count? Well, now she would have someone her own age to share secrets with, to run and skip with. Gran wasn't very good at that part. "Papa," Katie asked, "what's a maid?"

"That's a girl who helps a lady get dressed and fix her hair and such."

"You mean that poor girl has no arms of her own to dress herself?" Katie's eyes nearly bugged out.

Both Papa and Gran broke into laughter. "No, no, my Katie," Papa continued, "it's just that ladies don't work anymore than they have to, so they hire people to do their work for them."

"But Papa," Katie went on, "since when is getting dressed work?"

"Well, Katie, there is truth in that, all right."

There was a lot to do to get ready. Gran went about scrubbing Katie's best dress. She only had two, so it was a mystery to her how Gran could figure out which one was the better. They were both worn, but Gran would say, "We may be poor, Katie Elizabeth, but we are clean." So after her dress was scrubbed, Katie was scrubbed.

Fear tugged at her heart along with the excitement. "Gran," she whispered, "what if I don't do things right? Where do I go once I get to the Brick House?"

Gran looked at her granddaughter with great tenderness. "I know ya be afraid, Katie dear, but don't e'er let fear keep ya back from where God wants ya to go. Just trust."

A sigh of frustration escaped. As much as she loved Gran, it was hard to get a real answer from her. She always gave those tricky answers that Katie tried to figure out but seldom did. "Gran, I need a good answer! I don't know what you mean."

Gran merely smiled and gave her a hug. "Simply, Katie, there be no need to worry about where God is taking ya, as long as ya trust in Him."

Gran was wonderful, but at times she was no help at all. Katie wondered then if all old people talked like that. Was it because they knew they would be dying soon and needed to talk about God a lot so they could get to heaven? She didn't like to think about Gran "going to dust," as the old ones called it. Katie made her decision. She may be frightened a little, but no one would know. She would hold her head up and be brave...or at least try.

Early the next day she went to work with Papa. It was the first time she was allowed to go to the Brick House. It had always been a distant thing of beauty. Coming closer to it took Katie's breath away. *Grand* was not the word for it. She could not imagine the money a person would need to live in such a place. She'd always thought it looked like a castle, so it only made sense her new, soon-to-be best friend must be a princess!

When Papa stopped right before entering, Katie knew more instructions were coming. "Remember, Katie dear, to curtsey like Gran showed you, and be ever mindful of your manners. Oh, and don't forget to always say 'sir' and…"

"Papa," Katie whispered, "I know, I know. You told me over and over last night!"

"All right, Katie girl, I guess you're ready. Now don't forget to smile."

Katie rolled her eyes, causing Papa to chuckle to himself.

They stepped through the door into a large warm kitchen. Katie was amazed at the size of it. The whole of their little cottage could fit in this room alone. The aroma of bread baking made her mouth water. At one end of the room were large windows and a table full of flour and bowls. "Flour fairies" danced in the sunshine pouring through the windows. A plump woman in a neatly pressed dress and crisp apron stood by the stove. She turned to see who was invading her kitchen and broke into a big grin. "Well, look who's here. Mr. Brady, is this the wee girl you've been braggin' on?"

Katie shyly smiled at the woman.

"This be my Katie," her father said with pride. "She's here to work with Miss Tess. Is Lord Wilson here or out riding the grounds?"

Wiping her hands on her apron the woman went to retrieve two cups from the cupboard. "Sit, Mr. Brady, and have a cup of tea. Aye, Lord Wilson is out riding and Lady Wilson is resting, so you have a few minutes. Come, Katie, have some milk and a warm slice of bread with jam."

Papa led Katie to the table. "Katie, this is Miss Maggie Gray. She's the best cook in the county."

Katie curtsied.

"Why, what a perfectly fine little lady you are. I can see why your papa would be so proud. Now, Katie, you can call me Maggie. Come sit and rest yourself."

Katie liked her immediately. She seemed kind and was squishy looking like Gran. Her face was smooth and her cheeks rosy. When she smiled, which was a lot, her nose turned up a little, and she smelled good.

Suddenly a loud voice came from the next room. "I don't have to listen to you. You aren't my mother!"

"Oh-oh," Maggie whispered, "brace yourselves. 'Tis the shrew coming."

With that, the kitchen door flew open. In stepped one of the prettiest girls Katie had ever seen. *I was right,* thought Katie. *There is a princess living here.*

The girl stopped dead in her tracks, staring at Katie. "Who are you, and why are you eating my father's food?" she bellowed.

Katie, with a bite of bread half in her mouth, froze. Lowering it to the plate, she turned to look at Papa.

"I invited Mr. Brady and his daughter, Katie, to sit a spell," Maggie said, struggling to sound cordial. "She is your new companion, Miss Tess."

"I wasn't talking to you, Maggie. Can't she speak for herself?" the girl snapped. "And, Maggie, she's not my companion; she's my servant."

"Now, Tess, ladies don't speak that way," corrected a very plain-looking woman who stood behind Tess.

The girl's ringlets bounced as she pivoted to glare at the woman. With great flare, Tess stalked through the door she had come from. That was the first meeting Katie had with her new—at least she had hoped—best friend. Disappointment flooded her heart as she realized the pretty girl wasn't going to be all that easy to like. She had no doubts now; she didn't want to stay. It had never entered her mind that any princess living in such a grand castle would be mean. Katie decided the princess wasn't all that pretty after all.

"I apologize for our young lady," stated the plain woman. "She is quite high-spirited, and of course that's to be expected. It's just sometimes she seems to forget herself. Let me introduce myself. I am Miss Simms, the governess. I have been looking forward to meeting you, Katie."

Katie wasn't sure what to say but managed, "Thank you."

"I must attend to Miss Tess, but as soon as you are finished with your milk, Maggie can bring you upstairs to properly meet your new mistress." Miss Simms nodded, then went out the kitchen door.

Katie couldn't help but think how the woman looked like she had swallowed a lemon whole after chewing on it awhile. All the excitement that had been building was gone, replaced with uncertainty.

"Don't you worry yourself," Maggie cooed, "you'll be fine. You won't be alone here. I'll be here, and so will your papa." Pouring more tea, Maggie turned her attention to Papa. "Miss Simms is new here, too. It was decided that Tess would stay home from school, so a governess was hired. I suspect the school decided that."

Papa nodded in understanding.

Katie couldn't finish her treat of bread and jam. She couldn't swallow the lump in her throat, let alone food. Tears threatened as her disappointment grew, but Papa and Gran had been so excited. She could never disappoint them....

Katie's thoughts crashed back to the present and the gaol. What if she had never stepped foot in the Brick House or met Tess? What if she had stayed home with Gran?

Yet what good did it do to wonder what if? Despair wrapped her like a heavy cloak. Her life was now a never-ending nightmare. How could she ever feel safe again? Never again would she feel the security of someone taking care of her. Her beloved family was gone now. She was truly on her own...in the pit of hell.

Mary excitedly whispered to Katie, "Come, or it all be gone."

Katie went to jump up, but her body screamed its objection. Sitting and sleeping on the cold dank floor had stiffened her body. She was about to complain to Mary but bit her tongue. If Mary, the old man across the cell, and the two wee ones didn't complain, she wouldn't either.

By the time she got to her feet a crowd was already at the gate to get their meager portions. She doubted there would be anything left, but she had to try for the children. They were so thin.

Just then she heard a deep voice. "Get away; let me through!" It was the big man. The group of people parted out of his way.

Katie felt disappointment. For some reason she had expected better of him, but what did she know about him? *Maybe he has motives of his own. Maybe...*

Before she could finish her thought, the big man handed her a wooden bowl. It was full of gruel, and there was a slice of bread as well. "For you and the little ones," he said. Then he turned to get food for the old man and the women. After they had their share, he went back for himself.

Katie noticed his bowl wasn't nearly as full as the one he had gotten for her. It was funny how even the gaoler dishing the gruel seemed in a hurry to do his bidding. The other men in the cell glared at him, but nary was a complaint made. Katie watched as the crowd of people stepped aside for the big man as he made his way back to "his" corner. He didn't speak to anyone, yet the people parted for him like the Red Sea for Moses. Katie smiled. The "red" man and the Red Sea. It was clear to Katie that the man's heart was as big as his body, and she felt shame for her earlier ponderings. Sitting, she gave the bowl to the two children. As they began to eat, Katie tore the bread into two pieces, giving half to Mary.

"Why, bless me soul. First ol' Mary has a lad waitin' on meself, and now a sweet lass gives me bread. Bless ya, darlin', for thinkin' of me. Ya have a good heart to go with that pretty face."

Katie smiled and slowly chewed her bread. Everyone grew still as they ate their meager meal. Katie peeked at the big man. He seemed gentle. His kindness to others touched her deeply. He wasn't loud, nor did he demand any attention. He didn't complain or shout his innocence to anyone who would listen. He simply served others any way he could. By watching him, Katie felt hopeful in a strange way. His acts of kindness seemed to confirm that the future would somehow get better. Then and there she made a decision. No matter what, she would hold her head up. She wouldn't let herself become bitter. No matter what the future held for her, she would be strong. She would make it through—somehow.

At least she would try.

2

Blood Red

Once everyone had a little food in their stomachs, all settled down to rest. Except for an occasional cough, and the faint trickle of water through the wall somewhere, it was quiet. Katie stole another peek at the big man. He was huge, bigger than Papa had been. She couldn't get over his large hands. There was no mistaking his red hair and beard, even though they were dirty and matted.

One thing puzzled Katie. She saw the way the other men in the cell treated him, as as if they were scared to death of him. They kept their distance and their eyes on him. She wondered if something had happened in the cell between the men before she got there. She had not yet heard the rumors about "Blood Red."

If one was to listen to the other men, Red was the foulest, most depraved man ever to walk the earth. It was said he ate flesh! Word came down that a man and Blood Red had a fight. Before it was over, Red took a bite out of the man…and swallowed! It all made sense if you looked at him. He was huge, and all that red hair! After conferring with one another, they had no doubts as to Red's liking of flesh. Taking no chances, they took turns watching all through the night. That man-eater wasn't gonna sneak up on any one of them.

Red had noticed the other men watching him. They would murmur amongst themselves, then nod toward him. He sensed their fear but wasn't sure why they feared him. It really didn't matter as long as they left him and the others alone. He reflected on the mistakes he'd made that had landed him in Newgate. He was just one of many without a home or family. With shame he realized how he had stopped trusting in God and had taken matters into his own hands. There were hundreds without homes, families, or direction for their lives who had not ended up in a gaol. Red had direction and hope in the Lord, yet here he was.

He had traveled all over working wherever there was a job to be had. Being large for his age and very strong, he never had a problem finding work. As long as a body was willing to work hard, there was work to be found. James Patrick, or Red as he was called, was on his own since he was twelve years old. His parents died when their cottage caught fire. His father had taken him out and returned for his mother. He never made it out again. The boy was left alone with nothing. How old did that make him now? Red figured about twenty-six or seven. He had done everything from harbor work to being a stable boy. The longest lasting job he had was working on a farm for over eight years. It had been the closest thing to having a home of his own after losing his parents. He now understood it was the Lord who brought him and his second family together.

He was fourteen and, once again, looking for work. He saw a man in the fields trying his best to hoist a boulder from the soil. As quickly as possible, Red ran to help, and before too long the rock was out of the way. When the farmer asked what pay he wanted, Red responded, "Just a bit of bread would be appreciated."

He was invited to a hardy meal of beef, potatoes, carrots from the garden, biscuits right out of the oven, and tea. When he was certain it couldn't get any better, he was served hot apple slab! He hadn't eaten like that in months. Along with the food he was offered a job, and he thankfully accepted. Red wasn't sure how to respond when the farmer announced that the younger man was an answer to prayer. Since the man's only son was a toddler and his two daughters only seven and ten, he had been praying for help with the farm. Red had been called a few things in his short life but never "an answer to prayer."

The kind couple shared what they had with him, as did their three children. Roy O'Malley worked hard on his farm, gladly teaching Red all he knew. Picket O'Malley was a wonderful Christian woman. She was a cheerful wife and gentle mother. She treated Red as one of her own.

Each night after chores, the children were given reading and writing lessons. There were times when Red felt uncomfortable being older, but he was thankful for the chance to learn. Just before bed they were told Bible stories. It was then that Red became a Christian. He probably would have stayed with them forever, except they lost the farm to a crooked banker. In the midst of being forced off their land, the O'Malleys had told Red of the plan God had for their lives. Oh, they were angry for sure, but once they sought the Lord, they asked for His blessing on the banker. They encouraged Red to do the same—to trust in the Lord as they would do. The eight years he spent with the O'Malleys rooted him for what lay ahead of him…or so he thought.

Red was a man of twenty-two when they lost the farm. Had that terrible day never occurred, Red would probably still be there. When they had to leave the farm, Red knew it was time for him to go out on his own. What a hard and sorrowful parting it had been. He was given kisses, hugs, and a small amount of money. After being sent on his way, he found a large tree and lay beneath it, crying his heart out. When his tears were gone, he curled up and slept. Once he was awake, he dusted himself off and found another job.

He wondered where his "family" was now. How disappointed they would be in him if they knew where he was. It had all started when he had stopped trusting in the Lord. It was after losing another job with no prospects that he began losing hope. It was bitter cold, and he found himself drifting once again. His belly had not been full for over a week. He happened across an open door, exposing a table with bread and cheese. Before thinking about it, he grabbed it and ran. It wasn't long before a few men chased him down. He received a beating and a place of his own…in the gaol. Times were tough before, so why had he turned to stealing? He couldn't answer, because there was no answer. At the time he was bone-weary, empty with loneliness, and weak.

Red shifted to ease the pain in his back. The wall wasn't nearly as hard as admitting his failure. Something stirred within him, a familiar longing. It had taken him a while to figure out what that longing was. Over the years he had tried to tell himself that one day he would have his own land and family. One day he would have a family who wouldn't leave him. Without money to buy the land or a family to give it to him, there was little chance of that happening. So he had given up… given up on himself, his dream, and given up on God. He had tried to save some money, but wages were small. He worked mostly for his food and lodging. Irritation replaced longing, irritation at himself. The world was filled with the starving and deprived. All he had to do was look around the cell to see that. Yet his mind continued to chase the elusive and impossible dream. The wanting it wouldn't go away. Shame came over him until he heard that wonderful, soft voice within: *"Trust in Me."* Red had to smile. The Lord was not about to let him sit there and feel sorry for himself.

Forgive me once again, Father, he prayed. He felt peace knowing the Lord would not leave or forsake him. He would never feel alone again.

Another three weeks went by before the day of rescue came for the children. Keys rattling brought everyone's attention to the door. The gaoler unlocked the door and turned to look as if waiting for someone. A moment later a man and woman stepped through the door holding their arms out. "Patty, Michael, we're here!"

The two children looked up with the calling of their names. With squeals of joy and relief they ran as fast as they could toward the couple.

"You poor babies, we came as fast as we could. We just heard about your mother. Look how filthy you are!"

As soon as the children reached the woman, they buried their faces into the folds of her skirt. By what Katie could make out, the couple was likely the children's aunt and uncle.

"Oh, Arthur, let's get these poor children out of this horrid place. Who would lock innocent children in a place like this?" the woman questioned as she placed a hanky over her nose and mouth.

"I don't know, dear, but I intend to find out. This is an outrage." Turning to the little girl, her uncle spoke softly. "Don't worry; you will never be left alone again."

Tears of relief ran down Katie's cheek. Knowing the children would have a place to live, and with people who seemed to love them, comforted her. Envy also tugged at her heart. How she wished someone would rescue her. She wanted to be brave, but what difference would it make? Who cared if she were brave or not?

Gran would have cared. How many times did she tell Katie to, *"Be true to yourself and God"?* No matter what circumstances surrounded Gran, she walked in peace. Katie didn't have that same assurance. *Well,* she thought, *maybe not, but I did have more than most.* She had come from a family of love, deeply rooted and solid. She may not know where she was going, but she knew from where she came. She still had more than most, and no one could take that away from her. Strength surged through her, bringing hope in its wake. Things would somehow work out.

"Get up with yas! Come on, tarts, time to move into yer new 'ouse." The gaoler chuckled at his poor joke.

"What's going on?" one of the male prisoners asked.

"Nothin' tha' concerns the likes of ya. Sit back an' mind yer own business. All right, girlies, line up to be moved."

They did as they were told. The gaoler and several other turnkeys took the ten women down to another cell. Fresh hay covered the floor while blankets lay neatly folded. The women were relieved. They wouldn't have to worry about the men. The big man called Red seemed to protect the women, but they could never be sure of his intentions either. No one really knew him. After all, he was a prisoner too.

As the other women settled in, Katie ran her fingers through her long hair. The tangles were many and tight. "Will we ever get out of here?" she asked.

Mary shook her head, "Not sure, lass."

"What's to happen next?"

Mary's brow crinkled. "I be 'ere twice afore. It be a 'ard thing to say. One time they jest let me out with nary a word said. The next time a gaoler 'isself said 'e would have me quartered if I come back, then 'e let me out again. I think they 'ave enough to worry 'bout sides an ol' woman such as I be, but now I be 'ere again. My mind worries a bit, Katie. If they know I be 'ere afore, they could keep me 'ere a long time."

This new cell became home to the women for quite some time. Other good things came their way. The women were assigned jobs, making the days more bearable. At daylight a bell would ring, and the women went out to another room to wash and dress. After they straightened up their makeshift beds, they were led to work. They were assigned to various jobs. Some worked in the kitchen; others cleaned corridors, sewed, or did laundry, depending on their capabilities. Some of the women were taken to factories, but Katie and Mary were ordered to do kitchen work. They were relieved to find they would be together. It was hard work but satisfying. It was such a relief to have something to fill the long hours.

Katie, Mary, and other kitchen workers were first to rise in the morning to get food ready. They worked through breakfast, which consisted mostly of gruel and dry bread. After breakfast and clean up, they went to chapel for thirty minutes. Afterwards they went back to work through lunch…more gruel. When cleanup was finished, they were allowed to walk a bit outside in the "pen," taking in fresh air. There was a short rest period before the evening meal had to be prepared and served. Finally, after all the meals were done for the day, the kitchen was cleaned and set up for the next day. After the day's work, some of them had visitors, but most were locked up until the next morning.

Their routine was the same day after day. Sleep came quickly in spite of the harsh conditions. Time wore on endlessly, and the women forged friendships. They found strength in one another and safety in numbers. They took it upon themselves to pester the gaoler for brooms and buckets to clean up their areas. Once they were given those things, they insisted on getting clean hay.

The gaoler would complain but usually gave in to their demands. "Blimey, I gets this job ter get away from my ol' woman at 'ome 'cause she nags me ter death. Now I got ten more women naggin' after me 'ere! Be enough to drive a man to rum."

Katie experienced a strange sense of contentment in her daily life. She wasn't nearly as frightened as she had been. The days ran together, and time was of no significance. She had no idea what day or month it was. She focused on keeping fit but noted she was getting thinner. She knew that was because of the physical work, but mostly because of the lack of proper food. Although she worked in the kitchen, she was watched closely. No one received extra food…no one.

A good piece of time passed until a different day from the rest dawned. The women were not let out for work or chapel.

As they stood around speculating, they were startled when a man came to the gate and yelled out, "All right, come forward and step out! Step to; ain't got all day! Line up 'ere and stop that blabberin'."

The gaoler lined the women up, then led them down the long dank hallway. They made a sharp turn into another room. Everyone was surprised to see the room clean and bright. Sunshine washed over the walls, floors, and their faces. As soon as their eyes adjusted, they saw buckets of water on a heavy table. A second table held folded material. They stood together, not knowing quite what to do.

Again the gaoler barked, "Line up 'ter git yer 'eads shaved!"

"No!" one of the women shouted. A few others protested as well. They had been taught all their lives that their hair was their glory. Many had never had their hair cut before.

"Yas ain't got no choice in the matter, an' I ain't got all day. This be done whether yas wants it to be or not. Now somebody better go sit in that chair."

One of the older women slowly walked over and sat down. Another man stepped forward. He had scissors, razor, soap, and a razor strap in hand. After cutting the woman's hair short, he proceeded to shave her scalp. The room grew quiet.

"Why would they do that to us?" Katie whispered Mary.

"Ain't got no idea, Katie, girl. Ne'er 'ad it done afore the other times I be 'ere."

Katie wanted to bolt as panic seized her, but there wasn't anything she could do. How many other humiliations would they have to endure?

A few of the women protested again until the gaoler threatened them. Others just cried softly. One by one the women's heads were shaved. Once that task was completed, they were instructed to bathe and put on clean clothes.

"Ain't ya ever seen water afore?" the gaoler barked when the women didn't move. They were not about to undress with him there.

"Git away with ye now, ya filthy bloke!" Mary snapped.

The jailer sniffed, spit, then wiped his mouth on his sleeve. Turning to Mary, he snarled, "Tain't as though I want to be lookin' at an ol' heifer such as ye."

The women informed him they would only bathe after the men left. Once the women's heads were shaved, the gaoler started to walk out, only hesitating enough to make sure the women weren't already undressing.

"I be just outside the door if ye tarts get any ideas 'bout runnin'. Or could be yas want me ter wash yer backs fer yas?" His lips curled back in a sneer, showing his blackened teeth.

The women touched their heads. It was true; their long locks were gone. The high pile of hair verified that. Their "glory" lay there in the hay. They stood staring at the pile for a time. Slowly, one of the women kneeled to pick some of the hair up. "Seems like I've just lost an old friend," she whispered.

Mary, seeing a blanket, picked it up. "Come, lass, and 'elp me 'old this," she spoke to the woman kneeling. "Katie, come and bathe while we 'old this up fer ya."

Each woman took her turn holding the blanket. There were only three buckets of water along with a sliver of soap to wash, so they had to share. Katie took great pleasure in feeling a little cleaner. She made a mental note never to take a bath for granted again. They found the material on the table to be clean shifts to replace their filthy dresses. All were the same size, causing some women to drown and some to squeeze into them. When one of the women found an extra shift, she tore some material from it for a scarf. Katie made herself a scarf along with a belt.

Time dragged by as they awaited news of what would happen next. There had to be a reason for the clean clothes and bath.

"Could it be we are going to be set free?" one of the women whispered with hope in her voice.

"Nay." Mary shook her head. "They not shave our 'eads or give out clothes and water last time I was 'ere. They jest open the door and shew ol' Mary out."

"Maybe we are to be taken to see the magistrate," another woman offered.

That was the better guess, Katie thought.

Just then the gaoler came back with two other men. "All right, ya tarts; come this away and make it quick!"

The women formed a line, but this time they were shackled together. The gaoler led them out with two other turnkeys bringing up the rear. The women labored up some stairs, then turned out to a courtyard. Everyone visibly straightened once they stepped into the fresh air and sunshine. How sweet the air smelled. They had breathed in stench for so long their lungs couldn't seem to fill enough. Katie couldn't believe how chilled she felt without her hair. Turning, she looked back at where they had just come from. It was amazing to have such filth and freshness so close together. The softness of a bird singing caused a tear to fall. How she loved being outside. A deep longing gripped her heart as she once again thought of home…her home that was no more.

The women were instructed to get into a cart. It proved to be difficult with the shackles, but they helped one another. Once all were loaded, the horses plodded along.

"Wesley," the gaoler barked, "watch the ol' lady. She's crazy and mean. She almost castrated one of the men with her bare hands a time ago."

The man called Wesley turned to eye Mary. "Don't worry; she gives me any trouble, and we'll rope an' drag 'er."

Mary stared straight ahead.

The cart lumbered through tall gates onto a city street. People scurried out of the way. Katie would never get used to the noise of the city. The sounds of people and horse's hooves echoed off the stone buildings. Filth ran in the streets, but it could not compare to the gaol. Even so, this was a rare treat for the women. It would have been most enjoyable, had it not been for the situation they were in. Stares and jeers from some of the people didn't help either. One thing they did know for sure: they were going to find out what their futures held soon. Little comfort was found in that knowledge.

3

Victoria

"For heaven's sake, Peter," Victoria quipped, "stop pacing the floor. You are truly working up my nerves."

Peter Reeves pivoted toward his wife. As long as he could remember she loved to make decisions regarding his business. He could sidestep her for the most part, but this time she had him against the wall. He took a long drag off his cigar and slowly blew the smoke before speaking. "I just don't think it is realistic, Victoria. You must realize that women placed in these gaols are not the same caliber as yourself. Besides, my dear, you really do not need to worry your little head about such matters."

"Peter, why do you insist on talking to me as if I were a child?" Victoria moved with grace toward him.

Peter knew "it" wasn't over by the lift of her dainty chin. "All I mean, Victoria, is that these women are not decent thinking. They do not live by the standards you do. The same rules do not apply to them as to women such as you."

"What does it matter if a woman has learned gentle and feminine ways? Women are women, so how can you even think of sending single women on ships? It isn't decent. I can't believe you would even consider such a thing, let alone agree to it."

Peter ran his fingers through his hair. He wasn't about to tell her that women had been shipped out unmarried for many years now. Victoria gave her husband *the look*. He knew he had two choices: he could do as she said, or lie and tell her he would do as she said. "Must we speak of this right now? We'll be late meeting our guests for dinner." Hoping to divert her attention, he gently touched her cheek.

"All right, Peter. We can discuss this later, but be assured I will be satisfied on this matter." Turning, she called her maid to attend to her.

Putting up with his wife's self-righteousness was a source of great irritation. Her chin was raised, but not her morals. Oh, Peter wasn't the most moral man either, but he didn't pretend to be by dictating to others…except for prisoners, of course.

After leaving her husband's suite of rooms, Victoria headed toward her own. As her maid brushed out her heavy black hair, she thought of Peter. How she loved being

421

married to him. He always gave in to her wishes, but that was because she knew how to handle him. She enjoyed the attention and prestige that came with her husband's position. Being married to a Common Law Judge had benefits indeed. Peter had to travel to many different towns to sit the bench, giving her freedom to do as she pleased. She accompanied people she enjoyed instead of the many stuffed shirts they had to socialize with. With Peter's appointment on the bench and her inheritance there was more than enough money for the lifestyle she loved so much.

Yes, Victoria was very happy with her life. She only had two fears: growing old and boredom. It was the second fear that caused her to help the needy. When she heard Peter talking about those wretched women, she knew she had to step in. Men couldn't understand what a woman needed. Every woman wanted a man to take care of them, to give them a home and some stability. Certainly she understood it would be difficult to marry a stranger, especially a criminal, but the women were criminals themselves. That made it right. At least they would have someone to help them. Yes, it was the best way, the only way. Victoria planned on talking to her father to make sure he would convince Peter of that fact.

The ride to the dining hall was peaceful. Once arriving, Peter and Victoria spotted their friends and quickly walked over.

"So, Peter, how is the world of law and order?" Crowley offered his hand.

"I think we are all safe for now," Peter answered.

The women hugged, then sat after their husbands pulled out their chairs. They ate a light dinner due to the theater date afterwards, but found they still had time before the opening.

"You see, Peter, Lydia agrees with me concerning the female prisoners." Victoria smiled at her husband.

"Now, Victoria, must we bring that up again? I was looking forward to a more uneventful evening. I prefer not to talk about prisoners or court matters of any kind."

Victoria could not be so easily swayed. "What do you think, Brent? Do you feel that women should be shipped off to…God knows where? They would have no safety in marriage with men all around!"

Brent squirmed, as if he hated to be thrust between the couple's disagreements. "I'm sure Peter will have the right answer whatever he decides," he answered tactfully.

Victoria sighed. "Leave it to men to stick together on an issue that concerns the welfare of women."

Peter glanced at his pocketwatch. "It's time to be off. We don't want to be late, do we, ladies?"

Once in the carriage the talk again turned to crime.

"Did you hear that poor Mrs. Pike was accosted on Newberry Road, and the thugs got away?" Lydia stated.

"It wouldn't matter if they did catch them," Victoria said. "There is no room to put any of these people. Our gaols are full, and so are the prison hulks in the harbor."

"It almost sounds like you have more sympathy for these ruffians than for the victims," Lydia replied harshly.

Bristling, Victoria bit back, "Don't misunderstand me. It's just that with so many criminals abounding, and nowhere to go with them, things could get much worse."

"Hallelujah!" Peter yelled. "Now, my dear, you have it: the reason we are sending these prisoners to Australia."

"Peter, I never said I didn't want these people sent away. But we need to make sure the single women are sent with husbands. I believe it's our Christian duty. I've never wanted to keep these prisoners here. I, like everyone else, want them as far away from us as possible."

Peter scowled in the shadows. *So much for Christian duty.*

"Oh, what a wonderful idea!" Lydia exclaimed. "Can you imagine marrying a stranger, especially a convict who did only God knows what?"

"Lydia!" Her husband jumped in. "Try to calm yourself. I'm not sure ladies should be discussing such things!"

Lydia, properly chastised, sank back against the seat.

"Oh, for heaven's sakes, Brent," Victoria said, "she is only stating a fact. These women are prisoners and have questionable character. They need our guidance in moral and spiritual matters. It may be difficult for them to marry a stranger, but think of the alternatives...actually, I don't want to think of the alternatives."

Peter's dark mood deepened. Once his wife sunk her teeth into something, she wouldn't let go. He would be forced to take steps to satisfy her. That, or suffer, and suffer he would.

Victoria, perhaps sensing she had overstepped when the only thing coming from her husband was silence, tried to smooth things a bit. "These people can thank whoever it is they thank that Peter is their judge. At least you know they will get justice for their acts. If it were up to Earl Pierson, they would all be hanged. It's said he's hung more people than a woman hangs laundry."

Peter had to give her credit. She was good, but he knew she was "handling" him. A master manipulator, she practiced on him constantly, and he hated it. His wife had been taught by the best, his father-in-law. Every chance he got, the old man used his daughter to let Peter know what he wanted done in the court. Since he had handed Peter his position, the old man expected Peter to judge in accordance to his will.

Victoria continued her stroking. "Father knew when he stepped down that his recommendations would carry a lot of weight. He knew Peter was the best man for the job."

There it was. Peter expected it to come sooner than this but knew it would come. Victoria had to remind him and everyone else that her father gave him his position. Deep down he felt envy for the men being shipped out. Given a second chance, he wasn't sure he would make the same choices he had, in business or marriage. The best thing about his position was the traveling, being away from the constant dickering of his wife. It brought him peace and a chance to explore the pleasures he wasn't able to when at home. Tomorrow he would be leaving again. It couldn't happen soon enough.

Victoria couldn't wait until tomorrow. Her husband would leave and be gone a couple of weeks. This would give her enough time to put her plan into motion. She would have satisfaction in regard to these women and their situation. This would also give her enough time to see her latest male friend. A thrill sent shivers through her body. She felt sorry for anyone who wasn't her. She had the perfect life, and all that went with it—beauty, intelligence, money, and power. Oh, and her Christian duty, as well. That was important too. Those women were lucky that she was looking out for their best interest. They should all be on their knees thanking her. Yes, life was good.

But after the rush of pleasure left her, she was left with a sense of emptiness. If her life was so perfect, why did she feel so empty? *I'm just being silly,* she chided. *I am the luckiest woman in the world.*

Yet the emptiness remained.

The females were led to an underground floor of a large building where other women were already held. The gaoler turned, locking the heavy door behind him. One small lantern did nothing but send dark shadows across the room. The room itself was long and narrow with wood planks for them to sit on. Hay lay on the floor with a few blankets scattered about. The women snuggled together, trying to fight off the chill. The darkness matched their mood. Despair was their constant companion. The uncertainty about their future lay heavy on them.

Mary whispered, "Katie, I be hearin' the women talk and 'tis afraid I am. They be speakin' of ships and sailin' away to some far-off place."

Katie despaired even more. If Mary was afraid, Katie was petrified. "Before we get ourselves upset, let's ask them about it," she suggested.

Mary nodded.

"Aye, many ships have left already," one of the women shared. "Most of the ships don't make it, so I hear. Sea monsters get them for the most part afore they reach land."

"Why are ya frightenin' these women?" Mary said. "'Tis bad enough without ya runnin' yer mouth off!"

"'Tis true what I say! I be knowin' 'bout the sea. Me cousin sailed a time or two, and he told me of all the demons of the sea."

Mary eyed the woman. "'Ow can it be if yer cousin sailed a time or two, an' faced them demons, 'e came back ter tell tales?"

Shrilly the woman insisted her cousin had just barely escaped with his own life. Katie decided to listen but only believe about half of what she heard. Reality for Katie was frightening enough. "Where do the ships go, and who decides if you go or not?" she asked the woman.

Another woman spoke. "I 'ear different places. Some call it Owstraler or something like that."

"I think it's called Australia," another woman added. "I know of no monsters except the ones who keep this prison, but I have heard it is a great and terrible journey. If you make the journey at all, you then go to this foreign land to face unknown dangers. I have even heard there are black, ferocious men there."

Mary shrugged and quipped, "Sounds like all the men aroun' 'ere. Sounds like 'ome."

The women chuckled.

The same woman added, "I hear 'tis the magistrate who decides our fate to go or not." That made the most sense. The woman went on. "I do know that if you are married, your husband can't go with you. Your babes can, if your husband lets them. I know of a woman whose husband was sent out; she never heard from him again."

"Do you think if we get sent there, we'll ever get back home?" someone asked.

"Can't say, but from what I hear, I doubt it. I don't know if a lot of the ships make it. If they do, I don't know what happens next. I would guess those poor souls are worked to death." The woman seemed to forget she was now one of those poor souls.

Katie noticed that Mary pulled the old scrap of cloth from her pocket and ran it through her fingers. It seemed that whenever Mary was troubled, the cloth soothed her. Katie was about to ask her about it but thought better of it. If Mary wanted her to know, she would tell her.

"Wha' if ya can't swim?" Mary asked. Katie detected a quiver in her voice.

"What does that have to do with it? They don't care if we can swim or not," was the answer given.

Mary nodded.

Finally the women grew quiet. They faced another cold, damp, lonely night.

Suddenly men showed up with extra blankets and food. "'Ere be warm food for your bellies. I don't want no trouble tonight. Sleep 'cause yer gettin' hell on the morrow."

No one had the courage to ask what he meant by that.

They ate in silence, then tried to rest. Sleep was lost to them, all except for Mary. Her snores would have made a sailor proud.

A possibility had haunted Katie since they left the gaol. What if she was to be hanged? In some ways it didn't seem any worse or better than being shipped off to the end of the world. Fear was fear, and Katie feared them both. What a strange name…Australia. It sounded as if it wasn't part of this world at all. She couldn't comprehend how big the sea was, let alone another land. She had nothing to gauge her imaginings on, so was unable to calm herself. Were there really sea monsters, and who were those ferocious black men? She gave up trying to sleep, but somewhere in the night she did. She slept deep and dreamless, as if she did not have a care in the world.

Voices roused Katie, and for a split second she couldn't remember where she was. When reality hit, dread swept over her once again. Would she feel anything but fear and trepidation ever again? Katie stretched, trying to get the kinks out. Soon food was brought in. Most of the women stared at it, but Katie forced herself to eat. It was cold and tasteless, but there was no telling when she would get another chance. The others soon saw the wisdom in it and also ate.

A gaoler barked out, causing the women to jump, "'Urry up with yas now. Day of judgment fer ya sins be 'ere, and the judge ain't takin' a notion to wait on ya, so git movin'."

The women stood quietly, not knowing what they were supposed to do. Fear in their faces seemed to bring about a lighter mood in the man.

"Ah, don't want to face the music, does yas? Ya likes to play, but when it comes to payin' fer it, ya be afraid, ain't yas?" He didn't seem so innocent in life himself, Katie thought. "Line up now, and git yerselves ready to see the ol' judges," he added. "They don't take to ya being late, so 'urry!"

The day Katie had been waiting for had finally come. She felt relieved and fearful at the same time. Relieved, for the waiting was over. Soon she would know some of what lay ahead. Once again the women were lined up and shackled. The chains seemed heavier than before.

"The ol' men don't want no prisoners unchained in their courtroom, neither. Especially wild women," the man scoffed. "Ya be a dangerous bunch. I can sees it fer sure. I like wild women even without any 'air on their 'eads." He snickered, pinching one of them.

The women were led out into the sunshine, but it didn't seem quite as bright as yesterday. They crossed a courtyard filled with flowerbeds of brightly colored blooms and an ornate fountain. *Why put things of beauty in such an ugly place?* Katie mused.

Arriving across the courtyard, the women were shoved into some kind of backroom. Other women were there as well, so it was crowded and stifling. To Katie, it seemed that they were either freezing or barely able to breathe. The turnkeys left them shackled and alone. Some of the women whispered among themselves, but most were quiet.

Red, at the very front of the platform, watched Katie walk in with her head held high. He felt strangely proud of her. He calmly watched the proceedings until two turnkeys came to lead him toward the smaller platform. They released him from the common chains and put separate irons on him, doublechecking to make sure he was secure.

Magistrate Peter Reeves glanced at the prisoner being led forward. He was glad this man was chained. Usually one man guarded each prisoner, but they had two guards on this one. The size of the man was impressive.

After hearing the charge, Peter addressed the man. "Do you realize that by stealing that food you left those deserving of it hungry?"

"Yes, sir," Red answered.

"Do you have anything to say in your defense?" Peter added.

Red simply stated he was wrong in what he did.

"Do you have anything you would like to say, Barrister Boggs, in defense of this man?" Peter looked at the defender.

"No, sir. This man has stated that he is guilty of the theft, so indeed there is nothing more to be said."

Peter conferred with his partner, Magistrate Mathers, before sentencing Red. He looked down at his desk as if going over some information, but in reality he was thinking. It was unusual for a man to state he was guilty. He was more accustomed to hearing lies, pleading, and excuses. Again, Peter was impressed with this man. "Prisoner, are you married, or do you have family in these parts or own property here?"

"No, sir, no wife, family, or property."

Peter continued, "You are hereby sentenced to be transported to Botany Bay for no less than seven years. You will be given the privilege of making a new life for yourself there. At the end of your seven-year sentence, you can stay there or you may choose to be shipped back to England. I hope you will take advantage of this opportunity I am giving you to make a new home and life for yourself. Next prisoner, forward!"

Mathers cleared his throat and leaned toward Reeves with a lifted brow. "If it's not too much trouble, could you explain what this is about? Why ask if the man is married or not?"

Peter didn't like to explain himself to anyone. Trying to curb his irritation, he answered, "This is something new. We're allowing the single female prisoners to pick one of the men to marry. It's either that, or stay here in one of the gaols. We aren't transporting single women out."

"That's surprising to hear," Mathers responded. "When was this decision made, and by whom?"

"Can we discuss this later?" Reeves all but snapped.

"Certainly," Mathers stated.

Red expected his sentence. It didn't matter that he stole because he was hungry; stealing was stealing. What did surprise him was the way he felt…completely at peace. He heard the journey was survivable at best. He knew the new land was not much better, but he had decided never to doubt God ever again. He would have to face the consequences but knew the Lord would sustain him.

When one of the magistrates had read the big man's name, Katie leaned forward to hear it. *James Patrick Murphy. A fine Irish name,* she thought.

Katie's heart went out to the big man, but why? Why did she care about him? She knew she was accused of the same crime as he, so her punishment would probably be the same. Anger filled her. Why was she even here? She looked around, only to blush when many eyes turned in her direction. Why should she feel shame when she didn't do anything?

Lifting her chin, she stood straighter. Who were these people to judge her? How shallow were their lives that they needed to sit all day in a room, and see others judged and sentenced? Would she be able to convince the judge of her innocence? She had been shouting her innocence from the beginning, but no one believed her yet. Why would he? Only Tess and God knew Katie wasn't guilty. She certainly didn't expect either of them to show up anytime soon to speak on her behalf. Again she felt a longing in her soul…to be close to God like Gran had been. No, she wasn't going to do it; just call on God when she got in trouble. It wasn't right. It was too late now. She would have to get through this on her own.

Once the men were finished, the women were led, one by one, to the dreaded platform. Every once in a while the barrister would make a feeble attempt to defend the prisoner, but each time the prisoner was found guilty anyway. Katie wondered if this man got paid for being there. The one thing that puzzled everyone was the question that had been asked of each prisoner: "Are you married?" It had never mattered before.

One of the women was found guilty of killing her husband and sentenced to hang. She tried to explain that her husband had beaten several of their children so badly that one of them had died. She explained how she tried to protect her children from him, but it didn't matter. She had committed murder. She would hang. Katie wondered sadly what would happen to the children. Why was there so much suffering in this world? The hysterical woman had to be half carried out of the courtroom.

The day wore on, causing a woman to faint from the heat. About the time Katie thought she would die of thirst, buckets of water were brought in. The women were given a few minutes to sit and drink. The women collectively sighed in relief as they sat leaning against the back wall. After ten minutes all prisoners were led out in small groups for personal breaks. When they returned, the lanterns and chandelier were lit, and proceedings resumed.

Mary's name was the first called. The common shackles were removed, replaced by a smaller set. As Mary was being led, Katie noticed she was hobbling. *Probably from the leg irons.* She sent up a quick prayer for Mary. She hoped God would listen, even if it was her doing the praying.

Peter barked at Mary once she took her place, "Your charge is prostitution. What do you say, guilty or not?"

Mary looked him square in the eye. "I be as innocent as yourself be."

The spectators gasped. Katie's heart sank. Surely Mary had sealed her fate with that remark. Everyone turned to look at the man who held Mary's future in his hands. Katie expected him to be scarlet with anger, but after a second of surprise, he laughed. Soon most of the spectators were laughing along with him. Magistrate Mathers covered his mouth to hide a smile.

Barrister Boggs spoke up. "I find this lack of respect quite disturbing, sir!"

Peter leaned forward, causing the laughter to die. "I, on the other hand, find this woman quite refreshing," Peter turned his attention back to Mary. She squirmed a little under his gaze. He ruffled some papers. "I see that you have been arrested before. What do you have to say to the court?"

Casting her eyes down, she replied, "Aye, sir, I cannot lie 'bout that, yer Lordship. 'Tis truth told that it be a time or two I be locked up, but there be another truth, sir. I would ne'er be able to make it to that foreign land. I not be sayin' that I have not wronged anyone. It just be that I'm not strong to take the sea, 'tis all."

Mary had told Katie she'd been afraid of water all her life. The sea was the most frightening thing imaginable to her. She'd claimed she would drop dead of fear if she had to sail anywhere. Only her stiff old corpse would be left.

In a gentler tone, Peter spoke. "You have repeated arrests, and it would seem clear that you have no intention of turning yourself around. I have no choice but to sentence you to five years in service of the gaols. You will serve at Newgate. At least you will have a roof over your head and honest work."

Katie found herself holding her breath. She looked at Mary for her reaction. At first it seemed as if Mary had not heard the sentence. She stood there quiet, then looked up at the younger man and nodded. Five years in the gaol was far better than death at sea. Mary stepped down and was led out.

"Next!" the magistrate called out.

Katie watched Mary until the pulling of her wrist brought her attention back. Her turn had come. Queasiness threatened. She fought the sick feeling. All this was humiliating enough without getting sick too. Katie tried to steel herself. No matter what, she had to remember that she was innocent. She refused to feel shame. She placed her hands on the rail to steady herself. Tears threatened to flow, so she closed her eyes and clenched her teeth. She had never felt so alone and scared. She comforted herself by thinking, *I'll cry later.*

Peter was getting tired. The heat was worse because of his robes and wig. He fought the urge to run out of the room. With resolve he looked down at the paperwork for the next case. Another thief...would this day not end?

Peter hated the way they shuffled their feet when they walked. He seemed to forget about the leg irons. Yes, indeed, his contempt was harder and harder to hide when it came to these cowards. They wouldn't think twice of killing or robbing, but they had no backbone when it came to facing up to their deeds. He was starting to believe he was the one who had been given a life sentence. Having to face these miserable liars year after year was growing wearisome. His only reprieve today had been the old prostitute and the big man. Prisoners usually didn't tell the truth. It was quite refreshing indeed when they did. He studied a young woman standing on the platform. She'd held his interest when she first entered his court. She stood out from the others.

Katie looked back at him. Her eyes stayed fixed on him until he looked down, breaking the spell.

Peter spoke up. "It says here that you are a thief. Is that correct?"

Katie's tongue seemed twice its size, causing her words to stick in her throat.

"Well?" Peter questioned as he glanced up from his papers.

Katie swallowed. "I have never stolen anything in my life, sir."

"So you are completely innocent then?"

"No sir," Katie came back. "I'm not innocent in my life, but I did not steal what I am accused of."

"Do you have any proof you can offer?"

"No."

Once again Peter looked down at the papers on his desk, then let out a disgusted sigh. He picked up a paper and held it up for Katie to see. "I have sworn testimony here stating you did steal a necklace. Your word is of no value here. If that is all the proof you have, I am afraid I must find you guilty. Are you married, or do you have children?"

Katie shook her head.

"I sentence you to seven years. You will be transported out with the others. That is all."

Katie tried to will her eyes off this man who was about to change her life. She wanted to look away but could not. She opened her mouth to defend herself, but what could she say in her defense? Without asking, she knew who had written the statement of lies and then sworn them to be true.

She offered no resistance as she was led to the back room. Seething anger—and thoughts of strangling Tess—filled her.

The day wore on, causing many of the spectators to leave. Evening fell, and all were exhausted. Trying to speed things along, Mathers read the cases to Peter, letting him judge all the prisoners.

Finally the last woman stood before him. Even so this would not be the end to the day. Now he had to face the unmarried women, and ask them if they wanted to marry or not. Peter wasn't sure how this new procedure would work. He wondered how the female prisoners would take the ultimatum: work in the gaols, or marry a stranger. He was sure some would think of it as a double sentence. Of course they could refuse to marry. What did it matter really? Marriage wasn't a sacred thing to people like these anyway.

After the last prisoner was sentenced, he had the gaolers bring all the unmarried prisoners back inside the courtroom. They were led to the benches since all spectators had left.

Mathers excused himself. If Reeves wanted to play the "who's married and who's not" game, so be it. But Mathers said he had better things to do.

As the women and men were being seated, Peter came down from his desk to stand before them. Slowly he perused each prisoner. They would visibly straighten when his eyes fell on them. He wasn't sure how to present his news, so he just stood there looking at them for a few minutes.

Fear hung in the air. Clearly the prisoners wondered why they were brought back to court. Why hadn't they been taken out with the others? Something was amiss, but what?

Clearing his throat and placing his hands behind his back, Peter started pacing. He stopped at one point as if ready to speak but turned and began pacing again. Finally he decided to be direct. "I suppose you are wondering why you have been kept at court. As you can see, only those who have been sentenced to sail and are not married are here. It has been discussed at great length and decided that those unmarried women who have been sentenced to sail will need to be married."

A gasp could be heard throughout the group.

Peter continued, "I realize this is a surprise to you, but this has been decided for your best interest. To ship out single women is difficult on both them and the men. As you can see, there are only three women here that this applies to. We will not force this upon anyone. However, if you decide not to marry, you will be given the only other choice. You will have to serve your time in one of the gaols here.

"Women, you will be allowed to pick out a husband from these men. If the man is not willing, then you may pick another. If no man here will marry you, then you will be sent to a gaol to serve your time. The time spent in a gaol will be the same amount of time that you would have served at your destination. You will be brought back here to voice your decision tomorrow morning. If you decide to marry, then you will be shipped out with your husband. You need to decide now, so look the men over well.

"Guards, give these people fifteen minutes to talk with one another. After that, take them back to the cells below to be held until court tomorrow. I want to remind all of you that this could be an exceptional chance for you…a chance to have your own family and home. I would hope that you take advantage of this opportunity, and make a good life for yourselves. You may find your life can be quite rewarding when what you obtain is from honest work. Guards, watch them carefully. Let them speak to one another no longer than the allotted time." Turning back to the prisoners, Peter added, "I would suggest that you don't let shyness hinder your time."

With that, Peter turned and walked out. Tomorrow would be another long day.

Katie barely heard what was being said. Had she actually heard him say marry? Marry? Marry…who? She was still trying to make sense of his words.

Everyone turned to look at each other. Some of the men wore smirks, and others the same look of surprise as the women.

One of the gaolers shouted, "All right, snap to. Ain't got but a few minutes."

Katie was shaken. Fifteen minutes! How could a decision that big be given only minutes? She started looking at the men. Could she spend seven more years in that gaol? Things were a little better since she worked in the kitchen but still….

She recalled the magistrate's words—of having her own home and family. She had always dreamed of that, but not this way!

One of the women jumped up and grabbed one of the men's arms. "This bloke is mine, so don't be thinkin' otherwise!" she addressed the other women. She had surprised the man, but he smiled and nodded, letting her know it was fine with him. A few of the other men chuckled.

Suddenly a soothing calm came over Katie. She knew what she had to do. Stepping forward, she stood in front of James Patrick. He lifted himself off the bench with surprising ease as she approached. He towered over her. "Sir, I do not think I would live if I had to stay long in this place. I have seen your kindness and your compassion for others. It has touched me. If you marry me, sir, I promise I will be as good a wife as I can be. I'm strong, a hard worker, and in spite of being here, I am an honest person. I would not do anything to shame you." Katie couldn't think of anything else to say. Her mind raced. What if he turned her down? What if he accepted? What if…?

For a second Katie thought he would turn away from her. What would she do then?

A loud voice interrupted. "Don't be doin' it, miss!" a man with no teeth yelled. "He be a man eater! I 'ear say he eats the flesh of the innocent!"

"Shut up, ye crazy ol' goat!" the gaoler snapped.

Katie looked at the toothless man, then turned away.

The old man continued, "It be fine with me if you get kilt and done eaten by the bloke. Serves ye right fer not taken heed of my words, lass. Cannot say ya wasn't told of it."

Red looked down at her. How small and fragile she seemed. Dark circles lay under her eyes. Her skin seemed almost translucent. It had been a shock to see her head shaved. Where there had been silky brown hair, little peach fuzz now appeared. A feeling of protectiveness swept over him, and his heart pounded.

Red wondered what the old man was raving about. He stepped closer to Katie, speaking in hushed tones. "What I say is to you alone. I'm not sure what the future will be. I have been alone most of my life and struggle to care for myself at times. I don't know if I can properly care for you. Especially in the situation I'm in right now."

"I thank you for your honesty, sir, but I have no home or family left," Katie said. "Like you, I do not know what the future holds, but we could help each other. I will try not to complain or be a burden to you. I know I don't look strong now, but I am a hard worker. Usually I'm cheerful, when not in such a difficult place as this." She appeared to be holding her breath.

Red admired her strength. The thought of having someone to care for, and have them care for him, filled him with warmth.

"Make up yer mind, man," the chainer spoke up. "Ya got a minute left."

Red knew that what he was about to say would change both of their worlds forever…one way or the other. He felt something awaken within him—the knowledge that it was meant to be. She was meant to be his, and God was bestowing a rare and wonderful gift on him. Even though he didn't feel love now, he somehow knew that, given time, they would have it.

He reached for Katie's hand. There they stood, both in chains, while everyone gawked at them. He smiled at her. "Then so be it. We will wed, and I too give you my word that I will be the best husband that I can be." His look of tenderness made Katie blush. He continued, "Maybe I should tell you my name if we're to be married. My Christian name is James Patrick Murphy, but everyone calls me Red."

Katie whispered, "Aye, I heard your name in the courtroom. I also heard others call you Red. I will try to do my best to make you glad for your decision. I would like to call you by your given name, James Patrick. My Christian name is Kathryn Elizabeth Brady, but almost everyone calls me Katie."

Red repeated, "Katie."

In a second their "moment" ended, and they were thrust back with the others.

"Ye be sorry fer it all, lass," hissed the toothless man. "Ye don't believe it now, but I 'ear he does eat the flesh. He will surely put harm to ya."

"Shut up ya ol' fool, or I'll take a bite outta ya meself!" the gaoler yelled. "What about yerself, woman?" He turned to the third woman. "Best to git up to grab yerself one of these fine gents afore time is gone."

Everyone watched the woman. She kept her gaze on the floor.

"Fine, then. All ye prisoners on yer feet, and make 'er snappy. Me supper awaits me!" the gaoler barked.

5

Matrimony

Katie and the other two women were the only ones in the cell. Mary and the others must have been taken back to the gaol. Soon food was brought, and to their surprise it was hot and plentiful.

The other woman who had decided to marry came and sat next to Katie. "Tain't it something that we had to marry one of them blokes?" she asked with her mouth full. "My man was surprised I grabbed him, eh?" The woman giggled. "I had my eye on him afore, so the choosing weren't so hard."

Katie smiled at her, not knowing how to respond. She looked over at the other woman sitting by herself, noting she wasn't eating. Getting up, Katie grabbed some food to take over to her. "Aren't you hungry?" Katie asked her.

The woman jumped at Katie's voice. "Oh, I nary saw you standing there," she sputtered. "Aye 'tis hungry I am, but I have my mind on other things." After thanking Katie, she took the bowl. Katie turned to walk away but stopped when the woman began talking again. "Couldn't believe my ears when that judge said we would have to marry a stranger. Not me. I have had enough trouble from menfolk. At least here I know what to expect. How can you marry a stranger?"

Katie tried to sort her feelings out before answering. It was strange, but she wasn't afraid to marry James Patrick. In the depths of her soul she knew she would be safe. However, she was afraid of sailing far away to a land she couldn't even visualize. What amazed her was her sense of excitement about it all as well.

She turned to the woman and spoke softly. "We have been given only two choices. I feel I have made the best decision for myself. I am afraid of sailing far away, though."

"Aye, 'tis a hard decision to be sure. Well, may the good Lord watch o'er all of us," the woman added.

Katie nodded and then turned back to her food. Her mind roved over the events of the day.

After she finished eating, she lay down on a blanket. It didn't take long to fall into a deep, dreamless sleep. She was exhausted.

Red sat off by himself, resting his back against the cell wall. He couldn't keep his mind off his soon-to-be bride. He felt anxious to marry the gentle girl. Her name! What was her name? It was Kate. No, Kathryn. No, Katie. Yes, that was it—Katie Elizabeth Brady. He felt everything from excitement to fear to shyness. When would they be married? Would she have picked him for her husband in different circumstances?

What was he thinking? Of course not! She wasn't given much choice. Doubts filled him. How could he marry with nothing to call his own? Again he had to remind himself about the Lord being in control. He remembered how he felt peace with the decision to marry her. Soon sleep called him. Closing his eyes, Katie's face came to him, and once again he knew it was meant to be. She was meant to be his. He smiled in the dark.

The women were led back into the courtroom the following morning to give their decision. Katie's mind raced. Had she rushed into it? She almost began laughing out loud. Of course she had rushed into it...she had no choice. She knew she could change her answer, but she wouldn't. She looked around for James Patrick, but the men were not there yet.

A few minutes later someone barked out orders. "Git goin', blokes! Time be runnin', an' we best not keep the good magistrate waitin' on us."

Everyone knew the gaoler was saying that for the magistrate's benefit, but he could have saved his breath. The magistrate wasn't in the room yet. The gaoler led the two men toward the women, then went to stand over by the other chainer.

"Ain't like 'im to be late," the one said to the other. "Hope this be o'er soon. Gonna be a hot one again today."

The other chainer joked, "Don't want no cryin' from ya when the wedding comes. I ain't got no hanky." The two laughed, slapping each other on the back.

Magistrate Reeves finally stepped into the room wearing his robe but not his wig. He looked even younger without his hairpiece. Stepping up to his desk on the high platform, he spoke directly to the prisoners. "I see that you have made your decisions to marry since there are two couples in front of me. I would like all four of you to stand before me. Gaolers, remove their chains."

After their chains were removed, they stepped up to the front of the room. Red moved next to Katie. He gave her a smile of reassurance, and his eyes lingered on the scarf on her head.

The magistrate looked intently at the two couples, then addressed the women. "Have you thought this through?"

Katie couldn't believe he would even ask them that. He had given them no time to consider anything and pretty much no choice in the matter.

Both women simply answered, "Yes, sir."

Magistrate Reeves then turned to the men. "What about you? Are you both in agreement to marrying these women?"

They both answered, "Yes, sir."

Then the magistrate asked all four of them, "Are you prepared to marry now?"

They all nodded in agreement.

Magistrate Reeeves stepped down from his desk and instructed the two couples to step closer to the front. He married the two couples in one ceremony. Before they could say, "I do," it was finished. They stood looking uncomfortable, not sure what to do next.

The magistrate stepped back up to his desk and spoke to the couples. "Your marriages are legal and binding. I will have you sign these papers. If you cannot write, make your mark. You will not see one another until the time comes to set sail. I have decided to give you one hour to visit. Gaolers, take them to the back of the room. Let them sit, and bring them something to eat. Give them one hour before taking them back to the gaol. Do not chain them again until the hour is up, but I want them guarded well." He then led the two couples to a smaller table with official-looking papers.

Both Katie and Red signed their names. *So he, too, can write,* she thought.

Magistrate Reeves again turned to the couples. "I understand this must be difficult for you, but I want you to realize you have been given a wonderful opportunity. You now have family and will soon have a chance to make something out of your lives. It will be a hard life, but having someone to help you in your endeavors will make it easier. You are the first couples to marry by order of the court. I feel especially hopeful that you will succeed. God bless your marriages, and good luck." With that he disappeared into an adjoining room.

The gaolers shuffled up to the couples in the front, sputtering all the way. "Blimey, ya would think 'e be speakin' to the Queen 'erself, God blessin' ya and all. All right with yas, 'urry up to the back now. We best get yer food so we can serve ya like ye be the royals and all. Yas won't be getting chained, but be mindful now, we be watchin' yas. Now sit yerselfs down."

The couples sat at opposite ends of the row for privacy. Red turned toward his bride. "Are you all right?" he asked, concern in his eyes.

She could feel the flush on her cheeks. Nodding, she softly answered, "Aye, I am fine—just out of breath with everything happening."

Both sat quietly for some time until a strange noise resounded. Looking around, Katie saw the other couple engaged in a long, passionate kiss. Now she and Red both blushed.

Silence reigned until the chainers brought some food.

Red wondered if he should mention how nice Katie looked. She probably wouldn't believe him, not with her shaved head.

Katie wondered if she should mention how brave she thought James was, but thought better of it.

Both tried hard to think of something to say until both began talking at once. They burst out laughing. Katie liked his smile. Deep dimples creased his cheeks.

After their meal they spoke of everyday things. They discovered they had a lot in common. Neither had any family, except for each other now. They spoke of their fears and hopes for the future. Both confessed how they always wanted family of their own. Katie showed a great deal of knowledge in farming, which pleased James. They had another thing in common. Katie had lost Gran when their cottage burned to the ground just as James had lost his parents.

All too soon it was time for them to part.

They had only a moment more together, and Katie felt a strange disappointment.

"Take care of yourself, Mrs. Murphy," James Patrick said, smiling. "I'm not sure when I will see you again."

Katie inhaled in surprise. "Oh, that's right! My name is changed now!"

A minute later the gaolers gruffly placed them in chains once again. It always amazed Katie how some people preferred treating people roughly when given any degree of power. It seemed to annoy the gaolers that the magistrate spoke to them as human beings.

The four were hoisted up into a cart and soon were headed back to the gaol. During the ride back James would smile at Katie as if to let her know everything would work out. She realized she now had someone who cared for her. That knowledge gave her hope. *I will take care of you, too,* she thought.

Once at the gaol, James spoke softly to Katie. "I don't know when I will see you next, but you must eat as much as you can. You must take care of yourself!"

Katie nodded, keeping her eyes on him until he was led out of sight. Slowly she turned, letting herself be led the other way. Funny how alone she felt, separated from him. It would be a battle to keep her spirits up, but now she had someone else to think of. Maybe she didn't know what the future would bring, but at least her life was moving forward.

What a difference a day made…married! Tears welled as she recalled how Gran had talked about having a wedding for her one day. She had told Katie of the dress Mama had worn. It had been tucked safely away for so many years for Katie to use someday.

Sadly it had been lost in the fire. *Now I'm married!* It was not a wedding of her dreams, but life was nothing like what she thought it would be. She had to make some plans. She was determined to do her best to keep herself as strong as possible. She had to prepare herself for what was ahead. The loneliness lightened. Suddenly she was given a future and a family.

Katie and the other newly married woman were led to a different cell once at the gaol. Mary and the other women were already there. The two friends hugged after seeing each other. Katie shared everything that had happened to her since they had been separated, surprising Mary to say the least.

"Can't say I e'er 'ear such a thing as that as 'avin' to marry some bloke. Ya picked a man did ya, Katie?"

Katie told Mary it was the man who looked after them in the communal cell. "His name is James Patrick."

Mary's eyes teared up. "Aye lass, ol' Mary had a man such as that once. Surprised, are ya? 'Tis true and 'e be a good bloke ta me. Died, 'e did, and then I had to go to the streets. Yer man seems to be of a kind heart, handin' out food to us an' all."

Katie didn't push for any information about Mary's past life. She simply held the older woman's hand.

Time seemed more peaceful since the men and women were separated. The threat of violence was gone until a new prisoner was brought in. Bess was a large woman with a loud voice to match. It was obvious she wanted to rule the cell. Threats and coarse language were her weapons. They worked on just about everyone…except Mary.

There was tension in the air almost as soon as Bess came into the cell. She warned the others not to cross her. "Me name 'tis Bess, an' I be in gaols afore. I eat first, and if I want a spot, then I get it. Ya 'ear me? Don't be crossin' me, or it be bad fer yas." Without warning, she kicked a woman out of her spot as if to emphasize her words. The others weren't sure how to react. Some moved further away from her, but Mary just let out a "hmmph!"

Room was given to the woman until she pushed Katie out of pure meanness two days later. "Git away with ya, or ya hit the floor!" Bess yelled, making Katie jump.

Mary was on her feet in a split second. Everyone stood with their mouths gaped at her speed and agility. Without any noise, she grabbed a hold of the woman's hair. Before the woman could even react, Mary spun her around and kicked hard. Bess was knocked against the wall. Mary grabbed her again, pushing her against the opposite wall. Just as the woman turned to defend herself, Mary slapped her. The sound of it echoed through the cell.

"Want some more, tart?" Mary yelled. She braced herself for the counterattack.

After hearing the fight start, the turnkey watched through the gate, clearly enjoying himself immensely. Fights, especially between women, were a rare treat. It added excitement to an otherwise boring day.

Katie couldn't believe her eyes or ears. Mary had changed into another person. The sweet, caring person she knew was gone, replaced with a wild woman. Her hair, what she had of it, looked like it was standing on end. Her face was distorted. The snarl that came from her sounded inhuman.

Once the surprise of the attack wore off, Bess lunged at Mary. The two women rolled on the ground. Hay, dust, and the other women scattered everywhere. It looked like Mary was going to be bested until Katie jumped in to help. Now three women were rolling, and what a sight it was. Five of the other women jumped on Bess as well. Before too long she was subdued and pinned to the ground. Mary got up, spitting and sputtering hay from her mouth. She spun around, looking for her opponent. After completing a couple of turns punching air, she finally stopped. It took several seconds before she realized Bess was down with the others on top of her.

"That a way! Git 'er good! Let 'er 'ave it, lasses!" Mary yelled in excitement and anger.

"Git off me, ya bloody lout!" Bess yelled. "'Tis a sorry lot ye be if'n yas don't let me up!"

The women held her down. Katie was able to stand once the other women had a good hold. "Nay, you will stay there until you cool down," was Katie's reply.

Mary had to get in her two words. "Ya be bullyin' us since ya got 'ere. I be sick of it, and so be the others, it would seem. Ya want to be wearin' yer face on yer backside, keep it up, ya ol' hag!" Mary emphasized her words by pushing her bosoms up.

Katie was a little calmer. "Mary is right. We won't have you pushing us around any longer. You will wait your turn like the rest of us when the food comes, and no more pushing anyone out of their spot at night. If you start acting like a human being, we will let you up. Don't think of getting up to start more trouble. Do you understand?"

Bess glared but agreed. The women slowly let her stand. She swayed, having to brace herself against the wall. After catching her breath, she simply sat down. The other women sat down as well, keeping a keen eye on Bess.

Katie turned to Mary. "I've never been in a fight before. Are you all right?"

"I be fine and dandy. 'Tis been a long time since I ripped some 'air out! Good thin' she 'ad 'air to rip out. I be glad me 'ead be shaved so she cannot grab any of mine. Does the blood good fer sure, to ruckus." Mary laughed.

Katie smiled, shaking her head in response. There was only one like Mary. She seemed more like a child at times than a middle-aged woman.

Soon the women calmed down. Everyone was exhausted from all the excitement, except for the gaoler. He seemed disappointed it had ended so quickly. The gleam in his eye revealed he hoped it wouldn't be long until the next bout.

Weeks passed, and the women thought they would go mad with boredom. They made up games to occupy themselves or exchanged stories. They came to know each other better. Even Bess participated. Excitement swept through when word came down that they may be given jobs again. It would be an easier time if they had something to do.

By now, Katie sported a hairstyle resembling a boy. Mary challenged Katie by betting whose hair would grow the fastest. Mary was losing, for her head was still covered more in gray fuzz than hair. "I earned all those gray 'airs, every one," Mary boasted. She then proceeded to run a broken old comb over her head, pretending it was caught in a snarl. Everyone laughed. Katie was proud of Mary. In all the time they suffered hardships, she never complained. Well, she did complain about one thing—the fact that Bess was a friend now, ending the possibility of another good fight.

All Red thought about was Katie and all the things he wanted to talk to her about. He worried about her, too. Hopefully she would fare well. He prayed for her every time he thought of her. She seemed a dainty creature compared to some of the other women, but he knew he needed to trust in God for her safety. Since God had given her to him, He surely wouldn't take her away from him now. What a great comfort to know he could rest in the Lord.

The men were in a cleaner cell, but boredom lay heavy. Most of their ponderings turned toward sailing out. When would they leave? How long was the voyage? Would they be able to work land for themselves once they were there, or would they be used strictly for slave labor? If that was the case, why would they need wives? There were so many questions and no answers.

Again Red took comfort, knowing the Lord had the answers. He would direct their paths, and all would work out. Red had no qualms about going to Botany Bay; it was only the getting there that concerned him. He might not get land right away, but it sounded like hard work could earn him some land later on. He didn't care where the land was as long as it would be his to hand down to his children.

Children. What a strange thought. Just a few days ago he was alone in the world, except for the Lord, and now he had a wife. He'd never reflected on marriage much. He just figured he would meet someone someday, fall in love, and that would be it.

Weeks passed, and a few new men arrived in the cell. They were fair fellows, fitting in as best as anyone could. One of the men was a talker and openly shared his experiences. The experience that seemed to interest everyone the most concerned the prison ships in the harbor.

"I was there fer 'bout three months, be my guess," he began. "Foulest place I e'er be in, rats crawlin' all over. Lice nearly eat ya alive." With that statement the others stepped back. "This place we be in now is a heap better. Why, they had small boys chained with the foulest of men. Women cried mournfully, some with wee ones to boot. Cells are in the dank belly of the ships, weavin' back and forth 'til a man empties his belly. Only clean air was up top. If the weather be foul, then we be left chained and locked below."

"How did ya e'er get out of it?" ask one man.

"Seems one of my ol' cronies be up fer 'is trial soon. Needs me as a witness, so I be brought back to shore. Thank Mary, Mother of God."

This was just one of the many fears the men in the gaols had to face day in and day out. At any given time they could be brought to one of the prison hulks. It was no secret the gaols were bursting at the seams.

As bad as Newgate was, it wasn't the worst. Not like Kirkdale, where gaol fever ran rampant. If that wasn't bad enough, it wasn't unusual for cat-o-nine tails to be laid to the back. As long as you minded your own business, chances were someone else would get it. Stories were told how some of the young boys had to give the men their food for protection. At Kirkdale you had a good chance of going out in a coffin. Other prisoners said, "Newgate 'tis closer to heaven, while Kirkdale shimmies up to hell."

Red couldn't imagine how bad it had to be to consider this place closer to heaven. He prayed he would never need to find out.

The men asked the talker if he had heard about sailing out or what it was like in the new land.

"Only that if a body goes ter the new land, you don't 'ear of him no more. Seems they don't come back...ever. Don't know what be worse, the goin' or the stayin'."

The men all agreed on that. Finally they all settled in for the night. Snores, loud and soft, could be heard throughout the cell.

Red prayed well into the night, thanking God for His protection. Soon he slept, dreaming of his bride. He saw her sailing off without him. She was crying and trying to jump ship, but men held her back. Red wanted to swim to her, but he couldn't move. He fought to go to her. When he woke, he felt exhausted. When would he see Katie again? Had something happened to her? Why would he dream something like that? He had to remind himself to trust in the Lord.

As the days wore on, the uneasiness that settled around him wouldn't leave, no matter how he prayed. He felt he would go crazy unless he heard something of his wife, but he had no way to contact her. That was the true torture, the not knowing.

6

Freedom

"Come with me," was all Katie was told. She'd never been led out of the cell by herself and felt nervous about it. Grabbing her scarf, she looked back at Mary as she went out the door.

The gaoler fastened lighter chains on her wrist. She was led a few steps down a long narrow hall to a heavy door. The gaoler knocked. He opened the door wide, allowing Katie to see the magistrate who had married her to James sitting behind a desk. He wasn't wearing a robe or wig but was dressed casually. He was studying some papers.

Katie stood quietly in front of the desk, not knowing what to do. The man looked up from his desk and told her to sit down. She did as she was told, while trying to still her beating heart. *Now what is he planning to do to me?*

"Take those chains off this woman!" he barked at the gaoler. Once that was done, he had the gaoler leave. "Do you like tea, or is coffee your preference?"

Katie hadn't had coffee in so long. "Nothing, sir, but thank you."

"Nonsense, you look like you need some warming up. These gaols are damp. I'm having coffee myself, so would you like some or tea?"

She relented. "Coffee would be fine."

After calling the gaoler back in to retrieve their drinks, he began. "I'm sure you are wondering why I had you brought here. I was surprised by a visit several weeks ago by a man and his wife named Lord and Lady Wilson. Their concern was for you. Do you know them?"

Katie was surprised by the news. "Aye, I know them."

"Well, it seems they found out you are not guilty after all. I explained you had been sentenced and also married. I guess you could say they were quite shocked by the news of your marriage. After they left, I instructed the authorities to investigate their claims. They have done that, and it seems you are indeed innocent. This puts me in a very uncomfortable position."

Katie's heart began beating irregularly. "They really know I'm innocent? You finally believe me?" Relief flooded her; questions filled her. "What changed that they now believe me?"

Peter explained how Lord and Lady Wilson had caught their daughter, Tess, in a lie. After a time she admitted she had taken her own necklace.

"I questioned them about the sworn affidavit I was given in regard to your case. Their daughter had signed it. I also asked them if they realized their daughter could have certain charges brought against her. They were aware of it, but at this point are more concerned about you."

Katie's heart soared with the news. Taking a drink of her coffee gave her time to think. Setting the cup down, she looked at Peter. "What happens now? Does this mean I will be released?"

Peter had never encountered such a predicament such as this. Unfortunately, innocent people were sometimes charged and found guilty. It was bound to happen with the vast numbers of prisoners. This was the first time, though, that a high-stationed citizen had come to him personally and pronounced a prisoner's innocence. If that wasn't enough, there was the fact that he'd had her married off. Yes, this was a very uncomfortable situation indeed.

"I guess that is pretty much up to you. Of course you will be released. I have been given a letter for you. I will leave you alone to read it. Can I assume then that you can read?"

Katie nodded that she could.

"Then please take your time. When I come back, we'll discuss what we will need to do then." Peter opened his desk drawer, pulling out the letter. After handing it to Katie he stood, leaving the room.

Katie slowly tore at the seal. She began reading.

> *Dearest Kathryn,*
>
> *It is with great difficulty that I write. I cannot tell you what shame and pain we feel. I wonder if I can express to you how sorry we, Lady Wilson and I, are. We want to explain to you all that has transpired and how we learned of your innocence.*
>
> *Arrangements have been made to bring you to the Brick House whenever you are ready to meet with us…assuming, of course, you do agree to meet with us.*
>
> *Please give us a chance to earn your forgiveness if at all possible. We will do all we can to make up for your horrible experience.*
> *Lord Edward Wilson*

Katie sat staring at the letter for some time. She found herself blinking back tears of relief. Finally they all knew she was innocent! That was so important to her. She would not have to stay in this horrible place any longer.

Suddenly she thought of James. James Patrick, her husband! What was she to do? Could it be she *wanted* to be married to him? What about going off to a new land?

She knew what to expect at Brick House. She would rather be at Newgate with all its filth than spend one more day under Tess's thumb. What was she to do? They certainly didn't expect her to live there again?

Magistrate Reeves stepped back into the room. "Have you decided what you would like to do yet?"

"I'm not sure. How soon can I leave?"

"Today. There are papers that need to be filled out and signed. Do you have somewhere to stay, any family?"

It suddenly struck Katie that there was no home or family waiting for her. "No, sir, I have no family left. My father was killed in an accident, and Gran passed away almost five years ago. I lived at the Brick House with Lord and Lady Wilson after my father was killed. I was in their employment." Why was she telling him all this? Surely he wasn't really interested.

"Lord Wilson was informed that you would be released today," Magistrate Reeves said. "He has ordered a carriage to wait here, all day if necessary, if you decide to see them. Meantime I can make some inquiries into finding you temporary shelter."

Katie wasn't sure how to respond. Temporary shelter, where? How long? Once again her future seemed confused and frightening to her. She shrugged. "I guess I could speak to them." After hesitating, she added, "What do I do about my husband? I mean, I am married now, and we are to be shipped away. What is to become of him?"

The magistrate ran his fingers through his hair. "I'm not sure I have the answers, but why don't you meet with Lord and Lady Wilson and go from there? It will give you time to think of what you want to do. We surely will not force you to be shipped out since you are not guilty of a crime. As far as your marriage goes, since it hasn't been…well, a real marriage yet…it can be annulled."

Katie blushed, looking down at her hands.

The magistrate rushed on. "These decisions are the kind you need to think about for a time. Why don't I make arrangements for you to rest and change into some new clothes? Meantime I will send a messenger to Lord Wilson's estate to inform them that you are coming."

He called for his assistant to prepare a room for Katie and to ready clean clothes for her. Stepping around his desk, he leaned against it. "Miss, I cannot tell you what to do. I feel somewhat responsible for your predicament. I want you to know that I will do what I can to help you. You are not going to be left in the streets on your own."

A knock was heard as the magistrate's assistant stepped in to let them know a room was ready. As she was led out, she turned, giving a smile of thanks. Magistrate Reeves had been the only person who had shown any concern for her, except for Mary and James Patrick, of course.

Peter stared after the young woman. The smile she had given him made his heart lurch. A feeling came over him that he hadn't felt in a very long time. Shaking his head, he turned his mind back to business. It was one thing to promise help, but now what was he to do? Maybe he had spoken too soon, promising too much. But there was something about her that made him feel protective. He confessed to himself that he felt attracted to her. Maybe he just needed one of his ladies' companionship tonight. He had a line of them from town to town.

No, he decided, it was more than that, more than physical. Well, if nothing else, the young woman could stay in the room she occupied now. Rooms were available to the magistrates and their wives if the women chose to accompany their husbands. Victoria had yet to come with Peter, and probably never would.

Katie was amazed at how beautiful her room was. It looked like it belonged in a castle somewhere. Not even the Brick House held a room such as this. A large tub full of water was placed in the middle of the room while a fire burned brightly in the fireplace. A huge bed with a large peach-colored coverlet stood at one end. Two ceiling-to-floor windows with peach-colored drapes lined each side of the bed. A clean shift and a pair of slippers lay on the bed.

After the man closed the window curtains, he showed Katie where she could find all she needed. After he left, she went over to lock the door. She was used to being locked in, not locking others out. Only a few hours ago she had been in prison, and now here she stood in this grand room. Heaven and hell, guilt and innocence, beauty and ugliness all rolled together. *Have I died and gone to heaven?*

As she sank into the tub filled with hot water she decided she was right. She definitely had died and gone to heaven.

Red paced the cell, flexing his arm and leg muscles as best he could. He needed to be strong with a long voyage and new life ahead of him. Unlike the others sentenced to sail, Red was more than willing. There was an expectancy that made the everyday humdrum life in that cell bearable. He dreamed of the voyage and adventure…to work for his own land. Sure, he would be working for others for the seven years of his sentence, but after that…. He could only shake his head at the wonder of it all.

Thankfully the men had a break from their cell a few days later. They were given hard labor, breaking down an old stone wall just outside the city. Red welcomed the work and fresh air. His muscles ached, putting him in misery the next day, but he hoped for more work to come.

Slowly the other men began seeing Red in a new light. They saw how he worked and held himself. When others complained and cussed, he simply did his work. When others moaned and groaned under the pressure, Red kept his daily routine going. He prayed, exercised, ate, and exercised some more. The men witnessed this big man in prayer. At first a few snickered, but as time went on, they saw a new strength that had nothing to do with the physical. One by one the men came to respect him and began following his lead. Even the gaolers noticed.

When there was work to be done, it was the men in Red's cell who were chosen because of the good day's work done without complaint. Days passed more quickly, but it was still difficult. They were given hard work, but not extra food. Heat and filth still surrounded them. Fresh water was not to be found, and danger of other prisoners was still a concern. The others watched Red pray and exist in peace. They watched him very closely.

Katie stretched her muscles and decided to leave the bath. She stayed in as long as possible but now felt chilled. Grabbing a towel, she stood before the fire. She had not had a bath like this in over two years. *Now what do I do? Am I supposed to stay here?*

Katie looked longingly at the massive bed. She was exhausted. Walking over, she tested its softness. Her body and mind wouldn't let her resist. Turning the rich coverlet down, she slipped under the blankets and sank into its softness and warmth. She thought about James. What would happen to them, their marriage? The magistrate was right. It wasn't a "real" marriage.

It is too a real marriage! Katie realized angrily a minute later. *It was real enough yesterday before everyone found me innocent.*

Katie's head ached. In her mind she could see James standing in front of her, looking hurt and confused. What was she to do? Where would she go?

Suddenly a new idea was conceived. What had changed? She was still married to James. She must certainly be able to go with him! They had to let her go with him. She may be free, but she was still married and wanted to be.

Yes, she wanted to be married to James. She held her breath, knowing in her heart that she loved him. When did it happen? It didn't matter. Her decision was made. She would find a way to stay with him. She would go to Australia with her husband. Katie hadn't planned on asking Lord and Lady Wilson for anything, but now they could help her. They had influence. Yes, they owed her that, didn't they? Smiling, she snuggled down, and soon she slept soundly.

Lord Wilson took the note from the butler. Opening it, he turned and smiled at his wife. "She is coming," was all he said.

"Oh, thank God!" Lady Wilson brought her hand to her bosom. "Thank God!"

Lord Wilson sat next to his wife and placed his arm around her. Bringing her closer, he kissed her cheek.

She smiled up at her husband, whispering, "I should never have doubted you, Edward. You said she would come, but I had my doubts."

He gently touched his wife's cheek. "To be honest, I doubted as well, but we don't need to worry now. She will be here tomorrow, or so says the note."

"Thank God Tess isn't here," she replied. "Is the cottage ready? Did you get the bank draft?"

He chuckled. "Dear, you've asked me that several times now, and I keep giving you the same answer."

"I'm sorry. I guess I am being a twit. I just don't know what we'll do if she refuses. I don't know if I can ever forgive myself for what we did to her. She only served us with loyalty and with love. I cannot imagine going through what she did."

The man nodded sadly. "I know, dear, but she's a very special young lady. I can't say whether she'll forgive us or not, but we will try our best to make it up to her."

And with that Lady Wilson spent the rest of the day in preparation. She needed to stay busy so her nervousness wouldn't overwhelm her. A special meal had to be planned, and she needed to meet with the cook, Maggie. She wanted every detail of Kathryn's homecoming to be perfect.

Lord Wilson paced in his study. He had comforted his wife with the right words, but doubts still plagued him. How could Kathryn ever possibly forgive them? What innocent could ever get past her ordeal? He knew a little of what Newgate was like, unlike his wife. Could they really say, "So sorry, we were wrong," and expect her to forgive completely?

Opening his desk drawer he retrieved a cigar. Clipping the end, he lit it. This wasn't the first time Tess had gotten them into a mess. No, this was more than a mess. This had been the undoing of an innocent woman whose family had faithfully served his family for many years. The Brady name had been an honorable one, until Tess's lies.

Running his fingers through his hair, he drew on his cigar, then exhaled. Oh, it wasn't all Tess. He had a lot to do with it, too. By the time he and his wife had returned from their trip, Kathryn had been arrested. Tess had signed the affidavit stating the girl was guilty. It was too late to do anything. At the time he thought there might be a chance Kathryn had stolen the necklace. Deep in his heart he knew better, but he didn't want to expose his daughter for what she was, a liar and a cheat. It had all gotten out of hand so quickly.

You're a coward, Wilson. Tomorrow would be difficult to face, but face it he would. He only hoped he could make some of it up to the girl. He longed for her forgiveness. It was important to him because of her father. Brady had not only been a fine man and employee, he had been a true friend. Lord Wilson knew he had let him down. Thank God Brady wasn't around to see what happened, but things needed to be made right…if they could be.

Lord Wilson rose from his chair to gaze out the window. *Forgive me, Brady. Forgive me for what I've done to your daughter.* What more could he say?

7

Broken

Katie stepped in the waiting carriage to take her to the Brick House. It seemed so strange to be going there. She let her mind wander as the coach passed tree-lined streets heading for the outskirts of town. Now that she was out of Newgate, she felt amazed at how she had adjusted to the hardships. How strange to think her time spent there had passed so quickly. She clearly remembered how time crawled when she was sitting in Newgate instead of this comfortable coach. Smiling to herself, she knew much of her adjustment was due to Mary and the friendship they had forged.

Lifting her hand to her head, Katie adjusted the bonnet she was given. Her short hair poked out, and once again she fought to keep it neatly tucked. She wondered where the clothes she was given had come from. They fit a little loose, but there wasn't much to fill the dress. Her bones seemed to jut out everywhere.

Sighing, Katie couldn't help think how wonderful it was to be outside. The carriage ride soothed her. Suddenly she sat up straighter. What if she was dreaming? What if she was still in the gaol? She pinched her arm hard. No, she was sitting on the red velveteen-covered seat of the carriage. Smiling at her own foolishness, she again sat back in comfort.

Would the Wilsons realize she wasn't the same person she was the last time she had seen them? She wasn't the young innocent with no idea of life anymore. She had to learn fast and hard in the gaol, and she did. Katie had learned well and chose to be the better for it. What happened to her could not be changed, but she could choose how she would react to it all.

Gran's words once again came back to her. *"Ya know, Katie Elizabeth, life 'tis all about choices that are made. Whether by ya or someone else, it don't matter. What does matter is how ya decide to live through the choices made."*

"Aye, Gran, now I understand."

Her focus now turned to James and Mary. They had been her strength, her reason for going on. She was going to help them somehow. She wouldn't rest until she had done something to better their lives.

Before she realized it, Brick House loomed in the distance. Katie busied herself tucking her hair under her bonnet once more before the coach reached the front of the

Manor. She felt somehow detached from her surroundings. She didn't feel anxious or fearful. She was strangely calm when the footman opened the carriage door for her.

Lord Wilson descended the front stairs. He hesitated at the sight of her. The young woman looked thin and drawn. Her hair stuck out in the front and bottom of her bonnet. Dark circles lay under her once bright eyes. Guilt for her suffering stabbed his heart.

Lord Wilson extended his hand to her, and she took it. "Kathryn, we are so happy you have decided to come. Lady Wilson is in the parlor waiting for us."

Lady Wilson rushed over as soon as she saw Kathryn and wrapped her arms around the frail form. "Oh, Kathryn, how wonderful that you would come visit us."

Kathryn stood motionless. A maid came in with a tray of coffee, tea, and cakes.

Lady Wilson blinked back tears. "Thank you, Maud. Just put the tray on this table, would you, please? I'll serve."

The maid curtsied and turned to leave. Lady Wilson poured Kathryn coffee.

Lord Wilson sat on the couch facing Kathryn. "My dear, it was with great sorrow and shame we found that we had accused you wrongly. Our daughter was caught in a lie. That does not take away from our own guilt. We are willing to do anything we can to make this up to you. We realize the ordeal you have been through can hardly be worth any amount of money, but we will do whatever we can to lessen the pain."

The old familiar dread had washed over Katie as soon as she entered the house. Now she sat quietly wondering if they had any idea of the fear, pain, and suffering she had endured...not only that, but the day-to-day humiliation of it all. Would they understand her suffering began long before her imprisonment? That one prison had only been replaced with another? That their beautiful home had been a place of darkness and despair for her just as much as that cell she had been in? Because of their daughter's cruelty, and their blindness to it, Katie had suffered greatly. Oh, she knew they were sincere, caring people, but how could they not have seen their daughter for what she really was? What could they possibly give Katie to make up for any of it?

At Katie's silence, Lord Wilson stood. He walked to the mantel of the fireplace to pick up a sealed envelope and promptly handed it to her. "This is just a small portion of what we owe you. Please realize we know in our hearts no amount of money could make up for this. But we want you to have something to help you in your new life."

Katie slowly opened the paper. In her hands was a bank note for a tremendous amount of money. Not in her whole life could she possibly spend it all. Stunned, she looked at Lord Wilson, waiting for him to say, "Oh, Kathryn, this is just another cruel joke."

He waited for any kind of response. When there was none, Lord Wilson again spoke. "Along with these funds we have the papers of ownership to your father's house." He handed her another envelope.

"Papa's house?" Katie questioned. "Papa never owned a house."

Lord Wilson explained, "We never told you, but this house was given to your father for many years of faithful service. Along with it, he received seventy acres of land. I don't know if you knew this, but he saved my life once. I fell off my horse when it bolted. My boot became caught in the stirrup. I was dragged a great distance. Your father jumped in front of the horse, putting himself in danger. He was able to grab the reins and thus saved my life."

Katie vaguely remembered, as a little girl, hearing a lot of commotion about Lord Wilson getting hurt. She heard something about Papa being a hero, but Papa had always been a hero to Katie.

"Two weeks before you were supposed to move into the house is when he was killed. He was going to surprise you. We never mentioned it to you after he died because you were too young to live alone. By the time you were old enough we, well…" Lord Wilson looked down as if embarrassed. "…we were so attached to you, we couldn't bear the thought of you leaving us. That, and also we hoped some of your sweet nature would rub off on Tess. We kept your papa's house in good repair. We fully expected to hand it over to you, but the opportunity never came."

Anger filled Katie. So she was left to endure their daughter's abuse in hopes she would what? Teach their daughter to be a better person?

Lady Wilson added, "Kathryn, there are no words to tell you how devastated we are. We have always known that Tess is a troubled girl, but we never believed she would be capable of this. We wore blinders when it came to our daughter. We cannot lay all the blame on her shoulders. I know we are just as guilty, like Edward said. We have come to realize how selfish we have been. We ask…no, we beg your forgiveness, and ask only one other thing of you. Please tell us if there is anything else we could do to try and make things right."

Katie felt overwhelmed. Money and a house! What did it matter now without Papa and Gran to share it with? Why now? Why at all? Could she so easily take these things and call it even? Was forgiveness bought and sold? Was a year of her life and the ruin of Papa's name worth all this money and a house? Papa's good name was all he ever had. He sealed bargains on his word alone. Isn't that how she first got this position, on his word alone? Katie's throat burned; tears threatened. She tried blinking them away, but one slipped through.

The older woman knelt by Katie's chair. "Please forgive us, dear. The most painful thing for us above all was discovering our daughter was capable of such lies and deception. Not only to lie to us, but to have a heart capable of hurting you in such a terrible manner. We are not excusing our part in all this, Kathryn, but we were wounded as well. We felt it best to send Tess to her aunt's estate for a time. We are not sure what will become of her, but we are ready to face any charges made against Tess."

Katie nodded slowly and looked down at her hands folded in her lap. Did they really want her to feel bad for them because their daughter was a liar and cheat? Katie's anger grew a little hotter until she looked at Lady Wilson. The pain was so evident on her face. If Lady Wilson was guilty of anything, it was believing in her daughter.

Katie thought of Mary and James. Maybe there was a reason for all this. Gran used to say things didn't just happen. Katie's anger cooled as her heart softened toward the matronly woman. Reaching her arms out to Lady Wilson, both women began to cry. Lord Wilson shifted uncomfortably, looking toward the ceiling. The two women clung to each other, weeping bitterly. They had both lost so much.

Katie finally felt her throat relax enough for her to speak. "I guess a lot of people have been hurt by this. It was especially horrible in the beginning, but I forged friendships there. I became close to some of the other women. It is amazing how people can adjust when they have to. Gran used to say that unforgiveness was one of the quickest ways to hell. It is capable of killing a heart and putting disease on a body. I understand now what she meant."

Lady Wilson daintily blew her nose. "Kathryn, I must again confess we had selfish motives. We couldn't think of our home without you. We were very wrong for that. It's just that you were a ray of sunshine and laughter. We were hoping some of your wonderful qualities would rub off on Tess, as Edward has said. You had attached yourself to our hearts. We were so wrong to lay the responsibility of Tess's actions and attitudes in your young hands." Lady Wilson put her arm around Katie's shoulders. "We need to make plans. Do you think you will want to move into your own home?"

Katie looked into her kind face. "I'm not sure. I can't believe the change in my life in one morning. My mind is spinning." She thought about her beloved papa, how proud he would have been to have a home of his own. After losing Gran in the cottage fire, they were all that was left of their family. Papa had stayed in the men's quarters on the estate, and Katie had a small room of her own in Brick House. She closed her eyes to the memory of the most terrible time in her life except for the gaol. First Gran had died. Then Papa was crushed while cutting down a tree.

Lady Wilson's voice broke in. "Then, dear girl, why not move into your new home? Stay until you decide what you want to do. Whatever you decide, we will be here to help you. We have also heard of the circumstances in which you were forced into marrying some criminal. Needless to say, we were appalled. You can have the marriage annulled. We are willing to help you with that as well."

Katie wasn't sure if she should tell them of her plans to stay married to James, so she was silent.

"Enough for today. You look exhausted, dear. We'll have our carriage brought around to take you to Brady's Brick."

Katie's jaw dropped.

"Yes, that's what your father named his cottage. He said you would like that. We had it prepared for you just in case you agreed to go there. Write down anything you require, and we will have it brought over to you. In the meantime try to rest, and think about what you want to do with your future."

Katie remembered. "Magistrate Reeves agreed to help me find a place to stay temporarily. I should let him know I have a home."

"I'll have a message sent to him," Lord Wilson stated.

"May I ask you something?" Katie inquired.

"Of course, dear," Lady Wilson answered.

"Did you supply the clothes I'm wearing? The ones brought to me just after my release?"

The older woman smiled. "I took it upon myself to buy some things. I wasn't sure of your size. I hope you don't mind?"

Katie was relieved they weren't Tess's castoffs. "Not at all. I really appreciate your thoughtfulness."

Everyone rose to leave. Lady Wilson and Katie walked hand-in-hand to the carriage. Soon she was heading to her new home, Brady's Brick. Tears flowed freely once she was alone. It all seemed surreal—a new life, a new home, freedom. Her life seemed to be pushed and pulled every which way and none of it by her own actions.

Katie closed her eyes, letting her body rest in the gentle sway of the coach. She decided not to make any decisions for three days. By three days she would be rested and have some idea of where she was heading. For now she would just wait to see her inheritance. Brady's Brick was a gift from Papa, making her love it already. She could hardly wait to see it. Her own home, the home of Papa and of Gran too. Given the choice, the three of them would have lived there together, but they were not given choices. They were just given hardship and death.

A stab of self-pity bolted through Katie, but she didn't let it take hold. She wasn't going to waste time on that. This time yesterday she was locked up, but now…no more sleeping on a blanket covering hay, no more hunger or cold. Katie appreciated the sunshine like never before. She melted into the softness of the coach seats, rejoicing in the rhythmic clopping of the horses' hooves. She was thrilled at the femininity of her dress and bonnet. She felt weak with thankfulness for her freedom. Freedom she had not experienced since she had left her precious home with Papa after the fire.

The next time she opened her eyes she saw it…her home. The carriage pulled up in front. Her heart skipped a beat. It wasn't too long ago when she'd thought, *I'll never feel joy again.* She was wrong. Joy flooded her. For the first time in a very long time, she cried…tears of joy.

Red heard a group of men talking about the next voyage to Botany Bay. He stepped up to listen. He needed to learn as much as possible to prepare himself and Katie for the sail. He was disappointed, for there was nothing he hadn't heard already. The prisoners relied on new people coming in to give them any details, but few knew anything of the transport ships. Walking away from the group of men, Red began talking to others. They laughed and shared stories. It had taken a long time for Red to get people to trust him since that ridiculous story had come out about him. Now it seemed that God had given him favor in most of these men's eyes. Some treated him like their leader. Others resented it, but even those who didn't like him seemed to respect him. They saw gentleness and acceptance without being judged.

Days went by until he was once again summoned to the heavy locked door. Unconcerned, Red stepped out. It was probably another job for him and the "crew."

He was led into a room that was obviously an office and told to sit down. The gaoler stepped out, closing the door. Looking around, Red felt uneasy. He was alone with no chains or guard. That was unusual. He shifted to turn in his chair when the door opened. Red jumped to his feet at the sight of the man who had sentenced and married him and Katie.

"Why are you not in chains?" Magistrate Reeves barked. Before Red could respond, the magistrate opened the door shouting, "Gaoler!"

The man came running.

"Where are his chains?" The magistrate looked at Red's wrist, as if to find a clue to the answer.

"I be sorry, sir. I best forgot 'em. Big Red here be trusted, and we don't chain 'im none no more."

"Who told you to trust this man? Who made the decision to keep prisoners out of chains? I will be back in a few minutes, and this man will be chained! You will be guarding him! Understood?"

"Aye, sir!"

Magistrate Reeves left his office, wiping sweat from his brow.

Red was amused by it all. The gaoler had run out to get chains, leaving Red alone once more. Before too long the man returned, and to Red's surprise the man apologized for having to chain him. "Sorry, but ol' man Reeves is boss. If he says to put chains on ya, then chains it is. Ya best sit in the chair."

Red stood quietly while he was shackled, then sat as instructed. He tried to hide a smile, for it was quite the sight. The gaoler stood all of five feet tall, and sitting down Red was still taller. He could overpower the man by just blowing on him.

Soon Magistrate Reeves reentered his office. Seeing the guard and chains in place, he closed the door. "Stand up! Who told you to sit?" he barked at Red.

Red stood. Even the gaoler straightened a little. The magistrate started reading some papers to himself, making the prisoner stand for some time. Red recalled what he had read in the Bible about Jesus standing before his accusers. He had stood and offered no resistance, and he was innocent. *Help me to be more like You, Lord.*

Finally Magistrate Reeves glanced up with disdain. Red wondered if the man hated just him, or if he was like this to all prisoners. When they were in the court, Red had sensed fairness and compassion in this man. What had changed?

Peter was fighting a battle within himself. He was fighting jealousy, and he hated it. He was jealous of this prisoner, this nobody. It galled him. Kathryn Brady had picked this big lout as a husband, and Peter hated Red for it. Of course, the situation was Peter's doing in the first place. He had forced the young woman into her decision. It had been years since he'd felt his heart stir for a woman, and he'd found himself fantasizing about her. He couldn't get her off his mind.

"You are here only out of my good conscience to tell you that your marriage has been dissolved," Peter stated harshly. "You are no longer husband to Kathryn Brady. You will need to sign papers when they are ready. That is all."

Peter wasn't about to explain that this was his decision. The girl didn't even know about this meeting. She had not made any decision as far as Peter knew, but no matter. He was positive she wouldn't have anything to do with this man, given the choice. Now he was making the choice for her. How relieved she would be. He couldn't wait to tell her that she was not bound to this oaf any longer.

Red was stunned. It felt as if someone had hit him in the stomach with a hammer. He was frozen in place. It didn't take long for him to realize that he had been holding his breath. Once the words sank in, he responded, "Not married, but how…why?"

The magistrate appeared annoyed. "I said you are dismissed. I need not explain anything to you."

The gaoler stepped up, grabbing Red's wrist chains to lead him out. Once out of the room the gaoler whispered, "Don't worry yerself, man. There be nothin' I cannot find out. As soon as I 'ear anything, I will let ya know of it. Ol' man Reeves seem to not take a lik'n to you. It makes me want to find out even more what flies in the air."

The other men in the cell stood when Red was let in. "We got ourselves another job, Red?" was their question. All Red could do was shake his head. He walked over to his regular spot and sat down.

The men exchanged looks. Something was wrong. They decided to keep quiet.

Red was lost in angry thoughts and hurried prayer. *Why, Lord? Why would this happen? I believed in my heart You wanted me to marry Katie. You have made me feel for her, and now she is being taken away. Is this a test, Lord? Do You want to see if I will turn from You or stay on Your path? Lord, was I placing my hopes for my future on Katie, and not You? Is this why You've taken her from me?*

The big man closed his eyes and rested his head against the wall. The sigh that escaped said it all. He found himself fighting tears. So much of his future, hopes, and dreams had been due to Katie after they were wed. He had not realized how much she meant to him until he heard he had lost her.

Why, Lord? Why? Once again Red felt the vast emptiness that came with being alone in the world. No family, yet he knew better. He did have a Father and a Lord who cared. He would cling to Him, for He alone would get him through. What did people do who didn't have the Lord?

Red settled it in his heart. *I will wait on You and trust in You. I know You will not leave me or forsake me.*

But his heart still ached. He couldn't help but wonder what had changed Katie's mind. *Lord, why do I feel my heart breaking when I know You dwell within it?* A Scripture verse came to mind: *"When you are weak, then I am strong. Lean not unto thine own understanding."* His life was not his own. He had no control over it. Red did the only thing he could: he surrendered. He surrendered the pain, the emptiness, Katie, and his broken heart, once again, to the Lord.

8

Home

Katie could hardly take it all in. She was unable to take her eyes off the little cottage. More tears fell as she pondered how excited Papa must have been when he was planning to move into it. Emotions flooded her; excitement and sadness consumed her. Why, oh why, couldn't Papa and Gran have lived? How different things would have been. Papa had always been her champion, and Gran was just as tough when it came to protecting her. They would never have let her be put into prison. Papa would have been able to speak to Lord Wilson and convince him of her innocence. How wonderful it would have been if…

She was doing it again, the "what ifs." Sighing, she stepped down from the carriage. Only one thought remained: *Papa, I'm home.*

Katie slowly walked through an iron gate that was attached to a wooden fence covered with vines. The small stone cottage seemed to reach out to her, welcoming her. Color burst everywhere from the trees covered in their fall foliage. Mums and marigolds lined the fence. A stone path led to the arched front door. Small-paned windows graced each side of the front door. Under the windows hung little boxes with a variety of flowers adding to their charm. The stone path broke away from the main entrance curling around to the back.

Katie slowly opened the door and peeked in. Her eyes had to adjust to the dimmer light of the room. To the left of the entrance a large fireplace took up most of the wall. Two doorways stood on each side of it. Straight ahead were four cottage windows with criss-cross panes and, under them, a table with four chairs. Sunshine filtered through the trees, splashed onto the table, and overflowed onto the floor. To her right were steps that evidently led to a loft area. Furniture filled the cozy room. Everything was neat and tidy like the outside.

Katie heard a noise and turned to see a woman enter the main room. She was wiping her hands on her apron. Suddenly the two women squealed at the same time, for in front of Katie stood her dear friend, Maggie. The women ran and grabbed each other in great delight, jumping up and down like two little girls. Once they calmed down they stood back, looking at each other.

"Oh, Katie, I didn't hear ya come in! What a sight for me old eyes. How I've missed you, lass." Maggie hugged her again.

Katie was still in shock. "I can't believe you are here. I never expected you! It's so wonderful to see you." Suddenly Katie's tears of joy turned into uncontrollable sobs. She had fought the onslaught of tears for so long. The dam she had built to hold them back broke. Tears freely flowed—tears of joy, sorrow, fear, and shame streamed down her face. Embarrassed, she turned away, covering her face with her hands.

Maggie held the girl in her arms. As if comforting a small child, she cooed, "It be all right, lass, Maggie is here. You go ahead and cry."

Sobs wracked Katie as Maggie led her to a chair. After a few moments Katie's crying ceased. She wiped her eyes, blew her nose, and started to apologize for her outburst.

"I won't hear of it!" Maggie exclaimed. "Had I been there in that place I'd do worse than cry a few tears. So much has happened to you of late. No wonder you're overwhelmed. You are home now. I insisted on being here for you. I think Lady Wilson would give you anything, so she let me come. I wanted to surprise you. I'll stay until they call me back to the Brick House. Come, let me show you the cottage, and then you are to rest. After that, I'll finish supper."

Katie followed Maggie. The room off to the left of the large fireplace was a small bedchamber. Rose-colored curtains around a bed with a matching coverlet caught Katie's attention first. A small fireplace graced one wall along with a desk and chair. On the mantle of the fireplace was a small woodcarving of a dog. Katie gasped. She had forgotten about the little carving her father had given her one Christmas long ago. "Maggie! How did this get here? I thought it was lost in the fire!"

"It was in the things Lord and Lady Wilson kept for you. A few days ago I was told to unpack your trunks and ready the cottage. That's when I found it."

Katie went over to pick up her treasure. She noticed it was scorched on one side. "Look, someone must have found it after the fire, but who? It was probably Papa." After placing it gently back on the mantle, she scanned the room again. A wardrobe stood in one corner, and a rose-colored rug lay beside the bed. The lace curtains that covered the double windows fluttered in the soft autumn breeze. Fresh-cut flowers and an oil lamp sat on a small table next to the bed.

The two women turned back into the main room. On the other side of the fireplace was another doorway. Stepping through, Katie found herself in the cook's room, where another fireplace with a baker's oven next to it occupied the farthest wall. Colorful rag rugs covered the floor for warmth. Two small criss-cross windows graced the outer wall. They were also open, to let in fresh air. Underneath the windows were a small table and two chairs. Open-faced cupboards and shelves holding utensils and food occupied the wall opposite the door. The back door was divided into two halves with the top half open. Katie looked out to a beautiful flower garden planted on one side of a cobbled path. On the other side was a vegetable garden.

The two women turned toward the main room again. Katie walked over to the large table adorned with more fresh-cut flowers. Speckled sunlight danced on the high-gloss surface. Two overstuffed chairs, a small divan, and various-shaped tables were arranged to face the fireplace. Across the room was another door to a small room used for storage.

"How cozy!" Katie gushed. "Where do you sleep?"

"Up those stairs to the loft. It's warm up there. Come, I'll show you."

They went to the stairs that led up to Maggie's loft. It was a charming room with a low ceiling. A window was centered at the arch of the roof. A bed, bench, and a table with a lamp were all the room held. Wooden pegs for Maggie's clothes hung on the taller wall at the other end. A simple rag rug covered the floor.

After descending the steps, Maggie asked, "Katie, are you up to some tea, or would you rather lay down for a quick nap?"

"I feel wide awake. Do we have coffee?"

"Aye, I forgot you favor it. I can only imagine how you must be feeling, coming to your father's house after all you have been through." Maggie stopped after seeing Katie's downcast face. "I'm sorry, lass; I didn't mean to upset you again."

Katie raised her hand toward Maggie. "No need to apologize. You did nothing wrong. It was so terrible in the beginning, but then I started to look forward to the future once I was married. Isn't it funny how a day can change a life? Now I'm not sure what I will do. I feel like I've been going from a dream to a nightmare back to a dream again. My life has taken on so many strange twists and turns."

Maggie hadn't seemed surprised about Katie's marriage. Most likely Lady Wilson had already told her about it. As she made the drinks, she listened to Katie without judgment or questions. The two friends sat at the table in the cook's room, enjoying each other's company.

Maggie reassured Katie once more. "'Tis no dream, Katie, you are home. No one can take it from you, and I will stay as long as you want."

They spoke of Papa, of old times, and the events leading up to Katie being arrested. Katie had always known Maggie had deep feelings for Papa. It would not have surprised her if Papa had asked Maggie to marry him, if he had lived. They would have made each other happy.

"Now drink your coffee, then lay down while I fix our supper," Maggie ordered.

Katie did as she was told. She was used to doing that after all. She was sure she wouldn't sleep but needed to rest. Climbing in her soft bed, she curled up.

Within minutes Maggie could hear the girl's deep breathing. "Sleep the sleep of the innocent, lass," Maggie whispered as she peeled potatoes.

9

Struggles

It didn't take long for Katie to become settled in her new surroundings. It was time for her to make some serious decisions. The gaol seemed a distant bad dream, but she thought often of James Patrick. She saw his face everywhere. She should be relaxed and comfortable. Instead, uneasiness shadowed her spirit, as if something was expected of her.

It was a dismal day. Thunder crashed as lightning blazed across the sky. Maggie built a roaring fire to keep the dampness at bay. Katie curled up in her chair, staring at the same page of her book until Maggie interrupted.

"Katie, come get some fresh coffee."

Katie moved to the table to watch the rain. "Oh, Maggie, I don't know how to help James Patrick." It was the first time Katie had mentioned her husband.

"No one will fault you if you turn from the marriage. People don't expect you to stay married to him, lass." When Katie didn't respond, Maggie went on. "You aren't considering staying married to him, are you?"

Before she could answer, the clopping of horses coming up the lane caught their attention. Maggie went to look out the front door.

"Who is it, Maggie?"

"I don't know. Never seen the carriage around here before, but it's someone important. Sure is a fancy rig."

Once the horses pulled up, and the coachman opened the door, a gentleman dismounted. Since he wore a black cloak with his hat pulled low, his identity was hidden as he briskly walked through the front gate and up the path.

Maggie opened the door for him to step through. "Good day, sir." She curtsied.

"Is your mistress home?" he inquired.

"Aye."

Lifting his hat, he stepped inside. Katie was surprised to see Magistrate Reeves. Apprehension struck. What in the world could he want? Was her release a mistake? Did he come to take her back to the gaol?

"Forgive my intrusion, miss. I hope I haven't caught you at a bad time?"

"No...not at all. Please come and sit by the fire. Maggie, would you please get some fresh coffee?"

463

The man shook the rain from his hat and coat, handing them to Maggie, who scowled at the water on her clean floor.

Katie and Magistrate Reeves sat before the fire, nervously smiling at one another.

Peter couldn't help but notice how much the young woman had changed. She was attractive even in dirty rags and a shaved head, but now she was radiant. In this short span of time she glowed with health. Her simple dress only added to her charms.

He spoke first. "I just wanted to see how you were doing. I heard from Lord Wilson that you were living here, and the circumstances by which you acquired this home. It's quite a story indeed."

Clearing his throat, Peter pushed forward. "This is a very charming cottage. You seem to have started a new life. It suits you. I do have some news for you. It is of a delicate matter, so I felt I should speak to you myself." Peter felt irritated when his statement was met with silence. This one-sided conversation was difficult. "Since I was the one to perform your marriage, I took it upon myself to take steps to annul it. You are not obligated to the man. I have also informed the...ah...gentleman of these facts as well. I thought it best if you didn't see him again. You've been through enough. I thought it best to spare you any more discomfort."

Strange how rigid she holds herself, Peter mused. *What is the matter? Doesn't she understand what I've just said?*

Maybe he had not made himself clear. Wasn't she listening to him? He was doing all the dirty work for her. Smiling to hide his true feelings, Peter spoke again. "What I'm trying to say is that..."

From the first, Katie didn't like the idea of this man knowing her personal business. Then, as he'd proceeded, Katie wasn't sure she was hearing right. Wasn't this the same man who had sentenced her, then forced her into the decision to marry a stranger? And now he wanted to spare her discomfort? Was *he* actually telling her that *he* had decided she shouldn't be married at all? Anger surged through her.

She held up her hand to stop him and took a deep breath. This was a powerful man. She didn't want to anger him or take the chance that his wrath would fall upon James Patrick. Keeping her voice level, she started out slowly, picking her words carefully. "Sir, I cannot express how much I appreciate your concern for me. I am grateful for your offer of rescue when I thought I had nowhere to go and you offered me shelter. Again you show your thoughtfulness by coming to my home personally."

Maggie let out a sniff from behind the door, where she was listening.

"Things have been happening so fast in my life that I have not had a chance to think. I wish you would have informed me before taking any steps on my behalf. I have not been able to make decisions for myself for a long time now. I would like to begin doing so. I understand you were trying to save me from further distress, and I appreciate that. I hope you understand, but I must ask that you leave any changes regarding my life to me."

Magistrate Reeves frowned. "I understand, Miss Brady; however I felt somewhat responsible for your predicament. I was only too happy to oblige myself."

Katie almost corrected him about her name, but hearing the edge in the man's voice, she continued to tread softly. "Again, thank you for all you have done for me. You have gone out of your way to help me, and I appreciate your kindness. I feel I have burdened you more than enough. Is it safe to say that my marriage is…erased then?"

"I have been only too happy to help a lady in distress."

Again Maggie let out a sniff. Katie glanced toward the door to give her a "look."

He continued, "All I need is for you to sign this paper, and it will be over for you."

Katie looked down at the paper. There were two signatures required—hers and James Patrick's.

"I noticed that Mr. Murphy hasn't signed," Katie said a little too softly.

The magistrate gave her a quizzical look, then explained, "I tried to get the man to sign. He agreed to sign the paper if you were to sign first. I cannot fathom what the man was thinking."

Katie's heart leapt. "You mean to say he refused to sign?"

"Yes, he stated that if you wanted out of the marriage, then he would sign. It's not as if you had a real marriage, you know. I don't know why he had to make this more difficult for you."

Katie had to bite her tongue. The marriage was real enough only a few short days ago. Real enough that this man was willing to send them off together to a new land. "May I have the paper? I cannot think of this right now. There are so many new changes in my life. I do not want to make any important decisions about anything right now. I hope you can understand."

The magistrate scowled but said, "Of course I understand." He stood, handing the paper to her. "All you need to do is sign, and I will take care of the rest. My intention was not to pressure you into making any decisions. I know you have been through enough. Thank you for your hospitality. Here's my card, if you wish to contact me."

Maggie ran to get his coat and open the door for him.

"Thank you again for all you have done for me." Katie gave him her warmest smile.

"Good day," was all he said before going out the door.

Maggie was chomping at the bit. "Hmmph, what a dandy! Katie, are you thinking of staying married to that stranger?"

Katie sat down and stared at the papers. Looking up, she softly stated what was in her heart. "Yes, I am going to stay married to him…if he wants."

Maggie sat beside the young woman. Placing her arm around her shoulder, she replied, "You must think very highly of the man. Can you tell me of him?"

"I will tell you soon, Maggie. Suddenly I feel very tired. I think I'll go rest a bit before dinner." Katie stood to go into her bedchamber. Curling up under her blankets, she soon fell off to sleep. She dreamed about a large red-haired man with the bluest eyes, but there was something wrong. There were tears in those blue eyes. Katie stirred in her sleep as James Patrick stirred in her dreams.

Later that evening, as Katie ate dinner, she went over what Mr. Reeves had told her. James Patrick would only sign if she signed first. Did that mean he wanted to stay married to her? It had to mean that. Her future was just as unsure as before. Katie put her fork down. She sat by the window gazing out into the garden. The season was turning cold. All the flowers were dying. The thought of a long winter ahead deepened Katie's gloomy spirit.

Maggie came in to clear the table. When she finished, she sat beside Katie. "'Tis worried I am for you, Katie. I feel as if we are family. I don't know if you knew, but I had feelings for your father. He was such a gentle, kindhearted man. I believe, Katie, that had he lived we would have…well, who knows?"

Katie reached out to hold Maggie's hand. "I know he was very fond of you too."

With tears glistening Maggie explained, "The reason I'm bringing this up now is to let you know that if you would like to talk things over, I am here for you. Like I said before, I think of us as a family of sorts. I don't have a lot of answers about things, but sometimes it clears the mind to simply let the words pour out."

So Katie did just that. "Oh, Maggie, I have come to love James Patrick. He protected me while I was in the gaol. I felt safe being his wife even when we were apart. I've grown to trust and respect him. There was even a sense of pride knowing he was my husband. He isn't an evil man or a thief, but someone who was trying to fill his belly to keep from starving. When Mr. Reeves told me James Patrick wouldn't sign that paper unless I signed first, I was relieved. I was happy he wanted to be married to me. It was only a year ago that I felt all alone in this world. When James Patrick came into my life, I had family and purpose again. Even when we were to be shipped out, I felt secure, knowing I would be with him. I have seen him in a horrible place, and he proved to me how brave and compassionate he is."

Maggie listened quietly.

"I was told later," Katie said, "that when James first arrived, everyone thought he was some kind of monster. Less than a year later a lot of people respected him. After we were married, a gaoler brought me news about James. He told me that James and some other men were given extra jobs on the outside. My heart would actually flutter thinking about him. Maggie, can you understand what I'm feeling?"

"Aye, Katie. Remember what I said about your father?"

Dabbing her eyes, Katie continued, "Then of course you know how I feel. I also met this woman named Mary. She became a dear friend. I feel so guilty leaving her there in that dreadful place. Here I am sitting by a warm fire with food in my belly. Oh, Maggie, how can I help her and James Patrick while they're still in that gaol?"

Maggie didn't have all the answers, but she did have comfort to give. "Katie, I have listened, and you do sound like a woman in love. He fills your heart and your thoughts. That tells me how important he is to you. I don't think things just happen. I think they happen for a reason. If you want to stay married to this man, then don't let anyone tell you different. I guess the first thing you would need to do is go talk to the man…hear what he has to say about it all. You have after all, accepted him as your husband. Who better to talk to about your life together? As far as your friend in the gaol, you are in a better place now to help her. You have Lord and Lady Wilson. I think they would do anything for you. You could call on them for help. You also can take in extra food and clothing for her. I'm sure she would love you to visit."

It was as if a great weight was being lifted off of her. "Yes! I do want to stay married to him. I want to be his wife, Maggie. It will mean I will have to leave here. I would rather do that than stay in this lovely, safe home without him."

Yes, she cared deeply for James Patrick, but somehow she had gotten the idea that caring for him was wrong. It was all right as long as she had been in the gaol, but now that she was a free woman, it wasn't acceptable. That was what Mr. Reeves had tried to impress on her without actually saying it.

"Tomorrow I will go and visit James and Mary," Katie said. "Can you put some food together for me to bring?"

"Aye, two baskets full I'll have for you. Now make sure you tell him how you feel. Do it first thing." Maggie stood. "I'll go and make some coffee. I have a feeling we're going to be up for a while talking."

It was indeed very late before the two women went off to bed. Katie found sleep impossible once she climbed into bed. The sun wasn't going to rise quickly enough for her this day. She could barely wait to see James Patrick…her husband.

Red woke feeling stiff, but his mood was lighter. There was no reason for him to feel better, but he did. Maybe it was because he had poured his heart out to the Lord the night before. He admitted his love for Katie. He hadn't realized it until he found that she was taken from him. His anger and hurt had surprised him. There were no answers given to him, but he knew the Lord heard.

"Up and at 'em, Red. Ye got a visitor, and 'tis a fair lass to boot," the gaoler shouted for all to hear. "She be a-waitin' for ya, so up with ye now!"

Red knew it was Katie. His heart beat faster. He'd had all night to think it over and decided not to make this difficult for her. She had only married him because she was forced into it. He just wasn't sure he could sit and listen to her as she explained herself out of his life. He had faced many a fight, and even death a time or two, but this was a harder thing. Squaring his shoulders, he took a deep breath. If at all possible, the only two who would know his heart was breaking would be God and himself. He couldn't stand the thought of losing her. The only way it could be worse was if she knew how he felt, and she walked away from him anyway.

The gaoler led Red to a small room that was bare except for a small table with two chairs. Red was told to sit, and that his visitor would be there shortly. The gaoler added that he would give them privacy since he knew he could trust Red, but the chains would have to stay on. It wasn't but a minute or two when Katie stood in the doorway. Red couldn't take his eyes off of her. She was lovely in her simple gown. She had a healthy glow and had even filled out some. The lump in his throat threatened to do him in. He stood without saying anything. He didn't dare. His voice would fail, making him appear like a fool. He sent up a quick prayer for God's will.

Katie walked in and sat across from him. She noticed he had lost weight. He was beginning to look a little gaunt. She tried to read his expression, but his face was hard. His eyes caused her to hesitate, but determinedly she began. "How are you, James Patrick?"

He just nodded.

"I know you heard that I was released. Would you believe it if I were to tell you Mr. Reeves came to see me? You remember, don't you? He was the magistrate?"

"I know who he is." Red almost snapped the words.

Katie faltered but went on. "He told me he felt it best to annul our marriage. I was angered because I felt no one had the right to decide that except you and me. He had brought the paper for me to sign. I...I saw that you hadn't signed it yourself."

"You mean you weren't the one who wanted to annul the marriage?" Red straightened in his chair.

Katie noticed a small vein pulsating at James's temple. "No, James, I didn't know anything about it. We were thrown together by our circumstances, and I would understand fully if you feel it best for us to...well, not be married. But I felt you and I had an understanding of sorts. I would never do something like that without talking to you first. I really don't know how to say things except bluntly. Gran always used to say, 'If ye need to say something, then say it.' I had no knowledge of this paper until it was brought to me. I didn't sign it when I saw you hadn't either. I thought it best if we talked about it. Like I said before, if you feel it best..."

Before Katie could finish, Red jumped up from the table, startling her. Since he was chained at the wrists, he couldn't reach out to her but stepped forward. "You mean you want to stay married to me?" he blurted out. "Is that what you're saying?"

Katie blushed scarlet.

For a split second Red wondered if he had mistaken what she was trying to say and had made a fool out of himself after all.

Katie looked up at him with a twinkle in her eye. "I want you to know I hold no claim to you, James Patrick. You owe me nothing, and I understand that. But I have found that I care about you deeply."

Red's heart pounded.

"Even though we were pushed into getting married, I chose you myself. I thought we were forced to marry, but we weren't. No one made me marry you. I started to feel comfort in knowing that I had a family again. I felt safe knowing you were my husband, and pride too. I heard how people were talking about you. How the men respected you, and the ladies, well, a few let me know how they envied me. James, I want to stay married to you…if you will have me."

James grabbed her hands the best he could. The room they were in was barely big enough to hold the smile on his face. They started laughing and talking all at once. Katie told him of Papa's house and of the lands given by the Wilsons. James could scarcely take it all in.

"Katie, I will be shipped out, but not soon because winter is coming. Now that you have a home, are you sure you want to go with me?"

Nodding, she said, "I have thought it through. I want to stay with you. Would there be any way you could stay here now that we have a home?"

"I don't know. I remember Reeves asked me if I had family or land before he sentenced me, but I don't know if it would make a difference now."

Katie's face brightened. "Why don't I talk to Lord and Lady Wilson? Maybe they can help us! They said if I needed anything, all I had to do was ask."

James sighed. "If I stay, I would be locked up here until I've served my given years. I would rather be working the land than sitting in a cell all that time. Even if the land I'm working won't be my own."

Katie crinkled her forehead. "Then I will ready myself for the sail. I will also make arrangements for visits until it is time to go. What will we do with Brady's Brick?"

James lifted a brow.

"That's what Papa named our cottage," Katie explained. "I don't want to sell it, James. I know Papa would want me to keep it."

Red smiled at his wife. "Then you won't sell it. We need to make plans."

Katie nodded in agreement. "Aye, you are right. I will see if I can come see you again in one week's time. Is there anything I can get for you while you are here?"

"Some fruit would be nice if you can get some," was his reply.

"As a matter of fact, I already have that," Katie stated. Getting up from the table she walked just outside the door, stooping to pick up a large basket. It was loaded with food. "How about a picnic?" She smiled.

After the feast, James sat back, patting his stomach. They talked a little longer, but all too soon it was time for Katie to leave. She stood as her husband came around to her. He placed his arms around her. He had to lift his hands with chains over Katie's head. "You have made me a happy man, Katie Elizabeth. I thought I had lost you."

Katie lay her head on Red's chest, next to his heart. After a moment they stepped apart.

After Katie left, Red was led back into his cell. He told the men some of what had happened.

"Ye don't say," sputtered one of the men. "Ye mean that ol' man Reeves hisself told the lady she could not be married to ya?"

The night was spent talking about marriage and the joy, or lack of it. It all depended on who was doing the telling. Laughter could be heard as they shared their stories of wives trying to tame them. Red, for the first time ever, felt a part of it all. They talked well into the night about their lives and wives. Red stayed quiet for the most part. After all, he lacked experience.

10

Bon Voyage

Lord and Lady Wilson arrived for a surprise visit at Brady's Brick right before the noon meal. Fortunately Maggie had made enough stew and biscuits for all. After greeting one another, Lady Wilson spoke first. "We hope you don't mind, but we were shopping, and at the last minute decided to stop for a visit. We hope we aren't interrupting your lunch as I can see your table is set."

Katie smiled. "No, no, please stay for lunch. Maggie always makes more than enough, as you already know."

The couple accepted her kind invitation. Afterwards tea and fresh berry pie were served. Katie was asked many questions about how she liked her new home, and if she was settled in. She thanked them for keeping her trunk with her few treasures and told them how grateful she was for all they had done and were doing for her.

Lord Wilson grew serious. "I was called upon by the magistrate, Mr. Reeves, a few days ago. He was distressed when he heard you decided not to annul your marriage. He hoped I would talk to you and make you understand that you need not stay married. For some reason he feels you find yourself obligated to this man. You need not be. Mr. Reeves also informed me he was happy to settle things for you so you wouldn't have to be involved. Then he heard you insisted on visiting this person at the gaol."

Katie pushed her bowl away, knowing her meal was finished. Maggie all but ran into the next room for safety. Katie was a gentle soul, but this was a touchy subject. Anger threatened to rise until Katie studied both their faces. They spoke purely out of concern for her.

Gently she tried to explain her decision. "I know it is because you care that you are here. I have made some decisions that may surprise you, but I hope you understand. I want to stay married to James Patrick. Without going into great detail I need you to understand that being in the gaol was very difficult. This man cared for me and for others. He looked out for the weaker ones, and I came to respect and care for him, and he for me. No, more than that, I have come to love him."

"Are you sure of that, or is it gratitude you feel?" Lord Wilson questioned.

"Yes, I am sure. I had every opportunity to walk away from him but found I couldn't. I know it will be a hardship sailing to another land, but I feel I can face whatever comes with James Patrick. I want to be his wife."

Lady Wilson looked at her husband as if he could say some magic words to change Katie's mind. When he stayed quiet, she jumped in. "My dear, do you truly realize what you are saying? Not only do you want to leave this comfortable and safe home for the unknown, but to leave with a stranger! Think about what you are doing!"

"I do not wish to hurt either of you; however, I think you will understand when I tell you that I had to learn to trust strangers in my situation. I learned that just because people were locked up in a gaol didn't mean they were bad people. Many suffered from their circumstances. I saw horrible things, and I saw acts of courage and tenderness. My eyes were opened to many things. I found myself trusting people who were virtual strangers."

Lady and Lord Wilson did not have an answer to that. What could they say? For it was they who had let her down. They needed to trust her…and her judgment. Even if she were to make a mistake, it was her right to do so.

Lady Wilson spoke in a very contrite way. "Kathryn, you are right. We need to let you live your life. You know we are only thinking of you, but we don't have any right. I guess we have been trying to control your life again. That needs to end. It's just that we have come to love you as if you were a daughter, and we want you safe." Lady Wilson then leaned over the table to place her hand over Katie's. "Please, dear, I ask one thing: that you let us help you. We will keep your home open for as long as it takes for you to come back, even if it's for a visit. We will speak to the authorities and try to make the voyage more comfortable. Since you are free and your…husband is not, we may be limited as to what we can do, but we will try. You will always have a home here. If you ever need anything, simply ask. We have let you down once. It won't happen again."

Katie's heart overflowed from their kindness, but she could not completely lean on these people. She needed to lean on herself and James Patrick. It wasn't that she didn't trust them, but they would never be able to help her where she was going.

Katie thought of Mary. "There is one thing you could do for me if you would. There is a woman who is a great friend of mine. She's still in the gaol. She became as close to me as anyone could. She stepped in to protect me before she even knew me. I would wish that she could live here at Brady's Brick as long as she wants. Do you think we could meet with a magistrate on her behalf? Since she will have a home, they may let her leave. I believe she was given a hard sentence since she had nowhere to go. Mary is proud. She would never agree unless she could somehow pay her own way. She worked in the gaol kitchen with me. I can tell you she would be a great help to anyone given the chance. She is strong and intelligent, and even though she was in the gaol…"

Before Katie could finish, Lord Wilson interrupted her. "Dear Katie, you need not explain anything to us. Your friend will be welcomed. We would be happy to help. As far as her staying here at Brady's Brick, this is your home to do with as you wish. We will go tomorrow, and do what we can to have her released."

Katie jumped up with tears in her eyes and hugged them both. "You will never know how happy you have made me." She sniffled.

The Wilsons promised to pick her up in the morning to submit a petition of release for Mary. With a job and a home waiting, they were very hopeful. Then they bid Katie good-bye.

Maggie closed the door softly after they left. She had to wipe her own tears. "Blimey, can't say I ever heard the master and his wife sound so sad in all my days. They sure take a shining to you. It nearly killed them when all this first happened. I believe they knew the truth all along, but Miss Tess cornered them. She forced them to choose her over you. Of course they sided with their own blood. That young woman has a way of making people do what they don't want to do."

"What has become of Tess?" Katie asked. "I was told she was sent away."

Maggie shrugged. "She was shipped off for a time. Hiding out, I guess. I heard it cost his Lordship a pretty copper penny to keep her from the gaol for falsely signing papers and lying about you."

That old feeling of bitterness washed over Katie. She knew it was wrong to hate. Gran had taught her that, but she couldn't deny her hate for Tess. She would fanaticize about getting even with her. Katie felt uncomfortable with this feeling. It seemed to have power over her. Somewhere in the back of her mind she knew it could overtake her if she allowed it. For the most part she was able to fight it off, but once in a while it would raise its ugly head. Yes, hate was ugly, but at times it felt so good.

Victoria Reeves followed her maid to her room, throwing her hat and gloves on the bed. "Marie, put all my things on the table, and get my bath ready." Marie obeyed while Victoria began opening packages. Holding her new treasures, she admitted to herself that shopping was becoming a bore. She decided to get more comfortable by taking her hair down so Marie could brush it out.

Victoria reflected on her husband and his moodiness. After he had returned from his court rounds, he still seemed distant. Lately, he'd had little time for his wife. She sighed. Sometimes he could be so aggravating. She didn't want him around all the time, but when she required attention, he needed to be there.

She smiled in the mirror. His mood really didn't matter. She knew how to handle him. A little flattery, a little extra feminine attention, and her husband would melt.

Victoria only had one problem. She was getting as bored with her husband as with shopping. She needed someone or something new and exciting in her life.

Maybe a trip to America.

No, there were wild Indians there, and even the idea of them made her shudder.

Perhaps Paris. It had been a long time since she and Peter had gone anywhere.

Peter entered his wife's bedchamber and stopped to admire her beauty. He would never get tired of looking at her. Yes, he had to admit she was a beautiful woman, but empty inside: no substance, no depth. She couldn't or wouldn't meet his needs. Their lives revolved around her. He had once loved her deeply, but his desire for her had waned. He felt nothing for her anymore. When she tried to demurely force her will on him, it angered him. He was no fool. Peter suddenly felt that strange, restless feeling again. Although he had just returned from a long trip, he wanted to get away again.

Victoria jumped at seeing him out of the corner of her eye. "Peter! For heaven's sakes, you scared me half to death! How long have you been standing there?"

"I'm sorry. You seemed deep in thought, and I didn't want to disturb you."

"Well, now that you have, I want to talk to you about something that's been on my mind. I would like for us to take a holiday to Paris. It has been so long since we have traveled anywhere exciting. You have been working so hard, and I hardly see you anymore. What do you think?"

Going to Paris was the last thing he needed. "You're right. It has been some time since we traveled, hasn't it? I really can't get away right now, no matter how much I would like. Why don't you go? Ask Ruth to go with you and make it a shopping trip."

Victoria pressed her lips in an exaggerated pout. "Don't you want to be with me?"

Peter could see Victoria needed stroking. "Of course, darling, but because of the shortage of magistrates, I have to help pull the extra counties. I couldn't leave them strapped right now. We could wait until next year, if you're willing."

Victoria stood and walked over to her husband. Slipping her arms around him, she lay her head on his chest. "I don't want to wait that long. If you really can't come along, maybe I will see if Ruth can go. You wouldn't mind?"

Peter put his arms around her, setting his chin on top of her head. "I guess I could let you go if you promise not to put us so far in debt that I would have to work the next fifty years."

"Oh, thank you, Peter! I'll try to hold back a bit." Victoria lifted her head, considering him with a bright smile. "Now I must get in my bath before the water turns cold." Pulling away, she walked to the side room where her large tub was filled. She stopped and turned just before closing the door. "You realize, of course, I won't have as much fun without you."

Lady, you're not fooling anybody, Peter thought. He knew she didn't want him to go with her, but it worked out for him too. With Victoria gone for a time, he would have the freedom he desired, and that was something to look forward to. Even if it cost him a bundle with Victoria's spending, at least he would have some peace. The price was worth it. He hoped his lovely wife would be leaving soon.

Smiling, Victoria closed the door, then climbed into the warm water. Yes, she knew how to handle Peter. She knew he didn't want to go with her, and she didn't want him to. She would be free to really enjoy herself.

The harbor was a mass of humanity. Ships were loaded and unloaded. Huge crates and other materials were stacked everywhere. To one end of the harbor, carriages were dispatched to pick up incoming passengers and drop others off.

A young woman in a maid's uniform stumbled on the plank descending from one of the ships.

"Be careful, you twit! If you drop any of my bags in the water, you'll follow them!" Tess Wilson hissed.

The maid turned red with embarrassment as she held on tighter.

Tess lifted her skirts to keep from tripping herself. At the bottom of the plank she paused, waiting impatiently for her father's coach. "Where are they? You would think they would care if their own daughter came home."

The longer the young woman had to wait, the more agitated she became. Men carrying baggage from the ship brought the rest of her trunks. The two women stood, feeling quite uncomfortable in the middle of the noise and filth. If that weren't bad enough, a number of ruffians kept eyeing them.

The sound of harnesses and horses' hooves caused Tess to turn. She watched as a fine carriage, pulled by matching bays, stopped further down the pier. Fascination replaced irritation as she watched a man and woman stepping down. By looking at them, one could tell they were well off. The woman was dressed elegantly with a cape that matched her smart little hat. The man was handsome and dressed impeccably. All of his attention was on the beautiful woman.

Tess was mesmerized as she watched the couple. Jealousy crept in as she witnessed the tenderness between them. She wanted to be given that kind of attention. Tess thought she had a lot of baggage, but it was nothing compared to this other woman. Another carriage filled to the brim with trunks, boxes, valises, and other items followed. Soon several men were busy unloading the woman's trunks. Tess strained to hear what they were saying, but there was too much noise.

"I'll miss you, darling. As excited as I am, it won't be as fun for me without you. Are you going to miss me?" Victoria practically purred.

Peter held his wife, saying all the right words. He wondered why Victoria felt she had to overplay her departure. "Don't be ridiculous. You know how much I'm going to miss you. Please take care of yourself. Three months is a long time for you to be away. I just hope you don't forget me," he said, overplaying himself.

"Oh, Peter! How can you joke about such a thing? Of course I won't forget you. Are you sure you won't change your mind and come along?"

"Well, I expect we would end up with a chaperone once Ruth got here. You know I need to stay here to make some more money to replace all you plan on spending," he joked. They embraced once more and turned to see the Crowleys' carriage pulling up.

After greeting each other the two couples walked the plank to the ship. With great fanfare all the good-byes were said and kisses given. Soon the men headed back to their separate carriages.

"So, Reeves, what are you going to do with all this freedom now that the women are leaving?" Crowley smiled wickedly.

"I would suspect the same as you." Peter chuckled.

Shaking hands, the men parted.

Minutes later, peering out the window of his carriage, Peter noted an attractive, young woman by herself, except for a servant. Baggage was piled all around her. Frustration creased her lovely brow. Peter tapped the top of his carriage with his cane. "Digs, pull over," he ordered his driver.

"Yes, sir!"

As soon as the carriage stopped, Peter opened the door himself and jumped down. Stepping in front of the woman, he tipped his hat, introducing himself. "Hello, you appear to be in need of assistance. May I offer you mine? My name is Peter Reeves." Peter bowed.

The woman gave a demure smile, offering him her hand. "Mr. Reeves, I'm Tess Wilson."

"Wilson? You wouldn't happen to know Lord and Lady Wilson, would you?"

"Why, yes, they are my parents! You know them? I must say I'm angry with them right now since they were supposed to pick me up. I can't imagine where they are. I was about to hire a carriage, but you don't know who or what has been sitting inside one of those."

Peter studied the young woman. So this was the daughter who had so coldly lied to send an innocent woman to the gaols. He would have to be careful. If she was capable of that, she could be capable of anything. "Actually I'm glad they aren't here. It gives me a chance to meet you, and offer you my assistance." Peter once again bowed slightly. "I have met your parents on several occasions. I'm sure they wouldn't mind if I give you a ride home. That is…if you want."

"So you can be trusted, sir?" Tess smiled.

"Well, I never said that—only that your parents know me."

Tess laughed, stepping into the carriage as Peter held the door for her.

"Digs, you and Sacks hire a public coach. Sacks, you load the luggage in it. Make sure to leave room for the maid."

"Yes, sir, Mr. Reeves," the driver responded.

Victoria stepped onto the deck to get one last glimpse of her husband. What she saw made her blood boil. At that precise time, her husband was helping a young woman into their carriage. She gasped, then turned back toward the cabin, rage contorting her face as she swept by a sailor.

Pacing her cabin like an animal, Victoria hissed at the air, "I'm not even out of the harbor yet, and already he has a trollop! I'm not going to be made a fool of! Well, two can play that game." She had the time, and Peter's money to make sure she wouldn't suffer alone. "So be it. Let him have his fun now. He will pay dearly."

The angry woman on deck was so loud the sailor could hear her berating the air. He was glad he wasn't the target but could step out of her way. He walked off shaking his head. He didn't know who the man was she was muttering about, but by the look on her face, he was a dead man. As for himself, the sailor would rather fight the sea than a woman in such a foul mood.

Peter instructed his driver to head to the Brick House, then sat back to enjoy the ride.

Tess was the first to start the conversation. "I hope you don't think me bold, but I noticed you were escorting a woman to one of the ships. You seemed close."

"Ah, yes, she is my wife. She's traveling with a friend to Paris," Peter offered.

"Paris! Oh, I have always wanted to go there."

"Really? You obviously were traveling. Have you been gone long?" Peter questioned.

"Too long to suit me. I was just visiting my aunt for a time, and now I'm headed home. I don't consider that traveling, but I have been gone about six months. I was anxious to see my parents. That's why I was so disappointed when they didn't come. I appreciate your help, Mr. Reeves."

"Call me Peter. That is quite an extended visit. It would seem strange your parents wouldn't be here to greet you, but I'm happy to help a fair lady in distress." Peter could pour on the charm when he wanted to, as could Tess. They were a well-matched pair.

"Tell me, Peter. You said you've met my parents. When?"

Peter shifted in his seat. He had to be careful how he answered. "Why, there are few people in London who don't know your parents. When you said your last name, they just came to mind. Like I said, I've met them at several social occasions." Peter gave her a bright smile.

Tess nodded, smiling back. She seemed content with his answer.

They rode in silence until they stopped in front of the Brick House. Peter was always impressed with the wealth that gushed from the estate. He had only been there a few times before but appreciated the grandeur even more each time. As soon as the carriage stopped, the footman opened the door, helping the occupants down. They walked up the stairs to the entryway just as the door opened.

Lady Wilson stood with a look of surprise and question. "Tess! How? Why? Mr. Reeves!" Lady Wilson was so flustered she couldn't get a full sentence out.

Peter grabbed her hand, speaking quickly, "Why, Lady Wilson, how nice of you to remember me since it has been a while. Remember we met at the Grayson's Ball? I hope you don't mind that I offered your daughter a ride home. I was at the harbor seeing my wife off and spotted this young woman in distress."

Lady Wilson understood what Peter's intentions were and appreciated the fact that he obviously hadn't shared any information with Tess, especially about Kathryn.

Tess stepped forward. "Mother, where were you and Father? I waited and waited. Thank goodness Peter offered his help, or I might still be standing there in that awful place."

"We thought you were arriving next week. We had no idea you were arriving early, but I appreciate *Mr. Reeves* bringing you home." Lady Wilson emphasized his proper name, sending her daughter a message. She did not appreciate Tess calling a man by his given name after just meeting him…especially a married man. Surely Tess had heard him speak of having a wife. Lady Wilson was finding out more and more about her daughter that was disturbing.

Tess scowled. She wasn't even in the house yet, and she was being corrected. Pouting, she asked, "You didn't get my letter explaining my plans? Aunt Marilyn wanted me to stay a little longer, but I missed you and Father so much. I needed to come home." Tess melted into her mother's arms.

Lady Wilson clung to her daughter. "I have missed you too. I'm so glad you're home. Thank you, Mr. Reeves, for all you have done for our daughter. Please, come into the parlor and have some tea."

"Where's Father?" Tess inquired. "Shouldn't he be home by now?"

"Your father had business to attend to and won't be home until dinner."

The trio sat having tea, discussing all the news and tidbits Tess had missed out on. When it was time for Peter to leave, Tess felt a sense of loss even before he was out the door. "Must you leave so soon, Peter?" Tess cooed.

Lady Wilson's brow arched in disapproval.

Peter stepped back, distancing himself from Tess. "Thank you, Lady Wilson, for your hospitality. I enjoyed my afternoon, but I really need to attend to business. It was nice to see you again." Peter took his coat and hat from the servant. Bowing, he stepped out the door.

Tess pouted once more as she turned to go back into the parlor. "Why, he didn't even say good-bye to me. What kind of gentleman won't even acknowledge a lady?"

"A married gentleman, Tess… especially when a young lady is falling all over him."

"I only asked why he had to leave so soon!" Tess shouted.

"Tess, let's not fight on your first day back," her mother pleaded, looking overwhelmed.

Tess lifted her head slightly, showing her defiance. Her parents had no idea how she planned to make them suffer. She would never forgive them for forcing her to go away. How could they have stood up for that stupid servant girl over her?

Tess suddenly smiled at her mother. "You are right, Mother dear. Forgive me for being so curt with you. I'm tired from the trip."

In that moment Lady Wilson was filled with regret…regret that her daughter was back. Peace was once again gone from her home. Sadness washed over her as she realized her true feelings for her daughter. Having Tess home meant dread and anxiety instead of happiness and joy. Lady Wilson excused herself from Tess's presence to rest before dinner. She suggested her daughter do the same.

With a heavy heart the grand lady left the room before Tess could see the tears forming in her eyes.

11

Mary Willow

Mary bent over the scrub barrel to wash the pots. In spite of her aching back, she felt content with her life. Once her talents were realized, they were used. She was given the job as head cook shortly after she had started working in the kitchen. Some would have considered that a punishment in itself, but she was thrilled. She had never held a position before. Mary was given more freedom in her job and found the days flew by. She often fought to get decent food to work with but did the best she could with what was given her.

There was only one thing that caused her heart to ache, and that was the loss of her friend. Katie came to visit once a week. When it was time for her to go, it seemed to Mary that a small piece of her left with the girl. Mary was happy Katie girl was no longer made to stay in this "pit o' the devil," but how she missed her.

Sighing, she put the pot on the shelf where it belonged and bent her body backwards to get the kinks out. Talking to herself, she quipped, "Blimey, 'tis a better life in this 'ere kitchen than the streets. Who e'er think ol' Mary be 'appy in prison?"

Chuckling, she turned to check out "her" kitchen to make sure all was in place. The old girl hadn't felt pride in a long time, but she felt it now. She took great pride in her kitchen. She was first to work in the morning and last one out at night. As time passed, she had proven herself trustworthy, earning the freedom she needed to do her job right. The other cooks could care less about cleanliness or how the food tasted. They thought Mary to be a crazy old woman, but they didn't mess with her. If she wanted to do all that extra work, then let her.

"Eh, ol' Mary!" the turnkey named Henry greeted her. "Ye be gettin' in big around 'ere. Ye need to check in at the boss's office in the morn. 'Tis said ye got some high-and-mighty gents to sees ya on the morrow!"

Fear gripped Mary's heart. Things were going good now. She didn't want any changes. "Me? What for they need to be a-seein' me?"

"Nobody be tellin' me nothin' round 'ere. I jus' do what is told to me, an' I be told to fetch ye in the morn," came the answer.

Henry let Mary inside her cell. Trying not to disturb the others, she turned to her "spot." She carefully hung her dress and apron on the peg. Fear kept rearing its ugly head at her. All sorts of unpleasant things entered her mind. Was something missing in

480

the kitchen? If something came up missing, would she be blamed?

The night wore on for her as she tossed and turned. Sleep eluded her until she realized she was worrying for nothing. What could they do to her? She was already in prison, and she hadn't done anything to get hanged over. They could take her kitchen from her. Now that indeed would be a great loss. Well, she had no control over what happened around her. Others had her life in their hands. At any given time her world could be turned upside down just on someone's whim. Turning one more time to get more comfortable, she resolved that it would be a long sleepless night…and it was.

Finally the morning arrived. Why was it that sleepless nights were endless? Mary knew she was late in rising, but exhaustion ruled her. Bones could be heard creaking as she stood. Stretching, she reached for her dress and long apron.

"Mary! What are ye doin' 'ere so late in the morn?" one of the other women asked. "Ye always be in the kitchen long afore anyone."

Mary nodded in agreement. "'Tis truth ye speak. I slept hard fer sure," she lied.

The turnkey unlocked the door. "Are ye ready for yer visit today, Mary?"

Mary nodded. Once again, fear squeezed her heart. "When is it I go?"

"Not 'til later, but don't worry, I'll come to fetch ya when the time comes." The man smiled at her.

"Thank ye, 'enry," Mary nodded as she headed toward the kitchen.

"Ye got a visit from some other besides Katie?" one of the other women asked her as they walked together.

"Aye, but cannot say as to who it be. 'Twas told it be with gents."

One of the other women snickered. "Could it be that yer reputation followed ya 'ere? Could be the gents heard more than ye being a good cook."

Everyone laughed except Mary. She was afraid. Nothing good ever came out of people needing to see her. Life had taught her that…no good indeed.

The night had dragged on, but it was nothing compared to the day. Knowing she would be summoned made her edgy. One look at her and people stayed clear. Everyone knew by midmorning of her call to the office and assumed it was bad news. Finally the word came down that she had been summoned. Slowly she pulled off her apron and went to wash her hands and face. Poking wisps of hair back into her cap, she turned to leave the kitchen. The other workers silently stepped aside and faced her as if she were walking to the gallows. They all patted her shoulder as she passed.

Mary's feet felt like they were made out of lead. As she looked down the hallway, it seemed to lengthen and narrow. She wasn't sure, but she thought she spied a noose hanging at the end of it for a split second. Finally she stepped up to the door. The gaoler lightly knocked. After being asked to enter, she peeked in first. To her surprise she saw several men and a fancy looking lady. More surprisingly, Katie was there.

Katie sprang to her feet to greet her friend. "Mary, I'm so glad to see you!"

"Wha…why?" was all Mary could muster.

"Come sit down, Mary. We have good news for you." Katie took her hand, leading her to the chair next to hers. "Mary, this is Lady Wilson."

Lady Wilson extended her hand to Mary. "I've heard wonderful things about you from Katie."

Mary could only nod. She was dizzy with relief. She didn't know what was going on, but Katie said it was good news.

A man behind a desk peered at his papers, then over the rim of his specs at Mary. "I take it that you are Mary Willow?"

Mary nodded affirmative.

"I am Magistrate Withers. I have been given your case to review. You have been here at Newgate for over two years now. Is that correct?"

"Aye," Mary mouthed, although nothing came out.

"It would seem, Mrs. Willow, that you have some very good friends. A petition has been brought before me. I have reviewed your case, as I said before, and found you to be an exemplary prisoner."

Mary bristled. What did he call her? Exempla what? What did he mean by that?

"During this year of confinement you have earned a position as top cook, and by the looks of this report, an excellent one. Praise for a prisoner is not easily found here, Mrs. Willow. I must say, I am impressed with your accomplishments."

Mary felt herself blush to her amazement. She hadn't blushed in over forty years. Not since that boy, Tommy McNally had…why, of all things. Even though she wasn't sure what all the words the man was saying meant, she knew they were good. He was actually saying what a good cook she was.

"I also reviewed the crime committed that caused your confinement. I know many women of your um…station, shall we say, have been victimized by society. That can cause a woman to go astray." Now it was the magistrate's turn to blush. Clearing his throat, he went on. "I have a signed petition to free you at this time. I have been assured that you have a home and employment, so you can become a useful member of society. What do you have to say to that?"

Mary could scarcely breathe. Home, job, where? She looked around until her eyes fell on Katie. This couldn't be a joke. Katie wasn't cruel. She stared at the man behind the desk.

"Well, Mrs. Willow, do you understand what I've just said?"

Katie laid her hand on Mary's arm. "Mary, it's true," she said gently. "You can come home with me now!"

As their words sunk in, she loudly exclaimed, "Aye, aye, would be a fine day to leave 'ere, a fine day indeed. But what of my kitchen?"

Katie laughed. "Let's worry about you for today. I'm sure they can work something out in the meantime."

Tears slipped down Mary's cheeks. Sniffling, she took Katie's hand. "Nobody e'er came ta 'elp me afore ya come along, Katie girl." Katie held out a hanky. Mary loudly blew her nose. "Blimey, would ne'er have thought it to be me last morn in the gaol when I awoke. Katie girl, 'tain't dreamin', am I?" She handed the used hanky back to Katie, who only stared at it with a bemused look. Mary quickly tucked it in her sleeve.

Katie laughingly assured her it was not a dream and hugged her friend. "'Tis true, Mary. You are free. Free to come home with me. All we need to do is get your things."

Mary grabbed her friend once more. "I 'ad it in me mind that I be stayin' 'ere a long time, so I try to do the best I can. Ter get out o' 'ere is a fine thing. Oh thank ye, Katie girl. Thank ye!"

Laughing, Katie hugged her back. "Lady Wilson is the one to thank. She fought hard for your release."

Mary turned to the other woman. "Thank ya fer yer help and kindness."

Lady Wilson beamed. "Mary, how could a good lady such as you ever be kept in such a place?"

For the second time in one day the impossible happened: Mary blushed ear to ear.

As Katie and Lady Wilson signed papers, Mary went back to her cell to recover her meager belongings. Upon hearing her news, the others were excited but hated to see her go. "Blimey, Mary, who's going to cook fer us?" That seemed to be the big question.

"I don't know. 'Twasn't told of that."

"Where ya be livin' now, Mary?"

"Not too sure on that either, but I s'pect it be a piece better than this place be." Mary hugged some of the women before leaving. Looking back she couldn't help but feel bad for leaving them there. She felt a little sad to leave her kitchen as well, but not bad enough to stay. "Now ye girls be good, and don't go given' ol' 'enry trouble, 'ere?"

Henry shuffled his feet. "Don't ya forget us 'ere, Mary. Kinda got used to seein' yer face around."

"Why 'enry, yer face is all red," laughed a couple of the other women.

With a sniff, Henry led Mary back to the office. "God bless ya, 'enry," was all Mary could say for the lump in her throat.

Tipping his old cap, Henry turned and shuffled away sadly, muttering quietly about how there weren't a lot of women like Mary. He would miss her for sure. Full of spit and fire, that one was.

After Mary had left the office to get her things, Katie and Lady Wilson embraced. "Thank you, for all your help getting Mary released," Katie cried.

Lady Wilson fought tears herself. "Oh Kathryn, did you see her face? What a wonderful day for both of you. Have you everything ready for her at the cottage?"

Nodding, Katie wiped her tears and turned to Magistrate Withers, who stood looking rather uncomfortable, witnessing their emotional show of affection. "Thank you, sir, for all of your help. We could not have succeeded without your recommendation."

Magistrate Withers took Katie's hand. "You're very welcome, Mrs. Murphy. Good tidings don't come often enough with my job. I was greatly impressed with Mrs. Willow's record. It spoke volumes on its own. Now if you will excuse me, I must leave to attend other business. Good day ladies, gentlemen." Nodding to all, he left.

Katie and Lady Wilson turned to thank the others for all their help. Lady Wilson spoke to one of the barristers. "Mr. Jacobs, I appreciate all your time invested in this. I must say that Lord Wilson was pleased at how diligently you worked on Mary's release. I am to inform you that he will be stopping by your office to personally hand you a bonus."

A wide smile stretched the young man's face as he thanked Lady Wilson before leaving.

Mary timidly reentered the room, holding on to her pitiful bag of belongings. Once Katie saw her, she took Mary's arm and led her back out in the hallway.

"Come, Mary, let's get you out of here. Lady Wilson's coach is waiting for us, and I'm anxious for you to see your new home. There's so much to talk about! I can't wait for you to see your room, and Maggie has stew cooking on the stove."

"Where ya takin' me, an' why didn' ya tell me, Katie girl, ya was workin' to set me free?"

"I didn't want you to be disappointed if things didn't work out. It took longer than I had hoped. If it hadn't been for Lord and Lady Wilson, I don't know if you would have been released. As far as your new home, it's a surprise."

Mary turned to the fancy lady standing next to Katie once more. Tears threatened to fall once again, so Mary looked down at her shoes. "'Tis thankin' ya again, I am. Katie girl told me of ya when she come to visit. She said ya 'ad a kind heart."

Lady Wilson appeared touched by the words. "I am so happy I could help, Mary. Katie speaks highly of you, too."

With those words, the three women walked out, arm in arm, as if leaving church instead of one of the most notorious prisons in history.

Maggie stirred the stew once more. She then checked her bread before going back to the spare room. All the boxes had been removed and were replaced with furniture. Heavy curtains hung on the window now that winter was on its way. The bed was freshly made up with a warm coverlet in bright patchwork colors to match the curtains. Rag rugs covered the floor, and a small fireplace with a cheery fire warmed the room. The day couldn't be more perfect for Mary's arrival. Maggie checked on her stew once more when she heard a coach approaching. Glancing once more around the room, she nervously patted her hair into place. She stood at the door but didn't want to seem overanxious by opening it too soon. She turned back to stand by the fireplace, changed her mind, and ran back toward the door. *Blimey, I haven't been this nervous about anything in a long time.* She couldn't stand waiting any longer…she opened the door.

The coachman helped Katie down. He then turned to give Mary his hand, but Mary wouldn't have it.

"Been 'elpin' meself down all these years. Can do it now," was all she said.

The poor man looked at Katie, not sure of what to do. Evidently he decided it was best to step back, out of Mary's way.

Katie had to hide a smile as she observed Mary flounce to the ground on her own. Katie waited on the walk until Mary caught up. They turned to wave their good-byes to Lady Wilson.

"Here it is Mary, Brady's Brick. What do you think?" Katie asked.

Mary stood eyeing the cottage. A smile broke across her face. "'Tis one of the finest cottages I e'er see in me life, Katie!"

Seeing Maggie in the doorway, Katie turned to Mary to introduce the two women. After all the pleasantries, the three women went in.

Mary's eyes nearly bugged out as she looked around. "Blimey, Katie girl, this 'ere cottage be fanciful."

The two women went from room to room as Maggie set the table for lunch. It was when Mary saw her own room that she let out a shriek. "Cannot be! Me own room with the curtains? I ne'er, I swear I ne'er 'ad me own place such as 'ere even when me poor ol' Percy brought me in to 'is house." That was the first time Katie ever heard the name of Mary's dead husband.

"Why don't you get your things settled before we eat?" Katie suggested. She watched as Mary carefully set her torn bag of belongings on the bed. She carefully lifted out the only other dress she owned. Looking around she found a wooden peg for hanging. With her rough, red hands Mary smoothed the dress out as best she could. Turning back to her bag, she took out the half-toothless comb she always carried, and set it on the table by her bed. Once again she turned back to the bag, bringing out the worn, filthy piece of material that Katie had noticed so long ago in the gaol. With great tenderness, she placed it next to the comb. Closing the bag, she pushed it under the bed announcing, "I be moved in now."

Katie's heart swelled as she watched her friend. Mary had shared only a little of her life. In so many ways Mary was a mystery. She was one of the toughest, yet gentlest women she had ever met. What could Mary have accomplished in her life if only she had been given the chance? Katie was going to give her that chance now. She vowed to do everything she could to help Mary live her years remaining more comfortable and worry-free.

Once settled in, the two women went into the kitchen. They found Maggie standing off to the side, wringing her hands in anticipation of Mary's arrival. Katie watched with an amused look.

"'Tis a fine kitchen indeed," Mary announced. "So cheery with the wee windows. Smell the bread. Reminds me of the kitchen in me own house on Turnmill Street in East London. 'Twas not a fine place such as this, but to me 'twas a palace. 'Course it was not smellin' so sweet there even when the bread was bakin'. A stinkin' place 'twas the street we lived, but I 'ad me Percy. Why, Percy and me had a fine life there for a time." Mary lifted her apron she always wore to wipe a tear.

"Come sit and eat now. 'Tis been a busy day," Maggie stated. "Hope you like my stew. The mixins have been in my family for a long time now." Maggie set about slicing fresh bread and mixing up some hot tea and honey for Mary.

Katie served herself and sat back, listening to the two women. They spoke of the old ways to making stew, and how mutton was the best of all. It was as if she weren't there, not that she minded. It did her soul good to see her two friends together.

"Honey! Yer 'ave real honey fer the tea! 'Tis been a fine day fer sure. Ye bless ol' Mary with yer kindness. Why, Katie girl, 'tis been too long since I had me a speck of honey. 'Tis why ol' women such as I get crusty and sour. Never get enough honey." Mary laughed at herself.

As evening fell and dinner was put away, the three women enjoyed a crackling fire. Now that the sun had gone down the air turned very cold. Katie broke the silence that had enveloped them for a time. "Mary, you've mentioned your husband a few times today. In fact, I never knew his name before today. Can you tell us more about him, or would it be too painful?"

A faraway look came over Mary's face as she went back to the old times with her Percy. "'Twas a special time in me life when the hardness was made softer fer the love I 'ad with 'im. How I miss 'im still." Mary gripped her cup as if she once again felt the sharpness of her longing for him. "It's as if 'e died yesterday, instead of twenty years back." She took a sip of tea. "I haven't spoken of 'im fer so long." She sighed, as if memories of him were her treasure, and it was hard for her to begin the precious story.

"'Twas in Ireland where I met 'im. 'Twas a young lass when I first laid me eyes on 'im. Thought 'e was one of the most handsome men I ever did see. Black hair like pitch, and blue eyes that 'ad to be from an angel. No man could e'er have such blue eyes. 'Is laugh made me laugh too, and when 'e looked upon me 'twas if I was on fire. First time I e'er saw him, 'e was chasing down sheep for the shearin'. I member 'e was mad and swearin'. My Percy could put a red face on a sinner for the swearin' 'e did at times." Mary chuckled. "I remember 'is big hands. Biggest I e'er saw on a man."

Katie thought of James Patrick's hands.

"Percy told me 'e was wantin' to leave the island fer all the hardships. Said 'e had the passage for 'isself an' spare fer me if I be willin' to follow. Told 'im 'e eeded to marry me first, an' 'e did. Then we sailed. Seems to be a hundred years ago. Me Percy was a 'ard worker. Worked in a factory, 'e did, once we settled in London. 'Twas 'ard work, but 'e was thankful to 'ave it. Made nothing fer all the work 'e did."

Taking another sip of her tea, she continued. "Weren't long afore he begin to 'ave coughin' fits. 'Twas bad spells 'e 'ad. Afore too long 'e begin ter spit up 'is own blood. They called it Black Lung. Killed 'im outright, it did. Me poor Percy, 'ardly drank the rum either. 'Twas a good man." Sniffling, Mary wiped her face on her apron.

"Mary, I'm so sorry," Katie said, laying a hand on Mary's arm.

Blowing her nose, Mary shook her head. "'Tis sad fer sure but needs to be remembered. Can't forget my Percy. We 'ad a wee one, a boy. Tiny as could be. Poor little one not be strong enough to live in this 'ard world. Named 'im baby Jimmy, we did. Died small, but 'twas best that 'e did because 'e was sick from the start. Percy took it the hardest. I be glad 'e was in God's 'ands, and not in this cold world. I saw hardships fer the wee ones. They worked j'st as 'ard as the men did. King George is said to 'ave blood on 'is throne from all the wee ones workin' in those cotton mills. 'Tis a fact, our babe's better off in 'eaven then 'ere. How it be fer me to care fer 'im, if I cannot care fer meself? All I 'ave of baby Jimmy now are the memories, an' a small piece of 'is blanket."

So that was the tattered piece of cloth Katie saw in Mary's room. No wonder she handled it so tenderly.

"I forgot to tell you some important news," Katie said, swiftly changing the subject. "You did such a fine job as cook at the gaol that they are willing to hire you for wages. You have a day or two to think it over before they select a prisoner for the job."

"Blimey, getting paid doin' what I was doin' afore? 'Tis a blessin' indeed. Was that the job the judge mentioned afore lettin' me out?"

"No," Katie answered. "Originally, Lady Wilson was going to offer you a position at Brick House. I received word from Newgate this morning about the job and meant to tell you sooner. I thought you might like 'your' kitchen back, but the choice is yours. Lady Wilson said that her offer is still open."

"'Tis a fact ol' Mary took pride in 'er own kitchen. Done, will do it I will! I like ter take me kitchen back. I 'ave friends there an' all. Ter 'ave a 'ome and place to work…God be good ta ol' Mary fer sure. Did the price to be paid get told?"

"Well, he said if you were willing to start out at a half crown per month you could have the job." Katie smiled at her friend.

"Ne'er had half a crown afore. How much that be?"

"Two shillings and six pence."

Beaming, Mary finished her tea. "'Tis a rich one I'll be!" Suddenly her smile disappeared. "Won' be 'urtin' the lady's feelin's if'n I take the other offer, do ya think? She be good ter me."

"Of course not," Katie assured her. "She is going to be happy for you."

"Praise be the Almighty! Then I'll take it fer sure!"

It had been an exciting day for all. It wasn't long before Mary's head began bobbing.

"Mary, why not head for bed?" Katie gently shook her.

"Aye, I think I will. Good night ta yas now." Mary headed for her room.

Getting into the fresh gown she was given, Mary gently picked up baby Jimmy's piece of tattered blanket. Stroking it, she tenderly placed it next to her cheek. It was hard to remember back, but good too. It had been a magical day that Mary would never forget. Things would never be the same for her...thank God.

After tossing and turning for a time, Mary gathered her bedding and placed it on the board floor. Tucking Jimmy's cloth under her pillow, she covered up and was soon asleep. It would be a long time before she would get used to a soft mattress.

Katie and Maggie sat by the fire, enjoying their time together. They talked about Mary and the events of the day.

"What of Mary once you leave the house? Have you told her your plans yet?" Maggie questioned.

"No, so much has happened today. If she wants, she can stay here to watch over Brady's Brick when I'm gone. She'll be able to make a living with cooking for the gaol. They don't pay anyone to cook there. Why should they? They have enough prisoners to do the work. I told a fib, but Mary is proud. She would never take charity. I had to make arrangements to pay her myself after the warden agreed to my plan. He said it was the best run kitchen he ever had when Mary was in charge. He agreed to keep my secret. I gave the bank instructions to give her a draft each month. She'll think it's from the gaol, and that's what I want. I don't like deceiving her, but she would never take money from me. This way I know she will be all right, and it gives her a sense of purpose. The money will pay for her looking after the place for me, but she won't know it."

"You are a good friend, Katie," Maggie stated quietly.

"I owe her my life. She is one of the bravest, kindest people I know, but you wouldn't ever want to get her mad. I saw her take a woman, much younger than herself, and teach her some respect." Katie's eyes crinkled with amusement at the memory of the fight. "Then one time she stood between me and two men. Defended me, she did, as if I were family instead of a stranger—and won! Of course James Patrick stood behind her, and that really was the reason those men backed down. She didn't know that, though. She was brave for just standing up to them."

"I don't think I could ever do that. I'm not that brave. It all sounds so awful. I cannot imagine being in one of those places…all those poor people. Mary has lived a hard life, yet look at her gentle and kind spirit. 'Tis a hard thing to hear of all her troubles," Maggie added.

"She is someone special, that's for sure," Katie answered as she headed to her room. "Thank you, Maggie, for making her so welcome today. It was important to me."

"It was important to me too. I'll be heading for bed myself. Good night, Katie. Have sweet dreams."

Katie lay on her bed unable to sleep. She had tried to speak to several people about her husband, but his guilt was without question. In fact, remembering back to their trials, James was the only one who confessed his guilt. Katie sensed that James wanted to leave England. It held nothing for him, and his heart was turned to the new land. He hoped to earn his own land one day. It was said ten acres would be given to a prisoner who was willing to work it. It wasn't a lot, but enough. Even though she had land from her father, it seemed important to James to earn his own. They both knew it would be years before that happened, though.

Katie got up and cracked the window open. Quickly she added more wood to the fire. Fall was her favorite time of year. She loved the crisp air. The curtains lifted at the breeze. She hurriedly jumped back into the bed. Watching the curtains move, and listening to the leaves rustle in the wind, she turned her thoughts back to James. She knew he held his belief in God very seriously. He didn't push her into what he believed but instead encouraged her and comforted her. She whispered a prayer to God, the unknown, invisible God of James Patrick and Gran. *Please, watch over him and keep him safe. Let us soon be together, and thank You for bringing Mary home.*

Katie reflected for a time about what she had just done. Why did she pray? It just seemed to come out of her without thinking about it. She was too tired to figure it out and snuggled down into her blankets. Without realizing it, she thanked the invisible God once more for her soft warm bed.

12

The Kiss

The door opened to the room, and Red rose to his feet at the sight of his wife. She smiled and handed him a basket. Red grabbed it in spite of the chains.

"I wish you didn't have to be chained like that. I don't know what they think you're going to do."

"They probably know I would grab you and not let you go." He smiled.

Katie blushed. Red put the basket on the table, then waited for Katie to show him what she had brought.

After removing a towel from the top, Katie handed him a package wrapped in brown paper. "Mary made you a fine shirt, and I knitted you more socks. I hope they fit. They look a little big to me, but try them and see." Next she lifted out cheese, apples, and slices of fresh bread. "I have some roasted beef for you too."

Red's mouth watered. "Tom! Would you like some of this here food?" he asked the guard. "My wife brings enough to feed this whole place." The gaoler stepped into the room with a sheepish grin and nodded to James. Katie placed some beef on a slice of bread and handed it to him. He took it, tipped his cap to her, and stepped out the door. "I think the men get almost as excited as I do when you come to visit. They keep asking if my 'saint of a wife' is coming in. Are you sure you can afford to be bringing all that extra food each week?" Red inquired.

"Saint indeed! I have more than enough. I'm just thankful I'm allowed to give it to you."

"Speaking of being thankful…" James bowed his head in prayer. "Heavenly Father, I thank You for all the wonderful blessings in my life and especially Katie. Thank You, Lord, for bringing her into my life. Bless this food, and help us to always remember who our blessings come from. In Jesus' name, amen."

It always amazed Katie how a man in chains and locked in a gaol could be thankful for all his blessings. Yet she had to admit she felt her life being led by a power greater than herself. She had been aware of it for some time now, and it gave her a strange sense of peace. Lost in thought, she started eating an apple.

His gentle voice prompted, "Where are you?"

Katie smiled. "Oh, I was sailing off to the New World on a mighty ship. Have you heard when we leave?"

"No, I would think you would be able to get more information than I would. Did you speak to Lord Wilson about sailing to Botany Bay?"

Katie hesitated, unsure whether to tell him her news.

Red stopped chewing. "What is it? What's wrong?"

Katie sighed. "James, I talked to Lord Wilson a couple of days ago. He came over and brought two men with him. One was a marine and had been to Botany Bay. The other man worked on one of the prison ships in the harbor. Oh, James, it was horrible what they told me, and I feel they were holding back some of what they told."

"What did they say?"

"The man who guarded prisoners gave me a short history of the prison ships. How the overcrowding of the gaols forced them to put prisoners on old ships in the harbor. Those ships quickly became so overcrowded that they decided to send the prisoners to Botany Bay. They used to send them to America, until the war. He said that it's not as bad aboard those prison ships now as it used to be years ago."

"Do you know what kind of ships they are?"

"Aye, they are old troop transports with their masts and riggings gone. He told me that typhus has claimed many a prisoner and marine alike. Rats run the ships, and the men are chained together in the hulks. They are only brought up for fresh air when the weather is fair. Many die, and I heard the food is not sufficient to stay healthy. I never thought I would be truly thankful that you are in here, but I am. How dreadful to think you could be on one of them. If they consider the conditions better now, what must have it been like before?"

"It could still happen, Katie. You never know. I could be taken to one of those ships yet. Besides, look around. Gaol fever has struck here, but God has protected me. If it weren't for you, I would be getting a lot less food, and not near as good. You and the Lord take good care of me." He sighed. "I will just pray for God's will. I can't ask God to spare me the hulks, and have others go." He studied her intently. "Was that all the man said?"

"He said if the men were lucky, they would be picked to do harbor work on shore or dredging. The men are usually weak and cramped up from being chained for so long. James, what are we going to do? I didn't know what to expect, but I never dreamed anything like this. If being on a ship anchored in the harbor is that horrible, then what will it be like sailing thousands of miles on a rough sea? If that isn't bad enough, I have heard of many hardships once we reach the land. Hunger and danger threatens. People struggle to survive in a place so far away that help is not to be found."

As Katie talked, her voice lifted with agitation, and her lower lip trembled.

Covering her hand with his, he tried to comfort her. "Katie, I knew all along it wouldn't be easy. I don't know all the facts, but I have heard that the colonies are better settled now. I've been thinking about all this and need to ask you something. I've been asking myself if it's fair for me to put you through all of this. Why should you pay for my crime? I think it would be a good thing if you were to stay here. Maybe the magistrate was right about getting the marriage annulled. You have a home here, and friends. I think it would be best."

Red opened his mouth to say more, but Katie's expression stopped him cold.

She jumped up, knocking her chair over. With her dainty hand, she jabbed her finger into the big man's chest. "James Patrick Murphy! How dare you try and ditch me! Just because I may be a little afraid of the unknown, that by no means makes me a coward! And what makes you think you can tell me what to do? How do you know what is best? I have had men telling me how to run my life long enough. No more! Don't ever think you can tell me that I am going to stay here while my husband sails off! I am not going to have our marriage annulled! Whatever happened to all that faith you're always talking about? Is your God so weak He won't be able to watch over us?"

Red's eyes bugged out, and his mouth hung open.

Katie's chest heaved, and sweat popped out on her brow as she retrieved her chair. She couldn't remember feeling so angry. Actually, she couldn't remember ever talking to anyone like that before. Pushing loose hair from her face, she took a deep breath. She felt dizzy. It was as if a dam had let loose, causing all her fears and frustrations to pour out. She was so worried about Red. At least he was gaining weight with the food she brought. But she wished she had his faith. She couldn't understand her husband's relationship with God. How could he so easily dismiss the thought of being taken aboard one of those horrible ships...or dismiss her?

The gaoler rushed into the room at the sound of Katie's raised voice. After seeing everything was all right, he left. Clearly, he wasn't about to step in between a man that size and a wife that mad.

With a shaky hand Katie wiped her face with her hanky and proceeded to let out a loud sigh. Red was still sitting with his eyes bugged out. He looked so ridiculous; she couldn't help but stare at him. Without warning, she burst into laughter.

Red jumped with surprise at the sound. He looked at her as if she had just lost her mind, which caused Katie to laugh even more. After a moment Red began chuckling. Soon his body shook with laughter.

Even the gaoler joined in after hearing them. It made quite a scene.

Once Katie caught her breath, she spoke. "Oh, James, I don't know what came over me. I am not a high-tempered person. When I saw your face like that, I couldn't keep myself from laughing. You looked so silly."

James chuckled again. "My face! You should have seen yours! It was so red and puckered up! I feared you were going to throttle me."

"I was thinking about it," Katie stated before breaking into laughter again.

Laughter gave way to a more serious mood as Red spoke. "I want you to know that, while I was saying the words, my heart was telling me to stop. I don't want you to suffer through all the hardships, but I hate the thought of losing you even more. I guess

I'm selfish, but I'm greatly relieved you won't even consider it."

Katie stepped around the table and knelt before his chair. Placing her hands on his knees, she looked up into his eyes and spoke from her heart. "You will never get rid of me, James Patrick. Not unless God himself decides otherwise."

They both stood. Red lifted his chains over her head, drawing her closer. Lowering his head, they shared their first kiss, a kiss of promise. Katie drew back for lack of breath and lay her head on his chest. She could feel his heart pounding, matching her own.

"Mrs. Murphy, I love you," Red whispered.

"I love you too, Mr. Murphy."

A few moments later Katie walked back into the sunshine with her basket empty and her heart full. She decided then and there to start working toward the future. Part of that was doing what she could to make changes in that prison. Some changes had occurred, but too few and far between. There was much to do. Who else could better understand what the gaol needed than someone who had lived in it?

She felt different—changed somehow from a girl to a woman. She felt stronger and not as afraid of the future. Hardships were coming. Of that, she had no doubt. But people could live soft and still have a hard life. Hardships were not something to fear, but to live and work through. She knew in her heart that somehow they would make it, for they had each other. Yes, she and James would make it. That was the promise of the kiss they shared.

"I can't believe you let those men tell Kathryn about all the horrors aboard those ships. I think that was cruel. That wasn't like you at all, Edward!" Lady Wilson scolded.

"My dear, it is best that she realize what she's getting herself into. It won't be easy, especially for an innocent such as Kathryn."

"But to let them give her gory details that only served to frighten the poor girl…well, she has been through enough. You said you wanted to help her!"

"I do, but she needs to know what can happen. How else will she prepare for such a journey? I hear it's very difficult. I don't want to tell her otherwise. Besides, after hearing all this, she may change her mind. It would be best for her to do that now, rather than when she's halfway across the ocean."

Overwhelmed with fear and grief, Lady Wilson dabbed her eyes. "Why in the world would she want to do this in the first place? I truly have tried to understand, but I can't. To marry a stranger, and go off to some godforsaken place? At best all they can do is to scratch out a living—if they survive at all. It's beyond me."

"Now, now, Barbara, there's no reason to get yourself all worked up. Have you forgotten that you and I were virtual strangers when we married? That ours was an arranged marriage? We have come to love each other deeply. I know that it isn't quite the same, but we need to let her make her own decisions. I wasn't trying to be cruel, but to prepare her for some of what she may face." Lady Wilson nodded in agreement, and he continued. "She has her mind made up, so all we can do is try our best to help her. Since she is going to be so far away, it will be next to impossible once she is there. You will need to trust me, my dear. I promise you, we will do everything in our power to help her. Now, go rest before dinner. We don't want Tess to know that you've been crying. How would you explain it?"

Lady Wilson let her husband lead her to the staircase and obediently went to her rooms to rest. Sleep eluded her as her mind went from Kathryn to Tess. Once again she had to admit that she had enjoyed her relationship with Kathryn more than with Tess. This knowledge caused her much pain and guilt. She couldn't help it. She had come to love Kathryn as much, if not more, than her own daughter. Her fear for the girl's future was very real. She knew she had no control over her own future, let alone anyone else's. It was futile to worry. Nonetheless, she felt panic whenever she thought of Kathryn sailing away. She decided to indeed trust her husband and promised herself something. She would watch to make sure as time passed that her husband's concern for Kathryn wouldn't ebb away. Once that was decided, she was able to rest.

Lord Wilson stepped out into the garden. Although the temperatures were dropping, the sun had not fully set, leaving the temperature still pleasant. Soon it would be time to close the house up and move to their summer home. He felt tired. His age was catching up with him. Knowing that made him feel melancholy. This should have been an easy time for him and Barbara. He had expected to have grandchildren by now. It had been his intention to see Tess married and settled into home life. He had hoped that would curb some of her wild nature.

He knew his wife was also feeling agitated due to their daughter's return. Her health seemed fragile. He needed to take steps to ease his wife's worries, but what could he do? He was a man of action, which was easy if you had the money. He did, but money wasn't the answer this time.

He had expected to hear from the detective he had hired any day now. He should have hired him sooner to check on James Murphy. He would have to know what kind of man Murphy was if he was to help them. It all depended on the detective's report. Kathryn may have decided to stay married to the man, but if he turned out to be a rogue, Lord Wilson would not spend his time or money on him. Being in the gaol in the first place was cause for mistrust. However, Kathryn had been in the gaol for no fault of her own; perhaps something similar had happened to the man, though he doubted it.

Lord Wilson's brow creased as his thoughts returned to his daughter. He knew it was only a matter of time before she once again got herself into a "situation." Barbara could never know what he knew about Tess. He had spent a lot of money keeping their family name cleared of any scandal. However, he was never sure what Tess was up to. Barbara told him how Tess had practically thrown herself at a married man.

Deeply troubled, he walked back into the house. After closing the French doors, he stepped to the side table to pour some brandy. Arrangements to move to the summerhouse would have to be postponed. He had too many irons in the fire to leave and questions that needed to be answered. It was time to give George Day the answer he had been expecting. If George's son was truly interested in marrying Tess, he would give his permission. If she wouldn't settle down on her own, he would arrange a good match for her. That decision made, he belted down the brandy, pouring another. Tomorrow would be a difficult day. He didn't want to face it, but face it he would, and so would Tess.

"Lord Wilson, you have a visitor, sir. A Mr. Grimes." The servant stepped aside to show the man into his employer's study.

A young man stepped over the threshold smiling, bowing ever so slightly.

"Grimes, thank you for coming. Sit down." Lord Wilson extended his hand. The man took it. "Graines, fetch some tea, and brandy."

Once the two men were settled, Grimes took out a small notebook from his pocket and opened it. "I have some interesting information for you. What do you want first?"

"What do you have on Murphy?"

"He was orphaned and traveled from job to job. Ended up with a family for about eight years, but they lost their farm. As far as I could find out, he was once again on his own. Seems he's a hard worker. Except for stealing bread and cheese from a shopkeeper, he was never in trouble before. He fared better than most of the gutter pups here in the city. I checked him out at Newgate. Seems when he first arrived most of the men were afraid of him. Probably from his size; he's huge. The gaolers even use him on jobs with a team of men. Seems he gets the job done, and done right. I came across something interesting. Many of the turnkeys respect him. That's unheard of."

Lord Wilson listened intently.

The man went on. "I also found many of the other prisoners are quite loyal to the man. They treated me with great suspicion and were quick to defend him. I find myself quite amazed by it. They usually tell any and all if they think it will help them. Many times they offer information I don't ask for. But not on this man."

Lord Wilson lit a cigar and leaned back in his chair. Taking his time, he puffed, blowing the smoke over his head. "What was all the stealing business about?"

"I guess he was hungry. Stole bread and cheese and got caught."

"That's it? I still can't believe they will transport a man for as little as that." Lord Wilson snorted.

"I hear tell of a lad, twelve years old, who was sent out for stealing pants for himself. He was cold and half-naked. They want these thieves gone. It doesn't matter what they stole."

"Taking food because you're hungry or clothes to cover yourself doesn't make you a thief. If he worked all those years, it shows that it's not his nature. I can't fault anyone for trying to eat. Is that all the information you have on him?"

"Yes, sir, I had trouble finding out anything else since he has no family, and the tight-lipped cronies wouldn't talk."

"What other information do you have for me?" Lord Wilson picked up his ornate cigar box and offered one.

Taking a cigar, the man clipped it and waited for a light. "Your daughter, well, has been seen on several occasions with Magistrate Reeves. Seems his wife is on an extended trip to Paris with a friend of hers. Reeves and your daughter have been seen at the gambling house and out to a few plays."

"Gambling house! Her mother would faint dead away if she knew her daughter was frequenting such an establishment *and* with a married man! What else?"

The man squirmed in his chair. "That's about all. It seems they are…well, shall we say, becoming close friends? The man's wife is due back in another month."

"So there seems to be a marriage of convenience between Reeves and his wife?"

"I was told Reeves got his title of magistrate from his father-in-law. Was a barrister making less than he is now. Met his wife and fell into money."

Lord Wilson leaned back in his chair once more. He had much to think about. "Anything else?" was all he said.

"That's about it for now. I'm still working on getting a meeting together for you with those men I told you about. Grayson is free now, but I'm having trouble getting in touch with Brice and Knotts."

"Contact me when you are able to set something up. If there are any new developments, contact me immediately." Lord Wilson rose from his chair, dismissing the younger man. "Good job, Grimes. You answered many of the questions I had. Thank you for coming."

The two men left the study, stepping into the massive foyer to the front entrance. Once again they shook hands before Grimes left.

Lady Wilson descended the stairs smiling at her husband. "Business, Edward? Seems a lot of people have been coming and going lately."

Lord Wilson took his wife by the hand and led her into the parlor to sit before the fire. "Nothing you need to concern yourself over, dear. I've decided to stay in London instead of going to the summerhouse. I have some important business I need to finish, and I thought it would be nice to have the holidays here this year. What do you think?"

"Of course, Edward, I don't mind if you need to stay. I will need to get word to the staff not to open the summerhouse."

"I've already taken care of that. Would you like to have a Christmas ball this year?"

Lady Wilson looked surprised. Normally he was not one for such social functions. "It's been such a long time since we entertained like that, Edward. I would love it! It would give me a chance to show off the house dressed in its Christmas finest. Tess will be excited too, I'm sure of it."

"I think you will be the one most excited, my dear," the man said.

"Why, Edward? Is there more to all your surprising news?"

"Oh, yes, but I'm not telling you yet. You must wait and see. I don't want to spoil it." He failed to mention to his wife that it would be more than a Christmas ball. She didn't know it yet, but she was about to plan her daughter's engagement party. "Start making the arrangements and make sure Tess helps. Spare no expense, Barbara. Christmas comes only once a year, and who knows when we will ever do this again."

Lady Wilson's eyes twinkled with merriment. "Oh, Edward, what a wonderful ball it will be. Thank you!" Off she ran to make her plans.

Lord Wilson smiled at his wife's excitement and at his cleverness. Soon all would be set, and he would not have to worry about his daughter any longer. Let another man have the job.

13

Family

Mary held the back door of the cottage open for Henry as he pulled at the pine tree. Snow followed, leaving a wet trail on Maggie's clean kitchen floor. "Blimey, 'enry, Maggie will cuff ya if she sees that snow all over," Mary warned.

"Well, git a rag, woman, and wipe it up afore she sees it," Henry quipped. The fragrance of cookies baking along with the aroma of pine filled the warm kitchen. Mary was amused, watching Henry struggle with the tree. "Ya think maybe ya could help some, putting this monster up?" Henry leaned forward as his chest heaved.

"Are ya alright there, 'enry?"

"Aye, just need some more breaths of air, and I'll be fine."

Between the two of them the tree was soon standing in front of the windows, ready to be decorated.

Maggie came in to check on her cookies and gave her approval. "'Tis a fine tree. Katie will like it. Come and have some tea now. Sit and rest yourselves."

"Don 'ave to ask me twice." Mary smiled, grabbing Henry's arm. "'Ave we any honey left, Maggie?"

The three old friends sat in comfortable silence for a time, sipping tea. The rest of the afternoon was spent sewing lace onto the cloth decorations they had made earlier. They strung cookies for the tree. As they placed all the decorations, Maggie asked, "When did Katie say she would be back from seeing James?"

"Don't know but won't be too long now. It be gettin' dark." As if to answer, a horse whinnied, and the sound of a carriage pulling up was heard.

"I'm home! Anyone here?" Katie shouted breathlessly.

"Aye, in the kitchen, Katie. Are ya hungry?" Mary shouted.

"Aye, famished. What's on the stove?"

Supper was pleasant, and Katie raved about the tree.

Henry finished eating, then said his good-byes before heading home. "Let me walk a piece with ya, 'enry," Mary said before running for her cloak. The two old lovebirds left, leaving the house quiet.

"I think it's sweet that Henry started courting Mary after she left the gaol. The way they act, you would think they were kids." Katie laughed.

Maggie chuckled. "Remember the day the old rogue came to the door with that handful of wilted flowers, all red-faced and stammering? I thought Mary was going to bust with pride. She was more flustered than him, I believe. Never saw her at a loss of words before. Probably never will again neither. Do you think he'll ask her to marry him?"

"I don't know. Would be grand if he did, but I don't know if Mary would go through with it. Still talks of her Percy a lot and says she's too old for such things. It's fun to watch, though."

"How have your meetings been going with the Lady's Society? Have you been able to help those poor souls in the gaol? Any more changes made?"

Katie shook her head. "Not really. It can be so frustrating. Trying to make any kind of changes in this old system is like dragging a dead horse. Everyone agrees the changes need to be made, but they seem to drag their feet. Laws are born, not written, and labor can be hard and painful. Elizabeth Fry has struggled for years for reform, but it comes slow."

"Who is Elizabeth Fry?"

"She's the one who has fought for changes for the women at Newgate. She visits them, brings them food and clothing. She has given them hope when they had none."

Soon the two turned their conversation toward other things, enjoying each other's company. Katie picked up her bag of knitting and began working on it.

"What are you knitting now, Katie?" Maggie questioned as she finished washing the dishes.

"Another sweater for James. You would not believe how damp it is in that place. I thought I was going to die from the cold when I was there. I wouldn't be surprised if James gives this one away too. He always says that he finds someone whose needs are greater than his."

"A rare man he is, Katie. A glorious find he is. Not too many men like him around. Wouldn't mind finding one such as him for myself."

"Who says you won't? You never know, Maggie. Just like Mary, you could get a man knocking on your door."

"Won't hold my breath—or anything else—waiting," Maggie joked. "Maybe if your papa had lived....well, you know."

The two sat quietly after that. Katie thought of her beloved papa, while Maggie remembered her lost love...the same man.

Christmas was approaching fast. Katie needed to stay up late each night to finish making her presents for her "family." There was a sweater for James, warm socks for Henry, and a new warm covering for Maggie's bed. She had finished sewing the two new aprons for Mary the previous week. The hardest of all was what to give Lord and Lady Wilson. They had everything, and there was nothing they couldn't buy. Katie wanted so much to give them something special for all they had done. The Wilsons had more than made up for any past mistakes. Katie thought of them now as part of her family. She never went to the Brick House because of Tess, but they came to see her on a regular basis. What could she make for them? Time was running out, and she was feeling panicky.

Suddenly it dawned on her. She would give Lord Wilson her father's watch. It had meant the world to Papa, for it had come from his father. It was one of her treasures, but she wanted Lord Wilson to have it. He had not only given her father a job when most people hated and mistreated the Irish, but he took her father into his heart. If it hadn't been for the Wilsons, her family would not have been able to have a comfortable life. Oh, her father worked hard earning what he made, but he was happy because of it. For that, she had to credit Lord Wilson. Katie had thought of giving the watch to James, keeping it in the family, until she reminded herself that the Wilsons were her family, too.

For Lady Wilson she would give her the most valued prize of all—a beautiful shawl made by Gran, given to her mother. It was a delicate knit, the color of cream, and made when Gran lived in Ireland. Gran had saved it for Katie, keeping it in one of her trunks. Thank God, the Wilsons kept Katie's things for her when she was locked up. It was because of them that she still had her treasures. She became very excited now that she had gifts for them. She knew they would like anything she gave, but it was important to her to give them something special. She was almost finished, and Christmas was only two weeks away.

There was only one thing that could have made her Christmas perfect—having James there with her. Sighing, Katie slipped out to the kitchen for some milk. Returning to the main room, she stirred the fire. She began thinking how much her life had changed since Gran had died. More changes were to come, and perhaps there would not be a time like this again. Would she ever sit at a warm fire on a cold night, and feel safe and secure again once she left?

Katie felt apprehensive about the future, but it was too late to worry about it now. The decision to go was made, and go she would. Hopefully it wouldn't be the nightmare she kept hearing about. After all, she had heard terrible things about Newgate, too. While it certainly wasn't pleasant, she had found she could endure.

Finally, as the clock chimed three in the morning, Katie lifted herself out of the chair, stretched, and headed for bed. As she lay watching the flames in her fireplace, she thought of her family. Family, yes, she once again had a family besides James, and it would be hard to leave them. She was as close to those around her now as she was to Papa and Gran. Blessed she was, and she knew it. As she lay in her bed, she again whispered a soft prayer: *Thank You, God. Thank You for my family.*

"Father, you wanted to see me?" Tess bounced into her father's study.

"Come sit down, Tess. I need to talk to you. Where's your mother?"

"Didn't she tell you that she had to run to do some shopping for the ball?"

"Yes, but I wanted to make sure she was gone. I need to talk to you, and what I have to say may upset you. I do not want your mother to hear."

Tess leaned forward in her chair. "Is Mother all right? She isn't ill, is she?"

"No, she's fine. What I need to speak to you about concerns your future."

The hair on the back of Tess's neck stood up. She knew this wasn't going to be good. Her father never called her into his study. Something was wrong…wrong for her. She braced herself.

"Tess, I hired a detective to look into your activities. What he found greatly disturbed me. You have forced me to make some hard decisions."

"You what? A detective? Who?" Tess blurted out.

As calmly as possible, Lord Wilson answered her questions. "He's a friend of mine. His name isn't important, but what he found out is. Seems you are 'seeing' a married man, and you have been frequenting some unsavory places. Tess, what are you thinking? Don't you know a lady doesn't go to the gambling houses?"

Tess leaped to her feet, thundering, "How dare you! I'm not a child to be dictated to! You side with some servant, sending me off to Aunt Marilyn's, and now you have me followed? I'm not going to stand for it." Tess pivoted to storm out.

"If you don't sit down, you will never get another cent from me."

Tess stopped in her tracks. Pulled between her pride and greed, she teetered in the doorway. Finally greed won out. She turned back toward her father.

"Good. Now I want you to listen to what I'm going to say. First of all, we've been through all this about Kathryn. You lied, sending an innocent person to the gaol. Your mother and I couldn't believe you would do such a thing. I had to pay a great deal of money not to have you arrested for falsely signing those papers, but that is past. I now have new concerns. The reason I told you about the detective in the first place was to avoid your denial and save time. I had hoped by now that you would accept one of the proposals that had come in for you. Instead, you decide it's more to your liking to run with a married man and show yourself a loose woman."

Tess opened her mouth to respond, but her father raised his hand. "I will have my say. I had hoped you would have settled down by now and possibly have a couple of children. It has been your mother's hope as well. Since that is not the case, I have taken steps to make it happen."

Tess's eyes widened. "What do you mean you've taken steps? What steps?"

"The party your mother is preparing for is going to be more than a Christmas ball. It will be your engagement party as well. Your mother doesn't know about this, but after our talk, she will." Lord Wilson waited for the words to sink in.

Tess's mouth opened, but nothing came out.

He continued. "I have been corresponding with George Day. His son, David, has asked my permission to marry you. I said yes, and you shall also. They will be coming for a visit in a week, and I want you to be ready for it."

"You what! You can't do this, Father! Give me away as if I were a puppy! David Day! I've never met the man, and you expect me to marry him?"

"You have met him, but it has been years. His father is a ship builder. He owns a large estate just outside London. The family is old blood. Your future husband has his own estate in Kent. He has asked for your hand, and I am giving it to him. He will be taking over his father's business and feels it is time to settle down. I've had him checked out and found him to be an excellent catch."

Tess sat paralyzed. How could this be happening? She'd had her father wrapped around her little finger for as long as she could remember. What had changed? How could he even talk to her like this, as if she were some kind of harlot off the street? "I know who he is, Father, but I don't remember ever meeting him, just hearing about him. I heard he was dull and dim-witted."

Lord Wilson lit a cigar. "Tess, I can see that you are in shock. You must realize I'm doing this for your own good. You are heading into disaster, and as your father, I feel inclined to take the necessary steps to secure you a future. David Day is far from dim-witted. He's a great businessman."

Tess spoke as if to herself. "I can't believe you're doing this to me. Have I been that horrible that you would throw my life away as if it meant nothing?" Tears threatened as she looked up at the man who had always been her protector.

For the first time, doubts clouded Lord Wilson's mind. Maybe she was right. What if he was doing the wrong thing? After all, Tess at least had had the decency to be concerned about her mother in the beginning of their conversation. Perhaps there was hope for the girl after all.

No, he chided himself, he had to concentrate, and remember all that she had been involved in lately. Her tears were not going to work to change his mind this time.

His chin firmed in determination. "You have no choice in the matter. You have proved you are not capable of making your own decisions. Before you ruin your reputation, and our name, I will see you married! That is the end of it, except for this: your mother will be home soon. You will not say anything to her. *I* will tell her the news, and *I* will also let her know that you were in on the surprise. She must think that you and I planned to surprise her as a Christmas present. Do you understand?"

She crossed her arms. "And what if I refuse?"

"Then you will leave this house, never to return. You will have to rely on your lover's money and help, which I doubt will come after his wife returns."

Could he, would he really do that? Tess wasn't sure, so she simply nodded. Slowly she opened the door, waiting for her father to say, "I'm only joking," but it didn't come.

She advanced the staircase, heading for her rooms. Locking the door, she curled up in the chair before the fireplace. Putting her hands over her face, she cried. Her life was over. She would marry some stranger and get fat having his brats. She would probably die in childbirth. Tess considered suicide for a minute, but not seriously.

A soft knock was heard at her door. "Miss Tess, 'tis Betsy. I 'ave a bit o' tea fer ya."

Tess unlocked the door. "Leave the tea, and don't bother me anymore. Tell my mother when she gets back that I have a headache and went to bed early. Make sure no one bothers me anymore tonight. Now get out!"

Betsy quickly headed out the bedroom door after Tess locked herself in once more. Going into the kitchen, Betsy couldn't wait to tell the others that Miss Tess was in some kind of trouble again. Why else would her eyes be red from crying? No one on the staff would feel pity for the girl. It was always a time to gloat whenever she was in one of her "tragedies."

With great exaggeration Betsy told of the goings-on upstairs, then concluded gleefully, "Miss Tess is 'ard to work for, but she sure keeps things excitin'."

All agreed before returning to work. They couldn't wait to see what would happen next.

"We 'ave a letter!" Mary shouted as she came through the door. "'Tis a 'ard winter's day out. Wind darn near blew the letter from me 'ands."

Katie smiled at Mary's excitement. As time passed, Mary seemed to become more comfortable with her surroundings. It was fun to watch her take such great pleasure in simple things…like a letter. Mary handed it to Katie, then waited with expectation to hear the news it held.

"Oh, it's from Lord and Lady Wilson. They will be able to come for our Christmas gathering after all. Mary, we have so much to do. We only have three days left!"

Katie's excitement at the news was contagious. Mary beamed at the idea of planning something this important. "'Tis grand news fer sure. Well, Maggie an' me put our 'eads together, an' thought long an' 'ard 'bout what ter be serving for Christmas. We 'ave decided on lamb an' red potatoes. I can make me best puddin', some sausage, an' wine sauce. What ya think, Katie?"

"It all sounds wonderful. You have done a beautiful job at decorating already. I want to use the linen cloth for the table, and our best dishes, of course. They may be Lady Wilson's hand-me-downs, but they are still beautiful. I also need to finish wrapping gifts. Do you think we should hang some pine boughs on the fence outside?"

The two friends talked over their plans for Christmas. "Ne'er dreamt I would be sittin' in such a fine cottage as this, 'avin' cider. Life is funny, ain't it, Katie girl?"

Katie smiled as she sipped her cider. "It sure is. It wasn't so long ago that we were sitting in filthy hay. Now look at us on soft chairs in front of a warm, bright fire." She sighed, thinking of all the changes in her life in such a short time.

Mary, too, was quiet, staring at the fire.

At last Katie broke the silence. "When I went to visit James Patrick last, he told me there was to be another hanging. That could have been us they were leading from Newgate. James said there will be three women hanged along with seven men next week. Remember the woman who killed her husband trying to protect her little ones? I suspect she'll be one of them. I wish we could do something for those poor souls."

"Aye, 'tis a sad thing indeed. I 'ad a friend taken' out an' 'anged. Did I tell ya that?"

"Oh, Mary, I'm sorry. When was this?"

"Oh, 'twas a long time now. 'Er name was Rosie Meggens, a good friend 'o mine. Lost 'er man an' two of 'er babes to the fever. She became a Pure-finder after that."

"Pure-finder? What in the world is that?"

"Pickin' up dog turds. She got a few shillings a bucket fer 'em from the tanneries."

"Oh, how awful. What did the tanneries do with it?" Katie asked.

"Rosie told me it were used in makin' the bindin' of fancy leather books. Can ya believe it? Ole Rosie worked 'ard to find them turds. After a while it all got ta her. She took to stealin' an' got caught. They 'anged 'er. Couldn't go an' see 'er 'anged meself. That's when I turned to the streets. 'Ard times hit me, but I weren't going to be no Pure-finder. All stealin' got yas was swingin' from the gallows."

Katie rose from her chair to go over and put her arm around Mary. "Mary, I'm so sorry you lost your friend that way."

"Ya, it be a 'ard thing fer sure, but I wanna ferget it now. That's why I don't go to no hangin'. 'Enry does when 'e can, but I don't go with 'im."

For a while the only sounds were the ticking clock and the crackling fire.

Bang! The front door flew open, startling them. "Blimey, ye scared ten years off me!" Mary shouted at Maggie.

"Sorry, I couldn't grab hold of the door. Wind is picking up."

Katie rose to take some of the packages from her. "Were you able to find what you were looking for?"

"Aye, it took me some time, but it was worth the search," Maggie answered as she removed her cape.

"What yer lookin' fer, Maggie?" Mary asked.

"Never mind with you! I needed a gift for a friend, and you don't need to know more." Maggie spoke with a twinkle in her eye.

Mary crinkled her brow until she understood Maggie was talking about her. Smiling, Mary got up, turning toward the kitchen. "Well, fine. Ol' Mary 'as some secrets of 'er own, ya know."

Katie poured Maggie hot tea. "Come and warm yourself. Mary and I were just talking about our Christmas gathering. Lord and Lady Wilson will be coming. We got a letter from them today."

"Good. Did Mary tell you what we were thinking about serving for dinner?"

"Aye, and it sounds wonderful. I'm really getting excited. It has been a long time since I celebrated Christmas with family," Katie said.

"'Tis true of meself as well," Mary stated as she came back into the room.

"We are going to have a fine Christmas this year," Maggie added. "What are you giving James Patrick?"

"I've crocheted a blanket, a sweater, and more socks for him. He keeps giving his away, and I can't make them fast enough. Mary is going to bake a rum cake, and I'll pack a fine lunch. We'll make it as merry a Christmas as we can."

The women talked into the night, of their plans for the holidays until Katie stood. "Well, I best be off to bed. We have much to do in the next few days, and I want to have an early start tomorrow. Good night."

The other two rose as well, saying their good nights. They all settled in, but sleep wasn't to be for a while. Too much knitting was going on until the wee hours.

After much tossing and turning, Mary sat up from the floor, looking at her bed. *'Tis time ter try out this soft bed.*

Picking up her blankets, she smoothed them on the mattress along with the coverlet. Setting her pillow at the head of the bed, she lowered herself gingerly, as if on a bed of nails. Covering herself up, she lay there stiffly, quickly deciding she was not yet ready. She doubted she would ever get used to a soft mattress. But since it was so cold, and the bed was warming from her body, she decided not to get up right away. She would lie there a little longer before climbing back onto the floor.

But soon she was fast asleep.

14

Christmas Eve

Christmas Eve was here! The cottage smelled of roast lamb, fresh pies, rolls baking, and pine. Mary and Maggie were up early with all the excitement of the day ahead. A fire crackled in each fireplace, helping to warm the cottage with Christmas spirit.

Aromas reached Katie's nose, waking her. Yawning, she rubbed her eyes and stretched. Realizing what day it was, she jumped out of bed, grabbing her robe and slippers. She flew into the main room, where Mary and Maggie already waited for her.

"Merry Christmas Eve!" all shouted at the same time. The three friends sat at the table laughing, eating rolls, and telling of Christmases past.

"Let's open some presents," Katie suggested.

"Ain't ne'er opened presents on Christmas Eve morn," Mary whispered as if they were all about to commit some mortal sin.

"I know, but let's just open one. I can't wait!" Katie laughed after seeing Mary's serious expression. Carrying their cups, they went by the tree and sat down. Katie sat cross-legged on the floor while Mary and Maggie pulled up chairs. "Here's one for you, Mary." Katie laughed as she handed the gift over.

"'Tis been a piece o' time since I got me a present. We were jest happy if'n we 'ad any food on Christmas Day."

Katie nodded in understanding. She watched as Mary opened the box.

"Blimey, 'tis two aprons! None so grand I e'er see! Don't know fer sure if I be wearing 'em. They be too pretty to mess up wearin' cookin' and cleanin'."

"You better wear them, Mary Willow! The head cook at the gaol should look the part."

"'Tis a fine present, Katie girl. Thank ye." Mary blinked as her eyes misted.

"Here, open mine, Mary!" Maggie laughed.

"What? Thought we were to open only one!" Mary beamed, reaching for the gift. She carefully pulled back the paper and sucked in her breath as she stared at a new dress with lace at the collar. "Oh, I ne'er saw such a fine dress as this! Ya made it fer me, did ya, Maggie?"

Maggie nodded as she helped Mary hold it up. "I snuck in yer room and copied the size from one of your dresses hanging there. I hope it fits."

"'Tis a pretty blue color, an' there be lace at me throat! Well, where will I e'er wear it?" Mary questioned.

"Don't forget that we're invited to several Christmas celebrations. I was going to ask you both to go to Chapel with me tonight," Katie asked.

"Blimey, Katie girl, 'tis you that people was invitin' to Christmas. Not ol' Mary."

"No, the invitations were for all of us, and I won't go if you don't."

"Then best we all go. Don't want ta ruin yer fine Christmas by keepin' ya at 'ome." Mary laughed. "I be thankin' ya, Maggie, fer the fine blue dress. I ne'er 'ad such a dress in me life! I want yas to open me gifts. Such fine gifts as these they are not, but I 'ope yas like 'em anyway."

After both women assured Mary that her gifts were special to them, they began unwrapping. Katie received a beautiful linen hanky with her initials embroidered on it. For Maggie, there was a knitted hat that would keep away the winter cold. They were both thrilled.

"Now open your gift from me, Maggie," Katie said as she handed it to her.

"Oh, 'tis lovely. It's going to look beautiful on my bed. So much work you've done on it. Now I know what Mary means about not wanting to wear those pretty aprons. I'm tempted to hang this coverlet on the wall instead of putting it on my bed. Now ain't that silly. Can you imagine anyone hanging their bed coverlet on the wall? Thank ya, Katie. Now open my gift to you."

Katie opened the package to find a soft nightgown with matching robe. Maggie was pleased when Katie stood, holding it up. She twirled around the room several times. After thanking each other once more, the women sat before the fire, drank their warm drinks, and talked.

"Well, so much for self-control. Who said we had to wait to open gifts on Christmas Day anyway?" Katie smiled.

"You did!" came the answer at the same time. All laughed.

"'Tis it time now?" Mary asked Maggie.

"Time for what?" Katie inquired.

"One more gift to be opened," Maggie answered. She nodded to Mary. "'Tis a gift from your husband."

Katie sat up straighter in her chair, setting her drink down. She watched Mary as she went into her room. After pulling the small package from its hiding place, Mary came back and laid it in Katie's lap. Katie sat staring at it for several moments.

"Blimey, Katie girl, ain't goin' to open itself!"

Katie gently lifted the small package and began tearing away the paper. She uncovered a small box. There was a note attached. Katie opened the note first.

Dear Katie,
   Merry Christmas! I know we can't spend it together, but please know that you

are in my heart as you read this. You will always be in my heart. I want everyone to know that you are my lovely wife, and so I give this ring with all my love.
   James

Katie's hands trembled as she slowly opened the box. There, wrapped in purple velvet, was a small gold band. The firelight danced off of it. "Oh my, oh my," was all she could say.

Maggie and Mary giggled with pleasure as they watched her. "Ain't ya goin' ta put it on, Katie?" Mary asked.

Katie nodded, never taking her eyes off the ring. Holding her hand out, she pushed it on her ring finger. She stared at her hand, flexing her finger. Without warning, she burst into tears.

The two women rushed over to Katie. Not quite knowing what to do, Mary grabbed the hanky she had made for Katie and handed it to her. Maggie just stood shifting her weight from one foot to the other. Mary patted Katie on the back, cooing as if comforting a babe.

Before too long Katie sniffed, wiped her eyes, and blew her nose. "How in the world did he ever get a ring for me? How did he know it would fit? Did you two have something to do with this?"

Smiling, both nodded. "Aye, but Lady Wilson was part of it too," Maggie stated.

"'Twas surprised were ya now, Katie?" Mary laughed.

"*Surprised* isn't the word for it. Isn't it beautiful?" Katie held her hand up to examine the ring once more. "Thank you for this!"

"No need to thank us. James would have done it himself if he was able. We just did his footwork for him," Maggie replied.

"'Tis the truth, Katie girl. 'Twas the first time I e'er be in a fancy store fer such things. Ne'er been in a shop jest for baubles. Didn't know there be such a thing. Should 'ave seen the sparklers. Ne'er saw anythin' like it! Why, there be jewels the size of me big toe, an' some bigger still!"

Maggie stared at Mary as if she had grown another head. "Calm down, Mary. You're starting to sweat; it was only a store. Katie, I wish you could have seen her in there. I almost had to tie her down for all the commotion she was making."

"Hey, 'twas all new ta me. Just lookin' I was," Mary teased back.

"Where in the world did he get the money to pay for it?" Katie mused out loud.

"Don't e'er ask a man such a question. His pride will bruise for it," Maggie warned.

"'Tis truth she speaks," Mary added. "A man's pride is somethin' fearful. If'n ya wants to be knowin', ask Lady Wilson and not James."

"Oh, Mary! I dirtied the beautiful hanky you gave me already."

"'Tis a grand thing when it be used fer tears o' joy, an' not sorrow. A grand thing indeed."

The women spent the rest of the morning talking, laughing, and enjoying their time together. It went by fast, and before too long it was time to get ready for their visitors. They set the table with their finest dishes, making sure all was in order. Soon the Wilsons' carriage pulled up.

Katie ran to open the door, catching sight of the footman struggling with many gifts. "Goodness, what is all this? It looks like you bought out the stores."

Lady Wilson hugged Katie. "Don't say that. Edward always says I overdo it, but I can't help myself. It's my favorite holiday. I love to shop."

Lord Wilson patted his wife's hand. "I've given up trying to hold you back, my dear. We've been together long enough for me to know that I've lost the battle. I surrender."

They had a grand day. The dinner turned out wonderfully. Maggie, along with Mary, beamed with pleasure at all the compliments given them. Gifts were exchanged along with laughter and a few tears of joy.

Lady Wilson gasped as she opened the shawl Katie gave her. "It truly is beautiful, dear. It really belonged to your mother, and you want me to have it? I feel honored that you would give me such a wonderful gift. Edward will treasure your father's watch, won't you, dear?"

"I certainly will. Your father meant a great deal to me. He was more than a worker to me. He was my friend. Thank you, Katie, for such a heartfelt gift. I don't think anyone, except my dear wife, has ever lavished on me such a thoughtful gift."

Katie, Mary, and Maggie were heaped with gifts from the Wilsons. Katie noticed that all the gifts for her were practical things. She was given warm clothing, blankets, bedding, and such. One thing stood out for Katie—a beautiful picture with their sweet faces smiling at her. The frame was exquisite. She would treasure it forever.

"I see you received a very special gift from your husband," Lady Wilson said.

"Isn't it beautiful? I was so surprised to get it. I know you had a lot to do with my receiving it. Thank you both for all you've done, and for your love and support."

Mary broke in. "If ya ever need to shop in one of them fancy sparkler stores again, Lady Wilson, jest let me know. Ol' Mary will be happy ta help."

Katie turned toward Lady Wilson. "How is it going with your Christmas ball?"

"Fine, just fine. I haven't had a chance to tell you that it's more an engagement party for Tess than a Christmas ball."

Katie flinched at the mention of Tess. Her stomach flip-flopped, but she held her composure. "Oh, how interesting," was all she could say.

"Yes, what a shock it was for me when Edward and Tess told me about her engagement. I used to think a mother was the first to know, but I guess they wanted to surprise me. They certainly did. David, Tess's fiancé, and his father arrived a few days ago. We've had a splendid time getting to know each other."

Katie only acknowledged with a nod.

Lady Wilson shared some of her plans for the party, which was to be held the night after Christmas. "We have wreaths hanging in every window, and next to the orchestra will stand a fifteen-foot tree."

Mary exclaimed. "A fifteen-footer? Yas can be fittin' such a tree in your room?"

"Yes, it happened to be a Christmas surprise. David had it shipped in, and it arrived the same day as they did. He talked to Edward and planned to surprise Tess and myself with it. It is breathtaking! I wondered why Edward fought me so when I wanted to get a tree ready for their arrival. Now I know. David is such a thoughtful young man. He and his father have some relatives here in London, and they wanted to spend the day with them. It worked out so nice since that gave us a chance to be here with all of you. Tess went with them. They seemed so happy. I've asked Tess how she met him, and how they could have had a courtship without me knowing about it. She just laughs, saying she'll explain later. I'll never know how she kept this from me. Between being surprised with the engagement and the tree, I wonder how many more secrets my husband is keeping from me." Lady Wilson laughed. "But it's a dream-come-true for Tess to at last be engaged," she admitted.

Her husband cleared his throat, taking a drink offered him, and eyed Katie.

Soon it was time for church. Mary flounced about, showing off her new dress. Everyone oooed and aaahed, making her feel special. Maggie wore the hat Mary had crocheted for her.

They all loaded up in the carriage and were off. The team of horses wore sleigh bells, although they pulled a coach instead of a sleigh. Still, it added to the magic of Christmas. The cathedral was filled to capacity, but Lord and Lady Wilson led the others to their private booth. The music filled the ornately built structure with beauty and the feeling of goodwill. Mary couldn't keep the wonder of the place to herself. Pointing and declaring appreciation at the sight of the statues and stained-glass windows, she caused many a smile. As Katie looked around, she sadly thought of those who didn't have a warm cottage, food to fill their bellies, or family. Guilt tugged at her. No, she would not feel guilty but would enjoy her Christmas. It could be the only one she would ever spend with these dear ones.

The music spilled out of the cathedral onto the streets, where two children stood and listened. They had stopped picking up loose coal that had fallen from the wagon that was heading down the street.

"Listen ter that, Sadie! Sounds like angels singin'!" the young boy said to his smaller sister.

"Real angels? Do you think so, Tommy? What a wondrous thing it would be to hear angels sing!"

The two began running after the coal wagon once more. "Mum will be 'appy fer sure with all the coal we got! She be cookin' up a fine hen fer dinner. What a Christmas we will 'ave. Let's go home."

And the two skipped off with their wealth of coal and hearts full of all that Christmas held.

Finally, the day of the ball had arrived. Only three days after Christmas, it was an exciting time for all. Tess stood gazing at her image in the mirror. The gown she wore was a beautiful emerald green with puffy sleeves. Filmy red material was ornately tucked in at the bodice. Her hair was pulled back with curls cascading down her back. Holly sprigs were pinned amongst the curls. She knew she looked beautiful. She tried to think of the evening ahead, but her mind kept drifting to Peter. He would be there tonight, since he had responded to her personal invitation. The guests did not know it was going to be an engagement party, including him. She was afraid to tell him, afraid he wouldn't come if he knew. The announcement would come during dinner.

Looking out her window, she watched as carriages of all shapes and sizes pulled onto their road. Tess tried to ignore the nagging feeling of fear in the pit of her stomach. Of late she had enjoyed her fiancé, his father, and the new attitude her parents had toward her. They treated her like a mature adult instead of a child.

Her feelings toward Peter had also begun to change as of late. He wasn't as attentive as he had been. She wanted to see his reaction to the news of her engagement. Would he get angry or be relieved? Would there be a confrontation between Peter, David, or her father? If so, she knew her parents would be mortified. Still, it would be interesting to watch his reaction. Secretly she wanted men to quarrel over her in front of all the guests. It would serve some of those snooty women right. She smiled to herself. She would be the talk of the season.

Tess turned as her mother knocked on her door. "Oh, Tess, you look beautiful! Isn't this the most exciting Christmas we've ever had? Everything is happening so fast! Since David has been here, I can see how much he truly cares for you. Oh, honey, you look gorgeous!" she repeated. Lady Wilson was simply gushing with excitement.

The young woman smiled at her mother, saying nothing. Tess was struggling with her feelings. She felt trepidation about her upcoming marriage mixed with some degree of excitement. Then there was the shame she felt, knowing her father knew about her liaisons with Peter. She was angry with him for his interference and for how easily he cast her off on to another man.

Lady Wilson went on. "You seem happy with David. What do you think of his father? He seems honorable and pleasant. He is taken with you, but how could he not be? Look at what a beautiful daughter-in-law he is getting. Just think, Tess, by next

Christmas I could be a grandmother! What a wonderful present that would be! We should go downstairs. David is waiting for you, and our guests have been arriving."

"I'll be down shortly, Mother." Tess kissed her mother's cheek. Once alone, again she sat in front of the fireplace trying to compose herself. That was just like her mother. To make her feel pressured to have a child right away. She was trapped into this and didn't like it. But she had no choice. Peter never promised her anything. Then there was his wife. Tess heard the woman could be ruthless. She didn't want to explain to Victoria why she was taking up a lot of her husband's time of late.

David was very handsome and seemed kind. He was also intelligent. She remembered their first meeting when she was much younger. It was at the theater. She remembered flirting with him, but he hardly took notice of her. She was as surprised as anyone that he had made a bid for her hand.

A horrifying thought surfaced. Did her father offer David money to marry her? Tess's face burned with humiliation. *How can I ever face David again if my father has paid him?* She had to know the truth. She would not start a marriage like this, even if it meant losing her father's support. She pulled the cord to summon her maid.

When Betsy knocked, Tess drew her in. "Go downstairs and tell my father I need to speak to him right away. Tell him it's very important, and hurry!"

Soon her father knocked. "Tess?"

Tess opened her door to let him in. "I need to know one thing, Father, before I go through with this. Did you pay David to marry me? Did you tell him I had to get married, and then offer him money?"

Wrapping his arms around her, he held her close. "Oh, Tess, don't you know that I have done this because of my concern for you?"

"And Mother," she simply stated.

"Yes, that's true, but I do love you, and I have been gravely worried about you. The answer to your question is no. I did not bribe him into it. I had a business meeting with his father, and he mentioned that David had asked about you. He said his son was seeking out a suitable wife and had been struck by your beauty, good humor, and family. I lied and told him you had mentioned his son from time to time as well. One thing led to another, and here we are. I'm sorry I had to do this against your wishes. I would not have embarrassed you by paying someone to take you. You are a worthy wife. David is honored that you have consented. He believes this is all his idea. Of course he doesn't know it was me who consented for you. Tess, this is an extraordinary chance for you to be happy in the way God meant women to be…married and, hopefully, a mother. People have been arranging marriages since the dawn of time. You know my marriage with your mother was arranged, and look how much we love each other. You need to give it a chance. By the way, you look lovely."

Tess could hear her father's heart beating as she kept her head on his chest. "I thought you didn't love me anymore."

Gently pushing her away from his chest, he looked down at his only child. "How could I not love you? You are my daughter. Besides, I can only stay angry with you for a short time. You must understand what a great marriage you are entering into. David is a young suitable man with a good family name…and money. Most women would give anything for a marriage such as this. Please promise me you will work hard to make this marriage work. Will you make me proud?"

Tess felt irritation at her father's words. This wasn't about him. It was about her life, but she knew she was stuck. Why alienate him from her by getting angry? Instead of expressing her true feelings, she looked up, trying to give her most innocent gaze. With a pout she nodded. "Yes, Father, I will work hard and make you proud."

Lord Wilson beamed down at her. "Come now, Tess. Let's greet your guests who have already begun to arrive."

Tess held tightly to her father's arm as she descended the staircase. Holding her head high, she made quite the entrance. She only hesitated for a second when she saw David and Peter standing together at the bottom of the staircase…waiting for her.

It was Katie's second visit to her husband after the holidays. James held his wife tenderly. As they embraced, he prayed silently, *Thank You, Father, for Katie. Bless her, and help me to be the kind of husband You want me to be. Amen.*

"So, have you given your Christmas presents away yet?" Katie teased.

Smiling, James shook his head. "I couldn't after all the hard work you put into them. I've been enjoying them myself."

Katie giggled. "I still can't believe you got me a ring. I'll have to remember that you are quite the schemer." She laughed.

"So, are you still meeting with the women's group? What dragons are they fighting now?" James asked.

"Aye, and don't tease about it, James. We have done much to help prisoners in various gaols. It's important what we do. Especially to you, who are still locked in this place. You know Newgate and Kirkdale are the worse prisons, but the others are not much better. Think of those who don't have families to comfort them, or bring them extra food and clothes."

"Scolding me, are ya? Don't forget that I know exactly how it feels to be alone as you do. I thank God every day for you, and the blessings He gives. I don't take your work for the prisoners for granted one bit."

Katie relaxed. "I'm sorry, James. I guess I have been fighting so long for the prisoners and arguing against the wrongs done them that I get a bit touchy when talking about it."

Smiling, James told his wife how happy he was to have her on his side. "I wouldn't want you against me, Katie Murphy."

Katie went on to tell of the blankets and Bibles that her group had passed out. "We have been able to successfully argue for better conditions on the prison ships. The prisoners are getting more exercise time and surgeons to help with their ailments. Now we're working on getting them more blankets and food. More matrons are needed for the women as well. Most of them are attacked within days of arriving. With matrons on board, it keeps everyone in their place, if you know what I mean. We don't have time to rejoice in our winning small battles. There is so much more needed. "

James nodded in understanding, then turned the subject. "I believe when spring comes, we will sail out. I could be wrong, but I know a man on one of the harbor crews who knows they like to pull out in spring."

It was Katie's turn to nod in agreement. "Aye, I think you may be right. When I think about it, I get such mixed feelings. I think I'll have myself worked up into a tizzy when the time comes to set sail."

Like so many times before, they made small talk, got to know each other better, and became closer. In one way this time was different, for they began to share together the importance of God in their lives. They laughed, held hands, and shyly kissed good-bye. As always, Katie walked out alone. Loneliness covered them both each time they had to separate, but they were thankful for having each other. They knew it wouldn't be long before they could be together…in every way.

Yes, a time of change was coming for them.

15

Changes

Lord Wilson leaned back in his chair and smoked his cigar, content to listen to the four men telling of the prison hulks. Grimes was there as well. Lord Wilson wanted to hear more. If he was to help, he would need more information. Some of what they said he already knew from the men who had talked to Katie, but some information was new. But he didn't like the fact that they were in his office, where his dear wife could come knocking at his door at any moment. There was much of what was being said that he didn't want her to overhear.

"The hulks are necessary, Lord Wilson. What with the war ending and the population doubling, crime increases. There's been an increase in transports over the last five years with no end in sight," a man named Trace informed the others. "I can tell you stories well into the night about when I was quartermaster on the *Liberty*. Fine name for a prison hulk, wouldn't you say? *Liberty*, ha!"

Lord Wilson detested this brass braggart of a man, but he had a wealth of knowledge when it came to this subject. Lord Wilson told Grimes to find him a man who lived in the thick of it, and he did.

Trace went on, "These people aren't any better than dogs on the streets, maggots one and all. If they make it alive, fine. If not, there are more to replace them."

Brice interrupted, "It has gotten much better than it was, but it's still a hard journey for sure. Takes from four to six months before dropping anchor off of New South Wales. Most of the prisoners are half dead before they even leave Langston, Portsmouth, Deptford, or Woolwich Harbor. Don't make any difference what hulk they're on, they are all treated pretty much the same. If the lot is lucky, they'll work ten hours a day on the docks while they wait to sail. If they aren't lucky, they are left on board chained up, starved, beaten, and sick of heart and body."

"What do you expect? You think we should pat them on the wrists, and feed them good beef? It be best for everyone to be rid of them. They deserve to be punished. That is my job," Trace bragged.

"And I hear you do it well." Grayson narrowed his eyes at the man.

"I assure you, sir, I do the job I'm hired for. After a week in that hell's pot, you'd not fair any different."

Lord Wilson jumped in before an argument erupted. "What about the families left behind? Can they be transported with their husbands or wives?"

"Not often," came the answer from Brice. "There have been thousands of letters written by families. They often ask to sail along with their mates, but unless they have a ticket-of-leave, chances are they stay behind."

"What's a ticket-of-leave?"

"It would show that the convict could somehow support his family once transported. If a person had money to do that, he probably wouldn't be in a gaol in the first place. Usually it's all they can do to survive, let alone bring a wife and brats in tow. Sometimes letters are written, beseeching the authorities on behalf of the convict. If funds follow, they may let the family go then, but that is a rare thing indeed. Once in a while a husband and wife are convicted together and transported out, but not always to the same place. The brats are shipped out with the mothers, though. We have no need to keep them. The foundling homes bulge now."

"And it only gets worse," replied Grayson. "Any time a new prisoner comes on board one of the hulks, the 'old-timers' steal from him. They take whatever is of value after one of the marines attaches a fourteen-pound iron to his right ankle. They aren't likely to try to swim away with that on their leg. Once the irons are removed, their legs jerk up uncontrollably when the prisoner tries to walk. It depends on how long the iron is left on. It takes a long time to get over that, if they ever do."

"Tell me about the food on these prison ships. Why did you say they were starved?" Lord Wilson asked, sitting forward.

It was Knotts' turn to share his knowledge. "The Naval agent assigned to the transports mostly determines whether prisoners see the food they're supposed to get. They're usually issued an 'institutional pound' of raw meat but..."

"Institutional pound? What's that?"

"About fourteen ounces, but before the prisoners get it, it gets picked off. The agents, cooks, inspectors, and boat crew help themselves first. They're lucky to get six ounces. Salt horse is a staple. It's brined beef. Then they usually get rice, plum pudding with suet, pork with peas, and the like. Of course, scurvy was a problem a while back, but they have a handle on it now. At times they are given small beer, a brewery byproduct. Ale and real beer are never allowed. Poorly filtered river water caused dysentery and typhus, but there aren't as many outbreaks now that the cause has been discovered."

"That's exaggerated," Trace quipped. "You sound like you favor the convicts over authority."

"Just stating the truth as I found it to be," Knotts said.

"What about the trip itself? How bad is it?" was Lord Wilson's next question.

"It's a hardship for sure. Hard for the captain, crew, and their families that go, but hell for the prisoners. They're chained below; don't see the light of day sometimes through the whole voyage. Sick and laying in their puke. They get bloated and suffer starvation. If the bloke next to you kicks, you hope nobody finds out until the body begins to swell and stink. That way you can have his ration of slop along with your own. It's bad. You sail from Portsmouth to the Canary Islands, where you pick up supplies and water. Then to the Cape Verde Islands. After that it's the long haul to Rio de Janeiro, then Cape Town, which is 3,300 miles itself. From there you travel 6,500 miles to Botany Bay. Once there, it's a whole different story. Surviving there in the past made the trip look like an outing on the pond, but things are better, like I said."

Throughout the afternoon the men shared what they knew. Much of it was not encouraging. The conditions weren't as bad as in the past but were far from good. There had been vast numbers of prisoners lost on the prison hulks and on the journey. Even though all the information shared by Trace was one-sided, he did give some insight to the horror faced by the poor, wretched souls.

All this tragic talk was taking its toll on Lord Wilson. Certainly he had seen the poor on the streets his whole life—the beggars, prostitutes, orphans—but he never gave them any serious consideration. They were a part of the scenery, castoffs of society who were given as little notice as possible. At Christmas time he would give to the workhouses and hospitals...enough to ease his conscience for another year.

Lord Wilson abruptly stood. "Gentlemen, I just realized the time. I fear I need to end this. Thank you for coming to share your insights and knowledge."

After everyone but the detective had left, Lord Wilson sat back in his chair. "Grimes, how can I allow Mrs. Murphy to go on such a terrible voyage? How would she ever survive? I never realized the horror going on outside my door."

"How could you, sir? If something hasn't touched your life, then how would you know of it?"

"I don't think that's any excuse. How will I ever be able to, in good conscience, allow Mrs. Murphy to walk innocently into such a horrible situation? She's going because her husband is being transported, and she's only married to him because she was forced to. It was my daughter who lied having her locked up. Tell me I'm not responsible. And yet aren't we responsible even if we don't know these people? Who is responsible for those who can't help themselves? Do you really want to live in a world where no one looks out for anybody but themselves? What hope is there then?"

Grimes was surprised by his employer's words. Wilson was a shrewd businessman, a caring family man, but not given to sentiment. For him to show such emotion meant he must have been touched deeply by what he had heard. Nonetheless, this conversation was becoming a little uncomfortable for Grimes.

"Get me a list of the prison ships and all of the prisoners' names," Lord Wilson ordered, "then find out what transports are listed to leave for Botany Bay. When you've done that, get me the names of the captains, and who they are contracted with to sail. I want to know if they are private or government contracted. I want to know everything about these men. How many times they've sailed, their past records, what their crews think of them. That's important, you know, and if they are family men. Give me the names of any agencies that help these prisoners and their families. Please do this as soon as possible. I'll write the governor of Botany Bay, letting him know that I am interested in helping the colonies over there. I'll tell him that I realize there is much to do, so I'll ask him to prioritize the needs. I need to be realistic. Perhaps there is some good that can come out of all this."

Grimes thought about the gargantuan task setting before him, but also about the money he was about to make. One thing was sure: Wilson kept him busy, and in money. He extended his hand to the older man as he got up to leave. "You've got it. I'll contact you as soon as I have any information."

After Grimes left, Lord Wilson needed to decide how much he would tell his wife. Protecting her from the truth was tricky at times, but necessary. He would have her help him plan what they could do for the prisoners. She would need something to occupy her time after Tess was married. He didn't feel any better even after making his decision to help others. He had a nagging feeling as if someone was pointing a finger at him, blaming him for all the misery in the world. He decided he would give a lot of time and money to his new cause. That would ease any guilt he may have for not acting sooner to help others. He knew it would. It had eased his guilt before…many times.

"We're leaving, Katie. We're leaving soon," Red told his wife.

Katie's heart skipped at his words. "Are you sure, James? Lord Wilson didn't tell me anything."

"I got the news from Flores. He's one of the gaolers here. He was on the docks the day before last. The ships are here and being loaded up with provisions."

"But are you sure one of them is our ship?"

"Best as I can tell, yes. We've been waiting all winter long. Now a fleet has arrived and anchored in. Why wouldn't it be for us?"

Katie was torn between excitement and dread. They had waited for so long that she often forgot they would be leaving at all.

"Flores also said there are two naval vessels set to sail with the transports," James added. "He said they are fine-looking ships, sturdy too. He is going to try to find out if we're being shipped out. He said he would let me know by tomorrow, if possible."

"James, I'm afraid. Knowing we would leave at some point in the future is so much different than knowing we're going to be leaving soon."

"I know, Katie, but God knows all about it. He is our refuge and strength. We need to put our trust in him. Remember what I told you? Jeremiah 29:11 says, 'For I know the thoughts that I think toward you,' saith the Lord. 'Thoughts of peace, and not of evil, to give you an expected end.' As long as we trust Him, whatever happens to us will be for our good."

"James, you know I believe in God, but I've never felt the assurance you talk about. Many of the other women in my women's group have that same assurance, but I'm not sure how to get it."

"Katie, I've told you that you only need to accept Jesus Christ as your Savior. Confess that you are a sinner; that only through Him is there hope for our salvation. We've talked about this many times."

"Yes, I know, James, but I don't feel any different."

"Feelings have nothing to do with salvation, Katie. Do you believe that Jesus Christ is the Son of God and that He died on the cross for you? Do you believe He rose again and lives?"

"I guess so."

"Pray, Katie, that He will reveal himself to you. I cannot convince you, and your friends cannot talk you into salvation. It has to be between you and the Lord. He loves you so much that He died for you, so I know if you ask Him to reveal himself to you in a very real way, He will."

"All right, James. I'll start to pray that He speaks to me, and that I will know it is Him."

Soon it was time for Katie to once again leave her husband behind. Before heading home, there was one more stop to make. Katie instructed her driver to go to the cathedral. As she stepped through the door, the quietness of the place wrapped itself around her. It was nothing like Christmas, when it had been filled with people singing. The echo of her steps vibrated off the walls.

Easing into one of the pews, Katie knelt, then bent her head in prayer.

Lord, I've been talking to You more and more, but I don't feel like You are there or that You hear me. James says I can't go on feelings, but I need to know You are there. I never felt close to You like Gran and James. I want to, but I don't. James said I should ask You to reveal Yourself to me. Part of me is afraid You won't, and part of me is afraid You will. I'm afraid, Lord. Afraid of the unknown, afraid of my future in the far-away place, and afraid of You. How can You love me enough to have died for me? Everyone says You love me, but Lord, I want You to tell me that. If You are real, and I do believe You are, then tell me yourself that You love me. I need to know. I need to hear. I need You. I know I'm a sinner, and only You can save me. Please, Lord.

Before Katie could lift her head, a comforting sensation ran from the top of her head to her feet, as if warm oil was being poured over her. Every fiber of her being knew, really knew that God loved her. He loved her! He knew her, and loved her! Katie couldn't move. The beating of her heart sounded in her ears. She took a deep breath when she realized she had been holding it. Katie started to laugh and cry at the same time. Her heart spilled over with joy.

A man standing off to the side stared at her. By his robes she could tell he was a priest. Wiping her eyes, she smiled at him.

Uncertainty crossed his face, but he stepped closer to her. "Are you all right, miss?"

Katie laughed again. "Oh, yes, yes, I'm fine! I was praying, asking God to tell me if He really loved me, and He did! He did! He loves me! Isn't that amazing?"

The priest nodded in bewilderment while backing up a little. "Yes, He does love us. He loves us all."

"I know, but He told me himself! He loves me!" Laughing again, Katie couldn't help but jump around in her excitement.

The priest stepped back even further.

After a few moments, Katie turned to pick up her cloak. She needed to go home to tell Mary and Maggie. They had to know, to find out the truth. He loved them too, and she needed to tell them. "Thank you, Father," Katie called back to the priest as she ran down the aisle. "Thank you so much!"

The priest scratched his head, wondering whether it was rum or if the Lord truly did speak to the young woman. He decided it must be rum for he was a priest, and God never told him. He knew God loved him, but still he wondered why he never felt the excitement of it as the woman did. *Surely must be the drink*. He turned back toward the altar. He had work to do.

Tess yawned, stretching out her long legs. It was late morning, time to get up. She rang for the maid. Once she arrived, Tess instructed her to ready a bath and bring breakfast. She then set about the most arduous task of the day, picking out what she would wear. Once she finished eating, she stepped into the hot tub, sank back, and let her mind wander. Of late she found herself thinking more and more of her husband-to-be instead of Peter.

She smiled as she remembered back to her engagement party, and the moment she was descending the staircase with her father. Her eyes had found Peter and David standing next to each other. Peter had stepped forward to claim her hand from her father's, but David cut him off, taking it instead. Peter looked at him with surprise and at her with question. She had liked David's aggressiveness in claiming her hand. It was her father who had stepped in, guiding Peter away from them. She was curious as to what her father had said to Peter, for shortly afterwards he left the ball.

What an enchanting evening it was in that beautiful setting. She had been the center of attention, having David hang on her every word. She could tell he did his best to please her. She had seen envy on many of the young women's faces, but best of all was the way her parents acted. They were so puffed up with pride, her father strutting around like a Banty rooster. Her mother seemed like a young girl herself. She laughed and danced the evening away.

Tess let a giggle escape as she remembered the stolen kiss she shared with David out in the garden. He was so charming and handsome. She hadn't felt this happy in a long time. It was almost like her very first love. Could it possibly be that she was falling in love with him? It had been a long time since she felt like this.

Tess was jarred out of her daydream by a knock at her door. "Who is it?"

"'Tis Betsy, miss. I 'ave a letter for ya."

"Bring it to me, then hurry and fetch me that towel. I may as well get out since you're here to help me."

"Aye, miss."

Sitting by the fireplace in her warmest robe and slippers, Tess ordered Betsy to get her fresh tea. After Betsy left, she started to read but stopped to see who signed it. In delicate script, Kathryn Brady Murphy appeared at the bottom of the page. She stared at the signature, trying to figure out who the name belonged to. It escaped her for the moment.

When it finally dawned on Tess who Kathryn Brady was, she was dumbstruck. *Why in the world would she write a letter to me? Why is her last name Murphy now? Don't tell me she got married!*

Tess knew nothing that had happened to the servant girl except she had been released from prison. Tess knew her parents had something to do with it. She knew she was being punished when she was sent off to her Aunt Marilyn's. Everyone, including Tess, was very careful not to mention the Brady girl's name. She turned the letter over and began reading.

Dear Miss Wilson,

    I'm sure you are surprised to hear from me, but I feel that I must write to you. I would like to meet with you. There is something important I need to speak to you about. I could come there, or we could meet somewhere else if you wish.

    Please say that you will come. I feel it would benefit us both if we spoke together.

    Sincerely, Kathryn Brady Murphy

Tess's first instinct was to tear the letter up, but something held her back. She re-

read it several times. *Why would she want to talk to me now? So much time has passed since she was in prison. Does she still hold me responsible? Is she out for revenge? Wouldn't she have done something before now?*

Tess rang for Betsy. "Who brought this letter?"

"It came by coach, miss."

"Do you know where to send a response?"

"I was told by Graines that he was given instructions on where to take any reply."

"Then go down to the kitchen and ask the butler what instructions he was given. Come back and tell me."

"Aye, miss."

Tess felt impatient waiting for the maid's return. Soon Betsy came back with the answer. "Graines said he was told to either have a reply mailed or brought to 750 Courtney Road here in London."

"Stay here while I write a response, then take it to Graines." Tess quickly penned a note, sealed it, and handed it to Betsy. "Give it to Graines, and be sure he has it taken to that address immediately! Come back to help me dress afterwards."

"Aye miss."

Kathryn read the note that had just arrived.

I received your letter and must say that you were right: I was very surprised to hear from you. You have aroused my curiosity, so I will meet you at the Hill Café for tea on Grignon Street. I'll be there tomorrow at noon. If that doesn't work out for you, please reply. Otherwise I will see you then.

Tess Wilson

So there it was. She would finally see Tess, the black princess. Katie's heart raced. She still wasn't sure what she would say to her when she saw her. The last few weeks had been a blur of joy and blessings. She'd never felt such happiness. It was a freedom she'd not experienced previously. She felt like she had been drowning, and a strong hand lifted her out of the water. Except she didn't know she was drowning.

She'd made several attempts in the past week to explain how she felt to Mary and Maggie. Poor Mary just watched her closely as if she had lost her mind. Katie shared what had happened in the cathedral with them. They said they understood, but how could they? She still didn't understand it all herself.

The most wonderful thing of all was seeing James the next day and telling him. He laughed and cried with her. She knew that he truly understood. He shared how he felt when he realized that God loved him, and forgave his sins. They rejoiced together; then

James prayed a thankful prayer for his "new" wife.

The only thing that hindered her happiness was the knowledge that God wanted her to forgive Tess. She wasn't even sure when God had laid it on her heart, but He had. Oh, how she struggled with that. She felt angry, for her newfound joy was tainted now with the knowledge of what was required of her. A spiritual battle raged on within her soul one night. Alone in her bedchamber, the Lord gently spoke to her. She knew what she had to do but simply couldn't or didn't want to.

How can You ask me this, Lord? Katie prayed. *You know all she did to me. She lied and had me imprisoned. She treated me worse than dirt when I only tried to serve her well. She talked awful about Papa and Gran. She teased me about who I was, and where I came from. Every chance she got she made my life miserable. But that wasn't enough for her! She had to steal those years away from me when I was locked up!* She repeated her prayer. *Lord, how can You ask me to do this?*

Hour upon hour she wrestled in prayer. She decided to give up and went to lie down. She wasn't going to forgive Tess; she couldn't. God must understand that. She was miserable tossing and turning throughout the night. Getting up, she stoked the fire, then picked up her new Bible. Opening it, she read a few verses. They didn't mean anything to her. She had a hard time understanding some of what she read. She laid her head back on her chair.

Everything was fine, Lord, until You asked me to forgive Tess. You must know I simply can't. I don't want to. I hate her. She's evil and mean. I don't plan on revenge; isn't that enough?

Nothing…only silence.

How come I heard You speak to my heart to forgive Tess just fine, but I can't hear You now? I need You!

Katie fought hard for *her* will to be done. The hatred she felt for Tess was entangled around her very soul, and she wouldn't let it go. It was all impossible. She could never…no, she didn't want to forgive her. She didn't want the Lord to forgive Tess either. The Lord was hers and not Tess's. Katie began to cry in frustration.

The battle of wills continued on through the night, lasting until the early morning hours. A fight for her very soul was fought that night. Yes, she had accepted Jesus Christ as her Savior, but there was more required of her. Her hate for Tess had no room in her heart now that He abided within it.

Katie felt compelled to open her Bible once more. She began to read Matthew 5:44: "But I say unto you; love your enemies, bless those who curse you, do good to them that hate you, and pray for them which despitefully use you, and persecute you." Her eyes then fell on Matthew 6:14: "If ye forgive men their trespasses, your heavenly Father will also forgive you." Katie flipped back to Proverbs 16:7: "When a man's ways please the Lord, he maketh even his enemies to be at peace with him."

Katie knew the Lord was speaking to her through His Word. She knew He was instructing her. Eagerly she continued reading even though she was not familiar with her Bible. She knew He was leading her on to His Truth. She read of the account of Jesus' trial and crucifixion. Who knew better than He of being unjustly and cruelly treated? She then turned to the book of John.

John 15:10: "If ye keep my commandments, ye shall abide in my love; even as I have kept my Father's commandments, and abide in his love."

John 14:21: "He that hath my commandments, and keepth them, he it is that loveth me and he that loveth me shall be loved by my Father, and I will love him, and will manifest myself to him."

Katie read on and on. Scriptures seemed to jump out at her, and she drank deeply of the Living Water. The hatred she held in her heart seemed to melt away, and she made her choice. Just like the choices Gran had told her about, she made the choice to obey, to allow Jesus to cleanse her from all unrighteousness. It was as if she could float. She never realized how her hatred of Tess had weighed her down. As she rejoiced in her newfound freedom, she heard a soft whisper inside her heart: *Go and tell of your love for her…and Mine.*

Lord, You want me to tell her I love her? Isn't it enough I forgave her? You see my heart! You know I have forgiven her. Isn't it enough?

"Go."

I'm afraid! What will she say? What will I say? She'll probably laugh at me!

Hebrews 13:6: "So that we may boldly say, The Lord is my helper, and I will not fear what man shall do unto me."

Again and again her eyes fell on His promises. "Fear is not of the Lord….I will never leave nor forsake you." With great joy, Katie finally relented. *Okay, okay…I get it. Thank You for loving me, and speaking to me. I will trust You, Lord.*

Exhausted but full of joy, Katie went to lie down. She was awestruck. Almighty God, Creator of heaven and earth had just spoken to her…to her! He knew *her* name, and He loved *her!* A tear of gratitude slipped down her cheek as she slipped into slumber.

A couple of times Tess had almost changed her mind. Why should she meet with Brady? She didn't owe anything to this girl. Why should she even bother? But her curiosity got the better of her. That's why Tess arrived at the café early. She would have the advantage if she were the first one there. Requesting a table by the large window, she watched for the girl. Sipping her tea, she saw a carriage pull up. The driver helped a young woman as she stepped down from the coach. Tess did a double-take leaning closer to the window. *Is that really her? Where did she get such a fine rig and horses?* The young woman carried herself with ease and grace. Gone was the scrawny girl with the big doe eyes. Jealousy gripped Tess as two gentlemen tipped their hats and held the door for her.

Katie looked around the crowded room until she saw Tess. Smiling hesitantly, she walked over. As she reached to pull out one of the empty chairs at the table, a waiter pulled it out for her. Thanking him, she turned her attention back to Tess.

Tess coolly tilted her head. "You're looking well. It has been a long time."

"Hello, Tess. Yes, it has been a long time. You haven't changed."

The waiter walked up to their table to take their orders. "Tea, miss?"

Katie declined. "No, I prefer coffee if you have it."

"Certainly."

Once their order was taken, the two women looked at each other, waiting to see who would speak first.

Clearing her throat, Katie started, "Thank you for coming. I wasn't sure you would." When there was no response, she continued. "I'm sure you are wondering what this is all about. I'm not sure how to say this, so I will come right out with it. Will you please...forgive me?"

Tess had steeled herself for any words Katie had to say, except for those. In her mind she had played out every scenario, but this one. Not too often did she feel unsure of herself, but this was one of those rare moments. Shocked, Tess blinked a couple of times, then focused on her lap. She looked back up at Katie, then down again.

Katie went on. "I have had bad feelings toward you in the past. I no longer feel that way. I'm asking your forgiveness for how I've felt about you in my heart. I'm truly sorry. A lot has passed between us. Even when you were not near me, I sensed your presence. We have been a part of each other's lives for some time now. Years ago, when we first met, I was hoping we could be friends. I don't know if it's too late for that, but I would like to try to be friends now."

Tess searched her mind for words, but none came. She had never been in a situation such as this. She had never asked forgiveness from anyone, and no one had ever offered it to her...until now.

Katie placed her hand gently on Tess's arm. "Do you think that could be possible? Can we be friends, Tess? Can you forgive me?"

Tess reacted on raw instinct. She pulled away. "What...friends? Are you jesting? I have friends. I don't need any more!"

"I know you have many friends," Katie said softly. "I just thought you could use another one. I know we have never liked each other, but I want you to know that I feel differently now."

"So what's changed?" Tess said suspiciously.

Katie went on to tell Tess about her new life in the Lord. To her own amazement, Tess sat quietly and listened. Katie spoke with a boldness that surprised her. She told of her experiences in the gaol, of James and her marriage. She told of Brady's Brick and how her papa had left it for her. Katie spoke of the love she felt in her heart since she had become a Christian, and of the love she felt for Tess.

Something stirred Tess's heart. She looked into Katie's eyes and saw how sincere she truly was. Her hard heart cracked. Tess had lied; she'd never had a true friend, and she longed for that. Other women were to be avoided. She needed to protect herself from them; they could be so hateful. But at that moment her eyes were opened. She realized how hateful she was…and how much she longed for acceptance from others. She had no one except her mother and father to share things with, and David. Now she was being offered a true friendship, for the very first time in her life. Any friendships in the past had been shallow and used for gain. She had paid dearly for her folly. Having no one close to share her life with meant loneliness. Maybe that was why she was so drawn to David. He would be someone to share her lonely life. It came as a shock to realize how lonely she truly was. Her face burned; she had to fight back tears.

"Are you all right?" Katie asked with concern.

Tess wiped the corners of her eyes and sniffed. "There's not much that surprises me anymore, but you about knocked me off my chair. I thought you came to rail on me, to tell me what a horrible person you think I am, but instead…" Tess tried to swallow the big lump in her throat. New feelings overwhelmed her. Her heart had been hard for so long that once it cracked, there was no stopping it from crumbling.

"Does this mean you forgive me?" Katie whispered.

"I…guess so, but I'm not sure what I'm forgiving. Shouldn't I be the one to ask forgiveness from you?"

Katie smiled. "I have forgiven you, and that's what I wanted to tell you. It must be overwhelming for you right now. Are you sure you're feeling all right? You look a little pale."

"I don't know what I'm feeling. I feel strange. Can I ask you something? You became a Christian and felt you needed to see me?"

Katie explained what had happened the night the Lord had spoken to her about Tess.

Tess wasn't sure what to make of it. "Are you telling me that God Almighty told you to forgive me, and then come and tell me?"

"That's exactly what I'm saying. I know it sounds strange. I wouldn't have believed it either, but it happened!"

"I'm not sure I could ever forgive you, if things were reversed," Tess said hesitantly.

"I understand, but it doesn't matter now."

Tess started to pour her heart out to Katie. She told how she resented the relationship Katie had with her parents. Her jealousy in knowing they cared for her. She had felt so insecure and vulnerable growing up.

"You were jealous of me?" Katie was astounded. "I thought you had everything. I even thought you were the prettiest girl I had ever seen when I first saw you. I believed you to be a princess."

"I've been called a lot of things, but never a princess."

Both laughed at that.

The two young women talked as equals, sharing what was happening in their lives. Old hurts and scars melted away. Tess was greatly surprised to hear about the circumstances surrounding Katie's marriage to James. Katie also shared how she and James would be leaving soon…on a prison ship!

Guilt washed over Tess. "It's because of me you are leaving."

"No, you're wrong, Tess. God had a plan for James and for me, and He used you as one of his instruments to accomplish that plan."

Tess wasn't sure she understood all of what Katie was saying. "I don't know what to say to you. I can't believe we are here talking like this, as if we are old friends. For the first time in my life, I feel sorry for my actions. I always felt justified in what I did, until now. Oh, Katie, please forgive *me!*"

Katie was quick to assure Tess that all that had happened was in the past. "Let's begin anew, as if none of this ever happened."

"How can you do that?"

"With God's help, and knowing that I am not without guilt myself. We all sin, Tess. No one is better or worse."

Overwhelmed with gratitude, Tess felt heady from what was transpiring. "Yes, let's begin anew, like you said. Thank you, Katie."

The two young women hugged and laughed in their joy. They spent another hour listening to one another and the stories they had to tell. Katie listened intently as Tess talked about her upcoming wedding. To anyone sitting close to their table it would seem as if two old friends were simply catching up on each other's news, and by the grace of God, they were.

"Look at the time!" Tess exclaimed. "My mother will think I've been kidnapped, or worse. She's such a worry wart."

Getting up to leave, she found that she genuinely did not want to leave. The two young women made plans to meet again soon. Shyly they took each other's hand and squeezed.

As her coach moved away, Tess pinched herself to see if she was awake. Did all of that really happen? Exhausted, she longed for sleep. Her mind was so befuddled she couldn't think anymore. She felt different, and it frightened her a little. *I'll go home, sleep, and figure it all out later.*

Katie smiled from ear to ear. Only God could have made their meeting as perfect as it was. Never had she dared believe that she and Tess could forgive each other. Katie caught her breath as she remembered the passage of Scripture where it said God would give her the desires of her heart. Even before she had met Tess, she had hoped they would be friends. *Oh, Lord, only You could do this.* Katie was just grateful that she had obeyed and gone to see Tess. *Help me to always be obedient.*

"What do you think, Mary? Is she losing it? After all the poor wee girl has been through?"

"Do not know, Maggie. Would seem the girl's got Jesus all right. I knew of a man who got holy and goofy in the 'ead. 'Is poor wife didn't know what ta think, what with 'im prayin' all the time instead of workin' for 'is family and her 'avin' to work so 'er little ones could eat."

Maggie went on. "I just can't believe the change in her. She has always been a happy person, but she seems downright giddy. Don't seem normal. I can remember when her father first brought her to the Brick House. She was such a shy little thing, but once she got to know a person she wouldn't stop smiling. Except for when Tess was around, of course, and to find out she actually went to see the snit today! I don't know that any good can come from it, Mary."

"Aye, 'tis a strange thing all right. I don't trust that Tess anymore than I trust the devil hisself. Got a shifty look 'bout 'er. I saw 'er one day while at the Brick 'ouse visitin' Lady Wilson. Made me blood run cold knowin' what she 'ad done to Katie girl. I 'twas surprised when Katie girl told of wantin' to go see the she-devil."

"I know. You could have knocked me over with a feather when she told me too!" Maggie added.

The two women talked about the changes in Katie. They didn't know what to make of it all. "We need to keep an eye on her. If she gets out of hand, we'll need to speak to someone," Maggie stated matter-of-factly.

"Who?"

"Don't know, but someone."

That was all that was decided before Katie returned home. She only confirmed their suspicions with her humming and light step. She hugged them both, exclaiming how good God was. She proceeded to make their supper, telling them "to rest themselves." It was a tough time for the older ladies. They didn't like change.

16

Sally Mae

"What do you mean you already belong to the Prison Reform League?" Lord Wilson was incredulous.

"What's the matter, Edward? I told you of it a while ago. Mary, Maggie, Kathryn, and I all joined to help James and the other prisoners."

Lord Wilson stared at his wife as if she had just grown a second head. He thought the idea of helping prisoners was his alone.

"Honestly, Edward, I've told you and told you that you don't listen to me."

He had to admit she was right. He never took interest in his wife's activities. He just went along with what she was doing as long as it made her happy.

"Why do you ask about it now?" his wife questioned.

"I want to help in some way and thought we could do it together is all."

Barbara Wilson was touched by her husband's words. Putting her arms around his neck in a rare show of playful affection, she nuzzled him. "Why, dear Edward, has your heart been moved by those poor wretched souls in the gaols?" She smiled up at him.

He looked down at the only woman he had ever truly loved. "I must say it has shocked me how so many people just trying to take care of themselves and their families have been caught up in such hardship. Taking clothing or food to survive and being sentenced to hell is quite sobering. I have come to realize how blessed I am. I cannot imagine being pulled away from my family to another part of the world, never seeing them again." He held his wife close. He buried his face in her neck. "I love you, Barbara. I have loved you my whole life."

They held onto one another for some time, thanking God for each other.

Captain Miles Warwick stood watching as provisions and livestock were brought on board. He was an impressive man in his forties with fine features and a solid build. He could be a hard taskmaster when needed, but most of the men had been with him for a long time. They had learned to respect his fairness and his knowledge of the sea. It was not beneath him to work alongside his men, and because of it his men held him in high regard.

"Get that cargo below! I want this ship ready by the end of the week!" Above the shouts of men working, and the terrified bawling of cattle and sheep, the man's deep voice rang out. Men scurried about the deck as if their lives depended on it. When their captain gave an order they obeyed.

Addressing the Naval agent, the captain gave a slight smile. "Richards, make sure that the food, water, and especially the port are under lock and key. Remember, I know how much port we are loading."

"Yes, sir!" The man saluted and grinned.

The two men were old friends. The captain counted it fortunate to have this Naval agent on his ship. Lieutenant Gaylord Richards was diligent, caring, knowledgeable, and experienced in transporting large numbers of prisoners. It was his job to outfit the transport ships with provisions of water, clothing, and other materials. He then supervised the loading, which was no small task. Each ship carried 160 gallons of water, huge barrels of rice, wheat, salt pork, beef, butter, raisins, suet, sugar, flour, and other foodstuff. Live animals, clothing, material, medicines, along with tools, cooking utensils, and bedding were also brought aboard. The supplies were endless. He had to check every bale, barrel, and flask on all three ships. It was imperative for him to keep careful records.

At least they did not have to carry a vast amount of extra supplies to the colonies since they were well established and self-sufficient. Trade ships sailed on a routine basis, lightening the load considerably for the transports.

Richards was also in charge of overseeing the prisoners taken from the gaols and prison hulks to the transport ships. He inspected the tween decks. They needed to be fumigated since that was where the prisoners were housed on arrival. He issued each male prisoner new clothes, consisting of a jacket, waistcoat of blue, duck trousers, a coarse linen shirt, yarn stockings, one woolen cap, and one pair of shoes. The women were given a brown "serve" jacket, one petticoat, two linen shifts, a linen cap, one neck handkerchief, one pair of worsted stockings, and one pair of shoes.

Although Richards was in charge of supplying and loading the full fleet, he could only sail on one ship. He chose the *Sally Mae* whenever he could. Warwick ran a tight ship when most did not. Once sails were hoisted, the fleet of ships rarely sailed together. The weather saw to that. At times the ships were left to the wind while the provisions and prisoners were at the mercy of the ship's captain.

In all the chaos Jules Crane, the Surgeon-Superintendent, came aboard. His knowledge and aggressive care of the prisoners made a vast difference in the number of healthy convicts at the end of the journey. Captain Warwick smiled after spotting Crane. Having Richards and Crane on board helped him sail successfully time and time again. That was why the British government eagerly contracted the *Sally Mae*.

Warwick turned once more to eye his ship. With pride he had made her into one of the most successful convict transports. No ship had ever been built for the express purpose of transporting prisoners, and the *Sally Mae* was no exception. She was all of 672 tons and one of the larger convict ships running. Being built in India made her a solid ship…a prize indeed.

The ship was divided into three decks with part of all of them used for holding the prisoners. The men were kept down in the orlop—the very bottom of the ship. It held eighteen secure bays, nine on each side of the ship. A corridor ran down the center of the deck with iron bars separating it from the bays. The two end bays housed the livestock, leaving the air pungent. The light was dim at best. The sway of the ship was the only real difference between the lower bays and a dungeon in Newgate.

Of course, Captain Warwick didn't see it that way. His job was to get as many prisoners as he could safely to Botany Bay. Warwick was a fair and compassionate man, but in his business life was hard. He treated the convicts and his crew with a lighter hand and some humor. He found it made a vast difference to morale, but he was tough when he needed to be. He did all he could to make the voyage just as safe for his prisoners as the marines, their families, and his crew.

The transport was almost ready to sail. Along with the *Sally Mae* were two other transport ships and two naval vessels. They were set to sail together if the weather held.

Warwick, Richards, and Crane fought and won to keep the number of convicts transported on the *Sally Mae* to a manageable number. Many fleets were overloaded with convicts, but the *Sally Mae* was able to ask for special favors because of her record.

The other convict ships of the transport were called the *Greystone* and *The Clip*. They also tried to keep the number of prisoners down to 624, which averaged out to 208 convicts per ship. Less crowding meant less disease and discomfort for everyone. The sad truth was that, no matter how much effort was taken, hardships were had by all. It was such a long and arduous voyage. Most times overcrowding was a fact of life, and few ships were given special attention.

Warwick also made it a habit to meet with the commander of the guards, his officers, warders, along with the matrons to head off any trouble. Communication was vital and welcomed between the captain and service personnel. Since the warders and matrons were in charge of the prisoners, Warwick felt it was important to keep communications open with them.

It was one such meeting that Kathryn Murphy's name was first spoken. It was with great interest that Captain Warwick listened to his First Officer, Marks, read a letter regarding Mrs. Murphy. It was a common occurrence that a free woman would ask to follow her convict husband. Most were turned down. This letter was not a request, but more of an order given by top government officials. That was the reason for such interest. An Irish woman given any consideration at all was a rare thing. To be given special favor was unheard of.

"What do you think, Captain?" Marks asked.

"I think it's strange that we would get a letter like this in the first place. We will do as the letter says. One more woman on board will make little difference. If the British government wants her on this ship, then on this ship she'll be."

"Aye, sir."

The cabin boy entered after knocking on the captain's door. He stood silent until Warwick acknowledged him. "Yes, Fred, what is it?"

"A man named Smith is asking for you. Says you needed to talk to him about the marines and their family's quarters."

"Yes, yes, send him in, Fred. Bring some port." Warwick reached for his pipe to light it. He continued his instructions to his men. "Well, everything is pretty much ready to set sail. Remember, I still want the rest of that information on the convicts. Make sure there are enough matrons on board to help the females."

"Aye, sir." The men left their captain to finish their tasks.

Warwick had a moment alone before his visitor arrived. He yawned and stretched his heavily muscled legs. He felt good about the progress made; he was sure all would be ready to set sail in time. The more trips he made the more was learned, and the easier it was to ready his ship. The hard times were coming once they left the harbor.

A knock was heard, and Warwick acknowledged. One more person to deal with, and his day would be done. "Smith, good to see you. Let me get you some port." The door closed behind the two men, and business was taken care of.

"Oh, Edward, isn't that the most exciting news!" Lady Wilson beamed at her husband. "Who would have ever dreamed that Tess and Kathryn could become great friends, after all that has happened?"

"Are you sure you heard Tess right, my dear? Maybe you misunderstood her."

"No, she even sent a dinner invitation for tomorrow night to Kathryn."

"Well, I must agree this is exciting news. Too bad it couldn't have happened years ago. What brought all of this on in the first place?"

Lady Wilson repeated everything to her husband as it was told to her. "Haven't you noticed a…softening in Tess since she's been engaged to David? She genuinely seems to love him."

They spent a long time talking, expressing their hope in the changes in their daughter. Lord Wilson took his wife's hand tenderly, holding it. He didn't want to spoil her happy moment, but he needed to give her the news. He waited until the last possible moment to tell her. "I have some news that may upset you, Barbara. Kathryn and James will be leaving very soon. The fleet is being loaded up as we speak."

Surprise and then sadness crept across Lady Wilson's face. Tears formed as her husband pulled her to his chest. "There, there, we knew it was coming. I want you to know that I have had the captain investigated, and he runs a tight ship. He is a fair man, and his crew respects him. I've written letters, and even bought extra provisions for the voyage. All that can be done for Kathryn is being done."

Wiping her eyes, Lady Wilson lifted her head. "I know you are doing everything in your power to help her, Edward. I just wish she wasn't going. What a horrible, dangerous journey it is going to be for her. I can't even imagine all she will face."

"Just remember dear, there are other women on board—marines' wives and families, along with matrons for female prisoners. The ship is sound, and like I said, the captain and crew are experienced."

"What about when they get there? Where are they going to live? How in the world will there be enough food? Oh, Edward, I feel so helpless. What if Tess and Kathryn had become friends long ago? We wouldn't be having this discussion now. What if she wasn't forced to marry James?" Tears spilt down her cheeks.

"Don't do this to yourself, Barbara," Lord Wilson said gently. "It won't help anything. We've been through this. Kathryn could have backed out of her marriage but chose not to. I've been corresponding with the governor of Botany Bay. That's where Kathryn and James are sailing to. The colony is established and strong. I told the governor about James being a farmer. He said they have great need for men who know how to take care of land. If he does well, he can farm his own place. Life is hard there, but after what these two have been through, I think they will be fine." He held his wife a little longer.

The couple talked until they came to the conclusion that God would have to watch over Kathryn and James. After all, James was a hard-working, capable man. He would take good care of their girl. There were many things in the world they couldn't control, and this was one of them.

It was late as they climbed the staircase. They both turned toward their separate bedchambers. Ever since Barbara had given birth to Tess, she thought it best to have her own rooms so as not to disturb her husband. After all these years, they still kept separate rooms. Tomorrow was going to be a hard one, and they needed to be strong, strong for Kathryn, and for each other.

Hesitating at the top of the stairs, Edward turned toward his wife. He decided to stay the night with her. She looked so vulnerable…how he hated to see her suffer. After climbing in her bed, he held her in his arms until she slept. Looking into her sweet face, he drew her closer, to ward off any evil.

Katie left early with Lord Wilson to go to the harbor. Lord Wilson stayed close to answer all of her questions. Katie could not help but think the ships seemed small for transporting so many, yet they did look sturdy. The docks buzzed with activity. Men were loading and unloading; others were barking orders. Katie saw prisoners in their telltale filthy rags. They were working on the docks and in long boats heading out to the harbor. They all looked so thin and sickly. Nothing at all like James, thank God! She was surprised James had not been brought to work on the docks.

Katie turned her attention to the prison hulks anchored out further in the harbor. They were a far cry from the transport ships. They reminded her of the filthy tenements of London. What looked like bedding hung on makeshift lines. The hulks were in great disrepair. Lean-tos stuck out at all angles from the original hull. Waves slapped the hulks, heaving them to and fro in the water. A few of them looked as if they would sink at any moment. Lord Wilson explained to her that some were French war ships captured in battle, and some were obsolete first-raters. Rusty chains and rotted wood were all that was left of their glorious service to England.

Lord Wilson appeared concerned as he caught her watching the prisoners working the docks. She knew he wanted to shield her from the harsh realities in the world, but he couldn't…and she wouldn't let him. "I've made arrangements to visit your husband this afternoon. I thought he would like to hear the news on the fleet. Would you like to come too?" he asked.

"Yes, thank you, Lord Wilson. What would we have done without you?"

They walked along the harbor, taking in all the sights and sounds.

"I'm not afraid anymore," Katie stated bluntly. "I used to be, but I'm not anymore…not right now, anyway. I know God is going to take care of us. I have to remind myself of that from time to time, but just because I falter in my faith doesn't mean He falters."

Lord Wilson looked dubious. "Yes, life is hard, but when you came into our lives, you made things easier for us. We will miss you dreadfully."

"You really don't have to worry," Katie went on. "We will be fine. It may be hard, but life is hard all over, isn't it?" Katie placed her hand on his arm and squeezed. She would miss the Wilsons too. She fought hard to keep that feeling of excitement about leaving, but right now it was anything but exciting. Reality shouted at her: that her husband was a prisoner with no rights or say in their future. Their lives were in the hands of strangers.

No! Our lives are in Your hands, Father, Katie silently and stubbornly declared. Harder still was leaving these people, her family. Just thinking of it tore at her heart. She prayed again. *Lord, help me to remember that You know all things, and we are in Your hands. Fear is not of You, Lord. Ease our grief and help us to trust You in everything.*

Her thoughts turned to God's Word and promises for the future.

Katie and Lord Wilson kept walking along the docks. He couldn't help but think of all the horrors and danger this young woman would be facing. He wished he could feel as assured as she appeared to be. This newfound faith of hers seemed to give her strength. She would need that on the journey ahead.

Lord Wilson couldn't help but marvel at this girl. Her concern had always been for others. Here she was leaving soon, yet she was trying to comfort him.

Mary wailed uncontrollably while Maggie patted her shoulder. "I can't bear that Katie girl be leavin'! I be knowin' she was to leave, but not now."

Maggie nodded, wiping a tear of her own. The time seemed to come far too quickly.

"We ne'er see 'er again," Mary howled, burying her face in her apron.

Maggie could only nod and pat her friend's shoulder.

"What 'appens if she sinks in the sea or is killed in the jungle where she be goin'?" Mary asked between sniffles. "What if she gets eat up alive from those black heathens I 'ear 'bout there? What if?"

Maggie couldn't listen to any more. "Don't be thinkin' like that, Mary! It will only cause her leaving to be harder. It was Katie's decision to go. There are others there to help, and James will take care of her. Now stop the cryin' before she comes home. We don't have much time to spend with her, so let's not fill it with tears."

Mary lifted her head. "And what will 'appen to ol' Mary when my Katie is gone?"

"You will stay with me. I've gotten used to your sour old puss."

Mary smiled weakly at her friend, then blew her nose. "Ya be right. Time ta stop wailin' 'bout it. Cannot be doin' anythin' 'bout it, 'tis true. We needs to be strong for Katie girl. 'Tis feelin' better I am. Aye, a good hard cry 'tis good fer the soul."

A knock sounded, and Henry stepped inside the door. Before he knew what hit him, Mary flew into his arms, letting out a howl. She held onto him with all her might, burying her face in his shirt. Poor Henry looked bleakly at Maggie. His eyes begged for help. There was none. Maggie simply shook her head and went into the kitchen…so much for being strong.

Lord Wilson had never met Kathryn's husband. He'd heard about him being a big man in size but was caught off guard nevertheless. Kathryn walked around the table to give her husband a hug, then turned to introduce the two men. "Lord Wilson, this is my husband, James."

Red offered his hand to Lord Wilson even though it was chained. "Sir, I'm glad to finally meet you. Katie has told me all that you have done for her, for us. Now I can thank you in person."

Lord Wilson shook the big man's hand. He did not usually feel awkward, but he did now. Standing with this stranger who just happened to be a prisoner and was bigger than a mountain made him feel uneasy. Lord Wilson pulled out a chair for Kathryn, then said, "I've wanted to meet you, Mr. Murphy."

"You can call me James, or Red. That's what most call me."

"James, then; news has come of a voyage. Kathryn and I thought you would like to hear it."

"I've wanted to meet you too. What of the ships in the harbor? I've heard rumors, but there are always rumors flying here. I know there is a fleet anchored in the harbor. Several have come and gone, yet here we are. It was said we were leaving, but I don't know. I was beginning to believe I would spend my seven years here at Newgate. Since it is late May, I thought I would be here at least another year."

"Actually you could have left two weeks ago on another fleet, but I requested that you be held back."

Katie and her husband both appeared surprised. They looked at each other, then quietly waited for his explanation.

"Fact is, I had both captains and fleets investigated. I found Captain Miles Warwick to be outstanding. He's one of the best, as far as a transport captain is concerned. The first fleet was questionable, but Captain Warwick's record is impeccable. It would seem that he has over twenty successful voyages credited to him. His crew respects him, and he treats his prisoners humanely. I hope you don't feel I was overstepping. I know you were not able to do any investigating yourself so I took it upon myself. My family cares deeply for your wife, and my wife would not be able to rest if Kathryn was put into more danger than necessary. If my wife doesn't rest, I don't rest."

James smiled at that. "Sir, I would not question any decisions you make regarding my wife. I know you have only her best interests in mind. That is all I need to know."

Lord Wilson was surprised. He didn't expect Murphy to be an educated man. Oh, he knew the man could read and write, but Murphy held himself with confidence. Where most men would have balked at someone else making decisions for their family, this man understood. Yes, Lord Wilson was surprised indeed. Grimes said this man gained respect from everyone he fell in contact with. Now he understood what was meant when he heard Grimes say, "It seems he's not just big in stature."

After a few minutes Lord Wilson continued, "I have a few details you may want to know. There are five ships in the fleet—three transports, and two naval vessels. The entire transport can hold 1,730 prisoners, but they are loading fewer than that. It's one of the stipulations of Captain Warwick. He'll hold the number of prisoners to just fewer than 300 per ship. The ships are stout, and I heard they are fast as well. Life on board is going to be very difficult. The ships were loaded a couple of weeks ago and are now anchored, waiting for the prisoners to arrive. If the weather holds, you should leave at the scheduled time."

"I'm sure we'll be fine," James said, looking at his wife. "Our trust is in the Lord."

"Of course," answered the older man.

They continued to talk about the voyage ahead—what to expect and how long it was going to take to reach their destination. Lord Wilson explained that Kathryn would share a cabin with several of the matrons. He explained that matrons helped with the women prisoners. He surprised James by telling him of his request to have James part of the crew instead of a prisoner. It wasn't to be. James would be transported same as the others. There would be no privileges there.

"I was able, however, to keep you off one of the prison hulks, or forced to do any dock work while waiting to be transported out."

"I was wondering why I wasn't taken out. Most of the men who work with me have been kept here as well. Again I see that I need to thank you, sir."

Lord Wilson cleared his throat. "No need to thank me, young man. I personally think it's a crime to sentence a man to seven years for being hungry. Whoever made that law should be the one locked in here. I must admit, I had you investigated. If I was to help you, I wanted to know what kind of man I would be dealing with."

Kathryn broke in. "I told you that James is an honorable man."

"Yes, I know, but love is blind sometimes."

Katie blushed.

James spoke up. "He was right to question, Katie. I would have done the same thing." Turning to Lord Wilson, he continued, "So when do we leave?"

"If the weather holds, and all goes well, the end of next week."

Kathryn and James looked at each other. "That soon?" they said in unison.

Kathryn jumped up. "I didn't realize there was so little time left. I've waited and waited, and now...well, I don't know what to do first! I must go, James. There's so much I need to do."

Lord Wilson and James stood watching her as she began to pace the room, talking to herself. "I have to decide exactly what I need to take, and I have to sign those papers at the lawyer's, and I have to..."

"Katie," James said as he caught her arm, "there is plenty of time. Don't worry, everything will get done."

"Oh, James, next week! We're leaving next week!"

James turned to the older man. "Would you mind if I speak to my wife a moment? Thank you again for all you have done for us. I'll never be able to repay you. I give you my word that I, along with the Lord, will take good care of Katie."

Lord Wilson shook James's hand once more. Smiling, he leaned forward. "Don't worry, my boy; women always panic at any news they get. I will see you before you leave. Now that I have met you, I know she'll be fine. Kathryn, I'll wait outside."

Kathryn nodded. "Thank you, Lord Wilson. I'll be out shortly."

James took Katie's hands. Gazing deeply into her eyes, he said, "Katie, are you positive you want to do this? It's not too late to change your mind." Katie started to speak, but James rushed on. "I know we talked about this before, but that was when the voyage was somewhere in the future."

A doubt crossed Katie's mind, but it went away as fast as it came. "No, absolutely not, we are going together. God will be with us whether we sail or stay. I thought we decided to trust Him and each other."

"Yes we did, and I do, but if—"

"James, you're wasting time and words."

James hugged his wife. "Well, then, you best go so you can get ready. It will be hard for me to sit here waiting to go when I feel I should be helping somehow."

Katie wrapped her arms around her husband. "I love you, James. I know we will be fine." Katie kissed him good-bye.

Once outside she mouthed a quick prayer. *Father, give us strength, and help our faith grow. Give me wisdom to know what things I need to do to prepare for the voyage. Help me to say good-bye to all the people I love.*

Lord Wilson stepped down to help Katie into the coach. "Are you all right, Kathryn?"

"I'm fine. I knew we would be going soon, but I didn't think it would be next week. I guess I wasn't sure what soon really meant."

"He seems to be a fine man, Kathryn. I've always wondered what attracted you to him. Now I understand. I'm a pretty good judge of character. The little I've talked to him I can see he is a man of integrity and strength. You will be just fine."

Katie smiled. "I wish we could have met under different circumstances, but the Lord works in mysterious ways."

The rest of the ride home was quiet. It would not be long before they would be saying good-bye. It would be a difficult thing to do, for it would likely be good-bye forever. Katie smiled when Lord Wilson took her hand in his. He didn't say a word, simply held her hand gently in his own.

17

Good-byes

The chandelier in the dining hall cast soft light over the room. Servants walked around the massive table while Lord and Lady Wilson engaged their guests in conversation. Lady Wilson planned a very special evening since there was precious little time left. She was intent on making it perfect, but the mood was still subdued in spite of all her efforts.

Tess, and her fiancé, David, sat next to each other with Kathryn across from them. Great care was taken on everyone's part to keep the conversation light and interesting. It was difficult to say the least.

After dinner everyone strolled into the parlor, each finding a seat in front of the fire. Shortly after, the men excused themselves, going into the den for brandy and cigars. The ladies stayed to talk about the upcoming wedding and sip their tea. Lady Wilson marveled as she watched her daughter. It was if someone else who looked like Tess sat across from her. In a short time Tess had turned into a new person. Her daughter had even gone so far as to ask forgiveness from her parents. What a wondrous time it was for this small family.

Tess addressed Kathryn. "I wish you could be here for my wedding. I was going to ask you to stand up with me. I'm just being selfish, I know, but I don't want anyone else. I want you to share in the biggest day of my life. Then again, it is my fault you're leaving in the first place."

"Tess, that's all over and done with. The decision to leave was mine. I could have chosen to stay here. It's all water under the bridge so, please, don't mention it again," Kathryn stated firmly.

A sigh escaped from Tess. "I feel free and happy for the first time in my life. Yet my heart is breaking at the thought of losing you. When I think of all the years I've wasted…"

"Now stop; didn't you hear anything I just said? You need to forgive yourself. That's the only thing holding you back. Everyone has regrets. We can't change that. As far as wasted years, they weren't wasted. It took all that happened to bring us to the Lord, and our friendship. We will always be friends. Distance can't change that, nor can time. I still can't believe the changes in our lives. How grateful I am for new beginnings."

Tess nodded, then bent forward to hug Kathryn. The two women clung to each other. Just then a maid entered to announce more guests were waiting in the great hall.

"Show them in, Esther." Just as Lady Wilson stood, Maggie and Mary came in. "Ladies, I'm so glad you could make it. I was sorry you couldn't make dinner, but at least you are here now."

Katie was pleasantly surprised. Neither had mentioned they were coming. In fact, she was a little disappointed when she thought they had not been invited. She noticed Maggie carrying a package.

"Here's the package you wanted, Lady Wilson."

"Thank you, Maggie. I'm glad it came in time."

"What's this?" Katie questioned.

"Well, dear Kathryn, we all have a going-away gift for you." Lady Wilson handed the wrapped package to Katie.

Again Katie asked, "What is it?"

"Blimey, Katie girl!" Mary laughed. "Open it up. I can't wait 'til ya sees it!"

Maggie placed her hand on Mary's shoulder. "Easy, ol' girl."

Everyone laughed at Mary's excitement.

Katie slowly unwrapped the package, then drew in her breath. "Oh, they are beautiful!" She lifted three pewter framed mini-portraits out from the wrapping. One was of Lady and Lord Wilson, one of Tess and David, and one of Mary and Maggie.

Mary tittered, "Ya like 'em, Katie girl? See me? I ne'er 'ad a picture of me drawn afore. They be tellin' me ta smile so I tried ta make it a good one." She beamed with pleasure.

"Oh, how beautiful," Katie repeated. "I don't think I could ever treasure anything so dearly as these. Thank you so much." She choked back a tear.

Mary broke in. "Cannot be cryin'! Won't be havin' it! Ya start, an' we be startin' right behind ya."

Lady Wilson explained to Katie they thought small portraits would be easier for her to take. She continued, "We have a friend whose cousin is Randolph Case. He's an accomplished artist and just happened to be in London a few months ago for a show. We were so lucky to get him to do these for us. He did some quick sketches of all of us, and just finished the portraits a day ago. Randolph sent them to his cousin's house, and we sent a coach with Mary and Maggie to pick them up."

Mary added, "'Twasn't goin' to let nobody else pick 'em up. Sure didn't want 'em to get lost."

"Katie, I've never seen anyone as excited as Mary over these portraits. I wish you could have seen her." Maggie laughed.

"'Tis important is all I be sayin'," Mary broke in. "Whene'er ya look at me picture, ya won' ferget ol' Mary."

Katie got up from the couch and walked over to her. Squeezing Mary's shoulders, she murmured, "I would forget to breathe before I would forget you, any of you."

"When David and I have our wedding portraits finished, I'll send you one," Tess promised.

"I would love that!"

The evening went all too quickly, and soon Katie, Mary, and Maggie had to leave for home. The women planned to gather at her cottage the next day to help pack. After saying good night, the ladies climbed into their coach. Sadness fell on Katie, thinking of the short time they had left. She also recalled the days of Gran and Papa. She had believed her whole life would be lived with those two special people. It had all been so simple back then, before her life had taken so many twists and turns. What would Gran think if she knew all that was going on in her life now?

Katie smiled. Maybe Gran did.

Her thoughts turned to Maggie and Mary. After discussing Maggie's future with the Wilsons, she'd had papers drawn up to give Maggie and Mary co-ownership of the cottage. It would belong to them, along with her and James. She knew they would be happy there. It did her heart good to know that if she and James did ever come back they would have something, and someone, to come back to.

Soon the coach pulled up in front of Brady's Brick. The driver jumped down to help them out. Katie hesitated on the front walk, looking at the cozy cottage. Smoke from the fireplace gently rolled from the chimney, leaving a curly line reaching for the sky. Buds on the few trees in front promised to open soon, and flowers peeked out from the earth. She wanted to remember the warmth, love, and promise this little cottage held for her. It was her father's dream, passed on to her. In turn she would pass it on to her family.

"Ya be comin' in, Katie girl?" Mary asked as she passed Katie on the walk.

"I'm coming. I was just thinking how pretty the cottage looks from the outside at night. All cozy and warm. I'll surely miss it."

The three women promised each other that there was not going to be another crying session. They all made a valiant effort, but tears still fell. They talked long into the night, pledging to always write and pray for one another.

James ran his fingers through his hair in frustration as he paced up and down his cell.

"Sit down, boy, or there will be a rut in the floor where ya be walking," Ben stated.

"I can't sit down. Now that I know we're leaving, I want to do something to get ready, but what?"

Ben, much older than Red, stepped up, placing his hand on the big man's shoulder. Red turned at his touch.

Ben gently reminded him, "Be careful for nothing; but in everything, by prayer and supplication with thanksgiving, let your requests be made known unto God. And the peace of God, which passeth all understanding, shall keep your hearts and minds through Christ Jesus."

"You're right as usual, Ben. It seems I need a daily reminder of those things."

"We all do," Ben assured Red. "I have some good news too. I will be transported on the same fleet as you."

"How do you know?"

"I just talked to my sister today. She had a list of prisoners leaving, and both our names are on it. So are Hayes, Thomason, O'Hare, and Jameston."

"That is good news!" Red slapped Ben on the back. "How did she get that list?"

"Her husband knows someone who had access to it."

"Hey, men, we're all sailing on the same ship to Botany Bay!" Red announced.

All the men who had been a part of the work crew with Red gathered to discuss the voyage. Their talk became more excited by the minute until the cell was full of men's voices lifted in excitement over their departure.

One man sitting watching the group blurted out, "Blimey, ya bunch of patties. Don't ya knows yer all gonna die? Ya talk as if yas goin' on a trip ter Paris or somethin', but it be hell yas goin' to. Don't ya realize it, or is the whole bunch of yas daft in the head?"

"Ya! Yer all be nuts, ya are!" added someone else.

The group of men stood silently for a few minutes, then all eyes turned to Red. Since they all seemed to expect him to say something, he did. "You are right! We're daft all right, but at least we have enough brains to know we want out of here."

The other men laughed and began talking again. Now that they knew they were leaving, expectancy filled them. At last, the men settled down. They were not fools. They knew dangers were coming, but these men had known danger all their lives. Hardship and hunger had been companion to most of them since they were lads. If anything frightened them, it was the sea…the sea with its black water and monsters just under the surface. Not hunger or hardship, but the unknown was the enemy, the fear-giver. Hope was lost to them early in life, and they had learned to live without it.

Then this large man with the large heart had told them of a new hope. In the beginning many wanted to believe, but some felt foolish, and some were doubtful. As the days, weeks, and months went by, they watched Red and Ben walk in faith. That was why most of the men turned to Red in the first place. He replaced their fear of the unknown with hope in the absolute…God's Son.

Ben and Red prayed by themselves, but one by one the others joined them. The rest of the afternoon was spent talking about God's promises and of the hope only He could give. Some expressed a longing to know that kind of hope and asked the Lord into their hearts. Several men on the other side of the room scoffed, making coarse jokes, but some quietly watched. When a sweet fragrance descended upon the cell, Red knew the presence of the Holy Spirit had entered. Suddenly, the men cracking jokes fell silent. Men started to loudly praise God with tears streaming down their faces. Those who knew something powerful was happening, but didn't understand what, were inspired to awe.

The afternoon was spent in fellowship. Ben shared many Bible verses he had memorized over the years. Several others came to listen and accepted Jesus as their Savior. In that filthy, cold, damp cell men were transformed. Hearts were broken, only to be healed anew. Spirits rose along with voices of praise.

Red looked at the men who remained on the other side of the cell. "Would you like to join us?"

"Ya mean fer yer little girly tea party?" one man scoffed. The others laughed.

"This journey is going to be difficult. God will care for you and protect you if you let Him," Red said.

"Ahhh, I'll give ya a week an' ya be at each other's throats. Ya be scrappin' fer bread and blanket 'fore ya even leave the harbor in that hulk. Yas talkin' freedom, but yas ne'er have freedom. The rest of you men listenin' to him will be hatin' him afore the week is out."

"God don't love us!" another spoke up. "He only loves the rich an' stupid. Blimey, He may love yas after all!" Laughter once again rang throughout the cell.

Red could see it wouldn't do any good to talk to them. Maybe once they were on their way, and it became harder, they would be more open to listening. For now he was going to concentrate on the others. He leaned against the wall closing his eyes. He felt refreshed and strengthened. A new chapter was opening in his life while the old one was being closed. How would this chapter read? Would it be success or failure, happiness or grief? Whatever the future held, Red knew he would not face it alone. He had the Lord and Katie. He felt bad for the others who were leaving loved ones behind. Many had children they would probably never see again. He couldn't understand how they could face all that without the Lord. He felt gratitude for his salvation, his wife, and yes, for the difficult journey ahead.

One day at a time, Lord. Help me to live just one day at a time.

Katie went through her bag for what seemed the thousandth time. Space was limited, and she had to leave a lot behind. Only two trunks were allowed to go with her, and they needed to be filled with the things that would be most important to her and James in the future. But what was the most important? Katie didn't know what would be available to buy once they reached Botany Bay. She had brought material, needles, thread, medicines, garden tools, and even some seeds for planting. For the household she packed blankets, soap, candles, wicks, pots for cooking, and extra clothes. Along with Mary and Maggie, she had made extra socks, pants, and shirts for James. For her there were dresses, aprons, under things, shawls, and bonnets. She purchased an extra pair of shoes and boots for both her and James along with warm coats, hats, and gloves for the cold. Her trunks were stacked to the top. The bag she now packed bulged, threatening to tear. Katie had her most prized possessions in the center of her bag with clothing around to protect them—her Bible and the small portraits of her "family."

She and James had gone over a list of items to bring, but she was so afraid of forgetting something that she had packed and repacked many times. A soft knock sounded at her door. "Come in," she called.

Maggie opened the door, followed by Mary, carrying a tray of tea and coffee. "Thought you would like a break," Maggie said as Mary set the tray down.

"Oh, that sounds good. I need to stop for a while."

The women talked over any possible items that might be forgotten, but each item was accounted for. Katie decided her packing was done. Lady Wilson and Tess planned on coming over later in the day to take all of them out to dinner. Lord Wilson would meet them after work. The ladies finished their hot drinks, then proceeded to get themselves ready for dinner.

Once the other two left Katie washed up, putting on a clean dress, and fixed her hair. She wondered if she should chance taking a mirror on her journey but decided against it. Hopefully there would be one available to buy. She had a feeling she would not care much about her hair once there. When she was ready, she pulled Gran's shawl out of her bag, placing it around her shoulders. It had seen better days, but it gave her comfort.

"Ya be ready, Katie girl?" Mary shouted. "Lady Wilson and Tess be 'ere with the coach."

"Aye, I'll be right out." After checking her reflection in the mirror once more, she dabbed on a little cologne.

The women loaded up in the coach and were off. All spoke in excitement of the evening.

"'Ere we are," Mary murmured as the coach pulled up.

Lady Wilson led the procession to a large table in the dining hall. It was only a few minutes before Lord Wilson arrived, and their orders were taken. It was a lovely evening of good food and friends, but Katie longed to have James there.

The talk around the table was light until Katie broke in, "Lord Wilson, do you think James will be able to get a homestead once we get there?"

He looked at her with surprise. "Well, I wrote to the governor. He said they needed men who knew their way around a farm. He also said it was hard work, and many just gave up. I can't guarantee anything, but by the sounds of it there's more than a chance of it."

"James knows everything about farming. His dream has been to own land, and farm it. I know that this may be a strange way to obtain it, but like I said before, God works in mysterious ways. Well, I keep saying I'm going to trust in the Lord so I need to trust Him in everything, right?"

Through the rest of the dinner, conversation was kept light. All too soon it was time to leave.

"The captain wants everyone on board early," Lord Wilson said, "so I better get everyone home. We leave at dawn for the harbor. It's drizzling rain now, but hopefully it will clear by morning."

Soon everyone was in their own carriages, heading for Brady's Brick.

"It is getting late, but I don't want to go to bed as soon as we get home. We have such little time left," Katie said to Mary and Maggie.

Once at Brady's Brick everyone sat in front of the fireplace talking. All too soon it was time for Lady and Lord Wilson and Tess to leave. Lady Wilson would not accompany them to the ship in the morning. It was too painful, so she said her good-byes to her sweet Kathryn.

"As long as you live, remember that you have many people who love you. If ever you get a chance to come back to either stay or visit, please do so. I love you for your good heart and your sweetness."

Katie hugged the older woman. "I promise that, as soon as possible, I will do my best to come back and see you. Thank you for being the mother I needed all this time. I love you."

Tess and Katie walked outside arm in arm. They planned on saying their good-byes in the morning. Tess wasn't about to miss out seeing her one more time, she said. Lord Wilson gave Kathryn a hug, telling her he would be there bright and early.

So here it was—her last night in the cottage. It had threatened to come too quickly, and it did. Mary, Maggie, and Katie lingered together a while longer, but all too soon it was time for bed.

As Katie lay in her room, she went over the contents of her baggage once more in her mind. She tried to think of anything she may have forgotten. Finally she decided she had done all she could and would trust the Lord in the rest.

Sleep came quickly, along with disturbing dreams….

Dark waters swirled around her, and people were screaming. Wood splintered as she frantically looked for James. She saw him sink under the depths of the sea. But when she tried to scream, nothing came out. Katie swam as fast as she could to grab onto James before he sank farther down into the waters.

Suddenly she was pulled away from James by a horrible sea monster. The monster opened its mouth to devour her….

Katie jerked awake.

Mary stood over her with concern on her face. "Katie girl, are ya all right? It be dreamin' ya be doin'. Wake up now, wake up."

Katie slowly sat up in her bed, wiping the tears from her eyes. "It was awful, Mary. The ship was sinking, and James was drowning. I went to grab him, and a monster came up from the depths and—"

"Hush now, jest be a dream, Katie girl. Jest be a dream." Mary sat with Katie until late into the night. They talked about the dream, the voyage to come, and what it all meant.

Katie finally lay back on her pillow, closing her eyes as Mary watched over her.

Soon Mary could hear Katie's deep breathing. "Keep 'er safe, God. Let 'er be 'appy and blessed," Mary whispered.

She quietly slipped out of Katie's room. Sadness filled her as she shuffled off to bed. *'Tis the last day afore she be gone. May be the last I e'er see 'er again.*

Mary got into bed, but sleep didn't come. She was afraid to sleep. She didn't want to miss any time remaining with Katie. She just waited to hear the first stir of someone in the kitchen. She didn't have to wait long.

Katie lay awake, determined not to cry. Mary had just tiptoed out of her room thinking she was asleep, but she wasn't. They all would have a hard enough time at her leaving. Katie determined she would not break down again, but that dream had left her shaken. For the thousandth time Katie set her mind and heart on trusting the Lord. He was leading the way for her and James, so she would trust. At least she would keep trying. Excitement, along with dread, swept back and forth within her. A spiritual battle raged throughout the night.

By early morning Katie felt the wounds of that battle in her numbness. She was exhausted. Trust was an easy word on the tongue, but the heart was a different matter. Trust would have to be a choice she would make minute by minute, if necessary.

Katie gave up on any notion of sleep. This was to be the first day of her new life. She got up and knelt beside her bed.

Lord, You see my heart. I want to walk boldly in faith, and sometimes I do, but many times I stumble. Forgive my lack of faith, and help me to be strong. I know You will take care of us. It's just I'm afraid of the unknown, and of the sea. I've heard such awful things. Help me not to be afraid, to keep my eyes on You. Give me strength to help others on the voyage.

Katie continued to kneel when she felt His words in her heart.

"I will never leave you nor forsake you. The sea is My creation, as are you."

Katie barely breathed as His words washed over her. Tears moistened her eyes as she rested in His love for her. She would never stop being amazed when Almighty God, Creator of Heaven and Earth, the living, sovereign God of the universe, spoke to her! His love astounded her, and His words revived her strength. There were no words to express her love and gratitude so she simply whispered, "Thank You, Father."

Maggie stumbled into the main room to see the clock sitting on the mantle. It was just about to chime 4 a.m. She returned to her room to get dressed, hoping she would get more time with Katie. Lord Wilson would arrive before too long. As Maggie returned from getting dressed, she ran into Mary coming out of her room. Whispering as not to wake Katie, Mary leaned over to Maggie, "'Tis she up yet?"

"Don't think so. I want her to get her rest, yet I want to wake her."

"Aye, it won't be long afore Katie girl be gone." Mary sniffed.

"Now, don't you start your howling. You know once you start, there's no stopping you," Maggie warned.

As the two women went into the cook's room they were surprised to see Katie already sitting at the small table.

"About time you two showed up," Katie teased. "Come sit down while I pour your tea. There's something I need to talk to you about. I put it off until the last minute because I didn't want any arguments from you."

The two older ladies looked at each other, then back at Katie.

"I have some papers for you. They are co-ownership of the cottage and lands. I had them made out in both your names, along with James and mine."

Maggie was shocked. She would not have been surprised to learn the cottage was given to Mary, but why her too? She was here as a servant, though Katie never treated her as such.

"Blimey," Mary sputtered. "Ya be given me an' Maggie the cottage? Yer father gave it ter ya, Katie girl. What do ya think 'e would say 'bout that if 'e knew 'bout it?"

"My father isn't here, but he would agree with me. This decision is mine and James'. You and Maggie are my family, so it will stay with my family. If and when James and I return, we want a home and family to come back to. This is selfishness on my part."

It was Maggie's turn to question Katie. "Why me, Katie? I was brought here to work for you. Mary is more family than I."

"You are both family to me, and will always be." She then handed another envelope over to the women. "This is an account that has been set up at the bank for you. Each month there will be monies in there for you to live on, and for the maintenance of the cottage. Lord Wilson's lawyer will help oversee the account. If there is anything you need, just go to him. If there are repairs that need to be done, just contact him, and he will arrange for the workers to come. The land will be rented out to other farmers, and money will come in from that, along with some produce."

Pausing for only a second, Katie continued. "I know that in a few hours we will be saying good-bye. I really don't want to discuss business, so please accept this with no arguments. Like I said before, I'm being quite selfish because I could never leave if I had to worry about the two of you. This way I know you have each other to look after, and the cottage will be loved and cared for."

Any arguments the women had dissolved with Katie's words. Wiping tears, they thanked her and tried to enjoy the remaining time they had together.

Lord Wilson arrived and had Katie's trunks loaded. "Lord Wilson," Katie asked, "when will the ship be leaving?"

"I was told this very morning. Everyone is to be boarded by 7:00, so we don't have much time."

"Do you think I'll be able to see James?"

"I doubt it. There are no women allowed near the men prisoners the entire trip. The captain makes sure that even his crew stays away from the women prisoners. There are no exceptions according to Captain Warwick."

Lord Wilson left shortly after that, saying he intended to make sure Kathryn's luggage was delivered safe and sound.

Soon Tess arrived with her mother in tow. Lady Wilson had planned to stay away but could not. The women treasured the remaining time they had.

18

Awestruck

It was still black as pitch when James and seven other men were transported to the harbor. They were manacled together, then placed in an open cart. James had talked to Katie the evening before but had not known then that he was being brought aboard ship today. He hoped she wouldn't worry once she found out.

James heard a scuffle a few feet away. When one of the men tripped, causing four others to fall, one of the turnkeys kicked them and swore. "Git up, yer pieces of filth! Git up now!" The men struggled to stay on their feet.

James could see in the dim light of glowing torches women also being loaded into open carts. Their heads were shaved, and they looked half starved. A few had children holding on to their skirts. All were in rags, and many had no shoes. The children whimpered as they clung desperately to their mothers. A cold mist fell, adding to their misery. By the time the carts were loaded, the prisoners were soaked and shivering.

Ben whispered to James, "Seems a tough beginning."

Another man added, "Told yas, I did, that it were no holiday yas were goin on. Don't see yas laughin' and praisin' the Almighty now. Yas think cause yas say so, God will make it easy fer ya?"

A guard ended his tirade by switching the man across the mouth. "Shut up! No talking!"

It took longer for the carts to arrive at the harbor than expected. The gaolers were anxious to get out of the rain. People were pushed and pulled toward the long boats. The waters were rough, causing the loading of shackled prisoners to be treacherous. One of the small children nearly fell in when he tripped on his mother's skirt. Chaos ruled, and the gaolers took their discomfort and foul mood out on the prisoners. Finally, the long boats were loaded and heading out to the transport ships.

James noticed many boats. The prisoners loaded off the prison hulks appeared to fare worst of all. The rags they wore barely covered them. The prisoners were so thin, a good wind could have knocked them into the water. Once they reached the transport ships, they were hauled aboard and made to stand on the deck.

One man stood aside from the rest. James figured it was the captain. When another man pushed a prisoner down, kicking him for not getting out of his way fast enough, the captain commanded, "Barrett!"

"Yes, sir!" The crew member snapped to attention.

"What did I tell you about mistreating the prisoners? See it doesn't happen again!"

"Yes, sir!"

"Get these prisoners below, starting with the females and children. Make sure you hand out proper clothing, and everyone gets a blanket once they are deloused!"

"All right, women, down the hulk with yas! Git a move on. Ain't got all day," one of the sailors barked. Two matrons came forward to lead them down.

It took some time to settle the women before the men were led to their bays. The warder in charge of the orlop designated eight men per bay and had their shackles replaced with leg irons attached to rings in the bay. Each man was severely restricted in movement, having to mostly sit or lay on his wooden berth. It was not much more than a plank of wood.

The sound of frightened animals at the end of the bays filled the air. So did the smell of them. James noted the lack of fresh air. With all the bodies coming in, he knew it would soon be unbearable.

Captain Warwick ran a tight ship, with careful forethought. Iron bars had been put in to replace solid wooden doors throughout the corridors on the *Sally Mae*. This gave the prisoners more air, but "fresh" air was another matter. Between all the humans and animals alike, there was none to be had.

The deck above the orlop, also called the lower deck, was set up similar to the orlop. The only difference was a few cabins for marines and their families added between bays. Between those cabins and a chapel, which occupied a great deal of the space, was room for only fourteen bays. The upper deck had twelve bays and storerooms at the aft. It also held the captain's quarters, the surgeon's quarters, and a few other cabins at the forefront. The captain's quarters held a bedchamber, a pantry, and an open living area. A huge table in the center of the room took a lot of the space. The captain's massive desk was placed near the windows. Cook rooms and wash rooms were in the forecastle, along with one large cabin used as the sick room or hospital.

The women were held on the upper deck located at midship. The tall, thin head matron, Annie Hill, appeared hard but had a big heart. As she directed the women to their bays, she unlocked their manacles and placed the chains through heavy rings bolted in their bays. After being deloused, given clothes and blankets, they settled down, grateful to be out of the cold, damp weather. The children cuddled close to their mothers for warmth. It was hard to sleep, but exhaustion claimed many of them.

Once all the men were in place they were given a blanket to ward off the chill. In each bay were several slop jars for personal use and nothing else. It was sparse, dark, and stuffy. The pitch of the ship in the rough waters didn't help. It felt as if they were already on the high seas instead of anchored in the harbor. Before the day was out, a few people used the slop jars frequently.

James and the seven others in the bay sat on their wooden berths watching the warder. Several marines were there to help get the other bays settled. At one point the warder came back to one of the bays and had a young boy removed.

"What is he doing here?" the warder yelled at another. "You know we got the young ones on the upper deck. Take him out, and bring a man back here."

Once everyone was settled, the warder and marines left. Many of the prisoners sat upright, trying to sleep, while others quarreled and swapped stories. It would be a few more days before they set sail. They sat in the dim light, fighting off panic, nausea, and anger. This was it—no turning back. Some hoped for a last-minute reprieve or pardon, but it was not to be. Some were in shock, others in denial, but all were now on board the ship that would take them from their homeland. Most would never see it again.

James felt peace. He knew without a doubt that God was using this for His purpose and plan. He was determined to be open to God and His direction. He had to smile at that. To see James chained up, one would think God wasn't any part of his life, but they would be wrong. Yes, he had gotten himself here, but God would use it for His glory. James looked around. He saw the suffering and the hopelessness in men's faces. *Oh, Lord, help me to help them. Give me words, and let Your Spirit fall on us to comfort us. Lord, let us sense Your joy. Open these men's hearts to take Your Holy Spirit in. Give me wisdom, Lord, to know when to speak, and when not to. In Jesus' name, amen.*

Kathryn waved to her "family" standing on the dock.

Mary was jumping up and down like a little girl. "Bye, Katie, girl! Ol' Mary be a prayin' fer ya! Love ya, I do!"

Lady Wilson and Tess could be seen wiping their tears. Lord Wilson looked concerned as he waved. Katie waved and blew kisses as tears streamed down her cheeks.

The women standing on the deck of the ship were shooed off. "All right, ye women, git in yer cabins where ye belong!" a scruffy man barked.

Katie looked around her. About twenty women were scattered along the deck. They all looked lost, except for one woman who stepped forward, barking right back at the crewman. "You are not speaking to prisoners, but ladies, sir. You will not use that tone with us!"

The man spit on the deck, scowled, and muttered about women not belonging on ships in the first place. It was bad luck. He disappeared around some scaffolding.

The woman holding some papers called out, "Ladies, come together. My name is Annie Hill. Please follow me, and watch your step."

Stepping around rope and canvas, the women followed in obedience. Katie turned once more to catch a glimpse of her family. She waved again before joining the others. It didn't seem like much of a glorious departure. Not like she had imagined it would be. Of course, what did she expect? She was to get on the ship, wave, and leave.

"Our cabins are this way. Matrons will be sharing cabins." Holding out a piece of paper, she continued, "Is there a Mrs. James Murphy here?"

Katie stepped forward. "Aye."

"You will share a cabin with matrons Bess Tills, Jenna Knolls, and Grace Key."

Annie led all the women to their perspective cabins. Katie, along with the other three, stepped into a small, dark cabin. On each side of the room were two wooden planks, one above the other, covered with thin mattresses and blankets. Several trunks and one chair were next to a table on one side. Another small table with a lantern set alongside a dry sink on the other side. A curtain hanging from the ceiling provided privacy for the chamber pot. A tiny window eked out a miniscule portion of light.

"Ladies, we need to settle the other women, so please drop off your bags and follow me."

"May we return to the deck once more to say good-bye to our loved ones?" Katie inquired.

"Captain Warwick prefers you stay in your cabin once you are assigned. His crew has much to do, and they don't appreciate women in their way, as you witnessed earlier."

Closing the cabin door the four matrons left Katie alone. She walked over to light the lantern, then sat on one of the beds. Looking around, Katie decided to read until the others came back. She pulled her trunks near her bed and opened one to find a book. She would offer to help with female prisoners once things were settled.

Soon the other women were back. Bess Tills offered the first bit of information about herself. "Well, here we are at last. I didn't think we would ever get aboard. In case you don't remember, my name is Bess, Bess Tills." Katie warmed to the young woman's smile and easy manner. "I'm a matron to the women prisoners. My husband is a marine in the Royal Navy. He's in Botany Bay as we speak. That's why I signed on. It's been two years, and I don't mind saying, this ship isn't moving fast enough for me. Oh, and one more thing. I tend to chatter on and on."

The other ladies smiled, helping to break the ice. Soon they were all chattering away. Jenna Knolls and Grace Key were not new to sailing to Botany Bay. They had served as matrons for some time. Katie and Bess were anxious to hear all about it.

It was Katie's turn to tell of herself. She told how she came to marry and how her husband was in one of the bays. She told how she was released after being imprisoned for some time. She even shared a little of her faith.

"You mean to tell me you spent time in Newgate, and you were found to be innocent? You poor girl! Then forced to marry, and now because of him you have to sail from your home? Why didn't you leave him?" The other women were incredulous.

Katie shared how she had come to love James, and what an honorable man he was. How he struggled for many years to survive and then ended up at Newgate for stealing food. She had not intended to share so much about herself, but everything just poured out of her once she got started.

"Bless yer soul," Jenna quipped. "I don't think you know what you're in for, but you seem to have a good head on your shoulders and a healthy body. You'll do fine." The other women seemed to like Katie's openness and her sweet spirit.

Katie smiled, feeling more at ease. Although she had just met all three women, she liked them. She also felt drawn to Jenna Knolls for her matronly concern for the others. Grace Key was quiet, but not timid. She seemed self-assured and intelligent.

Soon each had claimed a bed and began setting up housekeeping. It didn't take long with their meager belongings. The chattering stopped as the women at last lay on their beds. Katie couldn't believe she was on board the ship. It had seemed like the time for her and James to leave was far away, and now here she was.

Turning toward the wall, she let her tears fall. *Lord, I hope You know that if I cry, it's not because I don't trust You. I feel a little overwhelmed, even though we haven't left the harbor yet. Please take care of Mary and Maggie, and Lord and Lady Wilson. I've told them about You, and they listened out of love for me, but I don't think any of them really understood what I was saying. Help them all to find You, and love You.*

The ship tossed in the choppy waters of the harbor, causing Katie's stomach to lurch. She fought hard not to be sick. It didn't work. Before she knew it, she had to lunge for the chamber pot.

"Ah, you poor girl!" Jenna jumped up to pour some water onto a towel for her. Dabbing Katie's forehead, she helped her to her cot.

"Some get sick and some don't," Grace said. "I used to, but not no more. Guess I got my sea legs now."

Katie would have been horribly embarrassed any other time, but right now she didn't care. She hadn't felt this sick ever. If she was this ill anchored off shore, what was it going to be like out in the open sea? She thought of the story in the Bible where Jesus walked on the water and held out His hands to Peter. In her mind she held her hands out to Jesus, and the waters seemed to calm. Soon she was sleeping.

"Come with me!" the man barked, yanking on James' chains.

Once his leggings were thrown off, James was led outside of the bay. He gave Ben a look of question but said nothing. The man led James up the steep steps to each deck until they were on the top. Men scurried about, giving the feeling of total chaos when actually they were time-tested sailors. They were simply doing the work they had to do to get *Sally Mae* ready for sail.

James was being led to the man he assumed to be the captain. James towered over him, but the man had an air of confidence. The man gave orders, and the men responded quickly without question.

"Here 'e is, sir!" the man leading James stated.

"Thank you, Pratt. You may leave us."

"Yes, sir!"

James' mind raced, wondering why he had been summoned. He stood for a few minutes before the man turned to speak to him.

"Murphy is your name, correct?"

"Yes, sir."

"I've been told you can read and write. Is that correct?"

James repeated, "Yes, sir."

"While in the gaol, you led a team of men in work who are now aboard this ship with you. Is that also correct?"

"Yes, sir."

"Good, then follow me."

James was surprised that the man would have him walk behind him. He could easily lay the metal of his chains around the man's neck if he had the mind to. Along the way to his cabin Captain Warwick gave a few more orders. Walking up to a young lad, he placed his hand on the cabin boy's head as he spoke. "Fred, I'm going to my cabin. Bring tea, enough for two, and make sure it's piping hot."

"Aye, sir."

Shortly after entering his cabin he ordered one of the marines to take the chains off of James. Shortly Fred came in and served tea.

Only when they were left alone did the captain speak. "I guess by now you know I'm the captain, Captain Warwick."

James nodded, saying nothing.

"I've heard many things about you. Quite frankly, next to the pope himself, I don't think I've heard men praise a man as much. I know the reason for your sentence and that your wife is aboard. I also know she is a free woman. What I don't know is whether you have any plans, sir, to rile your men once at sea and try to take my ship."

James was stunned. That had never entered his mind. "I would never do that."

"I thought not, but I wanted to see your reaction to the question. I need a clerk, and since you can read and write, I called on you. I don't trust you. I want to say that up front, but high words have been spoken on your behalf. I trust the men who told me of you, and they have earned my trust. You have not. If you fail me one time, it will go hard on you, understood?"

"Is that why you had me walk behind you? To see if you could trust me?"

"I heard you were intelligent. That was the first test. There will be others. I keep duplicates of my log. One is given to the governor of New South Wales when we arrive. The surgeon superintendent, Crane, also needs a duplicate of his records. He will speak to you regarding what he needs. I expect you to write word for word my instructions, or any information I give you. It needs to be legible. Is that understood?" James nodded, standing silent. "Well, do you want the job?"

James nodded again, but this time said, "I appreciate your trust in me to do the job, sir."

"I didn't say I trusted you yet. I do not, but I will give you a chance. Because you have agreed to be my clerk, you will receive special compensations. You will have your own cabin, and your wife may join you there. It is quite small, but private."

James's heart leapt at his words. "Alone...with my wife?"

"Is she so hard to look at, man?"

James didn't know what to say. Stammering a bit, he tried to explain. "Captain, my wife and I were married after we were both sentenced, and...we never ah...well, we've never been alone except to visit in the gaol, and ..."

"I understand. No need to explain. I don't think I've ever seen a man with a more panicked look." Warwick's laughter filled the cabin. "Actually, I know all about your situation. It was made known to me when a letter arrived, requesting me to take your wife on board. It was more of an order than a request. It would seem life has handed you some surprises. You are a prisoner, yet I get letters from important people requesting special attention and favors."

"I'm not looking for any special favors for myself, sir."

"Don't get your hackles up. I owe you no favors and don't intend to give you any. It just happens that I need a man who can read and write. My clerk decided to stay landlocked while his missus has her belly full of babe. The cabin is usually his, and near to mine. I need to have you close in case I need you. I know you have a motley crew of men who have worked with you in the gaol. Heard they do fine work at whatever is given them. I can use them as well. There may be times I call for you, and your men for work. If they do a fitting job, they will get extra rations. Is this acceptable to you, sir?"

James was thanking Almighty God as the man spoke. He was awestruck how the Lord worked everything out so he and Katie could be together. He wouldn't have to sail in that bay all the while! There was a sense of guilt at the thought. His friends were stuck there when he was not, but maybe he could help them more in this position.

"Well, I know you can talk. What will it be: cabin or back to the bay?"

"Cabin, sir."

"You are indeed a smart man. Now pour me some more tea. I cannot express how important it is to keep concise records. We will keep records of the weather, the ship's position, my steering orders, sickness, deaths, births, and any other out-of-the-ordinary occurrences. Right now I need to go over the Indent Papers. There should be a listing with all of the prisoner's names, where they come from, and the crime they committed. Let us begin."

James stood until summoned to sit and, with that, became the captain's clerk.

Mary, sniffling and blowing her nose, headed for her room to lie down. Maggie could tell she was overwhelmed with grief.

After the Wilsons left, Maggie stoked the fire and sat on the settee, staring at the flames. The cottage felt empty without Katie. It even seemed colder, though the fire roared. Maggie was concerned for Mary. She had thought the old girl might even collapse before getting home from the ship. She decided to give Mary a few days to grieve, but then she would have to do her best to snap her out of it. If Mary didn't, then Maggie was afraid she would not be able to physically bounce back from it.

Sighing, Maggie walked to Katie's room. Standing quietly, she closed her eyes, picturing the young woman's smile, her laughter. Covering her face with her hands, she wept. How lost she felt without Katie there. She sank to the floor, her shoulders shaking as her heart broke. She only looked up when Mary sat next to her. On Katie's bedroom floor they put their arms around each other. The two women clung to each other and cried until there were no more tears. Then they got up, wiped their eyes, and helped each other into the kitchen. They proceeded to make tea.

Many were the days and nights to come that they would reminisce about their lives with Katie. Many would be the days to come that they would be thankful they had each other.

The Wilsons sat in their parlor, staring at the fire. Lady Wilson had stopped crying a while ago but was left with a headache. Rising, she gave him a peck on the cheek. "I need to lie down. I hope you don't mind if tonight we have dinner in our room?"

"Not at all. In fact, I'll inform Tess we'll be spending the rest of the evening there."

After giving Graines instructions for dinner, the couple climbed the staircase. It would take time to get over their grief of losing Katie, but they had their daughter's wedding to arrange. Holding hands, they climbed the staircase and softly closed the door to Lady Wilson's bedchamber. They didn't want to be alone in their own beds tonight. In fact, they made the decision never to sleep apart again. Life was too short.

19

Voyage

The month of May was the birth of their voyage—the beginning of a new life for James and Katie. The anchor was pulled, and the ships headed for the open, endless waters. Excitement filled the men on the upper deck while fear and trepidation held the men in the lower.

James sat in his newly acquired cabin, impatiently waiting for Katie's arrival. When a knock sounded on the door, he expected to see her, but instead it was the same little man who had led him earlier to the captain.

"Yes?" James stated.

"I'm Pratt. Captain sent me to fetch ya, but I want to tell you something first. Don't think just because the captain made you 'is clerk that I won't be a-watching ya! One wrong move, and the whole ship will have yer head." Pratt emphasized his words by hitting the wall while glaring at the big man.

When Pratt left, James wondered if he had really been there. If anyone else were standing there, they might have found the whole scene funny. There was Pratt, bent over by years and maybe all of 150 pounds verbally protecting his captain. James thought Pratt resembled one of those leprechauns Katie had told him about—mystical, tiny men with upturned noses and twinkling eyes, except that Pratt's eyes were dark with warning.

Instead of feeling threatened by the man's words, though, James felt hope. Surely to earn such loyalty from the rowdy bunch that worked this ship, the captain had to be honorable and fair.

A few minutes later James was summoned to the captain's quarters. The little time spent with the captain proved to be valuable. James saw that the man was kind in the way he treated Fred, the cabin boy. Captain Warwick summoned one of his crew to show James around the *Sally Mae*. Then James was introduced to Crane and Richards.

Soon he was back in the small cabin, still awaiting Katie. James scanned the room. It seemed even smaller because of his size, but it was more room than he had in the bay. He wasn't sure when Katie would be brought to him, but the captain said he would arrange it. His hands were sweating so badly he had to wipe them on his pants.

Easy, Red. You faced your time in the gaol and the idea of being transported with less nervousness than the thought of being alone with your wife. He smiled to himself.

The berth was made for a single person. James couldn't imagine how in the world two people could fit. He doubted he could fit on it by himself, let alone with Katie. When he realized his thoughts, his heart fluttered. He wiped his hands on his pants once more. *Husband and wife at last.* He never thought they would be together until they reached their destination. James looked around, trying to think of some way to make it seem a little less bare. It was next to impossible to make a bare cabin into a "home" when there was nothing to work with. There was a small table with a water pitcher and a chair. A slop jar sat in the far corner with a curtain. A tiny window was all there was on one wall, and one blanket covered the bed. That was it.

A knock sounded on the door, causing James to jump. A man stood on the stoop. "Lieutenant Richards wants to see you on top!" He quickly disappeared before James could follow him.

James was left peering out his cabin door. At this rate he would never be with Katie. He was not used to roaming around on his own. It had been a long time since he could walk around freely. He wondered if this was another of the captain's tests. Once on the top deck, he spotted Richards and waited quietly until the man turned toward him.

"Murphy, come with me. We need to go over supplies. Once we land in the Canary Islands we will need to restock. I want to recheck my list as to what we have then on a weekly basis, check to see how low we are. Rationing is a must, and you will help me with that as well."

Richards took James to one of the supply bays. Unlocking the door, the lieutenant lit two hanging lamps, giving James vague instructions. Richards told him to stay in the bay until someone came to get him. Turning toward the doorway, Richards stopped suddenly. "By the way," he added, "I am to inform you that your wife is on her way to your cabin." Richards left the door wide open as he exited.

So she would be waiting for him when he was finished! James's heart beat jubilantly. He fought the urge to tear into the supplies, to finish the work hurriedly. The bay was in such disarray. Different food stuffs had been thrown around, and many bags, barrels, and boxes lay in no particular order. He knew nothing about sailing or how ships were run, but he had a hard time believing they didn't have a list somewhere of all the supplies. What capable captain would go on such an arduous journey without knowing what he carried? The captain had sailed many successful voyages. Isn't that what Lord Wilson had told him?

Warwick was intelligent and seemed to be an orderly man, so James knew there was more behind this. After all, it was the captain who stressed the need for proper records. James was given a lot of freedom all of a sudden, and to what purpose? This seemed to be another arrangement made by the captain to test him, but for more than just a job as a clerk. Clerks did bookwork, not cleaning and straightening supplies. The captain had more than enough crew to clean the bays out if need be.

This was just another example of trusting in the Lord. Men had many motives.

Mind reading wasn't a talent James had acquired, so trusting in the Lord was far better than guessing. James rolled up his sleeves and started to work. He prayed that he would do a good job...for God's glory. He didn't know what the captain was up to, but God did.

Katie woke, feeling much better. The others must have felt she needed the rest, for they let her sleep. She was grateful. Since she was alone, she looked out the window. It was still daylight, but gloomy. Re-lighting a lamp, she sat back on her bunk and prayed. Afterwards she wrote in a book Lady Wilson had given her. She described all the events that had happened since she came aboard.

It wasn't long before the others came back to the cabin with plates of gruel and some dried fruit. Bess carried one for Katie, who ate sparingly. She was afraid of becoming ill again. She smiled at Bess. "I'm feeling much better, but I'm afraid to eat too much. My stomach is sore from being sick, but thank you."

A knock sounded, and Annie Hill stepped into their room. "Mrs. Murphy, I need to talk to you alone. Do you mind coming with me?"

Katie followed her out into the corridor.

"Mrs. Murphy, I have just been given some news."

"Please call me Katie."

"You can call me Annie. The captain summoned me to his cabin to discuss your husband."

"James, why?"

"It would seem that because your husband can read and write, he has been made captain's clerk. It's not all that unusual to have a prisoner given that position when his regular clerk is not on board. The good news is that you, and your husband, have been given the clerk's cabin. I'm to help you settle into it."

Katie didn't know what to say. Her heart felt like it was about to tear out of her chest. This meant so much more than just having a cabin to herself.

"I know your husband is working right now, so I peeked in. I'm afraid there are no frills at all about the place, but who would expect frills on a prisoner transport, right?" Annie gave Katie a sheepish look. "I also heard this is your honeymoon."

Katie blushed, hoping Annie wouldn't see it in the dim light.

"Oh, Katie, I didn't mean to embarrass you. Please don't worry. No one else has to know it's such a special night. Now let's go see what we can do to make it a little cozier before your husband gets back."

Captain Warwick sat back in his chair lighting his pipe. Propping his feet up on his desk, he thought of Murphy and his wife. He couldn't help but smile at the big man's reaction when he told him of his cabin. Warwick thought for sure the man was going to try and bolt at the news. Laughing softly to himself, Warwick recalled a time, long ago, when he was as naïve about women. Murphy would have to wait to see his wife until his job in the bay was finished; then the captain would know what kind of man Murphy was. Would he do the job asked of him or leave the bay to go to his wife?

Captain Warwick drew on his pipe, then watched as smoke circled his head. Once again he smiled to himself. What he would give to have his own wife there with him. As much as he loved sailing, and having his own ship, he hated being separated from his Elizabeth. She was the most important person in his life. It was times like this he missed her most…at the beginning of the sail.

A knock came at the door, pulling his thoughts away. "Enter."

"Captain, I checked on Murphy without him seeing me. Seems to be working all right, and it looks like he'll be finished soon."

"Thank you, Richards. What about his wife? Is she settled into the cabin yet?"

"The women are all fluttering about the cabin. Sounds like a bunch of hens nesting in there." They both laughed.

Dragging on his pipe once again Warwick made a face, discovering it had gone out. He rose from his chair and headed out of his cabin to check on his crew, ship, and prisoners. He was determined to keep busy. It would help keep his mind off his wife.

Richards followed closely behind.

James worked all afternoon; still no one had come to get him. He had made an accurate count, for he counted twice out of sheer boredom. Did they forget about him? He thought about locking the door and going to his cabin, but Marks told him to stay there until someone came to get him. So that is what he would do. Why was time so slothful when you watched it?

He was anxious to see his Katie. It seemed like a lifetime since their last visit. He thought of her, but mostly he spent time with the Lord. He would have his own cabin, his wife with him, and work to do to lessen the strain of the voyage. How good God was to him. Looking about, he decided to make a bed in one of the corners until someone came for him. He pushed some heavy bails up against the wall, placed a blanket on top, and then reclined on them. He was exhausted from lifting all the heavy barrels and sorting through everything. The rocking motion of the ship had him dozing in no time, and soon he was with Katie in his dreams. That was a fine thing indeed.

A few matrons and marines' wives flocked around Katie with suggestions to add comfort to the cabin. Katie was amazed by their friendliness. They seemed genuinely excited for her. Katie wondered how many knew it was to be her honeymoon cabin. The ladies had men bring in a double plank to replace the single bunk. When Annie had the men brace it for strength, Katie blushed scarlet. Next a thick, feathered mattress was placed on the plank. Katie asked Annie where it came from.

Annie whispered, "It's a wedding present."

One woman sat on the only chair in the room sewing curtains for the small window while other ladies went in and out, sprucing up the room. It didn't take long before the little cabin was cozy and inviting. The curtains were hung, a couple of rag rugs lay on the floor, and candles were lit. Soft pillows lay on the heavy coverlet on the big bed. Even a crocheted doily lay on the table. The women soon left. Katie stood alone in her new "home." She felt such joy. She had prayed the Lord would help her bring joy to these women, and look what they had done for her and James instead.

A knock sounded. Thinking it was James, Katie rushed to open the door. Annie stepped in, carrying a pot of steaming water. "Here's some hot water for you to wash with. I'll be bringing you supper tonight. Isn't much to eat, but since this is a special night for you we'll bring it to you this one time."

"No need! You've done enough!"

"Let me do this, Katie. On these voyages we have little to bring us joy or celebration. I haven't seen these ladies laugh and work together like this in a long time. We all needed it."

"I just don't know what to say. I can't believe how hard everyone worked to fix our room up. It's lovely. All of you have been so kind."

"You can count your lucky stars you got on Captain Warwick's ship. He's a decent and honest man. He watches out for his crew and prisoners."

"I am blessed, I know," Katie stated. "I would like to help some way if I can…with the women prisoners, I mean."

"Can you sew?" Annie questioned.

"Aye, and I can cook too."

"Well, tomorrow is soon enough for you to begin, but tonight you relax. I best be going. I don't want to be here when your husband gets back. I'll be back in about an hour with supper."

"Good night, Annie, and thank you again for everything." Katie looked around once more at her cabin. She straightened an imaginary wrinkle in the coverlet and wiped off dust that wasn't on the furniture. She decided to wash up and put on a clean nightgown. She wrote in her book until she began to nod off. It was strange that James wasn't back yet. It must be very late. She wasn't sure what James's duties as a clerk were, so she had no idea when he would get back.

Katie retrieved another book from one of her trunks, along with her watch bobble. She had forgotten to wind it, so it had stopped. She sat at the table and read in the dim light until her eyes started to blur.

A soft knock had Katie's attention. She bolted toward the door, hoping for James to be standing there. Instead, Annie stood with a tray of food and stepped over the threshold once the door was opened. She proceeded to set it on the small table. Just as quickly as she had come, Annie left. Katie wasn't sure whether to wait for James or not. Her stomach was empty and her will weak, so she ate. Covering the remaining food for James, she glanced at the bed. The soft mattress and warm covers beckoned to her. She couldn't resist any longer. She didn't want to mess the bed up before James came in, but her weary body won out. Lying in the middle of it, she soon fell asleep.

It was good she didn't wait up any longer for James, for he was sound asleep.

Fred knocked on his captain's cabin door. After hearing the captain's bidding, he stepped in. He was balancing a tray of food and hot tea.

"Fred, get me Richards as soon as you're finished serving me, and I need Dr. Crane here as well."

"Yes, sir."

Once the men arrived and were seated Captain Warwick lit his pipe, then ordered more tea from Fred. "Richards, is Murphy still in the bay?"

"Yes, it seems he made a bed and stayed all night."

"Send one of the crew down to release him to his cabin. I want you to check the supplies. See if there's anything missing, or if he arranged the foodstuff in wrong containers."

"Yes, sir, but I didn't tell him certain foods need certain containers."

"I understand," Warwick answered, "but I want to see if he has common sense and uses it."

James quietly opened the door to his cabin, stopping midstep. He backed out, shutting the door, and looked around in confusion. He could have sworn this was his cabin. Standing there for a minute, he tried to get his bearings. Maybe he was on the wrong deck. He looked around again, only to see that he was on the right one. He took a couple of steps back to see if maybe he had gone too far down the corridor. No, this had to be his cabin.

Katie stirred, sensing a presence, but just as she lifted herself up from her pillow, she saw the door close. Frightened, she quickly climbed out of bed and grabbed her robe. She looked around for a weapon. Maybe the lamp? No, it could start a fire. Bending down she picked up one of her shoes. That would have to do.

A soft knock sounded. "Who is it?" Katie gasped.

"James."

"James?" Katie ran to the door, flinging it open. "What in the world are you doing? Why didn't you just come in?"

James surveyed the once-bare cabin. "I did, but I thought it was the wrong one. I saw someone lying on the bed but didn't know it was you. What in the world? Where did you get all these things, and why are you holding up your shoe?"

Katie giggled. "I was going to use it to protect myself. I awoke to see the door close and didn't know who was outside."

"So you were going to have someone sniff your shoe, hoping they would pass out or what?" It was James's turn to laugh.

"Oh, aren't we the funny one. Where have you been? Did the captain have you working all night?"

James explained to Katie what had been going on and where he had been. "I suspect the captain was testing me to see if I would do as I was told, or come to you."

"You mean that a bunch of barrels won out over me?" Katie teased.

"Some of those barrels held port!"

"James!" They both broke out in laughter.

Katie told James of all the ladies and what they did to get the cabin ready for them.

"You mean perfect strangers did this for us?"

"Aye, but they are friends now."

"Yes," was all James said.

Katie left to find Annie to get hot water for James to wash and have some hot tea. He said he hadn't eaten last night so the food left on the tray was a welcome sight.

James scanned the cabin while he ate. He stared at the big bed, which took up most of the width of the cabin. There was just enough room to climb in, and that was all. When he finished eating he stretched, yawned, and lay on the bed. Soon Katie was back with a tea kettle of hot water. After James washed, they both had a cup of hot tea.

"I bet you are missing your coffee, eh, Katie?"

"I'm thankful for everything. How could I miss coffee when God has blessed us so abundantly?" Suddenly Katie felt shy as she looked at her husband. It was the first time they had ever truly been alone together.

A knock sounded and the man named Pratt entered when invited in. "Captain wants to see ya," was all he said before leaving.

"Is everything all right, James?" Katie was worried.

"I'm sure it is. I did what I was told, so there's nothing to be frightened of. Just say a prayer, and I'll be back as soon as I can." James bent to kiss Katie, leaving her again.

Within minutes, James stood in front of the captain's desk, waiting for him to look up from his log.

"So, Murphy, I had Richards go over your work. You did a fine job organizing and logging all the supplies. I needed to see if you would follow orders and if you were a man of your word. I'm glad to see you are. How do you like your new quarters?"

"They are fine. Thank you, sir."

"Tomorrow I have a job for you and some of your men, but today you rest. Spend time with your wife. You will find that I reward good work. You and your wife may join the marines and their wives in the quarter's dining hall at dinner hour. That's all."

After thanking the captain once more, James quickly returned to Katie. They had the whole day! His heart beat double-time. He knocked on the cabin door so as not to frighten his wife.

Katie put her book down when she saw him. Once he explained what the captain wanted, James shyly placed his arms around Katie, whispering in her ear, "I've missed you terribly."

Katie responded by pressing her body against James. "I've missed you too."

James wondered if she knew what effect she had on him. "Katie, I want you to know I love you more than I thought possible. I know this is awkward as far as a honeymoon goes. I, well I mean, well…"

Katie smiled. "James, it's all right. I love you, too, and you are my husband. I guess all newlyweds are a bit nervous about…things."

They both had waited so long for this moment. James took Katie in his arms, gently kissing all her doubts away. With tenderness he replaced the fear with a longing that slowly grew more intense. Finally they could be complete as God had intended, and they had waited such a long time for.

Waking with a start, Katie gazed lovingly into the face of her husband. Her heart skipped a beat as she thought of what they had just shared. She quickly dressed, then ran to get more hot water for tea. It was still early afternoon, so once James woke, they sipped their tea and snuggled. Afterwards they strolled along the top deck. It was getting hot, so they decided to go back to their cabin. They lay in each other's arms until, once again, passions stirred.

It was dusk before they decided to see about dinner. They entered the marines' dining quarters just as most of them were finishing up.

One of the men came over to James. "My name is Brandon Rogers, and this is my wife, Doris. Come join us."

James and Katie introduced themselves as they walked to a plank that held food. Gruel, the staple, was cold, but there were some vegetables, dried fruit, and potatoes…a feast. Once their plates were full, they sat across the table from their new acquaintances.

"I thought your name was Red. Did your wife call you James?" Rogers questioned.

"Many call me that. In fact, until Katie and I were married, no one called me James. How did you know I was called Red?"

"Well, let's just say there is little that is unknown aboard a ship."

Katie wondered if that meant everyone knew it was their honeymoon. She looked down at her plate, trying to hide the fact that once again she was blushing.

A man jumped up from the same table, wiping his mouth on his sleeve. "'Tis a sorry day when good, honest men got to sit and eat with the likes of prisoners," he hissed in the direction of James.

"Ah, don't start up, Lark," another man retorted.

"Ya can eat with 'im if ya wants, but don't be telling me what ter do."

After the man left, the others turned to James and Katie to apologize. James eased the tension by joking, "I don't blame him. I've seen the way some of the prisoners eat."

Laughter rang out.

"So the captain made you his clerk, I hear, Murphy," Rogers stated.

"Yes, to my surprise."

"Why would you be surprised? The captain is a smart man. He uses everything and everyone to the best advantage to ensure a safe, smooth voyage."

"I was just surprised he knew I could read and write; that he knew anything about me at all. There are hundreds of prisoners. For him to know about me was surprising."

"I can assure you the captain knows about everyone or most everyone aboard his ship. He prepares months before the sail to know who he is dealing with. It's important to him for the safety of his crew and ship."

"I can understand that. He seems like a fair man."

"He is, but don't ever cross him. I saw what happened to a man who did. Let's just say that the sharks didn't go hungry that day."

Katie swallowed, putting her fork down.

"Now see what you've done, Brandon?" Doris Rogers scolded. "I'm sorry, Mrs. Murphy. My husband forgets his manners from all the years around sailors."

Katie smiled. "No, please don't apologize. I'm all right, and please call me Katie."

"I do need to apologize Mrs. er, I mean Katie. My wife is right. I tend to forget my manners in front of ladies. I apologize to you as well, my dear." Rogers smiled at his wife. She tenderly touched her husband's arm to let him know all was forgiven.

Doris turned to Katie. "Would you both like to join us for a night stroll on deck? It's beautiful tonight."

The evening was beautiful, but a little chilly. James went to retrieve Katie's shawl, leaving her with the Rogers. Once back, the foursome strolled along the deck, admiring the moonlight on the water. All stopped by the rail to look at the beauty of the sea.

"It's beautiful and so calm," Katie whispered.

"I've sailed twice before with Brandon," Doris said. "The sea is treacherous. One minute it can be beautiful, and the next...well, thank God, we are safe aboard a sturdy ship."

"I don't think I've ever seen the moon so large or so many stars. It's breathtaking." Katie stood with her hands on the rail, looking up into the night sky.

James caught his breath at the sight of Katie gazing heavenward. Her long hair, blowing in the soft breeze, trailed down her back. She held a sweet expression of awe on her lovely face.

Rogers cleared his throat, taking his wife's arm. "Come, dear, I think we need to leave these two alone for a time. Good night, James, Katie."

"Good night," the two said in unison.

James and Katie stood by the rail in silence. The creaking of the ship along with the gentle roll of the waves was calming. James took his eyes off of Katie long enough to see a couple of sailors eyeing them. James took Katie by the arm, leading her back to their cabin. "It is getting late. I think it's time to go."

"All right, James."

James entered the cabin first so he could light the lamp, then closed and locked the door behind his wife. They stood looking at each other shyly for a few moments. Then Katie went across the room by the bed to disrobe. James turned his back, doing the same. Blowing out the lantern he climbed into bed with his bride. James reached for her, and she eagerly went to him.

Laying her head on his massive chest, Katie could hear his heart beating furiously. She shivered, causing James to hold her closer, but she hadn't shivered from the cold. James gently lifted Katie off his chest. Leaning over, he kissed her deeply.

Something else besides nervousness stirred within her....

20

Murder

Tess rolled over to snuggle with her husband. He was still sleeping but stirred to hold her as she pressed in on him. She lay there content and thankful for him. Where had he been all her life? She thought she would never fall in love, not real love anyway. She had been determined never to be forced into marrying anyone. She would be forever grateful for her father's bullheadedness in this matter.

Tess closed her eyes, reliving the beautiful wedding. Her parents had spared no expense. She had the best of everything. The long, cream-colored gown shimmered with pearls in the soft candlelight of the cathedral. Her full skirt was covered with several different lengths of lace. She wore a long, matching veil with a diamond tiara. Silken ribbon and lace fell in a long train from her bouquet of cream-colored roses mixed with tiny pink rosebuds. The altar was lined with cream-colored roses and candles. Her father marched her down the aisle with his chest puffed out. She heard her mother crying even before she could see her. David looked so regal waiting for her at the altar. He was so handsome! It had been a wonderful day.

Even more wonderful was their honeymoon. Yawning, Tess extended her fingers, admiring her wedding ring. She smiled as the diamond caught the early morning light. Tess remembered when Kathryn received her wedding ring. She had been so excited. Their rings were vastly different, but the importance was the same to both women. She wished she could share her happiness with Kathryn right now. *How I miss her,* she thought, letting out a long sigh. It was amazing to Tess that she and Katie were now friends. She didn't understand exactly how it happened but was thankful it *did* happen.

"Are you bored with me already, dear wife?" David smiled down at her.

"Never! I'll never get bored with you. I was just thinking of Kathryn and wondering how she is doing."

David continued, "What do you want to do today now that we are back from Venice? I have to think about going back to work. My father will disown me if I let you keep me away from the business much longer."

Tess laughed. "I think you are the one bored. Actually I want to go over to my parents. I've missed them. Since we arrived home late last night, they don't have any way of knowing we're back. I would like to take them the gifts we brought them."

"Why don't I drop you off there and go to the office so I can get some work done in time to come home for dinner? In fact, why don't you invite them over for dinner tonight? Just tell the cook, and she'll have everything ready for you."

"That would be wonderful! What do you want me to serve?"

"It's time you make those decisions yourself since you're the mistress of the house."

Tess watched as David got up to stoke the fire. She reached over to ring for Betsy to bring them tea. Tess had brought Betsy along to her new home. One evening before the wedding Tess had asked the young girl's forgiveness for treating her so badly. The girl was speechless at first, then broke out into a big smile. She informed Tess that she was more than happy to come along. Tess was relieved. Somehow knowing that Betsy was there made her new home seem more "her home." Tess couldn't believe the change in Betsy. She seemed to know what Tess wanted before she asked.

It never occurred to Tess that it was she who had done the changing.

Waiting for the young servant, Tess quickly jotted a note to her parents, letting them know she would be coming to visit that morning. Just as she sealed it, a knock sounded. Sure enough Betsy came in with a tray of tea, biscuits, and jam. She then set about preparing the bathtub and informed Tess that water was already being warmed.

"Betsy, please send someone over to Brick House with this note as soon as possible."

"Aye, miss, I mean mistress." Betsy smiled shyly when the handsome master looked at her. She curtsied, then left the room.

Tess sat up against her pillows, sipping tea and smiling. She dreamily thought of her future. How wonderful everything was. She felt a stab of fear at the thought that all was too perfect. Something was bound to go wrong. Things didn't last forever.

"Darling, you're scowling. What's wrong?" David said as he poured himself a cup.

"Oh, I was just thinking how happy I am, and how wonderful our lives are."

"So you're scowling?"

"It's too perfect! Something will change and ruin it."

David gave his wife a blank look before breaking into laughter. "I've never heard of someone worrying before about having nothing to worry about."

"I know I sound silly, but I'm so happy, David. I can't help feeling something is bound to go wrong."

Sitting on the edge of the bed, David set his cup and saucer down. "Things will change, and they need to. We can't stay in this room for the rest of our lives worrying about changes. We need to have faith that whatever changes come, we will face them together."

"Tell me that you will always love me. Promise me that will never change."

David took his wife's cup, then set it down to reach for her. She let him draw her close. "I already promised you that when I stood in front of God and all those people in the cathedral."

They kissed, then talked about their plans, hopes, and dreams.

It took less than a month to reach the Canary Islands. By that time there was a routine about the days for Katie. She kept the prisoners' welfare uppermost on her mind. Guilt seeped into her happiness with James. She had a cozy cabin while many suffered the heat and confinement of a small bay. She and James had a varied diet while the prisoners were fed exact portions consisting mostly of gruel. Adding to her guilt was the knowledge that she had her husband. Many of the women prisoners, and men as well, were forced to leave their mates behind. Katie thanked the Lord often for her many blessings and prayed continually for the prisoners. She worked hard to do what she could for them. She prayed that her heart was motivated for the right reason, for the love of God, and not out of guilt.

James was kept busy writing logs and ledgers of numbers for the captain. He helped Richards keep track of the rations and worked with the other men on repairs. It was a much needed reprieve from the dark, dank bay for the men. They were happy to do any and all work, and the ship's crew was happy to oblige them.

The suffering of prisoners was great in spite of all considerations. Seasickness and lack of sun seemed to take their toll. Many of the men and women became lethargic and weak. It was apparent that all were losing weight. It was easier to shave heads to get rid of the "hair bugs." The prisoners were a sorry sight indeed.

Supplies were bought at the islands, and fresh water was brought aboard. There still wasn't an overabundance of fresh water since it was worth gold on board ship, but with rationing, it would be enough. The layover allowed the prisoners to be taken on shore and housed in a large storehouse where they could have more room. They enjoyed fresh air, sunshine, and exercise. The bays on ship were fumigated and scrubbed down once again. But the day quickly came when the prisoners were brought back on board.

Katie was just as busy as James with helping the woman prisoners. She obtained permission from the captain to teach reading and writing. It helped keep the women out of trouble. A few of them proved difficult, but nevertheless they touched Katie's heart. She knew their exteriors were hard but suspected they were only protecting tender hearts. When she looked at them, she thought of Mary. Oh, how she missed her friend.

After leaving the Canary Islands, they headed toward the Cape Verde Islands. Hot breezes filled the sails, pushing the ship along. Down below the prisoners lay on their hard plank beds sweating and longing for more water than they were given. It was better to be a little thirsty than completely out of water in the long run. Even the captain and crew were given rations of water. For a time tea was not allowed to be brewed. Finally they anchored off Cape Verde, and again they loaded up with fresh supplies. This was the time of plenty. There was water to wash with and to drink. It was especially important for them to stock up since they were in for one of the hardest and longest parts of their voyage. They would not stop again until Rio de Janeiro. That would take them another couple of months to reach, and it was indeed a treacherous stretch. There was still a lot of ocean to cross.

Once again the ship hoisted anchor, and soon Cape Verde was behind them. After leaving, the weather took a turn for the worse. High winds and rain kept the prisoners below. Many prisoners found themselves unable to eat with the pitch of the ship. In good weather prisoners were brought up in small groups to take in the fresh air and exercise. If the weather was bad, the wait for exercise and sunshine could be weeks. It was during these times that arguments broke out, and a few prisoners had to be separated. The prisoners lost even more weight and suffered terribly in their closed, cramped quarters. Despair fell heavily on many of them, to the point that several men and women tried suicide. After a full week of bad weather, the sun finally broke through the clouds, leaving a brilliant rainbow across the sky.

Katie and some other women took advantage of the good weather by hanging wet clothes on the ropes. Laundry had piled up, and trying to hang it to dry below was useless. Laundry was a daily chore and a difficult one to be sure. Seawater was hard on the skin and cloth. It tended to take away any moisture from the hands and strength from the material. During the day the women washed, hung, and folded clothing and bedding; in the evening they mended.

Between that and teaching the women their letters, Katie had busy days. She helped them wash their hair once it grew out. With the doctor's help they worked hard to clear up any "head bugs." If it proved too difficult to get rid of them, the prisoners' and children's heads were once again shaved. Katie enjoyed her time with the women convicts. How misjudged they were. Very few turned out to be violent or guilty of a crime worthy of this punishment. They were women with hopes and dreams similar to her own, who had found themselves in difficult circumstances that landed them aboard a convict ship.

Katie would listen to their stories, nurse the sick, and many times care for some of their children. The children were allowed a small section of the deck in which to play. They played in the sunshine and fresh air they so badly needed as long as they never got in the way. It was especially important to keep them away from the crew. It was not unheard of, some said, for a crew member to throw a wee one overboard if underfoot. So far that hadn't happened on Captain Warwick's ship, but it wasn't a promise that it wouldn't.

Sometimes the mothers could accompany their children, but most times not, so Katie stayed with them. The mothers were indeed appreciative and found themselves drawn to the caring, young woman.

It was still horribly hot and humid, but Katie tried not to complain. She knew how awful it was in the bays. The water was rationed, and although it was warm and close to becoming stagnant, it was appreciated.

In the third month of the voyage another storm hit. It was amazing how quickly the blue sky could turn black. Clouds swirled, and the wind blew so hard that waves crashed over the deck, threatening to spill men into the ocean. Sails were lowered, and the crew rushed to latch everything down.

Katie was teaching several women their lessons when it became impossible to concentrate. The gentle rocking motion of the ship disappeared and was replaced with great lifts; then a deep, thunderous drop threatened to break the ship apart. Thunder crashed while lightning lit up the sky. Fearing the lanterns would swing and break, Katie blew them out, leaving everyone in the darkness. One woman vomited from the rough-and-tumble pitch of the ship. Wood creaked all around. Children cried in fear, clinging to their mothers. Thoughts of drowning frightened most, but the unknown mysteries in the black waters terrified them more. Mental pictures of being cast into the vast, swirling waters filled their heads. They knew they were about to be dragged down by some slimy, scaly monster.

Katie started to pray. One by one the women encircled her and listened. Her soft, barely audible prayer changed into a more powerful, faith-filled talk with her Savior.

"Father, protect us and help us not to be afraid. Help the crew know what to do and protect them from falling overboard. Let these women, all of us on board, know You hold us in Your hand. Heavenly Father, You are our Creator and the Creator of the seas, wind, and rain. I know You love us and care about us. I ask that You place Your hand upon us and this ship along with the other vessels. Calm our fears, and help us know in our hearts the peace and joy only You can give. In Jesus' name, amen."

The women seemed calmer, but still they huddled close together, waiting for the storm to subside. A few more hours went by before the storm lost some of its intensity. Except for some of the children, all crying ceased. Katie turned to help the sick woman and began cleaning up after her as best she could. She stayed with the women until late.

James wasn't in their cabin when she entered, so she lay on the bed, turning her thoughts to her dear old friends in London: Mary, Maggie, and the others. What were they doing right now? Were they well? Had they by now given their hearts and lives to the Lord? She felt homesick for her cozy cottage and friends. Curling up on her bed, she let her tears wet the pillow. She missed their smiling faces.

When her thoughts turned to James, it dawned on her that he should have returned by now. Was he all right, or had something happened to him during the storm? Just as Katie swung her legs off the bed to go check on him, James entered the cabin.

"Katie, darling, what's the matter? Is it the storm? It's almost over now. We're safe and sound. No worse off from it."

"Oh, James, I was about to come looking for you. I was just feeling a little homesick. I've been wondering how everyone back home is doing."

James put his arms around his wife. "I understand; you are very close to them. An ocean can't change that. Of course you miss them."

Sniffling, Katie told James about the woman prisoners. "You're right, James, God is blessing us every day, and here I am crying."

And so the days and nights went on and on. It took longer for them to reach Rio de Janeiro since the storm had blown them off course, but they did arrive...safely. Some major repairs had to be done, which held them up even longer.

Captain Warwick informed everyone that *Sally Mae* wasn't in a race. They made good time in the beginning of the voyage, and time was not as important as safety. They did what they needed to do to make the ship safe and secure once more. *Sally Mae* was anchored for three full weeks before leaving to sail to Cape Town. It was now mid-October.

They pressed on and so did the days.

Magistrate Peter Reeves was dead. He had been dead for days before anyone was notified. His body was stuffed in some alley doorway in the seedy side of London. Many probably saw it there, but what did it matter? It was a common occurrence to find bodies. If any notice was taken at all, it was the richness of his clothes and whatever else could be picked off the body.

Some were shocked at the news, and some were not. Peter had quite the reputation with women, causing many a jealous man to seethe with anger when his name was mentioned. But all wondered who had been brave enough or stupid enough to kill him. He had been a powerful man.

Victoria made a beautiful grieving widow. She had several bereavement gowns made. It had taken a lot of planning and arrangements to have him killed. She had entrusted Justin, her lover, to find someone to do the deed. Even more good news, Justin informed her that the man he had hired was found a few days later beaten to death. No one knew but them. How perfect.

Sitting by the window in her room, she let her mind wander back to when she and Peter were first married. Oh, she knew he didn't intend to marry her at first. She was just another one of his conquests, but she had loved him in the beginning. Knowing that a high position would come along with her hand in the marriage tipped the scales. She and Peter were wed with great fanfare.

It wasn't long before she discovered that Peter was not content with just one woman. She had threatened him for years to stop his late-night rendezvous with his trollops. He thought he was clever enough that she wouldn't find out. But Victoria certainly wasn't one of those women who simply turned and looked the other way. He had rubbed her face in his infidelity long enough. Yes, he had made her look the fool for too long. But what had pushed her over the edge was when he openly pined for that Wilson snit.

They fought violently, and he said some unforgivable things to Victoria. How she and her father ran his life. How her father paid him to marry her, then kept his position as a magistrate over his head to keep him married to her. How hateful he had been. Worse, he'd even confessed his love for the Wilson girl. He planned to have her as his own. What did that…that female….have that could ever compare to Victoria?

When Victoria saw Peter with the girl the day she left for Paris, she hired the usual men to have him investigated. She might even have forgiven him one more time if he had not voiced his love for the girl. It was too much to bear. That's when the idea was conceived. She would make Peter pay…the girl, too.

When she heard that he was found dead, it was a relief. The stress of not knowing when it would happen was unbearable, but now only half her plan was accomplished. She needed to set things in motion to throw suspicion on the Wilson girl. Oh, it wasn't Wilson anymore. What was her last name…Day? Yes, that was it, Tess Day. That was her married name, but Victoria knew her by only one name: whore.

"The captain will 'ave yer liver if yas get caught."

"How will I get caught unless you tell someone?"

"Ain't sayin a word to nobody, but I ain't goin' in on it neither. I've been flogged once. Ain't goin' ter git it again."

The two men whispered in the dark as they slithered along the rail. Making sure there were no warders or matrons patrolling the women's bays, the men sneaked down to the last bay.

The man leading the way pointed at a woman asleep and whispered, "She's the one; 'er name is Betty. Don't unlock 'er until I be gone. If someone 'ears ya, I don't want to be 'ere." Leaving his partner, the man tiptoed out and went back to lie down, covering his head. If hell was going to let loose, he didn't want to be a part of it.

The remaining man unlocked the bay and stepped in. Some of the women snored softly, but one leaned up on one elbow. "What ya want 'ere?" she spat.

"Looking for Betty," is all he said.

The woman leaned over to push a finger into the side of the woman across from her.

"What? What's the matter?"

"Seems there's a man fer ya here."

Betty turned and peered into the darkness. "What ya want?"

"Heard ya is willing to give a man a little fun fer some extra considerations."

"Ya," was all she said.

Another woman whispered, "You're going to get all of us into trouble."

"Shut up, ya old hag," Betty hissed. "Yer mad cause ya can't get a man of yer own."

The woman only shook her head and turned away.

After they both crept out, he relocked the bay door. "Keep your head down now, or we both get caught," the man instructed.

"Don't worry. I can be as quiet as a mouse when I needs ta be."

Sneaking into one of the proper boats the two felt safe and secluded, but they should have known better. Very little went unnoticed on board a ship. It was only a matter of time....

Katie flew out from under the bedcovers and tried to dive over James to get to the chamber pot, but she didn't quite make it. Instead she landed on his stomach, startling the man out of a sound sleep. He grabbed her, not realizing what was going on.

"James, let me go!" She made it just in time before she vomited.

Setting his feet on the cold floor, he grabbed a blanket, draping it around her shoulders. Concern creased his brow as he wet a towel for her. Katie let James lead her back to bed.

"Are you seasick again?"

"I don't think so. It's been a long time since I was seasick. Maybe it's something I ate."

"Maybe I should get Dr. Crane."

"Not yet, James. Let's see how I feel later on. It's so early I don't want to disturb him."

"Fine, but you stay put in bed today. Don't even think of heading out to do laundry. I told you that you've been overdoing it. You're overworking yourself."

"James, I'm not working any harder than the others."

"The others don't do laundry, mending, and then teach the women. If that's not enough, you help them with their children. You need rest. Now I'm telling you to stay put. I'm going to go get you some tea, and hopefully that will help your stomach."

"Yes, sir!" Katie smiled up at her husband.

"Huh," was all he said as he got dressed. "When I come back, you better still be in that bed." Then he was gone.

Katie's stomach lurched again, and she hit the floor running. This wasn't seasickness. She didn't feel dizzy or lightheaded, just sick to her stomach. Snuggling down into bed, Katie yielded to the fact that she would be there for a while.

James brought her tea before leaving to answer a call from the captain. He admonished her once again to stay in bed. She did feel tired, so she didn't argue with him at all. Lying in a soft bed was more tempting at the moment than facing the day. Soon she was fast asleep.

Annie knocked on the cabin door, then opened it slowly when she didn't get an answer. James had asked her to peek in on Katie. Seeing her sleeping, Annie crept over and placed her hand on the young woman's forehead. No fever, her color was good. The girl took deep breaths in her sleep. Maybe she should get Dr. Crane like James suggested. She had a hunch of what was going on but thought it best to talk to the doctor first.

Annie was able to leave without waking Katie. She found the good doctor frowning as he put salve on one of the men's ankles.

"Shackles rub a man's skin raw; then it gets infected. Where do they expect these men to run to?"

"Doctor," Annie began, "Mrs. Murphy is sick and throwing up. She's sleeping sound right now. She doesn't have a fever, but I would feel better if you were to look in on her."

"How's her color?"

"Looks good. There's no telltale signs of sickness, just the vomiting."

"I'll see her when I finish with this man."

"Thank you, Doctor."

When Dr. Crane knocked on the cabin door, Katie first asked who it was, then invited him in. She said she'd just gotten up. She was sitting, wrapped in a blanket, at her small table.

"Mrs. Murphy, I've heard you aren't well."

"I don't know what's wrong with me, Doctor. I was quite sick this morning but feel much better now. I wonder if it was something I ate?"

"I'll be able to tell more after I examine you." Dr. Crane touched Katie's cheek for fever. There was none. He checked her throat for redness and listened to her heart and lungs for any telltale rattling. No, her lungs were clear, and her heart beat steady and strong. It wasn't long before he had completed his examination.

"Doctor?"

"Mrs. Murphy, have you noticed any changes in your body of late?"

"Changes?"

"Yes. When was your last monthly?"

Katie blushed at the question. "A few months ago, but I thought it was stress. Is everything all right?" She frowned, then realization seemed to hit her. "You mean...I could be expecting? I'm going to have a wee bairn?"

"I think it's safe to say that you will have a summer baby. July is my guess."

"It's so soon. I must of...I've, we've...I must be just pregnant. I didn't think women knew so soon."

"Every pregnancy is different. Some women can tell sooner than others."

Katie was silent, as if in shock.

"Mrs. Murphy, I've noticed you are an industrious person. I hear from others of your involvement in the female prisoners' lives. I see you always washing clothes or helping with children. All of that is fine, but I feel you should confine yourself to bedrest for the time being."

"You sound like my husband, Doctor. For how long?"

"No, I sound like your doctor. A week for now. I will see how you're faring after that, but for now you need your rest. I will also speak to the cook and the captain. You need extra food."

"Please don't tell my husband about our wee bairn, Dr. Crane. I would like to tell him myself."

"Of course. I wouldn't want to spoil your surprise for him."

Crane left to speak to the cook and the captain. He felt sad for the young woman. She had enough hardship to face, but to be pregnant now would be doubly hard on her. The chance of her baby surviving was questionable. Over half the babies born on board a ship died, but of course they would be at their destination by the time she gave birth. Still, with the dankness and the close confinement of humans, it wasn't hard to catch something. Three of the women prisoners and one wife of a marine had already miscarried. Chances were Mrs. Murphy would do the same. Of course, having her own cabin might help. Well, time would tell. Such was life on ship. No one knew that better than he.

After the doctor left, Katie sat on the bed in quiet shock. She'd always wanted children but didn't expect to have a child so soon. What would James say? Would he be happy about the bairn or disappointed in the timing? How was she to tell James? Did he suspect? Why hadn't she known herself? Strange, but it had never crossed her mind that she was going to have a baby!

Excitement and dread consumed her at once. Her heart beat faster as she gently lay her hand on her stomach. Staying as still as possible, she tried to feel the life within her. There was nothing, no movement or any indication of a body growing inside her own. It was early, after all. She was not bound to feel the bairn yet. A boy, a girl, names, clothes? Oh, she felt overwhelmed. She wasn't ready for a wee one, but how did you prepare yourself for that? Her mind swirled with emotions until she felt exhausted. Suddenly, as if a feather brushed against her, a thought entered: *The Lord is my fortress.* Katie concentrated on remembering part of a psalm that she had read.

"My soul finds rest in God alone;
my salvation comes from him.
He alone is my rock and my salvation.
He is my fortress; I will never be shaken."

Excitement flooded her. Of course! God knew all about this wee one. He knew she was pregnant! He had a perfect plan for her. He would take care of her. Why did she always panic every time something happened? It was as if she forgot the Lord in her day-to-day life until something happened to turn her back to Him.

Katie lifted her heart toward heaven. *Lord, forgive me for being so afraid. I keep fighting fear over the future when I know my future is in Your hands. Build my faith, Lord, and thank You, thank You, thank You for this new life. Help James to be happy about the news, too. Amen.*

The man's screams filled the air. He pulled at the leather binds around his wrists. He was to be given forty lashes. After less than half, he could stand no more. Blood dripped from the open wounds on his back. His mangled flesh hung in strips.

Many were there to witness the flogging. Some of the men looked down at the deck, remembering the searing, flashing pain they experienced when it was their misfortune to be flogged.

Captain Warwick stood stiffly watching the proceedings. He hated it. This was one of the few things he hated about being captain. He had no choice. Any orders given to his crew that were not enforced threatened the voyage; it also threatened lives. But more than that, it threatened his authority. He could have ordered different punishment. He considered doing so, but he'd had trouble with these two before. The flogging would cause them to think twice before giving any trouble again.

The crewman had begged for mercy. The woman standing off to the side cried and had to be held up, for she was to be next. Fear took all strength from her legs.

Warwick once again thought about changing the punishment for the woman, but it was too late. He couldn't show any kind of weakness. Besides, the woman had been trouble from the start. She was caught trying to steal rations from other prisoners and fought with the matrons. Now she had been found with one of his crew. It was almost impossible to keep the crew from the females, but he had to try. His crew knew before signing on that it was a stipulation of his. No chasing the female prisoners. Free women were different. If one of his men wanted to meet one of the matrons, that was up to them, but female prisoners were off limits.

As the lash bit into the man's flesh for the last time, Betty was brought forward. She wailed, fighting against the two men who were trying to bind her. She glanced over at poor Jake. He had mercifully blacked out, hanging from his wrists. Men cut the ties to free him. Betty felt a tugging, then heard the ripping of her shirt being torn from top to bottom in the back. Only the collar helped to keep the material together covering her.

"We didn't do nothin' wrong! We jest 'ad a little fun was all!"

Her words fell on deaf ears. A marine stood at attention until Betty was bound tightly. A slow rhythmic beating of the drum began. Captain Warwick nodded to the commander, who stepped forward to read off the charges.

"Betty Johnston, you are charged with mischievous and criminal behavior."

"Criminal? What? What is criminal 'bout lovin' a man? What is criminal 'bout not wantin' ta be alone?" she shouted.

The commander continued. "You will be given fifteen lashes for your crime." He then stepped back, which was indication for the man to begin.

"NOOO!" Betty screamed, throwing herself backwards, trying to release herself from the post. Blood ran from her wrists as she fought the ties.

The man stood, waiting for the captain's consent to continue. After hesitating for a moment, Captain Warwick nodded, and so it began.

Tears ran down Betty's face as the lash bit her tender flesh on her side. It would have been better had she held as still as possible, letting her back take the blows, but she found it impossible to do so. Her body writhed in pain, twisting away as if it had a mind of its own. Betty had never felt such pain, even in giving birth to the lifeless body of her babe months ago.

The man lifted his arm to strike again. He had only flogged one man in his life before today, never a woman. He had only volunteered to be the one to use the lash on this voyage for the extra money the job offered and had hoped he would not have to actually do the job he was hired for. He heard many in his position enjoyed their labor, but he did not. Sweat glistened on the man's face as his body labored in his task. He tried to lessen the blows, but it was impossible. There was no such thing as a soft whip.

Another blow resounded, along with another scream. It seemed endless, but finally it was over.

Whimpering, Betty hung by her wrists. Her eyes were rolled back in her head, and she had soiled herself. Men came forward to untie her. They carried her back to her bay. Thankfully, she had blacked out.

James stood off to the side, wishing he didn't have to witness this torture. He had tried to speak to the captain on the woman's behalf but was rebuked soundly. It came as a surprise that Warwick would order such a punishment. The captain had only shown great care and compassion toward the prisoners up until now. James had prayed for the man and now silently prayed for the woman. Every blow of the lash cut his heart. He was furious with himself and with the man who ordered such inhumane treatment. James knew he should have stepped in, but what good would that have done?

He imagined Christ being whipped and beaten. If James had been there, would he have stood watching? The tears he fought sprung to his eyes as he conceded that he probably would have watched then too. Disappointment, rage, and shame swamped him. He needed to leave the deck before his tears fell. Pride added to his already heavy heart. What would everyone think of him if they saw his tears?

James turned and left the deck without the captain's permission.

Warwick watched the big man walk with purpose toward the steps leading to the lower decks. He let him go, for the man's body language spoke loudly. The captain understood only too clearly the anger the man was feeling, for he felt it too.

Warwick straightened his spine. He did not have the luxury of giving in to his feelings. He was the sole master on this ship, and his decisions could mean life or death. Any other time he would consider reprimanding Murphy for his lack of control, but enough people had been punished this day. He would speak to him later.

Prisoners were brought forward to swab the blood and filth off the deck.

21

Fallen

Katie awoke from a scream that seemed far away, but by the time she was fully awake there was only silence. Probably another dream. More by sensing someone at the door than any noise, Katie walked over and opened it.

James stood there. By the look of her husband, she knew something was terribly wrong. "James, what are you doing standing outside the door? What's wrong?"

James hesitated to enter. He didn't want Katie to see how upset he was. But he also desperately needed her gentleness and kindness right now. Anger surged through him, anger toward himself and the captain. How could he claim to be a Christian when he stood by and let something like that happen? James stepped in and stared at the floor. Before he could stop them, tears streamed down his cheeks. His broad shoulders shook from his sobs as he fell to his knees. He grabbed Katie, holding her close.

"James, oh, James, what's wrong?"

It was a few minutes before he could answer. His heart ached; his soul was crushed. With everything else, his pride was hurt from crying in front of Katie.

Katie just held him. It was what he needed more than anything. Once he released her, she brought him a clean handkerchief. "I'm going to step out to get some hot water, but I will be back shortly."

He knew she was allowing him a moment alone.

James was sitting at the small table holding his head in his hands when Katie returned. Carefully she poured his tea, then sat on the edge of the bed waiting for him to speak. He didn't right away, so she silently prayed.

After a few minutes, James turned the chair around to face his wife. He then told her what had happened.

"Why wasn't I made aware of it?" Katie asked. "Neither Annie nor Jenna told me of the lashing."

"I asked them not to. I knew it was going to be ugly. I wanted to protect you from it. Oh, Katie, it was horrible. I've seen cruelty in the world, but not like that. And I just stood there. I didn't lift a hand to stop it. I tried to talk to the captain about it when I first learned it was to happen, but he let me know I was to stay out of it. As I watched, I kept thinking about Jesus. Of how He was beaten and whipped. I asked myself, if I were there, would I have done anything to help Him? I knew in my heart that I would probably have just stood and watched like I did today. How can He ever forgive me or love me? How as a Christian could I have stood by and just watched?"

Katie realized at that moment it must have been their screams that woke her. She could see her husband's heart and spirit was broken but didn't know what to say. She had never seen him so vulnerable. Protectiveness washed over her. She wanted to soothe him. She stood and embraced him, holding his head gently against her breast. Stroking his hair, she asked the Lord to give her wisdom and to give James comfort. He held on tight, as if his very life depended on it.

"James, what would have happened if you stepped in to help? Would it have done any good?"

"That's not the point. I didn't even try. I was afraid. How do you feel about your husband now?"

"You did try. You talked to the captain. You did what you could. As for my feelings for you, I love you as much as ever. The Lord's love for you has not changed, either. You know that. Remember when you told me that yourself? Nothing that we ever did, or will ever do, will stop Him from loving us. He knows our weaknesses. He also knows how you would have behaved if you were there when He was beaten. You are right. You probably would have acted the same as everyone else. We all would. That's why He came to us in the first place, because we are so weak and need Him. There is no hope without Him."

"Yes, but I am a Christian, and I still did nothing!"

"As was Peter when he denied Christ three times. We are all weak, James. You know it is not what we do that earns our salvation, but His grace. We are to rely on His strength, not ours. Yes, having Jesus in our hearts should make a difference in how we live, but we do and will fall short. It is only by grace, James, His grace. How many times have you told me that yourself? Remember when I didn't want to turn to Him in the gaol? I felt guilty about calling on Him only in my time of troubles. You told me that was a lie of Satan's, and that the Lord wants us to call on Him. That is when most people come to recognize their need of Him. Well, you believe in a lie of Satan's right now. Whether you stopped the punishment or not does not decide how God feels about you. He loves you unconditionally. Don't doubt His love for you or mine either because your human nature reacted to a difficult situation. You couldn't do anything about those people getting the lash, but you can do something to help them now."

"What do you mean?" James questioned as he lifted his head.

"This poor man and woman need their backs tended to and probably their spirits as well. You and I can go to them. We can try to ease their pain and suffering as Christ would. Not out of guilt, but out of His love."

James was quiet for a minute. "You're right. I didn't do anything then, but I can do something now. I just pray my motives are right. By the way, how did you get so wise?"

"I don't know about being wise, but He knows we're trusting in Him. I don't know your heart, James, but God does. Pray about it."

Katie thought of telling him her news, but it wasn't the time. She wanted James to be happy about the baby, and right now there were other things on his mind.

James couldn't pray. He still felt shame. He got up and washed his face. They both left to help the two wounded prisoners. They separated to go to the different decks, but not until Katie gave him a quick hug. "I love you, James."

He smiled down at his wife, but his heart was still heavy. He nodded, then turned to go. He didn't dare answer. The tightness in his throat threatened to bring more tears.

Betty lay on her berth in excruciating pain. Her nails were dug into the thin mat. It was drenched with tears…tears of anger, hatred, and pain. No one understood why she did what she did, nor did they care. No one had ever loved her. She'd never had a family except for the people she'd worked for. What a laugh—she had slaved and prostituted herself for them. It wasn't of her own choosing, but what difference did it make? She was never given a choice. She was so grateful to have a place to live and food to eat, but the price was high. She slaved for the woman during the day and prostituted herself to the man at night. No wonder they were happy to have her live with them. She hated it.

When she ran away, she took a few coins and the babe in her belly with her. She had earned the coins. She was cursed with the babe from the man she hated. Only a few coins were taken. She should have taken more, but it didn't matter since she was caught.

Now here she was, beaten and bloody for reaching out to someone for kindness, for security. She had to look after herself. No one else would. She was once again beaten down by so-called "decent people." Whenever she reached out for some human kindness, for love, she ended up hurt.

Katie searched for Annie to ask permission to tend the hurting woman.

Annie smiled when she spotted Katie. "How are you feeling? Still ill, or better?"

Katie didn't want to say anything to anyone about the baby until she had told James. "I'm feeling much better, thank you. I've come to ask if I can tend to that woman who was lashed today."

"You mean Betty? So you heard about it, eh? Why do you want to do that? She would rather spit at you than look at you."

"I just found out from James what had happened, and I want to help."

"I'm surprised you didn't hear their screams. It was horrible. It's never a good sight to see."

"I was resting this afternoon and woke when I heard screaming," Katie said. "I thought it was a dream. I'm surprised to hear such punishment is still handed down. It seems so extreme."

"Captain Warwick doesn't usually use the lash for punishment and especially on women. I must say I was surprised as well, but he must have had a good reason for it."

"Where is she now?"

"In her bay. The surgeon, Mr. Crane, was going to have her stay in his hospital at the foreport of the ship, but several men are already housed there. There isn't room to separate the men and the women. He felt it best for her to stay here. He already put a plaster on her back."

"I still cannot believe they would do this to a man, let alone a woman."

"Like I said, Captain Warwick usually doesn't. Usually women are placed in the coal hole—that's the darkest part of the ship—for days, or they're made to wear the wooden jacket."

"Wooden jacket? What is that?"

"The top of a heavy flour barrel is cut away; then holes are made for the woman's arms. Her hands are locked in chains together once it is in place. She wears it until she can't stand it no more. She can't sit nor lie down. It proves to be a deterrent in their causing trouble."

"It all sounds terrible, but they must have done more than be together to get the lash. Only thing is, I can't think of anything bad enough to have that done to them."

"Well, if you feel you need to help Betty, go ahead. Be warned, though. She's a spitfire. She hates everybody, especially decent folks. She seems to hate them most of all. Do you know which bay she's housed in?"

Katie nodded and made her way there after getting the key. Praying as she went, she tried to still her uncertainty. She was afraid, but of what? Rejection from the woman? Being verbally attacked? What? Katie had read that fear was not of the Lord, so she prayed for His peace.

When she saw Betty, Katie's heart went out to her. The other women were up on the deck exercising, leaving Betty alone. She looked like a little girl lost instead of a supposed hardened criminal. Her hair was matted and dirty. She was dreadfully thin. She lay on her stomach while the torn shirt still hung around her neck.

"Hello, my name is Katie Murphy." Katie found a stool and sat next to the berth.

"What ya want?" Betty cringed in pain as she turned her head toward Katie.

"I came to see if I could help you." Katie bent down so Betty could see her.

"Help me what? Can ya take me chains off and set me free? Can ya stop the pain or help me to git 'ome? Wha ya want fer yer 'elp? I ain't got no money."

"No, I can't give you those things you asked, and I'm not looking for payment from you. I thought if you would like I could carefully brush and clean your hair, or maybe feed you some broth."

There was silence, then Betty asked again, "Why ya want ter 'elp me?"

"I just do. Can I brush your hair?"

"Me back's on fire. What I want me 'air brushed fer?"

"I guess you're right. I'm sorry. I wasn't thinking. It's just that I want to ease your pain somehow."

"What fer? Ter make yerself feel better and ease your decent conscience for me gettin' the whip?"

"I do feel terrible about what happened to you. I'm sorry for your pain. Do you think you could eat something, maybe some broth? You need your strength to get better."

"Better," she spat. "Better fer what?"

"I'll get some warm broth. I'll feed it to you and make sure the flies stay off."

"You be doin' that fer me?"

"Aye."

"Cannot think of eatin'. Me back is on fire, like I said. I feel sick ter me stomach. Surely could use a drink o' water, though."

"All right, I'll be right back." Katie was surprised at how easily Betty responded to her. *Thank You, Lord,* she breathed. Retrieving some water, she headed back. She ran into Dr. Crane. She needed to see if he had any powders to ease Betty's pain.

"I've already given her some for her pain. She can have more later. When I tried to get her to eat something, she refused. Getting her strength up to fight off infection is the most important thing right now. If you can get her to eat, let her eat her fill," Dr. Crane stated.

"I asked her, but she's in too much pain to eat."

The doctor only shook his head in understanding.

Soon Katie was sitting on the floor next to Betty. Holding a cup to her lips, she let Betty drink. Katie sat quietly, chasing any flies away. After a time she placed rags under her so Betty could relieve herself. Katie then gathered the soiled material and began bathing her, avoiding her back. When finished, she then laid a clean sheet over her just up to her waist. Once again she sat next to Betty's berth, making sure no flies landed.

Soon Betty breathed deeply in sleep. Compassion and love filled Katie for this woman. Deep down Katie knew the feelings she had were from the Lord. How much He loved Betty. Even when people didn't realize it, God loved them. He sent people to help them in their time of need…if they would only accept it.

"What proof do you have that my daughter killed the man?" Lord Wilson bellowed.

"Enough proof to have her put in the gaol, and there she will stay until her trial!" the man bellowed back.

Lord Wilson did not intimidate Joseph Potter. Potter's family was very old and established with many positions within the government. Being Victoria's father and Peter's father-in-law only made him more forceful. "We even found a letter written in your daughter's hand, stating she intended to have him murdered."

"I saw that note, and you must realize it was too convenient. She would have to be crazy to leave something like that around her house. It was made to look like she did it."

"She is crazy for what she did, and she'll pay for it. Now I must take care of some business." The man departed, leaving Lord Wilson alone.

Never in his life had Lord Wilson felt so out of control, so beaten down. He had tried everything in his power to have Tess released, but met resistance on every side. Why did this have to happen now? His daughter was truly happy for the first time in her life. She was settled in with her new husband and home. He and Barbara had high hopes for grandchildren, and now this. Barbara was inconsolable with worry and grief.

Lord Wilson stood to leave. It was amazing how old he felt. He would go to Grimes to see if he had found out anything yet. Hope flickered in his heart. If there was anyone who could find the truth, it was Grimes.

Tess sat on the bench near the wall. She was in a tiny cell alone. Bringing her shawl closer about her, she leaned her head back. Tears ran down her cheeks. She believed that she deserved to be there. Oh, she was innocent of the murder, but she was there for what she had done to Kathryn. It must be God paying her back for her wickedness. She had treated Kathryn horribly for many years and then lied. Just because they became friends later, and Kathryn forgave her, didn't mean God did. It had to be Him punishing her now.

Words from Kathryn came back to her. *"The Bible says that when God forgives our sins, He forgets them. He doesn't remember them."*

So if God forgives me and forgets, why am I being punished? she wondered.

Noise filled the air. She heard crying, swearing, and a low hum of voices that never ceased. *There must be rows of cells full of people,* she thought. *Father must have requested I be placed in a cell alone.* She couldn't see anything from where she was except a plain wall across from the locked door. David and her father had left a few hours ago, promising to get her out. She clung to that, but as time went on, hope faded.

Wearily she went to lie on her mat. Sleep eluded her so far, but she would try again. Doing nothing threatened to drive her crazy. If she could only sleep to pass the time, it would help. Again she lay down, thinking of Kathryn locked up for over a year. How in the world did she endure? Other troubling thoughts crowded in. Who placed that written note in her home, and when? Someone took a lot of time and trouble to make the signature look like hers. Someone planted it, but who?

There seemed to be no answers, no hope, and despair set in. Was this how Kathryn felt...alone and desperate? At least Tess had family to help, but Kathryn had none at the time. Shame flooded her. She had never considered what Kathryn was going through at the time. Yes, she most certainly deserved to be here. God may have forgiven her, but the world found out about her sin. This was payment for her deceitfulness. This would be her life from now on. If only she could curl up and die.

Victoria basked in the attention. Flowers, notes, and requests for visits poured in for the grieving widow. Some gentlemen she knew were ready to pursue her had also sent notes. This was working out so well. She never thought she could be so clever. She was able to trick that dimwitted maid Betsy into planting that confession note in Tess's room. How did she word it again? Oh, yes:

> *Peter has left me to go back to his wife. I could kill him...no, I will kill him. I know someone who will do it for me.*

What looked like scribbling from a rejected, jealous lover made a beautiful confession. Yes, she was clever.

Victoria stretched her long legs. The hard part was having to stay locked up in her house, acting the bereaved widow. It was getting increasingly harder to work up widow's tears. Not able to go to any social functions or outings was difficult. She was not afraid at all of being found out. No one would ever suspect her. Her only fear was she might feel guilty after Peter was dead, but that proved false. With all she'd had to endure with that man, he'd forced her into it. That made it more his fault. And, after all, she didn't actually do the killing. Her hands were not bloodstained.

Victoria sighed heavily at the thought of spending another day closed up in her house with only her parents to keep her company. She thought of walking in the garden but decided against it. Maybe she would play the piano for a while. No, she decided on reading instead. Maybe a book about high adventure. After that, she would go over all the notes she'd received and pen some replies. She was anxious to respond to the gentlemen most of all, but she must be tactful. Oh, how she loved the game of "catch and release" when it came to men.

Smiling, Victoria turned to head downstairs. *Maybe I will plan another trip to Paris.* The world had opened up…now that she was free. Had she realized the benefits of widowhood she might have tried it sooner. Finding a book that looked interesting, Victoria curled up before the fireplace in the parlor. She summoned the maid for tea. Yes, if she could fight the boredom, she would be all right. *I wonder how that snit is doing in the gaol right now.* Smiling to herself, she began to read.

It took two weeks before Betty could sit up. Her wounds had begun to heal nicely during the time Katie had taken care of her. Katie had faithfully cleaned her hair and body and applied plasters. Betty was looking more robust than before from all the good care and food given her.

The other women in the bay also found a change in Betty. Her tough exterior started to crack. She smiled at times. In fact, the mood of all the women was getting better for the presence of Mrs. Murphy. She entertained them with stories and continued teaching them to read and write. To fight off the long hours of idleness they took up sewing shirts. They would be sold for a small profit once they reached their destination.

Betty began to open up to the others and, before long, friendships blossomed. Katie was able to share God's Word with them, and they listened eagerly to the Bible stories.

"Ya mean to say, God forgived that King David fer sleepin' with that married lady and fer killin' 'er 'usband?" Betty inquired.

"Yes, he did. We're all sinners, Betty, all of us. We are born into sin."

"Ya think maybe 'e can forgive somebody like me?"

"Absolutely. He looks at all of us equally. When we ask Jesus Christ into our hearts, we are new creatures, the Bible says. We are clean and whole."

"He sees me and someone like yerself as the same? Yer sure 'e forgives everythin'?"

"Yes, Betty. I'm a sinner like everyone else. Nothing you ever did or thought of doing is bigger than God. Jesus' blood covers it all."

Betty grew very quiet, trying to take it all in. After a moment she asked, "Is that yer words or the Bible's words?"

Katie opened her Bible to 1 John 1:9 and read out loud: " 'If we confess our sins, he is faithful and just to forgive us our sins, and to cleanse us from all unrighteousness.' "

"What does all that mean?"

"If you talk to God in prayer, and tell Him your sins, He will forgive them."

"Don' 'e know 'em already if 'e's God?"

"Yes, He does, but He wants you to tell Him. He wants us to talk to Him, communicate, and spend time with Him. I think too, if we tell Him about what we've done in our lives, it opens us up inside to allow Him to begin to heal us. We all have had things done to us that scar us and cause us a lot of pain."

"Did ya know I 'ad a wee bairn and it died? I didn't want it. I hated it afore it was even born. When it died, I was glad. God will forgive me on that?"

Katie was shocked by Betty's confession but didn't react. "Yes, Betty, He'll forgive that."

Betty went on to tell Katie about her life and the circumstances that surrounded her pregnancy. She told how she ended up on the *Sally Mae*. Katie felt such sadness for all the sorrow Betty had endured in her young life. She felt troubled for the lost bairn, who wasn't at fault.

"What 'appened to yerself to be 'ere? It would seem yer life to be perfect with a 'usband and being a lady and all," Betty asked.

Katie began telling the women of being locked in the gaol for over a year. Of her being a maid, of having been accused of stealing. She shared how she had met and married James, at how he was a prisoner on board. Some of them now remembered seeing her in the gaol, but had forgotten. The very idea Katie could be in the same situation as they gave them hope. In their minds it was easy to be religious when you were not hungry, cold, or abused. It was surprising that she had been all of this, yet she loved God. Knowing she had suffered many of the same things as they helped them see that God could accept them. They came to believe He would help them and actually save them as He had done her. God was not the God of the rich, but the God of all.

"Blimey, ne'er thought ya ter be a maid. Thought ya ter be a grand lady and all," one of the women stated.

Katie answered, "Did you know that when we accept Jesus Christ as our Lord and Savior we become princesses? He is King of kings and God is our Father, so that makes us His daughters—princesses!"

The women were speechless. They all looked at each other, then back at Kathryn. All began laughing at such a thought. Katie was able to share more amazing, wonderful things from the Bible. By the time the afternoon was over, there were a few more "princesses" of the Kingdom of God and the angels in heaven rejoiced.

22

Hardship

James was summoned to Captain Warwick's to answer for his behavior on the deck. He told James he was never to leave his presence again without permission. If he did, he would lose his position and be locked up along with the others. James tried to explain how he felt about the punishment inflicted on the two prisoners. The captain let James know that any decisions he made were law, and he did not need to explain anything to him.

It was unheard of for a prisoner to question a captain and not get the lash himself. Fortunately for James, Captain Warwick liked him and understood him. He knew he was not trying to undermine his authority but was a compassionate, moral man. Men like Murphy were rare. If the man had voiced any objections in front of the others, then he would have had to be punished. Lucky for him, he had walked away quietly. No matter how the captain felt about the character of the man, he could never let him question or interfere with the running of his ship. Too much was at stake.

James walked out of the captain's cabin with a decision made. He would never stand aside again while another human being was given the lash. He would have to do something. He could not stand to see another person punished like that. He just hoped and prayed it would never happen again…and that he would have the strength to do what he knew to be right if it did.

James kept busy, giving his time and energy to others. It helped him to stay busy. He tended Jake's wounds, helping him recover. He was even able to get the captain to let some of the prisoners work on board the ship doing more repairs.

When the ship's carpenter became ill, James found one of the prisoners to take his place until he recovered. There were a few who could not be trusted, but most of the prisoners, given the chance, wanted to work. James was becoming a trusted liaison between the captain, crew, and the convicts.

Rio de Janeiro took two months to reach. The biggest battle for ship and passengers was the heat. Water, though plentiful, was still rationed out. The wounded, sick, and children were the first consideration when it came to cleanliness. Fresh water could not be wasted on washing clothes or bodies. Rations of salt pork and beef were given out. In the evenings when the temperatures cooled, singing and dancing were encouraged to bring up the spirits and kill the monotony.

When finally the lookout sounded, "Land ahead," it was an exciting time for all. Once anchored and quarantine time was over, the prisoners were loaded into boats and taken ashore. They were placed inside lockhouses, where they were given fresh food and water. Fruit was given out freely, along with more salt pork, beef, and even some nuts.

Though the heat was heavy, fresh water was now readily available, and both men and women took advantage of bathing. Even the prisoners were allowed to wash up.

Dr. Crane kept his eyes open for any signs of fever. It had run rampant a few years back, almost wiping out the *Regal* and her sister ship, *Whirlwind*. The fever was not such a threat of late because of better conditions. The ships were fumigated regularly, and fresh food was supplied. Dr. Crane, however, never took any disease for granted. He always kept a wary eye out for those killer fevers.

Sally Mae was again fumigated and washed down once she was emptied of prisoners. It didn't take long for her to dry out. Fresh supplies were brought on board and repairs were made.

A week before *Sally Mae* was to leave, one of her sister ships, *The Clip*, arrived and anchored. The late ship was in desperate need of provisions and repairs. Prisoners on board were in worse shape than the ship itself. Eight men and two women prisoners had perished, and it looked like there would be more. It was found that their ship's surgeon-superintendent had also died, leaving no one to tend the sick. The authorities decided to keep *The Clip* under quarantine longer than usual. They had to be sure that no contagious diseases were carried by her occupants.

The *Greystone* had not been sighted nor heard from. Perhaps she was held up on the Islands or blown off course. No one knew for sure. But *The Clip* needed help fast or more lives would be lost.

"If you go over to her, you will have to stay," Captain Warwick warned Dr. Crane and Richards.

"I want to know what happened to all the provisions that were loaded," Richards barked. "If I find the captain sold them to make a profit, I'll have his head!"

"Take it easy; you'll only get yourself shot," Warwick warned.

Dr. Crane voiced his own feelings. "Everything is ready here, and I feel I'm needed on *The Clip*."

The captain was concerned. "I don't want to have to wait until the quarantine is lifted before picking you up and leaving. If you board her, you both may have to stay and sail her." It wasn't a threat, but a fact. Warwick had no intention of holding up because of another captain's blunder or misfortunes. Trouble was, he hated to lose these two men.

"It is my duty to go aboard," Dr. Crane said.

"Mine as well," added Richards.

"So be it. Take one of the longboats and a few crewmen with you. If you need any assistance, signal with the flags."

The two men loaded a few supplies and were soon boarding *The Clip*. She was indeed in dire need of help. Many of the people were quite sick with dysentery and scurvy, but nothing contagious. It didn't matter to the authorities on land. If there was any sickness aboard any vessel, it would be held in quarantine.

When he had a chance, Richards questioned the captain. "Where are the limes I ordered for you?" When the captain didn't answer, Richards knew they had been sold. It was typical of many of the prison hulks' captains to sell provisions to line their own pockets. The almighty coin took precedence over the health of the crew and convicts.

Even though Dr. Crane was confident there were no contagious illnesses, he could not be entirely sure. He had the crew signal the *Sally Mae*, who sent some of her crew ashore to buy more supplies. Once on shore they brought their long boat as close as possible, and by rope and pulley brought the supplies on board.

Dr. Crane rationed everyone an ounce of lime juice and sugar daily. In addition they were given rice, oatmeal, peas, bread, and a portion of wine and tea to help strengthen them. To many of the wretched souls on board, Richards and Dr. Crane became their saviors. Some were very close to death. Everyone had as much fresh water as they wanted. *The Clip* was cleaned, fumigated, and ventilated. Each bottom board of all the berths was carried on deck, washed with salt water, and thoroughly dried before being replaced. All the bedding was aired on deck or replaced, depending on the condition. Everyone had to have their clothes fumigated with the vapor of burning brimstone and oxygenic gas. Many had their heads shaven.

Much of the extra clothing the women of the *Sally Mae* had made was given to the prisoners of *The Clip*. Materials for repairs were brought on board, and so *The Clip* was made seaworthy once again.

Richards checked each barrel and flask of fresh provisions and carefully logged in every item and amount in his ledger. How he wished Murphy was there to help him.

Along with Dr. Crane, Richards planned on turning the captain of *The Clip* in for gross misconduct once in New South Wales. Of course he wasn't about to let the captain know this, or his throat would be cut before journey's end. Richards ordered the captain of the guard to appoint men to guard the new supplies. These men were not under the captain's authority. They seemed relieved to have someone of competence in charge of the provisions.

After ten days the quarantine was lifted, letting Dr. Crane return to the *Sally Mae*, but repairs were not finished on *The Clip*. Richards had no choice; he had to stay behind. He was disappointed he could not finish the journey with his friends.

Three days later *Sally Mae* weighed anchor and left.

By the time all the repairs were done and supplies loaded, *The Clip* was lagging behind two full weeks. Once they began their journey to Cape Town, South Africa, the prisoners were fit to sail. Richards decided he would see they stayed that way. He wasn't a doctor, but all they needed was to be treated like human beings. Dr. Crane gave him a crash course in the everyday ailments before leaving. Hopefully nothing serious would crop up. Any babes born would have to be left to the women. He didn't want to witness that mess. He knew one thing for sure: the "good" captain wouldn't be selling supplies for profit anymore. Richards wondered who the real criminals were sometimes.

Lady Wilson, Maggie, and Mary all looked at Tess with deep concern. She was pale and becoming quite thin.

"Are you eating all right, dear?" Lady Wilson inquired.

"Yes, Mother, thanks to you. If it weren't for you bringing me food, I wouldn't be. The food here isn't fit for animals. I can't believe people are treated this way. I had no idea."

Lady Wilson sadly shook her head. "I brought the books you wanted. Is there anything else we can do?"

"Just pray, Mother. Pray the truth will come out. Funny, isn't it? That is probably what Kathryn prayed for when she was locked in here. I bet you never thought you would be visiting your own daughter in this place. Not when you were working in the Ladies' Prison League."

Lady Wilson wrapped her arms around her daughter.

"At least I can testify that there is justice in this world after all. Look at me now." Tess sniffed.

"Don't be goin' over that again, Miss Tess. That be over an' done with. Ye cannot be blamin' yerself anymore fer that," Mary offered.

"That's right, Tess. What happened with Kathryn is over. You must stop thinking about that and concentrate on getting through this," Lady Wilson added.

"I'll try, but how perfect is the justice of all this? Experiencing this nightmare brings the blackness of my soul in view for doing such a thing. I wonder what Kathryn would say if she knew I was here now."

Maggie spoke up. "She would say the same as your mother and Mary: 'Tis over and done with.' You aren't being punished by God. You are forgiven by Him and Katie. You are being blamed for something you didn't do by someone who has it out for you. You truly have no idea who that could be?"

The three other women exchanged glances. Lady Wilson had given the others strict instructions not to tell her daughter that today was Peter Reeves's funeral. Many people would be there to witness his poor widow burying her murdered husband.

"I don't know who would do this," Tess said slowly. "I've thought long and hard but have no idea. I have many enemies. I've hurt a lot of people, especially my family. Truth be told, I can't blame anyone for putting me here. Now that I'm experiencing the other side, I'm even more ashamed for what I did to Kathryn than before."

Tess was almost inconsolable. Not because of her situation, but for what she had done to Kathryn.

The three visitors tried their best to comfort and assure Tess, but all too soon the visit was over.

Loneliness descended after her mother, Maggie, and Mary left the prison. Tess tried to read one of the books her mother brought but couldn't concentrate. It was all too coincidental to be accused falsely as Kathryn had been. She truly felt she was being punished—and deservedly so. She knew God had forgiven her, but she also learned He allowed things to happen for a reason. She would have to trust in Him, and that did not come easy. Tess knew consequences for actions were a reality in life. This was the end result of her lies and deceit.

Walking around her small cell, Tess tried to turn her thoughts in another direction. She began to pray, which was still a bit awkward, but she felt comforted.

Tess gazed at a streak of sunshine hitting the floor. She walked over and stood in it. Lifting her head up, she tried her best to feel its warmth. Strange how people took such simple things for granted. She certainly had. Sighing, she thought about David and how hard this was on him, too. She knew that her father and husband had been unsuccessful in their efforts to have her released. Too much time had passed.

Better get used to all this, Tess, she thought. Then she gave herself the one luxury she had left. She cried and cried.

23

Valley of the Shadow of Death

Betsy shook in terror. She knew this man meant what he said he would do to her if she wasn't truthful. He had her arm in a vise-like grip. There was no escape. All she had to do was answer his questions truthfully and he would let her go, or so he said. Why had she let him trick her into coming here?

"'Twas Mrs. Reeves that be a-givin' me the invitation! I swear it!"

"Invitation?"

"Aye."

It was just what Grimes wanted to hear. Walking the young servant over to the divan, he sat her down. Bending over her, he questioned her further. "Tell me what Mrs. Reeves told you."

"She says it be a note fer 'er friend, Miss Wilson. Says it be an invite."

"Don't you usually have one of the coachmen deliver notes?"

"Aye, but she be wantin' to be sure Miss Wilson be gettin' it, and it was ta be a surprise. She told me ta take it meself and to hide it in Miss Wilson's room."

"How did she contact you?"

"'Er maid Patty be my friend."

"Why did Mrs. Reeves want you to hide it?"

"It be fer a 'hiding party,' and Mrs. Reeves say it be part of the fun. Me and Patty hid it."

"Hiding party? What do you mean by 'hiding party'?"

"Ya know, when you get a bit of paper with things on it and gotta go and find it all."

"You mean a scavenger hunt?"

"Aye, that be it!"

"So Mrs. Reeves wanted you to hide the 'invitation' in Miss Wilson's room, and not say anything to her, hoping she would find it herself?"

"Aye, but she told us ter hide it so's Miss Wilson could find it easy. If she not find it by the week's end, Mrs. Reeves would call on 'er. Then she said she would tell Miss Wilson ta hunt for it. Told us not ta say nothin' so we didn't wreck 'er surprise."

"Didn't you think that was a little strange?"

"Everything they do is strange. I work for rich folk all me life, and none of 'em be normal."

"Oh," was all Grimes could say to that. "Did Miss Wilson tell you she had found the invitation?"

"No, 'twas Patty that told me."

"So Patty is the maid at the Reeves's house, right?"

"Aye, remember I told you she be Mrs. Reeves's maid? I told ya she be a friend. She be the one ta tell me to come see Mrs. Reeves in the first place. She come o'er one day ta say Miss Wilson found the invitation. She 'ad told Mrs. Reeves, so I didn' 'ave to worry 'bout it."

"So Mrs. Reeves sent her maid over to tell you specifically that Miss Wilson found it, and you didn't have to think about it again?"

"Aye." Betsy was getting impatient with him repeating what she'd said.

"Didn't you think it strange that Miss Wilson didn't say anything to you about it, and that Mrs. Reeves would bother to contact you?"

"I told ya afore, all they do is strange to me. Why would anyone wanta go lookin' for lost stuff at a party jest to say ya found it first? I ne'er could figure out the fun in that. Besides, Miss Wilson be mean ta me for a long time. She got nicer lately, but she still don't tell me anythin'."

"I see." Grimes had heard all he needed.

He had spent weeks investigating Peter Reeves's murder, getting nowhere. He knew Victoria Reeves was involved, and any evidence was probably hidden in her bedchamber. He needed to find a way in.

He had watched the estate almost a week and was about to give up when he noticed Tess's maid, Betsy. She arrived one day at Victoria Reeves's, and a woman let her in the back door. He wondered what she was doing there. He wondered if she had a part in the conspiracy. He couldn't believe his luck when he saw her enter the Reeves house. Betsy was young and could be easily intimidated. Any information she might have would be easy to obtain. He had to wait until she left the house.

When she finally did leave, he approached her, saying he had some important papers for her mistress, and would she give them to her? She fell for it. He led her to his office, but now he needed to find a way in the house. Grimes decided to change his tactics by charming the girl into helping him further.

"Betsy, you've been a great help to me. I hope I didn't frighten you. I am going to take a chance and tell you a secret. You know that I work for Lord Wilson and have for a long time. Well, I'm investigating Mr. Reeves's murder. I believe that Miss Wilson didn't kill him."

"Ya know it for sure? Then who? Ya don't think it be me! I ne'er do nothing like that in me life!" Betsy looked panicked.

"No, no, Betsy, not you! I didn't mean to make it sound like I was accusing you." Grimes could see the girl start to breathe again. He had to be careful. She was ready to bolt. "I have an idea, but I can't say in case I'm wrong. However, I'd like you to be my partner if you would. I will even be willing to pay you."

Betsy's eyes nearly bugged out of her head. "Blimey, ya pay me? 'Ow much?"

"It depends on how much information you can get me."

Betsy was suspicious. "Will it be dangerous? I ain't a-goin' ta do anything dangerous!"

"No, I won't let you get hurt. I'll do all the 'dangerous' work myself."

"If that be the case, I'll do it. I'll be yer partner. What ya want me ta do?"

"Just be yourself, but if anything unusual happens, come and tell me. If I'm not here, you can give any information you have to my clerk. The more information you give me, the more money you will make. In fact, I'm so pleased with what you told me today that I'm willing to pay you a pound now."

"A pound! Ne'er 'ad a pound all at once in me life!"

"Just don't tell anyone. Someone may think you stole it, and whatever you do, don't spend it all right away. They'll wonder where you got all the money. If anyone finds out you are helping me, then you won't be able to be my partner any longer."

"What kind of information are ya lookin' to 'ear 'bout?"

"Anything your friend Patty can tell you about Mrs. Reeves. Who she sees, who comes to her parties, where she goes when she leaves the house. Things like that."

"Ya can count on me! Patty don't like the lady, and she be 'appy ta tell anything I want. A pound! I got me a pound in me pocket!" Smiling from ear to ear, Betsy took it and hid it in her dress. Thanking him and bowing all the way out the door, she turned to do her errands.

Grimes was excited to bring news, any news to Lord Wilson. They had both suspected Reeves's wife, but proving it was another matter. If Grimes had learned anything in this business, it was two things: people usually slipped up somewhere leaving evidence, and people were willing to talk for a price. He knew Betsy would have been happy with a lot less but knew by giving her more she would dig deeper for information.

Now came the hard task of putting the information he learned today to work in proving Tess Wilson's innocence. How ironic—this was probably the only time in Tess Wilson's life that she was truly innocent. No matter how much time or money it took, he would find the evidence to free the Wilson girl. He smiled to himself as he thought, *Even if it comes down to planting my own evidence against the Reeves woman.* Two could play that game, and he knew he was better at it than she.

Annie and Katie struggled to hold on in the midst of the storm that threatened to capsize the ship. The wind howled, causing great waves to wash over the deck. The crew was forced to close the air-scuttles, leaving the lower decks dark and full of foul, hot air.

"Hold on to her, Katie!" Annie shouted over the noise.

"I will, but we need more towels now!"

Another woman lying on the berth writhed in great pain about to give birth. Jenna held a lantern as steady as possible while Annie went to find more towels.

With wide, frightened eyes the young woman looked at Katie for strength and comfort.

She looks so young, Katie thought. "It'll be all right. The baby will be here soon and…"

Another piercing scream filled the air. Katie looked around for Annie to return. Why didn't she go and get the towels? She didn't know anything about babies. As she witnessed the tremendous pain of birth, Katie's heart filled with fear.

Annie returned with a clean towel for the baby soon to be born. Kneeling at the end of the berth, Annie encouraged the young woman, "One more push and you'll be there! I see the baby's head! Push! Push!"

The young woman pushed with all the strength left in her body. Quite suddenly the baby slid out into Annie's hands. Covered in blood and a milky film, the baby lay still. Annie immediately turned the baby over and began to clear the mucus from its mouth. Once that was done, she gave a good slap on the tiny behind. With that, the baby let out a howl. Relief filled all…followed by laughter. Annie instructed Katie on how to tie off the cord, then proceeded to cut it. Gently Katie laid the baby into a towel. After wrapping the tiny human in it, she started to clean it up. Not ever in her life had Katie held such a tiny bairn. Emotion flooded her as she cleaned the child.

"What is it? What is my baby?" the exhausted mother cried.

"It's a boy," Annie told her. "A beautiful boy with lots of dark hair and a robust cry."

"I want to hold him, please!"

Katie brought the bairn over and settled him in his mother's arms. It was a miracle to see. Katie, of course, had seen animals give birth, but never a woman. Her fears turned to wonder as she watched the tenderness of the mother holding the baby to her breast. Everyone laughed at the hungry, suckling noises of the newborn.

"What are you going to name him?" Annie questioned.

"Stormy William Hughes," was the answer.

"'Tis fitting," Annie answered.

Once mother and baby were comfortable, the other women went about gathering the soiled sheets. The storm seemed to slack off, giving the women steadier steps. Jenna offered to watch over the little family while Annie and Katie took the dirty linen out. After putting it in a barrel full of cold seawater to soak, they made themselves tea.

"I've never witnessed a birth," Katie shared.

"'Tis a wondrous thing, isn't it?"

"Aye, but a bit frightening, too."

"'Tis the most natural thing in the world. Do you think women would keep giving birth through the ages if it was so bad?"

"I guess not, but they don't have much choice, either."

Annie looked at Katie. "You're going to have a baby, aren't you, Katie?"

"How did you guess?"

"Oh, I've seen the fear in your eyes before. I won't lie to you. The pain is awful as you saw, but you soon forget it after your babe is in your arms. Coming into the world is a hard thing, but so is living in it. If you think on your baby instead of the pain, it helps. You're healthy, Katie, and if you don't mind me saying, you have full hips. You aren't overly large, but you will be fine."

"Thank you, Annie. I watched that woman suffering. It did scare me a little."

"It's only normal to be afraid a little, but God built us to handle it. Now if it were a man pushing out a babe, well, let's just say they would do more than the Irish jig." Both laughed at the thought. "Have you told your husband about the babe yet?"

"No, I didn't mention it to anyone because I thought he should be the first to know. He's had a lot on his mind lately, and there simply hasn't been a good time to tell him."

"Don't wait too long. I can see your belly begin to round already. He may not guess it, but others will. He'll wonder why everyone else knew except him."

"Aye, you're right. I'll tell him very soon."

The women finished their tea, then Annie sent Katie to her cabin. "You better rest yourself. It's been a long, tiring night. Thank God that the storm is easing up."

"I am tired. Thank you, Annie, for calming my fears. I must have sounded like a tiny bairn myself."

"Not at all. Just a friend who needed some comfort."

Katie made her way to the cabin. James had been there when she was summoned to help with the birth. Maybe it would be a good time to tell him her news. Once she closed and locked their door, she crept over to the bed. Her husband was sleeping soundly. Deciding not to wake him, she quietly got ready for bed. She couldn't sleep. She kept seeing that bairn being born...the wonder of it. The pain kept filling her mind as well. She prayed for the Lord to ease fears of giving birth. Suddenly she recalled the love on the woman's face, erasing the torment and fear that had filled her expression only moments before.

Katie remembered what Gran had said about giving birth: *As easy as breathing, and as hard as dying.* Katie never understood what Gran had meant until tonight. Placing her hands over her belly, she tried to feel life, but only her breathing moved her body. Katie fell asleep trying to think of names for her baby. Arthur, like her father, or if a girl, Ida, like Gran....

Grimes watched behind the bushes as the carriage left, carrying Victoria and her parents away. Heading to the back of the house, he crept toward the window. Seeing Betsy and Patty waiting, he lightly tapped. Betsy quickly opened the door for him. Patty stood anxiously twisting her apron. Once Grimes entered, she whispered, "Come up the back stairs!"

"Which room is hers?" Grimes asked.

Patty pointed a shaky finger. "'Tis the door on the right. Don't make no noise! If the other servants 'ears ya, they'll shoot ya, and kick me into the streets."

"Don't worry, Patty, Mr. Grimes knows wha' he is doin'," Betsy assured her friend.

Once he was in Victoria's bedchamber he slipped his shoes off. He wasn't sure where to begin looking. Where would a woman hide her diary? Patty had told him and Betsy that Victoria kept a diary, but she didn't know where. As he scanned the room, he tried to guess the most likely place. Under the mattress? No, that was too obvious. He walked over to a bookcase filled with dainty figurines and books. He then turned to look at the fireplace. Perhaps behind the pictures on the wall? Something told him there had to be a secret panel somewhere.

Betsy stood outside, guarding the door while Patty watched the stairs on the first floor. It was only the promise of money that got Patty to help. Both girls were extremely nervous about the whole thing. If they got caught, they would never work in any house again. It wouldn't take long for word to get out that they couldn't be trusted.

Grimes felt along the walls until he noticed a small, almost invisible line running vertically to one of the window panes. Had Grimes not lifted the heavy drape panel he would not have noticed it at all. Running his finger over it, he tried to feel the opening. Whoever built the narrow panel next to the window pane had done a masterful job. Taking out his pocket knife, Grimes placed the end of the blade in the crack, causing it to pop open. Inside the narrow opening stood a book and a velvet bag. Grime's heart began pounding. Opening the book, he found it was what he was looking for. Placing it inside his coat pocket he turned to the velvet bag. Inside he found a diamond necklace and matching earbobs. For a second he was tempted to take the bag along with the book but decided against it. Making sure the secret compartment was closed and the drape pulled over, he turned to leave.

Betsy jumped a full foot in the air, letting out a yelp when Grimes opened the door.

"Is it safe?" he questioned.

"Blimey, ya scared me out of ten years. What took so long?"

"It doesn't matter. I found it."

"Ya found what?"

"The diary you told me about."

"Oh!"

Sneaking out of the house proved easy. After paying the two girls, Grimes was on his way to Brick House to see Lord Wilson. He couldn't seem to get there fast enough. After arriving, he explained what he had found.

"I've had Betsy helping me."

"Betsy? You mean Tess's maid, Betsy?"

"Yes, and it was because of her I was able to get my hands on this diary."

"I'm grateful for that, but I'm not sure I appreciate you involving my staff. Then again, I did tell you to use whatever means to find the truth."

"I can assure you, sir, she was never in any danger. When she told me her friend worked at the Reeves's estate, it was the only way. Once I found out that Victoria Reeves kept a diary, I needed help getting into the house to look for it."

"How did you find out she had a diary? That's personal information."

"Betsy is friends with Victoria Reeves's maid, Patty. She told Betsy about the diary."

"Well, I hired you because you're the best. I've never questioned your methods as long as you got the job done, and I won't start now."

The two men began reading the diary.

"This is better than one of those dime novelettes. You wouldn't have guessed that 'fine' Mrs. Reeves could be no better than one of the bargirls, would you? Not by the looks of her at least," Grimes commented.

"Just goes to show you—fine clothes and jewelry don't make a lady," Edward Wilson agreed.

For nearly an hour they went over the diary. They found it to be very interesting reading. They discovered many familiar names on the pages, including Tess's. The diary read:

I found out her name. It's Tess Wilson. I saw that little trollop today. She was coming out of the dress shop. I don't care who her parents are; she has taken up with the wrong man this time. I will not have her and Peter making me the laughingstock of London.

That was all that was said about Tess until ten pages later.

Peter came to me tonight and told me he wants a divorce! I can't believe he wants to marry that little snit. That he would pick her over me after all I've done for him. I won't have it! I won't. Justin said he can help me take care of it. I've decided to do it. It's time to free myself of Peter. Justin is willing to find someone to do the job for a lot less than I was willing to pay. He says he can find someone who would be willing to kill his own mother for the right price. Sounds horrible, but I guess that's the kind of man we're looking for.

"I wonder who Justin is," Grimes stated.

"I can't be sure, but I heard rumors of Lord Reynolds and the Reeves woman taking up with each other. His first name is Justin."

They read on.

It wasn't easy, trying to figure out how to make it look like the Wilson snit planned the whole thing, but I had a stroke of genius. It's too much to write about, and I don't have time now. Let's just say I have a "party" to plan for. Hopefully I will be a grieving widow within the week.

That was all the men needed to read. They had her! Lord Wilson pounded Grimes's back in congratulations and shouted, "Hallelujah, man, you did it! Barbara, Barbara!"

Grimes watched Lord Wilson run up the staircase to find his wife. He was surprised at the older man's agility as he took two stairs at a time.

"Barbara! Where in blue blazes are you?" he called at the top of his lungs.

Lady Wilson met him at the top of the stairs. "Good heavens, Edward, what has come over you? What are you yelling about?"

"I've got it! We can go get Tess! She can come home!"

"Edward, what are you talking about? You've got what?"

After explaining everything, Lord Wilson ordered their carriage to be brought around. All three headed off to their lawyer's office.

Tess's door creaked open, stirring her awake. Irritation at being wakened was replaced with fear when a large man with missing teeth grabbed her arm. He lifted her to her feet as if she weighed nothing. His breath was foul and so was his body.

"Git up with ya now!" the man snarled.

"You're hurting me! Let go!"

"Shut up with ya, and come with me!"

"Where are you taking me?"

"I said ter shut up."

The man led Tess down a long, dank hallway. Rats scurried to and fro, causing Tess to shrink back against the man. It seemed to please him greatly. Before too long they faced a thick wooden door. The man stopped to light a torch left by the door.

"Come with me now, 'urry up."

"Where are you taking me?" Tess questioned again.

The man just grunted, not answering.

Tess found herself being led down a long winding stairway made of stone. It looked as if it hadn't been used in years. The hairs on the back of Tess's neck stood up. She looked behind her, hoping someone would be there to help her. Sensing she was in grave danger, she thought of running but didn't have any way of escaping. She was in a mass of black nothingness except for the light the torch threw out. Past the light, Tess couldn't see anything. The stairs wound endlessly until Tess thought they must be close to hell itself. Finally they reached the bottom. Turning to the left, the man led Tess to a small room that had no door.

"Git in 'ere!" he snarled once more as he shoved her into the room. It was no larger than a small closet. "Go sit on that there bed."

Tess saw a half-rotted plank sticking out of the wall. Did he mean for her to sit there? She walked over to it, sitting on it gingerly to make sure it would hold her. A shiver ran through her as the scurry of something along the wall reached her ears. She shivered from the dampness of the dungeon and peered about in the dim light. The walls appeared to be covered in slime of some sort. The odors of mildew and decay were pungent. Tess let out a squeal when she saw what made the scurrying sound.

The man laughed as he stepped out of the room, taking the torch with him.

Tess was petrified. Was he going to leave her there?

"I told ya I would bring 'er 'ere."

Tess strained to see who the man was talking to.

A calmer, softer male voice spoke, then the burly man asked, "What ya want me ter do with 'er now that I got 'er 'ere?" came the question.

Again, the softer voice spoke in answer. Tess could not make out what he was saying.

Once more the brute spoke. "All right with ya now. Pay me, an' I'll be on me way."

Tess heard coins clinking together, then the rough man speaking. "Take the torch. 'Old it fer me to see the stairs."

Tess heard a shuffling noise and noticed the torch light move away from the room.

Should I try to run now? she wondered but decided against it. Tess's heart was hammering. *Maybe someone has come to get me out!* The thought soothed her for mere seconds. Why would they bring her to such a dank place as this? Holding her breath, she waited to see who would enter.

Footsteps sounded at the doorway. Squinting, she tried to see the man's face. All she could see was a man's torso dressed in a fine velvet jacket, riding pants, and boots. The torch was held low, making it impossible for Tess to see her captor.

"Do you remember me?" The voice was soft and vaguely familiar. "Do you need a hint?"

Tess leaned a little closer, trying her best to see him but could not. "Who are you?" she asked in a shaky voice.

"So you are frightened, are you?" the man softly stated. "I never thought you were frightened of anything."

"Of course I'm frightened. I'm led to this vile place for whatever reason, I don't know!" Tess was becoming hysterical.

"Calm down, Tess."

"How do you know me?"

"I know you very well. You could almost say…intimately."

"What are these games you're playing? Take me back to my cell at once or my father will…"

The voice chuckled. "Your father will…what? He doesn't know where you are. Besides, you're the last person who should be talking about games. You're the biggest game player of all. You are at my mercy, and mind you, Tess, you had better change your tone. It's beginning to irritate me."

Tess tried to sound brave, but she felt anything but. Once again she asked, only a little calmer, "What do you want of me? Who are you?"

"Just one of your long-lost lovers."

"I refuse to continue like this. If you do not tell me who you are, I will scream."

"Scream away, my lovely. No one can hear you down here. These old rooms were abandoned years ago. They used to be for storage, and at times for…well, let's say 'special punishment.' Most have forgotten about this part of Newgate. Those who do remember wouldn't come down here for anything."

"So what do you want of me?"

"Much."

"What do you mean?"

"First, let's see if you can remember who I am. A couple of years ago we met at the Spencers' Harvest Ball. We danced, and you led me to believe you enjoyed my company. Do you remember the ball?"

"Yes, but I danced with many gentlemen that night."

"Yes, you do love to play the field, don't you? Anyway, I'll give you another hint. Do you remember the dark corner of the Spencers' garden, the corner with the lovers' bench? We shared some interesting moments there. After that night, we saw each other frequently until you…grew bored."

Tess searched her memory. She had many rendezvous with many different men in her past. Pinpointing one separate night was difficult. She remembered having a spectacular time at that particular ball. There had been many eligible men there that night, including a couple of married men she had danced with. Suddenly a name and a face came to mind. Tess's head snapped up as she remembered who she had shared an intimate moment with in the garden. "Justin Reynolds?"

The man stood quietly for a moment. "Very good, you do remember me."

"Why…why are you doing this to me?" Tess pleaded.

"You know the lovely grieving widow of Peter Reeves, don't you?"

"Of course, but what does she have to do with this?"

"Haven't you wondered who planted that confession letter or pointed the finger at you for Reeves's death?"

"Yes, I've wondered. You mean to tell me it was you and Victoria Reeves?"

"It does take you time to figure things out, doesn't it? Of course I was attracted to your beauty and money, certainly not your brains. It would seem, my dear Tess, that you latched onto the wrong married man with Reeves. Since I am her lover, Victoria contacted me to have him killed. Of course, she had no idea that you and I had...a past. This turned out to be the opening I was waiting for."

"Why are you telling me all this? What do you want?"

"Like I said much, but for right now I think you need to hear me out. I've waited a long time for this moment. Don't you remember when I called on you a few months after the ball, and you laughed in my face? You told me not to be ridiculous, that you were just having fun and were tired of me. I poured out my soul to you and offered any and all love I had. You laughed at me. If that wasn't bad enough, you went around telling everyone how I came to lick your boots. You kicked me aside like some dog. Do you remember what I said to you? I told you that I wouldn't be treated like a fool. You would pay. It has taken some time, but now I'm calling your debt."

"You can't be serious! It was an affair that happened years ago! What are you going to do to me?"

The man held out his hand toward Tess. She cringed backwards against the dank wall. "I would suggest you take my hand, or it will go worse for you."

Hesitating, she reached her hand out to him. Tess was surprised at his strength.

"I've waited for this a long time."

"I wanted you to call on me again, Justin, but you never did. I thought you knew I was teasing." Tess spoke much too rapidly.

"And I suppose you're about to tell me that you love me?"

Horrifying fear had Tess by the throat. Her mind raced for a way out of this nightmare. *Help me, Lord!* came her plea.

The man laughed loudly, tightening his grip. "Do you really think I'm that stupid? I do realize that Victoria is going to be angry after she hears she has been cheated out of seeing you hang. Oh, well, she'll get over it. Then again she will never really know what happened to you, will she? No one will."

Tess panicked; she lunged at the man, digging her nails into his face, ripping and tearing. He let out a howl, turned on her, and hit her as hard as he could. Tess flew back against the wall, and all went dark.

Tess's head hit the wall with a sickening sound. Time seemed to stand still. The man wheezed from the effort. Blood ran down his face where Tess had torn his skin. He looked down on her, waiting for her to move, but she didn't. Her head was twisted in a bizarre manner, verifying what he already knew.

"Well, sweet, I had hoped to have a little fun before killing you, but the ending is still the same." Justin leaned the torch against the wall. Kneeling, he picked up her lifeless body. He went back into the small room she had first been taken to and laid her on the plank. She could lay there and rot. Who would ever know?

He turned to leave, never giving her a second glance. He walked out, angry over his own wounds. He hadn't expected her to fight. Wiping the blood from his face, he cursed her and walked away.

The once-promising life of the young woman was over. Her father, mother, husband, and all who knew her would never know what happened to their beloved Tess. The consequences for her past had killed her future. Her friend Kathryn had given her a gift worth much more than one lifetime; she had shared Christ with Tess.

And now Tess was home.

Tess was missing from her cell. No one knew where she had gone. A full search was done. Gaolers were questioned and threatened. Other prisoners were held in suspicion. Some speculated that she had escaped, but her family knew better. They had a full investigation launched into her disappearance. Lord and Lady Wilson spent a lot of time and money searching for her, but to no avail. They would never know how close they had come to taking their daughter home, if they had only arrived an hour earlier. If only…

Their grief and fear turned into anger for the woman who had framed her in the first place. They had Victoria Reeves taken into custody. It was the biggest scandal in years. All the people Victoria considered friends now spoke in hushed tones and biting words. All of London was buzzing about the "beautiful killer widow."

Justin Reynolds was not to be found. He had slipped away, but Lord Wilson swore he would have him hunted down. Reynolds was named in the diary as Victoria Reeves's accomplice. Lord Wilson knew they had something to do with his daughter's disappearance. He felt it in his bones. He thought Tess might even be with Reynolds. That the man had taken her out of prison and held her as his captive.

Time would prove him wrong.

Victoria could only endure three days in the gaol. She was found with a scarf around her neck, hanging from a beam. The humiliation was too great. When she heard her diary had been found, she knew there was no hope. Many people asked why she would keep such a diary in the first place. Victoria asked herself that same question before stepping off the chair into a dark eternity.

James and Katie walked the deck, looking at the beautiful sunset. It had been three days since the storm. Finally all had returned to normal. "So how are the new mum and babe doing?" James asked his wife.

"James, it's so sad. Ruth, that's her name, told me that her husband had left her right after he found out she was going to have a baby. She said they had been so happy up until that time. She had no family in London since her husband had moved them there, looking for work. She had no money or way to make a living. She ended up stealing and getting caught. She was scared to death that she would hang, but thankfully she was transported out instead. I can't speak of the menfolk, but most of the women are not criminals. Many were forced into stealing to survive, just like you! I've heard such sad stories, James. It would break your heart to hear them."

James shook his head slowly. "I can't imagine a man leaving his wife and babe like that."

"That's because you are a godly man, James."

"Also because I love you," he whispered as he hugged her. "Any man would be blessed to have a wife like you."

Katie's heart skipped a beat. "I want to help her, James. Can you imagine being all alone, not having anyone to help you? I feel we need to do something. If we were to get our own farm, do you think we could have Ruth and her baby stay with us and help?"

"We can't have every person who has problems stay with us, Katie. I think we need to wait and see if we are to get our own place. I know we've heard that capable farmers get their own land, but we really don't know if that is true. Besides, it will be a long time before that happens. I have to serve my time. It will be years before we acquire land, if ever. It doesn't hurt to dream, though." James chuckled. "The Lord has blessed us in so many ways. Sometimes I forget that I'm still a prisoner. We really shouldn't hang all our hopes on one man's statement about farmers being needed. We can't count on that."

Katie smiled. "You're right. We sure have lofty plans, don't we? Not only do we have our own land in our minds, but we have people to work with us already."

"We are getting ahead of ourselves. If God wants it for us, then it will happen. If not, then He will have something better for us."

"Know what else I want to find out about when we get there?" Katie teased him.

"What?"

"If they have a school and a church."

"School? Do you plan on teaching the women once we get settled?"

"No, I think I'm going to have my hands full with working alongside you. We will want a school for our children."

James laughed. "That's pretty far in the future. Why worry about it now?"

"It could affect us sooner than you think, James."

James stopped and looked at his wife. "You mean, you're going to have a…I mean, you and I are going to…how, when?"

Katie couldn't help but giggle. "In the summertime."

"Is it a girl or a boy?"

"Yes."

"What do you mean? Both?"

"No, I mean it's a girl or a boy."

"You can't tell?"

"Of course not, James. How would a woman be able to tell that?"

"I don't know. I just thought women knew what they were going to have. I wasn't told anything different. I guess I thought women could tell somehow. Is that why you've been getting sick?"

Katie nodded. "Yes, that's why I've been sick in the mornings and no, women can't tell what the baby is."

James hugged his wife gently. "A baby! You will never know how long and hard I prayed for my own family. Thank you, Katie." He lifted her into his arms, hugging her furiously. "A baby, a baby!" Just as suddenly as he had started his jubilee, James stopped. With panic in his eyes he carefully set Katie down. "Katie, are you all right? Are you in pain? Does it hurt?"

Katie laughed so hard she held her stomach. "James, I can't believe you. You are too funny. Of course I'm fine! No, it doesn't hurt to have you hug me. I'm just happy that you are happy. I was a little worried you wouldn't be happy with the news."

"Why would you think I wouldn't be happy about us having a baby?"

"I guess it's because we have a lot to worry about right now."

"God doesn't make mistakes, and I know children are a blessing and a miracle. Let's trust Him."

Katie nodded in agreement.

"Just think, Katie, we have our own little family already."

Katie only wished she felt peace about it all. *Help me to trust in You, Lord, no matter what,* she prayed silently.

24

Promises Ahead

It was now the month of December. Christmas was two days away. Katie and a few of the matrons planned to make it special for the women. Because of the kindness of the captain and careful planning by Richards they would be able to serve fuller rations for Christmas dinner to the prisoners.

Katie, the matrons, and the officers' wives had made rag dolls for the little girls. James and his men worked on wooden farm animals for the boys.

Katie sat on deck, thinking of the holiday preparations and sewing baby things. Her mind went to the Christmas past. It didn't seem possible that a whole year had gone by. How different Christmas was this year. Soft, warm breezes and sunshine surrounded her. Feeling a pang of homesickness, she gazed down at her wedding ring. What a surprise it had been when she received it. She remembered the look on Mary's and Maggie's faces when she opened it. She couldn't contain a giggle when she imagined Mary traipsing around the store looking at all the fine "sparklers."

She fought the threat of tears. How she missed everyone, and all the Christmas cheer. She missed the tree, snow, and the smells that only Christmas held. No, she refused to cry right now over anything. The voyage had been fairly smooth even with the few storms they had run into. Three new bairns were born and doing very well. Her wee one was growing and moving within her. Only months remained before they would be at their destination. God blessed her every day, and she wanted to pass it on to others.

Katie looked up to watch some of the women prisoners exercising and playing with their children. To look at them you would never guess they were ripped from their homeland with their futures in question. They were laughing and singing old songs of Ireland. They looked haggard and wore rags, but they seemed to be coping well. Some of their voices lifted in song...

> "We dance, we sing and live life in full
> We fish and plant the land that pulls
> Our hearts toward home and hearth and love
> Green Ireland, land from above..."

The tune was a favorite of Gran's. Katie closed her eyes, listening to Gran's sweet, quivering voice singing as she baked bread or hoed the dry earth. Katie laid her sewing down, deciding to join the women and children at their play. What a beautiful day.

Captain Warwick stood off to the side, watching some of the female prisoners playing with their children. Amusement crossed his face at their laughter. Hearing more laughter lift in the air, he turned to see Mrs. Murphy chasing a small boy. When she caught him, she lifted him in the air, making the boy giggle. It was a pleasant sight, causing his heart to pull. He missed his sweet Elizabeth and their sons. He had only spent four Christmases with his family out of twelve years of marriage. It was getting harder and harder for him as the years went by.

Christmas Day finally came. Someone played the squeeze box while others danced the jig. Many voices were raised in song. Captain Warwick ordered his crew generous portions of port for their holiday celebration, except for those on duty, of course. He and Dr. Crane stood watching the merriment. Many marines and their families joined in the Christmas celebration. When there was a lull in their merriment, they could hear the prisoners singing below. How lovely the sound of it was. It touched each and every heart. Those who sang below were locked up with uncertain futures, but they sang anyway.

"Silent night, holy night, all is calm, all is bright..."

All prisoners spent Christmas in their bays. It was easier for the crew and marines to enjoy their holiday that way.

"Round yon virgin, mother and child,
Holy infant so tender and mild..."

Katie visited each female bay singing, praying, and sharing the miracle of Christmas. The children were given their small gifts. Their eyes sparkled at the sight of the new toys. Little girls began naming their dolls while the boys played with their wooden animals. Many of the mothers sat with tears of gratitude as they watched their children enjoy Christmas.

James spent the evening with the men. Many of them seemed to open up to him more and more. He treated them with respect and genuine concern. They sang

Christmas songs of past. Old memories were shared, and laughter rang out from time to time. Even the men who were considered troublemakers sat quietly and listened. A few even joined in the singing. By the time the prisoners received their evening rations of gruel with sugar and butter, bread, salt beef, and rice, most of the joyous celebrations had wound down for the night. Quiet contemplation, memories, and regrets replaced them.

It was late when James and Katie met back at their cabin. They quietly talked, sharing their stories of the prisoners. Katie went to her side of the bed and lifted the blanket, revealing a bundle of cloth.

"What's that?" James asked.

"My Christmas present to you."

"Really, what is it?"

"Open it and see."

James removed the material, pulling out a new woolen shirt and scarf.

"It's for the cold nights when you're called to work."

"Katie, thank you. It amazes me how cold it can get at night when it's so hot during the day. These will work fine for me," he said as he tried the shirt on. Taking the scarf, he tied it around his neck. "So, how do I look? When did you have time to make them?"

"Very handsome indeed, sir. When the captain called you to his cabin, I would take it out and work on it for a while. You almost caught me with it one day, but I just casually laid it aside so you wouldn't notice. I'm always sewing something."

"That you are, Katie."

James gave his wife a hug and told her to stay put. He had to run to get his gift for her. He had hidden it out in the corridor. After a few minutes he was back, holding something small in his large hands.

"Oh, James, what is it?" It was Katie's turn to question.

James handed the object to Katie, warning her to be careful, for it could break. Very carefully Katie began to take off the cloth used to hide the treasure. James smiled as he watched her. She was like a child with a new toy. She took her time savoring the moment, then let in a sharp intake of breath at the sight of it. How glorious it was! The small globe was set on a wood base; inside the globe was sparkling "snow," water, a miniature castle, and tiny shamrocks.

"Oh, James, it's beautiful! Where in the world did you get it?"

"One of the marines and his wife bought some things in their travels. She asked me to build her a few small cupboards to store some things in their cabin. She wanted to pay me, but I asked if I could pick something out for you for payment. She thinks very highly of you, Mrs. Murphy. She told me she has never met anyone so kind or full of heart. I thought of you and your Gran when I saw this. I'm glad you like it. I wasn't sure how you would feel when you saw it, happy or sad."

"Definitely happy. It's perfect! Whenever I look at it, I will be reminded of Gran and her Ireland, and of my thoughtful husband."

The couple turned back the blanket and snuggled down. They prayed together, thanking the Lord for all their many blessings, especially the gift of His birth. The gentle lift of the ship and the sound of the waves lulled them both to sleep as they lay wrapped in each other's arms.

The *Sally Mae* was headed toward the end of her long journey. Sails billowed, bringing her ever closer to her destination. Katie and Annie talked excitedly about the coming end of their voyage. Annie shared that they were heading first to Botany Bay and then to Newcastle.

Katie added, "It seems like it all happened so fast now that we're almost there. In the beginning the voyage seemed endless. Botany Bay sounds so different. Tell me about it. You said you've been there a few times. What is it like?"

"The land is strange, but beautiful indeed, and so are the people. If you are a lazy man, it is hell. If you are industrious, it holds promise for you. There are people who live there who have the color of coal to their skin. They are savages who actually wear designs on their faces and bodies. They look like they are from the devil himself. Wait until you see the animals. Some are hard to describe. You probably won't believe me unless you see them for yourself."

"Like what?"

"Well, there's a thing called a kangaroo. The only way I can describe it is to say it looks like a huge hare, the size of a man. It has a long tail, long ears, and it sits back on its haunches. It has a pocket in the front of its belly to hold its young."

"You don't say? I cannot picture it in my mind. It must look very funny. You say it's as big as a man?" Katie added.

"Aye, I thought it was the funniest looking thing I ever did see. I saw one lay a big man, like your James, out in the dirt with one kick to the gut. Its feet are huge, and the legs on it are powerful. It nearly killed the bloke."

"Oh my, are there other dangerous animals?"

"More that would give you the willies than would harm you."

"Really?"

"There are snakes called pythons. They are huge and can weigh hundreds of pounds. Luckily, they shy away from people. The bogs are where you are likely to find them, so stay clear of them. Then there are crocodiles. Those are scariest of all, I think. They live mostly in the water but also like to lie on shore in the sun. They have a bumpy, tough hide and are low to the ground. They have teeth that can cut a man in half with one bite. They do not fear men. You will be warned where to go, and where not to go. You won't have to worry if you heed what they say."

"Are you making this up?" Katie questioned.

"No, I speak the truth. Like I said, they are the strangest creatures you will ever see."

"Annie, I'm afraid for the wee one. What if he wanders about?"

"It can cause concern for sure. Just keep your eyes and ears open. You'll both be fine. I don't mean to frighten you, Katie, but you need to know that there are dangers. There is beauty as well: birds of every color, and I saw a butterfly once that was as big as a bird. There are plants that are glossy green, and there's some that are poisonous. You will see flowers that will take your breath away. The sun shines mostly, but it rains enough for crops. It really depends on where in Australia you are. There is desert and lush land alike. "

"Tell me more about the people and how they live. Do they suffer, or do they prosper?"

After thinking for a moment she answered, "It depends on the person, Katie. Like I said before, if you are lazy and have a bitter heart, you will hate it. If you want to work hard and make a life for yourself, you will be fine. In the old days it was much worse. People were starving and murdering each other for food. It was awful. Some of the stories I've heard can cause your hair to curl. That is why everyone has to pull together. There is no tolerance for laziness or crime. Those who don't work don't eat. It's not all bad news, though. The colonies have been established long enough that they can take care of themselves. There was a time that a ship bringing provisions determined life or death. It's not like that any longer. Women live and work in factories or are used as domestic help. The men work the farms and build roads and bridges, things like that."

"What about those people you said come from the devil himself, the natives?"

"They are called Aborigines. They are very black and have flat noses. They are all heathen. Truth be told, you have to feel sorry for them. Many have been killed off. I heard a lot of them died when the first ships arrived, carrying diseases. Over the years they have been schooled, forced to learn English, and 'we' tried to change them into 'us.' They have fought against it. They are mostly peaceful now as long as we leave them alone and stay away from them. Once in a while a small band of them are spotted, but they pretty much stay off to themselves."

"Are there large prisons there like Newgate?"

"Yes, but only the worst prisoners are there. Men and women are needed to work. It is hard enough to feed yourself, let alone keep prisoners locked up and useless."

"I suppose. Do you think James will be hired out? Will I be able to be with him?"

"I don't know, Katie. The governor tries to keep families together. It's only common sense that people are happier with their families, but I can't say for sure."

"What are the farms like?"

"The ground is rich and fertile once it's cleared. That's the hardest thing—trying to keep the wild plants out once the crops are planted. Hard work for sure, but you can yield a bounty if the rain comes when it's supposed to. A lot of Merino is raised. That is where the money is."

"Merino? What in the world is that?"

"Those are sheep. They are especially bred to withstand the harsh, hot climate. We send wool to England and other countries as well. Merinos are what mainly feed and clothe some of the colonies, along with the lumber trade."

The two women talked a great deal more until it was time to feed the prisoners.

Katie stood to follow Annie, but saw James. She walked over to him. "James, Annie has been telling me about Australia. Some of it sounds frightening, and some exciting."

"I've been hearing about it too. I guess it's like any place you go, both good and bad."

"Aye, you're right."

James tried to lighten any fears she might have. "You don't have anything to worry about, Katie darlin'. We are going to do well in the new land. I think in a few years I may be running the place!"

"Oh, really, James? You plan on running the whole place? Isn't that the governor's job? I think you better ask him first if it's all right that you take over."

Both broke into laughter.

"You can always make me feel better after I talk to you." Katie hugged her husband. "I best get to work, or Annie will come looking for me," she added. Smiling back at her husband, she headed for the galley.

James thanked God for the thousandth time for his Katie and their baby. How blessed he was. He knew in his heart that God's hand protected him and Katie. He was so thankful knowing that it was God who provided the good captain, a sturdy ship, and crew. Yes, how blessed he was, and he let the Lord know how grateful he was.

Some of the crew snickered when they saw a big man kneeling on deck as if in prayer. It sure was a strange sight, but some hearts were touched.

As time passed, James and Captain Warwick seemed comfortable around each other. They formed a strange relationship. It was almost a friendship, but it would be denied if anyone asked about it. Captains never befriended prisoners.

"Well, sir, I've never heard of Sydney. Where is it?" James asked.

"It's between Botany Bay and Newcastle. It's a great port and well-established. Beautiful, too, with fertile land, and built up. We will be in Botany Bay in one month's time. A man can actually find a worthwhile life there if he has a mind to. Not saying it isn't a hard life, but tell me where a man doesn't find hardship."

"That's true enough. What will happen to the prisoners when we arrive?"

"You mean what will happen to you?"

"Yes, I guess I do."

"We stay on board for a week's time to make sure no one carries sickness, then once we go ashore the prisoners are taken to a communal hall. There you will be processed. You are checked over for health, and they look over your records. I have to hand in a report about you. How well you performed your duties and such. They will want to know what skills you may have. I don't think you have anything to worry about. The fact that you can read, write, farm, and work with your hands means a great deal."

James blurted out his next question. "Will my wife and I be able to stay together?"

"Not at first. Men and women are separated when they process you. Families are reunited before too long, though."

Relief flooded James.

"Murphy, I will put in a good word for you in appreciation for the fine job you have done."

"Thank you, sir." But James wondered if the captain's "good word" would be enough.

The night breezes caused Katie to pull her shawl tighter. James placed his arm around his wife as they stood at the ship's railing. The sea was calm, showing the bright, full moon. A low, eerie call of a whale resonated in the air.

"It sounds so alone," Katie murmured. "Do you think it's calling to another whale?"

"Probably," was all James said. He seemed to be deep in thought.

"It's so funny how quickly you can become used to something like the sound of whales. Not so long ago I had never heard of such a thing."

"Ah-hah," James answered.

Katie gave up on any conversation. She turned her gaze back on the sea. James seemed a million miles away. This was to be their last night of the voyage. The captain had announced the news to the matrons, warders, marines, and their families. Once anchored, they would spend a week in quarantine and make repairs on the ship. It would also give them a chance to ready themselves. They were warned that they wouldn't have their "land legs" for a time. It would be strange to walk without any swaying motion at first.

Glancing again at James's pensive face, Katie sensed his fears and concern about the unknown ahead of them. She placed one of her hands over one of his. "Look how the Lord has taken care of us, James. He will keep on doing so. I rather feel excited about our new life." Suddenly, Katie inhaled fast.

"What's the matter?" James asked in alarm.

"I felt the bairn kick me!" Taking James's hand, Katie placed it on her belly. "Can you feel him move?"

He left his hand there for several moments. "No, I don't."

"Maybe it is too small yet for you to feel, but I did! How strange and wonderful it is!" Tears gathered in Katie's eyes.

"Did it hurt you?"

"Not at all. It was a fluttering feeling, as if a butterfly touched my skin. It's not the first time I felt our bairn move, but each time it's a wonder."

James once again held his wife as they turned together to view all of God's glory revealed in the night and the sea.

The day they dropped anchor was sun-filled and kissed with soft breezes. The business of the harbor reminded Katie of London. From the ship she could see people bustling all about. Long boats were being loaded and unloaded. A few other ships were anchored off shore, but *The Clip* was not among them.

The captain barked several orders, and men jumped to do his bidding. He sounded stern, yet a light mood settled over the men. Another successful voyage under their belts, and few lives lost. It was a good sail for sure.

The prisoners were kept locked in their bays, wondering when they would see their new "home." Now that they had arrived, they felt expectant and restless. It would be a hard week of waiting before they could go on shore. The women were luckier, for they stayed busy mending and making new clothes. Everyone spoke in hushed tones, as if afraid of waking someone.

It was two days before the prisoners were allowed to come on deck to exercise. Small groups of them were told to walk around the deck. If they moved any slower, they wouldn't have been moving at all. Their interest lay solely in watching all the sights on shore.

Two nights before going on shore, all the "free souls" were called to have dinner with the captain and officers. Captain Warwick seemed in high spirits. He was heard laughing from time to time. "Ladies and gentlemen, may I present a toast?" Raising his glass of port, he continued. "It has been my great pleasure to sail with you. For those of you who have sailed with me before, you know this has been an 'easy' sail. For those of you who have never sailed before, I'm sure there were a few frightening moments, but we have come through grandly. God bless, and good luck to us all!"

Everyone stood and cheered. Once all quieted down, they sat to listen once more to the captain. "I feel saddened that a few of my passengers have lost their lives but grateful there were not more. In a couple of days we will go ashore. I want this transition to be as smooth as possible. Matrons and warders, there are specific instructions for you as to how I want the prisoners handled. See me later on this. I want to thank everyone involved who made this sail a good one. Now let's enjoy our last meal together. The next couple of evenings will be busy for all."

Later on Katie and James would remember how festive it all had been. "You would have thought we were at a family home having dinner," James replied.

Katie agreed. "Aye, it has been fun tonight. I almost feel sad about all of this ending. Isn't it funny? I mean, there has been a lot of sadness on this trip, but a lot of good memories for us, too. I guess it wouldn't have been so grand, had I been locked away in one of those bays. We had our cozy cabin. I still feel blessed by all the friends we made. I feel as if we've been traveling with family."

Quietness settled on both of them as their thoughts turned inwards. After a few minutes, Katie spoke as if more to herself, "We're going to be separated at first, you know."

James nodded. "I know, but it shouldn't be for too long. I have to remind myself sometimes that I am still a prisoner. I've been treated like a free man on board, but it stops as soon as we walk on land."

"Aye, I know. Have you noticed, though, that the fear we had in the beginning is now gone? I feel such hope and a deep joy. I know there will be hard times ahead, but I feel God's peace."

"So do I."

Katie and James spent a large part of the night talking about the Lord, and their future plans. They were without home or extended family. They were about to set foot on a strange new land. They had no job or way to make a living. James didn't even have his freedom. But even with all that, their joy was full.

James began quoting Jeremiah 29:11, a verse he had memorized. It had helped him in the hard times and in the good times as well:

" 'For I know the thoughts that I think toward you,' saith the Lord, 'thoughts of peace, and not of evil, to give you an expected end.' "

James and Katie were blessed.

Epilogue

James was assigned to work for Anthony Keys, a hard-working Scot with a fair heart. Keys and his wife, Bonnie, ran a large sheep ranch, and were successful at it long before James and Katie came to live there. The last of the five Keys children had left Australia to discover the world. The older couple was grateful for James's strong back and honest heart, along with Katie's gentle and giving nature. Oh, they didn't trust the convict and his wife that easily in the beginning. It took quite some time for James to prove himself.

Anthony Keys hated breaking in new prisoners. His experiences in the past had proven difficult. He had been lied to, stolen from, and even attacked. If it weren't for the free labor, he would have given up on the foulers a long time ago. But there was something different about this man. Instead of bragging about all he could and would do, he quietly went about his work and didn't stop until it was done well.

Bonnie watched how James treated his wife. A woman could tell a lot about a man by doing that. They were a novelty since he was a convict and his wife was not. Bonnie Keys was pleased to see the respect they had for one another, and when poor Katie lost their first babe at birth, James's gentleness and care touched the older woman's heart. She encouraged her husband to watch this couple closely, as they just might be the answer to their prayers.

And so it was that James and Katie came to live and take part in the lives of the Keys family and to contribute to the growth of the new land. With their lifeblood and sweat, they became as much a part of it as anyone. They lay their firstborn in the ground of Australia, soaking the grave with their tears. They plowed and planted, and grew to know more about sheep than they ever intended.

During their third year in Australia, Katie gave birth to a healthy baby girl they named Mary.

After seven years spent in service to the Keys family, James became a "freeman" and, with Katie's help, earned a small farm. They continued to manage the Keys ranch while building their own small place. They would grow and prosper, raise many more children, and have a ministry helping other prisoners.

They spoke often of going back to London to see their families but knew it would never happen. Australia was their home. As the years passed, they sent and received many letters from their loved ones.

The years stretched out and time passed as it always does. James and Katie lived their lives and become a part of the foundation of Australia.

Some called James a prisoner, an outcast, but he had never been freer in his life. God had plans and a purpose for their lives, and they lived it gloriously, walking hand in hand with each other and with Him.

About the Author

COLLIE MAGGIE, a self-proclaimed "throw-away" child, was abandoned by her mother after her father's death and entered foster homes at the age of four. She lived in seven foster homes before finding her true love with husband, Jack, and creating her own home, which has lasted for more than 40 years. They have three children—Susan, Aaron, and Jesse—as well as two grandchildren, Anthony and Olivia.

"My one and only dream as a child was to be adopted," Collie says. "It didn't happen until I became a Christian and read Ephesians 1:5: 'He predestined us to be *adopted* as his sons through Jesus Christ, in accordance with his pleasure and will.' My heart stood still after reading that verse. My dream came true that day."

Collie began writing to encourage those who are hurting and to remind readers of the hope in Christ and the promise He gave: that He has a purpose and a plan for each one of us. After researching *Chained to Your Heart*, she gained a tremendous respect and admiration for the pioneers of Australia—for their strength and courage in facing the voyage across the sea, as well as the challenges of that new land. "I have kept my story historically accurate, to the best of my ability. However, I added one detail that is not a part of history but from my imagination: that men and women convicts were forced to marry."

Collie has worked as a church secretary for her home church in Green Bay, Wisconsin, written many songs, poems, and short stories, and been involved in many ministries throughout the years.

www.oaktara.com